John Wade

**Junius Including Letters by the Same Writer**

John Wade

**Junius Including Letters by the Same Writer**

ISBN/EAN: 9783742830401

Manufactured in Europe, USA, Canada, Australia, Japa

Cover: Foto ©Andreas Hilbeck / pixelio.de

Manufactured and distributed by brebook publishing software
(www.brebook.com)

John Wade

**Junius Including Letters by the Same Writer**

# A CATALOGUE OF
# VARIOUS LIBRARIES.

PUBLISHED BY

## BELL AND DALDY,

STREET, COVENT GARDEN.

LONDON.

### I.

## Bohn's Standard Library.

A SERIES OF THE BEST ENGLISH AND FOREIGN AUTHORS, PRINTED IN
POST 8VO., AND PUBLISHED AT 3s. 6d. PER VOLUME
(EXCEPTING THOSE MARKED OTHERWISE).

Bacon's Essays, Apophthegms, Wisdom of the Ancients, New Atlantis, and Henry VII., with Introduction and Notes. *Portrait.*

Beaumont and Fletcher, a popular Selection from. By LEIGH HUNT.

Beckmann's History of Inventions, Discoveries, and Origins. Revised and enlarged. *Portraits.* In 2 vols.

Bremer's (Miss) Works. Translated by MARY HOWITT. *Portrait.* In 4 vols.
Vol. 1. The Neighbours and other Tales.
Vol. 2. The President's Daughter.
Vol. 3. The Home, and Strife and Peace.
Vol. 4. A Diary, the H—— Family, &c.

Butler's (Bp.) Analogy of Religion, and Sermons, with Notes. *Portrait.*

Carafas (The) of Maddaloni: and Naples under Spanish Dominion. Translated from the German of Alfred de Reumont.

Carrel's Counter Revolution in England. Fox's History and Lonsdale's Memoir of James II. *Portrait.*

Cellini (Benvenuto), Memoirs of. Translated by ROSCOE. *Portrait.*

Coleridge's (S. T.) Friend. A Series of Essays.

Coleridge's (S. T.) Biographia Literaria. [*Just Published.*]

Conde's Dominion of the Arabs in Spain. Translated by Mrs. FOSTER. In 3 vols.

Cowper's Complete Works. Edited, with Memoir of the Author, by SOUTHEY. *Illustrated with 50 Engravings.* In 8 vols.
Vols. 1 to 4. Memoir and Correspondence.
Vols. 5 and 6. Poetical Works. *Plates.*
Vol. 7. Homer's Iliad. *Plates.*
Vol. 8. Homer's Odyssey. *Plates.*

Coxe's Memoirs of the Duke of Marlborough. *Portraits.* In 3 vols.
*** An Atlas of the plans of Marlborough's campaigns, 4to, 10s. 6d.

—— History of the House of Austria. *Portraits.* In 4 vols.

De Lolme on the Constitution of England. Edited, with Notes, by JOHN MACGREGOR.

Emerson's Complete Works. In 2 vols.

Foster's (John) Life and Correspondence. Edited by J. E. RYLAND. In 2 vols.

—— Lectures at Broadmead Chapel. Edited by J. E. RYLAND. In 2 vols.

—— Critical Essays. Edited by J. E. RYLAND. In 2 vols.

—— Essays—On Decision of Character, &c. &c.

—— Essays—On the Evils of Popular Ignorance.

—— Fosteriana: Thoughts, Reflections, and Criticisms of the late JOHN FOSTER, selected from periodical papers, and Edited by HENRY G. BOHN (nearly 600 pages). 6s.

—— Miscellaneous Works. Including his Essay on Doddridge. Preparing.

Fuller's (Andrew) Principal Works. With Memoir. *Portrait.*

Goethe's Works, translated into English. In 5 vols.
  Vols. 1. and 2. Autobiography, 13 Books and Travels in Italy, France, and Switzerland. *Portrait*.
  Vol. 3. Faust, Iphigenia, Torquato Tasso, Egmont, &c., by Miss Swanwick; and Götz von Berlichingen, by Sir Walter Scott. *Frontispiece*.
  Vol. 4. Novels and Tales.
  Vol. 5. Wilhelm Meister's Apprenticeship.

Gregory's (Dr.) Evidences, Doctrines, and Duties of the Christian Religion.

Guizot's Representative Government. Translated by A. R. Scoble.

—— History of the English Revolution of 1640. Translated by William Hazlitt. *Portrait*.

—— History of Civilization. Translated by William Hazlitt. In 3 vols. *Portrait*.

Hall's (Rev. Robert) Miscellaneous Works and Remains, with Memoir by Dr. Gregory, and an Essay on his Character by John Foster. *Portrait*.

Heine's Poems, complete, from the German, by E. A. Bowring. New Edition, enlarged. 5s.

Hungary: its History and Revolutions; with a Memoir of Kossuth from new and authentic sources. *Portrait*.

Hutchinson (Colonel), Memoirs of, and an Account of the Siege of Lathom House. *Portrait*.

James's (G. P. R.) Richard Cœur-de-Lion, King of England. *Portraits*. In 2 vols.

—— Louis XIV. *Portraits*. In 2 vols.

Junius's Letters, with Notes, Additions, and an Index. In 2 vols.

Lamartine's History of the Girondists. *Portraits*. In 3 vols.

—— Restoration of the Monarchy, with Index. *Portraits*. In 4 vols.

—— French Revolution of 1848, with a fine Frontispiece.

Lamb's (Charles) Elia and Eliana. [*Immediately*.]

Lanzi's History of Painting. Translated by Roscoe. *Portraits*. In 3 vols.

Locke's Philosophical Works, containing an Essay on the Human Understanding, &c., with Notes and Index by J. A. St. John. *Portrait*. In 2 vols.

—— Life and Letters, with Extracts from his Common-Place Books, by Lord King.

Luther's Table Talk. Translated by William Hazlitt. *Portrait*.

Machiavelli's History of Florence, The Prince, and other Works. *Portrait*.

Menzel's History of Germany. *Portraits*. In 3 vols.

Michelet's Life of Luther. Translated by William Hazlitt.

—— Roman Republic. Translated by William Hazlitt.

—— French Revolution, with Index. *Frontispiece*.

Mignet's French Revolution from 1789 to 1814. *Portrait*.

Milton's Prose Works, with Index. *Portraits*. In 5 vols.

Mitford's (Miss) Our Village. Improved Ed., complete. Illustrated. 2 vols.

Neander's Church History. Translated; with General Index. In 10 vols.

—— Life of Christ. Translated.

—— First Planting of Christianity, and Antignostikus. Translated. In 2 vols.

—— History of Christian Dogmas. Translated. In 2 vols.

—— Christian Life in the Early and Middle Ages, including his 'Light in Dark Places.' Translated.

Ockley's History of the Saracens. Revised and completed. *Portrait*.

Pearson on the Creed. New Edition. With Analysis and Notes. [*Shortly*.]

Ranke's History of the Popes. Translated by E. Foster. In 3 vols.

—— Servia and the Servian Revolution.

Reynolds' (Sir Joshua) Literary Works. *Portrait*. In 2 vols.

Roscoe's Life and Pontificate of Leo X., with the Copyright Notes, and an Index. *Portraits*. In 2 vols.

—— Life of Lorenzo de Medici, with the Copyright Notes, &c. *Portrait*.

Russia, History of, by Walter K. Kelly. *Portraits*. In 2 vols.

Schiller's Works. Translated into English. In 4 vols.
  Vol. 1. Thirty Years' War, and Revolt of the Netherlands.
  Vol. 2. Continuation of the Revolt of the Netherlands; Wallenstein's Camp; the Piccolomini; the Death of Wallenstein; and William Tell.
  Vol. 3. Don Carlos, Mary Stuart, Maid of Orleans, and Bride of Messina.
  Vol. 4. The Robbers, Fiesco, Love and Intrigue, and the Ghost-Seer.

3

Schlegel's Philosophy of Life and of Language, translated by A. J. W. Morrison.

—— History of Literature, Ancient and Modern. Now first completely translated, with General Index.

—— Philosophy of History. Translated by J. B. Robertson. *Portrait.*

—— Dramatic Literature. Translated. *Portrait.*

—— Modern History.

—— Æsthetic and Miscellaneous Works.

Sheridan's Dramatic Works and Life. *Portrait.*

Sismondi's Literature of the South of Europe. Translated by Roscoe. *Portraits.* In 2 vols.

Smith's (Adam) Theory of the Moral Sentiments; with his Essay on the First Formation of Languages.

Smyth's (Professor) Lectures on Modern History. In 2 vols.

—— Lectures on the French Revolution. In 2 vols.

Sturm's Morning Communings with God, or Devotional Meditations for Every Day in the Year.

Taylor's (Bishop Jeremy) Holy Living and Dying. *Portrait.*

Thierry's Conquest of England by the Normans. Translated by William Hazlitt. *Portrait.* In 2 vols.

Thierry's Tiers Etat, or Third Estate, in France. Translated by F. B. Wells. 2 vols. in one. 5s.

Vasari's Lives of the Painters, Sculptors, and Architects. Translated by Mrs. Foster. 5 vols.

Wesley's (John) Life. By Robert Southey. New and Complete Edition. Double volume, 5s.

Wheatley on the Book of Common Prayer. *Frontispiece.*

## II.

## Uniform with Bohn's Standard Library.

Bailey's (P. J.) Festus. A Poem. Seventh Edition, revised and enlarged. 6s.

British Poets, from Milton to Kirke White. Cabinet Edition. In 4 vols. 14s.

Cary's Translation of Dante's Heaven, Hell, and Purgatory. 7s. 6d.

Chillingworth's Religion of Protestants. 3s. 6d.

Classic Tales. Comprising in One volume the most esteemed works of the imagination. 3s. 6d.

Demosthenes and Æschines, the Orations of. Translated by Leland. 3s.

Dickson and Mowbray on Poultry. Edited by Mrs. Loudon. *Illustrations by Harvey.* 5s.

Guizot's Monk and His Contemporaries. 3s. 6d.

Hawthorne's Tales. In 2 vols., 3s. 6d. each.

Vol. 1. Twice Told Tales, and the Snow Image.

Vol. 2. Scarlet Letter, and the House with the Seven Gables.

Henry's (Matthew) Commentary on the Psalms. *Numerous Illustrations.* 4s. 6d.

Holland's British Angler's Manual. Improved and enlarged by Edward Jesse, Esq. *Illustrated with 60 Engravings.* 7s. 6d.

Horace's Odes and Epodes. Translated by the Rev. W. Sewell. 3s. 6d.

Irving's (Washington) Complete Works. In 10 vols. 3s. 6d. each.

Vol. 1. Salmagundi and Knickerbocker. *Portrait of the Author.*

Vol. 2. Sketch Book and Life of Goldsmith.

Vol. 3. Bracebridge Hall and Abbotsford and Newstead.

Vol. 4. Tales of a Traveller and the Alhambra.

Vol. 5. Conquest of Granada and Conquest of Spain.

Vols. 6 and 7. Life of Columbus and Companions of Columbus, with a new Index. *Fine Portrait.*

Vol. 8. Astoria and Tour in the Prairies.

Vol. 9. Mahomet and his Successors.

Vol. 10. Conquest of Florida and Adventures of Captain Bonneville.

Irving's (Washington) Life of Washington. *Portrait.* In 4 vols. 3s. 6d. each.

—— (Washington) Life and Letters. By his Nephew, PIERRE E. IRVING. In 2 vols. 3s. 6d. each.
*For separate Works, see Cheap Series, p. 16.*

Joyce's Introduction to the Arts and Sciences. With Examination Questions. 3s. 6d.

Lawrence's Lectures on Comparative Anatomy, Physiology, Zoology, and the Natural History of Man. *Illustrated.* 6s.

Lilly's Introduction to Astrology. With numerous Emendations, by ZADKIEL. 5s.

Miller's (Professor) History, Philosophically considered. In 4 vols. 3s. 6d. each.

Parkes's Elementary Chemistry. 3s. 6d.

Political (The) Cyclopædia. In 4 vols. 3s. 6d. each.

—— Also bound in 2 vols. with leather backs. 15s.

Shakespeare's Works, with Life. by CHALMERS. In diamond type. 3s. 6d.

—— or, *with* 40 *Engravings.* 5s.

Uncle Tom's Cabin. With Introductory Remarks, by the Rev. J. SHERMAN. *Printed in a large clear type. Illustrations.* 3s. 6d.

Wide, Wide World. By ELIZABETH WETHERALL. *Illustrated with 10 highly-finished Steel Engravings.* 3s. 6d.

## III.

## Bohn's Historical Library.

### UNIFORM WITH THE STANDARD LIBRARY, AT 5s. PER VOLUME.

Evelyn's Diary and Correspondence. *Illustrated with numerous Portraits, &c.* In 4 vols.

Pepys' Diary and Correspondence. Edited by Lord Braybrooke. With important Additions, including numerous Letters. *Illustrated with many Portraits.* In 4 vols.

Jesse's Memoirs of the Reign of the Stuarts, including the Protectorate. With General Index. *Upwards of* 40 *Portraits.* In 3 vols.

Jesse's Memoirs of the Pretenders and their Adherents. 6 *Portraits.*

Nugent's (Lord) Memorials of Hampden, his Party, and Times. 12 *Portraits.*

Strickland's (Agnes) Lives of the Queens of England, from the Norman Conquest. From official records and authentic documents, private and public. Revised Edition. In 6 vols.

## IV.

## Bohn's Library of French Memoirs.

### UNIFORM WITH THE STANDARD LIBRARY, AT 3s. 6d. PER VOLUME.

Memoirs of Philip de Commines, containing the Histories of Louis XI. and Charles VIII. and of Charles the Bold, Duke of Burgundy. To which is added, The Scandalous Chronicle, or Secret

History of Louis XI. *Portraits.* In 2 vols.

Memoirs of the Duke of Sully, Prime Minister to Henry the Great. *Portraits.* In 4 vols.

## V.

## Bohn's School and College Series.

### UNIFORM WITH THE STANDARD LIBRARY.

Bass's Complete Greek and English Lexicon to the New Testament. 2s. 6d.

New Testament (The) in Greek. Griesbach's Text, with the various readings of Mill and Scholz at foot of page, and

Parallel References to the margin; also a Critical Introduction and Chronological Tables. Two fac-similes of Greek Manuscripts. (650 pages.) 3s. 6d.; or with the Lexicon. 6s.

8

## VI.

## Bohn's Philological and Philosophical Library.

### UNIFORM WITH THE STANDARD LIBRARY, AT 5s. PER VOLUME (EXCEPTING THOSE MARKED OTHERWISE).

Hegel's Lectures on the Philosophy of History. Translated by J. Sibree, M.A.

Herodotus, Turner's (Dawson W.) Notes to. With Map, &c.

—— Wheeler's Analysis and Summary of.

Kant's Critique of Pure Reason. Translated by J. M. D. Meiklejohn.

Logic; or, the Science of Inference. A Popular Manual. By J. Devey.

Lowndes' Bibliographer's Manual of English Literature. New Edition, enlarged, by H. G. Bohn. Parts I. to X. (A

to Z). 3s. 6d. each. Part XI. (the Appendix Volume). 5s. Or the 11 parts in 4 vols. half morocco, 2l. 2s.

Smith's (Archdeacon) Complete Collection of Synonyms and Antonyms. [In the Press.

Tennemann's Manual of the History of Philosophy. Continued by J. R. Morell.

Thucydides, Wheeler's Analysis of.

Wheeler's (M.A.) W. A., Dictionary of Names of Fictitious Persons and Places.

Wright's (T.) Dictionary of Obsolete and Provincial English. In 2 vols. 5s. each; or half-bound in 1 vol., 10s. 6d.

## VII.

## Bohn's British Classics.

### UNIFORM WITH THE STANDARD LIBRARY, AT 3s. 6d. PER VOLUME.

Addison's Works. With the Notes of Bishop Hurd, much additional matter, and upwards of 100 Unpublished Letters. Edited by H. G. Bohn. Portrait and 8 Engravings on Steel. In 6 vols.

Burke's Works. In 6 Volumes.
Vol. 1. Vindication of Natural Society, On the Sublime and Beautiful, and Political Miscellanies.
Vol. 2. French Revolution, &c.
Vol. 3. Appeal from the New to the Old Whigs; the Catholic Claims, &c.
Vol. 4. On the Affairs of India, and Charge against Warren Hastings.
Vol. 5. Conclusion of Charge against Hastings; on a Regicide Peace, &c.
Vol. 6. Miscellaneous Speeches, &c. With a General Index.

Burke's Speeches on Warren Hastings; and Letters. With Index. In 2 vols. (forming vols. 7 and 8 of the works).

—— Life. By Prior. New and revised Edition. Portrait.

Defoe's Works. Edited by Sir Walter Scott. In 7 vols.

Gibbon's Roman Empire. Complete and Unabridged, with Notes; including, in addition to the Author's own, those of Guizot, Wenck, Niebuhr, Hugo, Neander, and other foreign scholars; and an elaborate Index. Edited by an English Churchman. In 7 vols.

## VIII.

## Bohn's Ecclesiastical Library.

### UNIFORM WITH THE STANDARD LIBRARY, AT 5s. PER VOLUME.

Eusebius' Ecclesiastical History. With Notes.

Philo Judæus, Works of; the contemporary of Josephus. Translated by C. D. Yonge. In 4 vols.

Socrates' Ecclesiastical History, in continuation of Eusebius. With the Notes of Valesius.

Sozomen's Ecclesiastical History, from A.D. 324-440; and the Ecclesiastical History of Philostorgius.

Theodoret and Evagrius. Ecclesiastical Histories, from A.D. 332 to A.D. 427 and from A.D. 431 to A.D. 544.]

## II.

## Bohn's Antiquarian Library.

UNIFORM WITH THE STANDARD LIBRARY, AT 5s. PER VOLUME.

Bede's Ecclesiastical History, and Anglo-Saxon Chronicle.

Boethius's Consolation of Philosophy. In Anglo-Saxon, with the A. S. Metres, and an English Translation, by the Rev. S. Fox.

Brand's Popular Antiquities of England, Scotland, and Ireland. By Sir Henry Ellis. In 3 vols.

Browne's (Sir Thomas) Works. Edited by Simon Wilkin. In 3 vols.
Vol. 1. The Vulgar Errors.
Vol. 2. Religio Medici, and Garden of Cyrus.
Vol. 3. Urn-Burial, Tracts, and Correspondence.

Chronicles of the Crusaders. Richard of Devizes, Geoffrey de Vinsauf, Lord de Joinville.

Chronicles of the Tombs. A Collection of Remarkable Epitaphs. By T. J. Pettigrew, F.R.S., F.S.A.

Early Travels in Palestine. Willibald, Sœwulf, Benjamin of Tudela, Mandeville, La Brocquiere, and Maundrell; all unabridged. Edited by Thomas Wright.

Ellis's Early English Metrical Romances. Revised by J. O. Halliwell.

Florence of Worcester's Chronicle, with the Two Continuations: comprising Annals of English History to the Reign of Edward I.

Giraldus Cambrensis' Historical Works: Topography of Ireland; History of the Conquest of Ireland; Itinerary through Wales; and Description of Wales. With Index. Edited by Thos. Wright.

Handbook of Proverbs. Comprising all Ray's English Proverbs, with additions; his Foreign Proverbs; and an Alphabetical Index.

Henry of Huntingdon's History of the English, from the Roman Invasion to Henry II.; with the Acts of King Stephen, &c.

Ingulph's Chronicle of the Abbey of Croyland, with the Continuations by Peter of Blois and other Writers. By H. T. Riley.

Keightley's Fairy Mythology. Frontispiece by Cruikshank.

Lamb's Dramatic Poets of the Time of Elizabeth; including his Selections from the Garrick Plays.

Lepsius's Letters from Egypt, Ethiopia, and the Peninsula of Sinai.

Mallet's Northern Antiquities. By Bishop Percy. With an Abstract of the Eyrbiggia Saga, by Sir Walter Scott. Edited by J. A. Blackwell.

Marco Polo's Travels. The Translation of Marsden. Edited by Thomas Wright.

Matthew Paris's Chronicle. In 5 vols.
First Section: Roger of Wendover's Flowers of English History, from the Descent of the Saxons to A.D. 1235. Translated by Dr. Giles. In 2 vols.
Second Section: From 1235 to 1273. With Index to the entire Work. In 3 vols.

Matthew of Westminster's Flowers of History, especially such as relate to the affairs of Britain; to A.D. 1307. Translated by C. D. Yonge. In 2 vols.

Ordericus Vitalis' Ecclesiastical History of England and Normandy. Translated with Notes, by T. Forester, M.A. In 4 vols.

Pauli's (Dr. R.) Life of Alfred the Great. Translated from the German.

Polyglot of Foreign Proverbs. With English Translations, and a General Index, bringing the whole into parallels, by H. G. Bohn.

Roger De Hoveden's Annals of English History; from A.D. 732 to A.D. 1201. Edited by H. T. Riley. In 2 vols.

Six Old English Chronicles, viz.:—Asser's Life of Alfred, and the Chronicles of Ethelwerd, Gildas, Nennius, Geoffry of Monmouth, and Richard of Cirencester.

William of Malmesbury's Chronicle of the Kings of England. Translated by Sharpe.

Yule-Tide Stories. A Collection of Scandinavian Tales and Traditions. Edited by B. Thorpe.

1

## I.

# Bohn's Illustrated Library.

UNIFORM WITH THE STANDARD LIBRARY, AT 5s. PER VOLUME
(EXCEPTING THOSE MARKED OTHERWISE).

# JUNIUS:

INCLUDING

## LETTERS BY THE SAME WRITER UNDER OTHER SIGNATURES;

TO WHICH ARE ADDED

HIS CONFIDENTIAL CORRESPONDENCE WITH MR. WILKES,
AND HIS PRIVATE LETTERS TO MR. H. S. WOODFALL;

### A New and Enlarged Edition

WITH NEW EVIDENCE AS TO THE AUTHORSHIP,
AND EXTRACTS FROM AN ANALYSIS BY SIR HARRIS NICOLAS

BY

## JOHN WADE,

AUTHOR OF "A CHRONOLOGY OF BRITISH HISTORY
"THE CABINET LAWYER," ETC.

VOL. II.

CONTAINING THE PRIVATE AND MISCELLANEOUS LETTERS,
AND A NEW ESSAY ON THE AUTHORSHIP.

LONDON:

BELL & DALDY, 6 YORK STREET, COVENT GARDEN,
AND 186 FLEET STREET.
1865.

# PREFACE.

The present Volume comprises all the Letters known to be written by the Author of Junius under other signatures, or which have hitherto been ascribed to him. Several of these are now considered spurious; but it has been deemed advisable to republish every letter given in Woodfall's edition, rather than exercise any discretion in expunging what may have acquired interest with many, and, with some, is still matter of controversy.

The Private Letters of Junius, addressed to Woodfall, as printer of the Public Advertiser, are valuable not only for the light they throw on the progress of this remarkable correspondence, but also for the glimpses they afford of the movements and character of their long inscrutable author. The terseness and force with which these brief notes are penned, are strikingly significant of the energy and resolute purpose of the writer.

The Letters of Junius to Wilkes merit careful perusal. They are recommended by clearness and vigour of style, as well as excellent sense and a sound appreciation of constitutional principles. The replies of Wilkes place him in a favourable light, and evince a power of reasoning and a regard for enlightened principles of government, greater than might have been inferred from his giddy and dissolute career.

The Miscellaneous Letters possess several claims to notice. In them may be discerned the first agitation of public questions which Junius subsequently discussed more effectively, and in more elaborate and polished diction. They are not all, however, believed to be from the pen of Junius; and in the notes it has been attempted to distinguish such as are indisputably his from those which cannot be affiliated with certainty.

Newspaper correspondence had an authority and interest in the time of Junius which it no longer possesses, and the Miscellaneous Letters derive a value from the illustration they afford of this antecedent phase of journalism. At this period existed none of those leading articles or elaborate commentaries on public questions, which now occupy so prominent a place in our daily papers. The correspondents of the press were then the only writers of political communications which bore the character of leaders; and, as reports of the debates were not permitted, members of either house suffered equally with the people in possessing no common channel by which the one could learn, and the other convey, their sentiments. In consequence of this restrictive system, the correspondence of newspapers formed the most talented portion of their contents, influential men of all parties adopting this medium as the best for giving publicity to their opinions.

In the APPENDIX, with other elucidatory papers, will be found the letters privately addressed to the Earl of Chatham by Junius, and recently brought to light in the Chatham Correspondence.

But the subject in which the reader is likely to feel most interested is the identification of the author. The editor has pursued this inquiry to considerable length, under favourable auspices; he has not only been aided by the labours of numerous preceding investigators, but has conversed on the subject with several distinguished living individuals who were intimately acquainted with the remarkable person whom it seems now fair to acknowledge as Junius. He has also had the advantage of receiving much valuable information from the members and descendants of Sir Philip's family. From the courtesy and readiness with which his inquiries have been met, the impression appears to have become general, even among those most nearly concerned, that all motives for concealment have ceased, and that the time has arrived when a full disclosure may be made, without the compromise of any feeling, interest, or obligation.

In our Preface to the first volume, we promised to include, in the second, an Analysis drawn up by Sir Harris Nicolas; it therefore becomes necessary to explain why this is now omitted. It has been found, after a careful and minute examination of a mass of papers, greater in bulk than even the letters they are intended to illustrate, that no deductions are made, no conclusions drawn. They are mere materials, without any direct tendency, and could only be useful, or in the least degree interesting, in the event of further investigation, should any one still think the question not finally disposed of.

Sir Harris, some time before his death, told the Publisher, that he was engaged in posting up, ledger fashion, the pros and cons in the Junius Papers as given in Woodfall's edition, convinced that this was the likeliest mode of arriving at a satisfactory result. These postings, however, were never completed, and no *dénousment* is attempted. Indeed, Sir Harris confessed that he had not been able to arrive at any conclusion, but that less objection seemed to exist against the claims of Sir Philip Francis than those of any other candidate. He found, like some other astute critics, so happily bantered in Byron's stanzas *, that it was easier to prove that nobody wrote Junius, than to find a writer against whom there was no plausible objection. At that time Sir Harris was not in possession of some of the evidence which has since transpired. Bearing in mind that Archbishop Whately has ingeniously (and, were there any doubt on the subject, we might say successfully) proved that Napoleon never existed; we cannot wonder at the scepticism of those who, having once taken their stand, are determined that Sir Philip Francis shall not be the author.

The Analysis, we may here observe, was to have appeared in several successive papers in the *Athenæum;* and some of the preliminary remarks were there printed, Feb. 10, 1844, but were never continued. These, which form the introductory portion of our manuscript, together with a few extracts from the analysis itself, are annexed, that the reader may have a fair sample of Sir Harris's mode of treatment. We have not room for more, and even if we had, should hesitate to load our volume with what can have but little attraction for the general reader. The Index, however, has derived considerable advantage from Sir Harris's labours, and is in consequence much enlarged; the research occasioned by the operation of blending his materials with our own, has led us to discover the curious fact, that in the previous edition of Junius, published by Woodfall, the name of Sir Philip Francis is entirely excluded from the Index, which is the more remarkable, as in other respects it is singularly minute.

In the Preface to our first volume, the date of Woodfall's variorum Edition is, by a printer's error, stated to be 1813, instead of 1814. An error of more consequence occurs at page 95. The printer, intending to transfer a note respecting Woodfall's trial to the end of the volume, omitted it altogether. The import of it is given at page 324 of our present volume, and in a future edition we shall insert it in its place.

The labour and anxiety bestowed on the present volume have been very considerable, and if, after all, any trivial error should have escaped, the Editor consoles himself with the reflection that he has performed his task conscientiously, and has a considerate public for his jury.

* Vision of Judgment, canto 74, &c.

# CONTENTS.

## APPENDIX.

# JUNIUS AND HIS WORKS

## By Sir Harris Nicolas.

On the general question of the authorship of Junius's Letters my views coincide with those so ably expressed in the *Edinburgh Review*, that though the happiness of mankind may not be materially interested in its determination, and though it may not involve any great or scientific truths, yet, as a point of literary history, it ranks very high; and the fact of the community having long taken so extraordinary an interest in the subject, as to have given birth to at least a hundred volumes or pamphlets, besides innumerable essays and letters in magazines or newspapers, and that a great and universal curiosity is still felt to know who wrote the Letters, seem quite sufficient to justify a good deal of pains in the research, and satisfaction on the discovery. Perhaps we might add, that the obscurity in which the point is still involved, seems a reflection upon the critical acumen and literary industry of those who have investigated the subject; for it is almost incredible that means should not exist for removing the veil in which Junius has for nearly eighty years been shrouded. It has long been our conviction that the materials for ascertaining who Junius really was have not been so carefully nor so impartially examined as they might be; and that a mass of facts could be obtained from the Letters, which, when brought together and classed, would be found of infinite value to future investigators of this perplexing question. Though the Letters have been repeatedly read by all writers on the subject, two mistakes seem to have been committed. First (and which is fatal to almost any inquiry), the Letters have been critically examined by various persons, not to ascertain who the author *might have been*, but to establish some preconceived theory; and thus the same passages have been cited as conclusive proofs of totally different facts. Secondly, the passages and statements chiefly relied upon are such as Junius would naturally have used for the mere purposes of argument or illustration,—to give greater force to his attacks,—or to divert attention from himself. With these objects he evidently feigned representations of his own character, situation, and feelings; simulated disapprobation of men and measures; attacked or defended individuals, and expressed opinions according as the interests of his party or his own political views dictated, and which accounts for the contradictions and inconsistencies that appear in some of his writings.

To deny that Junius was a consummate actor, if even a stronger term would not be still more applicable, would be to deny that he wrote from political or party motives, and that he availed himself of the weapons which then disgraced party warfare. It is not, therefore, in studied phrases, elaborate metaphors, or well-turned periods; nor in the attacks upon or praise of individuals, that the author is to be traced. These were the materials of his business—the tools of his art—and are, consequently, of little other value for his identity, than as they afford evidence of his powers of composition. But even in this point of view their utility is materially lessened by the immense labour with which the Letters were written, and by the improbability of finding any other of his compositions after that time on which so much care was bestowed. But though great reliance should not be placed on those finished productions bearing the signature of Junius, they nevertheless afford some materials for identifying their author.

But Junius's private correspondence with Woodfall seems a far safer guide for tracing him ; for though he was probably almost as desirous of concealing himself from his publisher as from the public, and may have taken nearly equal pains to mystify both, yet those letters were necessarily of a much more personal nature than the others ; and they consequently exhibit many peculiarities of thought, feeling, temperament, and style, besides affording other facts of considerable importance for his identification.

Yet the difficulty of determining *what* passage or statement in any of his letters was *true*, is so great, that too much hesitation cannot be shown in fixing upon any one, as being the certain representative of a *fact*, unless it be supported by some corroborating circumstance. All inquirers into Junius's identity, must, we apprehend, have felt this difficulty ; for we find them adopting some parts of the Letters as true, and regarding others as feigned, though the grounds for belief in the selected passages seem equally uncertain.

For these reasons a complete *analysis* of the letters appears to be one of the most likely modes of ascertaining their author; for it is scarcely possible that some indications of *the man* should not be found in the dissection of several hundred of his letters, extending over nearly six years, and treating not only of all the political and party transactions of the period, but containing a quantity of personal matter altogether unprecedented in any political writer.

Hypocrisy cannot be consistent for a long period and under a great variety of circumstances ; nor can any one, be his skill what it may, altogether conceal the idiosyncracies of his nature when called into active life, whether as a speaker or an author. Though for these reasons we should place little weight on the tests usually relied upon for discovering Junius, yet his public as well as his private letters contain some minute peculiarities, as well as some statements, which are deserving of attention. Identity of an anonymous writer lurks in favourite words ; in repeated allusions to objects or sentiments with which he was familiar in early life, or which became habitual from professional avocations ; to feelings inspired by an unconscious but predominant passion ; in national or provincial phrases ; in dates and localities ; in accidental references to inconveniences, personal or local, arising out of his immediate labours, and which fall unconsciously from the pen ; in punctuation ; in the use of capital letters ; and, indeed in those numerous small but marked peculiarities by some of which each writer is distinguished from another, and which are rarely attempted to be concealed or suppressed, because he himself is usually unconscious of their existence.

Another equally strong, if not stronger peculiarity is *handwriting ;* and we think it as impossible for a person to disguise his writing in an effectual manner, as to change his features or his voice, unless, indeed, he be a professed mimic or ventriloquist. Most of Junius's notes to Mr. Woodfall, together with the *corrected* copy of Wheble's edition of the Letters, from which the first authorized edition was printed, are fortunately preserved.

It is here proper to remark that so far from having any theory of our own on Junius's identity, we are as entirely free from bias on the subject, and confess ourselves as profoundly ignorant of the authorship of those celebrated Letters, as if, instead of having for many years constantly had the question in our mind, and having read, we believe, nearly everything that has been written on the point, we had never bestowed a thought on the matter. We have indeed a strong impression that Junius was not any one of the numerous persons heretofore so confidently brought forward*; and we may at the conclusion of these papers, perhaps, "sum up" the evidence arising out of our analysis of the Letters, with the view of showing what *facts* must, in our judgment, meet in Junius. Our readers will have the goodness to bear in mind that our sole object is to bring together materials not hitherto collected, and parts of which only have hitherto been used, and then only to support some *preconceived* opinion. Having, on the contrary, no opinion to establish, we view the Letters, and the other circumstances which will be mentioned, as a mass of raw material, shall use them with the hope of enabling other inquirers to obtain from them some certain result. However startling the idea may be to the many pseudo-*discoverers* of Junius on both sides the Atlantic, we found much of the claim of our observations to attention in the very fact of our having *no Junius of our own*, and on our *disbelief in each of theirs*.

The analysis of Junius's Letters will consist of

1. The dates and signatures to all the letters in Woodfall's edition in 3 vols. 8vo, 1814 (now re-published in 2 vols.), arranged in chronological order.
2. Extracts from, or references to, letters containing indications of—
    Personal dislike to individuals.
    Personal approbation of individuals.
    Disapprobation of public measures.
    Approbation of public measures.
3. Indications of intimate knowledge of the proceedings of, or other matters relating to—
    The court,
    The ministry,
    The army.
4. Collection of statements as *alleged facts*, connected with Junius's identity, consisting of allusions to his own taste, opinions, proceedings, pursuits, habits, temper, age, movements, &c.
5. Indications of Junius being, if not a regular author, at all events a practised writer for the press.
6. Indications of his—
    Dislike of certain professions, country, &c.
7. Peculiar words or phrases, metaphors, style, &c., orthography, &c.
8. Remarks on the handwriting of Junius.

CHRONOLOGICAL LIST *of all the* LETTERS *attributed to* JUNIUS, *with the dates, signatures, and principal purport, distinguishing the private from the published Letters; and referring to the volume and page of Woodfall's edition wherein they occur. All the Letters were addressed " to the Printer of," or " for the Public Advertiser," except where otherwise stated:—*

I.—1767, April 28. "Poplicola."—A severe attack upon Lord Chatham, accusing him of aiming at arbitrary power, and charging him with having

* This essay was written in 1843.

"sacrificed" his brother-in-law, Lord Temple, and of promoting his "rancorous enemy," the Duke of Bedford. Lord Camden, the Chancellor, is called "an apostate lawyer, weak enough to betray the laws of his country."—(ii. 451.)

II.—1767, May 26.  " Poplicola."—A reply to Sir William Draper's defence of Lord Chatham, and supporting the charges against him.—(II. 458.)

III.—1767, June 24.  " Anti Sejanus, jun."—An attack on Lord Bute, and on Lord Chatham, for his " base apostacy."  " I will not censure him for the avarice of a pension, nor the melancholy ambition of a title"—" but to become the stalking-horse of a stallion"—[Lord Bute, then suspected of connection with the Princess of Wales] which is again alluded to in Letter V.— (ii. 465.)

IV.—1767, Aug. 25.  St. James's Coffee House.  " A Faithful Monitor." —Censuring the appointment of Lord Townshend as Lord Lieutenant of Ireland, and of his brother, the Hon. Charles Townshend, as Chancellor of the Exchequer.—" I have been some time in the country."—" I am not a stranger to this par nobile fratrum.  I have served under the one, and have been forty times promised to be served by the other."  Calls Lord Townshend a boaster without spirit, and alludes to his affairs with Lord (quær. Albemarle) and Mr. ——, " in which he set out with unnecessary insolence, and ended with shameful tameness."—(ii. 468.)

V.—1767, Sept. 16.  " Correggio."—On Lord Townshend's talents in caricaturing, and suggesting subjects for his pencil from the ministry, viz. the Duke of Grafton, Mr. Conway, Lord Camden, Lord Chatham, Lord Shelburne, Lord Northington, &c.  Several lacunæ occur in this letter.—(ii. 470.)

VI.—1767, Oct. 12.  " Moderator."—In reference to a controversy respecting Lord Townshend's courage, and supporting the attack on that nobleman. —(ii. 475.)

VII.—1767, Oct. 22.  (No signature.)—" Grand Council upon the affairs of Ireland, after eleven adjournments."  A satirical paper on the instructions to be given to Lord Townshend, as Lord Lieutenant of Ireland.  The speakers are, Lord Northington, President of the Council; Lord Camden, Chancellor; Conway and Lord Shelburne, Secretaries of State; and Lord Townshend himself, whose supposed want of personal courage is frequently alluded to, and he is made to say,  " I will consult Lord George Sackville, as he loves to be in the rear as well as myself."  This paper, which was imputed to Burke, was reprinted in the *Political Register*, where the coarse expressions given to Lord Northington occur at length.  The Chancellor observes of the Irish, that it "is their claim and birthright to talk without meaning, and to live without law."—(ii. 483.)

VIII.—1767, Oct. 31.  (No signature.)—Noticing another version of the Grand Council, which had appeared for the purpose of attacking Burke, offering to produce proofs which will gall " a Correspondent's patrons " that Lord Townshend could not obtain any instructions, and pointedly alluding to a conversation between Lord Townshend and one of the Secretaries on the subject.—(ii. 483.)

IX.—1767, Dec. 5.  " Y. Z."—Sending a copy of Mr. Burke's speech against the Ministry, but which the printer was afraid to insert, who apologized to his " valuable correspondent C." for the omission.—(ii. 498.)

X.—1767, Dec. 19.  (No signature).—Censuring the conduct of the American Colonies, and the repeal of the Stamp Act; and on the state of the country. Lord Chatham is called a lunatic, the Ministry abused, and Mr. George Grenville highly extolled.—(ii. 511.)

XI.—1767, Dec. 22. " Downright."—A short attack on Lord Chatham in answer to Mr. Macaroni.— (ii. 517.)

XII.—1768, Jan. 2. " To Lord Chatham " (without signature.) Lately printed in vol. iii. p. 302 of the Chatham Correspondence.—This remarkable letter (which is not in Woodfall's edition of Junius) commences thus : " If I were to give way to the sentiments of respect and veneration which I have always entertained for your character, or to the warmth of my attachment to your person, I should write a longer letter," &c. After saying he has " an opportunity of knowing something," and that the Earl may rely on his veracity, he states that during the Earl's absence from the administration, not one of the ministers had adhered to him with firmness, or supported his principles in the King's service—points out the conduct of his colleagues, and informs him of the plan of the Duke of Grafton to subvert him in the administration. The conclusion is in these words: " My Lord, the man who presumes to give your Lordship these hints, admires your character without servility, and is convinced that if this country can be saved, it must be saved by Lord Chatham's spirit, by Lord Chatham's abilities."

XIII.—1768, Feb. 16. (No signature.)—Censuring the Ministry, and especially the appointment of persons of no rank as Commissioners of the Privy Seal for six weeks, apparently during Lord Chatham's illness. In this letter Junius shows deep knowledge of the machinery of the constitution, and speaks with some respect of Lord Chatham himself.—(iii. 1.)

XIV.—1768, Feb. 24. " Mnemon."—Describes the English character as " somewhat phlegmatic " and patient under aggression, and applies the fact to Sir James Lowther having obtained a grant of part of the Duke of Portland's estate, " on the absurd and tyrannical principle, that no length of possession secures against a claim of the Crown." Calls Sir George Saville, who brought in a bill on the subject, " one of the ablest, most virtuous, and most temperate men in the kingdom."—(iii. 7.)

XV.—1768, March 4. " Mnemon."—An eloquent letter on the danger and injustice of the maxim " nullum tempus occurrit Regi"; calls Sir George Saville " a superior genius, a great light of the age," and attacks the Ministry for their conduct on the subject.—(iii. 13.)

XVI.—1768, March 24. " Anti Stuart."—Also on the nullum tempus maxim, in answer to a letter signed " Anti van Teague," who had defended the grant to Sir James Lowther. That signature seems to indicate that Junius was supposed to be an Irishman, and Mr. Burke. Junius signs " Anti Stuart," in reference to John Stuart, Earl of Bute, whose daughter Sir James Lowther had married. He then attacks the public character of the Duke of Grafton, the Prime Minister, and says he had not meddled with his private character, which he left for the Duke to curth in, whenever he is hard run, " according to the laudable example" of Lord North.— (iii. 22.)

XVII.—1768, April 5. " C."—Censures the conduct of the Ministry in respect to the proceedings at and after Wilkes's election for Middlesex. Wilkes himself is, however, severely treated, as " a man of most infamous character in private life," " without a single qualification, either moral or political;" " overwhelmed with debts, a convict and an outlaw ;" who " had wantonly and treasonably attacked" the King, who is spoken of in very respectful terms.—(iii. 27.)

XVIII.—1768, April 5.  "Q in the Corner."—On the same subject.
Suggests that the ministers tolerated Wilkes's conduct, in allowing him to
return to England and remain at large notwithstanding his outlawry, with
the object of terrifying Lord Bute, by producing their tribune once more
upon the stage.—(iii. 32.)
XIX.—1768, April 12.  "C."—Again on the maxim "*Nullum tempus
occurrit Regi.*"  Attack on the ministry for having acted upon it towards
the Duke of Portland.—(iii. 34.)
XX.—1768, April 23.  (No signature).—"To the Duke of Grafton."  A
severe attack on his public and private character, and especially for having
sat with his mistress (Miss Parsons, afterwards Lady Maynard) publicly at
the Opera.—(iii. 40.)
XXI.—1768, April 23.  "Bifrons."—Charges the ministry with duplicity as their general characteristic.  Attacks Lord Camden.  Adverts particularly to the Duke of Portland's case: says "he remembers seeing Bas-
sambaum, Saures Molina, and a score of other jesuitical books burnt at Paris,
by the common hangman."—(iii. 42.)
XXII.—1768, May 6.  "C."—The ministry censured for opening Parliament by commission.—(iii. 48.)
XXIII.—1768, May 12.  "Valerius."—On the Duke of Portland's case,
in reply to a defence of the grant to Sir James Lowther.—(iii. 51.)
XXIV.—1768, May 19.  "Fiat Justitia."—Censure of Lord Barrington's
(Secretary at War) letter, dated May 11, which he says he was informed of
by an officer of the Guards, conveying the King's approval of the conduct of
the troops in suppressing the riots in St. George's Fields, and promising them
the protection of the law and of the War Office.—(iii. 57.)
XXV.—1768, July 1.  "Pomona."—"To Master Harry, in Black Boy
Alley," [query        ] on his duplicity in promising a place to Lord
Rockingham and to another person.  Proposes to show how he can perform
his first promise, and "yet continue as great a rascal as you would wish to
be."  "You are a mere boy, Harry, notwithstanding the down upon your
chin." (iii. 60.)
XXVI.—1768, July 19.  "C."—On the appointment of a new Commission of Trade, which is ridiculed.—(iii. 63.)
XXVII.—1768, July 23.  "C."—Reply to a letter signed "Insomnis"
(iii. 66), defending the new Commission of Trade, supporting his former
letter.—(iii. 69.)
XXVIII.—1768, July 30.  (No signature.)—Attack on the "weak,
distracted, worthless ministry," for their proceedings towards America.  He
adverts to his letter of the 19th December, 1767 (No. X.)—repeats many of
his statements—praises Mr. George Grenville, whom the ministry "feared
and hated," because he had the "melancholy triumph of having truly foretold the consequences of their own misconduct," and preferred the rebellion of
half the empire to acknowledging his superiority over them—says the nation
is "on the brink of a dreadful precipice; the question is whether we shall
still submit to be guided by the hand that hath driven us to it, or whether
we shall follow the patriot voice [Mr. Grenville] which hath not ceased to
warn us of our dangers, and which would still declare the way to safety and
honour."—(iii. 73.)
XXIX.—1768, August 5.  "L. L."—Expressing indignation at the dis-

missal of Sir Jeffery Amherst from his government of Virginia, whose services and merits are strongly described. – (iii. 80.)

XXX.—1768, August 6. (No signature.)—A defence of Mr. Grenville's conduct respecting the Stamp Act, and towards the American Colonies, in answer to two writers in the 'Public Advertiser.' In reply to vague hints from one of them, he challenges him to "meet upon the fair ground of truth, and if he finds one vulnerable part in Mr. Grenville's character, let him fix his poisoned arrow there."—(iii. 83.)

XXXI.—1768, August 10. "Lucius."— In reply to "Virginius," a writer who had defended the appointment of Lord Botetourt, as successor to Sir Jeffery Amherst in Virginia; and exposing the motives and injustice of his dismissal.—(iii. 89.)

XXXII.—1768, August 19. "Atticus."—On the situation of the country. The decline of public credit had induced him to sell out of the funds, and invest his property in land; and concluding with a violent invective against the ministry. — (iii. 91.)

XXXIII.—1768, August 23. "Valerius."—The ministry were ordered to dismiss Sir Jeffery Amherst for the sake of giving Lord Botetourt, who is severely attacked, the situation. "It was proper not only to affront living merit, but to insult and trample upon the sacred ashes of the dead ;" i.e. the late Duke of Cumberland, "whose family was the great school of military knowledge," and under whose patronage Amherst first appeared.— (iii. 93.)

XXXIV.—1768, August 29. "Lucius."—"To the Earl of Hillsborough," Secretary of State for the Plantations, imputing to him the dismissal of Sir Jeffery Amherst, detailing every circumstance relating to it, and giving reasons for its not having been the act of any of his colleagues. He was not dismissed by the advice of Lord Granby or Sir Edward Hawke, the latter of whom had a pension, "nobly earned I confess, but not better deserved than by the labours which conquered America in America." "Military men have a sense of honour which your Lordship has no notion of." Speaking of Lord Chatham, he says, "his infirmities have forced him into a retirement where, I presume, he is ready to suffer, with a sullen submission, every insult and disgrace that can be heaped upon a miserable, decrepid, worn-out old man." He puts a series of questions to Lord Hillsborough about Sir Jeffery's dismissal, and says "they must and shall be answered."

"The W—g Company," mentioned in a note to this letter as "the enterprise," which Junius says had ruined Lord Botetourt (Sir Jeffery Amherst's successor), was the Warmly Company, for converting copper into brass, of which Lord Botetourt was the head. It is surprising that the object of that company had not furnished Junius with a sarcasm.—(iii. 105.)

XXXV.—1768, Sept. 1. "Lucius."—"To the Earl of Hillsborough," in reply to a letter signed "Cleophas," explaining the facts attending Sir Jeffery Amherst's dismissal, which letter Lucius assigns to the Earl himself, who has, he says, forfeited all title to respect, by the disingenuous and evasive nature of its contents. The facts of the case are fully discussed ; and the Duke of Grafton is bitterly and warmly attacked for refusing Sir Jeffery's proposition for recompense. Lucius shows much information respecting contemplated army arrangements.— (iii. 116.)

XXXVI.—1768, Sept. 6. "L. L."—In reply to a letter signed "Cleophas, Jun.," whose explanation of part of the Earl of Hillsborough's conduct towards Sir Jeffery Amherst is called "an absolute falsity." As the writer of *this letter* speaks of "Lucius" (certainly "Junius") as "a masterly correspondent," and as on the following day "Lucius" himself answered "Cleophas, Jun.," stating the same thing as "L. L." had done, it may, perhaps, be doubted if it were written by Junius.—(iii. 124.)

XXXVII.—1768, Sept. 7. "Lucius."—"To the Earl of Hillsborough," denying a statement of "Cleophas, Jun." in defence of that minister.—(iii. 126.)

XXXVIII. 1768, Sept. 9. "Lucius."—"To the Earl of Hillsborough," in answer to another letter of "Cleophas" on the same subject. He says his "authority is indisputable;" that the Earl's ostensible defence differs entirely from his private explanation; and that he is indebted to his forbearance for not exposing it. "You are sensible that the most distant insinuation of what the defence is would ruin you at once. But I am a man of honour, and will neither take advantage of your imprudence, nor of your situation."—(iii. 133.)

XXXIX.—1768, Sept. 10. "Lucius."—"To the Earl of Hillsborough," in answer to "Scrutator" on the same subject, in which "Lucius" made a mistake in the date of part of the transaction.—(iii. 139.)

XL.—1768, Sept. 15. "Lucius."—"To the Earl of Hillsborough," adverting to the same subject, but containing general charges of incapacity, especially in the instructions given by the Earl to governors in America. In a postscript he collects all the epithets heaped upon him by Lord Hillsborough's partisans, and corrects the mistake in dates in his preceding letter.—(iii. 145.)

XLI.—1768, Sept. 20. "Lucius."—"To the Earl of "Hillsborough." Draws a parallel between the case of Mr. Ford, who had been convicted of perjury, but escaped from an error in the date of the offence, and the mistake in the dates, above mentioned. He then answers a letter detracting from Sir Jeffery Amherst's military services, and "says the Earl, had left Amherst "poor in every article of which a false fawning minister could deprive him, but you have left him rich in the esteem, the love, and veneration of his country," and "concludes" the discussion.—(iii. 151.)

XLII.—1768, Oct. 6. "Atticus."—"Since my last letter (No. xxxii.) was printed."—On the state of France and this country, and the effect on public credit, in continuation of his letter of 19th August.—(iii. 156.)

XLIII.—1768, Oct. 12, "Temporum Felicitas."—Satirical praise of the correspondents who had supported the ministry, and again alluding to Lord Hillsborough and Sir Jeffery Amherst.—(iii. 160.)

XLIV.—1768, Oct. 15. "Brutus."—In answer to "A Friend to Public Credit," who had replied to Atticus's letter of the 6th October (No. xlii.), on the state of Foreign Affairs.—(iii. 162.)

XLV.—1768, Oct. 19. "Atticus."—On the state of affairs. He announces that Lord Shelburne's removal from office had "within these few days been absolutely determined," and unsparingly examines the conduct of the Duke of Grafton and the other ministers, *seriatim*. When discussing that of Lord Hillsborough, the case of Sir Jeffery Amherst is prominently mentioned, and the secret cause of his dismissal is stated. (Vide No. xxxviii.) Praises Granby's bravery, generosity, and good humour.

Grossly abuses Lord Shelburne, whose "life is a satire on mankind," in deserting a friend and attaching him to a declared enemy. "Of Lord Chatham," who had resigned on the 16th, then supposed to be worn out with the gout, "I had much to say, but it were inhuman to persecute when Providence has marked out the example to mankind."—(iii. 165.)

XLVI.—1768, Oct. 26. "Why?"—A high eulogium on the Earl of Rochford, pointing out his peculiar fitness for conducting affairs with France. He refers to the letter of Atticus (No. xlv.), and says the public reflect with horror on the intelligence he had communicated, and therefore asked why Lord Rochford was made Secretary of State, and for the Northern Department?—(iii. 177.)

XLVII.—1768, Oct. 27. "Brutus."—In answer to "Plain Truth and Justice," who had replied to his letter on the decline of public credit, supporting his former statements on that subject. It contains a compliment to Mr. Grenville,—"We may retire to our prayers, for the game is up."—(iii. 180.)

XLVIII.—1768, Nov. 14. "Atticus."—On the state of public affairs, and reviewing generally the conduct of the administration, its weakness and vacillation. "For my own part I am not personally their enemy." He particularly censures the Commander-in-Chief, Lord Granby, who looks no further than to the disposal of Commissions, and suffers the army to be robbed by way of pension to the noble disinterested house of Percy, and Sir Jeffery Amherst to be sacrificed." Most of the subjects noticed in his previous letters are touched upon. It is remarkable that he should state that "the Peerage which had been absolutely refused is granted" to Sir Jeffery Amherst, whereas he was not created a peer until the 20th May, 1776, eight years after.—(iii. 183.)

XLIX.—1768, Nov. 21. "Junius."—(The *first letter* bearing that celebrated signature, but it was not included in Junius's own edition of his Letters in 1772, probably because Wilkes was mentioned in a manner not consistent with their relations in that year.) On the violation of "all ties of honour, professions of friendship, and obligations of party" by the ministry to Wilkes, but clearly shows that he is not personally interested about him.—(iii. 190.)

L.—1768, Dec. 15. (No signature).—"To the Right Hon. George Grenville," "who possessed all the constituent parts of a minister, except the honour of distributing or the emolument of receiving the public money," containing general censure on the administration.—(iii. 192.)

LI.—1769, Jan. 21. "Junius."—On the state of the nation. General censure of ministers (including the Marquis of Granby, Commander-in-Chief), and review of their proceedings; but he compliments Sir Edward Hawke—to whom the navy is so highly indebted, that no expense should be spared to secure to him an honourable and affluent retreat. Praises the personal virtues of the king.—(i. 367.)

LII.—1769, Feb. 7. "Junius."—"To Sir William Draper." Reply to a letter from Sir William Draper, who had defended the Marquis of Granby. "I should have hoped that even my name might carry some authority with it." In support of his charges against that nobleman, Junius says, "he deserted the cause of the whole army when he suffered Sir Jeffery Amherst to be sacrificed.—(i. 410.)

# ADVERTISEMENT

## PREFIXED TO WOODFALL'S FIRST EDITION, OMITTED IN
### THE SECOND.

THE present edition contains, besides the letters published by authority of Junius himself, others written by the same author under various signatures, which appeared in the *Public Advertiser* from April, 1767, to May, 1772, together with his Private Letters, peculiarly curious and interesting, addressed to his printer, the late Mr. H. S. Woodfall, and his confidential correspondence with Mr. Wilkes. These latter papers only reached the proprietor's hands after a considerable part of the work had been printed off, which will account for the unavoidable omission of any notice of them in the Preliminary Essay.

It is in perfect consistency with the plan at first proposed by the author, but which he was compelled in some degree to depart from, as remarked in the Preliminary Essay, that the edition now offered contains, independently of his more finished compositions under the signature of Junius and Philo-Junius, letters under other signatures, bearing nevertheless characteristic and unequivocal marks of proceeding from the same pen; and which, though written perhaps with more haste than the former, exhibit merit enough to accompany them; while they possess no small portion of additional value as comments upon points that require elucidation.

The editor, in thus deciding upon materials which lie scattered through what he terms six "solid folios," will be found seldom to have relied altogether upon his own judgment, but to have availed himself of a variety of minute clues resulting from incidental references, or open acknowledgments in the Private Letters; direct charges of contemporary labourers in the same political vineyard, which were not disavowed by Junius himself, as was his custom whenever "other persons' sins," to adopt his own language, were attributed to him; or from numerous other casual hints, both in the acknowledged and more palpable Miscellaneous Letters, of which the reader, it is presumed, will meet with instances enough to satisfy himself as he proceeds.

To the author's explanatory notes, the present editor has added such others through the entire progress of the work, as the intervening lapse of time has seemed to render necessary, and though some of them are longer than he could have wished, yet from the circumstance of their having been written in answer to letters from Junius, he has thought it more desirable that they should appear in the form in which they are now offered, than be pressed into the text of the work, by which means its present size must have been very considerably extended; and the plan, as devised by the author, have been in some instances departed from. Many of these notes, moreover, selected from the *Public Advertiser*, will be found in themselves extremely curious and valuable, while at the same time they are nowhere else to be met with. The text has been carefully collated with the Journal in which the letters originally appeared, and very numerous errors, which have crept into all the editions, except the genuine one published by Mr. H. S. Woodfall himself, and which have been considerably multiplied in the later impressions, have been carefully corrected or expunged.

*The remainder of this Advertisement is of no interest.*

# HISTORY

# DISCOVERY OF JUNIUS.

To solve riddles is a leading propensity of man, and the more baffling they are the more ardent he becomes in research. Such dispositions of our nature. from their beneficial tendencies, may be commendably indulged. To persevering inquiry society is mainly indebted for its progress, and may look forward to continual advancement, till the utmost limits of discovery are reached, and philosophers, like Alexander at the close of his triumphs, sigh that no more victories remain to be won.

The phenomena of the material universe may challenge wonder and admiration, but what most absorbs sympathy are the mysteries of our own conduct. Hence the superior interest of inquiries that pertain to human genius; its grandeur, its perversions, and its eccentricities. History is replete with these themes; controversies on many of them seem interminable, and the combatants, like hardy warriors, retire from the lists, not because they are vanquished or convinced, but because they are exhausted.

It is this which has tended to leave undetermined many problems of a former period. Few would now care to renew the disputation whether Charles I. or Bishop Gauden composed *Eikon Basilike;* whether William or George Cavendish wrote the *Life of Wolsey,* or Lady Packington *The Whole Duty of Man.* The question revived in Queen Anne's reign, whether King James was the father of the old Pretender, has descended, with the young Pretender, into oblivion, and neither pen nor claymore is likely again to be drawn respecting any affinities of the Stuarts. Weariness of the dispute, if not greater decorum, precludes further scrutiny into the transgressions of Mary Queen of Scotland. Anne of Austria is similarly chartered, though her suspected derelicts were more numerous than those of the Scottish queen. All these are enigmas with which inquirers of the last century pertinaciously wrestled, as well as with the more melancholy ones pertaining to the death of Don Carlos of Spain, Alexis of Russia, and Count Königsmark at the electoral court of Hanover.

The truth of such dark passages of history might not be of use to mankind, if indubitably revealed; but there are inquirers who delight in their exploration as there are adventurers always forthcoming to brave the gloom and icebergs of the polar seas. On the other hand, there are men whose predominant taste is not to unravel mysteries but to create them. Hence the numerous impostors and literary forgeries that have appeared—Annius of Viterbo, Damberger, the pretended African traveller, and George Psalmanazar; the Rowley Poems, the Poems of Ossian, and the Shakspeare Papers. With rare exceptions, the authors of such fabrications maintained their genuineness to the last, and died without confession. Psalmanazar, indeed, after a long and successful career of imposition practised on bishops and church dignitaries, was at length unmasked, chiefly by Dr. Douglas —"the scourge of impostors, the terror of quacks,"—who pointed out the contradictions in his pretended missionary labours and nativity in the island of Formosa; but though Psalmanazar was brought to admit his deceptions, he could never be prevailed on to disclose his real name or birthplace.

Ireland too was an exception—he avowed the Shakspeare forgeries, after deceiving such recondite connoisseurs as the Earls of Lauderdale and Somerset, Sir James Burgess, Dr. Parr, Mr. Pinkerton, and Pye the poet laureate. But neither Chatterton nor Macpherson could be brought to admit the spuriousness of their productions. The "Poems of Rowley" were so adroitly executed, that no one, Mr. Malone affirmed, except the nicest judges of English poetry, from Chaucer to Pope, was competent to test their genuineness. As Chatterton died without acknowledging their composition, it is still open to controversy. Dr. Johnson believed that Chatterton was the author, but was astonished at his precocious ability. "This is the most extraordinary young man," said he, "who has encountered my knowledge—it is wonderful how the whelp has written such things." The "Poems of Ossian" have been an equally successful deception; deceived Gray, Home, and even Dr. Blair, a critic and writer on language by profession. But the acuteness of Mr. Hume, though willing to be converted, suggested a simple trial. "Shew us," said the historian, "the original Celtic poems from which the translations have been made, and tell us how they have been so wonderfully preserved during so many centuries." The appeal was a fair one, but Macpherson declined to join issue, and with affected disdain refused to answer.

These retrospective glances have been cast briefly to indicate the literary enigmas which have occupied a preceding generation, but except as pertaining to the mysterious, they have no relation to the subject of the present inquiry. In the depths of their secrecy the LETTERS OF JUNIUS have been unequalled, but stand wholly distinct from the class of literary forgeries. Rich in intrinsic excellence, they might have been safely left to their own merits to find a lasting place in public esteem. Unlike the fictions adverted to, they are a genuine production, commenced with a determinate purpose, resolutely persevered in, and in the main fully successful. The mystery in regard to them is, that a work of such undoubted claims, one which has commanded such universal admiration, should so long remain a waif—be so long astray in the world without any acknowledged claimant.

To unravel this mystery—to sever this Gordian-knot of the age—is the object of the present Essay. A task which has failed in the hands of so many, is not, it must be owned, either an encouraging or an easy one. Excess of false lights, in some degree, dazzles and perplexes the way. Junius has been profoundly invisible, but he is no myth of antiquity; he lived in an age when hardly anything that provokes curiosity can elude the searching blaze. For the result to be satisfactory, no disembodied spirit will suffice; it must be a being of flesh and blood, one that will bear to be challenged by facts, documents, and living witnesses. Despite of this array, I shall make the attempt. I shall show who Junius was, and the conditions and exigencies under which he acted. I will explain all that is most marvellous in him—all that most astonished his contemporaries—his apparently instantaneous and universal sources of intelligence; his meteoric career and sudden disappearance; the reasons of his concealment; and why he lived and died unavowed.

## WHO, THEN, WAS JUNIUS?

The lists are crowded with claimants, and this is the first difficulty which presents itself. The throng is embarrassing, but many combatants have no title to be placed, and the ranks must be thinned by settling the eligibilities of the tournament. This is a fair preliminary, allowed in every investigation. Geometricians always commence with axioms that are indisputable, by which the path is opened to theorems. In the trial of a judicial issue, certain descriptions of evidence are deemed inadmissible, and not entitled to be examined. By following this course, the ground is cleared, irrelevancies got rid of, and attention concentrated on essential points. It is a precedent I shall follow by describing certain denominations of candidates, none of whom can possibly have been Junius. Acting upon this rule, my first affirmation is,

*That Junius was not a Lawyer.*

In deciding this issue, I shall not trust to my own judgment, but appeal to higher authority: Lord Campbell, whose words have been quoted (p. 59), says distinctly that Junius could not have been a lawyer, or he would not have committed the serious mistake of denying the power of Chief Justice Mansfield to bail Eyre, charged with theft under peculiar circumstances [*]. A remark of like import I have heard made by a celebrated ex-chancellor. Indeed the mistake is held by the profession to have been an egregious one, and such as no barrister would have committed.

In his Dedication he falls into a further unprofessional error, when in speaking of the House of Commons, he says, "They are only *trustees*, the *fee* is in us." Upon this, Lord Campbell observes, "Those who are of the *craft* all know that the fee is in the trustee, not in the *cestuique trust*, or person beneficially interested."[†] But it is due to Junius to remark, that he never pretended to be of the "craft;" he disdained the connection; considered that it narrowed the mind and corrupted the heart. In a private letter to Wilkes, he says, "Though I use the terms of art, do not injure me so much as to suspect I am a lawyer. I had as lief be a Scotchman.

* Junius, vol. i. p. 440.        † Lives of the Chanc. vi. p. 344.

It is the encouragement given to disputes about titles, which
has supported that iniquitous profession at the expense of the
community." *  Judging, therefore, from this moral aversion,
his renunciation, and his legal mistakes, Junius must be concluded not to have been a lawyer.

The blank it creates in the roll of candidates is enormous.
Some of the brightest and best-supported names must be
struck off.  Dunning is one; subtle, able, honest, independent, so enamoured of the style of Junius that he once
essayed to imitate it, in answer to a City address, and so
successfully, that many were deceived.  Mr. Britton includes
him among his triumvirs, and Heron, the ingenious critic
of language and eloquence, finishes his learned essay by
announcing the "celebrated Dunning to be Junius."  A single
fact disposes of the conjecture.  Dunning was appointed
Solicitor-General in December, 1767, and held that office till
March, 1770.  In December, 1769, the famous letter of
Junius to the King appeared, in which he discharged those
fearful shafts at royalty that made the blood of Mr. Burke
"run cold;" and which, with other missiles from the same
quarter, must, if Dunning was Junius, have proceeded from
His Majesty's Solicitor-General!  Further, the Earl of Shelburne, with whom Lord Ashburton lived in confidential intimacy, often declared that Dunning did not "write a line of
Junius."

Other lawyers have been named.  A Mr. Sergeant Adair
was once produced, on the plea of certain ephemeral
pamphlets, but the feebleness they evinced caused him to
be quickly given up.  It appears almost ludicrous to note,
that the great Lord Camden was suspected, simply on the
ground of his dislike to the law and politics of Chief Justice
Mansfield.  William Gerard Hamilton, of *Single-speech fame*,
studied at Lincoln's Inn, but was not called to the bar.  He
was a man of worth and ability, the first patron of Burke, and
the intimate associate and correspondent of the leading men
of his day; but his nature was timid and retiring, and in the
latter days of his life he sank into an unambitious placidity,
irreconcilable with the energetic and indefatigable Junius.
When questioned on the subject by Earl Temple, he distinctly denied the authorship of the Letters†.  Just before his
death, the same question was asked him by a member of the

* Letter to Wilkes, No. 70, p. 91.	+ Dr. Good's Prelim. Essay, p. 56.

House of Commons; he repeated his denial, which it is quite unlikely he would have done if he had had any claim to the composition of writings so celebrated, so effective, and so accordant with his own principles.

In connection with Mr. Hamilton, an opportunity is afforded for a passing audit of the claims of Earl Temple; he was not a lawyer, but a volume has been written in his favour*. If his Lordship was Junius, it must have been a superfluous interrogatory, or a very poor joke, to ask Gerard Hamilton the question. Earl Temple was not reputed by a discern ing judge to be a writer of competent power to wing the shafts of Junius. A pamphlet which appeared in 1760, of some merit, was ascribed to him, but Lord Chesterfield remarked, that he thought it "above him." Besides, Temple was an active politician, a Peer of Parliament, and brother-in law of Lord Chatham, and had no need of the *Public Adver- tiser* to circulate his opinions. Although his claim is disal- lowed, it will appear probable in the sequel, that Earl Temple was one among the parties who contributed materials to Junius; and towards the close of the Letters, his Lordship may have confidentially known the author.

Other names, in addition to the above, have been adduced, but it is unnecessary to dwell on their claims. If any member of the profession be again brought forward under the visor of Junius, he may be readily disposed of either as a false Junius, or a bad lawyer. That Junius consulted lawyers, and able ones, has been admitted, but he could not have done this frequently without endangering his privacy. His argument, impugning Lord Mansfield's decision, he admits, cost him infinite pains, which is probable enough in the absence of professional acquirements and resources. Addressing Mr. Wilkes, he says, " No man writes under so many disadvan- tages as I do; I cannot consult the learned, I cannot directly ask the opinion of my acquaintances."† But enough of the legal character of Junius. Against the next class the proof is not so strong, but the probability is great

*That JUNIUS was not a Clergyman.*

If he were, he must have been a lax or insincere one, and that is inconsistent with his fiery and daring temperament. Some have held him to be without religion. This is inadmis-

* *Let. of Junius*, by Newhall, 1831.          † Letter to Wilkes, No. 79.

sible. Bigoted or sectarian he evidently was not; but that he
cherished real piety is attested by the grateful tenour of the
peroration with which he winds up his labours (vol. i. 470).
The priesthood certainly did not stand high in his estimation,
and by taunts and inuendoes he frequently attempts to cast
ridicule upon them. He was familiar with the language of
Scripture, but, as Heron has observed, often used it in mockery. Upon such *primâ facie* indications, it may with tolerable
certainty be concluded, that Junius was not in holy orders.

If this be correct, Philip Francis, D.D., descended from a
race of church dignitaries, richly beneficed, could not have
been Junius; and resting upon the like ecclesiastical objection, neither could the Rev. Philip Rosenhagen. He was
a chaplain in the army, and may have known something
of military men and affairs, but the Letters were beyond
his calibre. He wrote a pamphlet in answer to Dr. Johnson's *False Alarm*, in which the feebleness of the argument
was on a level with the meagreness of the style, and
very unlike the vivid flashes that illumed the columns of
the *Public Advertiser*. Mr. Woodfall knew him intimately;
he had been his schoolfellow at St. Paul's, and was quite
satisfied that he had no share in the production of the Letters.
The autograph of Junius was bold, firm, and precise; that of
Rosenhagen a feeble, half illegible scrawl. Besides, Rosenhagen was of foreign extraction, and could hardly be master
of the idiomatic phraseology, constitutional knowledge, and
British feeling that signalize Junius. But he was ambitious
of the honour, and in common with Hugh Boyd, and other
pretenders, decked in the plumage of the royal bird, sought to
profit by it; for, upon the authority of Gerard Hamilton,
it is related by Almon* that Rosenhagen tried to negotiate a
pension for himself with Lord North, on the stipulation that
Junius "would write no more."

Special reasons also exist against the claim of Dr. Butler,
Bishop of Hereford, who occasionally wrote political pamphlets, but they were mediocre productions, without either the
grace or fire of Junius. It could only have been an ironical
joke of Mr. Wilkes, to impute the authorship to this prelate.
The claim of the Rev. Dr. James Wilmot, in whose favour his
niece, the celebrated Olivia Wilmot Serres, ci-accvant Princess
of Cumberland, put forth a volume, with a portrait of the

* Letters of Junius, Preface, p. 10.

Doctor, Latin motto, fac-similes, &c., need only be mentioned. I advance to a higher sphere, comprising two estates of the realm, and proceed to show, that

> *Junius was neither a Peer nor Member of the House of Commons.*

A remarkable trait in our author is his knowledge of the great world. Whatever might have been his talents, the spirit of his language, the originality of his ideas, or the patriotism of his purpose, he evidently felt, that to exhibit a perfect and constant acquaintance with political and court life was absolutely essential to gain the *public ear.* In this object he completely succeeded, displaying such a mastery of facts, such an immediate knowledge of State secrets, and such superiority of style and tone, that he was always presumed to speak from a high position in society. "My rank and fortune," he artfully intimates, "place me above a *common bribe.*"[*] Perhaps a seat in the cabinet only could buy Junius. That he had some personal views to future honour and advantage he does not deny, but says, "I can truly affirm, neither are they little in themselves, nor can they by any possible conjecture be collected from my writings."[†] Then he had intelligence from every quarter. If a secret expedition was fitting out, he knew it; if war impended, he anticipated all the visitors of the Orange or Cocoa-tree[‡]. Were any official changes in train, Junius was the first to announce them. Were a nobleman affronted, he was the earliest to denounce it. "That Swinney," says he, "is a wretched, but dangerous fool, to address Lord George Sackville."[§] "Beware of David Garrick. He was sent to pump you, and went directly to Richmond to tell the king I should write no more."[‖] The Corporation of London, the cabals and clubs of the citizens,

---

[*] Let. No. 54, p. 265.    [†] Let. to Wilkes, p. 68.
[‡] Of the latter Gibbon gives the following description:—"That respectable body of which I have the honour of being a member affords every evening a sight truly English. Twenty or thirty, perhaps, of the first men in the kingdom in point of fashion and fortune, supping off little tables, covered with a napkin, in the middle of a coffee-room, upon a bit of cold meat or a sandwich, and drinking a glass of punch. At present we are full of king's counsellors and lords of the bedchamber, who, having jumped into the ministry, make a very singular medley of their old principles and language with their modern ones."—*Journal for November,* 1762.
[§] Private Letter, No. 5.    [‖] Ib., No. 40.

were equally open to him.  Neither were the precincts of the
Palace sacred ; with the secrets of the closet he was acquainted.
and even those of the kitchen did not escape him.  In one
place it is said, " a great personage had need of cordials ; "
in another, that a fit of chagrin had supervened over royalty,
and that it would be met by a " week's diet of potatoes."
Even the business of the printer would appear to have
been better known to Junius than to Woodfall.  " Your
*Veridicus*," says he, " is Mr. Whitworth ; I assure you, I have
not confided in him."*  " Your *Lycurgus* is a Mr. Keut. a
young man of good parts upon town."†  If oppressed by
power, he assures him that money shall not be wanted to
sustain him, and prevent loss.  He cautions Wilkes against
making himself " so cheap, by walking the streets so much.";
Perhaps Junius means it to be inferred that he had descried
the great agitator from his carriage.

Not content with creating an impression of rank and affluence,
and of a familiarity with both court and city, he sought to
clothe himself with the venerableness of age.  As one of the
fruits of his past life he strongly inculcates honesty to Woodfall.
'After long experience in the world," he tells him, "I can assure
you I never knew a rogue who was happy."  Wilkes tries to draw
him to a Mansion-house ball ; offers him tickets, and expresses
the joy he would feel to see him dance with Polly his daughter.
" How happy should I be." says he, " to see my Portia here
dance a graceful minuet with Junius Drutus !  But Junius is
inexorable, and I submit."  Junius replies, " Many thanks for
your obliging offer; but alas! my *age and figure* would do little
credit to my partner."  Would not any one infer that the
writer was an old man ; or, if not advanced in years, beyond
middle life. and somewhat portly ?

Under his circumstances it is but slight reproach to Junius
to have resorted to those illusive arts.  He had great practical
ends in view, which could only be realized by practical means.
Columbus, in quest of the New World, found himself compelled to resort to deceptions; and so too Napoleon, Hannibal,
Mahomet. and other great leaders or misleaders of mankind.  But few have been more triumphant than Junius.
His aims, as stated, were twofold—to give weight and
authority to his writings. and to conceal the writer.  His
success has been extraordinary in both.  His printer was

* Private Letter, No. 6.     † Ib., No. 5.     ‡ Page 73.

awe-struck by a sense of the great unknown with whom
he was in communion, and reverentially sought his guidance
in the discharge of his electoral duties*. The great demo-
gorgon of the city lay prostrate. " I do not mean," says
Wilkes, " to indulge the impertinent curiosity of finding out
the most important secret of our times—the authorship of
Junius. I will not attempt with profane hands to tear the
sacred veil of the sanctuary: I am disposed, with the inhabitants of Attica, to *erect an altar to the unknown god
of our political idolatry*, and will be content to worship
him in clouds and darkness."† To which the god replies,
first gently reproving the lax ethics of his worshipper,
" I find I am treated as other gods usually are by their votaries, with sacrifice and ceremony in abundance, and very little
obedience. The profession of your faith is unexceptionable;
but I am a modest deity, and should be full as well satisfied
with good works and morality.":   Even the sage Dr. Johnson
did not escape the Junius rage. He thought it was Burke's
thunder that rolled over him:—" I should have believed Burke
to be Junius," said he to Boswell, "because I know no man but
Burke who is capable of writing these letters; but Burke *spontaneously* denied it to me."§ Mr. Burke himself was carried off his
feet equally with the great moralist, and poured out the well-
known description already inserted (vol. i. p. 4), of the new
comet that blazed in the political firmament. The myrmidons
of the court, and the legal advisers of the Crown, were not less
astounded, and, according to Lord Campbell, many consultations were held between the Earl of Mansfield and his friends
to consider how "the mighty boar of the forest" could be most
adroitly ensnared in the network of the law. But they were
divided in opinion as to the most advisable course. In consequence the Chief Justice was left to his terrors, and for a long
time he was "afraid at breakfast to look into the *Daily Advertiser*, lest he should find in it some new accusation which he
could neither passively submit to, nor resent without discredit."||
In his extremity his Lordship is considered to have grappled
with his assailant in his own way, and to have entered the lists
against him in the *Public Advertiser* under the disguise of a
fictitious name. " There appeared," says Lord Campbell,

* Letter No. 64, p. 61.     † Letter of Wilkes, p. 83.     ‡ Ib., p. 87.
§ Life of Johnson, vol. iii. p. 402.
|| Lives of the Chief Justices, vol. ii. p. 402.

" in the *Daily Advertiser* [his Lordship's constant mistake for
*Public*] a very able paper signed 'Zeno,' in defence of Lord
Mansfield against all the charges Junius had brought against
him, which was supposed to have been written by Lord Mansfield himself; but it only drew forth a more scurrilous diatribe
from Philo-Junius, and all hope of refuting or punishing him
was abandoned."*

The excitement extended to an humbler sphere, and to
places distant from the metropolis. " Old people have told
me," says Lady Francis, " that we have no idea of the sensation created at the time in remote little towns. The post-
man would call out, as he rode through the streets, ' A letter
from Junius to-day!' and all who took in the *Public Advertiser*
were besieged with requests."

Amidst all this stir and *éclat* it does not greatly excite surprise that both the conjectures of contemporaries, and subsequent inquiries into the identity of Junius, have been so far
astray. It could not possibly be imagined, that letters replete
with so many indications of scholarship and station could
emanate from an ignoble source. Hence the telescopes
of observers swept the field at too great an elevation ; never
seeking the author in a less personage than a distinguished
peer or commoner, or some writer of established renown. This
was precisely the direction which Junius sought, with consummate art, to give to public scrutiny, and which enabled him
for half a century after to walk the earth in his invisible garb,
not only unknown, but unsuspected.

Misled by the fictitious character which Junius established,
the world has shut its eyes to a very palpable mode of narrow-
ing the circle of inquiry. Upon his own showing it has been
already decided that he was neither a lawyer nor a clergyman.
He also, in apparent unconsciousness of the conclusion that
might be drawn from it, raises the veil in another place, and
affords satisfactory evidence that he was not a member of
either house of Parliament. Anxiously and vigilantly he kept
watch to prevent detection† ; but, as Young truly remarks,—

" Man's caution often into danger turns."

---

* Vol. i. p. 421.

† That Junius took great pains to mislead inquirers into his identity is
evident from some of his contradictory statements, in cases where there is
no doubt of the genuineness of the letters ; thus, in Letter 111, vol. ii.
p. 106, he calls himself a Scotchman, and a right Scotus, while in Letter 70,

By referring to a subsequent page (p. 31), it will be seen that
Junius was extremely desirous of being present on the approaching debate on the Falkland Islands, and strenuously
exerted himself that the public might not be excluded.  For
this purpose he despatched a series of paragraphs to Woodfall,
to be successively inserted in his paper, with the aim of
shaming ministers into a compliance with his wishes.  But
why all this paragraphing to obtain open doors, and the admission of strangers into the gallery?  Had he been a member of Parliament he would have had the right of entry; but
that he was not, and sought admission only as one of the
broad public, may be safely inferred.  What a host of claimants are set aside by this consideration?  As elsewhere remarked (p. 35), the Duke of Portland, the Earl of Chesterfield, Earl Shelburne, Lord George Sackville, Mr. Hamilton,
Mr. Burke, Leonidas Glover, Colonel Barré, with sundry
others, could not have been Junius, since all these were members either of the upper or the lower House.

Against such conclusion it has been observed, that the object
of Junius on this as on other occasions may have been to mislead as to his identity.  But the paragraphs were not published under his signature; they were not meant to support
the Junius character; but were circulated as ordinary news to
advance a public object, and not to aid his disguise.  Besides,
it was not a direction in which Junius sought to deceive, his
aim, as already explained, being to augment the influence of
his writings by magnifying the impression of his political importance.

That the reader may at once perceive how few with any
pretensions have escaped suspicion, I subjoin a list of claimants with appendant notes.

| | |
|---|---|
| Colonel Barré, | Earl Shelburne, |
| Hugh Macauley Boyd [1], | Lord Camden, |
| Bishop Butler, | Earl Temple, |
| Lord Chatham, | M. Delolme [2], |
| Lord Chesterfield, | J. Dunning (Lord Ashburton), |

vol. ii. p. 91, and in other places, he manifests his dislike of the Scotch.
Again, in Letter 105, vol. ii. p. 393, he describes himself as a soldier, while
in another Letter he declares, " I am not a soldier."

[1] Preliminary Essay, vol. i. p. 67.
[2] A foreigner, author of an elegantly written Essay on the English

Henry Flood, the Irish orator,
Edmund Burke,
Edward Gibbon, the historian[3]
William Gerard Hamilton,
Charles Lloyd,
John Roberts,

Samuel Dyer[4],
George Grenville and
James Grenville[5],
William Greatrakes[6],
Duke of Portland[7],

---

Constitution, which for many years enjoyed great popularity, and is quoted by Junius. Delolme only arrived in England in the winter Junius began. He is Dr. Busby's hero; and his cause is maintained with considerable ingenuity by the usual appliances of fac-similes, identity of style and sentiment; also by reference to a letter that appeared two days previously in the *Morning Chronicle*, which letter the Doctor avers to have been written by Junius, *alias* by Delolme, and that Junius prevailed on Woodfall to reprint in the *Public Advertiser:* see No. 61 of the Miscellaneous Letters. But the statement proves nothing, except perhaps the industry of Junius, who, despite of his denial of the authorship to Woodfall, may have furnished Mr. William Woodfall with a rough copy in the way of encouragement in his newspaper adventure previous to its appearance in a more finished style in the *Public Advertiser.*

[3] Beyond holding a place it does not appear that Gibbon was greatly enamoured of politics. It was not till 1770 that he tried his powers in English composition, by a pamphlet in reply to Warburton on the Eleusinian Mysteries; and already his mind was absorbed in the noble task that has immortalized him.

[4] Of the claims of the last three named, see vol. I. p. 56.

[5] The brothers Grenville were two of the three sons of Richard Grenville, Esq. George Grenville, the minister, died in 1770. James, who became a Lord of the Treasury and died in 1783, established no claims to Junian honours.

[6] A notable example this of connecting small things with great. Greatrakes, a native of Ireland, died suddenly at Hungerford on his way from Bristol to London, and was buried there, with *stat nominis umbra* inscribed on his gravestone. The industry of Mr. Britton has collected some curious facts to prove that Greatrakes was the amanuensis employed by Junius to copy his letters for the *P. A.*; but it ought first to be shown that Junius employed an amanuensis. If he did, and Greatrakes was his penman, it could hardly give him a claim to the motto of his principal. That was a distinction which, if it has any significance, could be applicable only to the shadow of a shade that wrote the letters, not the copyist of them. Probably an affectation for the same device was the only affinity between them, and, in the case of Greatrakes, referred to the obscure place of his death, not to anything done in his lifetime.

[7] According to Mr. Johnston's interpretation, the entire aim of the Letters was the restoration of the Duke of Portland's estate, part of which had been taken from his Grace in the year 1767 and granted to Sir James Lowther, who had married the daughter of Lord Bute. It was the resumption of a royal grant, on the now exploded legal maxim that no length of possession will

Richard Glover[a],
Sir William Jones,
James Hollis,
General Lee[9],
Laughlin Maclean[10],
Lord George Sackville[11],
Rev. Philip Rosenhagen,
John Wilkes,

John Horne Tooke.
John Kent[12],
Henry Grattan[13],
Daniel Wray[14],
Horace Walpole,
Alexander Wedderburn (Lord Loughborough)[15],

bar the right of the crown, and is understood to have been the result of ministerial manœuvres to strengthen the election interests of the Lonsdale family in Cumberland. The transfer has been severely commented upon in the Letters; and the privation was keenly felt by the Duke of Portland, sufficiently so perhaps to make him a good lawyer, but not a Junius.

[8] The writer mentioned in the last note, who, in his " Letters to a Nobleman," bolsters up the pretensions of the Duke of Portland, treats with supreme contempt the claims of "Leonidas" Glover. Johnston declares that he has no faith in him, though his advocates, as corroborative facts, assert that Mr. Glover " wore a bag, with his wig accurately dressed, and carried a small cocked hat under his arm, before the year 1776, and in this costume constantly walked, in fine weather, from his house in St. James's Street, in Westminster, into the city," the writers thence inferring that he was the "tall gentleman" who threw the letter into Mr. Woodfall's office in Ivy Lane.

[9] At Warsaw pending the letter-writing.

[10] Vide vol. l. p. 77, note.

[11] Afterwards Lord George Germaine; a favourite and courtier of George III., and very unlikely to be his accuser. See also vol. i. p. 81.

[12] Wished to pass for Junius, but only a penny-a-liner, or, according to Almon, a newspaper editor at a weekly stipend.

[13] The suspicion fixed upon the Irish patriot induced Mr. Almon to address to him a letter of inquiry, to which Mr. Grattan, with characteristic manliness, returned the following explicit reply:—

" Sir,—I can frankly assure you that I know nothing of Junius, except that I am not the author. When Junius began I was a boy, and knew nothing of politics or the persons concerned in them.

" I am, Sir, not Junius, but your very good wisher and obedient servant,
" Dublin, November 4, 1805.                " H. GRATTAN."

[14] Many years a deputy-teller of the Exchequer by favour of the Hardwicke family. A good "fellow" at college and in society, and much devoted to letters, especially black. The pleasant biographical anecdotist, Mr. Justice Hardinge, contributed a curious Wray-ana to Nichols's "Illustrations of Literary History;" but the monument Mr. Falconar has sought to raise to his memory, by making Wray Junius, will not bear scrutiny.

[15] Lord Campbell repudiates the notion of Wedderburn being Junius. He and, however, his literary sponsors. Sir Nathaniel Wraxall remarks that "he had long nourished a strong belief that the late chancellor was the author, and that persons of credit had recognised the handwriting to be that of Mrs. Wedderburn, his first wife."

Philip Francis, D.D.[16],          James Wilmot, D.D.[17].

Junius has been a favourite theme of literary exercise, and there is not one of the above thirty-five names on which a book, pamphlet, review, essay, or disquisition has not been written, but almost the whole number are inadmissible under the general class-rules previously established.  As different persons, however, are impressible by different kinds of fact and reasoning, it may be more conclusive, in addition to the specific objections condensed in the accompanying notes, to add some further disqualifications.  Some of the candidates, as Laughlin Maclean, Lord Sackville, and Lord Chesterfield, appear to have possessed a tenacious vitality—have been slain, and buried repeatedly, and again been raised by ingenious operators.  To prevent similar reproductions, I shall, in respect of some leading names, subjoin a few supplemental notices, after which, I apprehend, the field will be cleared of pretenders up to the publication of Woodfall's Junius in 1812.

The Earl of Chatham has been mentioned; that neither he nor Lord Camden was Junius may at once be determined on the authority of the *Chatham Papers* and the facts stated at p. 52, elucidatory of the anxiety of Junius to obtain duplicate proofs from the printer to forward to the former statesman. Moreover, Lord Chatham, though most effective in oratory, was careless in literary composition; inexact, loose, and repetitionary: very unlike Junius, who not only polished his public letters to the highest finish, but never let the most brief or trivial private note escape him unmarked by the hand of a master.

Similar negligence of style is observable in the Earl of Shelburne.  His Lordship was a munificent patron of men of

[16] In the last note handwriting is assumed the cardinal point of proof. Mr. Taylor, in his first attempt to discover Junius, greatly relied on a long array of extracts, from which he concluded certain similarities of style made it probable Dr. Francis was the author of the Letters.  Both style and handwriting appear very uncertain criteria of authorship.  There have been, as the *Athenæum* has remarked, upwards of thirty Juniuses, and in favour of each the "respective patron has adduced similarity of style" in proof of identity.

[17] The late Mr. Beckford, of Fonthill, is said in a conversation reported in the *New Monthly Magazine*, to have given his opinion, that Dr. Wilmot was Junius, but he adduced no coincidences in the life, character, or abilities of the Doctor, who was a convivial divine, to prove identity.  In the sequel it will be shown who was Junius, and, this established, it ignores the claims of the above list of candidates.

letters and cultivated their society; was remarkably well informed on all public questions pertaining to this and other countries; used to select able men, like Dunning and Barré, to represent and enforce his sentiments in the House of Commons; and had special agents abroad for the purpose of forwarding authentic intelligence on the state of foreign affairs; but he was careless of language. Of this his letters in the *Chatham Correspondence* afford proofs; they are short and negligently expressed, manifesting an obvious desire of the writer to despatch what he had to say, in the fewest and readiest words—habits of composition not characteristic of Junius.

But his Lordship disclaimed the distinction, only a week before his death in 1804, on being personally applied to on the subject of Junius by the late Sir Richard Phillips. Sir Richard, according to the account he gave of the interview in the *Monthly Magazine*, told his Lordship, "that many persons had ascribed these letters to him, and that the world at large conceived that at least he was not unacquainted with the author." The Marquis smiled, and said, "No, no; I am not equal to Junius, I could not be the author; but the grounds of secrecy are now so far removed by death and changes of circumstances, that it is unnecessary the author of Junius should be much longer unknown. The world is curious about him, and I could make a very interesting publication on the subject. *I knew Junius, and I knew all about the writing and production of those letters.* But," said he, "look at my condition; I don't think I can live a week—my legs, my strength, tell me so; but the doctors, who always flatter sick men, assure me I am in no immediate danger. They order me into the country, and I am going there. If I live over the summer, which, however, I don't expect, I promise you a very interesting pamphlet about Junius. I will put my name to it. I will set that question at rest for ever." But there must have been misapprehension or inaccuracy in the report of this conversation, since it is doubtful whether Lord Shelburne, then the Marquis of Lansdowne, knew Junius. The present Marquis was appealed to some years later by Sir R. Phillips, and was informed by him that he had never heard Lord Shelburne say that he knew the author. "It is not impossible," his Lordship said, "my father may have been acquainted with the fact, but was perhaps under some obligation to secrecy, as he never made any communication to me upon the subject."—*Monthly Magazine*, July, 1813.

Thinking that in the long interval which had elapsed something further might have occurred to Lord Lansdowne. I reminded the Marquis of his answer to Sir R. Phillips. With his wonted courtesy his Lordship promptly replied, March 25, 1850, as follows :—

"Lord Lansdowne has much pleasure in answering the inquiry contained in a letter which he has received this morning from Mr. Wade, although he is afraid that answer will give him little information or satisfaction. He remembers to have answered a question put to him by the late Sir Richard Phillips, nearly in the terms mentioned by that gentleman ; but, although it was 'not impossible' that his father might have been acquainted with the name of the author of Junius, or known him personally, Lord Lansdowne's *belief is that he was not*, and his conviction is quite clear, at all events, that he was not, as has been sometimes supposed, though without the slightest proof, the author himself."

Upon the whole, the conclusion seems amply established that Lord Shelburne was not Junius; nor is it probable that he knew him.

I should not revert to the evidence against Burke, but from a recent occurrence. Within a few days I have heard a noble Lord, who, some thirty years past, had ably sifted the question. declare emphatically that he was "convinced that the *mind* of Burke was in Junius ; he did not care for the difference observable in their styles. Burke had wonderful powers of composition, and could imitate any style. He might have employed Francis, or any other person, as his amanuensis, or to do the 'conveyancing part;' but he was thoroughly convinced, upon as strong testimony as would convict any one at the Old Bailey, that Burke was the author of the Letters, and that there was no other contemporary of Junius capable of it." All this was doubtless uttered in momentary forgetfulness of his Lordship's masterly array of proofs to the contrary, and shows the need of keeping compact the evidence against Burke, to prevent similar error.

First against Burke are his own three separate denials . in one instance, to Lord Townshend ; next, when asked by Sir William Draper : these may be demurred to, on the plea of an author's admitted right to disavow, if interrogated, writings which he has published anonymously ; but his third denial to Dr. Johnson was not upon interrogatory ; it was spontaneous

c
.

(*ante*, p. xx.); and his standing answer to all who teased him on the subject of the Letters was, " *I could not if I would, and I would not if I could.*" Besides, how could Burke have described Junius in the transports he has done* had he been the author? How could he have depicted him as the bird of " daring flight," who came " souse upon both Houses of Parliament;" who carried off " their royal eagle [the Speaker] in his pounces;" who made " King, Lords, and Commons the sport of his fury;" and then conclude, or rather begin, with not much congruity of metaphor, by describing Junius as " the mighty boar of the forest," that had broke through all the toils of the law? No gentleman could have possibly indulged in such unmeasured praise of his own exploits. But what decisively negatives his complicity, is the fact that Mr. Burke, during the middle and all the latter period of his life, lived on terms of the closest intimacy and friendship with Junius; knew him, esteemed him, and always considered him to be Junius. Proof of this will be adduced in the sequel.

One of the wildest conjectures has been, the ascription of the Letters to the Earl of Chesterfield. An extreme of this pitch might have been passed unnoticed, were it not for the curious illustration it affords of the lengths to which literary ingenuity has been stretched for four-fifths of a century in quest of an author. But how could Chesterfield be the great unknown? That the Earl's talents were of a very superior cast; that they were solid as well as shining, may be unreservedly conceded: but these had become paralysed when the author of the Letters flourished. At the very time Junius was scattering his fiery darts, Chesterfield had sunk into the lowest abyss of misery. Extreme old age, physical maladies that excluded him from society, and the entire frustration of long cherished hopes, had overwhelmed him;—he was entombed in his great house in May Fair. His only son, on whom he had bestowed such anxious teaching in worldly arts, in which he himself excelled, but who was of a nature wholly different, had died; leaving mortifying evidence of a course of life directly the reverse of the paternal precepts. Amidst all these griefs is it likely that his Lordship could be urging onward the impetuous car of Junius? Is it possible that he could be occupied in a task requiring so many physical and intellectual resources, as by some have been thought beyond the

* Vol. i. p. 4.

powers of any single individual? Most assuredly not. Besides, the old Earl died when Junius was in full career*.

Despite of these stubborn facts, there have been and still are writers endeavouring to prove Lord Chesterfield to have been Junius. In 1821 a respectable volume appeared, headed with a motto from Lord Mansfield on the true nature of evidence, and with a specious show of facts, with the title " The Author of Junius discovered in the person of the cele brated Earl of Chesterfield." And at this moment I have before me the first part of a work in the press, apparently intended to be of considerable dimensions, kindly lent me by the author (Mr. Cramp), the object of which is to prove Chesterfield to have been Junius by a comparison of their writings.

The only other candidate upon whom I have remarks to offer in the present section is the celebrated Colonel BARRÉ. In the Colonel there were certainly materials to make a Junius with a fair show of probability, and Mr. Britton has advocated his claims with much ingenuity. Barré was the Danton of his day; an athlete in frame, with a stern, uncompromising countenance. His oratory was somewhat coarse but powerful, and flashed bold sententious truths, like Mirabeau's. His life, which has never been deservedly told †, was full of adventure and heroism. He was one of a group of officers round the gallant Wolfe when he fell on the Plains of Abraham, and was himself dangerously wounded. During Lord North's ministry he was a leading man in Parliament, and delivered his ablest speeches; defending the past conduct and present resistance of the American colonists, and severely reprobating the mistaken course of government. Still Barré was not Junius, though evidently endowed with many of his gifts, and nearly allied to him in political sentiment and party connection. It is not unlikely that he was the author of the Letter addressed in 1760 to "An Honourable Brigadier-General;" which has been twice brought before the public, from supposed resemblance of style, as a production of Junius: once by a correspondent of the *Gentleman's Magazine* in 1817; and again by Mr. Simons, of the library of the British Museum, in 1841. But the negatives against Barré may be soon stated. First, he was a member of Parliament, and did not require

* June 4, 1772, according to Debrett's Peerage.
† Mr. Britton's account of the Colonel, in his *Junius Elucidated*, is the fullest and most original. See Barré's Letters, Appendix, p. 417.

for admission, as Junius did, that the doors should be open to strangers. Secondly, he began his parliamentary life by a bitter personal attack on the Earl of Chatham, a statesman whom Junius always greatly admired. Thirdly, the incidents in the life of Barré do not coincide with the career of Junius. Had Barré been the author, the Bowood* politicians would in all likelihood have known him, and Dunning would have saved Junius from legal blunders. But if Barré was Junius, why should he deny it? What motives could he have for concealment, though, as will be shown hereafter, Junius had imperative ones? Why just come out in 1767, or 1769, and then disappear in 1773, and never be again heard of? Reasons must be given for all these eccentricities.

---

## II. AUTHORSHIP OF JUNIUS IDENTIFIED.

In the history of celebrated individuals, as in the history of nations, there is a fabulous era. Among the ancients a descent from the gods occupied the first pages of a hero's biography, but the moderns are satisfied with terrestrial honours—with tracing a pedigree to William the Conqueror, Charlemagne, or Iwan the Great. The genealogical chapter dismissed, the next is usually devoted to nursery tales of the auspicious omens that hovered over the birth of the future prodigy, or details of the extraordinary juvenile feats that shadowed the after warrior, statesman, or philosopher. As the life advances the wonderful diminishes; its meridian splendour may justly command admiration, but it seldom so far transcends the average of humanity as to leave unmixed impressions of supernatural genius or perfection.

A gradation of a similar kind pertains to the history of Junius. It began in fable, astonished in its midway progress, long perplexed in its inscrutable mystery, but at last all is unravelled, and shown to have been both possible and natural. The fictitious assumptions of Junius were essential to influence public opinion. That he accomplished his purpose triumphantly; that, under so many temptations, he preserved his

* Seat of the Marquis of Lansdowne.

incognito inviolate; that moving actively and conspicuously in society, he constantly eluded tho most eager search after him; and that, after more than half a century of diligent inquiry, there was not a single proximate guess at his identity, are remarkable facts in personal adventure, testifying largely to the extraordinary address and ability of the author. But everything must have an end, and why not the enigma of Junius?

The foundation of the discovery was laid by Woodfall's edition of 1812. Had the public never known any edition of the Letters except that revised by Junius himself, it is probable the author would have remained even unsuspected. But the "Private Letters" Nos. 61 and 62, and the "Miscellaneous Letters" subscribed *Veteran, Scotus,* and *Nemesis* afforded a clue, of which an ingenious inquirer successfully availed himself*. In these letters (No. 110) a name escaped, the name of one likely to be personally interested in the subject of some of the writings of Junius; that person still lived, was an eminent public character, known to possess superior abilities, greater than the world, and those not intimately acquainted with him, gave him credit for. Upon this person Mr. Taylor fixed, dragged him out, and was the first to challenge as the long sought Junius.

All, however, were not satisfied. The proofs were strong, and able judges acquiesced; still doubts were raised, mysteries remained unexplained, and certain superiorities were urged as distinguishing Junius from his assumed representative. The accused himself was silent; he was called upon to answer; he would neither confess nor positively deny the charge, but left the world to make the discovery. In this state the question has remained, and here I take it up, briefly recapitulating the leading points of Mr. Taylor's discovery, and supplying the needful links in the chain of testimony.

In two directions Mr. Taylor fell into error. First, in adopting the entire of the "Miscellaneous Letters" as from the pen of Junius, by which his investigation was embarrassed and he was led to conclusions inconsistent with the integrity of purpose and strict consistency which pervade the authorized letters of the author. Secondly, he fell into one of the snares Junius had adroitly laid for inquirers. Misled by one of those well-contrived feints that were meant to mislead, Mr.

* Mr. Taylor, in his *Junius Identified.*

Taylor inferred that Junius must be "an old man," or well stricken in years, and under this impression fastened on the father in lieu of the son*. Philip Francis, D.D., was not without weighty claims to the authorship. He was a classical scholar, celebrated for masterly translations of Horace and Demosthenes, lived on intimate terms with persons of rank, especially statesmen, was himself the author of several political pamphlets, and in his writings openly cherished liberal sentiments. Hence, in the first instance, he was naturally thought to be a competent Junius, and the younger Francis, whom Mr. Taylor had mistakenly concluded to be a minor, was supposed to have aided his father, by procuring intelligence, copying the Letters for the press, and doing perhaps "the conveyancing part" with Woodfall. But on discovering Mr. Francis to be ten years older than he had at first been led to believe, Mr. Taylor revised his calculations, and found, in the antecedents of his life, in his apt scholarship and superior talents, his position in the War Office, knowledge of public characters, and varied official experience, that he was adequate to fulfil every condition of the Junius problem; and this was further confirmed by his remarkable character and personal history. Under these new impressions Mr. Taylor resumed his investigation, and in the end relinquished the father to concentrate his labours on the son.

The proofs which Mr. Taylor has adduced to identify Sir Philip Francis with Junius are of three kinds †: first, the correspondence of dates and incidents in the life of Sir Philip, with the dates and incidents in the publication of the Letters ; secondly, the correspondence between the style, sentiment, and ability of the Letters, with the known writings and speeches of Sir Philip Francis; thirdly, the resemblance between the handwriting of Junius and Francis.

Sir Philip Francis was born in Dublin, in 1740. His father, Dr. Francis, has been adverted to as well known in the learned world, and among the great. His grandfather was Dean of Lismore, in Ireland. In 1750, Sir Philip came to England. In 1753 he was placed at St. Paul's School, and

* "A Discovery of the Author of the Letters of Junius." Lond. 1813. This first attempt of Mr. Taylor preceded the publication of *Junius Identified* by three years.

† "The Identity of Junius with a Distinguished Living Character established." Second edition. Lond. 1818.

he and Philip Rosenhagen, who was once thought to be Junius, were considered by Dr. Thicknesse. the master, his cleverest pupils. Mr. H. Woodfall, afterwards the printer of the Letters, was at the school at the same time. At this early period, Lady Francis relates that young Francis used to associate with men at the "table d' hote at Slaughter's Coffeehouse, when his father, who was Lord Holland's chaplain, used to dine out." In 1750 Lord Holland gave young Francis a place in the Secretary of State's office. The Earl of Chatham, who succeeded Lord Holland, continued to encourage him, and made him his Latin Secretary. Through this patronage he was appointed in 1758 secretary to General Bligh, and was present at the capture of Cherbourg. In 1760, by the same recommendation, he was appointed secretary to the Earl of Kinnoul, ambassador to Lisbon, and between this year and 1763 it is likely he paid the visit to the court of Louis XV. mentioned by Lady Francis *. In 1763, Lord Mendip, then Secretary at War, appointed him to a considerable post in the War Office, which he resigned in the beginning of 1772, in consequence of a difference with Lord Barrington, by whom he thought himself injured, his Lordship having appointed Mr. Chamier, instead of himself, Deputy Secretary at War. The greatest part of 1772 Mr. Francis spent in travelling on the Continent; he visited Rome, and had a long audience of the Pope, of which he sent a curious account to his friend, Dr. Campbell, and which is among the manuscripts of Sir Philip, in possession of his grandson. It would seem that Lord Barrington considered Mr. Francis to have been wronged, as his Lordship, in about half a year after his return to England, recommended him to Lord North as a fit person to be a member of the government of Bengal. In the month of June, 1773, Mr. Francis left England in company with General Clavering and Colonel Monson, the two other gentlemen who had been named in the Act of Parliament, to co-operate in the future government of India.

Farther than this period it is not essential at present to follow the history of Sir Philip Francis. The first authentic public letter of Junius is dated January 21, 1769, and his first private note to Woodfall, April 20, 1769. His last

* Junius alludes, in Letter 21, p. 175, to his presence in Paris at the burning of the Jesuitical books, August, 1761.

public letter, under the signature " Junius," is dated January
21, 1772, and his last miscellaneous letter, under the signature of " Nemesis," is dated May 12, 1772. The last private
note Junius addressed to Woodfall is dated January 19,
1773. He addressed no letter to Wilkes of a later date
than November 7, 1771. So that Sir P. Francis was passing
from his twenty-ninth to his thirty-second year during the
publication of all the Letters that are authentically avowed
or known to be by Junius.

In respect of age, therefore, I think no valid ground exists
for doubting the capabilities of Sir P. Francis to enact the
part of Junius. He was four years older than Pitt, when
he became Chancellor of the Exchequer and Prime Minister
of England. Napoleon, before he reached his twenty-ninth
year, had conquered Italy, and evinced administrative powers,
in the organization of the civil government of the Italian
Peninsula, fully equal, if not superior, to any he displayed in
after life. For political writing Francis had attained that
period of life when ambitious hopes and intellectual vigour
are usually the most efficient, provided, as was peculiarly the
case with him, there had been previous educational culture,
attention to public affairs, official experience, and general
intercourse with the world.

The circumstances which led Mr. Taylor to suspect Sir
Philip Francis, his reference to him in consequence, and Sir
Philip's reply, I shall let Mr. Taylor narrate.—

" Nearly at the end of the third volume I was struck with the unparalleled zeal which the writer displayed in the cause of two individuals belonging to the War Office. It appeared that Mr. D'Oyley, a clerk in that establishment, had a short time before been deprived of his situation, through the
interference of Lord Barrington ; and the writer of the letter to which I
allude desires Mr. Woodfall to inform the public, ' that the worthy Lord
Barrington, not contented with having driven Mr. D'Oyley out of the War
Office, had at last contrived to expel Mr. Francis.' * The Editor states in a
note, that this was the present Sir Philip Francis. Surprised at the occurrence of an intervention so extraordinary, I considered what grounds there
might be for thinking that either of the offended persons could have been the
writer ; or whether any one of their immediate relatives had thus volunteered
himself to advocate their cause. The political and literary character of Sir
Philip Francis caused my suspicions to fall on him. Upon reference to a
memoir of his life in the Public Characters, I saw sufficient evidence, as I
thought, to confirm my conjecture. The impression made by the facts there
related was strengthened by a comparison of style. From these materials I

* Miscellaneous Letters, No. 110, p. 405; signature, Veteran.

drew up my statement, and in agreement with my own opinion called it a Discovery of the Author of the Letters.

"Before it went to press I requested a friend to call on Sir Philip Francis, and informed him, that if he had the slightest objection to have his name connected with the investigation he might rely on the total suppression of the work. I am satisfied this communication was made in a way which must have convinced Sir Philip that it proceeded solely from respect to his feelings, and that what was proposed would be performed. It was, perhaps, due to him that not a step should be taken without his permission; nor could his refusal betray him into an implied admission of the truth of the charge. A simple negative would leave it still undetermined whether his aversion proceeded from a dread of the disclosure, or from a tender respect for his father's memory, or from a natural dislike to that free discussion of his own character and qualifications which the question of necessity required. His reply was such as might be expected :—' You are quite at liberty to print whatever you think proper, providing nothing scandalous be said respecting my private character.'

"Soon after the appearance of the pamphlet, the editor of the *Monthly Magazine*, intending to notice it in that work, wrote to Sir Philip Francis, to ask him whether the conjecture was correct. The editor did not recollect the distinction drawn by that strict moralist, Dr. Johnson, between spontaneous and extorted acknowledgments ; or, probably, he would not have taken the trouble to make this application :—

"'Boswell.—Suppose the person who wrote Junius were asked whether he was the author, might he deny it?

"'Johnson.—I don't know what to say to this. If you were *sure* that he wrote Junius, would you, if he denied it, think as well of him afterwards? Yet it may be urged, that what a man has no right to ask, you may refuse to communicate ; and there is no other effectual mode of preserving a secret, and an important secret, the discovery of which may be very hurtful to you, but a *flat denial* ; for if you are silent, or hesitate, or *evade*, it will be held equivalent to a confession. But stay, Sir, here is another case. Supposing the author had told me confidentially that he had written Junius, and I were asked if he had, I should hold myself at liberty to deny it, as being under a previous promise, express or implied, to conceal it. Now, what I ought to do for the author, may I not do for myself?' *

"Had the editor of the *Monthly Magazine* looked for an *affirmative* to his question, he should have recollected that he was not addressing one

"'Who would be wooed, and not unsought be won,'

to make the confession. Some obstacles, it might have been supposed, were still in the way of such an admission, or as soon as he was publicly affirmed to be the author, Sir Philip Francis would have owned the fact, without waiting for the decent opportunity afforded by the ingenious editor. If, on the other hand, a direct contradiction was contemplated, the reasoning of Dr. Johnson shows that not much faith was due to that. Of an evasive answer, it seems that no suspicion was entertained : the editor thought, 'good easy man, full surely,' that either *yes* or *no* would be the frank reply, and in his own opinion he obtained the latter.

"When Junius wished to disavow a letter published under his name, and

* Boswell's Life of Johnson, iv. 344.

*actually written by himself*, he would not suffer the printer flatly to deny its authenticity, but he instructed him to get rid of it by a side wind. He desired Woodfall to 'recall' the letter, but in such equivocal terms as would effect the purpose without directly committing the integrity of the writer. 'Suppose you were to say—We have some reason to suspect that the last letter signed Junius, in this paper, was not written by the real Junius, though the observation escaped us at the time.—Or, if you can hit off anything yourself *more plausible*, you will much oblige me, *but without a positive assertion.*'* Woodfall took the hint, and deprived that letter of its legitimacy by the following note:—'We have some reason to suspect that the last letter signed Junius, inserted in this paper of Thursday last, was not written by the real Junius, though we imagine it to have been sent by some one of his waggish friends, who has taken great pains to write in a manner similar to that of Junius, which observation escaped us at that time. The printer takes the liberty to hint that it will not do a second time.'†

"Assuming, for the sake of argument, that Sir Philip Francis was the author of the Letters, it would follow that, were he placed in the same dilemma in which Junius on this occasion found himself, his conduct would, in all likelihood, be similar to that which Junius adopted. Unwilling to acknowledge, yet unable to deny, he would doubtless seek shelter in ambiguous terms. He would strive to convey that meaning by the spirit, which in strictness would not follow from the letter, of his reply. He would disclaim the thing hypothetically. 'There is much virtue in an *if*.' It would be done, we may be sure, in a *plausible* manner, *but without a positive assertion*.

"Let it be observed, that it is only the author of the Letters of Junius who can be expected to act in this manner. No other man is bound by the precedent; nor have we a right to suppose that any man but the real author would hesitate to give a plain and unequivocal answer to the question, *Are you Junius?*

"It suits neither my purpose nor my inclination, to give a wrong colouring to this singular affair. The following extract from the *Monthly Magazine* will show the reader the exact nature of the question put to Sir Philip Francis, and in what guarded terms he couched his reply.

"Speaking of the pamphlet which contains the charge, 'We confess,' says the editor of the Magazine, 'we were at first startled by this hypothesis, from its temerity; because, if not true, Sir Philip Francis would be able, by a word, to disprove it; and it could not be supposed that so much labour and expense would be hazarded except on indubitable grounds. To be able, therefore, to render this article as conclusive as possible, we addressed Sir Philip Francis on the subject, in the way the least likely to render the inquiry offensive, and in reply received the following epistle, which we insert at length, in justice to Sir Philip and the public:—

"'Sir,—The great civility of your letter induces me to answer it, which, with reference merely to its subject matter, I should have declined. Whether you will assist in giving currency to a silly malignant falsehood is a question for your own discretion. To me it is a matter of perfect indifference.

"'I am, Sir,

"'Yours, &c.

"'To the Editor of the *Monthly Magazine*.'        "'P. FRANCIS.'

* Private Letter, No. 8, p. 22.    † Miscellaneous Letter, Note, post, p. 275.

"I need not ask the reader whether this letter is evasive or not. He will, perhaps, wonder how any one can have been misled by it for a moment. The editor, however, with a simplicity that does him honour, did not perceive the futility of this pretended disavowal, though he had just stated, properly enough, that if the hypothesis were 'not true, Sir Philip Francis would be able, by a word, to disprove it.' It certainly is not so disproved, and we are therefore authorized to conclude that it could not fairly be disputed. No man who had it in his power to give a simple negative to such a question would have had recourse to an innendo. The only surprising part of the transaction is, that any answer should have been returned by one who knew he could not send a better. But perhaps Sir Philip had no suspicion that it would be printed verbatim in the *Monthly Magazine*\*. He must have thought the editor of that publication would state the denial in his own way, and that if an impression was made on his mind in the first instance, the public would be convinced at second hand."

The patrician dignity in which Junius had masked himself had till now entirely screened Sir P. Francis from suspicion, but Woodfall's edition immediately brought into juxtaposition the important fact, that a distinguished living individual was known to have held a subordinate place in the War Office, and to have withdrawn from it at the time and in the manner Junius describes. What could be more natural than the precise inference that Mr. Taylor drew from this junction of occurrences?

As to the reply of Sir Philip, it is what might be expected from his character and anonymous position. If he were Junius, he was free to deny it if asked, agreeably with the conventional canon in such cases; but if he were *not* Junius he was not free to return such an equivocal answer as might lead the world to believe him such, or even have a doubt on the subject. This would have been directly and unfairly misleading for a personal object, and is wholly inconsistent with the integrity which in Sir Philip has never been impugned. But upon the import of his reply to the editor of the *Monthly Magazine*, I can state what Mr. Taylor was unable to do, namely, the construction Sir Francis himself put upon it. He explained to Lady Francis that his answer to Sir Richard Phillips "was no denial, and fools only could take it for one." His answers to other inquirers were of similar tendency, sometimes impatient and angry even to fierceness, but always evasive. To one he said, " I have pleaded not guilty, and if any one after that chooses to call me scoundrel, he is welcome." To another, who said, " I 'd

\* *Monthly Magazine*, July, 1813.

fain put a question to you," he exclaimed, " You had better
not, you may get an answer you won't like." To a third,
" Oh, they know I am an old man, and can't fight." Lady
Francis says, " He was very anxious to avoid either assent or
denial, lest he might implicate truth or honour." *

The personal movements of Sir Philip Francis coincide
exactly with the appearances and disappearances of Junius, of
which any one may satisfy himself by comparing the dates of
the Letters with the chronological summary previously given.
From 1763 to 1772 Sir Philip was in the War Office, and
must have resided in or near London ; and it is during this
period that all the Letters ascribed to Junius were published.
In Veteran's letter, written by Junius, and dated March 23,
1772, the expulsion of Mr. Francis from the War Office is
announced ; from this date till May 4, Mr. Woodfall received no communication from Junius. Coincident with this
interval is the fact, that Dr. Francis was then ill at Bath,
and it is likely that Sir Philip went to see him before going
abroad. All the subsequent communications of Junius, both
to the public and Woodfall, were concluded early in May, the
last on the 12th, and from this date the *Public Advertiser*
contained no more attacks on Bradshaw or Chamier, and even
Lord Barrington is seldom mentioned. The next communication he received from Junius was in January of the following year, and from that time Woodfall heard no more of his
correspondent. With this suspension Sir Philip's tour on the
Continent exactly tallies. He is supposed to have returned
either at the end of 1772 or beginning of 1773, and the last
letter the printer ever received from Junius is dated January
19, 1773. From this time Junius finally disappeared.
After returning from the Continent it is probable the attentions of Francis were again directed to his father's illness,
Dr. Francis dying at Bath, March 5, 1773. In June following, Mr. Francis received from Lord North, on the recommendation of Lord Barrington, as already stated, his appointment to the Supreme Council of Calcutta, and immediately
sailed for India.

The most sceptical person cannot fail to be struck by
these coincidences. Just as Francis moves Junius moves,
like substance and shadow. If Francis is in the country,

* Lady Francis's letter to Lord Campbell : Lives of the Chancellors,
vol. vi. p. 344.

Junius is away; if Francis is abroad, Junius is not heard of till his return. If Francis is aggrieved by abrupt dismissal from office, Junius suffers, and pours out the vials of his wrath against all the offending parties. If Francis finally disappears from the scene by removal to another hemisphere, Junius writes no more. The Siamese twins were not more closely conjoined, and if Junius and Francis were not identical, it seems a fair inference that they were allied by some inseparable tie.

Other correspondences between them may be traced. Junius evinces an intimate acquaintance with military transactions and the business of the War Office. The affair of General Gansel * is so minutely described and dwelt upon, that it might be inferred to have past under his own eyes. But what is most observable of him is his extreme dislike of certain officials in this department, comparatively much below the ordinary objects of his attacks, especially of Mr. Bradshaw and Mr. Chamier, both of whom he assails in terms indicative of considerable personal animosity. On the former person, in one place †, he particularly dwells, remarking that Bradshaw was too " cunning to trust to Irish security;" and traces his history from the time he was "clerk to a contractor for forage," till he found himself enabled to take the great house in Lincoln's Inn Fields, where Lord Chancellor Worthington had lived. In another place ‡ he is called the Duke of Grafton's "cream-coloured parasite;" and in Letters signed Domitian and Veteran he is familiarly mentioned as "Tommy Bradshaw," and tho "cream-coloured Mercury," whose "sister, Miss Polly, like the moon, lives upon the light of her brother's countenance, and robs him of no small part of his lustre." Against Mr. Chamier the fire of scorn is so bitter and incessant, that nothing less than personal hate and jealousy seem capable of producing it. He is termed "Little Shammy," the "wonderful Girgashite, a tight, active little fellow, that would wrangle for an eighth as if born in Jerusalem." A scene is figured between Lord Barrington, his patron, and a general officer, in which every possible ridicule is thrown upon Chamier. Among other opprobrious epithets ho is stigmatized as a "little grovelling broker," "little three per cents. reduced," "a mere scrip of a secretary," "an omnium of all that's genteel."§ Four

* Letter No. 30, vol. i. p. 239.     † Letter 36, and note, vol. i. p. 275.
‡ Letter 57.                         § Miscellaneous Letters, No. 105.

letters he addressed to Lord Barrington in the most abusive
tone of invective, in consequence of Chamier's promotion; and
it appears that his relationship with Bradshaw formed the
chief ground of his attack upon the latter.

To these ignoble feuds Junius did not, for obvious
reasons, condescend under the signature that had become
famous. First, Junius was a name, as he remarks in one
place, that " must be kept up." Secondly, had it been
known that Junius, Veteran, and Nemesis were all the same
writer, it might have fixed attention on the War Office as
the ambush whence the envenomed missiles were cast, and
where Junius himself lurked, and who might really be one
of the clerks in the War Department, mortified, perhaps, by
recent changes. Junius, therefore, had urgent motives to
prevent his identification with the authorship of the War-
Office letters, and hence his strict injunction to Woodfall to
keep the author a secret*; that is, keep the secret that Junius, Veteran, and Nemesis are the same writer. That such
was the case, and that Mr. Francis was implicated in it; that
he, in fact, was Junius, would seem probable, from what has
been previously extracted, but especially from the letter dated
March 23, 1772, in which he is distinctly named †.

But the War Office is not the only department in which
Junius evinced peculiar interest. With the transactions of
the Foreign Office he appears also to have been familiar,
from various passages in his public and private correspondence. Thus in his 23rd Letter he particularly refers to the
peace negotiation of 1763, and to the " callous pride," but
" English stuff," of Lord Egremont, and to the conduct of
the Duke of Bedford. In reference to the latter, he says,
in a private note, that, he " can threaten him privately with
such a storm as would make him tremble in his grave."‡
Now Sir Philip Francis was appointed a clerk in the Foreign
Office in 1756, and did not leave it for the War Department
till 1763; and it was during the latter part of this period that
Lord Egremont was Foreign Secretary, and the Duke of Bedford negotiated the peace of 1763.

Junius always shows great regard and much forbearance
towards the family of Lord Holland, even when most devoted
to Lord Chatham, their powerful adversary. In one place
he says, " I wish Lord Holland may acquit himself with

* Priv. Letter No. 62, p. 60.   † Miscell. Letters, No. 110.   ‡ No. 10, p. 28.

honour." In another: " I designedly spare Lord Holland."
Such forbearance agrees well with the relation in which Sir P.
Francis stood towards the Fox family. His father was Lord
Holland's chaplain, and also tutor to his second son, Charles
James ; to his Lordship Sir Philip owed his first official
appointment, and to the end of his life maintained friendly in-
timacies with Holland House. Junius seems always, by numberless proofs, to have had a singular personal kindness for, and
confidence in, Mr. Woodfall, and none at all for the other pub-
lishers through whom, under various signatures, he addressed
the country. " The spirit of your letter," says he to Woodfall, " convinces me that you are a much better writer than
most of those whose works you publish." Referring to his trial,
he says, " Let me know what expense falls particularly on yourself, for I understand you are engaged with other proprietors ;
some way or other you shall be reimbursed." Now, it appears
from what has been stated, that Woodfall had been a schoolfellow of Sir Philip, and that they were on friendly terms
through life, though they seldom met. Junius on one occasion
appeared to be apprehensive that the printer had found him
out, and he entreats him to be candid, and say " whether he
knew or suspected him."

There is reason to believe that Junius was known to Garrick.
He expresses himself much alarmed, by the exaggerated impression he had formed of the pryings of the latter*, and was afraid
lest Woodfall might have told him where the Letters were sent,
which he desires him to change. He writes a note to be sent
to Garrick, with the view of intimidating him, and to prevent him from meddling and endeavouring to trace the secret ;
and he desires Woodfall to copy it in his own hand. Such
extreme nervousness, bordering on terror, is easily accounted
for supposing Junius and Francis to be identical. Dr. Francis
was on intimate terms with Garrick, and dedicated his play
of " Eugenia" to him ; and most likely the younger Francis
was familiarly known to Garrick, and perhaps too his handwriting.

From several parts of the correspondence with Woodfall,
it is likely Junius frequently delivered the letters himself.
When he employed another hand, we may be well assured it
was that of a porter, or other ordinary messenger, as was
ascertained in one instance by Wilkes, who examined the
person, and learnt that he had received the packet from a

* Vide Private Letters, pp. 43 and 44.

gentleman. That he should entrust anybody with his secret for the mere purpose of conveying the Letters, appears highly improbable; and to have given a packet for Woodfall to a friend to carry would have been telling him the whole. Now, it appears from a statement already inserted, that Mr. Jackson once saw a "tall gentleman, dressed in a light coat, with bag and sword,"* thrown into Mr. Woodfall's office a Letter of Junius's, and that he followed the bearer, who drove off in a hackney coach. The account given by Mr. Jackson answers very well to the portrait preserved of the person of Sir P. Francis, and to descriptions I have heard of his person from gentlemen who knew him.

Besides these coincidences of personal appearance, of the history of Francis, and the publication of the Letters, with the other direct identifications, an important chain of corroborative testimony is derived from the fact that neither Junius nor Sir P. Francis was in parliament. Both, however, frequented the gallery of the House of Commons in 1770 and 1771, and both took notes of the same speeches at the same time and in the same words. It is next to impossible to account for such singular correspondences, except by concluding that the two were one and the same person. The most striking proof of this conformity is contained in the speech of Lord Chatham, at the opening of the session in January, 1770; this speech was reported by Sir P. Francis, who communicated it first to Almon, who published it in 1791, in his Life of Lord Chatham, and then to Hansard's Parliamentary History†. The publisher of the latter work informed Mr. Taylor that he received the speech from Sir Philip, who was present at the debate. Now, a comparison of the reported speech with some of Junius's Letters proves that either Junius must have heard the speech and taken notes of it, or received notes from somebody who was present; and not only so, but that the notes which he took or received were nearly the same with those taken by Sir P. Francis. The following are examples of coincidence:—

*Sir P. Francis's Report.*—"That on this principle he had himself advised a measure which he knew was not strictly legal; but he had recommended

---

* Preliminary Essay, vol. I. p. 24.
† Vol. xvi. p. 647. In a note the editor (the late Mr. Wright) says:—
"This important debate was taken by a gentleman who afterwards made a distinguished figure in the House of Commons, and by him it has been obligingly revised for this work." [1813.]

it as a measure of necessity, to save a starving people from famine, and had
submitted to the judgment of his country."
*Junius* (vol. i. p. 419).—"Instead of insisting that the proclamation was
legal, he (Lord Camden) should have said, 'My Lords, I know the proclamation was illegal, but I advised it because it was indispensably necessary
to save the kingdom from famine; and I submit myself to the justice and
mercy of my country.'"
*Sir P. Francis's Report.*—"He owned his natural partiality to America,
and was inclined to make allowance even for those excesses. That they
ought to be treated with tenderness; for in his sense they were ebullitions
of liberty which broke out upon the skin, and were a sign, if not of perfect
health, at least of a vigorous constitution, and must not be driven in too suddenly, lest they should strike to the heart."
*Junius* (vol. i. p. 302).—"No man regards an eruption upon the surface
when the noble parts are invaded and he feels a mortification approaching to
his heart."
*Sir P. Francis's Report.*—"That the Americans had purchased their
liberty at a dear rate, since they had quitted their native country, and gone
in search of freedom to a desert."
*Junius* (vol. i. p. 264).—"They left their native land in search of freedom,
and found it in a desert."

We have the distinct avowal of Sir P. Francis, that he
attended the debates and heard Lord Chatham. In his
pamphlet on the Paper Currency, are these remarkable
words:—"Let the war take its course, or, as I *heard Lord
Chatham declare* in the House of Lords, 'LET DISCORD PRE-
VAIL FOR EVER!'" That Junius also attended them may be
inferred from his own statement :—"The following quotation,"
says he, "from a speech delivered by Lord Chatham, on the
14th of December, is *taken with exactness.*" * Upon this
evidence it seems unnecessary to dwell : all is easily reconciled by supposing Junius and Francis to be one and the same,
but everything inexplicable on a contrary supposition.
The agreement and consistency in the person of any
other claimant are in no instance so complete as that which
can be traced between Francis and Junius; even in words and
peculiar phrases they coincide. Thus, "false fact," "I am
a plain man," "simplicity of common sense," frequently
occur in both. Both in Junius's and Sir P. Francis's private
notes this resemblance is observable. I subjoin parallel
instances :—

*Sir P. Francis.*—"*Pray* never mind anything I say. I slave myself to
death, and write and speak on instant impressions; so I am very sorry if I
have offended you."—*Junius Identified.*

---

* For the remainder of the quotation, see p. 324.

d

*Junius.*—"*Pray* tell me whether George Onslow means to keep his word with you;" and ends, "*and so* I wish you good night."—*Note to Woodfall*, vol. ii. p. 7.

*Sir P. Francis to Mr. Burke*, Feb. 19, 1790.—"I wish you were at the devil for giving me all this trouble; *and so* farewell!"

*Sir P. Francis*, August 20, 1804.—"My present intention is to visit you about the 10th of next month, or perhaps a little sooner; *and so*, dear children, farewell."—*Chatham Correspondence*, vol. iv. fac-simile No. 35.

Certain peculiarities have been remarked in spelling, which occur in both Junius and Francis; and neither of them has any such peculiarity that is not common to both. Of this class of confirmations, with other minor ones, the subjoined summary has been given by Lord Brougham in his able analytical review of Mr Taylor's work [*].

"Thus, they both write 'practise' with an *s*; 'completly,' instead of 'completely;' 'ingross,' 'intire,' 'intrust,' and many other such words, which are usually begun with an *e*; 'endeavor,' without an *u*; 'sixteen,' with a *k*, and several others. There may not be much in any of these instances taken singly; but when we find that *all* the peculiarities that belong to either writer are common to both, it is impossible not to receive them as ingredients in the mass of evidence.

"It is stated by a person who examined, with Wilkes, the arm and folding of the letters received by him, that they both agreed in 'thinking they could see marks of the writer's habit of folding and directing official letters.'

"Last of all, a careful examination has been instituted of the handwriting of Junius; and the specimens published by Woodfall have been diligently compared with letters of Sir Philip Francis. Those of Junius are known to be all written in a feigned hand; but its general character agrees well with Sir Philip's. Wherever, in the hurry of writing (for example, where a word is interlined), the natural hand, or something near it, breaks out, the resemblance is more complete, and certain peculiarities, preserved in the feigned hand, occur also in Sir Philip's. We cannot follow the comparison through its minute details; but we are confident that it must go far towards satisfying those whom the rest of the argument may have failed to convince. Some of the more remarkable coincidences are as follows:—

"When Sir Philip Francis signs with his initials, he draws a short strong line above and below them. The very same lines are uniformly drawn under and over the initials with which Junius signs his private letters to Woodfall. In correcting the press they both use, instead of the ordinary sign of deletion, a different and very peculiar sign, exactly the same in both. They both place the asterisk, or star of reference to a foot-note, at the *beginning*, and not at the *end* of the passage to which it belongs—contrary to what may be termed the invariable usage of other writers. They both write the words *you* and *yours*, in all cases, with a large *Y*, the form of which is strikingly alike in both authors. They also use a half large *e* at the beginning of a word, of a peculiar and characteristic formation. Their ciphers or numerals are all formed exactly on the same plan; as are most of their compound letters. Instead of a round dot over the *i*, they both invariably use an oblique stroke, sloping in the opposite direction to that of the general writing; and they mark their quotations, not by inverted commas, but by short perpendicular lines. They are both uniformly correct and systematic in the punctuation of their MS. Both write a distinct little a over '&c.', and connect words divided at the end of a line, not by a hyphen, but a colon, which is repeated, contrary to general usage, at the beginning of the second line as well as the end of the first."

Since the above was written, the evidence derived from handwriting, and the comparison of Sir P. Francis's ordinary hand, which was a remarkably fine one, with the studiously feigned hand of Junius, has been singularly strengthened by a late discovery. Lord Brougham states, in his "Lives of British Statesmen," that the late Mr. Daniel Giles obtained possession of a copy of verses addressed to his sister by Sir P. Francis, with a letter written in a feigned hand. Upon comparing this feigned hand with the facsimiles published by Woodfall, and one of which is affixed to the first volume, the two were found to tally accurately *.

With so many minute coincidences, the issue seems nearly wound up, and it is likely a judge in the summing up. in an ordinary trial, would be stopped at this stage by the jury declaring that they had heard enough, and were agreed upon their verdict. One eminent judge of the Court of Common Pleas, Sir Vicary Gibbs, affirmed, after the perusal of Mr. Taylor's book, that if the case had been argued before him as a judge in a trial for libel, he should have directed the jury to find Sir Philip Francis guilty. In the able review just quoted, Lord Brougham says, "We are half inclined to think, however, that the real author is at last detected."—"That it proves Sir Philip to be Junius we will not affirm; but this we can safely assert, that it accumulates such a mass of circumstantial evidence that it renders it extremely difficult to believe *he is not;* and that, if so many coincidences shall be found to have misled us in this case, our faith in all conclusions drawn from proofs of a similar kind may henceforth be shaken." But the case may be strengthened by further proofs; and after first disposing of certain objections to the foregoing identification, I shall adduce more recent testimony, and so strong that the writer of the cautiously-worded opinion just given will be constrained, I suspect, to admit that the issue is no longer in doubt, and that it is as certain Sir Philip Francis was Junius as anything human can be.

* I am enabled to add a little to the facts communicated by Lord Brougham. The verses Sir Philip addressed to Mr. Giles's sister are written

## III. REPLY TO OBJECTIONS.

It is the nature of truth to be consistent; every fresh discovery and more searching inquiry tend to confirm her immutable relations. After Sir P. Francis had been fixed upon, each succeeding step in the investigation helped to confirm the selection, till at length the cumulative proofs reached the extreme limit of circumstantial testimony. But since the appearance of Mr. Taylor's book, and Lord Brougham's review of it, there have been many revelations, all corroborative, and which, to complete the demonstration, it is essential I should bring under the reader's notice. Before I do this it will be best, in this section, to dispose, more definitively than has yet been done, of certain objections.

For instance, it has been urged *, that the greater part of the evidence is consistent with the idea that Sir Philip Francis was merely the amanuensis of Junius. The reasons against this construction are so obvious, that a glance at them will suffice. If Sir Philip had been only the copyist, how did it happen that the life and death of Junius, the commencement and close of the publication of the Letters, were wholly dependent on the movements of so subordinate an auxiliary? When Sir Philip was in the country, or travelling on the Continent, the Letters stopped; and after Sir Philip sailed for India Junius was no more heard of. How was this? Could not Junius compose because his amanuensis was absent? Was no copyist for the printer to be found except Francis? Had Junius been a person distinct from Sir Philip, and died, or gone abroad, the employment of his transcriber might have ceased; but that Junius should be stopped in his composition by the loss of his mechanical co-operative is as unlikely as that he should for ever cease to write because his pen wanted mending.

It appears most probable, from many facts already stated, that the composer of the Letters, their transcriber, and the bearer of them to the printer, were one and the same person. It is hardly possible on any other supposition to ac-

in his natural hand, but the address on the envelope, which is in the possession of my informant, Mr. H. R. Francis, is in Sir Philip's feigned hand. The subject of the verses is different, but the measure is similar to that of the verses referred to, vol. i. p. 152.

* Barker's Letters on Junius, p. 112.

count for concealment being so well preserved, and it agrees, too, with the declaration of Junius, that he was the "sole depositary of his own secret." For answering these different conditions Sir P. Francis, in the obscurity of the War Office, was aptly situated, not only for effectually masking the authorship, but for personally executing many of the active duties with which it would be unavoidably connected. A clerk only, he was not likely to be generally known, and this enabled him, without fear of discovery, to attend parliamentary debates, collect intelligence, deliver and call for letters, and transact other business with anybody, except Mr. Woodfall. Hence Junius instructs the printer, if he has anything for him, to leave it at the New Exchange Coffee-house in the Strand, or at any other coffee-house west of Temple Bar, "where it is absolutely impossible I should be known."* Francis might safely do this; he might call for any packet, and not be known by the waiters; but could Lord George Sackville, Colonel Barré, or other public character of eminence that has been fixed upon as Junius have done it? Certainly not; any more than Lord John Russell or Sir Robert Peel could appear at the Crown and Anchor or any other public tavern without detection.

Akin to the conjecture that Sir Philip Francis was only the amanuensis is the query, was Sir Philip the only person concerned in the production of the Letters? At all events he appears to have been the principal, since the others were governed entirely by his movements—began, proceeded, and finished with him. No doubt, like other political writers, he sought aid from books, newspapers, and individual communications. What his sources of intelligence were, I shall soon explain: they were peculiar and abundant, and quite adequate to the production of the Letters. But, to meet the question from internal evidence only, it may be remarked that the sentiments and style of Junius have been proved to be those of Francis; they pervade every letter to such an extent that no doubt can exist that a portion of them, at least, were derived from him; and, since there are in none of the genuine Letters any peculiarities, either of thought or expression. that may not be found in the acknowledged productions of Sir Francis, it is fair to conclude that he alone was engaged in their composition.

* Private Letter 5, p. 6.

A concluding and more difficult objection remains to be dealt with. Were the intellectual powers of Sir Philip Francis equal to the composition of the Letters, and do his after writings warrant their ascription to him? This demurrer may be met in two ways: first, by admitting the inferiority of the known writings of Francis to those of Junius, but tracing it to decline of mental energy or to special circumstances in his personal history; or, secondly, such alleged inferiority may be denied, and proofs adduced that no greater discrepancy exists between Francis and Junius than may be explained by the difference of age, difference of party or personal connection, difference in the subject and aim of the writings; or the fact that one was anonymous and irresponsible, and the other avowed or known. I shall deal with these objections under their several aspects, as well from their general interest as from knowing that with competent judges unsatisfied doubts resulting from these alone, give rise to hesitation as to the claims of Sir Philip Francis.

Admitting, by way of illustration, the inferiority of the later writings of Sir P. Francis to those of Junius, I reply that Francis was unquestionably a person of precocious gifts. His personal history attests this. He was the choice scholar of St. Paul's, and carried off the gold medal there; Lord Holland gave him "a little place" in the Foreign Office; Lord Chatham, succeeding his political opponent, continued to patronize him by making him his Latin secretary in the same department. He received other distinctions at an early age, all significant of high qualifications. It is possible, however, after these manifestations, that his intellectual ardour or powers may have abated, or have been diverted by other passions, or new circumstances. There is nothing in this supposition at all inconsistent with what is familiarly known of many eminent men. Some minds are weak and dull in infancy, but strengthen and brighten unexpectedly in later life; while others follow an exactly inverse ratio. Philip Duke of Wharton evinced extraordinary political talents almost in boyhood, and died exhausted before reaching middle life. Chatterton, Kirke White, Pascal, Hugo Grotius, and Mozart, were singular examples of precocious genius. All the great discoveries of Sir Isaac Newton were made prior to his twenty-fourth year; in after life he seems to have lost both the energy and ambition that had previously animated him in the pursuit

of science. Further examples seem unnecessary, or they might
be multiplied from a variety of sources, especially from Baillet's
"Enfans Celèbres,"* and the work of a learned German, who
has accumulated a whole volume on the subject of precocious de-
velopments†. The mind is subject to vicissitudes, like the body.
Men become feeble and decrepid at every age. Pitt died, according to the testimony of Lord Malmesbury, in exhaustion
of body, and perhaps of mind, at forty-seven, a period when
others are reaching their prime. It follows that if intellectual
inferiority were proveable in Sir P. Francis, such decadence
was compatible with the previous exercise of greater powers—
with the authorship of Junius. The difference of style, however, which is mostly dwelt upon is of little weight; but even
in this respect, none come nearer to the original than Sir
Philip Francis. But the style of Junius was feigned, like his
handwriting, his name, his character, and everything pertaining to him. It was an artificial style, well suited to his
purpose of inflicting deadly wounds, but it was not a style
which either Junius or any other is likely to have used in
ordinary. It would have savoured of as much affectation as
to write in heroic verse in domestic intercourse.

I leave, however, minor points to come to the great event
in the life of Sir P. Francis; that which is most likely to
have effected any perceptible change in his writings, and
lessened the fire and richness of powers evinced in the letters
of Junius.

The appointment of Sir P. Francis from a clerkship in the
War Office, with a stipend of 400*l*., to a seat at the council-board
of Calcutta, with 10,000*l*. per annum, probably appeared at
the time an auspicious occurrence; but it is likely that this
proved to be the most adverse event of his life, and more
than anything contributed to frustrate those ambitious aspirations which Junius evidently had indulged, when he told Woodfall he should "know him by his works." No two individuals
could have met more likely to destroy each other than Francis
and Warren Hastings; and this—paradoxical as it may seem—
not from the antagonism of their characters, but their homo-
geneity. Both had risen from humbler rank—Hastings first;
both possessed great natural and acquired gifts; both were

* Enfans Celèbres par leurs Études ou par leurs Écrits. *Paris*, 1688.
† Klefekeri Bibliotheca Eruditorum precocium, sive ad scripta hujus argu-
menti Spicilegium et Accessiones. *Hamb.* 1717.

of ardent and impulsive temperament; both were ambitious, brave, energetic, and indefatigable; both were warm in friendship, but unscrupulous and implacable in their animosities; lastly, both were capable of, and doubtless preferred, honourable warfare, but, upon occasion, could play a subtle, intriguing, over-reaching game. Separately, either was no doubt competent to achieve a name; but conjointly, fatal collisions were inevitable. Like gladiators in mortal conflict, both fell to the earth, mutilated and dead—dead to that which makes life precious—honour, riches, and unsullied renown—the melancholy victims of jealous rancour and uncompromising hatred. Which was the most in error, I leave history to determine. Ostensibly, they were mainly divided on the two great lines of Indian policy: the one, expediency, which Hastings patronized, as most conducive to individual and territorial aggrandisement; the other, the immutable principles of right and justice, which Francis advocated as the true principles of government. One may have been more available—more immediately gainful to British power and its agency; the other more honourable and enduring, but possibly impracticable in dealing with the native princes. So much were the two men identical in organism and aims, that it is not improbable, had it been possible for them to exchange places, that each in his altered position would have trod in the other's steps.

This could not be, and in the struggle that ensued Francis was worsted. He returned to England prematurely, dangerously wounded in a duel which his rival had provoked, probably as the shortest course to get rid of him, and, doubtless, burning with unquenchable resentment against the antagonist who had overpowered him. Mr. Hastings states*, that he did not " seek" a personal rencontre with Mr. Francis, but " expected it," as the consequence of the offensive minute† he had sent to him. Hastings was a good shot, and, according to Lady Francis, had he not been short in stature, and his opponent a " tall gentleman," the affair might have had a more fatal termination.

The effect of it, and the sudden destruction of cherished hopes and prospects, must, on a mind and spirit like that of Sir P. Francis, have been terrible. In the prime of life he became involved in a quarrel which endured for twenty-five years, and produced nought but disappointment and mortifica-

* Gleig's Life.                    † Appendix, p. 420.

tion. Generally, at the time, he was thought to have been
in the wrong, and when he arrived in England no one would
notice him, except the King and Mr. Burke. It is possible
that the big secret which he had carried in his bosom had
something to do with his errors and failures. The fame of
Junius—for such in the sequel, I apprehend, will be the
reader's conclusion—could not have been entirely inactive on
a nature like his; it could not but have inspired him with a
confidence, not to say haughtiness, of demeanour as offensive
as incomprehensible to those not in the mystery of his importance. There is a moral in this unravelment, in the retri-
butive influence resulting from the Junian secrecy apparently
so successful, that may have operated unfavourably on the
subsequent character and career of Francis.

However this may be judged, one conclusion is certain,
that Sir Philip cannot but have returned from India an
altered man. Indomitable as he was in spirit, it is unlikely
his energies would not abate under the severe repulse he had
experienced. But it was indispensable he should persevere;
his honour, future fame, and reputation in England, all depended on proving his Indian quarrel just. Upon this issue
all his powers hereafter had to be concentrated. He had to
convince the British public that Warren Hastings was an unprincipled treaty-breaker, a reckless spoliator, a crafty, corrupt,
avaricious, and tyrannical governor-general. For this end
very different accomplishments and exercises were needful
from those he had previously cultivated in the columns of
the *Public Advertiser*. He had the House of Commons to
address, upon which Burke's learned and fervid eloquence had
been unavailing; he had the Indian Board to memorialize;
pamphlets to write for popular conviction; conversations to
maintain, and explanatory letters to write, to gain patrons,
and satisfy private friends: all which was assuredly enough to
weary and dull the brightest and most untiring genius. In
this new field all beside plain facts, cogent reasoning, and
clear narrative, was out of place. Those excellences which in
a different character had challenged admiration—the studied
and lucid diction, the harmony of balanced periods, the elaborate sarcasm, dazzling metaphor, sparkling wit, epigram-
matic turns of style, and other classic elegancies, as well as
the fierce invective and cruel inuendo, which had at once
made the pages of Junius both beautiful and appalling, had

become of secondary moment. But such was fate. With
the fire of a Chatham in his bosom to electrify the senate,
and with the acumen, knowledge of human nature, and mastery
of language of a Hume, Robertson, or Gibbon, to adorn and
invigorate history, Sir Philip Francis was destined to leave,
as his avowed productions, only a pile of well-nigh forgotten
speeches, protests, pamphlets, manuscript notes on book margins, and fugitive verses.

But in this direction of his talents he was first-rate, if not
foremost. Vindication of his conduct and principles required
that he should become plainly didactive, or a dull matter-of-fact
narrator, in lieu of a brilliant declaimer; but he was supreme,
whether as Junius or a pamphleteer. This Mr. Burke admitted.
In oratory he laboured under a defect of utterance, caused by
an over-sensibility of temperament, alike incompatible with
public speaking and dramatic action. He has, however, left
admirable speeches, as well as written compositions of undoubted excellence.

But this being a question of taste, as well as judgment,
unanimity cannot be expected, and I shall not attempt
to elucidate at great length. One or two specimens I will
submit, perhaps not generally known, and which, both from
sentiment and style, import no inferiority inconsistent with
the conclusion that Sir Philip Francis was Junius.

The first example I shall give, and it is one which has been
much admired, is Sir Philip's reply in the House of Commons
to a coarse reflection of Lord Chancellor Thurlow:—

"It was well known that a gross and public insult had been offered to the
memory of General Clavering and Colonel Monson by a person of high rank
in this country. He was happy when he heard that his name was included
in it with theirs. So highly did he respect the character of those men, that
he deemed it an honour to share in the injustice it had suffered. It was in
compliance with the forms of the House, and not to shelter himself or out of
tenderness to the party, that he forbore to name him. He meant to describe
him so exactly that he could not be mistaken. He declared in his place, in
a great assembly, and in the course of a grave deliberation, 'that it would
have been happy for this country if General Clavering, Colonel Monson, and
Mr. Francis had been drowned in their passage to India.' If this poor and
spiteful invective had been uttered by a man of no consequence or repute—
by any light, trifling, inconsiderate person—by a lord of the bed-chamber,
for example, or any of the other silken barons of modern days, he should have
heard it with indifference. But when it was seriously urged, and deliberately insisted on, by a grave lord of Parliament—by a judge—by a man of
ability and eminence in his profession, whose personal disposition was serious,
who carried gravity to sternness, and sternness to ferocity, it could not be

received with indifference, or answered without resentment. Such a man would be thought to have inquired before he pronounced. From his mouth a reproach was a sentence, an invective was a judgment. The accidents of life, and not any original distinction that he knew of, had placed him too high, and himself at too great a distance from him, to admit of any other answer than a public defiance, for General Clavering, for Colonel Monson, and for himself. This was not a party question, nor should it he left to so feeble an advocate as he was to support it. The friends and fellow-soldiers of General Clavering and Colonel Monson would assist him in defending their memory. He demanded and expected the support of every man of honour in that House, and in the kingdom. What character was safe, If slander was permitted to attack the reputation of two of the most honourable and virtuous men that ever were employed, or ever perished, in the service of their country? He knew that the authority of this man was not without weight; but he had an infinitely higher authority to oppose to it. He had the happiness of hearing the merits of General Clavering and Colonel Monson acknowledged and applauded, in terms to which he was not at liberty to do more than to allude: they were rapid and expressive. He must not venture to repeat, lest he should do them injustice, or violate the forms of respect, where essentially he owed and felt the most. But he was sufficiently understood. The generous sensations that animate the royal mind were easily distinguished from those which rankled in the heart of that person who was supposed to be the keeper of the royal conscience."

According to the description of persons present, this philippic was powerfully delivered, bordering on the terrible in countenance, gesture, and vehemence. The next is a shorter extract from a speech in 1706; it is close, neat, and conclusive:—

"If I could personify the House of Commons, it would be my interest as well as my duty to approach so great a person with the utmost respect. But respect does not exclude firmness, and should not restrain me from saying, that it is the function of your greatness, as well as of your office, to listen to truth, especially when it arraigns a proceeding of your own. I am not here to admire your consistency, or to applaud the conduct which I am endeavouring to correct. These topics do not furnish any subject for applause. You have nothing like praise to expect from me; unless you feel, as I do, that a compliment of the highest order is included in the confidence which appeals to your justice against your inclination."

The next is an extract from a letter addressed by Sir P. Francis to Mr. Burke, on the publication of his celebrated "Reflections," and dated February 19, 1790. The discipline administered is severe, but not perhaps unwarranted by the occasion—the well-known extravagance of the orator on the Queen of France, and his lament over the fall of Chivalry.

"In a case so interesting as the errors of a great nation, and the calamities of great individuals, and feeling them so deeply as you profess to do, all manner of insinuation is improper, all gibe and nickname prohibited. In my opinion all that you say of the queen is pure foppery. If she be a perfect female character, you ought to take your ground upon her virtues. If she be the reverse, it is ridiculous in any but a lover to place her personal charms in opposition to her crimes. Either way, I know the argument must proceed upon a supposition; for neither have you said anything to establish her moral merits, nor have her accusers formally tried and convicted her of guilt. On this subject, however, you cannot but know that the opinion of the world is not lately, but has been many years, decided. But in effect, when you assert her claim to protection and respect on no other topics than those of gallantry, and beauty, and personal accomplishments, you virtually abandon the proof and assertion of her innocence, which you know is the point substantially in question. Pray, Sir, how long have you felt yourself so desperately disposed to admire the ladies of Germany? I despise and abhor, as much as you can do, all personal insult and outrage, even to guilt itself, if I see it, where it ought to be, dejected and helpless; but it is in vain to expect that I, or any reasonable man, shall regret the sufferings of a Messalina as I should those of a Mrs. Crewe, or a Mrs. Burke; I mean all that is beautiful or virtuous among women. Is it nothing but outside? Have they no moral minds? Or are you such a determined champion of beauty as to draw your sword in defence of any jade upon earth, provided she be handsome? Look back, I beseech you, and deliberate a little, before you determine that this is an office that perfectly becomes you. If I stop here, it is not for want of a multitude of objections. The mischief you are going to do yourself, is, to my apprehension, palpable. It is visible. It will be audible. I snuff it in the wind. I taste it already. I feel it in every sense; and so will you hereafter when, I vow to God (a most elegant phrase), it will be no sort of consolation for me to reflect that I did everything in my power to prevent it."

Sir Philip followed up his corrective admonition by strictures on the carelessness of his friend's diction, in the highest style of Junius:—

"Once for all, I wish you would let me teach you to write English. To me, who am to read everything you write, it would be a great comfort, and to you no sort of disparagement. Why will you not allow yourself to be persuaded that polish is material to preservation?"

Perhaps the reader will not be displeased with the following description of the oratory of Sir Philip, as given by Mr. Burke in a letter addressed to Mrs. Francis. It was on the occasion of opening the charges of corrupt administration against Warren Hastings, in which Sir P. Francis tried to lessen the natural impression that he was under the influence of personal animosity:—

"MY DEAR MADAM,        "Gerard Street, April 20, 1787.
" I cannot, with an honest appetite or clear conscience, sit down to my breakfast, unless I first give you an account which will make your family breakfast as pleasant to you as I wish all your family meetings to be. Then I have the satisfaction of telling you, that not in my judgment only, but in that of all who heard him, no man ever acquitted himself, on a day of great expec-

tation, to the full of the demand upon him so well as Mr. Francis did yesterday.   He was *clear, precise, forcible, and eloquent in a high degree.*   No
intricate brief was ever better unravelled; and no iniquity ever placed so
effectually to produce its natural horror and disgust.   It is very little to the
credit of those who are Mr. Francis's enemies, but it is infinitely to his, that
they forced him to give a history of his *whole public life.*   He did it in a
most masterly manner, and with an address which the display of such a life
ought very little to want, but which the prejudices of those whose lives are
of a very different character made necessary.   He did justice to the feelings
of others too; and I assure you, Madam, that the *modesty* of his defence was
not the smallest part of its merit.   All who heard him were delighted, except
those whose mortification ought to give pleasure to every good mind.   He was
two hours and a half or rather more upon his legs; and he never lost attention for a moment." *

Portions of the above accurately depict the style of Junius;
but I think enough has been adduced to dispose of the question
of literary or intellectual inferiority, and shall now enter upon
fresh proofs to connect the history of Sir Philip with Junius.


## IV   SOURCES OF THE JUNIAN INTELLIGENCE.

BESIDE the extraordinary talent evinced in the composition
of the Letters, one of their most remarkable features was the
authentic and prompt intelligence manifestly at the command
of the writer.   Invisible himself, Junius seemed the central
eye, to which converged the rays of light emitted from everything that moved in the political arena.   It was this univer-
sality of information that especially tended to preserve inviolate his secrecy, and to mislead inquirers into his identity.
How could it be imagined that a clerk in the War Office
could equal a cabinet minister, and even Royalty itself, in the
promptitude and accuracy of his official communications? that
the monarch, who, by virtue of his prerogative, receives from
his secretaries, chancellors, and spiritual vicegerents reports
of all transactions in Church and State, should be outdone by
so humble a retainer? that even the confidential whisperings
of the King's closet, and the gossip sacred to the privacy of a
ministerial dinner, could not escape this indefatigable scrutator?   The unravelment of this mystery in the Junius story
forms the purpose of the present section.
For the production of any important event, history shows
that the conjunction of two elements is indispensable—a quali-

* *Correspondence of the Right Hon. Edmund Burke*, vol. iii. p. 66.   Edited
by Earl Fitzwilliam and General Bourke.   Lond. 1844.

fied instrument and co-operating circumstances. The genius of Napoleon, fostered by the times in which he lived, constituted the phenomenon of his existence. Junius, in a less dazzling field of action, forms another signal example of the junction of means with ends; and in Sir Philip Francis we see exactly the man who, from his peculiar position, character, and acquirements, was competent to fulfil the conditions of the problem. Apparently open, communicative, and jocular, he was really a reserved being; self-dependent, communing much with himself, and subject to passions that might urge him to extreme courses, more or less elevated, according to the nature of the impulse. The Zanga of Young, or the Falkland of Godwin, offers the nearest dramatic presentment of his peculiar organization. Early in life, from unusual ability and trustworthiness, he obtained, as already stated, the confidential patronage of Lord Holland, and subsequently of the Earl of Chatham; and these noblemen, the ablest and most influential of their time, became the chief sources of the private information of Junius, through the intermediate agency, privity, or co-operation of Earl Temple, and perhaps of the Grenvilles, Mr. Calcraft, and Dr. Francis. These possessed ample opportunities to contribute all the parliamentary, court, and club news that rendered the Letters remarkable. The city intelligence partly passed through the same hands, especially Mr. Calcraft's, and was obtained first from Alderman Beckford, and after his death from Alderman Sawbridge. Wilkes also furnished fuel to the Junian furnace, but he seems to have been left to be dealt with by Junius, who received the civic contributions of the agitator through the medium of Mr. Woodfall. Such is the list of the *dramatis personæ*,—a body of intelligencers, it must be owned, amply sufficient to produce the Letters.

It will be necessary, however, to detail more fully the relations and positions of the individuals named, and refer to the public and private information upon which their complicity is established. I shall first speak of the Holland section, which was distinct in interest and political connection from the Chatham party.

But though Lords Holland and Chatham were the primary sources of intelligence, and through intermediate channels contributed to the Junian reservoir, it is doubtful to what extent these noblemen were privy to the Letters, or knowingly contributed information. That Lord Holland was

unacquainted with Junius, is highly probable : his Lordship
was a man of the world, of the Walpole school of politics, of
a kind, affable disposition, and associated much with those in
direct communion with Junius; but it is likely he himself had
no knowledge of the writer, and was unconscious that he was
aiding him by information. This will appear from a fact I
shall soon mention. As to Lord Chatham, he would probably
seek a communication with Junius on discovering that he was
his former Latin Secretary, but not till after the Letters had
become popular.

The position of Dr. Francis, as the chaplain of Lord Holland, living intimately with his Lordship, and as the author
of political pamphlets early in the reign of George III., has
been already described. At this period Lord Holland had
retired from the King's service, but continued a great favourite
at Court. He was, in fact, the confidential adviser both of
the King and Lord Bute, in the chief ministerial crises that
occurred from 1763 to 1770. Speaking of one of these junc-
tures in 1767, Mr. Adolphus says, " Lord Chatham's health
was now deemed irrecoverable, and the ministry were neither
benefited by his advice, nor supported by his popularity. They
wanted a distinguished leader of talent, character, and reputation, who could give efficacy to their measures, and by force
of superior powers enchain those minor pretenders who, in the
absence of such a chief, disdained submission and embroiled
the cabinet." It was in this disorder of his administration
that Lord Chatham wrote to the King, representing his health
as so bad that it was impossible he could afford further assistance to his Majesty, but recommending that the Duke of
Grafton should be prevailed upon to continue at the head of
the Treasury*. In this extremity Lord Bute applied to his
former associate, Lord Holland, who, as leader of the House
of Commons, had so materially assisted him in procuring a
parliamentary approval of the peace of 1763. Lord Holland
sent his advice, July 6†, and the result was an attempt to
strengthen the ministry by a union with the Bedford and
Rockingham parties. But it failed. On the 21st Lord Rockingham waited on the King, and immediately after his Lordship left the King's closet Lord Holland was introduced‡.
The final issue of the consultation was, that the Duke of

* Chatham Papers. † Almon's Life of the Earl of Chatham, vol. ii. p. 1167.
‡ Ibid. vol. ii. p. 130, note.

Grafton's ministry was reinforced by the friends of the Duke of Bedford; and it was this ducal union that subsequently rendered the Dukes of Grafton and Bedford the bitter objects of the attacks of Junius, when his patron, Lord Chatham, had recovered, and was eager to destroy the Grafton ministry.

Having given evidence of the private and confidential intercourse maintained by Lord Holland with the Court, I shall next show the intimacy subsisting between Lord Holland and his chaplain. It may be first remarked, that Dr. Francis was also chaplain of Chelsea Hospital, as well as the favourite chaplain of the celebrated Earl of Chesterfield, to whom he dedicated his play of *Constantine*. Besides his learned and dramatic accomplishments, he was a man of varied social intercourse, living in confidential communication with the highest personages. George III. used to honour him with audiences, probably from the fame of his classical translations. Gibbon the historian, who had been his pupil, bears testimony to the Doctor's attachment to the diversified society of London. He frequently met Garrick at the houses of Lord Holland, Foote, and other mutual friends. Garrick brought out at Drury Lane Dr. Francis's tragedy of *Eugenia*, and in the part of " Mercour" exerted himself greatly to promote its success. He was also on familiar terms with Mr. John Calcraft, the army agent, and who will in the sequel of this exposition be found to have acted a principal part. Speaking of Lord Holland, Mr. Heron says :—

" During the busiest period of his political life Mr. John Calcraft was his confidential clerk and humble friend. He lived much in the house of Calcraft, in Parliament Street, while Mrs. G. A. Bellamy presided at that gentleman's table. She introduced to him Dr. Philip Francis, the translator of Horace, who became his chaplain, was otherwise promoted under his patronage, was made the familiar companion of his convivial hours at the house of Calcraft, and was probably excited by him to undertake his translation of Demosthenes. Calcraft was enriched under Mr. Fox's protection till he aspired to an equality with his master. When he could not rise to the height of his ambition on the same side in politics with Fox, he deserted to Lord Chatham and the Grenvilles, was received into their confidence, and became an outrageous patriot."—*Letters of Junius*, vol. ii. p. 251.

With Dr. Francis moving in the circle I have described, it is obvious that the younger Francis, as Junius, would command a ready channel from which to draw court and political news, and whence, most probably, were derived those anecdotes of the private life of the King, of the Princess Dowager of Wales,

of the brutal behaviour of the Duke of Bedford to his Sovereign, of the intelligence conveyed by Garrick to Richmond,
and of those changes in the superior offices of the government
which he so promptly communicated. It also explains why
Junius spared the Holland family, he himself having received
favours from it, and his father continuing intimately identified
with it, and the origin of the wish he expressed to Woodfall,
that Lord Holland " may acquit himself with honour," in reply
to the charge of malversation.

But though Junius respected and spared the family of Lord
Holland, I shall in this place adduce a piece of information,
showing such relations of Junius towards it as will, I apprehend, be unexpected by the public. I have already stated,
that Mr. Taylor in his *Junius Identified*, in the first instance,
fixed upon Dr. Francis as the author of the Letters. But it
appears, and I state this on the best authority, that Dr. Francis
was entirely unconnected with the writings of Junius ; and he
was as much in the dark respecting the author as any reader of
the *Public Advertiser*. This information has been kindly communicated to me by the grandson of Sir Philip Francis, upon
the authority of a letter of Dr. Francis, in his possession. Mr.
Francis is in possession of his grandfather's curious collection
of MSS ; and further informs me that the views of Dr. Francis
differed from those of his son on many questions discussed by
Junius; and he conceives that " Sir Philip purposely concealed
the secret from his father, so long as it continued his exclusive
property." From this important explanation, I infer the probability that both Lord Holland and Dr. Francis were unconscious contributors to the Junius bulletins; and it is not
unlikely that certain disclosures in them may have led to such
discoveries and explanations between the elder and younger
Francis as stopped further supplies, and " the habits of the
closest intimacy, which had prevailed between father and son,
were finally broken off."*

I turn next to the Chatham branch of the connection as a
source of intelligence. Differing probably from his father in
this respect, Junius throughout his career was the ardent and
consistent admirer of the Earl of Chatham. From the *Chatham Correspondence*, lately published under the editorship of
the grandsons of Lord Chatham, it appears that Junius privately addressed letters to his Lordship. In the first of these
* Private Letters of H. R. Francis, Esq., dated April 26, and May 20, 1850.

letters, which is dated January 2, 1708, he says, "I have *an
opportunity of knowing something*, and you may depend on my
veracity." As Francis, Junius certainly had an opportunity of
"knowing something;" he then comments on the conduct of
Lord Chatham's colleagues in the ministry, and the treachery
of some of them, concluding with :—"the man who presumes
to give your Lordship these hints admires your character
without servility, and is convinced that if this country can be
saved, it must be saved by Lord Chatham's spirit, by Lord
Chatham's abilities."* The letter is marked "private and
secret; to be opened by Lord Chatham only." The second
letter was more remarkable, inclosing proof-sheets of the letters
which Junius was about to address to Lord Chief Justice
Mansfield and Lord Camden, the facts of which have been
already noticed†. A copy of Eyre's commitment accompanied
this letter, which Junius had obtained from Wilkes. The
letter is dated January 14, 1772, and is marked "most secret."
Junius concludes by saying, "Retired and unknown, I live in
the shade, and have only a speculative ambition. In the
warmth of my imagination, I sometimes conceive that, when
Junius exerts his utmost faculties in the service of his country,
he approaches in theory to that exalted character which Lord
Chatham alone fills up, and uniformly supports in action."‡
Facsimiles of both these letters are given in the *Chatham
Correspondence;* the handwriting more closely resembles the
natural than the feigned hand of Sir Philip Francis, and with
the former Lord Chatham must have been familiar, Francis
having been his secretary.

The exact time when Junius became known to Lord Chatham I have no means of stating, but that he did know him
I have the authority of Lady Francis§ for affirming, and that
his Lordship aided him with information. The object of
both, as stated, was to break up the Grafton Ministry, and
Chatham thought the writings of Junius would effect this.
The event occurred, but not so soon as was expected, and
when it did happen, the elevation of Lord North to the Premiership came on everybody by surprise.

The communications of Lord Chatham with Junius, it is
probable, were chiefly carried on by Mr. John Calcraft, the
army agent, and Lord Chatham's confidential secretary.

---

* Chatham Papers, vol. iii. p. 305.    † Private Letters, note, p. 62.
‡ Chatham Pap., vol. iv. p. 194.    § Let. from Lady Francis, Apr., 1850.

Calcraft was a member of the House of Commons, but, according to Junius, gave silent votes. He was, however, though not a speaker, an actor, extensively connected and well-informed in state transactions. In the higher departments of public affairs, as in the conduct of a lawsuit, a division of labour is unavoidable. It is sufficient occupation for a First Lord of the Treasury, Chancellor of the Exchequer, or Secretary of State, to exercise his patronage, attend cabinet councils, grant audiences, deliver speeches, sign despatches, and prepare budgets, of which the chief materials have been necessarily collected by assistants, but of which ministers have the honour and responsibility. Burke, on the commencement of his public life, filled a situation of this description under the Marquis of Rockingham, as did Mr. W. Gerard Hamilton under Lord Townshend, and Mr. Jenkinson, afterwards Lord Liverpool, under the Earl of Bute; Mr. Calcraft held a similar appointment, first under Lord Holland, and next under the Earl of Chatham. In 1763, under the Bute-Holland administration, he was deputy-commissary-general of musters, from which he was removed in December, in consequence probably of what had appeared in the newspapers on September 1 preceding, stating that, " Mr. Pitt and Lord Temple had, on the preceding day, paid a visit to Mr Calcraft, which lasted two hours." From this period, Mr Calcraft's connection with Lord Chatham began, and continued with unabated and mutual confidence till his death in 1772.

When Chatham was confined by gout at Hayes or Bath, Calcraft was his London correspondent, collecting court and city news, reporting debates and motions in Parliament, and apprising him of any royal audience at St. James's, or other party movement of his Lordship's political adversaries. His industry, fidelity, and varied sources of intelligence are amply attested in the *Chatham Papers*; the editors of which had placed at their disposal, by John Hales Calcraft, Esq., of Carlton Gardens, his grandfather's correspondence with Lord Chatham. The quarrel between Mr. Pitt and his brother-in-law, Lord Temple, in 1766, on the disposal of places, appears from this work to have been made up two years after by the intervention of their common friend, Mr. Calcraft. As a prelude to this amicable arrangement, Mr. Calcraft writes to Mr Pitt :—"July 15, 1766,—I have some reason to fear Lord

*e* 2

Temple's reception at Richmond was not the most flattering, of which I take the liberty to give you this hint, as you possibly may qualify it at your meeting. I can confirm what I said, that there are no engagements, and must do his Lordship the justice to add, his *sentiments towards you* are what I wished to find them."[*] But that which most concerns the present exposition is the interchange of intelligence between Mr. Calcraft and the author of Junius. That such communications were carried on, and the most friendly intimacy subsisted between Mr. Calcraft and Sir Philip Francis, I will adduce indubitable proofs.

First, as evidenced by the *Chatham Papers*. On the opening of the session of 1770, Mr. Calcraft informed Lord Chatham of the names of the members in both Houses that were to move and second the addresses. Lord Chatham delivered two speeches on this occasion; twenty-two years after, as already stated, they were printed by Almon from a report furnished by Sir Philip Francis, who was present, and they were by him revised and corrected in 1813, for the Parliamentary History: the remarkable fact connected with them is that the most striking passages in the speeches are nearly identical with passages in Junius. It is not improbable that Sir P. Francis composed those speeches for Lord Chatham; he certainly composed many of his Lordship's speeches. In Sir Philip Francis's copy of Belsham's History of Great Britain, vol. v. p. 298, sold at Evans's, in February, 1838, there appears the following manuscript note :—

"I wrote this speech for Lord Mansfield, as well as all those of Lord Chatham on the Middlesex election.— P. F."— *Vide* Evans's *Catalogue of the Library of the late Sir P. Francis*, p. 3.

The speech of Lord Chatham, March 2, 1770, was inserted in the *Public Advertiser*, March 5, and is known to have been reported by Junius from the letter that accompanied it in that Journal. Contemporary with his labour for the *Public Advertiser*, Junius contributed political papers for the *London Museum*, Almon's *Political Register*, and other periodicals. His industry is inconceivable, but all his untiring efforts had one great and leading aim—the glory of Chatham, for whom through life he cherished a grateful and unswerving admiration.

The noble name of Granby gave lustre and strength to

* Chatham Correspondence, vol. ii. p. 445.

the Grafton ministry, which never recovered the loss it suffered by his resignation of the command of the army, occasioned by the writings of Junius, co-operating with the personal solicitations of Lord Chatham's friends. Mr. Calcraft, January 20, 1770, writes to Lord Chatham,—" I can from authority assure your Lordship, that General Conway has refused the Ordnance, adding that he will take none of Lord Granby's spoils." On the 30th, Calcraft writes,—" I can from the best authority assure your Lordship the Duke of Grafton has resigned." To the surprise of the nation the Duke had resigned on the evening of the 28th, and Lord North, already Chancellor of the Exchequer, was appointed his successor. Mr. Calcraft continues.—" The Duke of Grafton has resolved on this step ever since Lord Granby's resignation, and the unreasonable demands of his Bedford friends have confirmed him in that resolution." This unexpected turn of affairs made the Chathamites furious; in the rage of disappointment even Lord Chatham lost his temper, and replies to Calcraft, April 10,—" The state of the House of Commons, from what passed last week, is certainly very critical, and the conduct of the more immediate *Bute faction there*, with the *Lord Deputy North* at the head of the illustrious band, glares more and more in the eyes of the world, and more augments the universal abhorrence."*

Mr. Calcraft despatched court gossip to Hayes, as well as weightier matters. March 24, 1770, he informs Chatham,— " The court thinks the ministers have stopped too short in the persecution of the city magistrates, and the language of Thursday was, ' *My* ministers have no spirit; they don't pursue measures with any spirit.' There is great confusion amongst them; and if we stand by the people as we ought, and take another early opportunity to show it, it will have the best effect, for, notwithstanding high words, there is great alarm." On the 29th Calcraft relates how their friends are moving in the city,—" I break my letter open to tell you Mr. Sawbridge has just been here. To my great concern he informs me that the Lord Mayor and the leading people of Middlesex are so offended by the half support given to the city remonstrance and total neglect of that for Westminster, that they mean not to remonstrate to-morrow. I have moderated the city warmth against any part of opposition for several

* Chatham Correspondence, vol. iii. p 443.

days; but fear it will break out at last."* On the evening
of October 19, Alderman Sawbridge called on Calcraft, and
reported to him that the Recorder's business had ended
satisfactorily. November 28, Calcraft writes to Chatham,—
" Your Lordship gave me great private satisfaction in what
you so generously said about my friend Sawbridge." Alderman Sawbridge was M.P. for Hythe. Mr. Beckford, the
fearless and patriotic magistrate, dying 21st June, 1770, he
was succeeded, as already stated, by Mr. Sawbridge in the
management of the Chatham party in the city.

I shall next show the co-partnership of Junius in these proceedings. Of the powerful aid he was affording by his pen,
his Letters in the *Public Advertiser* are sufficient proof, aided
by the explanatory private notes addressed to Mr. Woodfall.
But the public had no evidence of his transactions with Lord
Chatham's political attorney till the recent publication of the
*Correspondence.*

In the postscript of a letter to Chatham, dated April 22,
1770, Mr. Calcraft says,—" A servant has just brought the enclosed, which contains such very material intelligence that I
send it for your Lordship's perusal." The inclosure referred
to, the editors of the *Correspondence* state, " is in the handwriting of Sir Philip Francis," of which they give a fac-simile.
The inclosure gives Calcraft the particulars of the serious
riots in Boston in the preceding March, of which intelligence
had just arrived from America, which the writer says he had
" from very good authority." It concludes, " Pray let me
have notice of the day of Lord Chatham's motion. *Wilkes
will be there.*"† His Lordship's motion was made May 4 ;
it inculpated the King's answer to the city address and remonstrance ; and Lord Chatham's speech on the occasion, say the
editors, "bears internal evidence of being reported by Junius."‡
Perhaps he had previously composed it, and then the reporting
it afterwards would be easy enough, and likely to be faithful.
On a previous occasion (March 18) Mr. Calcraft writes to
Earl Temple, " Just as your Lordship left me a *friend* came
in, who says he hears a strong report that they [the minis-

* Vide Private Letters to Woodfall, No. 22, and notes, p. 301. To understand passing occurrences, and to save repetitions, it will be often necessary
to turn to the Letters of Junius, private, public, and miscellaneous, of the
corresponding dates, and the notes appended to them.

† Chatham Papers, vol. iii. p. 44?.     ‡ Ibid. vol. iii. p. 453.

ters] disagree among themselves or the difficulties they may
be involved in and have resolved not to proceed upon the remonstrance to-morrow." Upon this the editors of Chatham
ask, "Was not this 'friend' Sir Philip Francis?" Highly
probable ; but Calcraft was too conversant with the world to
lessen the importance of his intelligence, by informing Lord
Temple that the "friend" who had left him was young Mr
Francis, a clerk in the War Office.

A further, and remarkable contribution of the "friend" deserves to be noted. It is an extract from a letter addressed
to Mr. Calcraft, which he forwarded to Lord Chatham, and is
endorsed by his Lordship "Received December 9, and well
worth attention." On the 10th there was a warm debate
in the House of Lords, on the conduct of Chief Justice
Mansfield on the trial of Woodfall, of which an account has
been given *. Of the speech made by Lord Chatham on the
occasion two reports have been preserved, both taken by
Junius, and in both the above-mentioned extract is incorpo-
rated verbatim. For the extract, and the remark of Junius on
the report being "taken with exactness," see p. 324. In another communication of Mr. Calcraft to Lord Chatham, relative
to the speech of Lord North on the probability of war with
Spain, the words used by him are nearly identical with those
used by Junius †, and which it is likely he had received from
the same "friend."

Did not I fear exhausting the patience of the reader, I
could adduce other ramifications of intelligence and personal
connection elucidatory of the secret history of this period, and
intimately connected with the authorship of Junius. Lord
Temple, a man of literary tastes, an active politician, and by
some thought to be Junius, it is probable enough knew the
writer, and obtained the knowledge from his brother-in-law, the
Earl of Chatham. The probability of Lord Temple's privity
will appear from what I am going to relate. In a letter written
by Daniel Wmy, Esq., whom I have before noticed (*ante*, p
xxiv.), dated Nov. 22, 1772, and addressed to Lord Hardwicke,
is the following :—" The divisions are great in the enemy's
camp, particularly between Lords Temple and Camden, about
the author of Junius's Letters." Upon these lines the late Mr
Justice Hardinge, Solicitor-General to Queen Charlotte, in his
*Miscellaneous Works* remarks,—" These few words are of no

* Miscel. Letters, No. 82, p. 328.        † Miscel. Letters, No. 81, p. 319.

trivial import, and they wonderfully confirm a passage in a
conversation between Lord Camden and me. He told me that
many things in Junius convinced him that the materials were
prompted by Earl Temple, and he mentioned in particular a
confidential statement which had been made in private between
Lord Chatham, Lord Temple, and Lord Camden, which, from
the nature of it, could only have been disclosed by Lord Temple, through Junius, to the public." Whether the information
was communicated by Temple or Chatham, it shows that one
or both were at this period in correspondence with Junius, and
it is likely knew him as well as the Grenvilles, they being all
by marriage one family connection.

At this period Lord Temple maintained a constant intercourse with Mr. John Almon, the celebrated literary bookseller
and political writer. Mr. Almon enjoyed in a high degree the
confidence of his Lordship, who introduced him to the Duke
of Devonshire, Lord Rockingham, and other patrician leaders
of the liberal party. This acquaintance made Mr. Almon the
oracle of his day, and his shop the resort of the most distinguished public characters. Lord Chatham was also among
Mr. Almon's associates and correspondents. Indeed, it may
be observed of this great man, that he honoured and sought
out worth and ability in every grade of life, military or civil,
whether it was a bookseller, clerk in the War Office, or a jour
neyman printer*. The connections of Sir Philip Francis
with Almon have been repeatedly mentioned, and Calcraft
was a regular correspondent; but I must be content with
an extract from a letter dated Ingress, Jan. 1772   Calcraft
informs Mr. Almon, "My firm belief is, that Lord Shelburne
was at the Queen's house. I had it from one of his intimates.
Be assured that I never show a line to anybody that comes
from you. I have lived long enough to be caution itself, and
to no quarter more than where you allude. I send you some
Kentish brawn, which I hope you will find good."†

* When Lord Chatham was in the height of his power, Dr. Franklin
relates, in his "Life," that he often visited his Lordship at Hayes. On one
occasion Lord Chatham visited Franklin at his lodgings in Craven Street.
"He stayed with me," says Franklin, "near two hours, his equipage waiting
at the door; and being there while people were coming from church, it was
taken much notice of and talked of, as at that time was every little circumstance that men thought might possibly in any way affect American affairs."
† Found, with numerous other letters from public characters, among Mr.
Almon's papers, and published in the *Memoirs of an Eminent Bookseller.*

Ample indications have, I apprehend, been given to establish that Sir Philip Francis, pending the Junius era, lived in the centre of intelligence. The two great political divisions of the time were, the Court on one side, on the other the Whig nobility, often divided among themselves, but always united against the Bute-Holland coterie at St. James's. Although holding only a subordinate place in the War Office, without the possibility of exercising any direct personal influence on public affairs, it is hardly possible to imagine how any one could be more advantageously situated than Francis was, and with inclination and ability to make the most of his opportunities. He was placed at the central point of information. On the one hand he informed himself by intercourse with Dr. Francis and his friends of all that was most confidential at St. James's; on the other, by intercourse with Mr. Calcraft, a veteran placeman, with numerous and influential political ramifications. Francis himself must have been personally cognizant of the chief military transactions, and of a great deal that occurred in the public offices, from his position at the Horse Guards. Impatient of obscurity, possessed of extraordinary energy and great abilities, both natural and acquired, with vast sources of intelligence within his reach,—all these combined, most probably suggested to him the plan of his famous Letters.

In the preceding exposition, it may perhaps be thought that the links of connection between Calcraft and Sir P. Francis, and as deduced therefrom, the identity of Sir Philip with Junius, have not been sufficiently proved. This apparent deficiency I will proceed to supply. It is unnecessary to dwell on the apparently counter testimony drawn from the disparaging comments of Junius on Mr. Calcraft; these, in all likelihood, after the wonted fashion of the writer, were meant only for mystification, or it is possible that at the period Junius had not revealed himself to Calcraft. That they ultimately became known to each other, and intimate friends, I will establish; as well as that at a subsequent period of his life, Sir P. Francis took effective precautions to destroy the evidence of all pre-existing connection.

The reader has been apprized of the disappointment of Sir P. Francis in not being appointed Deputy Secretary-at-War*, which he esteemed his due from seniority of service, in preference to Mr. Chamier, and of Sir Philip's abrupt removal

* Ante, p. xxxiii., and the Letter of Veteran, Misc. Letters, No. 110.

from the War Office, immediately after, by Lord Barrington.
Pending these movements Mr. Calcraft appears to have strenuously exerted himself to serve Francis, and even to compen-
sate him for his official deprivation.   In a letter dated Ingress,
January 13, 1772, addressed to Mr. Almon, and inserted in
Mr. Almon's *Memoirs*, p. 83, Mr. Calcraft says,—" If you
put in paragraphs, put that Mr. Francis is appointed Deputy
Secretary-at-War, and continues his present employment also.
It will tease the worthy secretary [Lord Barrington], as I well
know, and oblige me.   I will give you my reasons, when you
will find more folly in that noble lord than even you thought
him capable of."   In another letter he adds,—" I was not
misinformed ; I knew Francis was not deputy, but *I wished
him to be so ;* and to cram the newspapers with paragraphs
that he was so.   For he is *very deserving.*"   These extracts
have a twofold value, as showing the lively interest felt by
Mr. Calcraft in the promotion of Sir P. Francis, and the high
opinion formed by him of his worth and public deserts.

But this was not the limit of Mr. Calcraft's endeavours in
favour of his friend, for whom he failed to obtain the appointment of Deputy, but compensated him for his loss.   On the
20th of March, 1772, Francis was dismissed from the War
Office, and on the same day Calcraft added a codicil to his will,
bequeathing to him the sum of 1000*l.* and an annuity of 250*l.*
for life to Mrs. Francis.   The intimate and friendly ties,
therefore, subsisting between Calcraft and Francis cannot be
doubted.   I shall next refer to the subsequent act of Sir P.
Francis, from which he was evidently apprehensive of unseasonable discoveries.   After perusing the *Chatham Papers*, and
the evidence they afforded of the confidential connection between Calcraft and Sir P. Francis, and knowing that the
present Mr. Calcraft had placed at the disposal of the editors
of that work, all the papers of his grandfather in relation to
Lord Chatham, it occurred to me that there might remain in
Mr. Calcraft's possession letters and papers which Sir P.
Francis had addressed to the Earl's secretary, and which would
throw light on the subject of my inquiries into the authorship
of Junius.   Under this impression, I wrote to Mr. Calcraft,
but, almost immediately after I had done so, I learned from an
unquestionable source, that my application would be fruitless,
as, nearly half a century ago, Sir Philip Francis, aware, no
doubt, that a mine existed in that quarter, had got back all his
private papers.

The intelligence I received of this transaction I relate in the words of my informant.

"It was to John Calcraft, the son of the army agent, that Sir Philip Francis applied for the private letters which he had written to his father. He was most solicitous to get them, and they were given up to him without perusal. This was in 1787, when the son came of age."—*Private Letter*, April 23, 1850.

Upon mentioning the information to Mr. Francis, the grandson of Sir Philip, and present possessor of his MSS., he replied,—

"I believe you have been quite correctly informed as to the restoration of papers by Mr. Calcraft's heirs. A remarkable expression used by Sir Philip Francis to a Lady of that family has led me to believe also that Mr. Calcraft was not only in the *secret* afterwards, but a purveyor of information at the time."—*Private Letter*, April 26, 1850.

Further exposition, I imagine, the reader will not desire on the subject. I shall only add that the anxiety of Sir P. Francis to get back his papers, in 1787, had a natural and obvious motive. He had become a member of parliament, and was in the midst of his great struggle with Warren Hastings. The impeachment of the ex-Governor-General was hotly in progress; and had it been discovered by the partisans of Hastings that his chief accuser had been Junius, it would have been advantageous to the defence, and a drawback to Sir P. Francis in two ways: first, by lessening, in the estimation of some, the trustworthiness of the charges urged by Francis against Hastings; and next, it would have tended to alienate from Francis many political friends with whom he was then in close co-operation to bring to justice the alleged Indian delinquent, whom in past times, as Junius, he had depicted in aggravating colours.

It is probable that Sir P. Francis, after getting possession of the Calcraft papers, destroyed them, as no trace of them can be found in the possession of his descendants. I may further add that the late Mrs. Godishall Johnson, the last surviving daughter of Sir Philip, used to say that "not only did she believe that Calcraft was in the secret, but also that his daughter was aware he had been so."

---

## V. RECENT AND CONCLUSIVE TESTIMONY

It seldom happens that absolute certainty can be obtained in human affairs; therefore reason and public utility require that mankind, in forming their opinions on the truth of facts, should be regulated by the superior number of probabilities on one side or the other.—LORD MANSFIELD.

THE laws of physical nature, depending on elements that change not, admit of no variety of results. We can no more believe the contrary respecting them than we can believe the converse of a mathematical truth; that a right line, for instance, is not the shortest distance between two points; or that the whole is not equal to all its parts collectively. Upon facts of this description there cannot exist any diversity of opinion, because there cannot be any diversity of experience.

But in moral questions the case is altered. These not being subject to any immutable relations, there cannot be uniform convictions respecting them. Conclusions will not only be different, from this cause, but also from differences in the perceptive powers. No two men can be found who see, feel, or observe, exactly alike, any more than they exactly coincide in features and expression. Men not only differ from each other, but the same individual is constantly liable to differ from himself under different influences. Hence, in inquiries pertaining to human conduct, we can rarely or never hope to reach absolute certainty, but must be governed, as Lord Mansfield says, by the "superior number of probabilities on one side or the other." "There are," as another learned judge has declared, "doubts, more or less, involved in every human transaction."*

The most direct and satisfactory portion of human testimony is that which a person gives of facts of which he has been personally cognizant, and has been the impartial observer. If he testify to his own actions, he is generally a still more competent witness, supposing the issue to be wholly indifferent to him; for he must be better acquainted with what he does himself than what he only observes in another. But the value of personal confession in regard to a man's own conduct is often overrated. It is in truth only circumstantial evidence, and may or may not be deemed credible, according to circumstances; its validity depending on the disinterestedness or credibility of the confessor, his powers of observation, his sanity of mind, and other conditions, open to proof or refutation like any other circumstantial detail. If a person confesses to an act that inculpates himself, which the law does not require him to do, it seems fair to take him at his word; but even

* Chief Justice Pollock.  Trial of the Mannings.  *Spectator*, Oct. 27, 1849.

this is not always to be relied upon; for examples are numerous of persons, under some delusive impulse or motive, accusing themselves of crimes they have not committed. On tho other hand, if a man testify in his own favour, it is proverbially said to be no recommendation, and without corroborative proof has little or no weight in a judicial trial.

Applying these distinctions to Junius, especially the remarks I have made on the value of confessional testimony, I will observe that, had Sir Philip Francis avowed the authorship of the letters, it would not have closed the controversy, nor greatly confirmed the conviction previously existing. Suppose he had declared " I am Junius; here are tho original letters I addressed to the *Public Advertiser*, and which Mr. Woodfall returned to me ; and here are the identical volumes, bound in vellum, that, according to my directions, I received from him." Would this confession have satisfied everybody? Certainly not. Might it not have been said, and with show of reason too, " His own confession of the authorship is not enough, nor even his proofs. He denied it before, and now ho avows it. Which are we to believe? Perhaps Sir Philip, like Hugh Boyd, General Lee, and other pretenders, only seeks an unearned honour. As to his documents, they may be fabricated ! Remember Shakspeare Ireland!" Doubtless a man so sagacious as Sir P. Francis foresaw this dilemma. He saw that an avowal would settle nothing, would tend little to strengthen the belief already entertained, and might expose him to great inconveniences. Wisely, then, did he act in screening himself from direct challenge by evasive denials, and yet respecting the truth (which he always said would be discovered) by abstaining from a positive abnegation of the authorship. In addition to these prudential considerations, it will be shortly seen that he was bound to secrecy, and that, as a man of honour, he could not act otherwise.

It is to evidence of this circumstantial nature that I now solicit attention, and which, to me, seems wholly conclusive. If a man's secrets are entrusted anywhere, it will most likely be to the wife of his bosom or to his descendants. I will first, therefore, insert some extracts from the remarkable letter lately addressed by Lady Francis to Lord Campbell, and communicated to him, as his Lordship informed me, by " his old and excellent friend the late Mr. Edward Dubois." The letter was written, as Lord Campbell states, " by the

amiable and intelligent widow of Sir P. Francis, for his information." It is inserted in his Lordship's "Lives of the
Lord Chancellors," vol. vi. p. 344.

\*       \*       \*       \*       \*

"Though his manner and conversation on that mysterious subject were
such as to leave me not a shadow of doubt on the fact of his being the author,
telling me circumstances that none but Junius could know, he never avowed
himself more than saying he knew what my opinion was, and never contra-
dicting it.    Indeed I made no secret of it to him, though not in a way that
called for any declaration either way; but I am certain he would not have
allowed me to continue in error, if it had been one, knowing my convictions.
His first gift after our marriage was an edition of Junius, which he bid me take
to my room, and not let it be seen, or speak on the subject; and his posthumous present, which his son found in his bureau, was *Junius Identified*, sealed
up and directed to me.   Sir Philip never did anything unadvisedly.   Edmund
Burke observed of him, ' He does nothing without a reason; there is thought
and motive in all he does, however trifling.'   You know Burke and he were
inseparables till the former left the Whigs; but their mutual regard, I believe, always continued.   Sir Philip told me that *Burke was convinced he
was Junius;* yet, before he was himself suspected, that is, before the 'Identification' came out, some people, discussing the question before him, asked
him if he thought Burke was the writer, as was generally believed at the
time:—' Faith, very likely,' answered Sir Philip, for I heard him, and considered it an ingenious evasion, like his answer to Sir Richard Philips, which
he took the trouble to explain to me was no denial, and said—' Only fools
could take it for one.'    He was very anxious to avoid either assent or denial,
lest he might implicate truth or honour, both of which he was very jealous of
committing.    He affronted poor Sam. Rogers, whom he liked much, to avoid
an ensnaring question.   On the 'Identified' appearing he withdrew his name
from Brooke's, when almost the father of the club, and petted and privileged
by all.    They entreated him not to desert them, and several wrote to beg
my intercession; but all in vain: he retired, and made no sign.   On consideration, I found the cause.   A club is neutral ground; it was not like the
Select Society, and protection of his own or his friends' houses, and he might
have been liable to meet with indiscreet or embarrassing questions.

\*       \*       \*       \*       \*

"But you will say, ' Why all this fear of discovery so many years after,
when the passions he excited, and the hearts they inflamed, had long been cold
in the grave?' I will tell you, in answer, what I collected from what he allowed
me to discover,—for so long as I asked no questions he would give me much
curious information, as of a third person,—from which I select the following
for Lord Campbell's satisfaction or amusement, prefacing, that my inferences
were known and uncontradicted by Sir Philip.   You know that he and
Philip Rosenhagen were declared by Dr. Thickness, the master of St.
Paul's School, to be the cleverest boys he ever educated.   At twelve and
thirteen years old he used to associate with men at a *table d'hôte* at Slaughter's Coffeehouse, when his father dined with the great.   At seventeen he
was Latin secretary to Lord Chatham; then to an embassy; then to General
Bligh; then clerk in the War Office, where he thought himself ill-treated.
He was at the Court of France in Louis the Fifteenth's time, when the

Jesuits were driven away for offending Madame Pompadour. Yet people say, at twenty-nine years old to thirty-two he was too young, and could not have gained the lofty tone to be the writer of these Letters, which bear all the stamp of what he must have been at that age, or even younger. But the fire and energy of youth lasted in him even when mature in experience and knowledge; and this union of youth and age not tempered by each other, but both in their extreme, is equally characteristic of Francis and Junius. The former passed his first years with his grandfather, the Dean of Leighlin, John Francis, who was a man highly considered in Ireland. Philip was an only and idolized son; he took the lead of his competitors at school, gaining the gold medal there. He was early accustomed to the lofty language and high thoughts of Lord Chatham, who, he told me, always treated him with consideration, discerning, no doubt, a spirit within worthy of an appearance greatly in his favour. Nor were the discussions his patron often carried on with his colleagues thrown away, when he was present, on the young secretary. So brought forward in the world, besides an innate loftiness of character, and a touch of Hotspur in him that would 'pluck bright honour from the pale-faced moon, or dive into the bosom of the deep' for it; when, therefore, he felt himself treated as a mere clerk in office, deprived of the promotion he expected, and even neglected by Lord Chatham, he wanted no stronger stimulus; but well aware of all the errors of government, which he had been trying to reform or stigmatize under different signatures for some time, his energy was roused, and vented itself in the first Letter of Junius. And here let me remark, that a writer who fears discovery should not write too much under one signature. He becomes at length an individual,—a character,—a living person; and adds so much to the danger of detection, that nothing but presence of mind, courage, and forethought like Sir Philip's, could parry it. This first letter, which was a kind of general attack and challenge, was intended, in bringing out a champion. The shield was struck, and the combat commenced! Sir W. D. gallantly wore no visor; but Junius could not imitate him! This was an advantage to him: but it was an embarrassment that Sir W. knew his father well, and himself slightly. This made him wish to close their controversy; and when his talents had been fully apparent in the castigation the K. B. had received, *a new and powerful ally came to his assistance.* Whether he knew that Junius was Francis I cannot say, nor whether he did more than slightly supply some facts that he could not have obtained without such aid; that some of the letters were submitted to him before they appeared, I have no doubt. Perhaps I have no right to mention that person's name; for Sir Philip was so anxious to guard it, that I had no doubt he had given his honour that the discovery should never come from him; nor did it; but he was not bound to volunteer an untruth if another found it out. When Junius says, 'I am the sole depository of my own secret, and it shall die with me,' I have no doubt he meant something that was like his reply to Sir Richard Philips. It might be a necessary evasion. Silence, sometimes, is consent. From the year 1805 to the end of 1816, I was either in constant correspondence with Sir P., or was his wife. Most of those beautiful letters were destroyed, as he would have *his* returned at the end of each year; but some few were spared at my earnest request. If these ever appear, they will make the world do him more justice. The situation he had in India, given by Government, of course involved a condition that he should never be known.  The King certainly told General Desaguliers—'We know who Junius is; he will write no more.'  I believe it was hoped he would see home no more: two out of the three collengues never did, and his return was all but a miracle.

\* \* \* \* \*

"No one that had any observation could be a member of Sir Philip's family without seeing that there was the 'volto sciolto, pensieri stretti,' in perfection,—not in his character, but produced by habit and necessity.  Many men have many secrets, but they are by nature cautious,—sometimes timid.  Sir Philip was daring and open on every other subject; but if the slightest thread of his web were touched, he was instantly on guard; not to me, certainly; yet he even kept within the compact that must have passed between the man who, he says, in a character of Fox, was the best-tempered public man he ever knew.  Some circumstances he always regretted.  One was losing the fame of being known; and, even if discovered, it might be said he had sold his power of guarding the liberties and rights of his country.

\* \* \* \* \*

"I must do Sir P. the justice to believe that he was driven into the measure of giving up the character, that is, the name of Junius; but though the conditions were both honourable and lucrative, he had to give up no principles or friends: he had not to approve the men and measures he once denounced; the most honourable of all offices was given to him.

\* \* \* \* \*

"Had Sir P. once said to me, 'I am not the writer of Junius's Letters,' I should have given up the belief immediately.  He would no more have volunteered a falsehood to me than he would have had the meanness of even leaving me in doubt.

\* \* \* \* \*

"He went once so far as to tell me that the truth will be known some time; and you remember the lines which I believe soothed him when he felt he had given up the purest of ambitions."

Lady Francis, in this interesting communication, forbore to inform Lord Campbell who the "new and powerful ally" was that "came to the assistance" of Junius and supplied him with information.  In subsequent letters to me her Ladyship has been more communicative, and I find that the "new and powerful ally" of Junius was the Earl of Chatham.  I have the same information from the grandson of Sir P. Francis, to whose obliging attentions, as well as those of Lady Francis, I feel greatly indebted.  As my inquiries of them were made accompanied with the intimation that information was sought publicly to elucidate more fully the mystery of Junius, there cannot be any impropriety in publishing the information I received.  But it will be best, in the first place, to consider the import of the letter addressed to Lord Campbell.

It appears to me almost demonstrative, and to render further inquiry unnecessary.  Sir P. Francis certainly does nowhere avow himself to be Junius; he could not do that, because he was bound to secrecy; but really the great secret seems ready to burst from his bosom; on every side it tries to escape; by every form of expression—by every symbol, save words, the mystery appears ready to be revealed.  What else could Sir Philip intend—what else could he mean, when on his marriage he presented Lady Francis with a copy of Junius, telling her to let no one know it, but that she had become affianced to the author?  But this was not enough; it seemed impossible for Sir Philip to die contented without a more distinct revelation.  His first gift might be construed as meant to win the favour of his young bride, but no such construction can be put on the second.  When Lady Francis received *Junius Identified*, Sir Philip had ceased to live; love and hatred, praise and blame, were alike indifferent to him.  No doubt he would fain have been more explicit: he seems indeed to have struggled with the secret, and been loth to leave the world without confession; but he could not with credit to himself act otherwise than he did.  Others had died—died nobly, without treachery; and should he—he who more than any was concerned in the bond, was most interested in observing it—should he alone prove traitor—traitor to those who had dealt so honourably by him, and who, long in their graves, could explain or defend nothing?  Impossible!  Honour fettered him inviolably—closed his lips to the last—and left him only the mute but expressive symbol of *Junius Identified*, to say that he was the MAN.

If, after resorting to this token—if, after employing so many indirect indications to impress upon Lady Francis the belief that he was Junius, Sir Philip had been discovered *not* to be the writer, he would, as her Ladyship has justly intimated, have been the basest of impostors.  He would also have been the weakest; for if he was not the author, how could he tell how soon the real author might be revealed upon unquestionable testimony, and then how supremely ridiculous and contemptible he would have appeared!  But Sir P. Francis was neither base nor imbecile; he was a man of powerful intellect, undoubted integrity, and sternness of purpose, as his life attested, and as many who knew him, and who are still living, confirm.

In old age, and near his death, Sir Philip seems to have become anxious that the truth should be known; but during

*f*

the active period of his existence, he was most vigilant to
preserve the secret, and took every precaution in his power to
prevent its discovery.  He got back the Calcraft papers, and,
for anything that can be discovered, destroyed them.  It was
the same with the copies of his public letters to Woodfall—
no traces of them remain.  Many reasons may be given for all
this caution, to which I shall advert in the concluding section,
and will only here remark, that, despite all his watchful endeavours, he did not escape the usual inconvenience or punishment of secret-keeping; for retribution, if I may so term it,
was on his track.  He then, as Lady Francis has related, retired from the world, withdrew his name from Brookes's, and
shrunk from the public scrutiny to which he foresaw he should
be hereafter subjected.

## VI. ARRANGEMENT WITH LORD NORTH.

THERE was nothing violent in the death of Junius.  He
lived his time, fulfilled his mission, and expired.  Before retiring from his labours, he duly executed his political testament; that volume of Letters which he collected, revised, and
dedicated to the English nation, with a fervid exhortation that
they would cherish its precepts, and, for the sake of their
children, watch over those glorious maxims of constitutional
freedom which in his last bequest to them he had sedulously
inculcated.  "When kings and ministers," says he, "are forgotten, when the force and direction of personal satire are no
longer understood, and when measures are only felt in their
remotest consequences, this book will, I believe, be found to
contain principles worthy to be transmitted to posterity."*
It is this legacy which constitutes the most precious portion of
the writings of Junius; the rest are chiefly preliminary, elucidatory, or extraneous, without distinct recognition by him
as the deliberate, authentic, and finished productions of the
writer.  That by which Junius sought to live in grateful remembrance—to be tried as a man, an author, and a patriot—
is the edition of his works corrected by himself, and which
forms the first volume of the present republication.
    The last public act of Junius was his letter to Chief Justice
Mansfield, January 21, 1772; his subsequent letters, under

* Dedication, vol. i. p. 67.

the signatures of Veteran, Scotus, and Nemesis, were unconnected with public questions; they were on private affairs, the
offspring of official pique or personal resentment. After the
letter to Lord Mansfield, the public never again heard of
Junius; and the last note Woodfall received from him, after
an interval of nine months, dated January 19, 1773, concluded
his correspondence with the printer.

By connecting these dates with the contemporary changes
in the personal relations of Sir Philip Francis, the silence of
Junius becomes perfectly intelligible, first, from the failure of
his sources of intelligence; and, secondly, because the one
great object of the Letters—the replacement of Lord Chatham
at the head of the Government—had ceased to be in immediate
prospect.

The year 1772 was a remarkable one to Sir P. Francis, in
connection with Junius. In March of that year he left the
War Office; in the same month his father died; in the same
year Mr. John Calcraft died; in 1774, Lord Holland; in 1776,
Lord Temple; and in 1778, Lord Chatham. In consequence
of Sir Philip's retirement from the War Office, and the deaths
of Dr. Francis and Mr. Calcraft, the three great channels of
information, by which he could alone hope to sustain the interest of the Letters, were at once stopped; and by a singular
casualty, within six years after, all the public characters who
had been contributors to, or interested in the Letters, had
ceased to exist. In addition, was the other change alluded
to, namely, the quiet, unpretending, but growing strength
and apparent permanence of the North ministry.

By attention to the dates of these occurrences, some of
the principal misrepresentations in the history of Junius
are at once disposed of. First, it is established that the
discontinuance of the Letters had nothing to do with the
appointment of Sir P. Francis to India; that appointment
not being received till June, 1773, full eighteen months
after Junius had ceased to write. Some intimation may have
been conveyed to Lord North that Junius would be resumed,
unless the author was provided for; but I have no authority
for this conjecture, nor do I believe any exists. The claims
of Francis on Government were independent of Junius,
though it is not improbable that, as the secret of his authorship had, previously to his appointment, been made known

*f* 2

both to the King and his Government, it may have had something to do with the precise mode adopted of disposing o
him, by sending him to the greatest possible distance.  But
the office was not given as purchase-money for the cessation
of the Letters: they had not only ceased long before Sir
Philip's appointment, but it is probable that the new
scheme for the government of British India had not been
thought of when the Letters were discontinued; for the
Act creating three new councillors, of which Sir P. Francis
became one, was passed in June, 1773, and the last letter
published was in January, 1772.

In his Dedication, Junius says, " I am the sole depositary
of my own secret, and it shall perish with me."  It appears
highly probable that, at the time, these words were written
in perfect sincerity.  I am inclined to think that, till then,
Francis was the sole depositary of the secret, and that, from
the fictitious character he had maintained, the secret means
by which he had obtained information, and the known hostility
of his nearest friends to the political sentiments of the Letters, he had resolved to remain unknown.  I have already
stated (p. lix.) on the best authority, that Dr. Francis
certainly did not discover his son to be Junius till after the
Letters were established in public favour.  Whether he ever
became acquainted with the fact, and when, I am not certain;
neither do I know when Mr. Calcraft or Lord Temple was made
privy to the secret; or when Lord Chatham first learned that
his former Latin secretary was Junius.  It is not impossible
that all the parties may have made the discovery about the same
period, that is, about 1770, or earlier *, and all of them after
Junius had written his Dedication; for Woodfall began to
think about a collective edition of the Letters as early as
August, 1769, when † only about twenty of them had been
published, and it appears that the complete edition of the
whole was out and on sale in May, 1772‡.

We thus see how beautifully, by simply attending to dates,
and getting hold of a few real facts of the case, things

---

* The late Mr. Dubois, who was an intimate friend, not amanuensis, as
sometimes stated, of Sir P. Francis, states in a letter dated Nov. 1, 1847,
that Lord Chatham began to correspond with Junius after the appearance of
his replies to Sir William Draper.

† Private Letter, No. 7, p. 21.   ‡ Private Letter, No. 61, p. 59.

reconcile themselves; and how all that is strange and unaccountable disappears.

An anecdote related by Sir N. Wraxall* has been often referred to by writers, to show that George III. became acquainted with the real name of Junius in 1772. Such may have been the case; Lord Holland may have confidentially learnt the name of Junius from Dr. Francis, and communicated it to the King: or the anecdote may have had its origin in the gossip of Garrick, and the information he had collected from Woodfall, and forwarded to Richmond, that Junius would write no more. That George III. was authentically in possession of the secret soon after will be presently shown, and that the King knowing Francis to be the author accounts for the fact that he was the only person, with the exception of Mr. Burke, who would speak to him on his unexpected return from India; his Majesty being among the few who were aware of the kind of subject that had re-appeared in his dominions, and unwilling perhaps to afford fuel for a new Junian warfare.

There is a piece of apocryphal intelligence that may be properly dealt with before coming to the real character of Sir Philip Francis's Indian appointment. In a recent work of Lord Campbell we find the following remarks respecting Junius:—

"At last 'the great boar of the forest' who had gored the King, and almost all his court, and seemed to be more formidable than any 'blatant beast,' was conquered—not by the spear of a knight-errant, but by a *little provender* held out to him, and he was sent to whet his tusks in a foreign land.'—*Lives of the Chief Justices*, vol. ii. p. 492.

From what has been stated, it is obvious that it was not a "little provender" that tamed, to keep up his Lordship's bovine metaphor. the terrible "boar." since Junius had retired from the field long previously, because the pasture was bare, and no fodder forthcoming from court or city, Hayes or Ingress, to keep up the stamina of the monster that had unsparingly devoured King and courtiers, lawyers, Scotchmen, and one of the greatest of chief justices.

* The following is the account of Wraxall:—"I have been assured that the King, riding out in 1772, accompanied by General Desaguliers, said to him in conversation, ' We know who Junius is, and he will write no more.' The General, who was too good a courtier to congratulate on such a piece of intelligence, contented himself with bowing, and the discourse proceeded no further."—*Memoirs*, vol. i. p. 455. [The son of Sir Nathaniel Wraxall, who is still living, lately stated to the publisher of the present volume that his father felt convinced that Sir Philip Francis was the author of Junius.]

I shall now state what appear to have been the preliminaries of Sir Philip Francis's appointment to the Supreme Council of Calcutta. About January, 1773, he returned from his continental tour, with very little to return to, being then out of office, and his father, after tedious illness, on the verge of dissolution. In this state of affairs Sir Philip was not likely to be indifferent about the future, and many ways were open to him. He might seek the friendly offices of either of his former patrons, Lord Holland or Lord Chatham; or he might submit, or a friend might submit, a temperate representation to Lord Barrington, setting forth the injustice he had suffered at the War Office, by the promotion over him of Mr. Chamier. The last is not unlikely to have been the course adopted, since it agrees with what Sir Philip Francis always stated of the influence that brought him under the favourable notice of Lord North. To this nobleman, previously to his Indian appointment, he was unknown; but Lord Barrington, who appears to have been of an easy, placable disposition, may have felt that he owed some reparation to Sir Philip, and, on hearing of his unprovided state, may, either under solicitation or spontaneously, have interested himself in his favour. Or Lord Chatham may have interfered, his Lordship, after becoming a peer, always continuing on the best terms with the King *. However this may be, it will be seen that the Earl of Chatham was one of the contracting parties with Francis, and in the secret.

And after all, the "little provender" bestowed on Francis was not of a very extraordinary character. He deserved it fairly, apart from every other consideration, for his personal merits and services. He was a man of first-rate talents; had filled many previous trusts, and must have been able to command the highest testimonials as to his oriental fitness. What wonder, then, that he should be selected for this "little provender," especially as, according to the editors of the *Chatham Papers*, it had been previously offered to, and declined by others?—for Indian nabobships, it must be remembered, though mostly lucrative, had not expanded into the safe and splendid proconsular appointments of a later period.

One important fact became known by all the parties to the transaction. It was on this occasion that Sir Philip Francis avowed himself to be the author of Junius, and his avowal was

* *Vide* Edinburgh Review, vol. lxx. p. 9?

made known to the King and the Government : whether to the
whole of the ministry, or exclusively to his Majesty and Lord
North, does not appear.   The only names that have been
mentioned to me as in the secret, and taking part in the
engagement of secrecy, are those of Lord North and the Earl
of Chatham.   This statement I make on the authority of
communications from Lady Francis and other survivors of the
family of Sir P. Francis ; and I feel a grateful pride in being
made the medium of communicating to the public the present information.   No feeling can be wounded, no confidence betrayed, no principle compromised, by this discovery ;
and doubtless the excellent sense of Lady Francis had suggested that the time had arrived, and the fit opportunity, on
the appearance of a new edition of the Letters, for terminating
this protracted controversy.

It must be borne in mind, that when Sir Philip Francis
avowed the authorship of the Letters to Lord North, he was
perfectly free to do so, his obligation to secrecy commencing
only after his engagement with the ministry.   Why the secret
continued so long may be explained by the consideration, that
all the contracting parties had an obvious interest in not divulging it.   Government could not wish it to be known that they
had taken into their service, and promoted to a lucrative
and highly responsible employment, a writer who was poli-
tically opposed to them, and had rendered many of them,
including even the King himself, the objects of bitter satire
and merciless inculpation.   Lord Chatham, as the confederate
of the assailant, secretly aiding him with information, was
under the strongest inducements to secrecy.   Lastly, Sir Philip
Francis, from natural pride and repugnance, as well as regard
to future personal objects and repute, must have been extremely loth the public should discover that the great Junius
had fallen, had deserted, in appearance (for it was only in
appearance), the cause of the people for a " common bribe,"
and joined the ranks of those he had so long reviled and held
up as the most dangerous foes of the constitution.   Such con
struction of his conduct would have been unavoidable, though
unfounded.   Sir Philip gave up no principle, nor, as he often
said, abandoned any friend ; and, in truth, his history attests
that there never was a more incorruptible, unflinching public
servant.   These merits Lord Brougham unreservedly con-

cedes to him *, though not among his warmest admirers. From the time he left the War Office, Sir Philip, as he once told the House of Commons, had never received a shilling of the public money, though many, under less urgent importunities, personally, and from family ties, had taken a "little provender."

That which must have held out the greatest temptation to unmask was the fame of the Letters, which augmented with time. Sir Philip knew, for Junius has said so, that mystery is a source of the sublime of authority, and sometimes of literary reputation: but the desire to wear a living crown must, to a mind like his, somewhat vain, and passionately fond of fame, have been overpowering. Lady Francis says he was fully sensible of the renown he was foregoing, and regretted it, but firmly resisted the temptation. Doubtless, his reasons, on reflection, and he did nothing without, were good and sufficient. Against a public avowal of the authorship was his contract of secrecy, which some may think to have been cancelled by the death of all the parties to it, except himself and George III., who was mentally defunct. But there were other and perhaps weightier reasons. The Duke of Grafton, whom Junius from political motives, for personal he could have none, had so relentlessly persecuted, lived almost as long as Sir Philip Francis, dying only in 1811, leaving a large family of surviving sons. There were also the numerous descendants of the Duke of Bedford, whom it would not have been pleasant, if safe, daily to have encountered, liable to be questioned as Junius (which they would have had an unquestionable right to do in case of open avowal) in the saloons or grounds of Holland House, or the still more free warren of a club-room. Discovery would have obviously and seriously endangered Sir Philip's peace, and would have weakened, if it had not destroyed, his political connection; and that at a time when he needed all the strength he could raise to fight his Indian battles, first against Mr. Hastings, and next against the Marquis of Wellesley. This is not all: opinions are not unanimous as to the *morals* of certain Letters. Junius thought himself justified in endeavouring to destroy the mischievous influence of public misdoers by damaging their private characters; but all are not agreed as to the integrity of this mode of political warfare. The sentiments of the present Chief Justice of

* Lives of British Statesmen.

England may be collected from his "Life of Lord Chancellor
Loughborough," in which Lord Campbell intimates that the
literary fame of Junius would be dearly purchased by the infamy of his libels. And this sentiment is by no means peculiar
to his Lordship; the question was lately put by the editor to a
distinguished leader of the Whig party, as to the probable
effect, according to his recollection, as a contemporary of the
writer, that an avowal of the Letters would have had on the
political connections of Sir Philip, and he emphatically declared that it would have entirely ruined him in their estimation. Junius foresaw this consequence, and has met it in
his own forcible and explicit way in what ho says on "measures, not men," denouncing it as the common cant of affected
moderation*. The equitable principle appears to be, that
private character ought to be held sacred till publicly ob-
truded; but if made a claim for public trust, or used as a
set-off against public misdeeds, then private history and character challenge scrutiny, and, if need be, censure.

Notwithstanding the fidelity of all the parties to the pledge
of secrecy of 1773, and the vigilance of Sir Philip Francis in
destroying evidence, the secret to a certain extent oozed out.
Throughout the latter part of the reign of George III. it was
commonly reported that the King, Lord North, and the late
Lord Grenville, had been made acquainted with the writer;
but the *name* of the author was never mentioned by any
one, nor suspected, till after the publication of the Woodfall
edition of 1812. Lord Sidmouth informed his son-in-law
on Lord Grenville's death, that "George III. and Lord
Grenville had both separately told him, that they knew
who was the author of Junius."† But no discovery was made
on the death of Lord Grenville; at least none has been
published. The "mysterious box with three seals," lately at
Stowe, has been rumoured "to contain secrets worth knowing"
with regard to Junius; but I can state on authority, that the
letters at Stowe were read not long since, and that they do
not reveal Junius. Probably they are of similar tenour to
those addressed to Lord Chatham about the same period, consisting of strictures on the contemporaries of Junius; and the
secret in respect to them, if not already anticipated, and to
which a factitious importance has been given by refusing to

* Vide Letter No. 26, vol. I. p. 224.
† Memoirs of Viscount Sidmouth, by the Dean of Carlisle, vol. iii. p. 449.

give any information of their contents, may be like that of the
Freemasons, and lose much of its value by disclosure.    Lord
Ashburton has recently purchased the Stowe MSS., but these
letters are said to have been withheld.

---

## VII. CONCLUSION, WITH CHARACTERISTIC TRAITS OF SIR PHILIP FRANCIS.

I INDULGE the hope that I have fulfilled the promises I held
out at the commencement.    Junius I undertook to make
known—to explain the necessities that enforced his fictitious
presentment to the public—the peculiarities in his personal
and official relations that prompted his enterprise, and enabled
him to support it with such extraordinary effect, power, and
resources—the circumstances that necessarily closed his career
of authorship—the events of his subsequent life that induced
a different style and character in his public writings—and the
obligations of honour, gratitude, future ease, party, and social
considerations, that afterwards bound him to preserve inviolate the secrets of his earlier career.

Beyond these revelations, I am not aware that anything
inexplicable pertains to the subject.    The mysterious spirit
that had eluded every grasp, and tortured general curiosity for
the best part of a century, has been fixed in the corporeal entity
to which it indubitably belongs.    There has certainly been no
avowal in words; but signs have been bequeathed, and a language that one whose lips were sealed could alone venture
to use has been employed—a language which cannot, and was
not meant to be misunderstood.    A confession less equivocal
was not allowable, consistently with past pledges; and, had
it been made, would hardly have contributed to the weight of
circumstantial evidence already adduced.

Believing that the great politico-literary mystery of the
age is solved, I shall merely add a few strictures on
the character of the singular person in whom it originated.
Sir Philip once remarked to the late Mr. Dubois, that he had
"spent so much time in writing, that he had almost forgotten
the art of speaking."    Notwithstanding the war of extermination waged by him against the Junius portion of his MSS.,

those which have escaped are numerous and curious; among these are the account of his long interview with the Pope at Rome, and the letters he wrote while attached to the British embassy in Portugal *.

Sir Philip Francis was a man of antique mould: it was the standard of his age, but of which examples are becoming rare under the influence of a more mild, equitable, and peaceful form of civilization.  His feelings, principles, and aspirations were all of the old Roman cast.  Partly he inherited them; they were fostered by the classic example of his learned and accomplished parent; but they found a congenial soil in his own temperament and vigorous mental organism.  From what he conceived to be the broad abstract right, either of individuals or communities, he never swerved, and no seduction of personal advantage could bend him.

This absolute inflexibility was exemplified at all times, in all places, and in all his private relations, whether on the banks of the Thames or the Ganges.  He held West India property, but undeviatingly advocated African freedom.  He steadily and to the last opposed the war with France, because he believed that the interference of the old European govern ments was a violation of the rights of Frenchmen to choose their own rulers.  His fatal Indian contests had a like origin; they were a pertinacious battle in behalf of right and justice towards the native princes, imperil as they might individual gains or British power.  The last effort of his pen † was a forcible appeal against the compulsory annexation of Norway to Sweden, to complete the arbitrary territorial demarcations of the Holy Alliance of despots.  And the last public speech he delivered was in his seventy-seventh year,

* His Portuguese letters have a strong resemblance to the style of Junius, though written antecedently, and refute the notion of Jaques and Coventry, that the natural style of Sir Philip was alien to that of Junius.  Speculation was right, however, when it was conjectured that Junius must be an Irishman from his Hibernicisms, especially his phrase, "the sophistries of a *collegian*," a term in use at Dublin for *governman*, not at Oxford or Cambridge. Heron, too, with singular tact, unconsciously threw out a hint applicable to the situation of Francis.  Criticising the composition of Letter 37, he says, " Its paragraphs seem to have been thrown out upon paper, without the preconception of any regular plan."  This is very likely to have been the mode in which Sir Philip worked off at intervals the first draft of many of his Letters at the War Office, and had not always time afterwards for polishing and best connecting their detached parts.

† Letter to Earl Grey.  Ridgway, 1814.

from the hustings at Brentford*, when he energetically denounced as unnecessary the suspension of the Habeas Corpus
Act, and the other Acts about to be passed, against the freedom of public meetings, writing, and speaking.

These are noble traits, which adequately fill up any outline
that fancy may have depicted of the Junius of old.   There
are other coincidences in minor matters, not undeserving of
notice.   Junius was obviously of a free, impulsive nature,
and Francis was a " very Hotspur."   To mystify Woodfall,
and avert recognition by his former school friend, he tells
him " I never am angry ;"† but the fact is, Sir Philip was apt
to be so, and violently.   I have heard a lady say of him that
when excited, his eyes, like Homer's heroes, emitted sparks
of living fire.   In connection with temperament, another incident forces itself on notice.   In his Dedication, Junius says
of the Letters, " To me they originally owe nothing but a
healthy, sanguine-constitution," a characteristic peculiarly
that of Sir P. Francis.   His personal appearance was im-
pressive.   He had large lustrous eyes, oval face, lips well
formed and strongly marked; was tall, thin, and of an
elegant figure : altogether the facial presentment was that of
an impassioned soul, with an active, acute, energetic intellect.

From what has been related to me, it would appear that Sir
P. Francis's musings in his fine library of Greek and Roman
classics (to which he was much attached, as his numerous
marginal annotations testify ‡), must have been seriously dis-

* June 22, 1817, at a meeting of Middlesex freeholders to petition against
the Six Acts.

† Private Letter, No. 47, p. 51.

‡ The following note is furnished me by the publisher, Mr. Bohn :—Sir
Philip Francis's library was sold by auction Feb. 3, 1838, and two following
days, by Mr. R. H. Evans, of Pall Mall.   It comprised 859 articles, including a very good collection of Greek and Latin classics, an extensive series of
political pamphlets and newspapers, and many of the principal works in
English and general literature.   The manuscripts were reserved by the
family, and not brought to the hammer.   Many of the books were annotated in the margins by himself, and nearly all bore evidence of having been
read or used.   Among the lots which more particularly concern the present
enquiry were several different editions of Junius's Letters, and some of the
printed enquiries as to their authorship.   These sold for rather high prices,
as the following quotations will show :—

" 416. Junius's Letters, 2 vols., with some MS. Corrections of the text,
        and Notes by Sir Philip Francis.  In calf; 1783.  12l. 12s.
                                                            Armstrong.

" 417. Junius's Letters, with Notes by Heron, 2 vols, with some MS.

:urbed by the movements of the author of *Junius Identified.* The first fix of Mr. Taylor upon Dr. Francis brought him close upon the real author of Junius, who could not help feeling apprehensive that the mistake of ten years in his age would in all likelihood be detected. In consequence, he attempted a diversion. He called upon Mr. Taylor, and intimated his surprise at the wild-goose chase in which he had learned he was wasting his time: said that so many years

Notes and Corrections of the Text, by Sir Ph. Francis, 1804. 2l. 2s. *Armstrong.*

"418. Junius's Letters, with Notes by Woodfall, 3 vols. A *presentation copy from Woodfall,* 1814. 2l. 2s. *Scott.*

"419. Junius Identified with a Distinguished Living Character, and the Supplement, with Facsimiles and Autograph Letter of Sir Philip Francis, 1816 17. 4l. *Armstrong.*

" 420. Junius. Discovery of the Author of Junius (via. Dr. and Sir Ph. Francis), 1813. The Pamphleteer, No. 54, containing Barker's Remarks on Sir P. Francis's Claims, 1827. Edinburgh Review, No. 57, containing the Review of Junius's Letters, with some MS. Corrections by Sir P. Francis. 2l. 10s. *Armstrong.*

" 421. Junius. A Collection of the Letters of Atticus, Lucius, and Junius; *with MS. Notes and Corrections, and Blanks filled up by Sir P. Francis,* 1769, and *other Tracts in the Volume.* 3l. 5s. *Armstrong.*

" 422. Junius. A Supplement to Junius Identified; with MS. Notes by Sir Ph. Francis, 1817. Discovery of the Author of Junius's Letters, 1513. 3l. 3s. *Armstrong.*"

It may be relevant here to quote the following article:—

" Sir Philip Francis's Speeches and Pamphlets, collected in 6 vols. 8vo, with numerous MS. Corrections and Notes, Extracts from Newspapers, &c. 14l. *Morton.*

" 515. Dalrymple's Memoirs of Great Britain and Ireland, 2 vols. 4to, 1771. *,* See a most curious note of Sir P. Francis, stating that the proof-sheets of this work were submitted for revision to George III. by Lord Rochford, " I know the fact," and a most severe note on Johnson's Character and Principles. 2l. 12s. *Armstrong.*"

These and most of the other annotated books were bought, under the pseudonyme of Armstrong, for Mr. H. R. Francis, then master of a Grammar School at Kingston-upon-Hull, in whose possession they still are. Lot 340, bought in the name of Morton, was for Mr. John George Francis, who then resided in Gower Street. The most curious illustration, perhaps, which could be collected from among them, was a letter found in lot 419, dated Bath, *Thursday morning, Dec.* 20, 1771, addressed to his wife, announcing his arrival at Bath "last night." It refers to the very feeble and helpless condition of his father, who had summoned the writer to his bedside. As, in Private Letter No. 47, Sir Philip gives peremptory orders that Woodfall should not write to him again until further notice, and as there are no letters of Junius under any of his signatures between Dec. 17 and Jan. 6, it is so far corroborative.

had elapsed, and so many fruitless attempts had been made
to discover Junius, that it now seemed perfectly hopeless
to expect he would ever be found out. "He would be
a lucky person indeed," continued Sir Philip, "who could
find out Junius;—why, it would make a man's fortune!"
Finding these discouragements had failed to make the desired
impression, Sir Philip observed at parting, "*If* you do persist in your purpose, I hope you will present me with a copy
of your book." With this the "tall gentleman" disappeared,—as he had done forty years before, after throwing a
Junius letter into Woodfall's office in Ivy Lane.

Sir Philip's first impression of greatness seems to have
been derived from the Earl of Chatham. The noble eloquence
of the Great Statesman—his pride—his lofty and independent
sentiments—his respect for national greatness and individual
merit in every station—his contempt for trivial things—his disdain of mere party objects—with his unstained private life—
deeply and ineffaceably impressed Francis with a sense of
human excellence, realizing all the visions he had cherished
in his early studies of the ancient models. He also thought
favourably of the Great Agitator of the city, on account of his
public services. Notwithstanding the private profligacy of
Wilkes, into which he appears to have been hurried, partly
by an uncongenial marriage, partly by his own unruly passions, but most of all, by his hearty contempt of hypocrisy,
he was not a man to be wholly despised. Like Junius, who
cautions Woodfall to be on his guard against "patriots," he
had no sympathy for democratic extremes, but he had a well-
grounded respect for constitutional freedom, and when it
was menaced by court judges and parasites rendered im
portant services intrepidly. It was the timely stand which
he made that put an end to general warrants, and his
fearless magisterial conduct that mainly contributed to procure a free publication of the parliamentary debates *. Junius
acted as his mentor, and the letters he addressed to him are
as valuable as any in the collection, replete with good common-
sense advice, as well as with sound political knowledge. The
active prying habits of Sir Philip, pending the Junius letters,

* Wilkes, too, appears to have had considerable claims to scholarship; he
edited Catullus and Theophrasti Characteres, upon a wager that he would
produce them without a single typographical error, and he began a History
of England from the Revolution of 1688, of which the Introduction (30 pages)
was printed (as a prospectus) in 4to., *Almon*, 1768.

makes it very probable that he was personally acquainted with so conspicuous a public character as Wilkes, and this would account for his referring the Dedication to him for correction. It is certain that Francis was on friendly terms with Mr. Wilkes after his return from India, if not before, and used to visit him at Kensington ; and at this latter period there is good reason for presuming that Wilkes knew Junius to be Francis.

The last conclusion is rendered probable by a letter addressed to the late Mr. E. H. Barker and inserted in his work on Junius. It was addressed to him by Mr. Sergeant Rough, from Sergeants' Inn, and is dated April 12, 1827. Mr. Rough had married a natural daughter of Wilkes, and in his letter remarks, " Mr. Wilkes used, I have been told, to say that he knew who the author of Junius was—that it was not Rosenhagen ; but he never said it was *not* Sir P. Francis. The latter used to dine at Kensington frequently, and once cut off a lock of Mrs. Rough's hair (she was then quite a girl). She had an obscure recollection that her father once said that she had met Junius."

Horne Tooke always appeared much perturbed when the subject of Junius was introduced. He was once asked if he knew the author ; on the question being put he immediately crossed his knife and fork on his plate, and, assuming a stern look, replied, " I do." After this, Mr. Stephen says, " his manner, tone, and attitude were all too formidable to admit fo any further interrogatories." *

The constancy of Sir P. Francis's attachments will appear from a rencontre he had with Lord Brougham on the merits of Mr. Wilkes. It was referred to some years since in the Edinburgh Review†, and adduced, as it had been before, as affording additional proof of the identity of Francis and Junius. I lately reminded Lord Brougham of this adventure, and his Lordship very good naturedly gave me an account of the affair. " It happened," says he, " at Brookes's, of which I was a member, though I am not a member of any club now. I had been commenting in the House of Commons on the profligacy of Wilkes's character, and the shame his popularity had brought on the people of England. Mr. Wilberforce complimented me, and confirmed my statement. Mr. Canning then took the opportunity to observe that Wilkes was by no

* Memoirs of John Horne Tooke, vol. ii. p. 358.    † No. 141, October, 1829.

means a singular instance of a demagogue not being respectable, and added,—

> 'He's knight o' th' shire, and represents them all.'

Next morning I was at the club, and Sir P. Francis was there, and had been reading an account of last night's debate. He immediately began to remonstrate with me, in company with other friends; observed that I ought to have said nothing in disparagement of Wilkes; he was fighting the public battles against the Court, and ought to be supported; it was the policy of the Court always to fix upon a bad man to run down, not a good one. He next turned upon Lord Mansfield; said he was a corrupt judge, and took bribes. I expostulated with him, remarking that such detestable practices would have been discovered and the chief justice impeached. He rejoined he 'knew it to be true; he took bribes in the Douglas cause, and he could prove it.'"—Here the sympathies and aversions of Junius are reproduced with pristine force and bitterness.

Sir Philip was impetuous, and somewhat abrupt in manner. He once interrupted George IV., at the royal table (and we are credibly informed that he frequently dined there), in the midst of a tedious story, with a "*Well, Sir, well!*" The prime of his life was wasted in a fruitless effort to arrest what he thought our unscrupulous career in India. His regrets on this account are painful to read. "I passed," said he in the House of Commons, "six years in perpetual misery and contest in Bengal, at the hazard of my life; then a wretched voyage of ten months, and two and twenty years of labour in the same cause, unsupported and alone. By so long endeavouring to maintain right against wrong, I have sacrificed my repose and forfeited all hope of personal advantage." It was truly the martyrdom of a life, and of a life that, with the brilliant gifts of Francis, might otherwise have been distinguished and prosperous. Who could help regretting the sacrifice? Others may learn prudence from his failures, but it was too late with Sir Philip. Yet the cause in which he failed was a noble one.

> —— "In man's cause I drew
> These evils on my head—but ills like these,
> My mind presaged them not."

# JUNIUS.

## PRIVATE LETTERS OF JUNIUS.

### LETTERS TO MR. H. S. WOODFALL.

#### No. 1.

SIR,                                                April 20, 1769.

I AM preparing a paper, which you shall have on or before Saturday night. Advertise it for Monday *. Junius on Monday.

C.

If any inquiry is made about these papers, I shall rely on your giving me a hint.

---

#### No. 2†.

SIR,                                          Friday, May 5, 1769.

IT is essentially necessary that the inclosed should be published to-morrow, as the great question comes on on Monday, and Lord Granby is already staggered ‡.

If you should receive an answer to it, you will oblige me much by not publishing it till after Monday.

* Junius, Letter 11, vol. I. p. 147.
† This note was addressed to Mr. Woodfall, with a desire that it should " be opened by himself only."
‡ The letter forms No. 55 of the Miscellaneous Collection, *post*, and the great question alluded to was upon the Middlesex petition against the seating of Colonel Luttrell for that county. The debate took place on Monday, the 8th of May, in the House of Commons, and continued from half-past one o'clock in the afternoon till half-past four the next morning, when, upon a division, there appeared for the petition 152, against it 221. The speakers

on this occasion, in favour of the petition, were Mr. Dowdeswell, Lord J. Cavendish, Mr. Wedderburne, Mr. Grenville, Mr. Cornwall, Mr. Burke, Mr. Seymour, and Sir George Savile; those against it, Mr. Stanley, Sir G. Osborne, Dr. Blackstone, Mr. W. Ellis, Mr. Thurlow, Mr. C. J. Fox, Mr. Moreton, and Sir F. Norton.

In consequence of the rejection of the petition to the House of Commons, the following was soon afterwards presented to the King, which we insert, as we shall also, in their due places, those of London and Westminster, upon similar subjects, with a view of giving some idea of the general politics of the day, and the warmth of the respective controversies that distinguished it.

### " TO THE KING'S MOST EXCELLENT MAJESTY.

" The humble petition of the Freeholders of the County of Middlesex.

" *Most Gracious Sovereign*,

" We, your Majesty's dutiful and loyal subjects, the Freeholders of the County of Middlesex, beg leave, with all affectionate submission and humility, to throw ourselves at your royal feet, and humbly to implore your paternal attention to those grievances of which this county and the whole nation complain, and those fearful apprehensions with which the whole British Empire is most justly alarmed.

" With great grief and sorrow we have long beheld the endeavours of certain evil-minded persons, who attempt to infuse into your royal mind notions and opinions of the most dangerous and pernicious tendency, and who promote and counsel such measures as cannot fail to destroy that harmony and confidence which should ever subsist between a just and virtuous prince and a free and loyal people.

" For this disaffected purpose they have introduced into every part of the administration of our happy legal constitution a certain unlimited and indefinite discretionary power, to prevent which is the sole aim of all our laws, and was the sole cause of all those disturbances and revolutions which formerly distracted this unhappy country; for our ancestors, by their own fatal experience, well knew that in a state where discretion begins, law, liberty, and safety end. Under the pretence of this discretion, or, as it was formerly, and has been lately, called, Law of state, we have seen

" English subjects, and even a member of the British Legislature, arrested by virtue of a general warrant issued by a secretary of state, contrary to the law of the land.

" Their houses rifled and plundered, their papers seized, and used as evidence upon trial.

" Their bodies committed to close imprisonment.

" The Habeas Corpus eluded.

" Trial by jury discountenanced, and the first law officer of the crown publicly insinuating that juries are not to be trusted.

" Printers punished by the ministry in the supreme court without a trial by their equals, without any trial at all.

" The remedy of the law for false imprisonment debarred and defeated.

" The plaintiff and his attorney, for their appeal to the law of the land, punished by expenses and imprisonment, and made, by forced engagements, to desist from their legal claim.

" A writing determined to be a libel by a court where it was not cognizable in the first instance; contrary to law, because all appeal is thereby cut off, and inferior courts and juries influenced by such predetermination.

" A person condemned in the said courts as the author of the supposed libel, unheard, without defence or trial.

" Unjust treatment of petitions, by selecting only such parts as might be wrested to criminate the petitioner, and refusing to hear those which might procure him redress.

" The thanks of one branch of the Legislature proposed by a minister to be given to an acknowledged offender for his offence, with the declared intention of screening him from the law.

" Attachments wrested from their original intent of removing obstructions to the proceedings of law, to punish by sentence of arbitrary fine and imprisonment, without trial or appeal, supposed offences committed out of court.

" Perpetual imprisonment of an Englishman without trial, conviction, or sentence, by the same mode of attachment, wherein the same person is at once party, accuser, judge, and jury.

" Instead of the ancient and legal civil police, the military introduced at every opportunity, unnecessarily and unlawfully patrolling the streets, to the alarm and terror of the inhabitants.

" The lives of many of your Majesty's innocent subjects destroyed by military execution.

" Such military execution solemnly adjudged to be legal.

" Murder abetted, encouraged, and rewarded.

" The civil magistracy rendered contemptible by the appointment of improper and incapable persons.

" The civil magistrates tampered with by administration, and neglecting and refusing to discharge their duty.

" Mobs and riots hired and raised by the ministry, in order to justify and recommend their own illegal proceedings, and to prejudice your Majesty's mind by false insinuations against the loyalty of your Majesty's subjects.

" The freedom of election violated by corrupt and undue influence, by unpunished violence and murder.

" The just verdicts of juries and the opinion of the judges overruled by false representations to your Majesty; and the determinations of the law set aside, by new, unprecedented, and dangerous means; thereby leaving the guilty without restraint, and the injured without redress, and the lives of your Majesty's subjects at the mercy of every ruffian protected by administration.

" Obsolete and vexatious claims of the crown set on foot for partial and election purposes.

" Partial attacks on the liberty of the press, the most daring and pernicious libels against the constitution and against the liberty of the subject being allowed to pass unnoticed, whilst the slightest libel against a minister is punished with the utmost rigour.

" Wicked attempts to increase and establish a standing army, by endeavouring to vest in the crown an unlimited power over the militia, which, should they succeed, must, sooner or later, subvert the constitution, by augmenting the power of administration in proportion to their delinquency.

" Repeated endeavours to diminish the importance of members of parliament individually, in order to render them more dependent on administration collectively. Even threats having been employed by ministers to suppress the freedom of debate; and the wrath of parliament denounced against measures authorized by the law of the land.

"Resolutions of one branch of the legislature set up as the law of the land, being a direct usurpation of the rights of the two other branches, and therefore a manifest infringement of the constitution.

"Public money shamefully squandered and unaccounted for, and all inquiry into the cause of arrears into the civil list prevented by the ministry.

"Inquiry into a paymaster's public accounts stopped in the exchequer, though the sums accounted for by that paymaster amount to above forty millions sterling.

"Public loans perverted to private ministerial purposes.

"Prostitution of public honours and rewards to men who can neither plead public virtue nor services.

"Irreligion and immorality, so eminently discountenanced by your Majesty's royal example, encouraged by administration, both by example and precept.

"The same discretion has been extended by the same evil counsellors to your Majesty's dominions in America, and has produced to our suffering fellow-subjects in that part of the world grievances and apprehensions similar to those which we complain of at home.

"*Most Gracious Sovereign,*

"Such are the grievances and apprehensions which have long discontented and disturbed the greatest and best part of your Majesty's loyal subjects. Unwilling, however, to interrupt your royal repose, though ready to lay down our lives and fortunes for your Majesty's service, and for the constitution as by law established, we have waited patiently, expecting a constitutional remedy by the means of our own representatives, but our legal and free choice having been repeatedly rejected, and the right of election now finally taken from us by the unprecedented seating of a candidate who was never chosen by the county, and who, even to become a candidate, was obliged fraudulently to vacate his seat in parliament, under the pretence of an insignificant place, invited thereto by the prior declaration of a minister, that whoever opposed our choice, though but with four votes, should be declared member for the county. We see ourselves, by this last act, deprived even of the franchises of Englishmen, reduced to the most abject state of slavery, and left without hopes or means of redress but from your Majesty or God.

"Deign then, most gracious Sovereign, to listen to the prayer of the most faithful of your Majesty's subjects; and to banish from your royal favour, trust, and confidence, for ever, those evil and pernicious counsellors who have endeavoured to alienate the affection of your Majesty's most sincere and dutiful subjects, and whose suggestions tend to deprive your people of their dearest and most essential rights, and who have traitorously dared to depart from the spirit and letter of those laws which have secured the crown of these realms to the House of Brunswick, in which we make our most earnest prayers to God that it may continue untarnished to the latest posterity."

Signed by 1565 Freeholders.

### No. 3.

Sir,                                        Saturday, July 15, 1769.

I HAVE received the favour of your note. From the contents of it, I imagine you may have something to communicate to me. If that be the case, I beg you will be particular; and also that you will tell me candidly whether you know or suspect who I am. Direct a letter to Mr. William Middleton*, to be left at the bar of the New Exchange Coffee House, on Monday, as early as you think proper.

I am, Sir, your most obedient, and

Most humble Servant,

C.

---

### No. 4.

(Private.)

Sir,                                             July 17, 1769.

MR. NEWBERRY having thought proper to reprint my Letters †, I wish at least he had done it correctly. You will oblige me much by giving him the following hint ‡ to-morrow. The inclosed § when you think proper.

"Mr Newberry, having thought proper to reprint Junius's Letters, might at least have corrected the errata, as we did constantly.

| Page | 1, line 13, for national | read national. |
| | 3, — 4, — was | — were. |
| | 5, — 15, — indisputable | — indispensable. |
| Letter 7, — 4, — in all masses | — in all the masses. |
| | 15, — 24, — rightest | — brightest. |
| | 48, — 2, — indiscreet | — indirect." |

* "Mr. William Middleton's letter is sent as desired." Answer to correspondents in the *Public Advertiser* of July 20, 1769.

† Newberry had thought proper at this time to publish a spurious and surreptitious edition of the first fifteen letters, as printed in the author's edition, under the title of *The Political Contest;* and it was these unauthorised publications that gave the first idea of publishing a genuine edition of the whole.

‡ This request does not appear to have been complied with, as the following answer to correspondents was inserted in the *Public Advertiser* of the 18th of July:—" Reasons why the hint was not printed are sent to the last-mentioned Coffee House in the Strand, from whence our *old* correspondent will be pleased to send for them."

§ Junius, Letter 16.

I did not expect more than the life of a newspaper, but if this man will keep me alive, let me live without being offensive.

*Speciosa quarro pascere tigres.*

---

## No. 5.

SIR,                                July 21, 1769, Friday Night.

I CAN have no manner of objection to your reprinting the letters, if you think it will answer, which I believe it might before Newberry appeared. If you determine to do it, give me a hint, and I will send you more errata (indeed they are innumerable), and perhaps a preface. I really doubt whether I shall write any more under this signature *. I am weary of attacking a set of brutes, whose writings are too dull to furnish me even with the materials of contention, and whose measures are too gross and direct to be the subject of argument, or to require illustration.

That Swinney† is a wretched but a dangerous fool. He had the impudence to go to Lord G. Sackville, whom he had never spoken to, and to ask him, whether or no he was the author of Junius—take care of him.

Whenever you have anything to communicate to me, let the hint be thus, O *at the usual place*, and so direct to Mr. John Fretly, at the same Coffee House, where it is absolutely impossible I should be known.

---

* In his Dedication (p. 67), Junius alleges the "encouragement and applause" of the people to have been the reason the letters were continued.—ED.

† "A correspondent of the printer's," Dr. Good says, but this does not throw much light on the subject, and it may be doubted whether Junius knew a great deal of the person he stigmatizes so outrageously. But the manifest aim of Junius was to impress his printer with the belief that he knew everything and everybody. Who Swinney was, however, is a question that has been often asked, and seems satisfactorily answered in the following extract, cited by Barker from Dr. Watt's *Bibliotheca Britannica*:—

"Swinney, Sidney, D.D., F.R. and A.SS. The *Battle of Minden*, a Poem, in Three Books. Lond. 4to, 10s. A Sermon. Lond. 1769, 4to, 1s."

The author of a poem on the *Battle of Minden*, if not on intimate terms with Lord George Sackville, was likely "enough to have spoken to him," especially if he had been, as has been stated, Lord George's chaplain.--ED.

I did *not* mean the Latin to be printed.

I wish Lord Holland may acquit himself with honour\*. If his cause be good, he should at once have published that account to which he refers in his letter to the mayor†.

Pray tell me whether George Onslow means to keep his word with you, about prosecuting‡. *Yes* or *No* will be sufficient. Your Lycurgus§ is a Mr. Kent, a young man of good parts upon town. *And so I wish you a good night||.*

Yours,

C.

————

A.

The " wish " expressed above, that "Lord Holland may acquit himself with honour," refers to a charge of peculation made in the City Petition presented to his Majesty, July 5, 1769, of which the following is a copy :—

" The humble Petition of the Livery of the City of London in Common Hall assembled.

" *Most Gracious Sovereign,*

" We, your Majesty's dutiful and loyal subjects, the Livery of the City of London, with all the humility which is due from free subjects to their lawful Sovereign, but with all the anxiety which the sense of the present oppressions, and the just dread of future mischiefs produce in our minds, beg leave to lay before your Majesty some of those intolerable grievances which your people have suffered from the evil conduct of those who have been intrusted with the administration of your Majesty's government, and from the secret unremitting influence of the worst of counsellors.

" We should be wanting in our duty to your Majesty, as well as to

\* It has been already observed, in the Preliminary Essay, that Junius appears to have uniformly entertained a good opinion of, or at least a partiality for, Lord Holland. The remark is not new; it was noticed long ago by several of his opponents. Thus, in a letter subscribed by our author *Anti-Fox*, and inserted in the *Public Advertiser* of October 16, 1771, he thus speaks of him : " I know nothing of Junius ; but I see plainly that he has designedly spared Lord Holland and his family." [The reason of Junius sparing the Fox family is apparent after the elucidation given of the authorship of the Letters, and it is now only surprising that so palpable a source of Identification was not earlier and more forcibly dwelt upon.—Ed.]

† See note A at the end of this letter.

‡ See note B, relative to Mr. Onslow, at the conclusion of the preceding note.

§ Lycurgus was a frequent writer in the *Public Advertiser* during the spring and summer of 1769 ; and opposed the ministry, but with less violence than most of his contemporaries.

|| See, in the Editor's remarks on the authorship of Junius, the extract from a Letter of Sir Philip Francis to his children.—Ed.

ourselves and our posterity, should we forbear to represent to the throne the desperate attempts which have been and are too successfully made to destroy that constitution to the spirit of which we owe the relation which subsists between your Majesty and the subjects of these realms, and to subvert those sacred laws which our ancestors have sealed with their blood.

" Your ministers, from corrupt principles, and in violation of every duty, have, by various enumerated means, invaded our invaluable and unalienable right of trial by jury.

" They have, with impunity, issued general warrants, and violently seized persons and private papers.

" They have rendered the laws non-effective to our security, by evading the Habeas Corpus.

" They have caused punishments, and even perpetual imprisonment, to be inflicted without trial, conviction, or sentence.

" They have brought into disrepute the civil magistracy, by the appointment of persons who are, in many respects, unqualified for that important trust, and have thereby purposely furnished a pretence for calling in the aid of a military power.

" They avow, and endeavour to establish a maxim, absolutely inconsistent with our constitution, that ' an occasion for *effectually* employing a military force always presents itself when the civil power is *trifled with or insulted;*' and, by a fatal and false application of this maxim, they have wantonly and wickedly sacrificed the lives of many of your Majesty's innocent subjects, and have prostituted your Majesty's sacred name and authority to justify, applaud, and recommend, their own illegal and bloody actions.

" They have screened more than one murderer from punishment, and in its place have unnaturally substituted reward.

" They have established numberless unconstitutional regulations and taxations in our colonies. They have caused a revenue to be raised in some of them by prerogative. They have appointed civil law judges to try revenue causes, and to be paid from out of the condemnation money.

" After having insulted and defeated the law on different occasions, and by different contrivances, both at home and abroad, they have at length completed their design, by violently wresting from the people the last sacred right we had left, the right of election ; by the unprecedented seating of a candidate notoriously set up and chosen only by themselves. They have thereby taken from your subjects all hopes of parliamentary redress, and have left us no resource, under God, but in your Majesty.

" All this they have been able to effect by corruption, by a scandalous misapplication and embezzlement of the public treasure, and a shameful prostitution of public honours and employments, procuring deficiencies of the civil list to be made good without examination ; and, *instead of punishing, conferring honours on a paymaster, the public defaulter of unaccounted millions.*

" From an unfeigned sense of the duty we owe to your Majesty and to our country we have ventured thus humbly to lay before the throne these great and important truths, which it has been the business of your ministers to conceal. We most earnestly beseech your Majesty to grant us redress. It is for the purpose of redress alone, and for such occasions as the present, that those great and extensive powers are intrusted to the crown, by the wisdom of that constitution which your Majesty's illustrious family was chosen to defend, and which, we trust in God, it will for ever continue to support."

Lord Holland, suspecting himself to be implicated in the last paragraph but one of the above petition, addressed the following letter to the Lord Mayor upon this subject :—

TO THE RIGHT HONOURABLE THE LORD MAYOR.

"MY LORD,

"In a petition presented by your Lordship it is mentioned as a grievance, *instead of punishing, conferring honours on a paymaster, the public defaulter of unaccounted millions.* I am told that I am the paymaster here censured; may I beg to know of your Lordship if it is so? If it is, I am sure Mr. Beckford must have been against it, because he knows and could have shown your Lordship in writing the utter falsehood of what is there insinuated.

"I have not the honour to know your Lordship, so I cannot tell what you may have heard to induce you to carry to our Sovereign a complaint of so atrocious a nature.

"Your Lordship, by your speech made to the King at delivering the petition, has adopted the contents of it; and I do not know of whom to inquire but of your Lordship concerning this injury done to an innocent man, who is by this means (if I am the person meant) hung out as an object of public hatred and resentment.

"You have too much honour and justice not to tell me whether I am the person meant, and if I am, the grounds upon which I am thus charged, that I may vindicate myself, which truth will enable me to do to the conviction of the bitterest enemy, and therefore I may boldly say to your Lordship's entire satisfaction, whom I certainly have never offended.

"I am, with the greatest respect, my Lord,

"Your Lordship's most obedient and most humble Servant,

"Holland House, Kensington,                             "HOLLAND."
    "July 9, 1769."

To this letter the Lord Mayor returned the following answer :—

"The Lord Mayor presents his compliments to Lord Holland, and in answer to the honour of his Lordship's letter delivered to him by Mr. Selwyn, he begs leave to say that he had no concern in drawing up the petition from the Livery of London to his Majesty ; that he looks on himself only as the carrier, together with other gentlemen charged by the Livery with the delivery of it; that he does not, nor ever did, hold himself accountable for the contents of it, and is a stranger to the nature of the supposed charge against his Lordship.

"Mansion House, July 10, 1769."

Mr. Beckford, seeing his name implicated in this correspondence, wrote from the country the following letter to a friend, who was a liveryman of the city.

"DEAR SIR,                                  "Fonthill, July 15, 1769.

"I AM as much surprised as you seem to be, at seeing my name and papers in my possession appealed to by a noble Lord. You and my friends in the city think it incumbent on me to vindicate (as they are pleased to express themselves) my honour and character, which is called in question. The only proper satisfaction in my power to give you and my other friends is to relate plain matters of fact to the best of my recollection.

"In the last session of parliament, on a question of revenue (as far as my memory serves), I did declare to the House that the public revenue had been squandered away, and that the money of the nation had not been regularly audited and accounted for.

"That in the department of the pay-office I had been informed there were upwards of forty millions not properly accounted for; that the officers of the King's exchequer were bound in duty to see justice done to the public; that process had issued out of the Court of Exchequer, and that all proceedings for a certain time had been suspended by the King's sign manual. I then did declare that it was an high offence for any minister to advise the King to stop the course of public justice without assigning a very good reason for such his advice. I desired the Chancellor of the Exchequer and the Lords of the Treasury, who sat opposite to me, to set me right if my information was not well founded; but not a single word was uttered in answer by any of the gentlemen in administration.

"After some days had elapsed I met my friend Mr. Woodhouse in Westminster Hall; he told me I had been misinformed as to what I had mentioned in the House of Commons, and that, if I would give him leave, he would send me a paper from a noble Lord which would convince me of my mistake. The paper alluded to is in London; I therefore cannot speak of the contents with accuracy and precision, but this I recollect, that the perusal of the paper did not convince me that all I had heard was false. It was a private paper, and I do not recollect having shown it to more than a single person. I have no doubt Mr. Woodhouse has a copy of the paper by him, and I hope he will submit the contents to the judgment of the public in vindication of an INNOCENT man.

"I am, dear Sir,
"Your ever faithful and affectionate humble Servant,
"WILLIAM BECKFORD."

In was in consequence of this letter that Lord Holland was induced to publish the account above referred to by Junius, and again by Mr. Beckford. Long as it is, it ought not to be omitted in this place.

FOR THE PUBLIC ADVERTISER.

*Letter to H. S. Woodfall.*

"MR. WOODFALL,                      "Kingsgate, July 20, 1769.
"LORD Holland, seeing in your paper a letter from Mr. Beckford to a liveryman, of July 15, 1769, and Mr. Woodhouse being at Spa, in Germany, sends you an authentic copy of the paper which he sent by Mr. Woodhouse to Mr. Beckford. He hopes the perusal of it will convince the reader that all is false that can impute any crime to Lord Holland.

"The reader will see that some of Lord Holland's accounts were then before the auditor, and there are two years' accounts since lodged there.

"He will see that Lord Holland's accounts (voluminous and difficult beyond example) have not been kept back from inclination, but necessity, and not longer than those of his predecessors.

"He will see (and is desired to observe particularly) that savings, so far

from remaining all in Lord Holland's hands, had been given in and voted in
aid of the public service to the amount of £910,541.  And £43,533 19s. 7d.
(upon some regimental and other accounts being adjusted this last winter)
have been since paid and voted.

"He will read in it that Lord Holland desired to be shown how he could
proceed faster than he did.  If nobody has shown or can show how that
might have been, or may be done, does he deserve either punishment or
censure?  And had he not a right to think himself sure that Mr. Beckford
must have been against the article in the petition relating to him, because
*Mr. Beckford knew, and could have shown the Lord Mayor in writing, the
utter falsehood of what is there insinuated?*

"Lord Holland prints the memorial examined by the Treasury, and the
sign manual it obtained; stopping process (not accounts) for six months,
which neither did nor could suspend or delay the paymaster's accounts an
hour.                                                   "HOLLAND."

### OBSERVATIONS ON THE ACCOUNTS OF THE PAYMASTER-GENERAL.

*Why were Lord Holland's accounts, as paymaster-general, for the years
1757, 1758, and 1759, not delivered to the auditors before the year 1763?*

#### ANSWER.

The paymaster-general's officers, being best acquainted with army accounts,
are employed in making up the account of the preceding paymasters.  The
accounts of the Earls of Chatham, Darlington, and Kinnoul, and Mr. Potter,
were made up by them, and regularly, and in due course, delivered to the
auditors.

Great as the army and its expenses were during the last war, beyond all
former example, dispersed in all quarters of the world, and difficult as it
must have been to keep the accounts in any tolerable order, it will be found
upon examination that the accounts of Lord Holland, as paymaster-general, are
not further back than those of his predecessors, and that his Lordship's accounts
are not kept back, as has been suggested, from inclination, but necessity.

The late Mr. Winnington's accounts, for two years and a half, from
December, 1743, to 24th of June, 1746, were declared the 15th of May,
1760.  The Earl of Chatham's accounts for nine years and a half, from the
25th June, 1746, to the 24th of December, 1755, are not yet declared.

The accounts of the Earls of Darlington and Kinnoul for the year 1756,
and the Earl of Kinnoul's and Mr. Potter's for six months, to the 24th of
June, 1757, are now before the auditors.

The accounts of Lord Holland for the years 1757, 1758, and 1759, likewise the accounts of his deputies attending the army in Germany from the
commencement to the end of the late war, are also before the auditors for
their examination; and his Lordship's account for the year 1760, is almost
ready to be delivered to them.

From the nature and extension of army accounts, it is most evident to those
that are best acquainted with them, that it is tedious and difficult to bring
even regimental accounts to a final adjustment; other parts of the accounts are
more so.  Lord Holland, in the course of the years 1759, 1760, 1761,
1762, 1763, and 1764, has paid to regiments and independent companies
£320,391 9s. 11d., whose accounts are at this time unadjusted for want of

proper authorities, and till those authorities are obtained the auditor will not allow one shilling of said sum in his Lordship's accounts. To obtain those authorities his Lordship has often repeated his solicitations.

*What is the balance of cash in Lord Holland's hands?*

ANSWER.

The meaning of this question can be no other than what savings[1] are in Lord Holland's hands? Or, in other words, how much has the expense in any case fallen short of the sum voted?

As to the savings: so far as the pay-office has been enabled to state the army accounts, they have been given into parliament.

From services that have fallen short of the sums voted, and from moneys paid in by army accomptants, Lord Holland directed accounts to be made up and laid before the House of Commons; and accordingly (out of these savings in Lord Holland's hands) parliament from time to time availed itself of the following sums, viz. :—

|  | £ | s. | d. |
|---|---|---|---|
| Voted in aid of extraordinaries, to December 24, 1763 . | 239,966 | 1 | 4 |
| Voted in the year 1764, in aid of German claims . . | 170,906 | 2 | 8 |
| Voted in the year 1765, in aid of ditto service . . . | 251,740 | 2 | 7 |
| Voted in the year 1766, in aid of extraordinary services | 60,838 | 2 | 10 |
| Voted in the year 1767, in aid of extraordinaries and other services . . . . . . . . . . . . . | 171,571 | 13 | 3 |
| Voted in the year 1768, in aid of the supply . . . . | 15,719 | 15 | 7 |
|  | £910,541 | 18 | 3 |

His Lordship could by no other means ascertain and give into parliament the savings on the votes for the army but by the final adjustment of army accounts; what further savings may be is very uncertain, as they cannot be known before the services are absolutely determined and closed.

His Lordship is very sorry to say it, that in the years 1759, 1760, 1761, 1762, 1763, and 1764, there are not less than fifty-six regiments and companies now standing open and unadjusted, for want of authorities, and in his ledgers there are accounts to a much greater extent, as the pay of staff officers, &c. &c.

It may be seen here, that though Mr. Winnington died in April, 1746, and his executor, Mr. Ingram, used all possible industry to close his accounts, they could not be closed till 1760, fourteen years. The Earl of Chatham went out in December, 1755; yet are not his accounts closed till 1768, thirteen years. The Earl of Kinnoul's are not closed yet, though he has been out of the office eleven years. Lord Holland has been out three years and a half. Where is the wonder his are not closed?

If those who complain will show Lord Holland how he can proceed faster

---

[1] It is hardly necessary to notice the difference between savings and a balance of cash in hand; the paymaster's answer, however, applies only to savings in military expenditure. Balances of public money are constantly held by the Bank of England, and the Bank uses them (as Lord Holland may have done his army balances), and pays for the use of them, which his Lordship appears not to have done.—ED.

than he does, he will be very much obliged to them. Let it be observed that he has before the auditors already accounts for more years than Mr. Winnington or Lord Kinnoul had to account for.

---

**MEMORIAL ADDRESSED TO THE LORDS OF THE TREASURY FOR LORD HOLLAND TO HAVE LONGER TIME TO MAKE UP HIS ACCOUNTS AS PAYMASTER-GENERAL.**

*May it please your Lordships,*

I beg to inform your Lordships that a process is in the hands of the sheriffs of Middlesex against me, to account to his Majesty for the moneys imprested to me as paymaster-general of his Majesty's forces.

I most humbly apprehend that the regular ordinary course of accounting in the exchequer was calculated (when established) for transactions at home, which are easily and readily to be collected and made up at short periods of time.

The accounts of the army, when employed abroad particularly, must unavoidably be much in arrear, from the nature of the service.

The army payments are necessarily in arrear; and articles, from accidents inevitable, are obliged to remain often open a long time before they can finally be closed.

The accounts of the last war are voluminous and difficult beyond example. The great variety of operations, and the very great distance of the troops, made and must make the correspondence, and adjusting those accounts with the paymasters and accountants attending them, very slow and tedious. These therefore will require longer time to make up, both from their bulk and difficulty.

During the course of a war, the troops constantly changing and moving, and the service in the utmost hurry, it cannot then be done with the order and regularity absolutely necessary. Since the war the utmost diligence has been used in them. The great intricate article of foreign expense (viz. the German), has been got together for the whole time (which, after the former war, was several years about); and one year and a half's general account is now made out, and ready to be laid before the auditors; the rest will regularly be laid before them as fast as it is possible to make them up. Though I have been two years out of employment, the payments for my time are not yet completed.

I therefore pray your Lordships will be pleased to obtain his Majesty's warrant, granting me longer time for making up my accounts as paymaster-general of his Majesty's forces.

Pay-Office, Horse Guards,   Which is, &c. &c.
25th June, 1767.                           HOLLAND.

---

**KING'S WARRANT, STAY OF PROCESS AGAINST LORD HOLLAND FOR SIX MONTHS.**

George R.

WHEREAS our right trusty and well-beloved Henry Lord Holland hath, by the annexed memorial, represented that, from several unavoidable causes and difficulties, he hath been prevented making up his accounts as late paymaster general of our forces; and we, having taken the said matter into our royal consideration, are graciously pleased to grant unto him a further time for making up his said accounts. Our will and pleasure therefore is, and we do hereby direct, authorize, and require you to cause all process against the said Henry Lord Holland for his accounts, as late paymaster-general of our forces, to be stayed for and during the term of six months, computed from the day of the date hereof. And for so doing this shall be your warrant. Given at our Court at Saint James's, the eighth day of July, 1767, in the seventh year of our reign.

By his Majesty's command,<br>
GRAFTON.<br>
C. TOWNSHEND.<br>
T. TOWNSHEND.

To our right, trusty, and well-beloved Samuel Lord Masham, our Remembrancer in our Court of Exchequer.

———

The charge against the Paymaster of the Forces, of being the "defaulter of unaccounted millions," was an exaggeration or invention of party warfare, virtually without foundation, got up by the city friends of the Earl of Chatham, to annoy his political adversary; and it was not creditable to Mr. Beckford's ingenuousness to reserve for the confidence of a "single friend" the explanatory paper that Lord Holland had communicated to him. It appears, however, strange at this day, that the paymaster's accounts from 1757 to 1764, should not have been closed with the Treasury in 1769; but this seems to have been no fault of his Lordship—it was the ordinary routine of public business; and the fact of having arrears of outstanding accounts long after withdrawal from office was a misfortune he shared with his official predecessors. At Lord Holland's death, some years later, the auditing of his accounts had not been completed; but he left with his executors a sufficient sum of money expressly for the discharge of whatever he should, in the end, appear to owe the exchequer. His Lordship's political character has been already adverted to in the exposition given of the authorship of the *Letters of Junius*. He had many qualities in common with his more celebrated second son, Charles James Fox, the Whig leader. He was a man of pleasure and practical politician; a good classical scholar, and a cultivator of the fine arts; an expert parliamentary debater, and a close, argumentative speaker; but he was lax in his public principles, after the fashion of the Walpole school, and amassed a large fortune—the proceeds of an active official life and parliamentary management.—ED.

———

B.

The Mr. Onslow spoken of at the end of Letter 5, as well as in various other parts of Junius, became Lord Onslow. The history of his dispute with Mr. Horne Tooke is as follows:—In the *Public Advertiser* of July 14, 1769, the following letter made its appearance, addressed

"TO THE RIGHT HON. GEORGE ONSLOW, ESQ.

"SIR,

"I HAVE heard from very good authority that one of the Lords of the

Treasury has lately gained a thousand pounds in a very common and usual manner, which is yet likely to be attended with a very uncommon and unusual consequence. Mr. —— applied to the right honourable Mr. —— for his interest for a certain lucrative post in America. The gentleman was informed that a thousand pounds, placed in the hands of Mrs. ——, would insure him the place. Mr. —— not having the money, prevailed on Colonel —— to join with him in a bond for that sum to the lady to whom he was directed. So far, Sir, all is in the common track: what follows is the wonderful part of the transaction. This Lord of the Treasury kept his word, and the gentleman was appointed to the office he had paid for! And stranger still, Lord ——, who discovered this bargain and sale, is offended at it, and insists on the dismission of this Lord of the Treasury. Now, Sir, I must intreat you to favour one of your constituents with the name of this Lord of the Treasury, for you, no doubt, who sit at that Board yourself, must be acquainted with him.

"Ash Court, July 11.            ANOTHER FREEHOLDER OF SURREY."

To this letter Mr. Onslow made the following reply, which was published in the same newspaper, July 18 evening.

"TO THE PRINTER OF THE PUBLIC ADVERTISER.

"SIR,            "July 16.

"HAVING just now read a letter containing, by evident insinuation, a most audacious attack upon my character, printed by you, in your paper of Friday last, asserting a gross and infamous lie from beginning to end; I do hereby publicly call upon you to name the person from whom you received the account you have presumed to publish. If you are either unable or unwilling to do this, I shall most certainly treat you as the author, and, in justice both to myself and others who are every day thus malignantly and wickedly vilified, shall take the best advice in the law if an action will not lie for such atrocious defamation, and if I may not hope to make an example of the author of it.

"The scurrility in general which has been of late so heaped upon me in the public papers I have hitherto treated with the contempt my friends and myself thought it deserved, and suffered it to pass with impunity; but this last is so outrageous, and tends so much to wound my character and honour in the tenderest part, that I am determined, if practicable, to see if a jury will not do me and the public justice against such a libeller, and whether they will not think the robbing an innocent man of his character is a robbery of the most dangerous kind, and that the perpetrators of it will stick at nothing.

"For the present I must content myself with only laying before the public the two following letters, which will explain to them all the knowledge I had of the detestable fraud, which has been taken advantage of to charge me with corruption; a crime which, of all others, I hold the most in abhorrence. I defy the whole world to prove a single word in your libellous letter to be true, or that the whole is not a barefaced, positive, and entire lie. That it is so I do assert, and I call upon any body, if they can, to disprove what I may.

"GEORGE ONSLOW."

Copy of a Letter to Mr. Onslow, received the 27th of June.

"SIR,                                        "New Bond Street, June 25, 1769.

" I beg you will pardon my thus addressing you, a liberty I could not think of, was any thing less than my family's bread at stake. Some weeks past my husband paid a large sum of money (which gave us inexpressible sorrow to raise) to a party who protest they are empowered by you to insure him, in return, the collectorship of Piscataway In New Hampshire. I have been told this day one Hughes is in possession of the same, and the Treasury books confirm the news. I beg leave most earnestly to intreat you will inform me whether Mr. Hughes is under any engagement to resign, or whether we are duped by those who have taken our money.

" Mr. Burns has had the strongest recommendations from persons of undoubted veracity, and I believe, on all accounts, will be found to be perfectly capable and worthy of the employment.

" Once more I intreat, good Sir, you will excuse this trouble, which is caused by a heart almost broken with the fear and terror of a disappointment. With the profoundest respect,

" I am, Sir,
" Your most obedient humble Servant,
" MARY BURNS."

Mr. Onslow's Answer.

" MADAM,                                     " Ember Court, June 27, 1769.

" YOUR letter was brought down to me hither only to-day, or I should have answered it sooner. Without having the honour of being known to you or Mr. Burns, it gives me much concern that any body should be so imposed upon as you have been, and as much indignation that my name should be made so infamous a use of. I should have been under an equal degree of surprise, had I not this morning had some intimation of the matter from Mr. Pownal and Mr. Bradshaw, and made some inquiry into it of Mr. Watkins at Charing Cross, with a determination to sift this shocking scene of villany to the bottom, and which I shall now be encouraged in by the hopes of getting you your money restored to you, as well as the earnest desire I have to bring the perpetrators of this roguery to the punishment and shame they deserve.

" For this purpose, might I beg the favour of Mr. Burns to meet me at my house in Curzon Street, about ten o'clock on Friday morning. I will go with him to Mr. Pownal's, of which I have given him notice; and I wish Mr. Burns would bring with him Mr. Watkins, or any body else that can give light into this unhappy and wicked affair.

" Till this morning I never in my life heard a single word of either the office itself, nor of any of the parties concerned. You will judge then of my astonishment, and indeed horror, at hearing of it to-day from Mr. Bradshaw.

" I am, Madam, &c.,
" GEORGE ONSLOW."

" Since writing of the above letters, more of this fraud has been detected, and further inquiry is making, in order to bring the actors in it to justice. A woman of the name of Smith, who lives near Broad Street, is the person who appears to be principally concerned in the fraud, the money being, it seems, for her use."

---

The writer of the first address, now authorizing the printer to give Mr. Onslow his name, (which he did, and which was that of the Rev. John Horne,) once more attacked the Right Honourable Gentleman as follows, in the same paper, July 26.

"TO THE RIGHT HONOURABLE GEORGE ONSLOW.

"GOOD SIR,

"IF with another INNOCENT man, Lord Holland, you were ambitious to add to the list of Mr. Walpole's right honourable authors, you might, like him, have exposed yourself with more temper, and have called names in better English.

"I should be sorry to libel you by mistaking your meaning, but the strange manner of wording your first sentence leaves me at a loss to know whether you intend that my letter, or —— your own character is '*a gross and infamous lie from beginning to end.*'

"You may save yourself the expense of taking '*the best advice in the law.*' Depend upon it you can never '*hope to make an example of the author, when the publisher is unable or unwilling to give up his name.*' And you need not wait for a jury to determine, '*that robbing a man is certainly a robbery.*' But you should have considered some months since that it is the same thing whether the man be guilty or innocent; and whether he be robbed of his reputation or —— of his seat in parliament.

"In the *Public Advertiser* of Friday, July 14, there is a letter FROM you as well as TO you. If that is the *scurrility* you speak of, I agree with you that it has been treated *with the contempt it deserves* by all the world; but how you can say that it has passed with *impunity*, I own I cannot conceive, unless indeed you are of opinion with those hardened criminals who think that, because there is no corporal sufferance in it, the being gibbeted in chains and exposed as a spectacle makes no part of their punishment.

"The letter written by you to Mr. Wilkes tends more '*to wound your character and honour*' than any other, and yet you pass it over in silence. But you shall, if you please, prove to the world that those who have neither character nor honour may still be wounded in a very tender part—their interest. And I believe Lord Hillsborough is too noble to suffer any Lord of the Treasury to prostitute his name and commission to bargains like that I have exposed; but will, if he continues to preside at the Board of Trade, resolutely insist either on such Lord's full justification or dismission. *Hinc illæ lachrymæ.*

"You '*defy the whole world to prove a single word in my letter to be true; or that the whole is not a barefaced, positive, and entire lie.*' The language of the last part of the sentence is such as I can make no use of, and therefore I return it back on you to whom it belongs: the defiance in the first part I accept, and will disprove what you say.

"My letter can only be false in one particular, for it contains only one affirmation, namely, that I heard the story I relate from very good authority. It then concludes with a question to you of—who is this Lord of the Treasury that so abhors corruption? Which question since you have

answered, I too will gratify you, and in return for yours do hereby direct
the printer to give you my name; which, humble as it is, I should not
consent to exchange with you in any other manner.

"Now, Sir, I do again affirm that I heard the story from the best authority,
and that it is not my invention your own letter is a proof, for I might have
heard it either from Mrs. Burns, or from Mr. Pownal, or Mr. Bradshaw;
but I heard it from better authority.  I go farther.  I do still believe the
story as I related it to be true; nor has anything you have said convinced
me to the contrary.  I do not mean to charge you or any one; but since
you have condescended to answer my former question, be kind enough to
explain what follows.

"Mr. Pownal is secretary to the Board of Trade.  Mr. Bradshaw is
secretary to the Treasury.  Why did these two secretaries come together to
you?  Were they sent by their principals or not?  Who first detected this
very scandalous though very common traffic?  Has not Lord Hillsborough
that honour?  And is not your exaggerated 'abhorrence of corruption,
your astonishment, and indeed HORROR, at this shocking scene of villany'
vastly heightened by the calm, and therefore unsuspected disapprobation of
his Lordship, who does not seem to think with you that every whore should
be hanged alive, but only that they should be TURNED OUT of honest company?

"How came you so instantly to entertain hopes of getting the money
restored to Mrs. Burns? when you declared that, 'till that morning, you
never in your life heard a single word of either the office itself, nor of any of
the parties concerned.'  Jonathan Wild used to return such answers, because
he knew the theft was committed by some of his own gang.

"You pretend to have given to the public 'all the knowledge you have of
this detestable fraud.'  I cannot believe it, because I find nothing in your
letter on which to found your hopes of restoring the money to Mrs. Burns;
and especially because in three weeks after this letter, i. e. from June 27 to
July 18, you have only discovered 'that Mrs. Smith appears to be principally concerned in this detestable fraud, the money being, it seems, for her
use.'  Sir, do you not know WHOSE wife Mrs. Smith is? and are you not
acquainted with that gentleman?  Have you caused Mrs. Smith or any one
else to be taken into custody?  Have you taken 'the best advice in law,
and are you determined to see if a jury will not do you and the public
justice' for this detestable fraud?  Or is there yet left one crime which you
abhor more than corruption, and for which you reserve all your indignation?
But why this anger?  He that is innocent can easily prove himself to be so,
and should be thankful to those who give him the opportunity by making a
story public.  Malicious and false slander never acts in this open manner,
but seeks the covert, and cautiously conceals itself from the party maligned
in order to prevent a justification.  If any person have done your character
an injury by a charge of corruption, they are most guilty who so thoroughly
believed you capable of that crime as to pay a large sum of money on the
supposition (an indignity which I protest I would not have offered to you,
though you had negotiated the matter and given the promise yourself): and
yet I do not find you at all angry with them when they tell you their
opinion of you without scruple.  On the contrary, you pity Mrs. Burns in
the kindest manner, which shows plainly that your honour is not like
Cæsar's wife.  Nay, you seem almost to doubt whether you 'might beg the

*favour of Mr. Burns to meet you at your house in Curzon Street;* that is, you humbly solicit Mr. Burns to do you the *favour* of accepting your assistance in the recovery of his money. Archbishop Laud thought to clear himself to posterity from all aspersions relative to popery, by inserting in his diary his refusal of a cardinal's hat; not perceiving the disgrace indelibly fixed on him by the offer. *'Mr. Burns has had the strongest recommendations from persons of undoubted veracity, and I believe on all accounts will be found to be perfectly capable and worthy the employment.'* The letter from Mrs. Burns to you does by no means declare her to be an idiot. Colonel ———— (whom you forbear to mention) is a man of sense, and well acquainted with the world. It is strange they should all three believe you capable of this crime, which *'of all others you most hold in abhorrence.'* Mr. Pownal, Mr. Bradshaw, and their principals, are supposed to know something of men and things, and therefore I conclude they did not believe you concerned in this business: though I wonder much that, not believing it, both the secretaries should wait on you so seriously about it but perhaps they may think, that when honour and justice are not the rule, of men's actions, there is nothing incredible that may be for their advantage. But, Sir, whatever may be their sentiments of you, I must intreat you to entertain no resentment to me; my opinion of your character would never suffer me to doubt your innocence. If indeed the charge of corruption had been brought against a low and ignorant debauchee, who, without the gratifications and enjoyments of a gentleman, had wasted a noble patrimony amongst the lowest prostitutes; whose necessities had driven him to hawk about a reversion on the moderate terms of one thousand for two hundred; whose desperate situation had made him renounce his principles and desert his friends, those principles and those friends to which he stood indebted for his chief support; who for a paltry consideration had stabbed a DEAR OLD FRIEND, and violated the sacred rights of that grateful country that continued to the son the reward of his father's services: if the charge had been brought against such an one, more fit to receive the public charity than to be trusted with the DISPOSAL and MANAGEMENT of the public money, small proof would have been sufficient; and instead of considering it as a crime the most to be abhorred, we might have suffered corruption to pass amongst the virtues of such a man. But yours, Sir, is a very different character and situation. In the clear and unincumbered possession of the paternal estate with which your ancestors have long been respectable; with a pension of three thousand, and a place of one thousand a year; with the certain prospect of Lord Onslow's large fortune, which your prudence will not anticipate; grateful to your country, faithful to your connections, and firm to your principles, it ought to be as difficult to convict you of corruption, as a cardinal of fornication; for which last purpose, by the canon law, no less than seventy-two eye-witnesses are necessary. Thus, Sir, you see how far I am from casting any reflection on your integrity; however if, notwithstanding all I have said, you are still resolved to try the determination of a jury, take one piece of advice from me: do not think of prosecuting me for an INSINUATION; alter your charge before it comes upon record, to prevent its being done afterwards; for though Lord Mansfield did not know the difference between the words when he substituted the one for the other, we all know very well now

o 2

that it is the TENOR and not the PURPORT that must convict for a libel, which indeed almost every student in the law knew before.

"ANOTHER FREEHOLDER OF SURREY."

The names of Lord Hillsborough and Mr. Pownal having been introduced into the preceding letter, they thought proper to deny any other knowledge of Mr. Onslow's supposed turpitude than that proceeding from common report, and accordingly inserted the following letters in the *Public Advertiser* on the day after their respective dates. Long as this note is, we cannot, in justice to Mr. Onslow, here omit them.

"TO H. S. WOODFALL,<br>
"<i>Printer of the Public Advertiser.</i></div>

"HAVING observed in a newspaper of the 28th of July last, that it is insinuated that I have been the detector of a supposed crime, imputed to the Right Honourable George Onslow, Esq., I do think it an act of common justice to declare in this public manner, that I am entirely ignorant of the said supposed crime, and of all circumstances relative to it, except that I have heard the story mentioned in common conversation, and constantly treated as a calumny propagated to injure Mr. Onslow's reputation.

"HILLSBOROUGH."

"Hanover Square, August 2, 1769.

———

"IT having been suggested in a letter addressed to the Right Honourable George Onslow, published in a newspaper dated the 28th of July last, that I was, together with Mr. Bradshaw, sent to Mr. Onslow on the subject of a scandalous transaction, in which Mr. Onslow is, in the said letter, stated to be concerned, it is become necessary for me, in justice to that gentleman, to declare that I never was sent to Mr. Onslow, on that or any other occasion; but having heard this story, I thought it but common justice to communicate it to Mr. Onslow, which I did through the channel of Mr. Bradshaw.

"J. POWNAL."

"Whitehall, August 2, 1769.

An action for defamation against Mr. Horne was brought by Mr. Onslow, agreeably to his menace, and the damages were laid at 10,000*l.* It was tried before Mr. Justice Blackstone, at the Surrey Assizes held at Kingston, April 6, 1770, and terminated in Mr. Onslow's nonsuit, in consequence of the word *pounds* being inserted in the record, instead of the word *pound*. The cause was re-heard before Lord Chief Justice Mansfield at the ensuing Summer Assizes held at Guildford, when Mr. Onslow was again nonsuited. The trial is supposed to have cost Mr. Onslow upwards of 1500*l.* in consequence of his having retained all the principal counsel upon the occasion.

## No. 6.

Sir,                                 Sunday, August 6, 1769.

THE spirit of your letter* convinces me that you are a much
better writer than most of the people whose works you
publish.  Whether you have guessed well or ill must be left
to our future acquaintance.  For the matter of assistance, be
assured that, if a question should arise upon any writings of
mine, you shall not want it.  Yet you see how things go, and
I fear my assistance would not avail you much.  For the
other points of printing, &c., it does not depend upon us
at present.  My own works you shall constantly have, and in
point of money be assured you never shall suffer.  I wish the
inclosed † to be announced to-morrow *conspicuously* for Tuesday.  I am not capable of writing anything more finished.

Your Friend,

C.

Your *Veridicus*‡ is Mr. Whitworth.  I assure you I have
not confided in him.

---

## No. 7.

Sir,                          Wednesday Night, August 16, 1769.

I HAVE been some days in the country, and could not conveniently send for your letter until this night.  Your correction was perfectly right.  The sense required it, and I am
much obliged to you.  When I spoke of *innumerable* blunders,
I meant Newberry's pamphlet; for I must confess that upon
the whole your papers are very correctly printed.

Do with my letters exactly what you please.  I should
think that, to make a better figure than Newberry, some
others of my letters may be added, and so throw out a hint
that you have reason to suspect they are by the same author.
If you adopt this plan, I shall point out those which I would

---

* The substance of Mr. Woodfall's reply to Private Letter No. 3 is not
known.

† Junius, Letter 20, vol. i. p. 197.

‡ *Veridicus* was a frequent writer in the *Public Advertiser* in the year
1769, and, as already observed in the Preliminary Essay, was Richard
Whitworth, Esq., M. P. for Stafford.

recommend; for, you know, I do not, nor indeed have I time
to give equal care to them all.

I know Mr. Onslow perfectly. He is a false silly fellow.
Depend upon it he will get nothing but shame by contending
with Horne*.

I believe I need not assure you that I have never written
in any other paper since I began with yours. As to Junius, I
must wait for fresh matter, as this is a character which must
be kept up with credit. Avoid prosecutions if you can: but,
above all things, avoid the Houses of Parliament—there is no
contending with them. At present you are safe, for this
House of Commons has lost all dignity, and dare not do anything.

Adieu,

C.

––––––––––

No. 8.

(Private.)

September 10, 1769.
Sir,

THE last letter you printed was idle and improper, and I
assure you printed against my own opinion†. The truth is,
there are people about me whom I would wish not to contradict, and who had rather see Junius in the papers ever so
improperly than not at all. I wish it could be recalled.
Suppose you were to say—*We have some reason to suspect that
the last letter signed Junius in this paper, was not written by
the real Junius, though the observation escaped us at the time;*
or, if you can hit off anything yourself more plausible, you
will much oblige me, but without a positive assertion. Don't
let it be the same day with the inclosed. Begging your
pardon for this trouble, I remain your friend and humble
servant,

C.

––––––––––

* This context is already related in the note to Private Letter, No. 5.
† It occurs in the Miscellaneous Letter, No. 59, *post*. In the genuine
edition it was omitted for the reason which the author has here specified.

## No. 9.

(Private.)

Sir,                                    Friday Night, September 15, 1760.

I BEG you will to-morrow advertise *Junius to another Duke in our next* *. If Monday's paper be engaged, then let it be for Tuesday, but not advertised till Monday. You shall have it some time to-morrow night. It cannot be corrected and copied sooner. I mean to make it worth printing.

Yours,

C.

---

## No. 10.

Thursday Night, October 5, 1769.

I SHALL he glad to see the packet you speak of †. It cannot come from the Cavendishes, though there be no end of the family. They would not be so silly as to put their arms on the cover. As to me, be assured that it is not in the nature of things that they, or you, or anybody else, should ever know me, unless I make myself known. All arts, or inquiries, or rewards would be equally ineffectual.

As to *you*, it is clearly my opinion that you have nothing to fear from the Duke of Bedford. I reserve some things expressly to awe him, in case he should think of bringing you before the House of Lords. I am sure I can threaten him privately with such a storm as would make him tremble even in his grave. You may send to-morrow to the same place without farther notice ; and if you have anything of your own to communicate, I shall be glad to hear it.

C.

---

## No. 11.

Sir,                                    November 8, 1769.

I HAVE been out of town these three weeks, and, though I got your last, could not conveniently answer it. Be so good as to

---

* This note accompanied the letter to his Grace the Duke of Bedford, Junius, No. 23, vol. I. p. 210, and was announced agreeably to the above request in the *Public Advertiser* for September 19, 1769.

† The nature of this communication is not known.

signify to Vaughan, either by word of mouth, or in your own hand, "that his papers are received, and that I should have been ready to do him the service he desires; but at present it would be quite useless to the parties, and might offend some persons who must not be offended." As to Mr. Mortimer *, only make him some civil excuse.

I should be much obliged to you, if you would reprint (and in the front page, if not improper or inconvenient) a letter in the *London Evening Post* of last night, to the Duke of Grafton†. If it had not been anticipated, I should have touched upon the subject myself. However, it is not ill done, and it is very material that it should spread. The person alluded to is Lord Denbigh. I should think you might venture him with a *D*. As it stands few people can guess who is meant. The only thing that hinders my pushing the subject of my last letter, is really the fear of ruining that poor devil Gansel, and those other blockheads.—But as soon as a good subject offers.—Your types really wanted mending.

C.

## No. 12.

SIR, November 12, 1769.

I RETURN you the letters you sent me yesterday. A man who can neither write common English, nor spell, is hardly worth attending to. It is probably a trap for me. I should be glad, however, to know what the fool means. If he writes again, open his letter, and if it contains anything worth my knowing, send it; otherwise, not. Instead of C. in the usual place, say only *A Letter* when you have occasion to write to me again. I shall understand you.

## No. 13.

Thursday, November 16, 1769. ·

As I do not choose to answer for any body's sins but my own, I must desire you to say to-morrow, "We can assure the

* Mr. Mortimer was either at this time, or shortly afterwards, employed by Mr. Woodfall to procure intelligence for the *Public Advertiser*.
† Miscellaneous Letter, No. 61.

public that the letter signed A. B. relative to the Duke of Rutland, is not written by the author of *Junius*."\*

I sometimes change my signature, but could have no reason to change the paper, especially for one that does not circulate half so much as yours.

C.

For the future, open all letters to me, and don't send them, unless of importance. I can give you light about *Veridicus* †.

---

## No. 14.

Sunday, December 10, 1769.

I WOULD wish the paper (No. 2) might be advertised for Tuesday ‡.

By way of intelligence you may inform the public that Mr. De La Fontaine, *for his secret services in the Alley*, is appointed Barrack-master to the Savoy.

I hope Vaughan has got his papers again.

---

## No. 15.

SIR, December 12, 1769.

YOU may tell Mr. Vaughan that I did not receive his letter till last night, and have not had time to look into the paper annexed. I cannot at present understand what use I can make of it. It certainly shall not be an ungenerous one to him. If he or his counsel *know how to act*, I have saved him already, and really without intending it. The facts are all literally true. Mr. Hine's place is customer at the port of Exeter. Colonel Burgoyne received 4000*l.* for it. To mend the matter, the money was raised by contribution, and the subscribers quartered upon Mr. Hine. Among the rest, one Dr. Brook, a physician at Exeter, has 100*l.* a year out of

---

\* Miscellaneous Letter, No. 61, and note \* appended to it.
† Note to Private Letter, No. 6.
‡ The paper here referred to is the letter of Junius, No. 34, vol. i. p. 250. The ensuing intelligence was published verbally in the *Public Advertiser* of the next day, Dec. 11.

the salary. I think you might give these particulars in your
own way to the public *. As to yourself, I am convinced the
ministry will not venture to attack you. They dare not
submit to such an inquiry. If they do, show no fear, but
tell them plainly you will justify, and *subpœnd* Mr. Hine,
Burgoyne, and Bradshaw of the Treasury—that will silence
them at once. As to the House of Commons there may be
more danger. · But even there I am fully satisfied the
ministry will exert themselves to quash such an inquiry, and
on the other side, you will have friends:—but they have been
so grossly abused on all sides, that they will hardly begin
with *you*.

Tell Vaughan his paper shall be returned. I am now
meditating a capital, and I hope a final, piece; you shall
hear of it shortly†.

-----

### No. 16.

December 19, 1769.

For *material* affection, for God's sake read *maternal*; it is in
the sixth paragraph‡. The rest is excellently done.

-----

### No. 17.

Sir,                                    December 26, 1769.

With the inclosed alterations I should think our paper might
appear §. As to embowelling, do whatever you think proper,
provided you leave it intelligible to vulgar capacities; but
would not it be the shortest way at once to print it in an
anonymous pamphlet? judge for yourself. I enter sincerely
into the anxiety of your situation. At the same time I am

* The facts were given to the public by Junius himself in Letter 34,
vol. i. ante, and are indeed touched upon more than once in his subsequent
letters.

† He refers to the Letter to the King, Junius, No. 35, vol. i. p. 255.

‡ Letter to the King, Junius, No. 35.

§ This paper is supposed to have been totally suppressed, the alterations
introduced into it not having perhaps satisfied the printer of his safety in
publishing it, as the signal of a private communication from him to the author
appeared in the *P. A.* of the next day.

strongly inclined to think that you will not be called upon *.
They cannot do it without subjecting Hine's affair to an inquiry, which would be worse than death to the minister.  As
it is, they are more seriously stabbed with this last stroke
than all the rest.  At any rate, stand firm (I mean with all
the humble appearances of contrition).  If you trim or faulter,
you will lose friends without gaining others.  Vaughan has
done right in publishing his letter.  It defends him more
effectually than all his nonsense.  I believe I shall give him
a lift, for I really think he has been punished infinitely beyond
his merits.  I doubt much whether I shall ever have the
pleasure of knowing you; but if things take the turn I expect, you shall know *me by my works.*

C.

---

## No. 18.

(Private.)

Sir,                                              January 12, 1770.

I DESIRED Vaughan not to write to me until I gave him
notice.  He must therefore blame himself, if the detention
of his papers has been inconvenient to him.  Pray tell him
this, and that he shall have them in a day or two.  I shall
also keep my promise to him†; but to do it immediately would
be useless to *him*, and unadvisable with respect to myself.
I believe you may banish your fears.  The information‡ will
only be for a misdemeanour, and I am advised that no jury,
especially in these times, will find it.  I suspect the channel
through which you have your intelligence.  It will be carried
on coldly.  You must not write to me again; but be assured
I will never desert you.  I received your letters regularly,
but it was *impossible* to answer them sooner.  You shall hear
from me again shortly.

* The printer was threatened by the minister with a prosecution for
publishing the letter of Junius, No. 33, vol. I. 249, and the Court of King's
Bench was actually moved on his behalf; but probably for the reason mentioned above, the threat was never executed.
† See Junius, No. 33, vol. i. p. 249, note, and Letter 86.
‡ The information was for publishing the Letter to the King, Junius, No.
35, for the particulars of which see the author's Preface, and note appended
to it, vol. i. p. 94.

No. 19.

(Private.)

SIR,                                    Beginning of February, 1770.

WHEN you consider to what excessive enmities I may be
exposed, you will not wonder at my caution. I really have
not known how to procure your last. If it be not of any great
moment I would wish you to recall it. If it be, give me a
hint. If your affair should come to a trial *, and you should
be found guilty, you will then let me know what expense falls
particularly on yourself; for I understand you are engaged
with other proprietors. Some way or other you shall be
reimbursed. But seriously and *bond fide*, I think it is
impossible.

                                                        C.

------

No. 20.

                                    About February 14, 1770†.

I HAVE carefully perused the information‡. It is so loose
and ill drawn, that I am pursuaded Mr. De Grey could not
have had a hand in it. Their inserting the whole, proves
they had no strong passages to fix on. I still think it will
not be tried. If it should, it is not possible for a jury to find
you guilty.

* For the trial referred to, see Appendix, vol. i. p. 471. The copy of the
information was procured in Hilary Term, 1770, and the trial took place
June 13 following. The costs to the printer in defending himself, though
ultimately successful, amounted to about 120l., a somewhat heavy fine for a
person not found guilty.

† It appears that this and the preceding note were undated when received,
and that Woodfall, or his editor, inserted the dates as near as they could ascertain or conjecture. Junius seems not to have had any fixed rule; sometimes the day is mentioned, sometimes the day of the month, and frequently
both. Some, both of his private and public letters, appear to have
been sent without date, and the day of the publication, or of receiving
them, to have been inserted by the printer. These irregularities preclude or
obscure any nice criticism founded on the dates of Junius's Letters.—ED.

‡ The information here referred to is that noticed in the note to the preceding letter.

------

## No. 21.

Saturday, March 17, 1770.

To-morrow before twelve you shall have a *Junius*, it will be absolutely necessary that it should be published on Monday. Would it be possible to give notice of it to-night or to-morrow, by a dispersing a few handbills? Pray do whatever you think will answer this purpose best, for now is the crisis *.

C.

---

## No. 22.

Sunday, March 18, 1770.

This letter is written wide, and I suppose will not fill two columns. For God's sake let it appear to-morrow. I hope you received my note of yesterday.

Lord Chatham is determined to go to the Hall to support the Westminster remonstrance†. I have no doubt that we shall conquer them at last.

C.

* The letter referred to is Junius, No. 37.

† Agreed upon at a general meeting of the electors of the city and liberty of Westminster, assembled in Westminster Hall, March 28, 1770, in consequence of their petition to his Majesty, requesting him to dissolve the Parliament which had expelled Mr. Wilkes, having been rejected. The following is a copy of the remonstrance:—

"The humble address, remonstrance, and petition of the electors of the city and liberty of Westminster, assembled in Westminster Hall the 28th day of March, 1770.

"We, your Majesty's most dutiful and loyal subjects, the electors of the city and liberty of Westminster, having already presented our humble, but ineffectual, application to the throne, find ourselves, by the misconduct of your Majesty's ministers, in confederacy with many of our representatives, reduced to the necessity of again breaking in by our complaints upon your Majesty's repose, or of acquiescing under grievances so new and so exorbitant, that none but those who patiently submit to them can deserve to suffer them.

"By the same secret and unhappy influence to which all our grievances have been originally owing, the redress of those grievances has been now prevented; and the grievances themselves have been repeatedly confirmed; with this additional circumstance of aggravation, that while the invaders of our rights remain the directors of your Majesty's councils, the defenders of those rights have been dismissed from your Majesty's service—your Majesty having been advised by your ministers to remove from his employment for his vote in Parliament, the highest officer of the law; because his principles suited ill with theirs, and his pure distribution of justice with their corrupt administration of it in the House of Commons.

" We beg leave, therefore, again to represent to your Majesty, that the House of Commons have struck at the most valuable liberties and franchises of all the electors of Great Britain; and by assuming to themselves a right of choosing, instead of receiving, a member when chosen, by transferring to the representative what belonged to the constituent, they have taken off from the dignity, and, we fear, impaired the authority of Parliament itself.

" We presume again, therefore, humbly to implore from your Majesty, the only remedies which are any way proportioned to the nature of the evil: that you would be graciously pleased to dismiss for ever from your councils those ministers who are ill-suited by their dispositions to preserve the principles of a free, or by their capacities to direct the councils of a great and mighty kingdom; and that by speedily dissolving the present Parliament, your Majesty will show, by your own example, and by their dissolution, that the rights of your people are to be inviolable, and that you will never necessitate so many injured, and, by such treatment, exasperated, subjects to continue to commit the care of their interests to those from whom they must withdraw their confidence; to repose their invaluable privileges in the hands of those who have sacrificed them; and their trust in those who have betrayed it.

" Your subjects look up with satisfaction to the powers which the constitution has vested in your Majesty—for it is upon them that they have placed their last dependance, and they trust that the right of dissolving Parliaments, which has, under former princes, so often answered the purposes of power, may, under your Majesty, prove an happy instrument of liberty.

" We find ourselves compelled to urge with the greater importunity this our humble but earnest application to the throne, as every day seems to produce the confirmation of some old, or to threaten the introduction of some new injury. We have the strongest reason to apprehend that the usurpation begun by the House of Commons upon the right of electing, may be extended to the right of petitioning; and that, under the pretence of restraining the abuse of this right, it is meant to bring into disrepute, and to intimidate us from the exercise of the right itself.

" But whatever may be the purposes of others, your Majesty hath, in your answer to the city of London, most graciously declared *that you are always ready to receive the requests, and to listen to the complaints of your subjects.* Your Majesty condescends likewise to esteem it a *duty to secure to them the free enjoyment of those rights which your family were called to defend.*

" We rely, therefore, upon the Royal word thus given, that our grievances will meet with full redress, and our complaints with the most favourable interpretation; that your Majesty will never consider the arraignment of your ministers as a disrespect to your person—a charge confined, by the very terms of it, to this House of Commons, as injurious to Parliament at large (the constitution of which we admire, and the abuse of which is the very thing we lament); or a request for the dissolution of Parliament, which your subjects have a right to make, and your Majesty to grant, as *irreconcileable to the principles of the constitution.*"

———

Junius at this period was busy and warm in the cause. The Westmin-

## No. 23.

(Private.)                          Friday Morning, October 19, 1770.

By your affected silence *, you encourage an idle opinion that
I am the author of the *Whig*†, &c., though you very well

star electors met on the 28th, unanimously agreed to a remonstrance, which,
in half an hour after, was presented to the King. But the whole affair was
an entire failure : Chatham did not attend, remaining quietly at Hayes on
his usual plea of the gout, trusting to Mr. Calcraft to report proceedings, and
who informed him next day that the Westminster remonstrance was carried
up " poorly attended and still worse received." Previously to the demonstration, the Lord Mayor had tried to secure the hearty co-operation of the
Whig grandees by a splendid entertainment at the Mansion House ; but they
did nothing beyond extolling the rich wines and viands of Beckford. In
consequence the reformers were dissatisfied, and Calcraft, in a postscript, tells
Chatham that Alderman Sawbridge had just called, informing him that the
Lord Mayor and leading people of Middlesex " are so offended by the half
support given to the city remonstrance and total neglect of that for Westminster " that they did not mean to remonstrate further.

, Junius's note to Woodfall is dated March 18, and on the same day Mr.
Calcraft addressed the subjoined to Earl Temple :—

" MY DEAR LORD,

" Just as your Lordship left me, a *friend* came in who says he hears a
strong report that they [the ministers] disagree amongst themselves, see the
difficulties they may be involved in, and have resolved not to proceed [in
the House of Commons] on the remonstrance to-morrow. Lord Chatham's
proposal about Westminster [attending the meeting, as Junius told Woodfall]
adds to their alarm. The greatest person requires cordials."—*Chatham Correspondence*, vol. iii. p. 430.

The editors ask, " May not this 'friend' have been Sir Philip Francis !"—
ED.

---

* " The printer really did not AFFECT a silence on a CERTAIN OCCASION,
with a view of encouraging his readers or correspondents in an idle opinion :
the motives for his conduct were, the fear of being thought impertinent by
declaring (without direction) what he knew ; and the probability of rendering himself liable to incur the displeasure of either of those who were pleased
to favour him with their correspondence."—*Answer to Correspondents*, Oct.
25, 1770.

† This letter was printed in the *Public Advertiser* under the signature of
" A Whig and an Englishman," Oct. 11, 1770, and refers chiefly to the
American Stamp Act, and the opinion of Lord Chatham, whom the author
panegyrized in very warm terms. The same writer had already published
several other letters in the same name ; and the printer, in compliance with
the request of Junius, gave the following notice :—

" October 20.

" The printer thinks it his duty to declare, that the letters which have
appeared in this paper under the signature of ' A Whig and an Englishman,'
were not written by the author of those signed Junius."

know the contrary. I neither admire the writer nor his idol.
I hope you will soon set this matter right.

O.

------

## No. 24.

Sir,                                    Monday Evening, November 12, 1770.
THE inclosed *, though begun within these few days, has been
greatly laboured.  It is very correctly copied, and I beg you
will take care that it be literally printed as it stands.  I don't
think you run the least risque.  We have got the rascal
down; let us strangle him if it be possible.  This paper
should properly have appeared to-morrow, but I could not
compass it, so let it be announced to-morrow, and printed
Wednesday.  If you should have any fears, I entreat you to
send it early enough to Miller to appear to-morrow night in
the *London Evening Post*.  In that case, you will oblige me
by informing the public to-morrow, in *your own paper*, that
a real *Junius* will appear at night in the *London*.  Miller, I
am sure, will have no scruples.

Lord Mansfield has thrown the ministry into confusion by
suddenly resigning the office of Speaker of the House of
Lords.

------

## No. 25.

Wednesday Night, November 21, 1770†.
I SHALL be very glad to hear from your friend at Guildhall.
You may, if you think proper, give my compliments to him,
and tell him, if it be possible, I will make use of any materials he gives me.  I will never rest till I have destroyed or
expelled that wretch.  I wish you joy of yesterday.  The
fellow truckles already‡.

C.

* Junius to the Right Hon. Lord Mansfield, Letter 41, vol. i. p. 305.
† On the outside of this note was written, "The inclosed strikes deeper
than you may imagine.  C."  The letter will be found in the Miscellaneous
Collection, No. 78, subscribed *Testiculus.*
‡ In allusion to the unanimous judgment of the Court of King's Bench,
on the verdict for printing the Letter to the King, given Nov. 20th, 1770,
by which Lord Mansfield lost his object, and the printer was granted a new
trial.

## No. 26.

Friday, 1 o'Clock, December 7, 1770.

I wish it were possible for you to print the inclosed to-morrow*. Observe the Italics *strictly* where they are marked. Why don't I hear from Guildhall? If he trifles with me, he shall hear of it†.

C.

---

## No. 27.

Sir, January 2, 1771.

I have received your mysterious epistle. I dare say a letter may safely be left at the same place; but you may change the direction to Mr. *John Fretly*. You need not advertise it.

Yours,

C.

---

## No. 28.

January 16, 1771.

You may assure the public that a squadron of four ships of the line is ordered to be got ready with *all possible expedition* for the East Indies. It is to be commanded by Commodore Spry. Without regarding the language of ignorant or interested people, depend upon the assurance *I* give you that every man in administration looks upon war as inevitable ‡.

* The paper referred to is Miscellaneous Letter, No. 79, signed *Domitian*, and was printed as requested.

† The allusion is to a communication between the writer and Mr. Wilkes, which had been promised by the latter, but had not been at this time received.

‡ Inserted in the *Public Advertiser*, January 17, nearly in the same words. The predicted war, however, did not follow, but the preparation was actually made, in the full belief, on the part of the cabinet themselves, that they would be compelled to go to war by the existing temper of the people, irritated by the dishonourable negotiation concerning the Spanish seizure of Falkland Islands, and that they should be accused of indolence, and even cowardice, by the approaching Parliament. The session opened only four days afterwards, and the question of hostilities was so much upon a balance, that in the Lower House not fewer than 159 members divided against the minister, upon the address of thanks and approbation.

---

It has been surmised that the ministers were better informed than to expect war, notwithstanding their preparations, but kept up the delusion for stock-

## No. 29.

Thursday, January 31, 1771.

THE paper is extremely well printed, and has a great effect *.
It is of the utmost importance to the public cause that the
doors of the House of Lords should be opened on Tuesday next.
Perhaps the following may help to shame them into it.

We hear that the ministry intend to move for opening the
doors of both Houses of Parliament on Tuesday next, in the
usual manner, being desirous that the nation should be exactly
informed of their whole conduct in the business of Falkland
Island.

### (Next Day.)

The nation expect that on Tuesday next, at least, both
Houses will be open as usual; otherwise there will be too
much reason to suspect that the proceedings of the ministry
have been such as will not bear a public discussion.

We hear that the ministry intend to move that no gentleman may be refused admittance into either House on Tuesday
next. Lord North in particular thinks it touches his character to have no part of his conduct concealed from the
nation.

The resolution of the ministry to move for opening both
Houses on Tuesday next does them great honour. If they
were to do otherwise, it would raise and justify suspicions
very disadvantageous to their own reputation, and to the
King's honour. Pray keep it up†.

C.

jobbing. Colonel Barré said, " The nation is a prey to stock-jobbers. A
French secretary, being in your secrets, has made near half a million by
gaming in your funds; and some of the highest among yourselves have been
deeply concerned in the same traffic." Whether Junius was knave or dupe,
or merely reported that which he had heard on what he conceived trust-
worthy authority, is more than we can decide.—ED.

* It refers to Junius, No. 42. For the nature of the subject alluded to,
see the Letter and the notes subjoined to it, vol. i. p. 316; as also, post, Mis-
cellaneous Letter, No. 38, and the note in explanation.
† These adroit flappers failed of the intended effect, and the anxiety of
Junius to be present in the Lords on Tuesday was not gratified. Lord
Chatham made his anticipated motion relative to the Falkland Islands, and a

## No. 30.

Sir,                                    Tuesday Noon, February 5, 1771.

I did not receive your letter until this day.  I shall be very glad to hear what you have to communicate.

C.

You need not advertise any notice.

---

## No. 31.

(Private.)

Monday, February 11, 1771.

Our correspondence is attended with difficulties.  Yet I should be glad to see the paper you mention.  Let it be left to-morrow *without further notice*.  I am seriously of opinion that it will all end in smoke *.

C.

---

## No. 32.

Monday, February 18, 1771.

If you are not grown too ministerial in your politics, I shall hope to see the inclosed announced to-morrow, and published on Wednesday †.

long debate ensued, of which no traces have been preserved, as strangers were rigidly excluded, and his Lordship's motion negatived by sixty-nine against twenty-two.  But the important conclusion already intimated, that Junius was not a member of parliament, may be drawn from his desire to have open doors.  Had he been a member of either house he would have had the privilege of *entrée* during the debate, and need not have been anxious about the admission of strangers.  What a host of claimants are disposed of by this single consideration?  Chatham, Dunning, Burke, Lord George Sackville, Colonel Barré, Lord Shelburne, Single Speech Hamilton, with numerous others, could not have been Junius, since all these were members of one or the other house of parliament.  But till recently nothing less than a peer or M.P. was deemed high or good enough to be Junius.—Ed.

* In reference to a note from the Attorney-General for publishing Letter of Junius, No. 42, but which was never further proceeded upon.

† This note accompanied *Finder*, No. 90, of the Miscellaneous Letters.  The printer had some scruples about publishing the whole of it; and in the *Public Advertiser* of Feb. 20 gave the usual mark, "A Letter," that a private letter was in waiting upon this subject.  In consequence of which the subsequent note was received, dated Feb. 21.

## No. 33

SIR,                                February 21, 1771.

IT will be very difficult, if not impracticable, for me to get your note. I presume it relates to *Vindex*\*. I leave it to you to alter or omit as you think proper;—or burn it. I think the argument about Gibraltar†, &c., is too good to be lost. As to the satirical part, I must tell you (and with positive certainty) that our gracious —— is as callous as stockfish to everything but the reproach of *cowardice*. That alone is able to set the humours afloat. After a paper of that kind he won't eat meat for a week‡.

You may rely upon it the ministry are sick of prosecutions. Those against Junius cost the Treasury above six thousand pounds, and after all they got nothing but disgrace. After the paper you have printed to-day (signed Brutus §), one

---

\* The following is a copy of the letter which Mr. Woodfall addressed to the author under the feigned name of Mr. John Fretly, and directed it to him at the New Exchange Coffee House in the Strand.

"SIR,

"To have deserved any portion of your good opinion affords me no small degree of satisfaction—to preserve it shall be my constant endeavour. Always willing to oblige you as much as lies in my power, I, with great avidity, open your letters; and sometimes without reading the contents, promise the publication. Such is my present situation, and I hope you will not be offended at my declining to publish your letter, as I am convinced the subject of it must, if I was to insert it, render me liable to very severe reprehension. That I am not grown too ministerial in my politics every day's paper will, I hope, sufficiently evince; though I rather hope some little regard to prudence will not by you be deemed squeamishness, or tend to lessen me in your opinion, as I shall ever think myself your

"Much obliged humble Servant.

"Feb. 19, 1771.            "HENRY SAMPSON WOODFALL.

"P.S. I shall wait your directions what to do with the paper in question, as I did not choose to trust it under cover till I was further acquainted with your pleasure."

† For the explanation of this passage, see Miscellaneous Letter 00, signed *Vindex*.

‡ See vol. i. p. 289, note †.

§ This letter was addressed to Lord North, and, as it is short, it is here transcribed, in proof that Junius was not severe in his opinion of it, nor singularly acrimonious in the phraseology originally adopted by himself.

"TO THE RIGHT HON. LORD NORTH.

"MY LORD,

"I never address your Lordship but I feel the utmost horror and indigna-

would think you feared nothing. For my own part, I can.very truly assure you that nothing would afflict me more than to have drawn you into a personal danger, because it admits of

tion; for I consider you as a man totally regardless of your own honour and the welfare of your country.

" The severity of a writer cannot be supposed to give your Lordship any uneasiness. A minister whose schemes extend only to the exigencies of a year but little regards his present or future reputation; yet it is a duty we owe to the public to trace out and expose the villain, wherever we can perceive him working up the ruin of his country.

" The choice of your friends is an eminent indication of your abilities and the blackness of your heart.

" *Nam quicunq; impudicus, adulter, ganeo, alea, manu, ventre, bona patria laceravit, quique alienum œs grande conflavit,* immediately flies into your arms, and reimburses himself with the plunder of his country.

" Such are the guardians of our liberties and law : such are the men to whom our constitution is entrusted : and cannot we then without any particular discernment, or any remarkable acuteness of observation, trace out the origin of our present di-contents?

" It would be needless to follow you through that maze of villany in which you have long delighted to wander; I shall only attack those measures which occur to our more immediate consideration.

" In what manner can you answer to your King for the scandalous prostitution of his crown and himself?

" In what manner can you answer to your country for the total disregard of its welfare and dignity?

" After all these formidable preparations; after all this expensive armament, you have made shift to patch up a temporary ignominious compromise, at the trifling expense of about three millions and the British honour.

" You imagine yourself sufficiently secured in the pursuit of your infamous intentions, and in the practice of every illegal and unconstitutional measure, by the countenance of the King. Rely not too much on that protection. His Majesty must not be suffered, through a blind and ridiculous attachment to an individual, or through a filial obedience which then becomes criminal, to ruin and subvert his infatuated kingdoms.

" Your late acquisition of Lord Suffolk will not do you much honour : he is of the same stamp with the rest of your adherents. His Lordship has given the world a very strong impression of his character and the disposition of his heart, by deserting his principal, and the cause in which he originally embarked, and by betraying that friendship which in the more early and virtuous time of his life he had contracted. His former party need not regret the loss of him, for they are by his desertion disencumbered of a ——.

" But I will now leave you, my Lord, to that mature insensibility which is only to be acquired by a sturdy perseverance in infamy.

" Every principle of conscience you have long ago been hardy enough to discard. There has not been an action in the last two years of your life but what separately deserves imprisonment. The time may come; and remember, my Lord, there is a very short period between a minister's imprisonment and his grave.—BRUTUS."

uo recompense.  A little expense is not to be regarded, and
I hope these papers have reimbursed you.  I never will send
you anything that *I* think dangerous, but the risque* is yours,
and you must determine for yourself.

C.

All the above is private.

———

No. 34.

Friday Noon, April 19, 1771.

I HOPE you will approve of announcing the enclosed Junius
to-morrow†, and publishing it on Monday.  If, for any reasons
that do not occur to me, you should think it unadvisable to
print it as it stands, I must entreat the favour of you to transmit it to Bingley‡, and satisfy him that it is a real Junius,
worth a *North Briton* Extraordinary.  It will be impossible
for me to have an opportunity of altering any part of it

I am, very truly, your Friend,<br>C.

———

No. 35.

Thursday, June 20, 1771.

I AM strangely partial to the enclosed§.  It is finished with
the utmost care.  If I find myself mistaken in my judgment
of this paper, I positively will never write again.

C.

Let it be announced to-morrow, Junius to the Duke of
Grafton for Saturday.

I think Wilkes has closed well.  I hope he will keep his
resolution not to write any more‖.

———

\* This peculiarity of spelling the word risk is the author's.
† Junius, Letter 44, which was printed as requested.
‡ The printer of the *North Briton.*
§ Junius, No. 49, to the Duke of Grafton.
‖ In allusion to the dispute between Mr. Wilkes and Mr. Horne, conducted with great acrimony, till the former resolved, as here advised, not to
answer after a definite period any additional letters, in consequence of the
total occupation of his time in his canvass for the office of sheriff of London,
for which he was then a candidate, and to which situation he ultimately suc-

## No. 36.

July 16, 1771.

To prevent any unfair use being made of the enclosed, I entreat you to keep a copy of it. Then seal and deliver it to Mr. Horne. I presume you know where he is to be found ".

C.

## No. 37

August 13, 1771.

Pray make an erratum for *ultimate* in the paragraph about the Duke of Grafton, it should be *intimate*. The rest is very correct†. If Mr. Horne answers this letter handsomely and in point, he shall be my great Apollo.

## No. 38.

Wednesday Noon, September 25, 1771.

The enclosed is of such importance, so very material, that it *must* be given to the public immediately‡.

ceeded. The following is the conclusion of the letter here spoken of, which was of course, addressed to Mr. Horne.

" Whether you proceed, Sir, to a *thirteenth* or a *thirtieth* letter is to me a matter of the most entire indifference. You will no longer have me your correspondent. All the efforts of your malice and rancour cannot give me a moment's disquietude. They will only torment your own breast. I am wholly indifferent about your sentiments of me, happy in the favourable opinion of many valuable friends in the most honourable connections, both public and private, and in the prospect of rendering myself eminently useful to my country. Formerly in exile, when I was *urbe patriâque extorris*, and torn from every sacred tie of friendship, I have moistened my bread with my tears. The rest of my life I hope to enjoy my morsel at home in peace and cheerfulness, among those I love and honour, far from the malignant eye of the false friend and the insidious hypocrite.

" I am, Sir, your humble Servant,
" John Wilkes."

* Note enclosing Junius's Letter to the Rev. Mr. Horne, No. 52, vol. i. p. 364.
† Junius, Letter 54, vol. i. p. 367. This letter appeared on the 13th of August, 1771, though in the author's edition it is by mistake dated the 15th.
‡ The Letter referred to is Junius, No. 57, and was printed in the *Public Advertiser*, Saturday, Sept. 28, 1771.

I will not advise ; though I think you perfectly safe : all I say is that *I rely* upon your care to have it printed either to-morrow in your own paper, or to-night in the *Pacquet*.

I have not been able to get yours from that place, but you shall hear from me soon.

------

## No. 39.

About November 5, 1771.

YOUR reasons are very just about printing the Preface, &c. It is your own affair. Do whatever you think proper. I am convinced the book will sell, and I suppose will make two volumes—the type might be one size larger than Wheble's *. But of all this you are the best judge. I think you should give money to the waiters at that place to make them more attentive †. The notes should be in a smaller type.

Pray find out, if you can, upon what day the late Duke of Bedford was flogged on the course at Lichfield by Mr. Heaton Homphrey ‡.

------

## No. 40.

Friday, November 8, 1771.

THE above to that Scotchman should be printed conspicuously to-morrow §. At last I have concluded my great work, and I assure you with no small labour. I would have you begin to advertise immediately, and publish before the meeting of parliament. Let all *my* papers in defence of Junius be inserted ||. I shall now supply you very fast with copy and notes. The paper and type should at least be as good as Wheble's. You must correct the press yourself, but I should be glad to see corrected proofs of the two first sheets. Show the Dedication and Preface to Mr. Wilkes, and if he has any

* The present proprietor and publisher of the *County Chronicle*, who took a conspicuous part in the dispute with the House of Commons respecting the publication of their debates, an account of which is in the Miscellaneous Letters.
† A coffee-house at which letters, &c., were left for Junius.
‡ Junius, Letter 23, vol. i. p. 214, note.
§ Junius, No. 66, vol. i. p. 441.
|| The Letters signed *Philo-Junius;* those numbered 63 and 64, and the extracts from the Letters to the Supporters of the Bill of Rights.

*material* objection, let me know. I say *material* because of
the difficulty of getting your letters.

C.

(Secret.)

Beware of David Garrick *. He was *sent* to pump you, and
*went* directly to Richmond to tell the King I should write no
more. The Dedication must stand first.

---

No. 41

TO MR. DAVID GARRICK

November 10, 1771.

I AM very exactly informed of your impertinent inquiries, and
of the information you so busily *sent* to Richmond, and with

---

* Garrick had received a letter from Woodfall, just before the above note
of Junius was sent to the printer, in which Garrick was told, in confidence,
that there were some doubts whether Junius would continue to write
much longer. Garrick *flew with the intelligence* to Mr. Ramus, one of the
pages to the King, who immediately conveyed it to his Majesty, at that
time residing at Richmond, and from the *peculiar sources of information*
that were open to this extraordinary writer, Junius was apprised of the whole
transaction on the ensuing morning, and wrote the above postscript, and the
letter that follows it, in consequence.

---

Both text and commentary in this instance are grievously wrong.
First, as to the text. From a letter of Garrick, which has been inserted
at the end of No. 43, it will be seen that Garrick neither *sent* nor *went* to
pump Woodfall, but that the communication of the latter to him was incidental and spontaneous. Second, that he neither " went *directly* to Richmond
to tell the King," nor visited Richmond at all; but, having occasion to write
to Richmond on the business of the theatre, he mentioned, as a piece of news,
as he did to other of his correspondents, that Junius would write no more.
On being better informed by Woodfall, Junius corrects his first error in his
next note by saying Garrick *sent* in lieu of *went* to Richmond. But in the
same note (No. 41) he falls into a third error in accusing Garrick of "impertinent *inquiries*," which he also corrects in No. 43, by directing Woodfall to
substitute " impertinent *practices*."

Dr. Good, from a love of the decorative, has expanded into poetical
licence. Dr. Good, not content with the prosaic errors of Junius,
that Garrick either *sent* or *went* to Richmond, says he "*flew* with the intelligence " to Ramus, who immediately conveyed it to the king. Next he
tells us that Junius was apprized of the actor's flight on the "ensuing morning," but Junius says, " next day ; " all which is intended by the doctor to
heighten the mystery of " the extraordinary writer," and to magnify the importance and promptitude of his peculiar sources of information.—ED.

what triumph and exultation it was received.  I knew every
particular of it the *next day*.  Now mark me, vagabond.
Keep to your pantomimes, or be assured you shall hear of it.
Meddle no more, thou busy informer!—It is in my power to
make you curse the hour in which you dared to interfere with
                                                    JUNIUS*.

* Mr. Garrick had, before this period, been threatened for his supposed
political bias to the court, as will appear from a charge which Mr. Horne
brought forward against Mr. Wilkes, during the personal altercation which
took place between them in the months of May and June preceding the
date of this letter, and which is more particularly noticed in the note to
Junius, Letter 52, vol. i. p. 305.    Mr. Horne's accusation is as follows :—
    " Whilst Mr. Wilkes was in the King's Bench, he sent a threatening mes-
sage to Mr. Garrick to forbid his playing the part of *Hastings* in the tragedy
of *Jane Shore ;* on account of some lines in that play which Mr. Wilkes
thought applicable to his own situation.    Mr. Garrick complained exceedingly of the cruelty of such an interdict, and wished to be permitted to proceed in his endeavours to please the public in the common course of his profession.    The patriot was inexorable ; and Mr. Garrick has not appeared in
that character since.    The Lord Chamberlain's control by Act of Parliament
over the pleasures of the public is exercised only over new plays."
    To this charge Mr. Wilkes replied as follows, offering several justly
merited compliments to the hitherto unrivalled genius of Mr. Garrick.

               "TO THE REV. MR. DORNE.

    "SIR,                    " Prince's Court, Thursday, June 6, 1771.
" Your ninth letter has relieved me not a little by taking me to the theatre,
and recalling to my delighted remembrance the amazing powers both of
nature and art in the most wonderful genius that ever trod the English,
or perhaps any stage, for his rival, Roscius, had a great defect, *erat
perversissimis oculis.*    You say, 'whilst Mr. Wilkes was in the King's
Bench,' &c.    The whole of this pompous tale is that some warm friends
of Mr. Wilkes imagined that Mr. Garrick acted the part of *Hastings* at
that time in a manner very different from what he had usually done, and
marked too strongly some particular passages, unfavourable to the generous
principles and to the friends of freedom.    They talked of expressing their
disapprobation in the theatre at the next representation of *Jane Shore,* and
likewise in the public prints.    Mr. Wilkes therefore thought it prudent to
state the case by two or three gentlemen to Mr. Garrick himself, and said
he feared the part of *Hastings* might bring on many disagreeable consequences to the great actor himself as well as to Mr. Wilkes and his connections, if continued in the manner then stated.    Mr. Garrick received the
friendly admonition in the most friendly way, but declared that the gentlemen, who had given Mr. Wilkes the account of his acting *Hastings,* had
greatly mistaken, that he had not made the least alteration in the usual manner of acting that part on account of the political disputes of the times, but
been solely guided by his own feelings : that he always had acted that part,
and always should play it in the same manner, not however slavishly

I would send the above to Garrick directly. but that I would avoid having this hand too commonly seen. Oblige me, then, so much as to have it copied in any hand, and sent by the penny post, that is, if you dislike sending it in your own writing. I must be more cautious than ever. I am sure I should not survive a discovery three days; or, if I did, they would attaint me by bill. Change to the *Somerset Coffee House*, and let no mortal know the alteration. I am persuaded you are too honest a man to contribute in any way to my *destruction*\*. Act honourably by me, and at a proper time you shall know me.

copying himself, but with all the variety which from time to time his genius might dictate, preserving still the cast and spirit of the original character. Nothing more passed on this subject between Mr. Garrick and me, nor has that gentleman ever expressed the slightest displeasure against Mr. Wilkes, or his friends: so far has he been from *complaining exceedingly of the cruelty of an interdict* which never existed.

"Did it escape your memory, Sir, that one of the objections made at that time by my friends was the peculiar emphasis Mr. Garrick was said to give to the following lines of *Hastings*, which some *thought applicable to your situation* :—

> 'Ill befall
> Such *meddling priests*, who kindle up confusion,
> And vex the quiet world with their *vain scruples* ;
> By Heaven 'tis done in perfect spite to peace.'

"You say, 'I think with half his (Mr. Garrick's) merit I should have had twice his courage.' If you mean *theatrical merit*, I can tell you of some parts in which you would infinitely exceed our great English actor. I mean all those parts from which—*fugiunt Pudor, Verumque, Fidesque. In quorum subeunt locum Fraudes, Dolique, Insidiaeque, &c. &c.* You would act and be *Iago* with success. Mr. Garrick has that in *him* which must ever prevent his acting well in that character. You have that in you which would make it easy and natural. *Shylock*, too, our Roscius must never attempt. The Christian priest of Brentford has no *vain scruples* to prevent his undertaking and being applauded in that part. He might then talk of *dying his black coat red with blood* in an innocent way on the stage, which at Brentford inspired a savage horror.

"The pleasing hours which Mr. Garrick gave me at the King's Bench I have deducted from the injury of a long and cruel imprisonment, and I think of him as Cicero did of the great Roman actor, *cum artifex ejusmodi sit, ut solus dignus videatur esse, qui in scena spectetur : tum vir ejusmodi est, ut solus dignus videatur, qui eo non accedat.*

"I am, &c.,
"JOHN WILKES."

\* The extreme alarm of Junius in consequence of the presumed exploratory movements of Garrick will be readily understood from the exposition now given of the authorship of the letters, coupled with the fact of Garrick being

I think the second page, with the widest lines, looks best.
What is your essential reason for the change*? I send you
some more sheets. I think the paper is not so good as Wheble's,—but I may be mistaken—the type is good. The aspersions thrown upon my letter to the Bill of Rights† should bo
refuted by publication.

Prevail upon Mr. Wilkes to let you have extracts of my
second and third letters to him. It will make the book still
more new. I would see them before they are printed, but
keep this last to yourself‡.

———

## No. 42.

November 11, 1771.

PRINT the following as soon as you think proper, and at the
head of your paper §.

a co-proprietor in the *Public Advertiser* (see Appendix, vol. i.), and well
known to Woodfall. Further, Garrick was on visiting terms with the elder
Francis, and probably Francis, junior (Junius?), was familiar to him, as well as
his handwriting. Hence the strict injunction of Junius to the printer to
withhold from Garrick a sight of his penmanship, and to copy in the writing of another the menacing note addressed to him. The fact of Woodfall
having informed Garrick of the "probability that Junius would write no
more," and the supposed celerity with which the intelligence was despatched to Richmond, has been adverted to in a former note; but nothing has
been said of the peculiar sources of Junius's information of Garrick's proceedings, and for this plain reason, that when Mason Good wrote, the claims of
Francis to the authorship had not been examined. But the source of intelligence may now be assumed on what seem sufficient grounds: Garrick may
have mentioned Woodfall's news to Dr. Francis, and be to his son; or Lord
Holland may have learnt it from George III. in one of his private interviews,
and made it a topic of conversation at the evening symposium with Dr.
Francis, Calcraft, the army contractor, and his mistress Bellamy.—ED.

* In allusion to a specimen of the intended genuine edition of the letters.

† In the correspondence which took place between Mr. Wilkes and
Junius, two of his letters related to the Bill of Rights Society, and were
written in disapprobation of several of their measures. These letters were,
in many respects, misrepresented to the public, and in his own opinion, purposely so by Mr. Horne. The explanatory extracts here referred to were
republished at the close of the second volume of the Junius edition, and will
be found in vol. i. p. 467. The letters are given at length in the private
correspondence between Junius and Mr. Wilkes, post.

‡ On the outside of this letter was written "private and particular."

§ Certain paragraphs relating to the marriage of the Duke of Cumberland,
inserted in the Preliminary Essay, p. 20.

I sent you three sheets of copy last night.

When you send to me, instead of the usual signal, say *Index shall be considered*, and keep the alteration a secret to everybody.

---

## No. 40.

About November 15, 1771.

IF you can find the date of the Duke of Bedford's flogging, insert it in the note*. I think it was soon after the Westminster election. The *Philos* are not to be placed as notes, except where I mention it particularly. I have no doubt of what you say about David Garrick, so drop the note. The truth is that, in order to curry favour, he made himself a greater rascal than he was. Depend upon what I tell you: —the King understood that he had found out the secret by his own cunning and activity. As it is important to deter him from meddling, I desire you will tell him that I am aware of his practices, and will certainly be revenged if he does not desist. An appeal to the public from Junius would destroy him.

Let me know whether Mr. Wilkes will give you the extracts†.

I cannot proceed without answers to those seven queries.

Think no more of Junius Americanus‡. Let him reprint his letters himself. He acts most dishonourably in suffering Junius to be so traduced; but this falsehood will all revert upon Horne. In the meantime, I laugh at him.

With submission I think it is not your interest to declare that I have done.

As to yourself, I really think you are in no danger. *You*

---

* See note to Letter 23 of Junius, *ante*, vol. i. p. 214.

† Referred to in the last paragraph of No. 41.

‡ Junius Americanus was a frequent writer in the *Public Advertiser* during the years 1769, 1770, and 1771. His letters chiefly related, as his signature readily suggests, to the disputes of the cabinet with the American colonies; and, in the course of his strictures, he attributed to Junius doctrines, in relation to their dependence on the legislature of Great Britain, which he had never avowed, nor even inclined to. At this time there was some idea of publishing them collectively. They were written by a Dr. Charles Lee, as may be seen by a reference to the private correspondence between Junius and Mr. Wilkes.

are not the object, and punishing *you* (unless it answered the purpose of stopping the press) would be no gratification to the King. If undesignedly I should send you anything you may think dangerous, judge for yourself, or take any opinion you think proper. You cannot offend or afflict me but by hazarding your own safety. They talk of farther informations, but they will always hold that language *in terrorem*.

Don't always use the same signal—any absurd Latin verse will answer the purpose *.

Let me know about what time you may want more copy.

Upon reflection, I think it absolutely necessary to send that note to D. G.†; only say *practices* instead of *impertinent inquiries*. I think you have no measures to keep with a man who could betray a confidential letter for so base a purpose as pleasing: * * * * * * * * * * * * * * *

* Preliminary Essay, vol. i. p. 22.

† David Garrick, *ante*, No. 41.

‡ This appears the proper place to insert Mr. Garrick's letter to Mr. Woodfall, first published in the Garrick *Correspondence* by Mr. Colburn in 1827, and which clears up the errors of Dr. Good, of Junius, and the latter's unfounded suspicions respecting Garrick.

LETTER FROM DAVID GARRICK TO H. S. WOODFALL.

"SIR,                                         "Nov. 20, 1771.

"I am obliged to address this letter to you and to appeal to your probity—in that, and my own, lies my defence against a most unprovoked and illiberal attack made upon me by your celebrated correspondent Junius. Had you not convinced me that the letter I received last Monday night was really written by that gentleman, I could not have imagined that such talents could have descended to such scurrility. However mighty the power may be with which he is pleased to threaten me, I trust with truth on my side, and your assistance, to be able to parry the vigour of his arm, and oblige him to drop his point, not for want of force to overcome so feeble an adversary as I am, but from the shame and consciousness of a very bad cause. In one particular I will be acknowledged his superior ; for, however easy and justifiable such a return may be, I will make use of no foul language. My vindication wants neither violence nor abuse to support it : it would be an unmanly to give injurious names to one who will not, as to him who cannot, resent it. Now to the fact which, till you had explained to me, had made no impression upon my mind. I am told in most outrageous terms, and near a month after the supposed crime was committed (for Junius was exactly informed of my *practices* the day after), that if the vagabond does not keep to his pantomimes, every hour of his life shall be cursed for his interfering with Junius. Is not this rather too inquisitorial for the great champion of our liberties? Now let us examine into the dreadful cause of this denunciation. Mr. Woodfall, the first informer, informs me in a letter in nowise

Tell me how long it may be before you want more copy. I want rest most severely, and am going to find it in the country for a few days. Cumbriensis* has taken greatly.

---

### No. 44.

November 27, 1771.

THE postscript to Titus must be omitted†. I did never question your understanding. For otherwise. The Latin word relative to the subject, without any previous impertinent inquiries on my part, or the least desire of secrecy on his, that Junius would write no more. Two or three days after the receipt of yours, being obliged to write a letter upon the business of the theatre to one at Richmond ¹, and after making my excuses for not being able to obey his Majesty's commands, I mentioned to him that Junius would write no more—but the triumph that succeeded this intelligence never reached me till I received Junius's letter: and so far was I from thinking there was a crime in communicating what was sent me without reserve, that I will freely confess that I wrote no letter to any of my friends without the mention of so remarkable an event. I will venture to go further, and affirm that it would have been insensible and unnatural not to have done it. I beg you will assure Junius that I have as proper an abhorrence of an informer as he can have—that I have been honoured with the confidence of men of all parties, and I defy my greatest enemy to produce a single instance of any one repenting of such confidence.

"I have always declared that were I by any accident to discover Junius, no consideration should prevail upon me to reveal a secret productive of so much mischief, nor can this most undeserved treatment of me make me alter my sentiments.

"One thing more I must observe, that Junius has given credit to an informer in prejudice of him who was never in the least suspected of being a spy before. Had any of our judges condemned the lowest culprit upon such evidence without bearing the person accused and other witnesses, the nation would have rung with injustice !

"I shall say no more ; but I beg you to tell all you know of this matter, and be assured that I am, with great regard for Junius's talents, but without the least for his threatenings,

"Your well-wisher and humble servant,
"D. GARRICK."—ED.

* See Miscellaneous Letter, No. 102. It was printed in the *Public Advertiser*, Nov. 13, 1771, upon the marriage of the Duke of Cumberland with Mrs. Horton, the sister of Col. Luttrell.

† His postscript addressed to Titus was added to his letter to Sir Wm. Draper of Feb. 21, 1769. It engaged to give Titus a severe castigation for

---

¹ " This alludes to his friend Ramus."—G. COVENTRY.

*simplex* conveys to me an amiable character, and never denotes folly. Though we may not be deficient in point of capacity, it is very possible that neither of us may be cunning enough for Mr. Garrick. But with a sound heart, be assured you are better gifted, even for worldly happiness, than if you had been cursed with the abilities of a Mansfield. After long experience of the world, I affirm before God, I never knew a rogue who was not unhappy.

Your account of my letter to the Bill of Rights astonishes me. I always thought the misrepresentation had been the work of Mr. Horne *. I will not trust myself with suspecting. The remedy is in my own hands, but, for Mr. Wilkes's honour, I wish it to come freely and honourably from himself. Publish nothing of mine until I have seen it. In the meantime be assured that nothing can be more express than my declaration against long parliaments. Try Mr. Wilkes once more. Speak for me in a most friendly but *firm* tone. That I *will not* submit to be any longer aspersed. Between ourselves, let me recommend it to you to be much upon your guard with patriots. I fear your friend Jerry Dyson will lose his Irish pension†. Say received.

having written with some degree of acrimony on the same side as the Knight of the Bath. The engagement, however, was not fulfilled under his signature of Junius, and hence the propriety of omitting the postscript in question in his own edition.

* Here he admits that he was mistaken in the conjecture that Horne had misrepresented the sentiments conveyed in his letters to the Bill of Rights Society. Yet as he published the same opinion in his own edition, which is now reprinted in vol. i. p. 467, he must afterwards have had fresh grounds for re-accrediting it, while in the present letter he seems more than half to suspect Wilkes himself.

† He feared with reason. Jeremiah Dyson, Esq., was one of the Lords of the Admiralty, and in Feb. 1770 resigned his seat in favour of the late lamented foreign minister Mr. Fox, upon an Irish pension of 1500*l.* per annum for his own life, and that of his three sons. The following is an account of the mode in which he lost it :—

"In a committee of supply of the House of Commons of Ireland, Nov. 25, 1771, after a long debate the question was put, and, on a division, it was carried against the pension by a majority of one, the numbers being, for it, 105, against it, 106 ; on which the House immediately resolved, 'That the pension granted to Jeremiah Dyson, Esq., and his three sons, is an unnecessary charge upon the establishment of Ireland, and ought not to be provided for.' Ordered, 'That the said pension be struck off the list of pensioners upon the establishment of Ireland.'" For Mr. Flood's speech upon this subject, see Preliminary Essay, p. 8d.

In page 25, it should be *the* instead of your*. This is a
wceful mistake;—pray take care for the future—keep a page
for errata.

David Garrick has literally forced me to break my resolu
tion of writing no more †.

---

No. 45.

December 5, 1771.

THESE papers are all in their exact order. Take great care
to keep them so. In a few days more I shall have sent you
all the copy. You must then take care of it yourself, except
that I must see proof sheets of the Dedication and Preface,
and these, if at all, I must see before the end of next week.
You shall have the extract to go into the second volume, it
will be a short one. *Scævola*, I see, is determined to make
me an enemy to Lord Camden ‡. If it be not wilful malice,
I beg you will signify to him that when I originally mentioned Lord Camden's declaration about the Corn Bill it was
without any view of discussing that doctrine, and only as an
instance of a singular opinion maintained by a man of great
learning and integrity. Such an instance was necessary to
the plan of my letter. I think he has in effect injured the
man whom he meant to defend.

When you send the above-mentioned proof sheets return
my own copy with them.

---

No. 46.

December 10, 1771.

THE enclosed completes all the materials that I can give you.
I have done my part. Take care *you* do yours. There are
still two letters wanting, which *I expect you will not fail* to insert in their places. One is from Philo–Junius to Scævola

---

* In the opening of the Letters of Junius, No. 3, vol. i. p. 416, it was
originally printed in the genuine edition, "Your defence," &c. In the
present edition the correction has been duly adopted.

† The letter alluded to is Junius, No. 67, vol. i. p. 441.

‡ For further particulars of this dispute, see Letters of Junius, No. 60,
vol. I. p. 417.

about Lord Camden, the other to a Friend of the People about
pressing*. They must be in the course of October. I have
no view but to serve you, and consequently have only to desire that the Dedication and Preface may be correct. Look
to it. If you take it upon yourself, I will not forgive your
suffering it to be spoiled. I weigh every word; and every
alteration, in my eyes at least, is a blemish.

I should not trouble you or myself about that blockhead
Scævola, but that his absurd fiction of my being Lord Camden's enemy has done harm. Every fool can do mischief;
therefore signify to him what I said.

Garrick has certainly betrayed himself, probably  *  *  *,
who makes it a rule to betray everybody that confides in him.
That new disgrace of Mansfield is true†; what do you mean
by affirming that the Dowager is better? I tell you she

* These two letters are numbered Philo-Junius, 60 and 62, vol. I. pp. 417
and 429.

† The allusion is to a cause which was tried at the Summer Assizes for
the county of Surrey, in 1771, Meares and Shepley against Ansell, for a
trespass, in which his Lordship was supposed to have given a very partial
charge in favour of the defendant, who thereby obtained a verdict. The
plaintiffs, however, on the Michaelmas Term following, moved the Court of
Common Pleas for a new trial, on the ground of the misdirection of the
judge. The judge was called upon for his report, which he could not make
without sending to the plaintiff's attorney for his affidavit of the transaction. He made his report at last, to which he subjoined that he was perfectly satisfied with the verdict of the jury. The Court of Common Pleas
was clearly of opinion that Lord Mansfield had acted contrary to every
principle of evidence, both in law and equity, in admitting Matthews and
Hiscox to give parol evidence, contrary to a clear explicit agreement in
writing, which they had attested—and asserted, that if such a practice was
to obtain, it would go a great way towards subverting the statute of
frauds and perjuries, and would be a most dangerous inlet to perjury, and
a means of rendering men's properties very precarious and insecure. The
court therefore set aside the verdict, and ordered a new trial; and it
appeared to the court to be so gross a misdirection that it dispensed with
the usual terms of payment of costs. Although Lord Mansfield, in his
direction to the jury, represented the trespasses as small and insignificant,
and the action as litigious, the Court of Common Pleas said the trespasses
were obstinate, wilful, and malicious.

Mr. Rowlinson, the plaintiff's attorney, felt so dissatisfied with the conduct of Lord Mansfield upon the occasion, that in the same term a motion
was made at his instigation to have his name struck off the Rolls of the
Court of King's Bench, which, as a motion of course, was acquiesced in,
when he was immediately admitted into the Common Pleas.

suckles toads from morning till night*. I think I have now
done my duty by you, so farewell.

---

No. 47.

December 17, 1771.

Make your mind easy about me. I believe your are an honest
man, and I never am angry†. Say to-morrow " We are desired to inform Scævola that his private note was received
with the most profound indifference and contempt."‡ I see
his design. The Duke of Grafton has been long labouring to
detach Camden. This Scævola is the wretchedest of all fools,
and dirty knave.

Upon no account, nor for any reason whatsoever, are you to
write to me until I give you notice.

When the book is finished, let me have a set bound in
vellum, gilt, and lettered Junius 1. 2. as handsomely as you
can—the edges gilt. Let the sheets be well dried before
binding. I must also have two sets in blue paper covers.
This is all the fee I shall ever desire of you. I think you
ought not to publish before the second week in January.

The London Packet is not worth our notice. I suspect
Garrick, and I would have you hint so to him.

---

* He refers to the following paragraph, which appeared in the Public
Advertiser, Dec. 6, 1771 :—
" We have the pleasure to assure the public, from the most undoubted
authority, that the repeated accounts of her Royal Highness the Princess
Dowager of Wales being very ill, and her life in great danger, are entirely
false ; such reports being only calculated to promote the shameful spirit of
gambling, by insurance on lives." The Princess Dowager was at this time
afflicted with a cancer, and died on the 8th of January in the following
year.

† He had received a note from Mr. Woodfall, vindicating himself from
any improper motive in his communication to Mr. Garrick, which has been
already referred to.

‡ The information to Scævola was duly communicated in the Public
Advertiser : and the flippancy of this writer's style, and the coquetry of his
political attachments, fully merited the contempt here expressed for him.

---

## No. 48

January 6, 1772.

I HAVE a thing to mention to you in great confidence. I expect your assistance, and rely upon your secrecy.

There is a long paper ready for publication, but which must not appear until the morning of the meeting of parliament, nor be announced in any shape whatsoever*. Much depends upon its appearing unexpectedly. If you receive it on the 8th or 9th instant, can you in a day or two have it composed, and two proof sheets struck off and sent me; and can you keep the press standing ready for the *Public Advertiser* of the 21st, and can all this bo done with such secrecy that none of your people shall know what is going forward, except the composer; and can you rely on *his* fidelity? Consider of it, and, if it be possible, say YES, in your paper to-morrow.

I think it will take four full columns at the least, but I undertake that it shall sell. It is essential that I should have a proof sheet, and correct it myself.

Let me know if the books are ready, that I may tell you what to do with them.

---

## No. 49.

Saturday, January 11, 1772.

Your failing to send me the proofs, as you engaged to do, disappoints and distresses me extremely†. It is not merely to correct the press (though even that is of consequence), but for another most *material purpose*‡. This will be entirely

---

* Letter to Lord Mansfield. Junius, No. 69, vol. i.
† Of Junius, No. 68, referred to in the preceding letter.
‡ Here Mason Good remarks, "He seems to allude to a promise or expectation of legal assistance from some friendly quarter." But what was only speculative conjecture in Woodfall's editor may now be spoken of as positive fact, the publication of the *Correspondence of the Earl of Chatham* having elucidated the "most *material purpose*" Junius had in view in obtaining proofs of his Letters to Lord Mansfield and Lord Camden. From this *Correspondence* (vol. iv. p. 190), it appears that proof sheets of these letters were forwarded by Junius to Lord Chatham at Burton Pynsent, together with a private letter to his Lordship stating and enforcing the chief points of his legal argument against the Chief Justice.

This letter has been inserted in the APPENDIX to the present volume. In

defeated if you do not let me have the two proofs on Monday morning.

The paper itself is, in my opinion, of the highest style of Junius, and cannot fail to sell. My reason for not announcing it was that the party might have no time to concert his measures with the ministry. But upon reflection, I think it may answer better (in order to excite attention) to advertise it the day before, *Junius to Lord Chief Justice Mansfield to-morrow.*

Quoting from memory, I have made a mistake about Blackstone where I say *that he confines the power to the Court, and does not extend it to the Judges separately.* Those lines must be omitted *. The rest is right. If you have any regard for me, or for the cause, let nothing hinder your sending the proofs on Monday.

his communication to the Earl of Chatham, Junius appears apprehensive lest Lord Mansfield may try to " whittle away his oversight" in bailing Eyre, and escape from the legal network in which he is confident he has enclosed him. To avert such result Junius is urgent that Lord Chatham and the Duke of Richmond should be present in the House of Lords, prepared to take down the words of the Chief Justice, and move for "committing him to the Tower."

Notwithstanding the firm belief of Junius that Lord Mansfield had exceeded his power in bailing Eyre, charged with theft, Lord Campbell remarks of the celebrated writer that he was " egregiously in the wrong—clearly showing that he was not a lawyer, his mistakes not being designedly made for disguise, but palpably proceeding from an ignorant man affecting knowledge."—*Lives of the Chief Justices,* vol. ii. p. 491. Junius, however, never pretended to be a lawyer; he admitted distinctly that he was not, and acknowledged himself " to be no more deeply read than every English gentleman should be in the law of his country."—(*Preface,* vol. i. p. 92). He cherished, indeed, an indifferent opinion of the morality of lawyers and their needful acquirements. " As a practical profession," says he, " the study of the law requires but a moderate portion of abilities. The learning of a pleader is usually upon a level with his integrity. The indiscriminate defence of right and wrong contracts the understanding, while it corrupts the heart."—*Junius,* vol. i. p. 449.

It does not appear from the Chatham Papers that the Earl left any remarks on the two communications Junius privately addressed to him, nor whether he had any knowledge or suspicion of his correspondent.—ED.

* " In the proofs now before us, corrected by Junius, this passage is erased. It may be added that the Greek ϴ is used for the sign of deletion instead of the more usual one of the Greek Σ. This trifling distinction would hardly be worth alluding to, did it not afford another instance of agreement with Sir Philip Francis, whose corrections for the press were made in a similar manner."—*Junius Identified.*—ED.

## No. 50.

January 16, 1772.

I RETURN you the proof with the errata, which you will be so good as to correct carefully. I have the greatest reason to be pleased with your care and attention, and wish it were in my power to render you some essential service. Announce it on Monday.

---

## No. 51.

(Private.)

Saturday, January 18, 1772.

THE gentleman * who transacts the conveyancing part of our correspondence tells me there was much difficulty last night. For this reason, and because it could be no way material for me to see a paper on Saturday which is to appear on Monday, I had resolved not to send for it. Your hint of this morning I suppose relates to this†. I am truly concerned to see that the publication of the book is so long delayed. It ought to have appeared before the meeting of parliament. By no means would I have you insert this long letter, if it made more than the difference of two days in the publication. Believe me the delay is a real injury to the cause. The letter to M. ‡ may come into a new edition.

Mr. Wilkes seems not to know that Morris published that letter §. I think you should set him right.

---

## No. 52.

January 25, 1772.

HAVING nothing better to do, I propose to entertain myself and the public with torturing that * * * * * Bar-

* Of this gentleman nothing is known.

† "*Mutare necessarium est.*" Answer to correspondents, Jan. 18, 1772.

‡ To Lord Mansfield, No. 68.

§ Mr. Robert Morris was a barrister, who took a very active part in the city disputes, and on the popular side, and was secretary to the Bill of Rights Society. For a further account of him see note in Miscellaneous Letter, No. 98. He occasionally wrote in the *Public Advertiser*. The publication of the letter alluded to Wilkes had attributed to a Mr. Cawdron. See Private Letter, No. 82.

rington. He has just appointed a French broker his deputy, for no reason but his relation to Bradshaw *. I hear from all quarters that it is looked upon as a most impudent insult to the army. Be careful not to have it known to come from me. Such an insignificant creature is not worth the generous rage of Junius. I am impatient for the book.

## No. 53.

Monday, February 3, 1772.

I CONFESS I do not see the use of the table of contents. I think it will be endless and answer no purpose; an index of proper names and materials would, in my opinion, be suffi cient. You may safely defy the malice of Mr. Wheble †.

---

* Mr. Chamier, brother-in-law to Bradshaw, the Duke of Grafton's private secretary, here, and elsewhere, so slightingly mentioned by Junius, is thus undervalued solely as a mode of attacking Lord Barrington. He was not a mere broker in the Alley, preferred only for the chicanery which may be learned there. We are told by Sir John Hawkins, in his entertaining *Life of Dr. Johnson*, that Mr. Chamier was selected by the sage as one of the original nine composing his club at the Turk's Head, in Gerard Street. " He was descended from a French refugee family. Having had a liberal education, his deportment and manner of transacting the business of a stock-broker distinguished him greatly from most others of that calling. He was well skilled in the modern languages, particularly the Spanish, in the study whereof he took great delight. He had acquired such a fortune as enabled him, though young, to quit business, and become, what indeed he seemed by nature intended for, a gentleman." This club was instituted in 1763.

Mr. Dyer, upon his return from Germany, where he had been a commissary with the army, was allowed to become the tenth member. Perhaps it may not be unimportant to show that thus Mr. Chamier was well known to Mr. Burke and to Mr. Dyer, at the time when Junius began to write, and was an esteemed member of the club, of which they were distinguished ornaments. The reader, even in a political work, may not be displeased to see the names recorded of men who thus met for social objects, and among whom politics never intruded.

| | |
|---|---|
| Dr. Johnson. | Sir John Hawkins. |
| Sir Joshua Reynolds. | Mr. Topham Beauclerk. |
| Mr. Edmund Burke. | Bennet Langton. |
| Christ. Nugent, M.D. | Anthony Chamier. |
| Oliver Goldsmith, M.B. | Samuel Dyer. |

† Wheble had already reprinted an imperfect edition of the Letters of Junius, but certainly without any intention of injuring the original publisher of them. The word malice, as applied to Mr. Wheble, merely meant rivalry. See Private Letter, No. 56.

Whoever buys such a book will naturally prefer the author's edition, and I think it will always be a book for sale. I really am in no hurry about that set. Purling, I hear, is to come in for Eastlow—a sure proof of the connection between him and government *. I would have you open anything that may be brought to you for me (except from Mr. Wilkes), and not forward it unless it be material.

That large roll contained a pamphlet.

## No. 54.

Monday, Feb. 10, 1772.

IF you have anything to communicate you may send it to the original place for once N.E.C.; and mention any new place you think proper, west of Temple Bar. The delay of the book spoils everything.

## No. 55.

Monday Night, Feb. 17, 1772.

SURELY you have misjudged it very much about the book. I could not have conceived it possible that you could protract the publication so long. At this time, particularly before Mr. Sawbridge's motion †, it would have been of singular use. You have trifled too long with the public expectation. At a certain point of time the appetite palls. I fear you have already lost the season. The book, I am sure, will lose the greatest part of the effect I expected from it. But I have done.

## No. 56.

About Feb. 22, 1772.

I DO you the justice to believe that the delay has been unavoidable. The expedient you propose of printing the Dedi-

* John Purling, Esq., one of the directors of the East India Company, who took a very active part in their affairs at that period.
† In favour of triennial parliaments, as already noticed in a note to the Preliminary Dissertation

cation and Preface in the *P. A.* is unadvisable. The attention
of the public would then be quite lost to the book itself. I
think your rivals will be disappointed. Nobody will apply to
*them* when they can be supplied at the fountain head. I hope
you are too forward to have any room for that letter of Domitian *, otherwise it is merely indifferent. The Latin I
thought much superior to the English. The intended bill, in
consequence of the message, will be a most dangerous innova-
sion in the internal policy of this country †. What an abandoned prostituted idiot is your lord mayor‡! The shameful
mismanagement which brought him into office gave me the
first and an unconquerable disgust. All I can now say is
make haste with the book.

C.

The appointment of this broker §, I am told, gives universal
disgust. That * ¤ * * * * * * * * * ‖ would never
have taken a step apparently so absurd if there were not
some wicked design in it more than we are aware of. At any
rate the broker should be run down. That, at least, is due to
his master.

———

## No. 57.

Saturday, Feb. 29, 1772.

I am very glad to see that the book will be out before Sawbridge's motion. There is no occasion for a mark of admiration at the end of the motto. But it is of no moment whatsoever. When you see Mr. W. pray return him my thanks
for the trouble he has taken. I wish he had taken more ¶.
I should be glad to have a set, sewed, left at the same place
to-morrow evening. Let it be well sealed up.

C.

* This letter, for the reason here stated, was not printed in the genuine
edition.
† The bill here spoken of is the Royal Marriage Act.
‡ In allusion to the partial and impolitic conduct of Mr. Nash, at this
time lord mayor, upon the common questions of city politics brought before
him, especially in refusing to call a common hall, agreeably to a request very
generally signified to him for this purpose.
§ Chamier.          ‖ Lord Barrington.
¶ Mr. Wilkes, at the request of Junius, perused and revised the Dedication
and Preface to the genuine edition of the letters.

## No. 58.

Tuesday, March 3, 1772.

Your letter was twice refused last night, and the waiter as often attempted to see the person who sent for it. I was impatient to see the book, and think I had a right to that attention a little before the general publication *. When I desired to have two sets sewed, and one bound in vellum, it was not from a principle of economy. I despise such little savings, and shall still be a purchaser. If I was to buy as many sets as I want, it would be remarked.

Pray let the two sets be well parcelled up and left at the bar of Munday's Coffee House, Maiden Lane, with the same direction, and with orders to be delivered to a chairman who will ask for them in the course of to-morrow evening. Farewell.

## No. 59.

Thursday, March 5, 1772.

Your letters with the books are come safe to hand. The difficulty of corresponding arises from situation and necessity, to which we must submit. Be assured I will not give you more trouble than is unavoidable. If the vellum books are not yet bound, I would wait for the index. If they are, let me know by a line in the P. A. When they are ready, they may safely be left at the same place as last night.

On your account I was alarmed at the price of the book. But of the sale of books I am no judge, and can only pray for your success. What you say about the profits † is very handsome. I like to deal with such men. As for myself, be assured that I am far above all pecuniary views, and no other person, I think, has any claim to share with you. Make the most of it therefore, and let all your views in life be directed to a solid, however moderate, independence. Without it no man can be happy, or even honest.

* The genuine edition of the letters was published on the 3rd of March, 1772.

† Woodfall made Junius an offer of half the profits of the book, or if he should decline accepting them for himself, to give a sum of money equal to their amount to any charity which he should choose to name.

If I saw any prospect of uniting the city once more, I would readily continue to labour in the vineyard. Whenever Mr. Wilkes can tell me that such an union is in prospect, he shall hear of me.

*Quòd si quis existimat me aut voluntate esse mutatâ, aut debilitatâ virtute, aut animo fracto, vehementer errat.* Farewell.

In the Preface, p. 20, line 7, read unseasonable,
            p. 20, —18, —— accuracy *.

---

## No. 60.

May 4, 1772.

IF *pars pro toto* † be meant for me, I must beg the favour of you to recall it. At present it would be difficult for me to receive it. When the books are ready, a Latin verse will be sufficient.

---

## No. 61.

Sunday, May 3, 1772.

I AM in no manner of hurry about the books. I hope the sale has answered. I think it will always be a saleable book. The enclosed is fact, and I wish it could be printed to-morrow. It is not worth announcing. The proceedings of this wretch are unaccountable. There must be some mystery in it which I hope will soon be discovered to his confusion. Next to the Duke of Grafton, I verily believe that the *blackest heart* in the kingdom belongs to Lord Barrington ‡.

---

* These errors are corrected in the present edition.

† A line in the printer's notice to correspondents, introduced as a signal that a letter, or parcel, was in waiting for him at the usual place.

‡ This was after Junius had quarrelled with Lord Barrington, for not being appointed his deputy in the War Office: it was, however, to the subsequent recommendation of his Lordship that Francis was indebted for his lucrative appointment in India. This note is still in possession of the printer of the present edition; It accompanied Junius's letter signed *Scotus*, addressed to Lord Barrington, and forms No. 111 of the Miscellaneous Letters.—ED.

## No. 62.

May 10, 1772.

Pray let this be announced, *Memoirs of Lord Barrington in our next**. Keep the author a secret †.

---

## No. 63.

January 19, 1773.

I HAVE seen the signals thrown out for your old friend and correspondent. Be assured that I have had good reason for not complying with them. In the present state of things, if I were to write again, I must be as silly as any of the horned cattle that run mad through the city, or as any of your wise aldermen. I meant the cause and the public. Both are given up. I feel for the honour of this country, when I see that there are not ten men in it who will unite and stand together upon any one question. But it is all alike, vile and contemptible.

*You* have never flinched that I know of; and I shall always rejoice to hear of your prosperity.

If you have anything to communicate (of moment to yourself) you may use the last address, and give a hint ‡.

---

## No. 64.

SIR,

I HAVE troubled you with the perusal of two letters, as that of the prior date accounts for the delay of not sending the books

* The annunciation, under this title, appeared in the notice to correspondents, *Public Advertiser*, May 11, and the *Memoirs* were printed in a letter bearing the signature of *Nemesis*, May 12, forming Miscellaneous Letter, No. 113. See also note at the end of *Nemesis*, for a notice of Lord Barrington.

† Junius (*Francis* ?) having done his work, set out, as already stated, on his continental travels, and did not, as appears from the date of his next and concluding note, again communicate with Woodfall till the January following. —ED.

‡ This letter was thus noticed in the answer to correspondents in the *Public Advertiser*, March 8, 1773. "The letter from AN OLD FRIEND and CORRESPONDENT, dated Jan. 19, came safe to hand, and his directions are strictly followed. *Quod si quis existimat, aut, &c.*"

sooner; and this acquaints you that I did not get them out of
the bookbinder's hands till yesterday; nor, though I desired
them to be finished in the most elegant manner possible, are
they done so well as I wished. But, Sir, if the manner of the
contents and index are not agreeable to you, they shall be
done over again according to any directions you shall please
to favour me with. With respect to city politics, I fear the
breach is too wide ever to be again closed, and even my friend
Mr. Wilkes lost some of his wonted coolness at the late election, on Sawbridge, Oliver, &c., scratching against him *. I
hope you will believe that, however agreeable to me it must
be to be honoured with your correspondence, I should never
entertain the most distant wish that one ray of your splendour
should be diminished by your continuing to write. Mr.
Wilkes, indeed, mentioned to me the other day that he thought
the East India Company a proper subject, and asked if I could
communicate anything to you, to which my reply was that I
could not tell (as I did not know whether you might choose
to be intruded upon). You will perceive by the papers that
two persons have forced themselves upon us who, without a
tithe of Mr. Wilkes's abilities, imagine the public will look up
to them as their deliverers; but they are most egregiously
mistaken, as every one who possesses a grain of common sense
hold them in almost utter contempt. You will probably guess
who I mean, and were I capable of drawing a parallel, I should
borrow some part of it from Shakespeare's Iago and Roderigo.
Should it please the Almighty to spare your life till the next
general election, and I should at that time exist, I shall hope
you will *deign to instruct me* for whom I should give my vote,
as my wish is to be represented by the most honest and able,
and I know there cannot be any one who is so fit to judge as

---

* Mr. Wilkes and Mr. Townshend were, after a sharp contest, returned to
the court of aldermen for them to make their election of one of these gentlemen to the mayoralty for the year 1772, when their choice fell upon
Mr. Alderman Townshend, in consequence of Sawbridge and Oliver
scratching against Wilkes. The candidates for that office, with the numbers
which they polled, were as under:—

| | | |
|---|---|---|
| Mr. Alderman Wilkes | . . . . | 2301 |
| „ Townshend | . . . | 2278 |
| „ Hallifax | . . . | 2126 |
| „ Shakespeare | . . | 1912 |

yourself. I have no connections to warp me, nor am I acquainted with but one person who would speak to me on the subject, and that gentleman is, I believe, a true friend to the real good of his country; I mean Mr. Glover, the author of *Leonidas*. As I thought Serjeant Glyn deserving of something more than the mere fees of his profession, for the pains he took upon my trial, I have made a purchase of a small freehold at Brentford by way of qualification, in order to convince him, if he should offer himself at the next election, whenever it should happen, that I hold his services in grateful remembrance. But I am since informed that it is not his intention, and that Lord Percy is to be joined with Sir W. B. Proctor, who is to be supported by the Duke of Northumberland's interest. I have heard much of a most trimming letter from Mr. Stewart to Lord Mansfield on the Douglas cause, but cannot possibly get a copy, which probably would be a good letter to print.

If, Sir, you should not disapprove of the Contents and Index I thought of advertising them in the manner of the enclosed form, if I have your permission so to do, but not otherwise. May I beg the favour of a line in answer? Believe me, Sir, to be, with gratitude and respect,

Your much obliged
humble servant to command,
HENRY SAMPSON WOODFALL.

Sunday, March 7, 1773.

# PRIVATE CORRESPONDENCE
## BETWEEN JUNIUS AND MR. WILKES.

---

### No. 65.

JUNIUS TO JOHN WILKES, ESQ.

London, 21st August, 1771*.

I PRESUME, Sir, you are satisfied that I mean you well, and that it is not necessary to assure you that while you adhere to the resolution of depending only upon the public favour (which, if you have half the understanding I attribute to you, you never can depart from) you may rely upon my utmost assistance. Whatever imaginary views may be ascribed to the author, it must always make part of Junius's plan to support Mr. Wilkes while *he* makes common cause with the people. I would engage your favourable attention to what I am going to say to you; and I entreat you not to be too hasty in concluding, from the apparent tendency of this letter, to any possible interests or connections of my own. It is a very common mistake in judgment, and a very dangerous one in conduct, first to look for nothing in the argument proposed to us but the motive of the man who uses it, and then to measure the truth of his argument by the motive we have assigned to him. With regard to me, Sir, any refinement in this way would assuredly mislead you; and though I do not disclaim the idea of some personal views to future honour and advantage (you would not believe me if I did), yet I can truly af-

* On this letter is written, in Mr. Wilkes's own hand, the following memorandum :—

"August 21, 1771.

"Received on Wednesday noon by a chairman, who said he brought it from a gentleman whom he saw in Lancaster Court, in the Strand.

"J. W."

firm that neither are they little in themselves, nor can they
by any possible conjecture be collected from my writings.

Mr. Horne, after doing much mischief, is now, I think,
completely defeated and disarmed. The author of the late
unhappy divisions in the city is removed. Why should we
suffer his works to live after him? In this view, I confess,
I am vindictive, and would visit his sins upon his children.
I would punish him in his offspring, by repairing the breaches
he has made. Convinced that I am speaking to a man who
has spirit enough to act if his judgment be satisfied, I will
not scruple to declare at once, that Mr. Sawbridge *ought to
be Lord Mayor*, and that he ought to owe it to *your* first
motion, and to the exertion of all your credit in the city. I
affirm, without a doubt, that political prudence, the benefit of
the cause, your public reputation and personal interest, do all
equally demand this conduct of you. I do not deny that a
stroke like this is above the level of vulgar policy, or that if
you were a much less considerable man than you are it would
not suit you. But you will recollect, Sir, that the public
opinion of you rises every day, and that you must enlarge
your plan as you proceed, since you have every day a new
acquisition of credit to maintain. I offer you the sincere
opinion of a man, who, perhaps, has more leisure to make reflections than you have, and who, though he stands clear of

* After the death of the patriotic magistrate, Mr. Beckford, in
1770, Mr. Sawbridge managed the Chatham interest in the city, and was
in constant communication with his Lordship's political attorney, Mr. Calcraft. Hence the declaration of Junius, that Alderman Sawbridge "ought
to be Lord Mayor." He in his election failed on the present occasion, but
in 1776 obtained the mayoralty. Writing to the Earl of Chatham, Oct. 19,
1770, Mr. Calcraft says:—" Mr. Sawbridge came here this evening, after
having attended the common council. The recorder's business has ended
much to the satisfaction of our friends." (*Chatham Correspondence*, iii.
474.) The recorder had given offence by declining to attend at St. James's
with the city remonstrance, and the common council, after first repealing an
old by-law that required them to consult the recorder and common sergeant in all city business, passed a resolution not to employ the recorder in
any city business, but to consult Serjeant Glyn. Mr. Calcraft writes to
Chatham, Nov. 28, 1770, " Your Lordship gave me great private satisfaction
in what you so generously said [in the House of Lords] about my friend
Sawbridge." (*Ibid.* iv. 33.) These excerpts are essential to elucidate the
origin of the city preferences of Junius, and the sources of his copious information relative to the movements of parties there. Alderman Sawbridge
died in 1795.—ED.

all business and intrigue, mixes sufficiently for the purposes
of intelligence in the conversation of the world.
Whatever language you in prudence assume to the public,
you cannot but be sensible that the separation of those gentlemen who withdrew from the Bill of Rights was of considerable disservice to you. It required, in my opinion, your
utmost dexterity and resolution, and not a little of your good
fortune, to get the better of it. But are you now really upon
the best ground on which Mr. Wilkes might stand in the
city? Will you say that to separate Mr. Sawbridge from a
connection every way hostile to you, and to secure him against
the insidious arts of Mr. Horne, and the fury of Mr. Townshend (if it could be done without embarrassing your leading
measures, and much more if it promoted them), would not give
you a considerable personal gratification? Will you say that
a public declaration of Mr. Sawbridge in your favour, and
the appearance of your acting together (I do not speak at
present of a hearty coalition or confidence), would not contribute to give you a more secure, a more permanent, and, without offence to any man, a more honourable hold upon the city
than you have at present? What sensations do you conceive
a union between you and Mr. Sawbridge would excite in the
breast of Mr. Horne? Would it not amount to a decisive
refutation of all the invidious arguments he has drawn from
your being deserted by so many of the considerable figures of
the party? The answer to these questions is too obvious to
be mistaken. But you will say to yourself, what you would not
confess to Junius :—" Mr. Sawbridge is a man of unquestionable probity, and the concurrence of his reputation would undoubtedly be of service to me; but he has not pliancy enough
to yield to persuasion, and I, Wilkes, am determined not to
suffer another to reap the harvest of my labours : that is, to
take the lead of me in the city." Sir, I do not mean or expect that you should make such a sacrifice to any man. But
besides difference in point of conduct between leading and going
foremost, I answer your thoughts when I say, that although
Mr. Sawbridge is not to be directed (and even this perhaps is
not so literally and completely true as he himself imagines),
on the other hand he does not mean to direct. His disposition, as you well know, is not fitted for that active manage
ment and intrigue which acquire an operating popularity and

direct the people by their passions. I attribute to you both the most honourable intentions for the public, but you travel different roads, and never can be rivals. It is not that Mr. Sawbridge does not wish to be popular; but, if I am not greatly mistaken, his virtues have not ostentation enough for the ordinary uses of party, and *that* they lead rather to the esteem of individuals than to popular opinion. This I conceive is exactly the man you want—you cannot always support a ferment in the minds of men. There will necessarily be moments of languor and fatigue; and upon these occasions Mr. Sawbridge's reputed firmness and integrity may be a capital resource to you—you have too much sagacity not to perceive how far this reasoning might be carried.

In the very outset you reap a considerable advantage, either from his acceptance or refusal. What a copious subject of ostentation!—what rich colours to the public! Your zeal to restore tranquillity to the city; the sacrifice of all personal recollections in favour of a man whose general character you esteem; the public good preferred to every private or interested consideration, with a long *et cetera* to your own advantage. Yet I do not mean to persuade you to so simple a part as that of contributing to gratify Mr. Sawbridge without a reciprocal assurance from him that, upon fair and honourable occasions, he will in return promote your advantage. Your own judgment will easily suggest to you such terms of acknowledgment as may be binding upon him in point of gratitude, and not offensive to his delicacy. I have not entered into the consideration of any objections drawn from the fertile field of provocation and resentment. Common men are influenced by common motives; but you, Sir, who pretend to lead the people, must act upon higher principles. To make our passions subservient to you, you must command your own. The man who, for any personal indulgence whatsoever, can sacrifice a great purpose to a little one, is not qualified for the management of great affairs.

Let me suppose, then, that every material difficulty on your part is removed; and that, as far as you alone are concerned, you would be ready to adopt the plan I propose to you.

If you are a man of honour you will still have a powerful objection to oppose to me. Admitting the apparent advantage to your own purposes, and to the cause you are engaged

in, you will te!] me "that you are no longer at liberty to
choose;—tnat the desertion of those persons who once pro
fessed a warm attachment to you, has reduced you to a situa
tion in which you cannot do that which is absolutely best;—
that Mr. Crosby has deserved everything from you and from
the city;—and that you stand engaged to contribute your whole
strength to continue him another year in the mayoralty."
My reply to this very just objection is addressed rather to
Mr. Crosby than to Mr. Wilkes.  He ought at all events to
be satisfied; and if I cannot bring him over to my opinion,
there is an end of the argument; for I do agree with you most
heartily, that it is as gross a breach of policy as of morals, to
sacrifice the man who has deserved well of us to any temporary benefit whatsoever.  Far from meaning to separate you
from Mr. Crosby, it is essential to the measure I recommend
that it should be your joint act.  Nay, it is ho who in the
first instance should open the communication with Mr. Sawbridge; nor is it possible for you to gain any credit by the
measure in which he will not of necessity be a considerable
sharer.  But now for considerations which immediately affect
Mr. Crosby.

Your plan, as I am informed, is to engage the livery to return him with Mr. Bridgen.  In my own opinion the court of
alderman will choose Bridgen; consequently the sacrifice I
require of Mr. Crosby would in effect bo nothing.  That he
will be defeated is to my judgment inevitable.  It is for him
to consider whether the idea of a defeat be not always attended with some loss of reputation.  In that case, too, he will
have forced upon the citizens (whom he professes to love and
respect) a magistrate, upon whose odious and contemptible
character he at present founds his only hopes of success.  Do
you think that the city will not once in the course of a twelvemonth be sensible of the displeasure you have done them?
Or that it will not bo placed in strong terms to your account?
I appeal to Miss Wilkes, whose judgment I hear highly commended—would she think herself much indebted to her favourite admirer if he forced a most disagreeable partner upon
her for a long winter's night, because he could not dance with
her himself?

You will now say,—" Sir, we understand the politics of the

city better than you do, and are well assured that Mr. Crosby will be chosen lord mayor;—otherwise we allow that upon your plan he might acquire credit without forfeiting any real advantage." Upon this ground I expect you, for I confess it is incumbent upon me to meet your argument where it lies strongest against me. Taking it for granted, then, that Mr. Crosby may be lord mayor, I affirm that it is not his interest, because it is not his greatest interest. The little profit of the salary cannot possibly be in contemplation with him. I do not doubt that he would rather make it an expensive office to himself. His view must be directed then to the flattering distinction of succeeding to a second mayoralty, and, what is still more honourable, to the being thought worthy of it by his fellow-citizens. Placing this advantage in its strongest light, I say that every purpose of distinction is as completely answered by his being known to have had the employment in his power (which may be well insisted upon in argument, and never can be disproved by the fact) as by his accepting it. To this I add the signal credit he will acquire with every honest man by renouncing, upon motives of the clearest and most disinterested public spirit, a personal honour, which you may fairly tell the world was unquestionably within his reach. But these are trifles. I assert that by now accepting the mayoralty (which he may take hereafter whenever he pleases) he precludes himself from soliciting, with any colour of decency, a real and solid reward from the city. I mean that he should be returned for London in the next Parliament. I think his conduct entitles him to it, and that he cannot fail of succeeding, if he does not furnish his opponents with too just a pretence for saying that the city have already rewarded him. On the contrary, with what force and truth may he tell his fellow-citizens at the next election, "for your sakes I relinquished the honour you intended me. The common good required it. But I did not mean to renounce my hopes that upon a proper occasion you would honour me with a public mark of your approbation."

You see I do not insist upon the good effects of Mr. Sawbridge's gratitude, yet I am sure it may be depended upon. I do not say that he is a man to go all lengths with Mr. Wilkes; but you may be assured that it is not danger that

will deter him. and that wherever you have the voice of the
people with you, he will, upon principle, support their choice
at the hazard of his life and fortune.

Now, Sir, supposing all objections are removed, and that
you and Mr. Crosby are agreed, the question is in what manner is the business to be opened to Mr. Sawbridge. Upon
this point, too, I shall offer you my opinion, because the plan
of this letter would not otherwise be complete. At the same
time I do very unaffectedly submit myself to your judgment.

I would have my lord mayor begin by desiring a private
interview between him, Mr. Crosby *, and yourself. Very
little preface will be necessary. You have a man to deal
with who is too honourable to take an unfair advantage of
you. With such a man you gain everything by frankness
and candour, and hazard nothing by the confidence you repose
in him. Notwithstanding any passages in this letter, I would
show him the whole of it: in a great business there is nothing
so fatal as cunning management; and I would tell him it
contained the plan upon which Mr. Crosby and you were
desirous to act, provided he would engage to concur in it *bond
fide*, so far forth as he was concerned. There is one condition, I own, which appears to me a *sine quâ non ;* and yet I
do not see how it can be proposed in terms, unless his own
good sense suggests the necessity of it to him—I mean the
total and absolute renunciation of Mr. Horne. It is very
likely indeed that this gentleman may do the business for
himself, either by laying aside the mask at once, or by abusing
Mr. Sawbridge for accepting the mayoralty upon any terms
whatsoever of accommodation with Mr. Wilkes.

This letter, Sir, is not intended for a correct or polished
composition ; but it contains the very best of Junius's understanding. Do not treat me so unworthily, or rather do not
degrade yourself so much, as to suspect me of any interested
view to Mr. Sawbridge's particular advantage. By all that's
honourable I mean nothing but the cause ; and I may defy
your keenest penetration to assign a satisfactory reason why
Junius, whoever he be, should have a personal interest in

* Mr. Crosby was, at the date of this letter, Lord Mayor, and Junius or
his printer has here, obviously through mistake, submitted his name for that
of Mr. Sawbridge.

giving the mayoralty to Mr. Sawbridge, rather than to Mr. Crosby.

I am heartily weary of writing, and shall reserve another subject, on which I mean to address you, for another opportunity.  I think that this letter, if you act upon it, should be a secret to everybody but Mr. Sawbridge and my Lord Mayor.

JUNIUS*.

---

No. 66.

JUNIUS TO JOHN WILKES, ESQ.

London, September 7, 1771†.

As this letter, Sir, has no relation to the subject of my last, the motives upon which you may have rejected one of my opinions ought not to influence your judgment of another. I am not very sanguine in my expectations of persuading, nor do I think myself entitled to quarrel with any man for not following my advice; yet this, I believe, is a species of injustice you have often experienced from your friends.  From you, Sir, I expect in return, that you will not remember how unsuccessfully I have recommended one measure to your consideration, lest you should think yourself bound to assert your consistency, and, in the true spirit of persecution, to pass the

---

* The plan recommended by Junius in the above letter was not acted upon by Mr. Wilkes, for the reasons assigned by him in his letter of Sept. 12, 1771 (No. 67).  The consequence was, that Mr. Alderman Nash, the ministerial candidate, was elected Lord Mayor, to the infinite mortification of Junius, who, in Private Letter No. 56, makes the following observation upon him and his election.  "What an abandoned prostituted idiot is your Lord Mayor!  The shameful mismanagement which brought him into office gave me the first, and an unconquerable disgust."  The subjoined is a list of the candidates for that office, with the numbers affixed to their respective names as they stood at the close of the poll :—

For Mr. Alderman Nash . . . 2199<br>
Mr. Alderman Sawbridge . . 1679<br>
The Lord Mayor . . . . 1795<br>
Mr. Alderman Hallifax . . 846<br>
Mr. Alderman Townsbend . 151<br>
Sir Henry Bankes . . . . 36

† Marked by Mr. Wilkes, "Received in Prince's Court, Saturday, Sept. 7, 1771."

same sentence indifferently upon all my opinions. Forgive this levity, and now to the business.

A man who honestly engages in a public cause must prepare himself for events which will at once demand his utmost patience, and rouse his warmest indignation. I feel myself, at this moment, in the very situation I describe; yet from the common enemy I expect nothing but hostilities against the people. It is the conduct of our friends that surprises and afflicts me. I cannot but resent the injury done to the common cause by the assembly at the London Tavern, nor can I conceal from you my own particular disappointment. They had it in their power to perform a real effectual service to the nation; and we expected from them a proof, not only of their zeal, but of their judgment. Whereas the measure they have adopted is so shamefully injudicious, with regard to its declared object, that, in my opinion, it will, and reasonably ought, to make their zeal very questionable with the people they mean to serve. When I see a measure excellent in itself, and not absolutely unattainable, either not made the principal object, or extravagantly loaded with conditions palpably absurd or impracticable, I cannot easily satisfy myself that the man who proposes it is quite so sincere as he pretends to be. You at least, Mr. Wilkes, should have shown more temper and prudence, and a better knowledge of mankind. No personal respects whatsoever should have persuaded you to concur in these ridiculous resolutions. But my own zeal, I perceive, betrays me: I will endeavour to keep a better guard upon my temper, and apply to your judgment in the most cautious and measured language.

I object, in the first place, to the bulk, and much more to the style of your resolutions of the 23rd of July\*; though

---

\* A copy of which is subjoined, to enable the reader the better to understand Junius's objections to them. They are as follow :—

London Tavern, July 23, 1771.

SUPPORTERS OF THE BILL OF RIGHTS.

SAVAGE BARRELL, Esq., in the Chair.

Resolved,

That the preamble, with the articles reported this day from the committee, be printed and published from this Society.

Whoever seriously considers the conduct of administration, both at home

some part of the preamble is as pointed as I could wish.  You
talk of yourselves with too much authority and importance.
By assuming this false pomp and air of consequence you
either give general disgust, or, what is infinitely more dan-

and abroad, can hardly entertain a doubt that a plan is formed to subvert
the constitution.

In the same manner, whoever attentively examines into the proceedings
of the present House of Commons must apprehend that such another
House for seven years, after the termination of the present parliament, would
effectually accomplish the views of the court, and leave no hope of redress
but in an appeal to God.

The Middlesex election, taken on its true ground; the employment of
the standing army, in St. George's Fields; the granting half a million,
without inquiring into the expenditure of the civil list money, and upon the
dangerous principle of considering the debts of the civil list as the debts
of the nation, and encroaching, to discharge them, upon the sinking
fund, the great support of public credit; the attempts made on juries,
the last sacred bulwark of liberty and law; the arbitrary and venal hand
with which government is conducted in Ireland; the new and most unconstitutional mode of raising a revenue on the people of America, without
asking the consent of their representatives; the introduction of an universal excise in America, instead of the laws of customs; the advancing
the military above the civil power, and employing troops to awe the legislature; all these are measures of so marked, so mischievous a nature,
that it is impossible they should be unfelt or misunderstood: yet these are
measures which the House of Commons have acquiesced in, countenanced, or
executed.

If the present House of Commons then have given such vital wounds to
the constitution, who is it can doubt, who is it can hope, that the conduct of
such another House will not be mortal to our liberties?

The trustees of the people should be pure of all interested communication with the court or its ministers; yet the corrupt correspondence between the members of the House and the court is as notorious now as
it is abhorrent from every great and good purpose of their institution.
Placemen, pensioners, contractors, and receivers of lottery tickets abound
to such a degree in the House of Commons that it is impossible a House so
constituted can do their duty to the people.

It must be plain to the most common apprehension that men deputed
by the people to watch over and guard their rights against the Crown
and its ministers, and, for that purpose, vested with the transcendant powers
of refusing aid to the one, and impeaching the other, can never duly exercise
those powers, or fulfil the intention of their election, if they are kept in pay
of that Crown and those ministers.  What is the plain and inevitable consequence, then, of entrusting such men with the guardianship of our rights,
but that our rights must be betrayed and violated?  Thus we have seen
a House of Commons infringing, as the court had pre-ordained, the sacred
birthright of the people in the freedom of election; erasing a judicial record;
committing to the Tower, and threatening with impeachment, the friends of

gerous, you expose yourselves to be laughed at. The English are a fastidious people, and will not submit to be talked to in so high a tone by a set of private gentlemen of whom they know nothing but that they call themselves *Supporters of the*

the people, and the defenders of the law ; while the favourites of the court are suffered to sport with the laws, and trample on the constitution, not only with impunity, but with approbation ; curbing the people rigorously, and without feeling ; while they uphold ministers, who are abhorred by the nation, in the most dangerous and alarming exertions of power; granting money with the most liberal, the most licentious hand to those ministers against whom the voice of the people calls loudly for impeachment. We have a suspecting people, and a confiding representative ; a complaining people, and an exulting representative ; a remonstrating people, and an addressing adulating representative—a representative that is an engine of oppression in the hand of the Crown, instead of being a grand controlling inquest in favour of the people. Such a representative is a monster in the constitution, which must fill every considerate man with grief, alarm, astonishment, and indignation.

It is corruption that has engendered, nursed, and nourished the monster. Against such corruption, then, all men, who value the preservation of their dearest rights, are called upon to unite. Let us remember that we ourselves, our children, and our posterity, must be freemen or slaves as we preserve or prostitute the noble birthright our ancestors bequeathed us : for should this corruption be once firmly rooted, we shall be an undone people.

Already is it fixed among the representative, and we taste, a thousand ways, the bitter fruit which it produces ; should it extend equally to the electors, we must fall, as Greece and Rome have fallen, by the same means, from the same liberty and glory, to slavery, contempt, and wretchedness.

Impressed with these ideas, the gentlemen who compose the Society of the Bill of Rights, have determined to use their utmost endeavours to exterminate this corruption, by providing for the freedom of election, the equal representation of the people, the integrity of the representative, and the redress of grievances. It is their great wish to render the House of Commons what it constitutionally ought to be, the temple of liberty. With these views they have drawn up the following articles, which they now submit to the electors of Great Britain. At the same time they, with great deference, take the liberty of recommending to the independent electors to form those articles into a solemn declaration, which the candidates whom they support shall be required, as the indispensable condition of their being supported, to sign and seal, publicly, at the general meeting, or at the place of election, binding themselves, by oath, to a due and sacred observance of what is therein contained.

The declaration so executed may be deposited in the hands of the coroner, clerk of the peace, or magistrate before whom the oath was made, as a public memorial of what the constituent has demanded, and the representative has pledged himself to perform.

*Bill of Rights.* There are questions, which, in good policy, you should never provoke the people in general to ask themselves. At the same time, Sir, I am far from meaning to undervalue the institution of this Society. On the contrary, I think the plan was admirable; that it has already been of signal service to the public, and may be of much greater; and I do most earnestly wish that you would consider of, and promote a plan for forming constitutional clubs all through the kingdom. A measure of this kind would alarm government more, and be of more essential service to the cause, than anything that can be done relative to new-modelling the House of Commons. You see, then, that my objections are directed to the particular measure, not to the general institution.

In the consideration of this measure, my first objection goes

1. You shall consent to no supplies without a previous redress of grievances.

2. You shall promote a law, subjecting each candidate to an oath, against having used bribery, or any other illegal means of compassing his election.

3. You shall promote, to the utmost of your power, a full and equal representation of the people in parliament.

4. You shall endeavour to restore annual parliaments.

5. You shall promote a pension and place-bill, enacting, That any member who receives a place, pension, contract, lottery ticket, or any other emolument whatsoever from the Crown, or enjoys profit from any such place, pension, &c., shall not only vacate his seat, but he absolutely ineligible during his continuance under such undue influence.

6. You shall impeach the ministers who advised the violating the right of the freeholders in the Middlesex election; and the military murders in St. George's Fields.

7. You shall make strict inquiry into the conduct of judges touching juries.

8. You shall make strict inquiry into the application of the public money.

9. You shall use your utmost endeavours to have the resolution of the House of Commons expunged by which the magistrates of the city of London were arbitrarily imprisoned for strictly adhering to their charter and their oaths; and also that resolution by which a judicial record was erased to stop the course of justice.

10. You shall attend to the grievances of our fellow-subjects in Ireland, and second the complaints they may bring to the throne.

11. You shall endeavour to restore to America the essential right of taxation, by representatives of their own free election; repealing the acts passed in violation of that right since the year 1763, and the universal excise, so notoriously incompatible with every principle of British liberty, which has been lately substituted, in the colonies, for the laws of customs.

SAVAGE BARRELL, Esq., Chairman.

to the declared purpose of the resolutions, in the terms and mode in which you have described it, viz. *the extermination of corruption.* In *my* opinion, you grasp at the *impossible,* and *lose the really attainable.* Without plaguing you or myself with a logical argument upon a speculative question, I will ingly appeal to your own candour and judgment. Can any man in his senses affirm, that, as things are now circum stanced in this country, it is possible to *exterminate corrup- tion?* Do you seriously think it possible to carry through both Houses such a place-bill as you describe in the fifth article; or, supposing it carried, that it would not be evaded? When you talk of contracts and lottery tickets, do you think that any human law can really prevent their being distributed and accepted, or do you only intend to mortify *Townshend* and *Harley?* In short, Sir, would you, *bonâ fide,* and as a man of honour, give it for your expectation and opinion that there is a single county or borough in the kingdom that will form the declaration recommended to them in these resolutions, and enforce it upon the candidates? For myself, I will tell you freely, not what I *think,* but what I *know;* the resolutions are either totally neglected in the country, or, if read, are laughed at, and by people who mean as well to the cause as any of us.

With regard to the articles taken separately, I own I am concerned to see that the great condition which ought to be the *sine quâ non* of parliamentary qualification, which ought to be the basis, as it assuredly will be the only support, of every barrier raised in defence of the constitution, I mean *a decla- ration upon oath to shorten the duration of parliaments,* is re- duced to the fourth rank in the esteem of the Society; and, even in that place, far from being insisted on with firmness and vehemence, seems to have been particularly slighted in the expression, *you shall endeavour to restore annual parlia- ments.* Are these the terms which men who are in earnest make use of when the *salus reipublicæ* is at stake! I expected other language from Mr. Wilkes. Besides my objection in point of form, I disapprove highly of the meaning of the fourth article, as it stands. Whenever the question shall be se- riously agitated, I will endeavour (and if I live will assuredly attempt it) to convince the English nation, by arguments, to *my* understanding unanswerable, that they ought to insist

upon a triennial, and banish the idea of an annual par
liament.

*Article* 1. The terms of the first article would have been
very proper a century or two ago, but they are not adapted
to the present state of the constitution.  The King does not
act *directly* either in imposing or redressing *grievances*.  We
need not *now* bribe the crown to do us justice; and, as to the
refusal of supplies, we might punish ourselves indeed, but it
would be no way compulsory upon the King.  With respect to
his civil list, he is already independent, or might be so, if he
has common sense, or common resolution: and as for refusing
to vote the army or navy, I hope we shall never be mad
enough to try an experiment every way so hazardous.  But,
in fact, the effort would be infinitely too great for the occasion.
All we want is an honest representative, or at least such a
one as will have some respect for the constituent body.  Formerly the House of Commons were compelled to *bargain* with
the Sovereign.  At present they may prescribe their own
conditions.  So much, in general, for grievances: as to particular grievances, almost all those we complain of are, apparently, the acts either of the Lords or the Commons.  The
appointment of unworthy ministers is not strictly a grievance
(that is, a legal subject of complaint to the King) until those
ministers are arraigned and convicted in due course of law.
If, after that, the King should persist in keeping them in
office, it would be a *grievance* in the strict legal sense of the
word, and would undoubtedly justify rebellion according to
the forms, as well as the spirit of the constitution.  I am far
from condemning the late addresses to the throne.  They
ought to be incessantly repeated.  The people, by the singular
situation of their affairs, are compelled to do the duty of the
House of Commons.

*Article* 2. I object to the second article, because I think
that multiplying oaths is only multiplying perjury.  Besides
this, I am satisfied that, with a triennial parliament (and
without it all other provisions are nugatory), Mr. Grenville's
bill is, or may be made, a sufficient guard against any gross
or flagrant offences in this way.

*Article* 3. The terms of the third article are too loose and
indefinite to make a distinct or serious impression.  That the
people are not equally and fully represented is unquestionable.

But let us take care what we attempt. We may demolish the venerable fabric we intend to repair; and where is the strength and virtue to erect a better in its stead? I should not, for my own part, be so much moved at the corrupt and odious practices by which inconsiderable men get into parliament; nor even at the want of a perfect representation (and certainly nothing can be less reconcilable to the theory than the present practice of the constitution), if means could be found to compel such men to do their duty (in essentials, at least) when they *are* in parliament. Now, Sir, I am convinced that, if shortening the duration of parliaments (which in effect is keeping the representative under the rod of the constituent) be not made the basis of our new parliamentary jurisprudence, other checks or improvements signify nothing. On the contrary, if this be made the foundation, other measures may come in aid, and, as auxiliaries, be of considerable advantage. Lord Chatham's project, for instance, of increasing the number of Knights of Shires, appears to me admirable, and the moment we have obtained a triennial parliament it ought to be tried. As to cutting away the rotten boroughs, I am as much offended as any man at seeing so many of them under the direct influence of the crown, or at the disposal of private persons; yet, I own I have both doubts and apprehensions in regard to the remedy you propose. I shall be charged, perhaps, with an unusual want of political intrepidity when I honestly confess to you, that I am startled at the idea of so extensive an amputation. In the first place, I question the power, *de jure*, of the legislature to disfranchise a number of boroughs upon the general ground of improving the constitution. There cannot be a doctrine more fatal to the liberty and property we are contending for than that which confounds the idea of a *supreme* and an *arbitrary* legislature. I need not point out to you the fatal purposes to which it has been and may be applied. If we are sincere in the political creed we profess, there are many things which we ought to affirm, cannot be done by King, Lords, and Commons. Among these I reckon the disfranchising a borough with a general view to improvement. I consider it as equivalent to robbing the parties concerned of their freehold, of their birthright. I say that although this birthright may be forfeited, or the exercise of it suspended in particular cases, it cannot be taken away by a general law for any real or pretended purpose of improving the constitution. I believe there is no power in this country to make such a law. Supposing the attempt made, I am persuaded you cannot mean that either King or Lords should take an active part in it. A bill which only touches the representation of the people must originate in the House of Commons, in the formation and mode of passing it. The exclusive right of the Commons must be asserted as scrupulously as in the case of a Money Bill. Now, Sir, I should be glad to know by what kind of reasoning it can be proved that there is a power vested in the representative to destroy his immediate constituent: from whence could he possibly derive it? A courtier, I know, will be ready enough to maintain the affirmative. The doctrine suits him exactly, because it gives an unlimited operation to the influence of the crown. But we, Mr. Wilkes, must hold a different language. It is no answer to me to say, that the bill, when it passes the House of Commons, is the act of the majority, and not of the representatives of the particular boroughs concerned. If the majority can disfranchise ten boroughs, why not twenty? Why not the whole kingdom? Why should not they make their own seats in parliament for life? When the Septennial Act passed, the legislature did what apparently and palpably they had no power to do; but they did more than people in general were aware of: they disfranchised the whole kingdom for four years. For argument's sake, I will now suppose that the expediency of the measure and the power of parliament were unquestionable. Still you will find an insurmountable difficulty in the execution. When all your instruments of amputation are prepared—when the unhappy patient lies bound at your feet, without the possibility of resistance, by what infallible rule will you direct the operation? When you propose to cut away the rotten parts, can you tell us what parts are perfectly sound? Are there any certain limits, in fact or theory, to inform you at what point you must stop— at what point the mortification ends? To a man so capable of observation and reflection as you are, it is unnecessary to say all that might be said upon the subject. Besides that I approve highly of Lord Chatham's idea of "infusing a portion of new health into the constitution to enable it to bear its infirmities" (a brilliant expression, and full of intrinsic wisdom), other reasons concur in persuading me to adopt it. I have no objection to paying him such compliments as carry a condition with them, and either bind him firmly to the cause, or become the bitterest reproach to him if he deserts it. Of this last I have not the most distant suspicion. There is another man, indeed, with whose conduct I am not so completely satisfied *. Yet even *he*, I think, has not resolution enough to do anything flagrantly impudent in the face of his country. At the same time that I think it good policy to pay those compliments to Lord Chatham, which, in truth, he has nobly deserved, I should be glad to mortify those contemptible creatures, who call themselves noblemen, whose worthless importance depends entirely upon their influence over boroughs, which cannot be safely diminished but by increasing the power of the counties at large. Among these men, I cannot but distinguish the meanest of the human species, the whole rneo of the *Conways*. I have but one word to add—I would not give representatives to those great trading towns which have none at present. If the merchant and the manufacturer must be *really* represented, let them become freeholders by their industry, and let the representation of the county be increased. You will find the interruption of business in those towns, by the triennial riot and cabals of an election, too dear a price for the nugatory privilege of sending members to parliament †.

The remaining articles will not require a long discussion—of the fourth and fifth I have spoken already.

*Article* 6. The measures recommended in the sixth are unexceptionable. My only doubt is, how can an act, *apparently* done by the House of Commons, be fixed, by sufficient legal evidence, upon the Duke of Grafton, or Lord North, of whose guilt I am nevertheless completely satisfied. As for Lord

* Possibly Lord Camden is the person here alluded to; as Junius, in Letter 69, vol. i. p. 467, seems to entertain some suspicion of this nobleman, from his renewed intimacy with the Duke of Grafton.

† The train of reasoning by Junius on constitutional objections to the disfranchisement of the nomination boroughs, and the transfer of representative rights to manufacturing towns, had little weight with the parliamentary reformers of 1832. The subject is well handled by Mr. Wilkes in his reply.—ED.

Weymouth and Lord Barrington, their own letters are a sufficient ground of impeachment.

*Article* 7. The seventh article is also very proper and necessary. The impeachment of Lord Mansfield, upon his own paper, is indispensable. Yet suffer me to guard you against the seducing idea of concurring in any vote, or encouraging any bill, which may pretend to ascertain, while in reality it limits, the constitutional power of juries. I would have their right to return a general verdict in all cases whatsoever considered as a part of the constitution, fundamental, sacred, and no more questionable by the legislature than whether the government of the country shall be by King, Lords, and Commons. Upon this point, an Enacting Bill would be pernicious; a Declaratory Bill, to say the best of it, useless.

*Article* 8. I think the eighth article would be more properly expressed thus :—*You shall grant no money, unless for services known to, and approved of by, Parliament.* In general the supplies are appropriated, and cannot easily be misapplied. The House of Commons are indeed too ready in granting large sums under the head of *extraordinaries incurred, and not provided for.* But the accounts lie before them, it is their own fault if they do not examine them. The manner in which the late debt upon the civil list was pretended to be incurred, and really paid, demands a particular examination. Never was there a more impudent outrage offered to a patient people.

*Article* 9. The ninth is indispensable; but I think the matter of it rather fit for instruction than for the declaration you have in view. I am very apprehensive of clogging the declaration, and making it too long.

*Articles* 10 and 11. In the tenth and eleventh you are very civil to Ireland and America; and if you mean nothing but ostentation, it may possibly answer your purpose. Your care of Ireland is much to be commended. But I think, in good policy, you may as well complete a reformation at home before you attempt to carry your improvements to such a distance. Clearing the fountain is the best and shortest way to purify the stream. As to taxing the Americans by their own representatives, I confess I do not perfectly understand you. If

you propose that, in the article of taxation, they should hereafter be left to the authority of their respective assemblies, I
must own I think you had no business to revive a question
which should, and probably would, have lain dormant for ever.
If you mean that the Americans should be authorized to send
their representatives to the British Parliament, I shall be
contented with referring you to what Mr. Burke has said
upon this subject, and will not venture to add anything of my
own, for fear of discovering an offensive disregard of your
opinion. Since the repeal of the Stamp Act, I know of no
acts tending to tax the Americans, except that which creates
the tea duty; and even that can hardly be called *internal*.
Yet it ought to be repealed as an impolitic act, not as an
oppressive one. It preserves the contention between the
mother country and the colonies, when everything worth contending for is in reality given up. When this act is repealed,
I presume you will turn your thoughts to the postage of
letters; a tax imposed by authority of Parliament, and levied
in the very heart of the colonies. I am not sufficiently informed upon the subject of that excise, which you say is substituted in North America to the laws of customs, to deliver
such an opinion upon it as I would abide by. Yet I am
easily comprehend that, admitting the necessity of raising a
revenue for the support of government there, any other
revenue laws but those of excise would be nugatory in such a
country as America. I say this with great diffidence as to
the point in question, and with a positive protest against any
conclusion from America to Great Britain.

If these observations shall appear to deserve the attention
of the Society, it is for *them* to consider what use may be
made of them. I know how difficult and irksome it is to
tread back the steps we have taken; yet, if any part of what
I have submitted to you carries reason and conviction with it,
I hope that no false shame will influence our friends at the
London Tavern.

I do not deny that I expect my opinions upon these points
should have some degree of weight with you. I have served
Mr. Wilkes, and am still capable of serving him. I have
faithfully served the public, without the possibility of a personal advantage. As Junius I can never expect to be
rewarded. The secret is too important to be committed to

any great man's discretion.  If views of interest or ambition
could tempt me to betray my own secret, how could I flatter
myself that the man I trusted would not act upon the same
principles, and sacrifice me at once to the King's curiosity
and resentment?  Speaking therefore as a disinterested man,
I have a claim to your attention.  Let my opinions be fairly
examined.

JUNIUS.

P. S.  As you will probably never hear from me again, I
will not omit this opportunity of observing to you that I am
not properly supported in the newspapers.  One would think
that all the fools were of the other side of the question.  As
to myself, it is of little moment.  I can brush away the
swarming insects whenever I think proper.  But it is bad
policy to let it appear, in any instance, that we have not
numbers as well as justice of our side.  I wish you would
contrive that the receipt of this letter and my last might be
barely acknowledged by a hint in the *Public Advertiser*.

No. 67.

TO JUNIUS.

Prince's Court, Monday, September 9.
Mr. WILKES had the honour of receiving from the same gentleman two excellent letters on important subjects, one dated
Aug. 21, the other Sept. 7.  He begs the favour of the
author to prescribe the mode of Mr. Wilkes's communicating
his answer *.

No. 68.

TO J. WILKES, ESQ.

September 10, 1771.
You may intrust Woodfall with a letter for me.  Leave the
rest to his management.

I expect that you will not enter into any explanations with
him whatsoever†.

---

* This note was inserted in the *Public Advertiser* of September 10, 1771.
† Mr. Wilkes has written on it, "Received by the Penny Post."

# No. 69.

## MR. WILKES TO JUNIUS.

SIR,                                     September 12, 1771.
I DO not mean to indulge the impertinent curiosity of finding
out the most important secret of our times, the author of
Junius. I will not attempt with profane hands to tear the
sacred veil of the sanctuary; I am disposed, with the inhabitants of Attica, to erect *an altar to the unknown god* of
our political idolatry, and will be content to worship him in
clouds and darkness.

This very circumstance, however, deeply embarrasses me
The first letter with which I was honoured by Junius, called
for a thousand anecdotes of Crosby, Sawbridge, and Townshend,
too tedious, too minute, to throw upon paper, which yet must
be acted upon, and, as he well knows, mark the character of
men. Junius has, in my idea, too favourable sentiments of
Sawbridge. I allow him honest, but think he has more
mulishness than understanding, more understanding than
candour. He is become the absolute dupe of Malagrida's
gang. He has declared that, if he was chosen mayor this
year, he would not serve the office, but fine, because Townshend
ought to be mayor. Such a declaration is certain, and in my
opinion it borders on insanity. To me Sawbridge complained
the last year that his sheriffalty passed in a continual secret
cabal of Beckford, Townshend, and Horne, without the communication of anything to him till the moment of execution.
Sawbridge has openly acted against us. Our troops will not
be brought at present to fight his battles. Mrs. Macauley
has warmly espoused the common cause, and severely con-
demns her brother. Any overtures to Sawbridge, I believe,
would have been rejected, perhaps treated with contempt, by
not the best bred man in the island. How could I begin a
negociation when I was already pledged to Crosby, who has
fed himself with the hope of that and the membership, by
which I overcame his natural timidity? Junius sees the confidence I place in him. Could there be a prospect of any
cordiality between Sawbridge and the popular party, at least
so soon as his mayoralty? I should fear the Mansion House
would be besieged and taken by the banditti of the Shelburnes.

G 2

But what I am sure will be decisive to Junius, I was engaged to Crosby before I received the letter of Aug. 21, and I have not since found in him the least inclination to yield the favourite point. The membership of the city is a security to the public for his steadiness in the cause. Surely then it would have been imprudent to have wished a change. My duty to the people only makes me form a wish for Crosby. To make Crosby mayor, it is necessary to return to the court of aldermen another man so obnoxious that it is impossible for them to elect him. Bridgen I take to be this man. While he presided in the city, he treated them with insolence, was exceedingly rude and scurrilous to them personally, starved them at the few entertainments he gave, and pocketed the city cash. As he has always voted on the popular side, we are justified to the livery in the recommendation of him, and the rest will be guessed. Crosby will probably be the *locum tenens* of Bridgen, if Bridgen is elected. I wrote the letter on this subject in the *Public Advertiser* of Sept. 5. The argument there is specious, although my private opinion is, the House of Commons will not again fall into that snare. Into another I am satisfied they will. The House of Lords too, will, I think, furnish the most interesting scene, in consequence of the powers they usurp, and the sheriff means the attack. I wish this great business, as I have projected it, could be unravelled in a letter or two to Junius, but the detail is too long and intricate. How greatly is it to be lamented that the few real friends of the public have so little communication of counsels, so few and only distant means of a reserved intercourse!

I have nowhere met with more excellent and abundant political matter than in the letter of Junius respecting the Bill of Rights. He ought to know from me that the American Dr. Lee (the Gazetteer's Junius Americanus) was the author of the too long Preamble, Articles, &c. They were, indeed, submitted to me on the morning of the day on which they passed, but I made few corrections. I disliked the extreme *verbiage* of every part, and wished the whole put again on the anvil. Sir Joseph Mawbey and I were of opinion to adjourn the business for a reconsideration, but the majority of the members were too impatient to have something go forth in their names to the public. It would have been highly imprudent in Sir Joseph or me to thwart them in so favourite a point, and the substance I indeed greatly approve. At all times I hate taking in other people's foul linen to wash. The Society of the Bill of Rights have been called my committee, and it has been said that they were governed entirely by me. This has spread a jealousy even among my friends. I was therefore necessitated to act the most cautious and prudent part. You cannot always do all the good you wish, and you are sometimes reduced to the necessity of yielding in a particular moment to conciliate the doubtful, the peevish, or the refractory. Junius may be assured that I will warmly recommend the formation of constitutional clubs in several parts of the kingdom. I am satisfied that nothing would more alarm the ministry. I agree that the shortening the duration of parliaments is the first and most important of all considerations, without which all the rest would be nugatory; but I am unhappy to differ with Junius in so essential a point as that of triennial parliaments. They are inadequate to the cure of destroying dependance in the members on the crown. They only lessen, not root out, corruption, and only reduce the purchase money for an annuity of three instead of seven years. I have a thousand arguments against triennial and in favour of annual parliaments. The question was fairly agitated at the London Tavern, and several of your friends owned that they were convinced. The subject is too copious for a letter. I hope to read Junius's mature and deliberate thoughts on this subject. I own that in the House of Commons sound policy would rather favour triennial parliaments as the necessary road to annual, but the constitutional question is different.

I am sorry likewise to differ with Junius as to the power *de jure* of the legislature to disfranchise any boroughs. How originated the right, and why was it granted? Old Sarum and Gatton, for instance, were populous places when the right of representation was first given them. They are now desolate, and therefore in everything should return to their former state. A barren mountain or a single farm-house can have no representation in parliament. I exceedingly approve of Lord Chatham's idea of increasing the number of Knights of Shires. If parliaments are not annual, I should not disapprove of a third part of the legislative body going out every year by ballot, and of consequence an annual re-election in part.

I am so much harassed with business at present that I have not time to mention many particulars of importance, and these three days I have had the shivering fits of a slow lurking fever, a strange disorder for Wilkes, which makes writing painful to me. I could plunge the patriot dagger in the heart of the tyrant of my country, but my hand would now tremble in doing it. In general I enjoy settled confirmed health, to which I have for some years paid great attention, chiefly from public views.

I am satisfied that Junius now means me well, and I wish to merit more than his regard, his friendship. He has poured balm into my wounds, the deepest of which, I sigh when I recollect, were made by that now friendly hand. I am always ready to kiss his rod, but I hope its destination is changed, and that it will never again fall as heavy upon me as towards the conclusion of the year 1769, when Thurlow said, sneeringly, the government prosecuted Junius out of compliment to Wilkes. I warmly wish Junius my friend. As a public man, I think myself secure of his support, for I will only depend on popular favour, and pursue only the true constitutional point of liberty. As a private person, I figure to myself that Junius is as amiable in the private as he is great in the public walk of life. I now live very much at home, happy in the elegant society of a sensible daughter, whom Junius has noticed in the most obliging manner.

I have not had a moment's conversation with Woodfall on the subject of our correspondence, nor did I mean to mention it to him. All he can guess will be from the following card, which I shall send by my servant with this letter. " Mr. Wilkes presents his compliments to Mr. Woodfall, and desires him to direct and forward the inclosed to Junius." After the first letter of Junius to me, I did not go to Woodfall to pry into a secret I had no right to know. The letter itself bore the stamp of Jove. I was neither doubting nor impertinent. I wish to comply with every direction of Junius, to profit by his hints, and to have the permission of writing to him on any important occasion. I desire to assure him

that in all great public concerns I am perfectly free from
every personality either of dislike or affection. The Stoic
apathy is then really mine.

Lord Chatham said to me ten years ago, " * * * * ** is
the falsest hypocrite in Europe." I must hate the man as
much as even Junius can, for through this whole reign almost
it has been * * * * * * *versus Wilkes*. This conduct will
probably make it *Wilkes versus* * * * * * *. Junius must
imagine that no man in the island feels what he writes on
that occasion more than I do*.

This letter is an emanation of the heart, not an effort of
the head. It claims attention from the honest zeal and sincerity of the writer, whose affection for his country will end
only with his life.

JOHN WILKES.

---

No. 70.

JUNIUS TO JOHN WILKES, ESQ†.

SIR,                                London, September 18, 1771.
YOUR letter of the 12th instant was carefully conveyed to me.
I am much flattered, as you politely intended I should be,
with the worship you are pleased to pay to the unknown god
of politics. I find I am treated as other gods usually are by
their votaries, with sacrifice and ceremony in abundance, and
very little obedience. The profession of your faith is unexceptionable: but I am a modest deity, and should be full as
well satisfied with good works and morality.

There is a rule in business that would save much time if it
were generally adopted. *A question once decided is no longer
a subject of argument.* You have taken your resolution about
the mayoralty. What I have now to say is not meant to alter
it, but, in perfect good humour, to guard you against some
inconveniences which may attend the execution. It is your

---

* These blanks, we suppose, may safely be filled up with the name of the
sovereign; but in extenuation of royal dissimulation—for that is what is
meant—it may be added that the King had a host of dissemblers of all
parties to deal with, intriguing for their own selfish ends.—ED.

† Written on by him, " Received Monday afternoon, September 18, 1771."

own affair, and though I still think you have chosen injudiciously, both for yourself and for the public, I have no right to find fault or to tease you with reflections, which cannot divert you from your purpose.

I cannot comprehend the reason of Mr. Crosby's eagerness to be Lord Mayor, unless he proposes to disgrace the office and himself by pocketing the salary. In that case he will create a disgust among the citizens, of which you and your party will feel the bad effects, and as for himself he may bid adieu to all hopes of being returned for the city. That he should live with unusual splendour is essentially your interest and his own; and even then I do not perceive that his merits are so distinguished as to entitle him to a double reward. Of the dignity or authority of a *locum tenens*, I know nothing; nor can I conceive what credit Mr. Crosby is likely to derive from representing Mr. Bridgen. But suppose Bridgen should be Lord Mayor, and should keep his word in appointing Crosby his lieutenant, I should be glad to know who is to support the expense and dignity of the office? It may suit such a fellow as Bridgen to shut up the Mansion House, but I promise you his economy will be of no service to Mr. Wilkes. If you make him Mayor, you will be answerable for his conduct; and if he and Crosby be returned, you may depend upon it the court of aldermen will choose him.

With regard to Mr Sawbridge, since I cannot prevail with you to lay the foundation of a closer union between you, by any positive sacrifice in his favour, at least let me entreat you to observe a moderate and guarded conduct towards him. I should be much concerned to see his character traduced or his person insulted. He is *not* a dupe to any set of men whatsoever, nor do I think he has taken any violent or decided part against you. Yet to be excluded from those honours which are the only rewards he pretends to, and to which he is so justly entitled, and to see them bestowed upon such men as *Crosby* and *Bridgen*, is enough to excite and justify his resentment. All this, Sir, is matter of convenience, which I hope you will consider. There is another point, upon which I must be much more serious and earnest with you. You seem to have no anxiety or apprehension but lest the friends of Lord Shelburne should get possession of the Mansion House. In my opinion they have no chance of success whatsoever. The real danger is from the interest of government: from Harley and the Tories. If, while you are employed in counteracting Mr. Townshend, a ministerial alderman should be returned, you will have ruined the cause. You will have ruined yourself, and for ever. To say that Junius could never forgive you is nothing \*;—you could never forgive yourself. Junius from that moment will be compelled to consider you as a man who has sacrificed the public to views which were every way unworthy of you. If, then, upon a fair canvass of the livery, you should see a probability that Bridgen may not be returned, let that point be given up at once, and let *Sawbridge* be returned with *Crosby;*—a more likely way, in *my* judgment, to make *Crosby* Lord Mayor.

Nothing can do you greater honour, nor be of greater benefit to the community, than your intended attack upon the unconstitutional powers assumed by the House of Lords. You have my warmest applause ; and if I can assist, command my assistance. The arbitrary power of fine and imprisonment, assumed by these men, would be a disgrace to any form of legal government not purely *aristocratical.* Directly, it invades the laws ; indirectly, it saps the constitution. Naturally phlegmatic, these questions warm me. I envy you the laurels you will acquire. Banish the thought that Junius can make a dishonourable or an imprudent use of the confidence you repose in him. When you have leisure, communicate your plan to me, that I may have time to examine it, and to consider what part I can act with the greatest advantage to the cause. The constitutional argument is obvious. I wish you to point out to me where you think the force of the *formal legal* argument lies. In pursuing such inquiries I lie under a singular disadvantage. Not venturing to consult those who are qualified to inform me, I am forced to collect everything from books or common conversation. The pains I took with that paper upon privilege were greater than I can express to you. Yet after I had blinded myself with poring over journals, debates, and parliamentary history, I was at last obliged to hazard a bold assertion, which I am now convinced is true (as I really then thought it), because it has not been disproved or disputed. There is this material difference upon the face of the two

* Note to Private Letter, No. 56, *ante*, p. 57.

questions. We can clearly show a time when the Lower House had not an unlimited power of commitment for breach of privilege. Whereas I fear we shall not have the same advantage over the House of Lords. It is not that precedents have any weight with me in opposition to principles; but I know they weigh with the multitude.

My opinion of the several articles of the proposed declaration remains unaltered. I cannot pretend to answer those arguments in favour of annual parliaments by which you say the friends of Junius were convinced. The question is not what is best in theory (for there I should undoubtedly agree with you), but what is most expedient in practice. You labour to carry the constitution to a point of perfection which it can never reach to, or at which it cannot long be stationary. In this idea I think I see the mistake of a speculative man, who is either not conversant with the world, or not sufficiently persuaded of the necessity of taking things *as they are*. The objection drawn from the purchase of an annuity for *three* years instead of *seven* is defective, because it applies in the same proportion to an annuity for one year. This is not the question. The point is to keep the representative as much under the check and control of the constituent as can be done consistently with other great and essential objects. But without entering further into the debate, I would advise that this part of the declaration be expressed in general terms, viz. to shorten the duration of parliaments. This mediating expedient will, for the present, take in both opinions, and leave open the *quantum* of time to a future discussion.

In answer to a general argument, by which the uncontrollable right of the people to form the third part of the legislature is defended, you urge against me two gross cases, which undoubtedly call for correction. These cases, you may believe, did not escape me, and, by the by, admit of a particular answer. But it is not treating me fairly to oppose general principles with particular abuses. It is not in human policy to form an institution from which no possible inconvenience shall arise. I did not pretend to deliver a doctrine to which there could be no possible objection. We are to choose between better and worse. Let us come fairly to the point—Whether is it safer to deny the legislature a power of disfranchising all the electors of a borough (which, if denied, entails a number of rotten boroughs upon the constitution), or to *admit* the power, and so leave it with the legislature to disfranchise, *ad arbitrium,* every borough and county in the kingdom. If you deny the consequence, it will be incumbent upon you to prove by *positive* reasoning that a power which holds in the case of Aylesbury or New Shoreham, *does not* hold in the case of York, London, or Middlesex. To this question I desire a direct answer; and when we have fixed our principles, we may regularly descend to the detail. The cases of Gatton and Old Sarum do not embarrass me. Their right to return members to parliament has neither fact nor theory to support it—"they have, *bona fide*, no electors;" consequently there is no man to be dispossessed of his freehold. No man to be disfranchised of his right of election. At the worst, supposing the annihilation of these pretended boroughs could no way be reconciled to my own principles, I shall only say, give me a healthy, vigorous constitution, and I shall hardly consult my looking-glass to discover a blemish upon my skin.

You ask me, from whence did the right originate, and for what purpose was it granted? I do not see the tendency of these questions, but I answer them without scruple: ‘In general it arose from the king's writs, and it was granted with a view to balance the power of the nobility, and to obtain aids from the people.’ But, without looking back to an obscure antiquity, from which no certain information can be collected, you will find that the laws of England have much greater regard to possession (of a certain length) than to any other title whatsoever; and that, in every kind of property which savours of the *realty,* this doctrine is most wisely the basis of our English jurisprudence. Though I use the terms of art, do not injure me so much as to suspect I am a lawyer. I had as lief be a Scotchman. It is the encouragement given to disputes about titles, which has supported that iniquitous profession at the expense of the community. As to this whole argument about rotten boroughs, if I seem zealous in supporting my opinion, it is· not from a conception that the constitution cannot possibly be relieved from them—I mean only to reconcile you to an evil which cannot safely be removed.

Now, Mr. Wilkes, I shall deal very plainly with you. The subject of my first letter was private and personal, and I am

content it should be forgotten.   Your letter to *me* is also
sacred.   But my second letter is of public import, and must
not be suppressed.   I did not mean that it should be buried
in Prince's Court*.   It would be unfair to embarrass you with
a new question, while your city election is depending.   But
if I perceive that within a reasonable time after that business
is concluded, no steps are taken with the Bill of Rights to
form a new, short, and rational declaration (whether by laying
my letter before the Society, or by any other mode that you
shall think advisable), I shall hold myself obliged, by a duty
paramount to all other considerations, to institute an amicable
suit against the Society before the tribunal of the public.
Without asperity, without petulance or disrespect, I propose
to publish the second letter, and to answer or submit to
argument.   The necessity of taking this step will indeed
give me pain, for I well know that differences between the
advocates are of no service to the cause.   But the lives of the
best of us are spent in choosing between evils.   As to you,
Sir, you may as well take the trouble of directing that Society,
since whatever they do is placed to your account.

The domestic society you speak of is much to be envied.
I fancy I should like it still better than you do.   I too am no
enemy to good fellowship, and have often cursed that canting
parson for wishing to deny you your claret.   It is for *him*,
and men like *him*, to beware of intoxication.   Though I do
not place the little pleasures of life in competition with the
glorious business of instructing and directing the people, yet
I see no reason why a wise man may not unite the public
virtues of Cato, with the indulgence of Epicurus.

Continue careful of your health.   Your head is too useful
to be spared, and your hand may be wanted.   Think no more
of what is passed.   You did not then stand so well in my
opinion; and it was necessary to the plan of that letter to rate
you lower than you deserved.   The wound is curable, and the
scar shall be no disgrace to you.

I willingly accept of as much of your friendship as you can
impart to a man whom you will assuredly never know.   Besides every personal consideration, if I were known, I could
no longer be an useful servant to the public.   At present

* George Street, Westminster, close to Storey's Gate, where Mr. Wilkes
then resided.—ED.

there is something oracular in the delivery of my opinions.
I speak from a recess which no human curiosity can pene-
trate, and darkness, we are told, is one source of the sublime.
The mystery of Junius increases his importance.

JUNIUS.

---

No. 71.

Prince's Court, Thursday, Sept. 19.

MR. WILKES thanks Mr. Woodfall for the care of the former
letter, and desires him to transmit the inclosed to Junius.

MR. WILKES TO JUNIUS.

SIR,                                    September 19, 1771.
I HAD last night the honour of your letter of yesterday's date.
I am just going to the Common Hall, but first take up the
pen to thank you for the kindness you express to me, and to
say that the Bill of Rights meet next Tuesday. I thought it
necessary not to lose a moment in giving you this information,
that whatever you judge proper may be submitted to that
Society as early as possible. Junius may command me in
everything. When he says, " my second letter is of public
import, and must not be suppressed. I did not mean that it
should be buried in Prince's Court,"—does he wish it should
be communicated to the Society, and in what manner? The
beginning of the second letter refers to a first letter, and some
other expressions may be improper for the knowledge of the
Society. I wait Junius's directions. I beg his free sentiments on all occasions. I mean next week to state a variety
of particulars for his consideration and in answer to his letter.
I had now only a moment to mention a point of business and
a feeling of gratitude.

JOHN WILKES.

---

## No. 72.

### JUNIUS TO J. WILKES, ESQ.

SIR,                                                  September 21, 1771 *.
SINCE you are so obliging as to say you will be guided by my
opinion as to the manner of laying my sentiments before the
Bill of Rights, I see no reason why the whole of the second
letter may not be read there next Tuesday, except the postscript, which has no connection with the rest, and the word
ridiculous, which may naturally give offence;—as I mean to
persuade and soften, not irritate or offend. Let that word be
expunged. The prefatory part you may leave or not as you
think proper. You are not bound to satisfy any man's curiosity upon a *private* matter, and upon my silence you may, I
believe, depend entirely. As to other passages I have no favour or affection, so let all go. It should be copied over in
a better hand.

If any objections are raised, which are answered in my
third letter, you will, I am sure, answer for me, so far forth,
*ore tenus*.

JUNIUS.

By all means let it be copied. This manuscript is for private use only.

———

## No. 73.

### JUNIUS TO J. WILKES, ESQ.

SIR,                                                  Monday †.
WHEN I wrote to you on Saturday, it did not occur to me
that your own advertisement had already informed the public
of your receiving two letters; your omitting the preamble to
the second letter would therefore be to no purpose.

In my opinion you should not wish to decline the appearance of being particularly addressed in that letter. It is calculated to give you dignity with the public. There is more
in it than perhaps you are aware of. Depend upon it, the

---

* Written on it by Mr. Wilkes, "Received Sept. 23, 1771."
† Written on it by Mr. Wilkes, "Received Sept. 23, 1771."

perpetual union of *Wilkes* and *mob* does you no service. Not
but that I love and esteem the mob. It is your interest to
keep up dignity and gravity besides. I would not make myself cheap by walking the streets so much as you do. *Verbum sat.*

---

## No. 74.

### MR. WILKES TO JUNIUS.

SIR,                                   Wednesday, September 25.

YESTERDAY I attended the meeting of the Society of the Bill
of Rights, and laid before them the letter, which I had the
honour of receiving from you on the 7th of September. The
few lines of the preamble I omitted, the word *ridiculous*, according to your directions, and a very few more lines towards
the conclusion. All the rest was a faithful transcript, the
exact *tenor\**. The season of the year occasioned the meeting
to be ill attended. Only eleven members were present. The
following resolution passed unanimously: "That Mr. Wilkes
be desired to transmit to Junius the thanks of the Society for
his letter, and to assure him that it was received with all the
respect due to his distinguished character and abilities."
Soon after my fever obliged me to return home, and I have
not heard of anything further being done: but Mr. Lee told
me he thought the letter capable of a full answer, which he
meant, on a future day, to submit to the Society, and would
previously communicate to me. The letter is left in the
hands of Mr. Reynolds, who has the care of the other papers
of the Society, with directions to permit every member to
peruse, and even transcribe it, on the promise of non-publica-
tion. Some particular expressions appeared rather too harsh
and grating to the ears of some of the members.

\* When Mr. Wilkes was prosecuted in the year 1764, for publishing the
*North Briton*, No. 45, Lord Mansfield issued an order for Mr. Wilkes's
attorney or solicitor to attend at his house on the morning previous to the
trial, "to show cause why the information in this cause should not be
amended by striking out the word PURPORT in the several places where it is
mentioned in the said information (except in the first place), and inserting,
instead thereof, the word TENOR." The Chief Justice was accused of having
suggested this alteration, and several objections were taken to it, which, in
argument, were overruled by the Court.

Surely, Sir, nothing in the advertisement I inserted in the *Public Advertiser* could lead to the idea of the two letters I mentioned coming from Junius. I entreat him to peruse once more that guarded advertisement. I hope that Mr. Bull's and my address of Saturday was approved where I most desire it should be thought of favourably. I know it made our enemies wince in the most tender part.

I am too ill to-day to add more.

JOHN WILKES.

---

## No. 75.

### JUNIUS TO J. WILKES, ESQ.

SIR,                                              October 16, 1771.

I CANNOT help expressing to you my thanks and approbation of your letter of this day *. I think it proper, manly, and to the purpose. In these altercations nothing can be more useful than to preserve dignity and *sang froid—fortiter in re, suaviter in modo*, increases both the force and the severity. Your conduct to Mr. Sawbridge is everything I could wish†. Be assured you will find it both honourable and judicious. Had it been adopted a little sooner, you might have returned him and Crosby, and taken the whole merit of it to yourself. If I am truly informed of Mr. S.'s behaviour on the hustings, I must confess it does not satisfy me. But perseverance, management, and determined good humour, will set everything right, and, in the end, break the heart of Mr. Horne. Nothing can be more true than what you say about *great*

---

* This was a long address from Mr. Wilkes to the livery of London, in his own defence, from an attack which had been made upon him by Mr. Alderman Townshend. We shall extract such parts of it as are more particularly alluded to by Junius in this letter.

† "Mr. Townshend asks, 'Does he (Mr. Wilkes) allow one man in the Court of Aldermen to be worthy of your confidence except himself and Mr. Crosby?' Let me state the question about Mr. Sawbridge. Mr. Wilkes has declared, under his hand, in all the public papers, 'No man can honour Mr. Sawbridge more than I do, for *every public* and private virtue which constitutes a *great* and amiable character.' Was this praise cold or penurious? Was it not deserving a better return than it seems to have found? Is not such a character worthy of your confidence?" *Mr Wilkes's Letter of October* 16.

*men\**.  They are indeed a worthless, pitiful race.  Chatham
has gallantly thrown away the scabbard, aud never flinched.
From that moment I began to like him.

I see we do not agree about the strict right of pressing†.
If you are as sincere as I am, we shall not quarrel about a
difference of opinion.  I shall say a few words to-morrow on
this subject, under the signature of *Philo-Junius.*  The letters under that name have been hastily drawn up, but the
principles are tenable.  I thought your letter about the military very proper and well drawn‡.

JUNIUS.

* "Mr. Morris told us at the Bill of Rights, that when he pressed Mr.
Townshend about the affair of the printers, his answer was, that he did not
find he should be supported by any *great man*, and otherwise it would be
*imprudent*, therefore did not choose to act in it.  The *prudent* Mr. Townshend may wait the consent of *great men*.  I will, on a national call, follow
instantly the line of my duty, regardless of their applause or censure.  Public
spirit and virtue are seldom in the company of his Lordship or his Grace.
For the printer's case, see *post*, Miscellaneous Letter, No. 92.

"Has not, by the conduct of your magistrates, a complete victory been
gained over the usurped powers both of the Crown and the House of Commons?  The two questions had been frequently agitated among the friends
of liberty, even while I remained at the King's Bench.  When the city and
the nation had clearly decided in favour of the cause, the *great men* followed,
as they generally do, joined the public cry, and thronged to the Tower to pay
their tardy tribute of praise to the persecuted patriots.  The business had
been completed without their assistance.  In all such cases I am persuaded
we shall find that the people will be obliged to do their own business; but if
it succeeds, they may be sure of the concurrence and applause of the *great*,
and their even entering the most loathsome prisons or dungeons—on a short
visit of parade."—*Mr. Wilkes's Letter of Oct.* 15.

† "As a good Englishman and citizen, I thanked my brethren Sawbridge
and Oliver for having so nobly discharged their duty as aldermen in the
business of press warrants, on which I expatiated as the most cruel species
of general warrants.—*Id.*

‡ A few days previous to Messrs. Wilkes and Bull entering upon their
office of sheriffs of London, they addressed a short letter to the livery, containing a paragraph respecting the military, of which the following is a
copy:—

"We have observed with the deepest concern that a military force has,
on several late occasions, been employed by an unprincipled administration,
under the pretence of assisting the civil power in carrying the sentence of the
laws into execution.  The conduct of the present sheriffs in the remarkable
case of the two unhappy men who suffered in July, near Bethnal Green, was
truly patriotic.  We are determined to follow so meritorious an example, and
as that melancholy part of our office will commence in a very few days, we take

## No. 76.

### MR. WILKES TO JUNIUS.

SIR,                                    October 17, 1771.

I AM not yet recovered, and to-day have been harassed with complaints against the greatest villains out of hell, the bailiffs; but so very polite and friendly a letter as Junius's of yesterday, demands my earliest and warmest acknowledgments. I only take up the pen to say, that I think myself happy in his approbation, that a line of applause from him gives the same brisk circulation to my spirits as a kiss from Chloe, and that I mean soon to communicate to him a project of importance. I will skirmish with the great almost every day in some way or other. Does Junius approve the following manœuvre, instead of going in a gingerbread chariot to yawn through a dull sermon at St. Paul's?

Old Bailey, October 24, 1771.

" Mr. Sheriff Wilkes presents his duty to the Lord Mayor, and asks his Lordship's leave to prefer the real service of his country to-morrow in the administration of justice here, to the vain parade on the anniversary of the accession of a prince, under whose inauspicious government an universal

this opportunity of declaring that as the constitution has entrusted us with the whole power of the county, we will not, during our sheriffalty, suffer any part of the army to interfere or even attend, as on many former occasions, on the pretence of aiding or assisting the civil magistrate. This resolution we declare to the public and to administration, to prevent during our continuance in office the sending of any detachments from the regular forces on such a service, and the possibility of all future alarming disputes. The civil power of this country we are sure is able to support itself and a good government. The magistrate, with the assistance of those in his jurisdiction, is by experience known to be strong enough to enforce all legal commands without the aid of a standing army. Where that is not the case, a nation must sink into an absolute military government, and everything valuable to the subject be at the mercy of the soldiery and their commander. We leave to our brave countrymen of the army the glory of conquering our foreign enemies. We pledge ourselves to the public for the faithful and exact discharge of our duty in every emergency without their assistance. We desire to save them a service we know they detest, and we take on ourselves the painful task of those unpleasing scenes which our office calls upon us to superintend. The laws of our country shall, in all instances during our sheriffalty, be solely enforced by the authority and vigour of the civil magistrate."

discontent prevails among the people, and who still leaves the
most intolerable grievances of his subjects unredressed." This
card to be published at length. Will Junius suggest any
alteration or addition? It is a bold step. The sessions will
not be ended on the 25th, and it is the duty of the sheriff to
attend. I will follow all your hints about Mr. Sawbridge. I
am sorry to differ so much from you about press warrants. I
own that I have warmly gone through that opposition upon
the clear conviction that every argument alleged for the legality of the press warrant would do equally well for ship
money. I believe Junius as sincere as myself; I will therefore be so far from quarrelling with him for any difference of
opinion, that when I find we disagree, I will act with double
caution, and some distrust of the certainty of my being clearly
in the right.

I hope the Sheriff's letter to Mr. Akerman has your approbation. Does Junius wish for any dinner or ball tickets for
the Lord Mayor's day, for himself, or friends, or a favourite,
or *Junia?* The day will be worth observation. Whether,
*cretd an carbone notandus,* I do not know, but *the people, Sir,
the people are the sight.* How happy should I be to see my
Portia* here dance a graceful minuet with Junius Brutus! but
Junius is inexorable and I submit. I would send your tickets
to Woodfall.

To-morrow I go with the Lord Mayor and my brother
Sheriff to Rochester to take up our freedoms. We return on
Sunday night.

I entreat of Junius to favour me with every idea which
occurs to him for the common cause, in every particular
relative to my conduct. He shall find me no less grateful
than ductile.

                                        JOHN WILKES.

* Probably the daughter of Mr. Wilkes, to whom he was tenderly attached,
and who till his death presided over his household. The affection was
mutual, and contemporaries concur in testifying to the many virtues and
elegant accomplishments of Miss Wilkes, who long moved in the highest
circles with an unsullied name.—ED.

## No. 77.

### JUNIUS TO J. WILKES, ESQ.

London, October 21, 1771.

MANY thanks for your obliging offer; but alas! my age and figure would do but little credit to my partner. I acknowledge the relation between Cato and Portia, but in truth I see no connection between Junius and a minuet.

You shall have my opinion whenever you think proper to ask it, freely, honestly, and heartily. If I were only a party man, I should naturally concur in any enterprise likely to create a bustle without risk or trouble to myself. But I love the cause independent of persons, and I wish well to Mr. Wilkes independent of the cause. Feeling, as I really do, for others where my own safety is provided for, the danger to which I expose a simple printer, afflicts and distresses me. It lowers me to myself to draw another into a hazardous situation which I cannot partake of with him. This consideration will account for my abstaining from * * * * * * * * * so long, and for the undeserved moderation with which I have treated him. I know my ground thoroughly when I affirm that *he alone* is the mark. It is not Bute, nor even the Princess Dowager. It is * * * * * * * * * * * * * * * * * * * * * * * * * whom every honest man should detest, and every brave man should attack.* Some measures of dignity and prudence must nevertheless be preserved for our own sakes. I think your intended message to the Lord Mayor is more spirited than judicious, and that it may be attended with consequences which (compared with the single purpose of * * * * * * * * * * * * * * * * * *) are not worth hazarding—*non est tanti*—consider it is not Junius or Jack Wilkes, but a grave sheriff (for *grave* you should be) who marks his entrance into office with a direct outrage to the * * * * * * * * * * * * * * *; that it is only an outrage, and leads to nothing. Will not courtiers take advantage? Will not Whigs be offended? And whether offended or not, will not all parties pretend to condemn you? If *measures and*

---

* The explanatory note, p. 87, is doubtless applicable to the blanks in the present letter.—ED.

not *men* has *any* meaning (and I own it has very little), it must hold particularly in the case of * * * * * * * *; and if truth and reason be on one side, and all the common-place topics on the other, can you doubt to which side the multitude will incline? Besides, that it is too early to begin this kind of attack, I confess I am anxious for your safety. I know that in the ordinary course of law they cannot hurt you; but did the idea of a Bill of Banishment never occur to you? And don't you think a demonstration of this kind on your part might furnish government with a specious pretence for destroying you at once, by a summary proceeding? Consider the measure coolly and then determine.

If these loose thoughts should not weigh with you as much as I could wish, I would then recommend a little alteration in the message. I would have it stated thus :—

"Prince's Court, October 24, 1771.

"Mr. Wilkes presents his duty to the Lord Mayor, and flatters himself he shall be honoured with his Lordship's approbation, if he prefers the real service of his country tomorrow in the administration of justice at the Old Bailey, to the vain parade of a procession to St. Paul's. With the warmest attachment to the House of Hanover, and the most determined allegiance to the chief magistrate, he hopes it will not be thought incumbent on him to take an active part in celebrating the accession of a prince, under whose inauspicious reign the English constitution has been most grossly and deliberately violated, the civil rights of the people no less daringly invaded, and their humble petitions for redress rejected with contempt."

In the first part, *to ask a man's leave to prefer the real service of his country to a vain parade*, seems, if serious, too servile ;—if jest, unseasonable, and rather approaching to burlesque. The rest appears to me not less strong than your own words, and better guarded in point of safety, which you neglect too much. I am now a little hurried, and shall write to you shortly upon some other topics.

JUNIUS.

## No. 78.

### MR. WILKES TO JUNIUS.

Prince's Court, Monday Morning, Nov. 4.

ON my return home last night I had the very great pleasure of reading the Dedication and Preface which Mr. Woodfall left for me. I am going with the city officers to invite the little great to the custard on Saturday. *Perditur hoc inter misero lux.* I shall only add, *accepi, legi, probavi.* I am much honoured by the polite attention of Junius *.

## No. 79.

### JUNIUS TO J. WILKES, ESQ.

November 6, 1771.

I ENTREAT you to procure for me copies of the informations against Eyre before the Lord Mayor. I presume they were taken in writing. If not, I beg you will favour me with the most exact account of the substance of them, and any observations of your own that you think material. If I am right in my facts, I answer for my law, and mean *to* attack Lord Mansfield as soon as possible.

My American namesake is plainly a man of abilities, though I think a little unreasonable, when he insists upon more than an absolute surrender of the fact. I agree with him that it is a hardship on the Americans to be taxed by the British Legislature; but it is a hardship inseparable in theory from the condition of colonists in which they have voluntarily placed themselves. If emigration be no crime to deserve punishment, it is certainly no virtue to claim exemption†; and however it may

---

* Upon this letter was written by Mr. Wilkes, "On returning Junius the dedication and preface he sent me."

† Whether emigration is meritorious, depends on the circumstances under which it occurs. The Greek colonists, who settled in Asia Minor, doubtless rendered a laudable service to themselves, the fellow-citizens they left behind, and the world in general, by their expatriation, whether it arose from strife at home, or the pressure of a redundant population. Corresponding benefits to all parties, from the wide scope obtained for industry and capital, may be

have proved eventually beneficial, the mother country was but
little obliged to the intentions of the first emigrants.  But, in
fact, change of place does not exempt from subjection:—the
members of our factories settled under foreign governments,
and whose voluntary banishment is much more laudable with
regard to the mother country, are taxed with the laws of consulage.  *Au reste*, I see no use in fighting this question in the
newspapers, nor have I time.  You may assure Dr. Lee, that
to *my* heart and understanding the names of American and
Englishman are synonymous, and that as to any future taxation of America, I look upon it as near to impossible as the
highest improbability can go.

I hope that, since he has opposed me where he thinks me
wrong, he will be equally ready to assist me when he thinks
me right.  Besides the fallibility natural to us all, no man
writes under so many disadvantages as I do.  I cannot consult the learned, I cannot directly ask the opinion of my acquaintance, and in the newspapers I never am assisted.

Those who are conversant with books, well know how often
they mislead us, when we have not a living monitor at hand
to assist us in comparing practice with theory.

---

### No. 80.

#### MR. WILKES TO JUNIUS.

SIR,                       Prince's Court, Wednesday, Nov. 6.
I DO not delay a moment giving you the information you wish.
I inclose a copy of Eyre's commitment.  Nothing else in this
business has been reduced to writing.  The examination was
before the sitting justice, Alderman Hallifax, at Guildhall;
and it is not usual to take it in writing, on account of the
multiplicity of business there.  The paper was found upon

---

safely attributed to the existing tide of emigration from the United Kingdom;
and the advantages that have ensued from the planting of the American
colonies in the 17th century, to which Junius specially refers, will hardly
at this time be deemed a debatable question.  But many unsettled points,
agitated when Junius wrote, have received their quietus from subsequent
events, and ceased to be controversial.—ED.

him. He was asked what he had to say in his defence, his
answer was, I hope you will bail me.   Mr. Holder, the clerk,
answered, That is impossible.   There never was an instance
of it, when the person was taken in the fact, or the goods
found upon him      I believe Holder's law is right.   Alderman
Hallifax likewise granted a search-warrant prior to the examination.   At Eyre's lodgings many more quires of paper
were found, all marked on purpose, from a suspicion of Eyre.
After Eyre had been some time at Wood Street Compter, a
key was found in his room there, which appears to be a key
to the closet at Guildhall, from whence the paper was stolen.
The Lord Mayor refused to bail Eyre, but I do not find that
any fresh examination was taken at the Mansion House.   The
circumstances were well known.   I was present at the examination before Hallifax, but as sheriff could not interfere,
only I whispered Hallifax he could not bail Eyre.   *Anglus*
in to-day's *Public Advertiser* told some particulars I had
mentioned.   I did not know of that letter; it is Mr. Bernard's
of Berkeley Square.   As to the Americans, I declare I know
no difference between an inhabitant of Boston in Lincolnshire,
and of Boston in New England.   I honour the Americans;
but our ancestors who staid and drove out the tyrant, are
justly greater in merit and fame than those who fled and deserted their countrymen.   Their future conduct has been a
noble atonement, and their sons have much surpassed them.
I will mention to Dr. Lee what you desire.   You shall have
every communication you wish from me.   Yet I beg Junius
to reflect a moment.   To whom am I now writing?   I am all
doubt and uncertainty, though not mistrust or suspicion.   I
should be glad to canvass freely every part of a great plan.
I dare not write it to a man I do not know, of whose connections I am totally ignorant.   I differ with Junius on one
point: I think by being concealed he has infinite advantages
which I want.   I am on the Indian coast, where, from the
fire kindled round me, I am marked out to every hostile arrow
which knows its way to me.   Those who are in the dark are
safe, from the want of direction of the pointless shaft.   I
followed Junius's advice about the card on the anniversary of
the King's accession.   I dropped the idea.   I wish to know
his sentiments about certain projects against the usurped
powers of the House of Lords.   The business is too vast to

write, too hazardous to communicate, to an unknown person. Junius will forgive me. What can be done? Alas! where is the man, after all Wilkes has experienced, in whose friendly bosom he can repose his secret thoughts, his noble but most dangerous designs? The person most capable he can have no access to, and all others he will not trust. I stand alone, *isolé* as the French call it, a single column, unpropped, and perhaps nodding to its fall.

JOHN WILKES.

---

## No. 61.

### JUNIUS TO J. WILKES, ESQ.

November 9, 1771.

I AM much obliged to you for your information about Eyre. The facts are as I understood them, and, with the blessing of God, I will pull Mansfield to the ground.

Your offer to communicate your plan against the Lords was voluntary. Do now as you think proper. I have no resentments but against the common enemy, and will assist you in any way that you will suffer yourself to be assisted. When you have satisfied your understanding that there may be reasons why Junius should attack the King, the Minister, the Court of King's Bench, and the House of Commons, in the way that I have done, and yet should desert or betray the man who attacks the House of Lords, I would still appeal to your heart. Or if you have any scruples about that kind of evidence, ask that amiable daughter whom you so implicitly confide in—*Is it possible that Junius should betray me?* Do not conceive that I solicit new employment. I am overcome with the slavery of writing. Farewell.

---

## No. 62.

### MR. WILKES TO JUNIUS.

Prince's Court, near Storey's Gate, Westminster,
Wednesday, January 15, 1772.

A NECESSARY attention to my health engrossed my time entirely in the few holidays I spent at Bath, and I am rewarded with being perfectly recovered. The repairs of the clay cottage, to which I am tenant for life, seem to have taken place very successfully; and the building will probably last a few more years in tolerable condition.

Yesterday I met the Supporters of the Bill of Rights at the London Tavern. Much discourse passed about the publication of Junius's letter. Dr. Lee and Mr. Watkin Lewes, who were both suspected, fully exculpated themselves. I believe the publication was owing to the indiscretion of Mr. Patrick Cawdron, a linen-draper in Cheapside, who showed it to his partner on the Saturday. The partner copied it on the Sunday, and the Monday following it appeared in the *Morning Chronicle.* The *Gazetteer* only copied it from thence. The Society directed a disavowal of their publication of it to be sent to you, and are to take the letter into consideration at the next meeting*. I forgot to mention that Mr. Cawdron keeps the papers of the Society.

* Perhaps Wilkes himself was the traitor: it certainly was his practice to make extracts from the private letters of Junius to circulate among his friends, for he was proud of his unknown correspondent and Mentor. A "card" of this description may be seen at the end of Almon's *Junius* (vol. ii. p. 342), given by himself to the aforesaid inculpated Dr. Arthur Lee, comprising the sentiments of Junius just referred to (p. 102) on the public merits of the primitive settlers of the American colonies. A copy of the card is subjoined.

"Junius desires Mr. Wilkes to present his compliments to Dr. Lee; his American friend is evidently a man of abilities, but I think it a little unreasonable that nothing will content him but a total surrender of the fact.

"If the ancestors of the Americans incurred no blame by their emigration, they deserved no praise; and though their emigration has been evidently useful, yet this country was not obliged to them for their desertion.

"You may assure Dr. Lee that to my heart and understanding the name of American and Englishman will ever be the same; but the Americans must not repine at being subject to an authority essential to the state of colonies, in which they have voluntarily placed themselves. British members of the factories abroad, who have more merit towards us, we subject to consulage. I think there is as great certainty that the speculative right will never again be drawn into action, as the highest probability can give.

"I do not see the necessity of fighting this question in the newspapers, nor have I time. I hope, as he corrects me where I am wrong, he will support me where I am right. My situation is * * * *."

Mr. Almon's correspondent, who subscribes himself R. M., says, "A copy from the original card was handed to Dr. Lee by Mr. Wilkes. That original ought to have been found among the papers of Mr. Wilkes; if it was not, we may conclude he had a motive to destroy it. The correctness of the copy in

The winter campaign will begin with the next week. I believe that the sheriffs will have the old battle renewed with the Commons, and I suppose the Lord Mayor and the courtly aldermen will commit the printer for us to release. Another scene will probably open with the Lords. Junius has observed, " the arbitrary power they have assumed of imposing fines, and committing during pleasure, will now be exercised in its fullest extent." The progress of the business I suspect will be this—a bitter libel against Pomfret, Denbigh, or Talbot, attacking the peer personally, not in his legislative or judicial capacity, will appear. His Lordship, passion's slave, will complain to the House. They will order the printer into custody, and set a heavy fine. The sheriffs the next morning will go to Newgate, examine the warrant of commitment, and, like the angel of Peter, take the prisoner by the hand, and conduct him out of prison; afterwards they will probably make their appeal to the public against the usurpation of their Lordships, and their entirely setting aside the power of juries in their proceedings.

Are there more furious wild beasts to be found in the upper den than the three I have named? Miller, the printer of the *London Evening Post*, at No. 2. Queen's Head Passage, Paternoster Row, is the best man I know for this business. He will print whatever is sent him. He is a fine Oliverian soldier. I intend a manifesto with my name on Monday to give spirit to the printers, and to show them who will be their protector. I foresee it will make the two Houses more cautious, but it is necessary for our friends, and the others shall be baited till they are driven into the snare. Adieu.

JOHN WILKES.

# MISCELLANEOUS LETTERS

## ASCRIBED TO JUNIUS.

## LETTER I.

### POPLICOLA TO THE PUBLIC ADVERTISER *

28th April, 1767.

Dictatura, quam in summis reipublicæ angustiis acceperat, per pacem continuata, libertatem fregit; donec illum conversus in rabiem populus et dii ultores de saxo Tarpeio dejecerunt.—LIVY.

" The Dictatorship, which had been confided to him during a period of extreme peril to the Republic, being continued to him after the peace, he abused it to the destruction of liberty, till the people turned upon him in their rage, and the avenging gods precipitated him from the Tarpeian rock."

THE bravest and freest nations have sometimes submitted to a temporary surrender of their liberties in order to establish them for ever.   At a crisis of public calamity or danger, the

* Both this and the next letter under the same signature are not equal to Junius in intensity and compactness of thought and diction, but have qualities in common with him in bitterness of invective, acuteness of stricture, frequency of classical allusion, and rigid construction of the English constitution.   They are a somewhat diluted reflex of what he might have produced ere practice and confidence had raised and invigorated his style. But that he was not the author of them is indubitably settled since the publication of the Chatham Papers.   Diversified and fertile as Junius undoubtedly was in his journalism, he was no Proteus, but hearty, sincere, and consistent.   These data alone ignore the assumption that he could in the same breath—and that too within the space of a few short months— be ardently occupied in alternately exalting and depreciating the same individual.   Yet such an inconsistency must be admitted were *Junius* and *Poplicola* to be regarded as one and the same writer.

Poplicola in April, 1767, depicts Lord Chatham as aspiring to a political dictatorship, and that the Tarpeian rock or a gibbet would be good enough prudence of the state placed a confidence in the virtue of some distinguished citizen, and gave him power sufficient to preserve or to oppress his country. Such was the Roman dictator, and while his office was confined to a short period, and only applied as a remedy to the disasters of an unsuccessful war, it was usually attended with the most important advantages, and left no dangerous precedent behind. The dictator, finding employment for all his activity in repulsing a foreign invasion, had but little time to contrive the ruin of his own country, and his ambition was nobly satisfied by the honour of a triumph, and the applause of his fellow citizens. But as soon as this wise institution was corrupted, when that unlimited trust of power which should have been reserved for conjunctures of more than ordinary difficulty and hazard was, without necessity, committed to one man's uncertain moderation, what consequence could be expected but that the people should pay the dearest price for their simplicity, nor ever resume those rights which they could vainly imagine were more secure in the hands of a single man than where the laws and constitution had placed them?

for the "carcase of such a traitor." But observe the contrast : Junius in a letter addressed to the Earl of Chatham in the following January, marked "private and secret, to be opened by Lord Chatham only," sets himself forth as a warm admirer of that statesman; and anxiously cautions him against the underhand practices of his colleagues, especially of Lord Northington and Mr. Conway, concluding as follows:—

　"My Lord, the man who presumes to give your Lordship these hints admires your character without servility, and is convinced that, if this country can be saved, it must be saved by Lord Chatham's spirit, by Lord Chatham's abilities."—*Correspondence of the Earl of Chatham*, vol. iii. p. 305.

So that the "dictator" of Poplicola is the saviour of Junius—both one writer. Impossible ! Who then, it may be asked, was Poplicola ? a question probably not very material to answer if he were not Junius. But I will mention one conjecture by an American editor, namely, that Poplicola was Horne Tooke, which seems not unlikely. About this period Mr. Horne Tooke returned from a tour in Italy as travelling tutor; on his way he spent some weeks with Mr. Wilkes in Paris, and imbibed his rancour against Grafton and Chatham; the latter, in the full bloom of place, peerage, and pension, having haughtily rejected Wilkes's application for compensation or public employment, and disowned his quondam friend "as the blasphemer of his God, and libeller of his king." In retaliation, Wilkes addressed a bitter inculpatory letter to the Duke of Grafton (see extract, p. 114), and Mr. Tooke is surmised to have lent his auxiliary aid by the two letters signed Poplicola.—ED.

Without any uncommon depravity of mind, a man so trusted might lose all ideas of public principle or gratitude, and not unreasonably exert himself to perpetuate a power which he saw his fellow citizens weak and abject enough to surrender to him. But if, instead of a man of a common mixed character, whose vices might be redeemed by some appearance of virtue and generosity, it should have unfortunately happened that a nation had placed all their confidence in a man purely and perfectly bad; if a great and good prince, by some fatal delusion, had made choice of such a man for his first minister, and had delegated all his authority to him; what security would that nation have for its freedom, or that prince for his crown? The history of every nation that once had a claim to liberty, will tell us what would be the progress of such a traitor, and what the probable event of his crimes *

Let us suppose him arrived at that moment at which he might see himself within reach of the great object, to which all the artifices, the intrigues, the hypocrisy, and the impudence of his past life were directed. On the point of having the whole power of the crown committed to him, what would be his conduct? an affectation of prostrate humility in the closet, but a lordly dictation of terms to the people, by whose interest he had been supported, by whose fortunes he had subsisted. Has he a brother? that brother must be sacri-

---

* This severe invective is aimed against the late Lord Chatham, formerly the right hon. W. Pitt. The reader, by a perusal of the preceding letters, is already acquainted with the utter aversion which Junius at first felt for this nobleman on various political accounts, and especially on the subject of the American dispute. His aversion, however, softened as their political views approximated, and was at length converted into approbation and eulogy.

[Dr. Good resorts to this forced construction by way of fixing Junius with the authorship of Poplicola's letters; but, so far as the writings of Junius can be authentically traced, he uniformly cherished favourable sentiments towards Lord Chatham, and never an "utter aversion." This is manifest from his private letter referred to in the preceding note, dated Jan. 2, 1768, and reprinted in the Appendix to the present volume. Junius has himself described the growth of his admiration of Lord Chatham in a passage of singular beauty (vol. i. p. 391). To have been the unvarying eulogist of that nobleman he must have been inconsistent with himself—more steadfast to an individual than to his own principles; and have been, as that statesman unquestionably was, the alternate advocate and opponent of measures of identical political import, to accommodate himself to the shifting vane of his Lordship's party movements. Upon this part of Chatham's career some strictures have been submitted, in the Editor's introductory Essay.]—ED.

ficed *. Has he a rancorous enemy? that enemy must be

* Lord Temple, brother-in-law to Lord Chatham. They resigned their respective offices, the former of privy seal, and the latter of principal secretary of state, in October 1761. Lord Temple was succeeded by the Duke of Bedford; and upon Lord Chatham's forming his administration in 1766 he took the post of privy seal himself. Lord Temple did not take part in any ministry arranged subsequent to his resignation of that office, and died Sept. 11, 1779.

The following letter from Lord C., before his promotion to the peerage, explains the motives of their joint resignation; it was addressed to a friend in the city¹ :—

"DEAR SIR,

"Finding, to my great surprise, that the cause and manner of my resigning the seals is grossly misrepresented in the city, as well as that the most gracious and spontaneous marks of his Majesty's approbation of my services, which marks followed my resignation, have been infamously traduced as a bargain for my forsaking the public, I am under a necessity of declaring the truth of both these facts, in a manner which I am sure no gentleman will contradict. A difference of opinion with regard to measures to be taken against Spain, of the highest importance to the honour of the crown and to the most essential national interests, and this founded on what Spain had already done, not on what that court may further intend to do, was the cause of my resigning the seals. Lord Temple and I submitted in writing, and signed by us, our most humble sentiments to his Majesty, which, being overruled by the united opinion of all the rest of the King's servants, I resigned the seals on Monday the 5th of this month, in order not to remain responsible for measures which I was no longer allowed to guide. Most gracious public marks of his Majesty's approbation of my services followed my resignation: they are unmerited and unsolicited, and I shall ever be proud to have received them from the best of sovereigns.

"I will now only add, my dear Sir, that I have explained these matters only for the honour of truth, not in any view to court return of confidence from any man who, with a credulity as weak as it is injurious, has thought fit hastily to withdraw his good opinion from one who has served his country with fidelity and success, and who justly reveres the upright and candid judgment of it, little solicitous about the censures of the capricious and the ungenerous. Accept my sincerest acknowledgments for all your kind friendship, and believe me ever with truth and esteem,

"Oct. 14, 1761.          "My dear Sir, your faithful Friend,
                                        "W. PITT."

[Long as this note is, it does not elucidate the text, namely, the "sacrifice of a brother" by the Earl of Chatham, an omission I shall endeavour to supply. The rupture between Chatham and his brother-in-law, Lord Temple, originated in a dispute on the distribution of cabinet council employments in 1766, Temple nominating Lords Gower and Lyttleton, from which Chatham dissented. "Upon this," says Lord Chesterfield, "Lord Temple broke up

¹ The "friend" was Mr. Beckford. — *Chatham Correspondence*, vol. ii. p. 188.—ED.

promoted *. Have years of his life been spent in declaiming
against the pernicious influence of a favourite? That favourite
must be taken to his bosom, and made the only partner of his
power †. But it is in the natural course of things that a despotic power, which of itself violates every principle of a free
constitution, should be acquired by means which equally violate every principle of honour and morality. The office of a
grand vizir is inconsistent with a limited monarchy, and can
never subsist long but by its destruction. The same measures
by which an abandoned profligate is advanced to power must
be observed to maintain him in it. The principal nobility,
who might disdain to submit to the upstart insolence of a dictator, must be removed from every post of honour and authority; all public employments must be filled with a despicable
set of creatures, who, having neither experience nor capacity,
nor any weight or respect in their own persons, will necessarily derive all their little busy importance from him. As the
absolute destruction of the constitution of his country would
be his great object, to be consistent with that design he must
exert himself to weaken and impoverish every rank and order
of the community which, by the nature of their property, and
the degree of their wealth, might have a particular interest in
the support of the established government, as well as power
to oppose any treacherous attempts against it. The landed
estate must be oppressed; the rights of the merchant must be
arbitrarily invaded, and his property forced from him by main
force, without even the form of a legal proceeding. It will
assist him much if he can contribute to the destruction of the

---

the conference, and in his wrath, went to Stowe." Lord Temple himself
explains the matter in a letter to his sister, the Countess of Chatham, dated
July 27, 1766, by stating that he had received the proposition of Pitt with
indignation, to be "stuck into a ministry as a great cipher at the head of the
Treasury, surrounded with other ciphers all named by Mr. Pitt," and with
the politics of several of whom he differed. He had acquiesced in the sacrifice of a brother, Mr. George Grenville's pretensions, but that he would not,
in the projected ministry, " go in like a child and come out like a fool."—
Chatham Correspondence, vol. ii. p. 468.

The wound continued open a couple of years, but through the mediation
of their mutual friend Mr. Calcraft, and repeated advances on the part of
Pitt, a reconciliation was effected. Further to strengthen the family compact, Mr. Grenville heartily acceded to the union.—Id. vol. iii. p. 349.—ED.

* The Duke of Bedford.

† Lord Bute.

poor by continuing the most burthensome taxes upon the
main articles of their subsistence. He must also take advantage of any favourable conjuncture to try how far the nation
will bear to see the established laws suspended by proclamation, and upon such occasions he must not be without
an apostate lawyer, weak enough to sacrifice his own character,
and base enough to betray the laws of his country *.

These are but a few of the pernicious practices by which a
traitor may be known, by which a free people may be enslaved. But the masterpiece of his treachery, and the surest
of answering all his purposes, would be, if possible, to foment
such discord between the mother country and her colonies as
may leave them both an easier prey to his own dark machina-
tions. With this patriotic view, he will be ready to declare
himself the patron of sedition and a zealous advocate for rebellion. His doctrines will correspond with the proceedings
of the people he protects, and if by his assistance they can obtain a victory over the supreme legislature of the empire, he
will consider that victory as an important step towards the advancement of his main design †.

Such, Sir, in any free state, would probably be the conduct
and character of a man unnecessarily trusted with exorbitant
power. He must either succeed in establishing a tyranny or
perish. I cannot without horror suppose it possible that this
our native country should ever be at the mercy of so black a
villain. But if the case should happen hereafter, I hope the
British people will not be so abandoned by Providence as not
to open their eyes time enough to save themselves from destruction; and though we have no Tarpeian rock for the immediate punishment of treason, yet we have impeachments;
and a gibbet is not too honourable a situation for the carcase
of a traitor.

POPLICOLA.

* This subject is fully explained in many parts of the Letters of Junius,
and in the notes now subjoined to them. The character alluded to is Earl
Camden, at that time Lord Chancellor.
† Lord Chatham, then Mr. Pitt, opposed Mr. George Grenville's Stamp
Act, and denied the right of the parliament of Great Britain to legislate for
America.

## LETTER II.

### TO THE PRINTER OF THE PUBLIC ADVERTISER.

SIR,                                                 May 28, 1767.

Your correspondent C. D.* professes to undeceive the public
with respect to some reflections thrown out upon the Earl of

* Poplicola, the writer of this reply, by some means or other mistook the
real signature, which instead of being C. D. was W. D.   The letter is dated
from Clifton, and is obviously from the pen of Sir. W. Draper; affording a
singular proof that the Knight of the Bath and Junius were political opponents under signatures mutually unknown, and so far back as May, 1767.
The subject of Sir William's observations was a defence of Lord Chatham
against some strong observations made upon his character by Mr. Wilkes, in
a letter addressed to the Duke of Grafton, relative to the illegal proceedings
of the Earl of Halifax.   The letter is dated Paris, Dec. 12, 1763 [1766¹],
and the part chiefly adverted to is the following :—

" I believe that the flinty heart of Lord Chatham has known the sweets
of private friendship, and the fine feelings of humanity, as little as even
Lord Mansfield.   They are both formed to be admired, not beloved.   A
proud, insolent, overbearing, ambitious man is always full of the ideas of his
own importance, and vainly imagines himself superior to the equality necessary among real friends, in all the moments of true enjoyment.   Friendship
is too pure a pleasure for a mind rankered with ambition, or the lust of
power and grandeur.   Lord Chatham declared in parliament the strongest
attachment to Lord Temple, one of the greatest characters our country could
ever boast, and said *he would live and die with his noble brother*.   He has
received obligations of the first magnitude from that *noble brother*, yet what
trace of gratitude or of friendship was ever found in any part of his conduct?
and has he not now declared the most open variance and even hostility?   I
have had as warm and express declarations of regard as could be made by
this marble-hearted friend, and Mr. Pitt had no doubt his views in even
feeding me with flattery from time to time; on occasions, too, where candour
and indulgence were all I could claim.   He may remember the compliments
he paid me on two certain poems in the year 1754.   If I were to take the
declarations made by himself and the late Mr. Potter d *la lettre*, they were
more charmed with those verses after the ninety-ninth reading than after
the first ; so that from this circumstance, as well as a few of his speeches in

¹ There is no species of evidence so conflicting as dates, which, without the
greatest care, are apt to be printed incorrectly.   In Woodfall's edition the
date is given as 1763 ; in Almon's *Correspondence of Wilkes* it is 1767 ; but
1766 is manifestly correct, judging from the dates of Wilkes's transitory
visit to England in the winter of that year, and his return to Paris on the
failure of his official suit to the Duke of Grafton.—ED.

Chatham in Mr. Wilkes's letter to the Duke of Grafton. Without undertaking the defence of that gentleman's conduct

parliament, it seems to be likewise true of the first orator, or rather the first comedian, of our age, *non displicuisse illi jocos, sed non contigisse.*

"I will now submit to your Grace if there was not something peculiarly base and perfidious in Mr. Pitt's calling me a *blasphemer of my God* for those very verses, at a time when I was absent, and dangerously ill from an affair of honour. The charge, too, he knew was false, for the whole ridicule of those two pieces was confined to certain mysteries, which formerly the *unplaced* and *unpensioned* Mr. Pitt did not think himself obliged even to affect to believe. He added another charge equally unjust, that I was the *libeller of my King*, though he was sensible that I never wrote a single line disrespectful to the sacred person of my Sovereign, but had only attacked the despotism of his ministers, with the spirit becoming a good subject and zealous friend of his country. The reason of this perfidy was plain. He was then beginning to pay homage to the *Scottish* idol, and I was the most acceptable sacrifice he could offer at the shrine of BUTE. History scarcely gives so remarkable a change. He was a few years ago the mad seditious tribune of the people, insulting his Sovereign, even in his capital city; now he is the abject crouching deputy of the proud Scot, who he declared in parliament *wanted wisdom, and held principles incompatible with freedom*; a most ridiculous character surely for a statesman, and the subject of a free kingdom, but the proper composition for a *favourite*. Was it possible for me after this to write a suppliant letter to Lord Chatham? I am the first to pronounce myself most unworthy of a pardon if I could have obtained it on those terms.

"Although I declare, my Lord, that the conscious pride of virtue makes me look down with contempt on a man who could be guilty of this baseness, who could in the lobby declare that I must be supported, and in the House on the same day desert and revile me, yet I will on every occasion do justice to the minister. He has served the public in all those points where the good of the nation coincided with his own private views, and in no other. I venerate the memory of the secretary, and I think it an honour to myself that I steadily supported in parliament an administration the most successful we ever had, and which carried the glory of the nation to the highest pitch in every part of the world. He found his country almost in despair. He raised the noble spirit of England, and strained every nerve against our enemies. His plans, when in power, were always great, though in direct opposition to the declarations of his whole life when out of power. The invincible bravery of the British troops gave success even to the most rash, the most extravagant, the most desperate of his projects. He saw early the hostile intentions of Spain, and if the *written advice* had been followed, a very few weeks had then probably closed the last general war; although the merit of that *advice* was more the merit of his *noble brother* than his own. After the omnipotence of Lord Bute in 1761 had forced Mr. Pitt to retire from his Majesty's councils, and the cause was declared by himself to be our conduct relative to Spain, I had the happiness of setting that affair in so clear and advantageous a light that he expressed the most entire satisfaction and particular obligations to my friendship. I do not, however, make this a

I 2

or character, permit me to observe that he was the instrument, and a useful one, to the party, therefore should not have

claim of merit to Mr. Pitt.   It was my duty, from the peculiar advantages of information I then had."

In answer to these strictures Sir William Draper, in the letter subscribed W. D., and which is too long to be copied verbatim, quotes several of Mr. Wilkes's previous declarations in favour of Lord Chatham while Mr. Pitt, and concludes as follows:—

" The letter asserts also that Lord Chatham is now the abject crouching deputy of Lord Bute, who he declared in parliament wanted wisdom and held principles incompatible with freedom.   The world knows nothing of this abject crouching deputed minister but from Mr. Wilkes's single affirmation; but we all know that his Majesty has been pleased to call Lord Chatham again to the ministry: if Lord Bute supports him in it, he gives the noblest proof of generosity and greatness of soul, and has revenged himself in the finest manner upon Lord Chatham for those expressions, and affords the strongest proof that he does not want wisdom or bold principles incompatible with freedom.   What greater proof of wisdom can he give than in supporting that person who is the most capable of doing good to his country, and has upon all occasions approved himself the most zealous protector of its liberties?   But I beg pardon; upon a late occasion, indeed, Lord Chatham showed himself to be no friend to liberty; he was so very tyrannical, as well as Lord Camden, that he denied some traders the right, liberty, and privilege of starving his fellow-citizens, by exporting all the corn out of the kingdom, for which he has met with his reward, and been as much abused as if he himself had been guilty of starving them.   Is there no Tarpeian rock for such a tyrant?

" Mr. Wilkes has now done with Lord Chatham, leaving him to the poor consolation of a place, a peerage, and a pension; for which, he says, he has sold the confidence of a great nation.   But I cannot take leave of, or have done with, Mr. Wilkes, without making a few observations upon this paragraph: Mr. Wilkes is a great jester; in this place he cannot possibly be serious; for as to the pension, I think I cannot explain it better to my countrymen than in Mr. Wilkes's own words, August 12, 1762.

" ' I must, in compliance with a few vulgar writers, call the inadequate reward given to Mr. Pitt, for as great services as ever were performed by a subject, a pension, although the grant is not during pleasure, and therefore cannot create any undue unconstitutional influence.   In the same light we are to consider the Dukes of Cumberland's and Marlborough's, Prince Ferdinand's, and Admiral Hawke's, Mr. Onslow's, &c. &c. &c.   I was going to call it the King's gold box; for Mr. Pitt having before received the most obliging marks of regard from the public, the testimony of his Sovereign only remained wanting.'

" Now as Mr. Wilkes has so fully set forth the nature of this pension, I cannot think it will at all lessen the confidence of the nation in Lord Chatham: it may very possibly lessen their confidence in Mr. Wilkes, who has contradicted himself so furiously, and perhaps destroy that idea of consistency which the gentleman boasts of in his letter to the Duke of

been sacrificed by it. He served them, perhaps, with too much zeal; but such is the reward which the tools of faction usually receive, and in some measure deserve, when they are imprudent enough to hazard everything in support of other men's ambition.

I cannot admit that, because Mr. Pitt was respected and honoured a few years ago, the Earl of Chatham therefore deserves to be so now; or that a description, which might have suited him at one part of his life, must of necessity be the only one applicable to him at another. It is barely possible that a very honest commoner may become a very corrupt and worthless peer; and I am inclined to suspect that Mr. C. D. will find but few people credulous enough to believe that either Mr. Pitt or Mr. Pulteney, when they accepted of a title, did not, by that action, betray their friends, their country, and, in every honourable sense, themselves. Mr. C. D. wilfully misrepresents the cause of that censure, which was very justly thrown upon Lord Chatham when the exportation of corn was prohibited by proclamation. The measure itself was necessary, and the more necessary from the scandalous delay of the ministry in calling the parliament together; but to maintain that the proclamation was legal, and that there was a suspending power lodged in the crown, was such an outrage to the common sense of mankind, and such a daring attack upon the constitution, as a free people ought never to forgive. The man who maintained those doctrines ought to have had the Tarpeian rock or a gibbet for his reward. Another gentleman, upon that occasion, had spirit and patriotism enough to declare, even in a respectable assembly, that when he advised the proclamation, he did it with the strongest conviction of its being illegal; but he rested his defence upon the unavoidable necessity of the case, and submitted himself to the judgment of his country. This noble conduct deserved the applause and gratitude of the nation, while that of the Earl of Chatham and his miserable understrappers deserved nothing but detestation and contempt.

POPLICOLA.

Grafton, where he assures his Grace that, 'however unfashionable such a declaration may be, consistency shall never depart from his character.' The reader has the proofs before him, and will judge of it accordingly. W. D."

## LETTER III.

### TO THE PRINTER OF THE PUBLIC ADVERTISER.

June 24, 1767.

*Accedere matrem muliebri impotentiâ; serviendum fœminæ, duobusque insuper nebulonibus, qui rempublicam interim premant, quandoque distrahant* [*].—*Tacitus 1° Annalium.*

THE uncertain state of politics in this country sets all the speculations of the press at defiance. To talk of modern ministers, or to examine their conduct, would be to reason without data; for whether it be owing to the real simple innocence of doing nothing, or to a happy mysteriousness in concealing their activity, we know as little of the services they have performed since it became their lot to appear in the *Gazette*, as we did of their persons or characters before. They seem to have come together by a sort of fortuitous concourse, and have hitherto done nothing else but jumble and jostle one another, without being able to settle into any one regular or consistent figure. I am not, however, such an atheist in politics as to suppose that there is not somewhere an original creating cause, which drew these atoms forth into existence; but it seems the utmost skill and cunning of that secret governing hand could go no further. To create or foment confusion, to sacrifice the honour of a king, or to destroy the happiness of a nation, requires no talent but a natural *itch* for doing mischief. We have seen it performed for years successively, with a wantonness of triumph, by a man who had neither abilities nor personal interest, nor even common personal courage †. It has been possible for a notorious coward,

---

* "To these reflections the public added the dread of a mother raging with all the impotence of female ambition : a whole people, they urged, were to be enslaved by a woman and two juveniles, who in the beginning would hang heavy on the state, and in the end distract and rend it to pieces by their own dissensions."

† The notion that the influence of the Earl of Bute, who is here alluded to, continued long after his retirement—that he formed the "influence behind the throne greater than the throne itself"—was long a popular delusion encouraged by faction. It was only suspected, never supported by any proof; and General Conway, while Secretary of State, denied that he "had ever seen, felt, or discovered," any such influence. The imputation was explicitly denied by Lord Mountstuart, the Earl's son, who, in a letter written

skulking under a petticoat, to make a great nation the prey of his avarice and ambition. But I trust the time is not very distant when we shall see him dragged forth from his retirement, and forced to answer severely for all the mischiefs he hath brought upon us.

It is worth while to consider, though perhaps not safe to point out, by what arts it hath been possible for him to maintain himself so long in power, and to screen himself from national justice. Some of them have been obvious enough; the rest may without difficulty be guessed at. But whatever they are, it is not above a twelvemonth ago since they might have all been defeated, and the venomous spider itself caught and trampled on in its own webs. It was then his good fortune to corrupt one man, from whom we least of all expected so base an apostacy *. Who, indeed, could have suspected that it should ever consist with the spirit or understanding of that person to accept of a share of power under a pernicious court minion, whom he himself had affected to detest or despise, as much as he knew he was detested and despised by the whole nation? I will not censure him for the avarice of a pension, nor the melancholy ambition of a title. These were objects which he perhaps looked up to, though the rest of the world thought them far beneath his acceptance. But, to become the stalking-horse of a stalliou; to shake hands with a Scotchman at the hazard of catching all his infamy; to fight under his auspices against the constitution; and to

in October, 1778, declared that "he (Lord Bute) does therefore authorise me to say, that he declares upon his solemn word of honour that he has not had the honour of waiting on his Majesty but at his levee or drawing-room; nor has he presumed to offer any advice or opinion concerning the disposition of offices, or the conduct of measures, either directly or indirectly, by himself or any other, from the time when the late Duke of Cumberland was consulted on the arrangement of a ministry in 1765 to the present hour." Lord Bute had neither the abilities nor the ambition of a statesman; his sympathies were chiefly limited to the Princess-Dowager of Wales and the purlieus of the court, and did not extend to national affairs.—ED.

* For the reasons assigned on the authorship of Poplicola's letters, this attack on the Earl of Chatham renders it unlikely that Anti-Sejanus was Junius. Chatham's peerage and pension appear for a time to have lessened his popularity, and this is said to have been the Machiavellian result Lord Bute intended by the grant of them. But it was only a temporary loss, and Pitt's great and popular talents soon raised him above the obscuration of his coronet.—ED.

receive the word from him, prerogative and a thistle; (by
the once respected name of Pitt!) it is even below contempt. But it seems that this unhappy country had long
enough been distracted by their divisions, and in the last instance was to be oppressed by their union. May that union,
honourable as it is, subsist for ever! may they continue to
smell at one thistle, and not be separated even in death!

ANTI-SEJANUS, Jun.

---

## LETTER IV.

### TO THE PRINTER OF THE PUBLIC ADVERTISER.

Sir,                     St. James's Coffee House, August 25, 1767.
I HAVE been some time in the country, which has prevented
your hearing sooner from me.  I find you and your brother
printers have got greatly into a sort of knack of stuffing your
papers with flummery upon two certain brothers*, who are
labour-in-vain endeavouring to force themselves out of the
world's contempt.  I have great good will to you, and hope you
are well paid for this sort of nonsense †, as indeed you ought
to be, for it certainly disgraces your paper.  It is in vain that
your friends assure the coffee-house that these things are
wrote by the brothers themselves; that you believe no more
of them than the rest of the world does; and that you only
put them in to show your extreme impartiality, which sometimes obliges you to insert the most improbable stories; I
would therefore advise you as a friend, to give up this noble
pair as *enfans perdus*.

I am not a stranger to this *par nobile fratrum*.  I have
served under the one, and have been forty times promised *to
be served* by the other.  I don't think it possible to characterize either without having recourse to the other; but anybody who knows one of them may easily obtain an idea of the
other.  Thus now: suppose you acquainted with the Chancellor, take away his ingenuity, and a something that at times

---

* Lord Townshend, and his brother, Charles Townshend, the former just
appointed Lord-Lieutenant of Ireland, and the latter at this time Chancellor
of the Exchequer. — ED.

† Of Charles, see note, vol. i. p. 155. — ED.

looks something like good nature, but it is not, and you have
the direct and actual character of the peer : a booster without
spirit, and a pretender to wit without a grain of sense; in a
word, a vain-glorious idler without one single good quality of
head or heart. I hope his affairs with Lord —— and Mr.
—— are the only instances of his setting out with unnecessary insolence, and ending with shameful tameness. But is
such a man likely to please the brave Irish, whose hasty
tempers, or whose blunders, may sometimes lead them into a
quarrel, but whose swords always carry them through it?
Are these the pair who are to give stability to a wavering
favourite, and permanency to a *locum tenens* administration?
Alas! alas!

> Non tali anxilio, nec defensoribus istis
> Tempus eget :

And is it by such a prop that Grafton thinks to stand, after
throwing down his idol Pitt, at whose false altar he had before sacrificed his friends? Is it for such a man that Conway
foregoes the connections of his youth and the friends of his
best and ripest judgment.—*O tempora! O mores!*

A FAITHFUL MONITOR.

---

## LETTER V*.

### TO THE PRINTER OF THE PUBLIC ADVERTISER.

SIR,                                          September 16, 1767.
HIS Excellency the Lord Lieutenant of Ireland† is said to
have a singular turn for portrait painting, which he willingly
employs in the service of his friends. He performs gratis,
and seldom gives them the trouble of sitting for their pictures.
But I believe the talents of this ingenious nobleman never
had so fair an occasion of being employed to advantage as at

* The following answer to correspondents in the *Public Advertiser* of
Sept. 16, identifies Junius to have been the writer of this letter : "Our
correspondent C. will observe that we have obeyed his directions in every
particular, and we shall always pay the utmost attention to whatever comes
from so masterly a pen."
† Lord Townshend.

present. It happens very fortunately for him, that he has now a set of friends who seem intended by nature for the subjects of such a pencil. In delineating their features to the public he will have an equal opportunity of displaying the delicacy of his hand, and, upon which he chiefly piques himself, the benevolence of his heart. But, considering the importance of his present cares, I would fain endeavour to save him the labour of the design, in hopes that he will bestow a few moments more upon the execution. Yet I will not presume to claim the merit of invention. The blindness of chance has done more for the painter than the warmest fancy could have imagined, and has brought together such a group of figures as, I believe, never appeared in real life, or upon canvas before.

Your principal character, my Lord, is a young duke mounted upon a lofty phaeton; his head grows giddy; his horses carry him violently down a precipice; and a bloody carcase, the fatal emblem of Britannia, lies mangled under his wheels. By the side of this furious charioteer sits Caution without foresight †, a motley thing, half military, scarce civil. He too would guide, but, let who will drive, is determined to have a seat in the carriage. If it be possible, my Lord, give him to us in the attitude of an orator eating the end of a period, which may begin with, *I did not say I would pledge my-self*—The rest he eats.

Your next figure must bear the port and habit of a judge The laws of England under his feet, and before his distorted vision a dagger, which he calls the law of nature, and which marshals him the way to the murder of the constitution ‡.

In such good company the respectable president of the council cannot possibly be omitted *. A reasonable number of decrees must be piled up behind him, with the word RE-VERSED in capital letters upon each of them; and out of his

* The Duke of Grafton.

+ Mr. Conway, Secretary of State for the northern department.

‡ Lord Camden. A scarcity of grain having been experienced during the recess, government had taken upon itself to stop the exportation of corn, in defiance of an act of parliament that granted a bounty for exporting it. The legality of this measure of a proclamation having been questioned, Lord Camden maintained that, in a case of necessity, the crown was possessed of a legal power to suspend the operation of an act of the legislature. See this subject further touched upon in Junius, Letter 60, vol. i. p. 417.

decent lips a compliment *à la Tilbury, Hell and d———n blast you all.* \* \* \* \* \*

There is still a young man, my Lord, who I think will make a capital figure in the piece. His features are too happily marked to be mistaken. A single line of his face will be sufficient to give us the heir apparent of Loyola and all the college. *A little more of the devil, my Lord, if you please, about the eyebrows; that's enough; a perfect Malagrida, I protest* †! So much for his person; and as for his mind, a blinking bull-dog ‡ placed near him, will form a very natural type of all his good qualities.

Those are the figures which are to come forward to the front of the piece. Your friendship for the Earl of Bute wil. naturally secure a corner in the retirement for him and his curtain. Provided you discover him \* \* \* \* \* §.

If there are still any vacancies in the canvas, you will easily fill them up with fixtures or still life. You may show us half a paymaster for instance, with a paper stuck upon the globe of his eye, and a lable out of his mouth, *No, Sir; I am of t'other side, Sir.* How I lament that sounds cannot be conveyed to the eye || !

You may give us a commander-in-chief ¶ and a secretary at war \* \* seeming to pull at two ends of a rope; while a slip-knot in the middle may nearly strangle three-fourths of the army; or *a lunatic brandishing a crutch* ††, *or bawling through a grate,* or writing with desperate charcoal a letter to North America; or a Scotch secretary teaching the Irish people the

---

\* Lord Northington, formerly Lord Chancellor, one or two of whose decrees had, at the above period, been reversed; a circumstance, however, which may possibly be as attributable to his not having sufficiently applied himself to the cases in question as to any natural deficiency of judgment. His manners had certainly not been studied in the refined school of Lord Chesterfield.

† Lord Shelburne, at that time Secretary of State for the southern department.

‡ Col. Barré, then vice-treasurer of Ireland.

§ A lady, who was thought to have considerable influence, is here alluded to.

|| Lord North and Mr. (afterwards Sir) G. Cooke, were joint paymasters, the former of whom is ridiculed.

¶ The Marquis of Granby.

\* \* Lord Barrington.

†† Lord Chatham.

true pronunciation of the English language. That barbarous people are but little accustomed to figures of oratory, so that you may represent him in any attitude you think proper, from that of Sir Gilbert Elliot * down to Governor Johnstone. They, however, are but the slighter ornaments of composition, and so I leave them to the choice of your own luxurious fancy.

The back ground may be shadowed with the natural obscurity of Scotch clerks and Scotch secretaries, who may be *itched* out to the life, with one hand grasping a pen, the other riveted in their respective * * * * * * *. Your southern writers are apt to rub their foreheads in an agony of composition; but with Scotchmen the seat of inspiration lies in a lower place, which, while the FUROR is upon them, they lacerate without mercy. By this delectable friction, their imaginations become as prurient as their * * * * * *, and the latter are relieved from one sort of matter, while their brains are supplied with another. Everything they write, in short, is polished *ad unguem*.

But amidst all the licence of your wit, my Lord, I must entreat you to remember that there is one character too high and too sacred even for the pencil of a peer, though your Lordship has formerly done business for the family. Besides, the attempt would be unnecessary. The true character of that great person is engraven in the hearts of the Irish nation; and as to a false one, they need only take a survey of the person and manners of their chief governor, if, in the midst of their distresses, they can laugh at the perfect caricature of a king †.

CORREGGIO.

* At that time Irish secretary.

† This is an amusing daub of scurrility, but assuredly not a Junius. He would not have described Chatham, for reasons already adduced, as " a lunatic brandishing a crutch, or bawling through a grate." Had Dean Swift been alive it might have passed for a dash of his satiric brush.—ED.

# LETTER VI.

TO THE PRINTER OF THE PUBLIC ADVERTISER.

SIR,                                October 12, 1767.

THERE has been for some time past a very curious altercation
carried on through your paper between *Philo-Veritatis* and
*No Ghost*. This altercation has hitherto been carried on like
other political disputes, by affirmatives and negatives, assertions and contradictions, good hits and smart repartees. This
is the kind of combat usually fought on, and indeed the only
one adapted to, the field of a public paper. But I perceive,
not without anxiety, that another species of battle is likely to
take place between the two champions whom I have mentioned *. In this I am too much concerned to remain neuter.

---

\* The following extract from the letter of *Philo-Veritatis*, in the *Public
Advertiser*, will enable the reader the better to understand the allusions in
the present letter.

"That his Excellency the present Lord Lieutenant of Ireland commanded
at Quebec is indisputable. Captain Schomberg, as gallant an officer as any
in the navy, and who, with the brave Captain Deane, burnt and destroyed the
French fleet, had the honour to convey him up the Gulph of St. Lawrence,
where his Excellency multiplied his military glory; and here I cannot omit
an anecdote relating to his Lordship, which occurred at Dettingen in Germany. In the very heat of the carnage of that day, and amidst the horrors
of almost universal desolation, a soldier, fighting near his Lordship's side,
was killed by a cannon ball; part of his brains flew out, and some on his
Lordship's clothes and in his face. The brave General G—— being near
him, said, 'My Lord, this is terrible work to-day.' 'So it is,' replied his
Lordship, wiping himself, with great calmness; 'but one would imagine,
General, this man had too much brains to be here;' at the same time tears
of manly pity filled his compassionate eyes.

"Now if humanity, intrepidity, and what the French justly distinguish
by the name of *sang froid*, be the characteristics of a valiant soldier, my
favourite Lord (and such I am proud to own him) can, as the lawyers say,
make out, even from this single story, a good title, and does deserve (as I
have before averred) to have his name inscribed in adamantine letters on a
column of eternal fame; and if Mr. *No Ghost* disputes it, I (in the ancient
style of the heralds) defy him: I accept his gauntlet, and stand forth his
Lordship's avowed champion, though a bad one, ready to fight in his defence,
either with pistol or pen, and desire *No Ghost* to accept of a Roland for his
Oliver in a scrap of Latin on my side.

"*Parturiunt montes; nascitur ridiculus mus.*    Bye bye, Mr. *No Ghost.*
"October 2.                                    PHILO-VERITATIS."

I have courage enough to draw my pen upon any man, but I should be very unwilling to draw my sword: the pop-gun of wit I can stand, but a pistol is what I dare not face. Somehow or other I have taken it into my head, that the dull and heavy argument of a pistol ball is more convincing than the most elaborate reasoning, or the keenest wit which can be delivered by a pen. Alas, Sir, what then shall I do? Shall I remain silent, whilst *No Ghost* affirms that the Lord Lieutenant of Ireland is a coward, and *Philo-Veritatis* (*è contra*) declares him a brave and undaunted soldier?—It is of little importance which side I am inclined to from judgment. If I declare in favour of *Philo-Veritatis*, I incur the danger of a pen which he himself seems to think very sharp—indeed so sharp, as to beg of his opponent to lay it aside, and take up a pistol; on the other hand, if I join with *No Ghost*, I have a pistol at my head, which may make a ghost of me. Thus circumstanced I will not take either part, but offer myself as a friend to both, to measure the ground, give the word, and carry off the body of whichever shall fall in the field of honour. In this character I shall beg (previous to their engagement) to state a few points not yet decided between them, and which they have not yet carried far enough in discussion to require the decision of powder and ball. Give me leave first (though I declare no prepossession in his favour) to compliment *Philo-Veritatis*, the *advocate* for his Lordship's *courage*, on his own bravery, who, under a fictitious name, challenges with the utmost intrepidity to single and mortal combat, a nameless opponent. I should spend some time, and take some pains, to turn this compliment and make it worthy of him, but that I dare say he is sufficiently applauded already, by those to whom he has revealed himself, for such an unexampled piece of heroism.

Now, to my purpose: *Philo-Veritatis* asserts that his hero, Lord Townshend, gave proofs of his *bravery* at Minden and Quebec. *No Ghost* denies the fact, upon the presumed impossibility of his transporting himself from one of these places to the other in the space of ten days, unless he could *fly*, and that very fast too. Now *flying* being a quality which *Philo-Veritatis* does not choose to ascribe (whatever belief it might gain with the public) to his hero, answers this in somewhat of a new way: "This objection," says he, "has no weight, and is made only to introduce a scrap of Latin and a witticism." This may be a very good answer at cross purposes; but is, I confess, a very whimsical one in the present case. Surely, Sir, this matter is not yet come so close to a point as to require the arbitration of a pistol. Let *Philo-Veritatis* again (for he has once already done it) affirm, that the hero was present at both actions; *No Ghost* denies it; *Philo* gives the lie; *No Ghost* knocks him down, and then the pistol enters as naturally as possible, and without the smallest breach of the rule which Horace has laid down on this occasion: *Nec Deus intersit, nisi dignus vindice nodus.*

*No Ghost* having denied that his Lordship was actually present at both places, *Philo* seems to fear lest we should doubt that he was at either. Minden he gives up; but being resolved to prove that he was at Quebec, he informs us that the brave Captain Schomberg had the honour of conveying him up the Gulph of St. Lawrence, where his Lordship *multiplied* his glory. These are the words. It is not my business to make remarks; but *Philo* will tell us where this multiplication table may be found; and I would recommend his Lordship to study it most attentively; he need go no further in this kind of arithmetic; the *next rule* will be quite unnecessary, as I presume no one will desire to *divide* with his Lordship. Now, if I guess right, the *No Ghost* will not deny that the brave *Schomberg* conveyed him up the gulph, and therefore this does not call very loudly for the pistol. Every one will acknowledge that Lord Townshend was at Quebec; for every one remembers his letter from thence; and perhaps *Philo* can tell who the secretary was.

To this multiplication of glory, *Philo* makes an *addition* of an anecdote, which, as he says, *occurred* to his Lordship in Germany; indeed, *occurred!* An anecdote occurred; a curious occurrence it was. First let us see the inference which *Philo* draws from, and then we shall relate the *occurrence* itself. It is, that the *humanity* of his *favourite* Lord (for such he is proud to own him) is established by it. The *occurrence* is, that a soldier being killed near, his brains were scattered upon his Lordship's clothes. A stander-by remarks, "that this is terrible work." "True," says his Lordship; "but one would have thought this fellow had too much brains to be here."——Reader, remark this, and if you doubt of his Lordship's humanity, you are infidel enough to doubt of his

courage.  Well, he burst into tears : and who could choose
but weep at a sentiment of such tender, compassionate, and
sympathizing humanity !  No one, that I know of, can suppose these tears shed from that depression of spirits which
the extremity of fear sometimes causes, and which finds some
ease from an involuntary overflow at the eyes.  Never had
such humanity such a panegyrist ; it does indeed deserve to
be inscribed on *adamantine pillars of eternal fame,* as *Philo*
elegantly expresses it.  Now, as he is such an admirer of
humanity in others, let me call on his own humanity not to
avail himself of the assistance of a pistol on this occasion ; as
I will venture to answer for Mr. *No Ghost,* that he will not
take up the gauntlet which *Philo* has so bravely thrown
down, offering him the choice of pen or pistol.  Alas, *Philo!*
at the first of these weapons you are by no means, indeed you
are not, a match for *No Ghost;* and for the use of the last, you
might chance to be hanged, and thus unfortunately frustrate
his Lordship's *humane* intentions of rewarding your courage
with one of those pensions which he will *multiply* on the *Irish*
establishment.                                   I am, &c.
                                                    MODERATOR.

-------

## LETTER VII.

FOR THE PUBLIC ADVERTISER.

October 22, 1767.

*Grand  Council upon the Affairs of Ireland after eleven Ad-
journments* *.

                                        Hill Street, 7th October, 1767.

PRESENT.

Tilbury . . . fuddled †.

* This paper was announced in the *Public Advertiser* in the following
words :—" The grand council upon the affairs of Ireland, after eleven ad
journments, is come to hand, and shall have a place in our next."  To which
was added by the printer himself:—" Our friend and correspondent C. will
always find the utmost attention paid to his favours."  C., as the reader
must already have observed from the Preliminary Dissertation and Private
Letters, was the secret mark in use between Junius and the printer, to
inform each other of the identity or receipt of communications.  The present
article, however, does not stand in need of this accidental proof of genuineness.  Its internal evidence is sufficient without it : especially the identity
of its style, and the peculiar nature of its political bearing.
† The Earl of Northington, President of the Council.

Judge Jefferyes *.
Caution ... without foresight †.
Malagrida ‡.
Boutdeville ... sulky §.

A chair left empty for the High Treasurer ‖, detained by a hurry of business at Newmarket.

*After a convenient time spent in staring at one another, up gets Tilbury.*

*Thus from my Lord his passion broke;*
*He ——— first, and then he spoke.*

TILBURY. In the name of the Devil and his dam, can anybody tell what accident brings us five together?

CAUTION. For my own part, my Lords, I humbly apprehend—though I speak with infinite diffidence—I say, my Lords, I will not pledge myself for the truth of my opinion; but I do humbly conceive, with great submission, that we are met together with a view, and in order to consider whether it might not be advisable to give some instructions to this noble Lord for his government in Ireland, or whether we should leave the direction of his conduct to the same chance, to which, under our Sovereign Laird the Earl of Bute (*they all bow their heads*) he owes his appointment. I may be mistaken, my Lords, but I—I—I—*looks round him, simpers, and sits down.*

TILBURY. D—t me if I care whether he has any instructions or not. But who the Devil's to draw them up?

MALAGRIDA, *with a complacent smile.* That's a task, my Lords, which I believe no man here is better qualified to execute than myself. Your Lordships well know that I am far from being vain of my talents; yet I believe I may affirm without presumption, that nature has done more for me, without any effort of my own, than other men usually derive from education and experience. My Lord Holland, who certainly had some reason to know me, has done me the honour to say that I was born a Jesuit, and that if all the

---

* Earl Camden, Lord Chancellor.
† Mr. Conway, Northern Secretary.
‡ Lord Shelburne, Southern Secretary.
§ Lord Townshend, Lord Lieutenant of Ireland.
‖ Duke of Grafton, First Lord of the Treasury.

good qualities which make the society of Jesus respectable
were banished from the rest of the earth, they would still find
room enough in the bosom of *Malagrida*.    His Lordship
sagaciously observed, that mine was a sort of understanding
more united with the heart than the head; and that my ideas
of men and things depended not so much upon the improvement of my brain as upon the original colour and consistence
of my blood; consequently—but this is a seducing subject,
upon which perhaps, I fear, I am too willing to expatiate.
To return then to the noble Lord's instructions.    I should be
happy to know what your Lordships' ideas are upon this most
important question, that, when I have heard all your opinions,
I may with greater decency follow my own.

TILBURY.    D—t me if I know anything of the matter.
*Falls asleep.*

CAUTION.    The very learned Lord who slumbers upon the
sofa, having, with his usual candour, confessed his usual
ignorance upon the arduous subject of our present debates,
it may seem presumptuous in a man of my inferior qualifications, even to form, much more to deliver, any opinion upon
it.    For this reason, my Lords, although I venture to speak
first, I shall take care not to hazard anything decisive.    I
have already had the honour of giving instructions to governors; and, excepting my noble colleague, with whom I agree
that he owes as much to nature for the accomplishments of
his mind as for those of his person, I believe few men succeed
better at the ambiguous.    It is my forte, my Lords;———I
always contrive to leave the person I instruct at full liberty
to act as he thinks proper, and entirely at his own .peril.
Positive instructions are too apt to endanger the safety of
those who give them.    Mine I am determined shall endanger
nothing but the safety of the state.    But since the noble Lord
absolutely insists upon being instructed some way or other,
my friendship for him, which he may believe is full as sincere
as what I felt for his brother—poor Charles ——* and art
thou gone!——so is my friendship;—I say, my Lords, since
his Lordship can have no doubt about the warmth of my
friendship for him, he may at all times rely upon my assis-

---

* The Hon Charles Townshend, Chancellor of the Exchequer, then lately
dead.

tance and concurrence, and—and—it is unnecessary I believe
to explain what ——*simpers at Sulky, and sits down.*

JUDGE JEFFERYES, *with dignity.* My Lords, your Lordships know that the greatest part of my life has been dedicated
to the study of the common and statute law of my country;—
you will not wonder, therefore, at my appearing a strenuous
advocate for the natural liberties of mankind, such as they
possessed them before the existence of positive laws in this
country, or any other. Now, my Lords, if I am not ill
informed, the Irish are already in this desirable state of
emancipation. By the most authentic accounts, they actually
approach as near to a state of nature as can be effected by the
absence of all legal restraints; and, for my own part, I will
speak boldly my Lords—I always do when the liberties of my
fellow-subjects are in question—I never consider my own
character in what I say either in council or Parliament—I
think, that to give any positive instructions to a chief governor,
might have the odious appearance of invading the natural
rights of the Irish. It is their claim, it is their birthright,
my Lords, to talk without meaning, and to live without law.
This is the sort of liberty which our ancestors fought for, and
which every true Englishman ought to revere. God forbid,
my Lords, that anything done by a British council should
tend to the diminution of privileges which the Irish justly
think invaluable. Besides, my Lords, I have too much
respect for the uncommon talents of the noble Lord himself
to wish to confine him by any opinions of ours. Let him but
follow the dictates of his own genius, and I will venture to
say that the Irish will have no reason to envy the government
of England;—at least he may be assured of our hearty endeavours and concurrence to prevent any ill blood, upon that
score, between the two nations.

SULKY, *in an attitude copied from Mr. Sparks\*.* I was
quiet enough at Raneham, when I was told I was Lord Lieutenant of Ireland. For a man to be told that he commands
a kingdom or an army, when he dreams of no such matter,
forms a situation too difficult for such a head as mine. My
Lords, I speak from experience. Upon another occasion,

* A comedian, thus characterized in Churchill's Rosciad :
  " Sparks at his glass sat comfortably down,
    To sep'rate frown from smile, and smile from frown."

K 9

Indeed, I found the business done to my hand, by a person
who shall be nameless. But alas! I find things in a very
different condition at present. I perceive that I am no more
a statesman than a general, and that my predecessor, instead
of doing anything himself, has only bequeathed to me the
disgrace of not being able to perform what he was so vain or
so simple as to promise. Then to be left to my own guidance!
If my poor dear brother had lived, you would not have
treated me so scurvily. Surely your Lordships forget that
these are a wild barbarous people, and how dangerous it is to
trust to their respect for the person of a lord lieutenant. In
short, my Lords, if you do not think proper to grant *them* a
*habeas corpus*, at least grant *me* one, and as soon as possible.
I shall never be easy until I find my body once more before
you. In the meantime, I believe I had best follow my Lord
Bute's advice.

OMNES.    Lord Bute! It must be followed. What is it?

SOLKY.    To carry over with me a battalion of gallant
disinterested Highlanders, who, if there should be any disturbance, may take to their broad swords. Where plunder's
to be had, they'll take to anything. I have seen it tried with
astonishing success: and sure never was a man in such a
*taking* as I was.

CAUTION.    The expedient, I confess, is admirable; but
pray, my Lord, how do you intend to provide for all these
sweet-blooded children?

SOLKY.    My secretary has got a list of the employments in
Ireland, and assures me that I shall be able to provide for as
many more.

JEFFERYES, *growing peevish and impatient*. To conclude,
my Lords. If what I have just now had the honour of
throwing out should not be consistent with the noble Lord's
ideas, or with his plan of government, he has my free consent
to adopt a very different system. Instead of permitting the
Irish to live without any law whatever, let him govern them
by edicts from the Castle. For my own part, I hate medium
in government. I am all for anarchy, or all for tyranny.
The Irish Privy Council are as good judges of the plea of
necessity, and I dare say as ready to make use of it, as any
other council. You have my authority and example, my Lord,
in support of suspending powers; and provided you are a

little cautious in the object of your first experiment, you may carry this wholesome maxim to as great a length in Ireland as, with the blessing of God (*turning up his eyes to heaven*). I intend to do here.

*A dog barks, and wakens Tilbury, who starts up.*

TILBURY.    Zounds, my Lord, do you keep bull-dogs in your house?

MALAGRIDA.    No, my Lord; it is but a mongrel. Your true English bull-dog never quits his hold; but this cur plays fast and loose, just as I bid him: he worries a man one moment, and fawns upon him the next *. But, my Lords, I hope you are not going away before I have finished my speech. It is a masterpiece, I'll promise you, and has cost me infinite labour to get by heart.

TILBURY.    No, damn me, 'tis a little too late, I thank you. *Aside:* This silly puppy takes me for his schoolmaster, and fancies I am obliged to hear him repeat his task to me. *Exit.*

CAUTION.    Pray spare me, my Lord; you know my friendship: I would stay to hear you if it were possible. *Aside:* I see this will never do; so I'll e'en try to renew with the Rockinghams. *Exit, talking to himself.*

JEFFERYES.    Change of place, my Lord, as well as change of party, is the indefeasible right of human nature†. It is a part of the natural liberty of man, which I am determined to make use of immediately. *Exit.*

MALAGRIDA *to* SULKY.    Won't you hear me, my Lord?

SULKY.    It is unnecessary, my dear Lord. I see your meaning written in your face. *Aside:* What the devil shall I do now? A sick man might as well expect to be cured by a consultation of quack doctors; they talk, and debate, and wrangle, and the patient expires. However, I shall at least have the satisfaction of drawing their pictures. I believe the best thing I can do will be to consult with my Lord George Sackville. His character is known and respected in Ireland as much as it is here; and I know he loves to be stationed in the *rear* as well as myself. *Exit.*

MALAGRIDA *solus.* What a negro's skin must I have, if this shallow fellow could see my meaning in my face!——

* The person here alluded to is Colonel Barré.
† Lord Camden had been Chief Justice of the Common Pleas, was now Chancellor, and was afterwards President of the Council.

Now will I skulk away to ——, where I will betray or
misrepresent every syllable I have heard, ridicule their
persons, blacken their characters, and fawn upon the man
who hears me, until I have an opportunity of biting even
him to the heart. *Exit \**.

* A writer in the *Public Advertiser*, in a pretended real account of what
passed at the council, having charged Mr. Burke with being the author of
this satire, and as the letters of Junius were during their publication attributed to that gentleman, we shall extract such part of it as more immediately
relates to him.

The council are supposed to have discussed the instructions to be given to
the Lord Lieutenant, and the Lord President is then made to address them
as follows :

PRESIDENT.  If nothing further occurs to your Excellency, nor to you,
my Lords, upon the present business, it will be time, I believe, for us to
break up.

(*As the Council are rising a Secretary enters.*)

SECRETARY.  My Lords, there is a person without who says he has business of a private nature, and earnestly desires to be admitted.

S. S.  Do you know who the man is?  Are you acquainted with his
person?

SECRETARY.  I am, my Lord; but as he desires, in case your Lordships
do not think fit to see him, that his visit may be kept a secret, I beg to be
excused mentioning his name.  I believe he is personally known to every
one present.

OMNES.  Let him come in.

(*The Secretary goes out and returns, introducing a tall, ill-looking fellow,
in a shabby black coat.*)

LORD PRESIDENT.  What are your commands with us, Mr. Brazen?

BRAZEN.  The business, my Lords, that has brought me thus unexpectedly into your company, will, I am persuaded, excuse the unseasonable-
ness of my intrusion.  I flatter myself I am known, well known, to every
one of your Lordships.  My part has not been an obscure one: I may say
with the *sublimest* of all poets,

"*Not to know me*," &c.

In short, my Lords, I think I have trod the public stage of the world
with some degree of applause; with a pen that can blacken the whitest
character, and a tongue that can *dash the maturest councils*, I hold myself
equipped at all points for the offices of party.  One in particular of this
right honourable company can bear testimony to my performances.  What
need of more words?

"*I have done the state some service, and they know it.*"

But, my Lords, to come to the point at once.  No man, I trust, in these
times, serves the state for nothing; yet such has been my pride or folly
(call it which you will), that I have got nothing for my pains but empty
praise.  Now, my Lords, this diet begins to grow too thin for my stomach.
I must own I expected to have reaped good interest for my self-denial, but

## LETTER VIII.

TO THE PRINTER OF THE PUBLIC ADVERTISER.

SIR,                                                    October 31, 1707.

YOUR correspondent, who has furnished you with what he calls a true account of a grand council in Hill Street, does not appear to me to have done much service to his patrons. The former dialogue had at least some pleasantry (though not enough, I

things have not come round as I looked for; the revolutions in government have not kept pace with those that have been made in my fortune; and the late unprosperous fatal negotiation has broken all my measures, and thrown me at length upon your Lordships' mercy, the humblest of your petitioners.

LORD PRESIDENT. Will your Lordships have the patience to hear this prating fellow any longer?

LORD CAMDEN. Mr. Brazen, you will please to contract your discourse as much as the matter will admit. A great deal that you have now been relating to us might, in my humble opinion, have been spared without any prejudice to your petition or to your principles. If you have any real business worthy being communicated to this company, we shall wish you to let us hear it without further preface.

BRAZEN. I should have thought that your Lordship at least, in the course of your high office, had been more patient under circumlocution than to correct me for the little I have now made use of; however, not to incur your displeasure, I will come at once to the point. Your Lordships see these two papers. This in my left hand, my Lords, contains the most important intelligence that was ever directed to ministers. It is, my Lords, the whole scheme and plan of opposition which you are shortly to encounter, concerted, modelled, and digested, according to rules logical, metaphysical, and mathematical. It is the most *beautiful*, as well as the *sublimest*, system of politics that ever sprung from the brain of man. I am here ready to consign it over to your Lordships upon the terms and conditions annexed to it; and with it myself, my faith, my friendship, and my conscience.

*Witness that here Iago doth give up*
*The execution of his wit, hands, heart,*
*To this great Council's service.*

(*The whole of the Council rise at once, and the High Treasurer speaks.*)

HIGH TREASURER. My Lords, I see the indignation with which you receive this proposal, and the just contempt with which you are about to treat this most infamous proponent. But I beseech you, let what I shall now say to him serve for his dismission, and hold him unworthy of any further reply. We reject your offer, Sir, with the most consummate disdain. Unfaithful to your own party, we scorn to admit you into ours; and though the bounty of the council holds forth rewards for merit, we have neither the will nor the means to bribe and seduce a villain. Amongst those gentlemen whom you thus offer to abandon, there are many for whose persons and characters we have the most absolute regard. Whatever their councils may

dare say, to draw a smile from the parties concerned), and
perhaps, in marking the characters, a little too much truth.
But this sorrowful rogue is too dull to be witty, and as for
truth, I suppose it would neither suit his argument nor his
disposition.  His raillery upon a shabby black coat is indeed
delicate to an extreme; but he forgets that wit and abilities
have as little connection with rich clothes as they have with
great places, and that a man may wear a fine suit, or figure
as a secretary of state, without a single grain of either.  But,
Sir, if facts asserted are notoriously false, the assertion of
them can do no mischief; if notoriously true, they are beyond
the reach of his wit, if he had any, to palliate, or of his
modesty, which I think is upon a par with his wit, to deny.

Now, Sir, if I were not afraid of distressing him too much,
I would ask him whether Lord Townshend did not openly
complain, only three days before his departure, that he could
not, by the warmest solicitations, prevail on the ministry to
agree upon any one system of instructions for him; that he
was left entirely to himself; and that the ministry could not be
persuaded to pay the smallest attention either to his situation
or to that of the country he was sent to govern.  Did he not

be, and however hostile to our measures, we scorn to look into them by any
indirect means.  Friends to the liberties of our country, and protectors of its
constitution, we wish not to destroy opposition by the force of corruption, we
seek only to confute it by the prevalence of reason; every proposal that has
the public welfare for its object, from whatever party it springs, shall have
our support; and while we have truth and justice on our side we have
nothing to apprehend from opposition, though all your genius and (which is
more) all your ill nature shall be drawn forth in its support.

BRAZEN.  'Tis very well, my Lords; 'tis mighty well; you have rejected
the olive branch, take then the sword.  This paper, my Lords, in my right
hand, holds a mine that shall blow you into the air.  It is a libel wrote in
gall.  Your present consultations are the subject; and every member here
present shall have a seat, except I think fit to dispatch your unimportant
Grace to Newmarket.  For you, my Lord President, I shall characterise
you under the name of Tilbury, because when that man kept an inn at
Bagshot, you put up at his house.  To my Lord Camden, I shall bequeath
the odious name of Jefferyes, by the old derivatory rule of *Lucus a non
lucendo.  Caution without foresight* shall be your title, Sir; and your noble
colleague's, Malagrida; when I have thought of any reason for either, I may
give it you.  To your Excellency, by way of contrast, I decree the name of
*Boutdeville*, or Sulky.

S. S.  Here; who waits there?  Take this fellow and put him out of the
house.

*Exit BRAZEN between two footmen.*

say this without reserve to every man he met, even in public court,' and with all possible marks of resentment and disgust? I would advise your second correspondent not to deny these known facts; for if he does, I will assuredly produce some proofs of them which will gall his patrons a little more than anything they have seen already. Let one of them only recollect what sort of conversation very lately passed between him and the Lord Lieutenant, how he was pressed, and how he evaded. But the facts, of which the public are already possessed, sufficiently speak for themselves, and the nation wants no further proof of the weakness, ignorance, irresolution, and spirit of discord, which reign triumphant in this illustrious divan, who have dared to take upon them the conduct of an empire.

One question more, and I have done. Did it become him, who has undertaken the defence of a whole ministry, to forget one of the principal characters of the piece? Why should he omit the dog? This mongrel, that barks, and bites, and fawns, has nevertheless a share in council, and, in the opinion of the best judges, cuts full as good a figure in it as his master.

*Here,* who waits *there?* — O charming antithesis! O polished language! and equally fit for the noble Lord who speaks, or for the footman who hears it.

## LETTER IX.

MR. PRINTER,                          December 5, 1767.

THERE are a party of us who, for our amusement, have established a kind of political club. We mean to give no offence whatever to anybody in our debates. The following is a mere *jeu d'esprit,* which I threw out at one of our late meetings, and is at your service, if you think it will afford the least entertainment to your readers*.

I am, &c.

Y. Z.

* As the debates in parliament were not allowed at this period to be given verbatim, they were usually detailed to the public under the guise of fictitious assemblies and opinions, through the medium of imaginary characters; and under this form the writer undertakes to canvass the

Mr. President. The condition of this country at the conclusion of the last spring was such as gave us strong reason to expect that not a single moment of the interval between that period and our winter meeting would be lost or misemployed. We had a right to expect that gentlemen who thought themselves equal to advise about the government of the nation, would, during this period, have applied all their attention, and exerted all their efforts, to discover some effectual remedy for the national distress. For my own part,

measures of government, on the opening of the session of parliament in November, 1767. Whether the printer was aware that the speech here detailed was actually spoken by Mr. Burke on the particular occasion to which it refers, or conceived it to have been merely fictitious, is uncertain. Since the former edition of this work, however, was put to press, a gentleman who still thinks Mr. Burke to have been the author of the "Letters of Junius," and who means to give his opinions upon this subject to the public, has discovered that the speech is genuine, and was actually delivered; and that the words *committee, society, chair,* &c., are here substituted for those of *administration, house, majesty,* with such other variations as are necessary to give it its present character. A passage was suppressed in the original publication, which has now been added in a note to p. 143. That this speech was sent to the printer of the *P. A.* by Junius, will appear obvious to the reader from its being thus announced for publication : " C.'s favour is come to hand, and we think our paper much honoured by his correspondence. He may be assured we shall take every possible means to deserve a continuance of it."

The severity of the speech, however, whether conceived at that time to be genuine or fictitious, is so pointed, that the printer was half afraid to insert it, and the next day made the following apology for its non-appearance : " We most heartily wish to oblige our valuable correspondent C., but his last favour is of so delicate a nature, that we dare not insert it, unless we are permitted to make such changes in certain expressions as may take off the immediate offence, without hurting the meaning."

This request appears to have been complied with; and hence, possibly, is to be attributed the turn given to the speech, as it appeared in the *Public Advertiser.*

---

[1] A pamphlet appeared accordingly in 1826, to prove Burke to be Junius, chiefly on account of this speech. But the writer begs the entire question, and the only facts that he proves are, that Burke spoke the speech; that the speech was published a few days after, as above, in the *Public Advertiser ;* and that a corrected version of it was published by Almon in 1772. But he adduces no proof that Burke was C., or that C. might not be *Corregio* or other correspondent of Mr. Woodfall; or conversely, Junius might be C., and have reported the speech, and still not be Burke. A remarkable fact about the speech is, that it was the first of Mr Burke's orations in parliament that has been preserved.—ED.

I had no doubt that, when we again met, the committee would have been ready to lay before us some plan for a speedy relief of the people, founded upon such certain lights and informations as they alone are able to procure, and digested with an accuracy proportioned to the time they have had to consider of it. But if these were our expectations, if these were the hopes conceived by the whole society, how grievously are we disappointed! After an interval of so many months, instead of being told that a plan is formed, or that measures are taken, or, at least, that materials have been diligently collected, upon which some scheme might be founded for preserving us from famine, we see that this provident committee, these careful providers, are of opinion, they have sufficiently acquitted themselves of their duty, by advising the chair to recommend the matter once more to our consideration, and so endeavouring to relieve themselves from the burthen and censure which must fall somewhere by throwing it upon the society. God knows in what manner they have been employed for these four months past. It appears too plainly they have done but little good; I hope they have not been busied in doing mischief; and though they have neglected every useful, every necessary occupation, I hope their leisure has not been spent in spreading corruption through the people.

Sir, I readily assent to the laborious panegyric which the gentleman upon the lower bench has been pleased to make on a very able member of the committee, whom we have lately lost*. No man had a higher opinion of his talents than I had; but as to his having conceived any plan for remedying the general distress about provisions (as the gentleman would have us understand), I see many reasons for suspecting that it could never have been the case. If that gentleman had formed such a plan, or if he had collected such materials as we are now told he had, I think it is impossible but that, in the course of so many months, some knowledge or intimation of it must have been communicated to the gentlemen who acted with him, and who were united with him not less by friendship than by office. He was not a re-

* The Right Honourable Charles Townshend, Chancellor of the Exchequer, who died Sept. 4, 1767, and was succeeded in that office by Lord North, the Chief Justice of the King's Bench, having, in virtue of his office, held the seals for a few days only.

served man, and surely, Sir, his colleagues, who had every
opportunity of hearing his sentiments in the committee, in
private conversation, and in this society, must have been
strangely inattentive to a man whom they so much admired,
or uncommonly dull, if they could not retain the smallest
memory of his opinions on matters on which they ought naturally to have consulted him often. If he had even drawn
the loosest outlines of a plan, is it conceivable that all
traces of it should be so soon extinguished? To me, Sir,
such an absolute oblivion seems wholly incredible. Yet, admitting the fact for a moment, what a humiliating confession is it for a committee, who have undertaken to advise
about the conducting of an empire, to declare to this society,
that by the death of a single man, all projects for the public
good are at an end, all plans are lost, and that this loss is
irreparable, since there is not a leader surviving who is in
any measure capable of filling up the dreadful vacuum!

But I shall quit this subject for the present, and as we are
to consider of an answer in return to the advice from the
chair, I beg leave to mention some observations occurring to
me upon the advice itself, which I think I am warranted, by
the established practice of this society, to treat merely as the
advice of the foreman of the committee *.

* The following are the passages in the King's speech more immediately
alluded to in this pretended discussion of it:—

"Nothing in the present situation of affairs abroad gives me reason to apprehend that you will be prevented by any interruption of the public tranquillity from fixing your whole attention upon such points as concern the
internal welfare and prosperity of my people.

"Among these objects of a domestic nature, none can demand a more
speedy, or more serious attention, than what regards the high price of
corn, which neither the salutary laws passed in the last sessions of parliament, nor the produce of the late harvest, have yet been able so far to
reduce as to give sufficient relief to the distresses of the poorer sort of my
people. Your late residence in your several counties must have enabled you
to judge whether any further provisions can be made conducive to the at-
tainment of so desirable an end.

"The necessity of improving the present general tranquillity, to the great
purpose of maintaining the strength, the reputation, and the prosperity
of this country, ought to be ever before your eyes. To render your de-
liberations for that purpose successful, endeavour to cultivate a spirit of
harmony among yourselves. My concurrence in whatever will promote
the happiness of my people, you may always depend upon; and in that
light I shall be desirous of encouraging union among all those who wish
well to their country."

The chief and only pretended merit of the present advice is, that it contains no extraordinary matter, that it can do no harm, and consequently that an answer of applause upon such advice is but a mere compliment to the chair, from which no inconvenience can arise, nor consequence be drawn. Now, Sir, supposing this to be a true representation of the advice, I cannot think it does the committee any great honour, nor can I agree that to applaud the chair for such advice would be attended with no inconvenience. Although an answer of applause may not enter into the approbation of particular measures, yet it must unavoidably convey a general acknowledgment, at least, that things are, upon the whole, as they should be, and that we are satisfied with the representation of them which we have received from the chair. But this, Sir, I am sure would be an acknowledgment inconsistent with truth, and inconsistent with our own interior conviction, unless we are contented to accept of whatever the committee please to tell us, and wilfully shut our eyes to any other species of evidence.

· As to the harmlessness of the advice, I must, for my own part, regret the times when advices from the chair deserved another name than that of innocent; when they contained some real and effectual information to this society—some express account of measures already taken, or some positive plan of future measures, for our consideration. Permit me, Sir, to divide the present advice into three heads, and a very little attention will demonstrate how far it is from aiming at that spirit of business and energy which formerly animated the advice from the chair. You will see, under this division, that the small portion of matter contained in it is of such a nature, and so stated, as to preclude all possibility or necessity of deliberation in this place. The first article is, that everything is quiet abroad. The truth of this assertion, when confirmed by an inquiry, which I hope the society will make into it, would give me the sincerest satisfaction; for certainly there never was a time when the distress and confusion of the interior circumstances of this nation made it more absolutely necessary to be upon secure and peaceable terms with our neighbours. But I am a little inclined to suspect, and indeed it is an opinion too generally received, that this appearance of good understanding with our neighbours deserves the name of stagnation rather than of tranquillity; that it is owing not so much to the success of our negotiations abroad as to the absolute and entire suspension of them for a very considerable time. Consuls, envoys, and ambassadors, it is true, have been regularly appointed, but, instead of repairing to their stations, have, in the most scandalous manner, loitered at home, as if they had either no business to do, or were afraid of exposing themselves to the resentment or derision of the court to which they were destined. Thus have all our negotiations with Portugal * been conducted, and thus have they been dropped. Thus hath the Manilla ransom, that once favourite theme, that perpetual echo with some gentlemen, been consigned to oblivion. The slightest remembrance of it must not now be revived. At this rate, Sir, foreign powers may well permit us to be quiet; it would be equally useless and unreasonable in them to interrupt a tranquillity which we submit to purchase upon such inglorious terms, or to quarrel with an humble passive government, which hath neither spirit to assert a right nor to resent an injury. In the distracted, broken, miserable state of our interior government, our enemies find a consolation and remedy for all that they suffered in the course of the war, and our councils amply revenge them for the successes of our arms.

The second article of the advice contains a recommendation of what concerns the dearness of corn, to our immediate and earnest deliberation. No man, Sir, is more ready than myself, as an individual, to shew all possible deference to the respectable authority under which the advice from the chair is delivered; but as a member of this society, it is my right, nay, I must think myself bound to consider it as the advice of the foreman of the committee; and, upon this principle, if I would understand it rightly, or even do justice to the text, I must carry the foreman's comment along with me. But what, Sir, has been the comment upon the recommendation made to us from the chair? Has it amounted to any more than a positive assurance that all the endeavours of the committee to form a plan for relieving the poor in the article of provisions have proved ineffectual? That they neither have a plan, nor materials of sufficient information to lay before

* The words " with Portugal " are not in the genuine speech.

the society, and that the object itself is, in their apprehensions, absolutely unattainable. If this be the fact, if it be really true that the foreman, at the same time that he advises the chair to recommend a matter to the earnest deliberation of the society, confesses in his comment that this very matter is beyond the reach of this society, what inference must we necessarily draw from such a text, and from such an illustration? I will not venture to determine what may be the real motive of this strange conduct and inconsistent language, but I will boldly pronounce that it carries with it a most odious appearance *.　　*　　*　　*　　*　　*　　*

With respect to the third and last head into which the

---

* The following is the passage suppressed at this place, and intimated to be suppressed by the asterisks. It is extracted from the genuine speech of Mr. Burke, as given in *Almon's Debates* for 1767, vol. iv. pp. 506, 507. Lond. Ed. 1792.

"It has too much the air of a design to exculpate the crown, and the servants of the crown, at the expense of parliament. The gracious recommendation in the speech will soon be known all over the nation. The comment and true illustration added to it by one of the ministry will probably not go beyond the limits of these walls. What then must be the consequence? The hopes of the people will be raised. They of course will turn their eyes upon us, as if our endeavours alone were wanting to relieve them from misery and famine, and to restore them to happiness and plenty; and at last, when all their golden expectations are disappointed, when they find that, notwithstanding the earnest recommendation from the crown, parliament has taken no effectual measures for their relief, the whole weight of their resentment will naturally fall upon us their representatives. We need not doubt but the effects of their fury will be answerable to the cause of it. It will be proportioned to the high recommending authority, which we shall seem not to have regarded; and when a monarch's voice cries havock, will not confusion, riot, and rebellion make their rapid progress through the land? The unhappy people, groaning under the severest distress, deluded by vain hopes from the throne, and disappointed of relief from the legislature, will, in their despair, either set all law and order at defiance, or, if the law be enforced upon them, it must be by the bloody assistance of a military hand. We have already had a melancholy experience of the use of such assistance. But even legal punishments lose all appearance of justice when too strictly inflicted on men compelled by the last extremity of distress to incur them. We have been told, indeed, that if the crown had taken no notice of the distress of the people, such an omission would have driven them to despair; but I am sure, Sir, that to take notice of it in this manner, to acknowledge the evil, and to declare it to be without remedy, is the most likely way to drive them to something beyond despair, to madness; and against whom will their madness be directed but against their innocent representatives?"

advice may be divided, I readily agree that there is a cause of discord somewhere; where it is I will not pretend to say. That it does exist is certain, and I much doubt whether it is likely to be removed by any measures taken by the present committee. As to vague and general recommendations to us to maintain unanimity amongst us, I must say I think they are become of late years too flat and stale to bear being repeated: that such are the kind sentiments and wishes of our chairman, I am far from doubting; but when I consider it as the language of the foreman, as a foreman's recommendation, I cannot help thinking it a vain and idle parade of words without meaning. Is it in their own conduct that we are to look for an example of this boasted union? Shall we discover any trace of it in their broken distracted councils, their public disagreements and private animosities? Is it not notorious that they only subsist by creating divisions among others? That their plan is to separate party from party, friend from friend, brother from brother? Is not their very motto *Divide et impera?* When such men advise us to unite, what opinion must we have of their sincerity? In the present instance, however, the advice is particularly farcical. When we are told that affairs abroad are perfectly quiet, and consequently that it is unnecessary for us to take any notice of them; when we are told that there is indeed a distress at home, but beyond the reach of this society's councils to remedy; to have unanimity recommended us in the same breath, is, in my opinion, something lower than ridiculous. If the two first propositions be true, in the name of wonder, upon what are we to debate? Upon what is it possible for us to disagree? On one point our advice is not wanted; on the other it is useless; but it seems it will be highly agreeable to the committee to have us unite in approving of their conduct; and if we have concord enough amongst ourselves to keep in unison with them and their measures, I dare say that all the committee's purposes, aimed at by the recommendation, will be fully answered, and entirely to their satisfaction. But this is a sort of union which I hope never will, which I am satisfied never can, prevail in a free society like ours. While we are freemen, we may disagree, but when we unite upon the terms recommended to us by the committee, we must be slaves.

# LETTER X.

SIR,                                    December 19, 1767.

If there be any man in this country who thinks that the combination lately entered into at Boston is merely a matter of interior economy, by which we are either not essentially affected, or of which we have no right to complain, I may safely pronounce that that man knows nothing of the condition of the British commerce, nor of the condition of the British finances. It might be happy for us if we were all in the same state of ignorance. To foresee a danger when every chance of avoiding it hath been wilfully cut off, is but a painful and useless sagacity, and to shut our eyes to inevitable ruin, serves at least to keep the mind a little longer in a thoughtless security

In this way I imagine any man must reason who is insensible of the consequence of the successive enterprises of the colonies against Great Britain, or who beholds them with indifference. I will not suppose that the bulk of the British people is sunk into so criminal a state of stupidity; that there does exist a particular set of men base and treacherous enough to have enlisted under the banners of a lunatic*, to whom they sacrificed their honour, their conscience, and their country, in order to carry a point of party and to gratify a personal rancour, is a truth too melancholy and too certain for Great Britain. These were the wretched ministers who served at the altar, whilst the high priest himself, with more than frantic fury, offered up his bleeding country a victim to America. The gratitude of the colonies shows us what thanks are due to such men. They will not even keep measures with their friends, for they hate the traitors, though the treachery hath been useful to them. The colonies are even eager to show that they regard the interests of the men (who to serve them gave up everything that men ought to hold dear, except their places) as little as they do the interests of their mother country, and will not comply so far with the promising engagements made for them here as even to con-

* Lord Chatham.

ceal their malignant intentions until their friends are out of place. Such is the certain effect of conferring benefits upon an American.

Whatever has been hitherto the delusion of the public upon this subject, I fancy we are by this time completely undeceived. Our good friends in America have been impatient to relieve us from all our mistakes about them and their loyalty, and if we do not open our eyes now, we had better shut them for ever.

It would be to no purpose at present to renew a discussion of the merits of the Stamp Act, though I am convinced that even the people who were most clamorous against it either never understood, or wilfully misrepresented every part of it. But it is truly astonishing that a great number of people should have so little foreseen the inevitable consequence of repealing it, and particularly that the trading part of the city should have conceived that a compliance which acknowledged the rod to be in the hand of the Americans, could ever induce them to surrender it. They must have been rather weaker than ourselves if they ever paid their debts, when they saw plainly that by withholding them they kept us in subjection. In the natural course of things, the debtor should be at the mercy of his creditor rather than a tyrant over him; but it seems that for these three years past, wherever America hath been concerned, every argument of reason, every rule of law, and every claim of nature, has been despised or reversed. We have not even a tolerable excuse for our folly. The punishment has followed close upon it; and that it must be so was as evident to common sense, as probable in prospect, as it is now certain in experience. There was indeed one man who wisely foresaw every circumstance which has since happened, and who, with a patriot's spirit, opposed himself to the torrent*. He told us that, if we thought the loss of outstanding debts and of our American trade a mischief of the first magnitude, such an injudicious compliance with the terms dictated by the colonies, was the way to make it sure and unavoidable. It was *ne moriare, mori.* We see the prophecy verified in every particular, and if this great and good man was mistaken in any one instance, it was, perhaps, that he did not expect his predictions to be fulfilled so soon as they have been.

* Mr. George Grenville.

This being the actual state of things, it is equally vain to attempt to conceal our situation from our enemies, as it is impossible to conceal it from ourselves. The taxes and duties necessarily laid upon trade, in order to pay the interest of a debt of one hundred and thirty millions, are so heavy that our manufactures no longer find a vent in foreign markets. We are undersold and beaten out of branches of trade of which we had once an almost exclusive possession. The progress towards a total loss of our whole foreign trade has been rapid; the consequence of it must be fatal. We had vainly hoped that an exclusive commerce with our colonies (in whose cause a great part of the very incumbrances which have destroyed our foreign trade were undertaken) would have rewarded us for all our losses and expense, and have made up any deficiency in the revenue of our customs. We had a right to expect this exclusive commerce from the gratitude of the Americans, from their relation to us as colonists, and from their own real interest, if truly understood. But unfortunately for us, some vain, pernicious ideas of independence and separate dominion, thrown out and fomented by designing seditious spirits in that country, and encouraged and confirmed here by the treachery of some and the folly of others, have cut off all those just hopes, those well-founded expectations. While we are granting bounties upon the importation of American commodities, the grateful inhabitants of that country are uniting in an absolute prohibition of the manufactures of Great Britain. To doubt that the example will be followed by the rest of the colonies, would be rejecting every evidence which the human mind is capable of receiving. To be mad is a misfortune, but to rave in cold blood is contemptible.

The enterprises of the Americans are now carried to such a point that every moment we lose serves only to accelerate our perdition. If the present weak, false, and pusillanimous administration are suffered to go on in abetting and supporting the colonies against the mother country, if the King should take no notice of this last daring attack upon our commerce, the only consequence will be that the contest, instead of being undertaken while we have strength to support it, will be reserved not for our posterity, but to a time when we ourselves shall have surrendered all our arms to the people with whom we are to contend—nor will that period be distant.

L 2

If the combination at Boston be not a breach of any standing law (which I believe it is) ought it not to be immediately declared so by an act of the legislature?   It is true that private persons cannot be compelled to buy or sell against their will; but unlawful combinations, supported by public subscription and public engagements, are, and ought to be, subject to the heaviest penalties of the law.  I shall only add, that it is the common cause of this nation, and that a vigorous and steady exertion of the authority of Great Britain would soon awe a tumultuous people, who have grown insolent by our injudicious forbearance, and trampled upon us because we submitted to them *.

## LETTER XI.

### TO THE PRINTER OF THE PUBLIC ADVERTISER.

Mr. Woodfall,                                    December 22, 1767.

Your correspondent of yesterday,' Mr. Macaroni†, in his account of the new ministerial arrangements, has thrust in a laboured bombast panegyric on the Earl of Chatham, in which he tells us, "that this country owes more to him than it can ever repay."   Now, Mr. Woodfall, I entirely agree with Mr. Macaroni that this country *does* owe more to Lord Chatham than it ever can repay, for to *him* we owe the greatest part of our national debt, and THAT I am sure we never can repay.  I mean no offence to Mr. Macaroni, nor any of your *gentlemen* authors who are so kind to give *us* citizens an *early* peep behind the political curtain, but I cannot bear to see so *much* incense offered to an Idol ‡ who so *little* deserves it.

I am yours, &c.
                                                     DOWNRIGHT.

* This letter was without a signature, and could not, therefore, be announced, but was thus noticed on the day previous to its publication: "O.'s favour is come to hand."  For a further continuance of this subject, see Miscellaneous Letters, Nos. 29 and 81.

† This writer had furnished the printer with a list of the supposed changes in administration.

‡ See the conclusion of Miscellaneous Letter, No. 4, and Private Letter, No. 23, in which the same term is applied to Lord Chatham.  But these inferences of Dr. Good are negatived by the knowledge subsequently obtained of the real sentiments of Junius in respect of Lord Chatham.  Otherwise *Downright* is short and pointed enough for a Junius.—Rd.

## LETTER XII.

### TO THE PRINTER OF THE PUBLIC ADVERTISER.

SIR,                                February 14, 1768.

A MINISTER who in this country is determined to do wrong should not only be a man of abilities, but of uncommon courage. To invade the rights, or to insult the understanding of a nation qualified to judge well, and privileged to speak freely, upon public measures, requires a portion of audacity unacquainted with shame, or of power which knows no control. Whether it be owing to a hardy disposition, or to the conceit of unlimited power, or to mere stolid ignorance, I know not, but it is too apparent that the present ministry, in everything they do, or attempt to do, are determined to set the understanding and the spirit of the English people at defiance. In a succession of illegal or unconstitutional acts, the instance of to-day ought at once to remind us of what they have done already *, and to alarm us against what they may attempt hereafter.  We have reason to thank God and the legislature that some of the most flagitious of their enterprises have been happily defeated.  Their endeavour to establish a suspending power in the crown met with all the contempt it deserved †; nor have they yet quite succeeded in emancipating the colonies from the authority of the British legislature.  But when open and direct attacks upon the constitution have failed, a bad ministry will naturally have recourse to some more artful measures, by which the prerogative of the crown may be extended, and the purposes of arbitrary power answered as effectually, and more securely to themselves.  When attempts of this insidious nature are made, it is the duty of every subject, be his situation what it may, to point out the danger to

* This appears to be the germ of the after amendment in the Dedication (v. L p. 87), on the danger of bad precedents; "what yesterday was fact, to-day is doctrine."  But this does not prove that the present communication is by Junius, as he may have either improved on his own first expression, or that of another.  Both the style and tenour of the argument, however, agree well with Junius, and the dissatisfaction evinced towards Lord Chatham further on, and noticed by Dr. Good, is not inconsistent with his known sentiments at an early period.—ED.

† See this subject further discussed in Junius, Letter 60, vol. i. p. 418.

his countrymen, and warn them to guard against it.  I shall
take another opportunity to inquire into the legality of the
appointment of a third secretary of state: at present let me
be permitted to rouse the attention of the public to a later
and to a still more flagrant stretch of prerogative.  A prostitution or corruption of old offices may be as fatal to the
constitution as the illegal creation of new ones.    In the
*Gazette* of Saturday se'nnight we are informed that the privy
seal is committed to the care of three persons, whose commission is to continue six weeks *.  From the names of these
persons we can collect nothing, but that two of them are of
Scottish extraction, and that the third is recorder of St.
Alban's; but from their insignificance and obscurity we may
easily collect, that there is some particular design in fixing
on such persons to execute one of the first offices of the state.
Why the Earl of Chatham should continue to hold an employment of this importance, while he is unable to perform
the duties of it, is at least a curious question †.   But it is

* Whitehall, Feb. 2.   The King has been pleased to issue his commission
under the great seal, authorizing and empowering Richard Sutton, William
Blair, and William Fraser, Esqrs., or any two of them, to execute the office
of Keeper of his Majesty's Privy Seal, for and during the space and term of
six weeks, determinable nevertheless at his Majesty's pleasure; and also to
grant, during his Majesty's pleasure, to the right honourable William Earl of
Chatham, the said office of Keeper of his Majesty's Privy Seal, from and
after the said term of six weeks, or other sooner determination of the said
commission.

† We have here another proof of the humility of Junius at one period to
this nobleman, a previous proof having already occurred in the Miscellaneous
Letter, No. 1, to the note appended to which we refer the reader.
    · In the Private Letter, No. 23, dated October 19, 1770, he still insinuates
his dislike; for in requesting the printer of the *Public Advertiser* to contradict his being the author of the letters subscribed *A Whig and an Englishman*, he adds, " I neither admire the writer *nor his idol*."   Who the writer
of these letters was we know not, but the *idol* was certainly Lord Chatham.
    In reality it was not till about the date of Letter 51, under his favourite
signature of Junius, that he began to think commendably of this nobleman.
"I am called upon," says he, in that Letter, "to deliver my opinion, and
surely it is not in the little censure of Mr. Horne to deter me from doing
signal justice to a man, *who, I confess, has grown upon my esteem*."¹

    ¹ All the needful elucidation of this commentary of Mason Good will be
found in notes, pp. 108-110.  It does not appear from any writing authentically identified with Junius, that he ever felt a strong aversion towards
Lord Chatham, but the reverse.—ED.

infinitely more material to inquire why the interregnum is not committed to people of a higher rank and character.

The establishment of the several high offices of state forms a natural and constitutional check upon the prerogative of the crown. No illegal or unconstitutional grant, charter, or patent of any kind, can take effect from the mere motion of the sovereign, but must pass through a number of offices, in each of which it is the duty of the officer, if the case requires it, to remonstrate to the crown, as he himself is answerable for the consequences of any public instrument which he has suffered to pass through his department. The delay of this progression has another good effect, in giving the subject time and opportunity to enter his protest against any sudden or inconsiderate grant, by which his own property, or the welfare of the country in general, may be affected, and to have the matter fairly discussed.

The precedence annexed to these high offices (exclusive of the importance of the several degrees of trust reposed in them) sufficiently proves that they ought to be confined to men of the first character and consequence. Men of that degree may safely be trusted, because they have a greater stake to hazard, and are answerable to the public with their lives and fortunes. The dignity of the lord privy seal's office (next in rank to the president of the council) would of itself be a sufficient reason for giving it to none but men of birth and character, and the great trust annexed to that dignity is a further reason for never committing such an office to any but men of the first rank and fortune. But in the choice of the present commissioners there seems to be something particularly and singularly improper. When a caveat is entered against a grant from the crown, and when a question of political and commercial importance is therefore to be discussed, can there be a higher insult to the public than to commit the determination of such a question to three persons very low in point of rank, and absolutely dependent in point of situation? Shall we not be justified in supposing that they are elected for no other quality but their insignificance? Whatever pretences may be alleged to the contrary, the public will have too much reason to suspect that these worthy commissioners are taught their lesson, and that the job is too dirty to be imposed upon gentlemen of a higher station than a clerk in office. I cannot believe that these persons could have been chosen by the Earl of Chatham. Whatever may be his faults, a man of spirit could no more lend his office than he could his mistress to the purposes of prostitution; much less would he descend to take either of them back again with a public mark of infamy upon them *.

Now, Sir, let us suppose these three respectable persons seated upon their tribunal, with two judges of England by their side, and the first lawyers of this country pleading before them upon a question of the first importance to this country: the judges, I doubt not, will sit in silent wonder at the judicial abilities of these great men, and silent they must be, unless a point of law should arise on which the triumvirate shall deign to ask their opinion; the lawyers will naturally exert their utmost efforts, when they consider that they have the honour to plead before three gentlemen of such profound knowledge, such distinguished rank, and such inflexible probity, that neither ignorance, nor ministerial influence, nor private corruption, can have any share in their decision.

I pity the unhappy Englishman, for he perhaps may blush for his situation.

* Lord Chatham, at this time, was suffering from severe indisposition, so much so that he was unable to use a pen. His continuing to hold the privy seal, while its duties were discharged by a commission, was justified by the earnest entreaty of the King, who was conscious of the influence of his name in strengthening the ministry. In a note, dated January 23, 1768, addressed to Lord Chatham by George III., he says:—

"I am thoroughly convinced of the utility you are to my service, for though confined to your house, your name has been sufficient to enable my administration to proceed. I therefore, in the most earnest manner, call upon you to continue in your employment; indeed my conduct towards you since your entering into my service gives me a double right to expect this of you, as well as what you owe your country, and those who entered into my service in conjunction with you."—*Chatham Correspondence*, vol. iii. p. 318.

But though Junius was partial to Chatham, he was not so to some of his colleagues, and cautions his Lordship against their underhand practices. See Appendix, Private Letter to the Earl, dated January 2, 1768.—ED.

## LETTER XIII.

### TO THE PRINTER OF THE PUBLIC ADVERTISER.

February 24, 1768.

Fluctus uti primo coepit cum albescere vento,
Paullatim sese tollit mare, et altius undas,
Erigit, inde imo consurgit ad aethera fundo.
VIRG. En. vii. 528.

SIR,

THE people of England are by nature somewhat phlegmatic. This complexional character is extremely striking, when contrasted with the suddenness and vivacity of many of our neighbours on the Continent. It even appears remarkable among the several kindred tribes which compose the great mass of the British Empire. The heat of the Welch, the impetuosity of the Irish, the acrimony of the Scotch, and the headlong violence of the Creolians, are national temperaments very different from that of the native genuine English.

This slowness of feeling is in some respects inconvenient: but, on the whole view of life, it has, I think, the advantage clearly on its side. Our countrymen derive from thence a firmness, an uniformity, and a perseverance in their designs, which enables them to conquer the greatest difficulties, and to arrive at the ultimate point of perfection in almost everything they undertake.

Their slowness to passion has also another advantage. No wise man will lightly venture to do them a real injury. Their anger is not suddenly kindled, nor easily extinguished: it is dark and gloomy; it is nourished to a gigantic size and vigour, under a silent meditation on their wrongs, until at last it arrives at such a mature and steady vehemence as becomes terrible indeed. It was on a consideration of this kind of character that a great poet says with a singular emphasis—"Beware the fury of a patient man."

It is surprising how much this character is exemplified in every part of our history. The long patience, amounting almost to tameness, with which the people of England have borne the outrages of evil ministers, has only been equalled by the irresistible force by which they attacked, and the

unrelenting severity with which they finally punished the
authors of their great grievances.

I wish with all my heart that our time may furnish no such
examples: and yet I confess my fears are excited by appearances that are sufficiently alarming.  The people of England
have seen an administration formed, almost avowedly, under
the direction of a dangerous, because private and unrespon-
sible, influence; and at the same time with an outward pre-
sidency of ministerial despotism, which by its very nature
annihilated all public council.  This they endured.  They
saw a course of the most scandalous and corrupt profusion of
public money that ever was known in the kingdom, attended
with such a neglect of every public duty as if an experiment
was intended, to try how far the state could subsist by its own
strength, without any of the usual aids of active government.
The people of England bore this likewise.

They saw the very first opportunity laid hold on to revive
the doctrines of a dispensing power, state necessity, arcana of
government, and all that clumsy machinery of exploded prerogative which it had cost our ancestors so much toil and
treasure, and blood, to break to pieces.  This we suffered
with our usual patience.  They saw an attempt made to render
all the monied property of the kingdom loose and insecure,
and to turn our national funds from being supports of public
credit into instruments of ministerial power, and to take away
that dependence upon law which had been in all ages the
great source of our domestic happiness, and that firm reliance
upon public faith which has been the means of making us
respectable to all the world.  The Englishman still continued
sullen and silent.

These very circumstances which strike terror into the
heart of a wise man are often such as inspire fools with
confidence and presumption.  Having had sufficient proof as
they thought of the passive disposition of their fellow-citizens,
and at a loss for precedents of despotism of a modern date in
any civilized country, they began to ransack the stores of
antiquated oppression, and ventured to perpetrate an act (by
a singular composition) of such consummate audacity and
meanness of spirit as it might well be thought impossible to
unite.

In subserviency to the odious influence under which they act, this administration dared—to an informer nearly allied to that very influence*; at the time, and for the purposes of an election; refusing to hear counsel; not daring to take the opinion of the King's law servants; denying access to the records in their possession—to pass a grant of the estate of a noble and most respectable person, derived from a king to whom we owe all our liberties; sixty-three years in undisputed possession, the subject of frequent settlements, and now actually a part of the jointure of the noble Duchess †.

The people of England at length began to break silence. They might indeed look upon the private wrong as a matter of inward meditation, and a further exercise of their patience. But the principle of this grant has given a SHOCK TO THE WHOLE LANDED PROPERTY OF ENGLAND.

Called upon by this practical menace to all landed property, and by many other detached grievances, arising from the same absurd and tyrannical principle, *that no length of possession secures against a claim of the crown*, one of the ablest, most virtuous, and most temperate men in the kingdom, supported by a steady band of uniform patriots, has made an attempt in a certain great assembly (without providing any remedy for this case of oppression), to secure the subject at least for the future against such wild and indefinite claims.

Such was the spirit which manifested itself upon that occasion that, though for the present, after a glorious struggle, they have failed, there is no sort of doubt that the cry of reason, justice, policy, and the general feeling of the people, will shortly prevail ‡; and the rather, as this discussion has brought to light further designs of the most extraordinary nature, and such as will, if not timely prevented, spread

* The informer was the late Earl of Lonsdale, at that time Sir James Lowther, who had married a daughter of Lord Bute, whose *influence* is here alluded to. The estate belonged to the Duke of Portland. See Letter 57, vol. i. p. 401, and note.

† Duchess of Portland.

‡ By a bill called the Quieting Bill, and which was again brought forward by Sir G. Savile in the following year, and carried. But see the subject further elucidated, and the final determination of the Court of Exchequer on the suit pending between Sir James Lowther and the Duke of Portland, in the note to Junius's Letters, No. 57, vol. I. p. 401.

distraction from one end of the kingdom to the other.  My
next will be on that important subject.

MNEMON.

---

## LETTER XIV.

March 4, 1768.

> " Oh, wretched state !    O bosom black as death !
>   O limed soul that, struggling to be free,
>   Art more encaged ! "

SHAKSPEARE.

SIR,

INNOCENCE, even in its crudest simplicity, has some advantages over the most dexterous and practised guilt.  Equivocal
appearances may, to be sure, accidentally attend it in its progress through the world ; but the very scrutiny which these
appearances will excite, operates in favour of innocence ;
which is secure the moment it is discovered.  But guilt is
a poor helpless dependent being.  Without the alliance of
able, diligent, and, let me add, fortunate fraud, it is inevitably
undone.  If the guilty culprit be obstinately silent, his silence
forms a deadly presumption against him.    If he speaks,
talking tends to discovery ; and his very defence often furnishes materials towards his conviction.

This has been exactly the case of those unhappy men (the
ministry), in that apology for their conduct, which they choose
to complicate with their opposition to the settlement of the
national property.    Nobody not originally acquainted with
the bottom of their proceedings was able to discern the true
nature and full extent of their crime, until we had seen upon
what principles they grounded their defence.

It is worth while to lay this affair a little more open.    The
maxim of *Nullum Tempus occurrit Regi* *, that *no length of
continuance, or good faith of possession, is available against a
claim of the crown*, has been long the opprobrium of prerogative and the disgrace of our law.    The ablest writers in that

---

* The commencement of the obsolete law which in this case was appealed
to by the minister ; hence called the Nullum Tempus Law.

profession have ever mentioned it with abhorrence; the best judges have always cast an odium upon it, as being fundamentally contrary to natural equity and all the maxims of a free government; and a superior genius, a great light of the age*, has not long since endeavoured to give it as great a check as judicature, unaided by legislative powers, is able to interpose.

The truth is, this prerogative has hitherto owed its existence principally to its disuse. It was an engine at once so formidable to the people and so dangerous to those who should attempt to handle it, that it never was considered amongst the instruments of a *wise minister*. It remained, like an old piece of cannon I have heard of somewhere, of an enormous size, which stood upon a ruinous bastion, and which was seldom or never fired, for fear of bringing down the fortification for whose defence it was intended.

But constituted as administration is at present, where real power is invested in one hand and responsible office placed in another, from the security of the former situation, and from the servile dependence of the latter, it is no wonder that hazardous measures should be commanded without fear, and that they should be executed, though with the utmost trepidation and reluctance. From thence arose that desperate proceeding which has given such an universal alarm to property.

Upon the first attack on that rotten part of prerogative (out of whose corruption the late northern grant was generated) the ministers found themselves entirely at a loss. To defend their *Nullum Tempus* upon principles of liberty, or even upon principles of justice, was a thing clearly impossible. To abandon it without reflecting on their past conduct, and without giving up their future projects, was a point of equal difficulty. It seems that they had hoarded up those unmeaning powers of the crown as a grand military magazine, towards the breaking the fortunes and depressing the spirit of the nobility, for drawing the common people from their reliance on the natural interests of the country to an immediate dependence on the crown, and principally for enabling ministers, public or secret, to domineer and give the law in all future elections. They thought their scheme would then

* Sir George Savile.

be complete if the votes of freeholders, the very means which our ancestors had provided as the great security to our freedom, could be converted into the most certain instruments of the public servitude.

It was evident that, when they refused to give up this barbarous maxim, it was their intention to make some sort of use of it. Such a conclusion could not in any way be evaded. In this strait they took the part of avowing that they did intend to find some employment for their favourite prerogative, which, after so long a trance, they had thought proper to disenchant and to set in action. It was then their business to find some excuse for themselves, and some pretence of public utility for their system.

On this occasion they built upon two grounds very well worthy of the reader's utmost attention. The first I shall now point out; the latter and most important would transgress the limits of your paper. It shall be reserved for another opportunity.

The first they did was totally to disclaim their own *free agency*. In the highest department of the state, they declared themselves to be mere creatures of execution. They asserted that they were, in all matters of this sort, entirely subservient to an officer hitherto little heard of, but from henceforth to be a name of dreadful note in this country, THE SURVEYOR GENERAL. It is their system that, if *informers* (be they who they may, in circumstances of indigence to make any desperate attempt, or of wealth and power to combat the great and crush the poor) can contrive to obtain the surveyor's report in their favour, ministers are *obliged*, without further inquiry, to grant to them patents to vex, harass, impoverish, possibly to ruin, any honest proprietor in the kingdom.

It is true that they supported themselves in this perverse doctrine by no one argument from law, usage, or common sense; but it is their system; and it is mentioned here, not to show the depth of their understanding, but the malignity of their designs: for if once they could come to establish this their favourite point, things would stand thus:—The *surveyor general*, who keeps all the crown titles (*inaccessible to the subject*), has a hint to find a weak part in some old possession—say of sixty, say of two hundred years. A court *favourite* has a hint to become an informer, a character no way incompatible

with his own; then all the rest follows of course.  The Lords
of the Treasury *must* obey the informer and make the reference; the surveyor *must* obey the Treasury and report; and
then the Treasury in their turn *must* obey the surveyor and
direct the grant.  The whole system moves, according to the
preordained laws of despotism, in a circle of strict *necessity* *.

In this procedure who can convict the *surveyor general*
of corrupt activity or obedience?  He is only bound to prove
that the lands in question have been, in some former age, in
the hands of the Crown.  This is not difficult; all the lands
of the kingdom have been so.  It is his duty, according to the
present prerogative doctrines, not to discover, or to suffer to
be discovered, anything which may tend to clear and settle the
right of the subject.  He may have that in his office which
would establish the very title he attempts to overthrow; but
fairness in *his* situation is held to be a breach of trust, because
the *Crown* is always considered by these gentlemen, with
respect to the *subject*, as an *adverse party;* and to exist in a
state of *unremitting and immortal litigation* with the people.

Thus a mutual obedience and a common impunity is established between these two great powers, the Treasury and the
surveyor, grounded on the favourite principle of *necessity.*
The only free agent in the whole transaction is the *informer;*
but he is not only as dispunishable as the others, but is highly
meritorious into the bargain, for discovering what, in their
prerogative jargon, is called a *concealment;* that is to say, in

* In a debate which took place in the House of Commons, February 27,
1771, on a motion made by Sir William Meredith, to repeal a clause in the
*Bill of Quiet*, which passed in the year 1768, Lord North thus defends himself from the grant in question :—
    "The honourable gentleman [Mr. Cornwall, afterwards Speaker of the
House of Commons] has revived in my memory a grant which passed since
I had the honour of holding the seal of the Exchequer, and which seal I am
proud to own was affixed by me to the grant in question.  This he calls an
abominable act; but in the situation I then was, and still am, I thought
myself bound to pass it by every principle of duty to the Crown, as the
servant of the Crown, and bound still more strongly by that duty which I
owe to the public as steward of the public estate, as far as it is entrusted to
me.  It is my glory that I passed the grant; and as often as mention of it
is made, so often shall I think that honour imputed to me."  Notwithstanding
Lord North's boast upon the occasion, the grant was ultimately set aside by
the Court of Exchequer, on the ground that a *quit-rent* of *thirteen* and *four-
pence* was not an adequate third part of its clear yearly value.

plain English, the ancient possession and inheritance of a valuable and loyal subject.  By all these means *an office of inquisition is established in the true inquisitorial spirit, and with genuine inquisitorial powers, over all the landed property of England.*  The use proposed to be made of it will be the subject of my next paper.

In the mean time it is a matter of very serious consideration to observe the growth of arbitrary and despotic principles in this country.  There is such a pernicious vigour in their vegetation, and such a rank luxuriance in the soil, that when they seem to be cut up even by the roots, they will suddenly shoot up in some other place, and under some other and perhaps more dangerous appearance.  Suppress them under the shape of *general warrants* or *seizure of papers*, they will start up in the form of *dispensing powers, forfeiture of charters, violations of public faith, establishments of private monopolies,* and *raising up antiquated titles for the crown.*  There is a consideration still more melancholy: that many persons\*, apostatizing from their principle, betraying their associates, and combining with their adversaries, make no other use of the credit they have derived from their former activity in the cause of freedom, than that they may approach it without suspicion, and wound it beyond all possibility of cure.

MNEMON.

---

## LETTER XV.

TO THE PRINTER OF THE PUBLIC ADVERTISER.

March 11, 1768

> What aileth thee, Mnemon ?
> Why art thou so disquieted ?
> And why is thy understanding troubled !

Is it not very extraordinary, Mr. Printer, that the parts and abilities of *Mnemon* should be prostituted to the licentious abuse of the highest and most honourable board in this king dom, composed of persons of the most unimpeached characters, because they have dared to grant some crown lands to Sir James Lowther, not comprehended in that of King William

* The Drke of Grafton is the person here alluded to.

to one of his Dutch imports, but usurped and illegally withheld by them?

Can any one review the parliamentary debates of that æra, and not be fired at the glorious spirit exerted by the Commons of England against the enormous grant of crown lands made to the Dutch favourites of that monarch? Was not the most scandalous partiality shown to them in prejudice to the people of this country? Were not honours and riches heaped upon them with unexampled profusion? Whence, in the name of God, all this clamour? What is it to the public whether a Bentinck or a Lowther succeeds? Are not the courts of law open to determine it? Can it be a subject for faction or a pretext for abuse? No, Sir; be assured the arrows wound not; the breast fraught with conscious worth feels not the shafts of envy.

ANTI VAN TEAGUE.

## LETTER XVI.

### TO THE PRINTER OF THE PUBLIC ADVERTISER.

Sir,      March 24, 1769.

Your correspondent, *Anti van Teague*, in your paper of Friday se'nnight, has undertaken a task far, I am afraid, above his abilities. His inclination I believe to be very good, but *non tali auxilio, nec defensoribus istis——Tempus eget*. If *Nullum Tempus* and the late most extraordinary and alarming use made of it is now to be defended, I would advise that most honourable board, composed (as *Anti van Teague* says) of persons of the most unimpeached characters, to hire abler advocates for its defence. Uncommon parts and no vulgar eloquence are required to subdue the fears and quiet the apprehensions of all the landed property of these kingdoms. When that most honourable board shall next think fit to bestow another estate upon a Lowther, or any other informer, wonderful no doubt will be the contented acquiescence of the person robbed when he is assured that what is taken from him to gratify the Scotch favourite of to-day, was given some hundred years ago by the Crown to a Dutch favourite of that time. Surely, Sir, the noble D—ke who is the present sufferer must feel great satisfaction in finding the sins of his ancestors visited upon him. A Stuart has at length risen up to avenge upon the memory of King William, and the descendants of all those who embarked with him in the once glorious cause, the injuries and sufferings of that once (but now no longer) hateful name.

We have lived, Sir, to see an advocate for the ministry of George the Third defending their actions and justifying their conduct by asserting, not that their actions are just and their conduct clear, but that their injustice falls heavy on the posterity alone of those who, by their arms and their counsel, assisted our great deliverer to effect that revolution to which, and which alone, we owe the establishment of his present Majesty's most illustrious and royal family on the throne of these kingdoms.

What *Anti van Teague* means by unimpeached characters I cannot readily guess. I suppose he means the public character of the ministers, or rather of the minister*. His private character I do not meddle with; but to call his character unimpeached who is not only charged with, but to the sense of every impartial person convicted of, the most daring and flagitious attacks upon the liberty and property of his fellow-subjects, is really surprising.

Is the revival of the suspending and dispensing powers of the Crown an experiment of curiosity alone? But for that he has in the most solemn manner been pardoned by an act of parliament, and therefore probably that will not make part of his impeachment. Is his open and wicked interference in elections, by threats and bribery, manifest to the whole nation (though his reverend instrument was acquitted), to be accounted no more than a good-natured solicitude for his friends?

Are his violent attacks upon the monied and landed property of the people nothing more than dutiful exertions of his power to pay on one hand the debts of the civil list, and on the other hand to raise support, and extend that hidden, pernicious, and unconstitutional influence, in which, and by which, he lives, and moves, and has his being?

Is his lavish and wasteful profusion of the public property

* The Duke of Grafton.

in pensions, reversions, grants, and monopolies, a decent and
becoming reward to those who have been, or are willing to be,
his tools and creatures?

Is his activity in corruption and oppression, and his perfect
idleness in, and neglect of, all public and national business, a
spirited exertion on one hand and a needful repose on the
other?

I have, you see, Sir, not meddled with his private character.
I leave that for him to *earth* in whenever he is hard run, according to the laudable example of his Chancellor of the Exchequer*. Let him resemble the great demi-gods of antiquity,
who had also two characters; and whilst one half of them was
taken up to heaven, the other half found its way to hell. I
shall only advise *Anti van Teague* to recommend it to his
patron not to trust too much to his double capacity, lest, at
some odd turn, he may find his *private person* so involved in
his *public character*, that the sharpest axe and the most dexterous operator may not be able to avenge the nation upon the
*last* without doing some small prejudice to the *first.*

I am, &c.,

Not yet an enemy to the revolution,

ANTI-STUART.

---

## LETTER XVII.

### TO THE PRINTER OF THE PUBLIC ADVERTISER.

April 5, 1768.

* Vivit I imò verò etiam in senatum venit : fit publici consilii particeps :
notat, et limis designat oculis ad cædem unumquemque nostrum."

CICERO in CATILINAM.

SIR,

THE return of Mr. Wilkes to England, and the measures he
has since pursued, have given the servants of the Crown an
opportunity of acting in a manner so becoming themselves,
that it would be ingratitude not to take notice of their extraordinary merits upon this occasion†. Our gracious Sovereign

* Lord North.
† The return of Mr. Wilkes was anything but agreeable to the ministers;
they had repulsed his first advances (p. 10?), and kept him at Paris by a
vote of £1,000 per annum, raised privately among themselves. It was

undoubtedly thinks himself highly indebted to his ministers for their uncommon care of his honour and dignity, as well as for their attention to the security of his house, family, and sacred person; and I may venture to assure them that the public in general have a just sense of the vigour and spirit with which they have administered the laws, and with which the peaceable part of his Majesty's subjects have been protected. What sort of thanks they will receive from their Sovereign I cannot tell; but, as far as my weak endeavours can reach, the nation shall not remain unapprised of the extent and species of our obligations to them.

A man of a most infamous character in private life is indicted for a libel against the King's person, solemnly tried by his peers according to the laws of the land, and found guilty *. To avoid the sentence due to his crime he flies to a

the divulging of this bargain by Horne Tooke that originated the bitter quarrel between them. But Wilkes was tired of exile, and eager to avail himself of the impending dissolution of parliament. Having failed on the former occasion with ministers, he resolved on this to try their royal master, addressing a supplicatory letter to the King. It was replete with loyalty and devotion, concluding as follows :—

"With a heart full of zeal for the service of your Majesty and my country, I implore, Sire, your clemency. My only hopes of pardon are founded in the great goodness and benevolence of your Majesty ; and every day's freedom you may be graciously pleased to permit me the enjoyment of in my dear native land shall give proofs of my zeal and attachment to your service."

Of course he received no answer ; indeed (Correspondence of Wilkes, vol. iii. p. 205) he neglected the established etiquette in the mode of transmission, sending his application by a common footman to the Queen's palace, in lieu of conveying it by the medium of one of the responsible ministers of the Crown, the only constitutional channel through which the King could receive or acknowledge it.—Ed.

* It has already appeared in several instances that Junius, subsequently to the present date, espoused the cause of Mr. Wilkes, or rather strenuously upheld him in the contest with the ministry upon the very subject adverted to in this letter. Yet the political conduct of Junius was perhaps strictly and unimpeachably uniform. He had at first, indeed, conceived a personal dislike to Mr. Wilkes, in consequence of his strenuous resistance to the general warrant which was served upon him during the administration in which Mr. George Grenville was Chancellor of the Exchequer, for whom, whether in office or out of office, Junius ever manifested the strongest partiality. But in the present instance, Wilkes is only adverted to as an instrument of attack upon an administration which Junius abominated ; and as soon as he found that he could support this attack better by enlisting this gentleman in

foreign country, and, failing to surrender himself to justice, is outlawed. By this outlawry he loses all claim to the protection of those magistrates and of those laws to which, by his evasion, he had refused to be amenable. After some years spent abroad, this man returns to England with as little fear of the laws which he had violated as of respect for the great person whom he had wantonly and treasonably attacked. Without a single qualification, either moral or political, and under the greatest disability, this man presumes so far upon the protection of the populace as to offer himself a candidate to represent the metropolis of the kingdom. Disappointed in this attempt, notwithstanding all the efforts and violence of the rabble, he has still the confidence to offer himself to the freeholders of Middlesex as a proper person to represent a county in which he has not a single foot of land; and, to complete the whole, we see a man overwhelmed with debts, a convict and an outlaw, returned to serve in the British parliament as knight of a shire. These, Sir, are the main facts of Mr. Wilkes's case. The circumstances with which they were attended are no less atrocious. We saw the other candidates, gentlemen of large fortune and of the most respectable characters, dragged from their carriages, and hardly escaping with life out of the hands of Mr. Wilkes's friends and companions. If the candidates were treated in this manner, you may imagine what sort of reception their friends met with in attempting to poll for them. The fact is that great numbers were driven back by main force or deterred by the threats of the populace, so that not a third part of the friends of Sir William Proctor and Mr. Cooke were ever permitted to approach the hustings. The conclusion of Monday and Tuesday night was perfectly consistent with the whole proceedings of the day. I need not enlarge upon this detestable scene, since there is hardly a family in London or Westminster which has not had reason to remember the day of Mr. Wilkes's

his favour than by continuing in opposition to him, he shrewdly took measures for such a purpose, and was fortunate enough to succeed.

There is the same apparent inconsistency in his being ultimately the friend of Lord Camden, who is here held up to public odium, and to Lord Chatham, after having as warmly opposed him. But his change of opinion concerning these noblemen was by no means a sudden flight; it grew upon him slowly, and was the result of their own change of conduct.

election.  The metropolis of the kingdom, the seat of justice, and the residence of the Sovereign and of the royal family, were left, for two nights together, at the mercy of a licentious, drunken rabble, without the smallest guard, either civil or military, to secure the King's person or to protect his subjects. Amidst all the horror and outrage of these transactions, is there one Englishman endowed with the smallest portion of reason or humanity, who can hear without grief and resentment that, even in some of the royal palaces, to avoid worse consequences, illuminations were made to celebrate the success of a ——, who, after heaping every possible insult on the person of his sovereign, returns in triumph to brave and outrage him again, even in the place of his immediate residence!

Such was the scene of which all the inhabitants of London and Westminster were witnesses to their cost.  Let us now inquire what has been the conduct of the ministry during the course of it.  Long before Mr. Wilkes appeared at Guildhall, it was well known that he was in London; and, if any measures had been taken by the ministry to secure him in consequence of his outlawry, it might undoubtedly have been done with the greatest facility.  Why no process was sued for out of the Court of King's Bench let the ministers answer if they can. But they have much more to answer for.  They are responsible for all the consequences of permitting this outlaw to appear at large, and for all the violences of which he has since been the author.  By their indolence and neglect, or perhaps in consequence of a secret compact with him, this man has been suffered to throw the metropolis into a flame, to offer new outrages to his Sovereign, and at last to force his way into parliament, where, if he were a man of any parliamentary abilities, I doubt not but he would reward them as they deserve.  In the midst of all this tumult and confusion, the Chancellor of Great Britain * and the first Lord of the Treasury † retire out of town, and leave the whole executive power of the crown to fall to the ground.  In the name of God and the laws, are such men fit to govern a great kingdom? To say that they are, is an insult to the common understanding of mankind, and I hope our gracious sovereign will do

---

* Lord Camden.                    † The Duke of Grafton.

justice to himself and to his people, by depriving them of a power which they have either not courage or not honesty enough to exert in his service.   I am persuaded there is not a man of property, sense, or honour in this country, who is not ready, heart and hand, to support the constitution, and to defend the sovereign, though his own immediate servants have deserted him.   We have hitherto taken no steps for our defence, because we expected the protection of government; but we are still strong enough to defend our lives and properties against Mr. Wilkes and his banditti; nor shall the treacherous example set us by the ministry, ever induce us to abandon our own rights, or those of the chief magistrate.

C*.

## LETTER XVIII.

### TO THE PRINTER OF THE PUBLIC ADVERTISER.

Sir,                                                April 5, 1769.

THERE is something so extraordinary in the conduct of the ministry, with respect to Mr. Wilkes, that I cannot help suspecting they have a secret motive for it, which the public is not aware of.   It is to me inconceivable that he should have been suffered to return to England, and remain at large, notwithstanding his outlawry; to offer himself a candidate for the metropolis; to appear the leader of violence and riot uncontrolled; and at last to succeed in his enterprise at Brentford; unless all this had been done with the connivance and consent of the King's servants.   My suspicions may perhaps be ill founded, but I think there is reason enough to apprehend that Mr. Wilkes would never have been permitted to go such lengths if all were well between the ministry and the Earl of Bute.   They certainly have a design to terrify the Scotchman, and to keep him in order, by producing their tribune once more upon the stage.   Let the Thane look to himself!   Mr. Wilkes, being a man of no sort of consequence in his own person, can never be supported but by keeping up the cry, and this cry can no way be maintained but by renew-

---

* The editor has already had occasion to observe in various places that C. was the signature adopted by Junius in his private correspondence with the printer of the *Public Advertiser*.   See more especially the private letters C. passim.

ing his attacks upon the Scotch favourite and his countrymen.
With this key we may, perhaps, account for the supineness
and indifference with which the ministry have seen the laws
trampled on, and the public peace and tranquillity destroyed,
by the respectable Mr. Wilkes, and his no less respectable
friends.

Yours,

Q IN THE CORNER.

---

## LETTER XIX.

April 12, 1768.

"The common law hath so admeasured the King's prerogatives that they
should not take away nor prejudice the inheritance of any."

COKE's INSTITUTES.

SIR,

THE extraordinary purpose to which an old maxim, or rather
dictum, of the common law, has lately been applied by the
commissioners of the Treasury, has led me to consider upon
what principles it was originally founded, and whether it be
applicable to the present circumstances of the British constitution.  A resumption of lands held under a supposed grant
from the crown, after a possession of near fourscore years,
was an alarming measure to every English gentleman of
landed property, but the principle on which it was defended
was formidable enough to strike a terror into men of all ranks
who had either estates or liberty to lose.  A ministry determined to invade the liberties or property of the subject,
may, in our law books, find antiquated maxims to support the
most violent stretches of prerogative; and if it be admitted
that no length of possession is good against the crown, I
hardly know that right or privilege, much less any tract of
soil possessed by the subject, which may not be disputed or
resumed at the pleasure of the sovereign.  It has been a
fashion with some writers to represent the feudal government
as a system of liberty; but I must confess that a constitution
wherein the king is supposed to be the original owner of all
the lands; wherein we have seen the nobility at perpetual
war with the sovereign, and bringing their vassals into the
field against him, or against one another; and wherein the
whole body of the people was held in absolute dependence

upon the petty tyrants, does not present to me the idea of
political liberty in any part of it. The greatest commendation it deserves is, perhaps, that it was capable of improvement. Accordingly it has been so altered and so mended
that a man must be well read in law to discover any trace of
it in the present form of our government; and I am justified
by modern statutes in asserting, that we never thought our
constitution completely settled upon the basis of freedom
until every mark of feudal services and dependence was
abolished by parliament.

But though great improvements have been made, there
remains yet a great deal to be done: and if the crown be
permitted to recur to maxims of law which prevailed when a
system of government subsisted very different from the
present, the most arbitrary measures may still pass for a
legal exertion of the royal prerogative. I am still the king's
liege man, and may be sent from one part of the country to
the other, from the care of my family and affairs, and perhaps
in my absence a *nullum tempus* may deprive me of my estate.
The argument alleged by lawyers in favour of their own rule,
that no delay shall bar the king's right, (viz. "because the
law intends that the king is always busied for the public good,
therefore has not leisure to assert his right within the times
limited to subjects,") will hardly bear a strict examination,
especially if referred to the present establishment. Either it
is not well founded in fact, or the reasoning on which it
depends will prove too much. It is not true at this day, and
I doubt whether it ever were true, that the law (which is the
solemn sense and opinion of the people) supposes the king so
continually employed about public affairs as to be entitled
to an extraordinary indulgence in the neglect of those precautions which concern the private interests of the crown. If,
indeed, the king were supposed to transact and govern the
affairs of the kingdom in his own person; or if he had not a
number of officers whose duty it is to take care of and transact
every business relative to his private rights, and private property, an indulgence of this nature to a chief magistrate, so
much employed, and so little assisted, might not be thought
very unreasonable. But when, on the one hand, the ministers
of the crown are alone responsible for the conduct of public
affairs; and when, on the other, it is the business of the
treasury, of the exchequer, of the land surveyors, and of a

multitude of other officers to oversee and manage the revenues
and distribution of the crown lands, I hold it to be highly unconstitutional, as well as absurd, to introduce the person of the
sovereign as claiming an indulgence to himself for neglects
which are properly the neglects of his servants.    But admitting the excuse of public employment for private negligence
to be valid, let us see how far it will reach.    If the sovereign,
on account of his high occupations, be entitled to such a
privilege, his ministers certainly have a claim to their share
of it.    The lords, who are hereditary counsellors of the crown;
the judges; every member of the House of Commons; and
ambassadors sent abroad, may all plead public employment;
nor can there be any good reason alleged why every officer
engaged in the public service, from the high chancellor down
to the bum-bailiff, should not be allowed his proportion of
*nullum tempus*, according to their several ranks, and the time
they continue in employment.    But it were endless to refute
arguments which have neither truth nor meaning.

The maxim, that *nullum tempus occurrit regi*, if ever, could
only be true under the feudal government *.    It was then a
national interest to preserve the royal demesne entire, because
the support of the royal dignity depended upon it.   The king,
out of this revenue, defrayed the expense of his family and
government, and never applied for aids to the people but
upon pretence of extraordinary emergencies.    By preserving
this separate property to the king, the people in effect preserved their own, and therefore admitted without reluctance
a maxim introduced by the lawyers of the crown, since it
tended to deter individuals from invading a branch of royal
revenue, any deficiency in which must have been made good
out of the public stock.    Nothing less than a reason of this
public nature could have procured submission to a doctrine
full of hardship and oppression to the subject, and which, in
favour of the crown, directly contradicted those rules of
common law by which the possession of property between
man and man was secured.

* The reasoning of this writer on the feudal consequences of the old law
maxim, that no " delay will bar the right of the Crown," is ingenious, but has
ceased to be of legal force.    In civil actions, relating even to landed property,
the Queen, like a subject, is limited to sixty years; and after fifty-five
years' possession a grant from the Crown may be presumed, unless a statute
has prohibited such a grant.—ED.

To revive and enforce a maxim of this sort, when not one
of the reasons subsist on which it was originally founded,
when the king's family and government are supported by a
fixed revenue of eight hundred thousand pounds raised upon
the people, is certainly a most unwarrantable and a most
dangerous attempt. Under the present board of treasury,
the reign of Empson and Dudley seems to flourish again;
and where is the man who can say his liberty or his property
is secure to him if antiquated doctrines and obsolete laws
may be brought to life at the breath of a young, inconsiderate,
arbitrary minister, and sent abroad to attack every subject
whom he shall think proper to call an enemy to government?
A minister capable of recommending such measures to the
crown, calls to my mind the idea which our ancestors had of
some black magician conjuring up infernal spirits from the
depths of the earth and of the sea, and letting them loose to
the destruction of mankind. Delusions of this sort have
indeed been long since exploded; but there are other diabolical arts, which certainly do exist, which ministers practise
but which I hope will be as little able to maintain themselves
against the improved understanding and well-directed firmness of the English nation *.

C.

---

## LETTER XX.

### For the Public Advertiser.

April 23, 1766.

#### TO HIS GRACE THE DUKE OF GRAFTON†.

Is it enough that Abra should be great
In the wall'd palace or the rural seat?
Oh, no ! Jerusalem combined must see
My open shame and boasted infamy.

My Lord,

Permit me to congratulate your Grace upon a piece of good

* This may or may not be a letter of Junius; but the general tenour of
its reasoning is congenial to him. He might be opposed to the ministry, and
yet not to Lord Chatham; although Lord Chatham was the chief cause of
ministerial weakness, his continued indisposition preventing his acting effi-
ciently in its direction.—Ed.

† This may be a letter of Junius, but not in his best style; it is redolent
of his sympathies and aversions, and its material was often re-dressed with
augmented piquancy.—Ed.

fortune which few men, of the best established reputation,
have been able to attain to.   The most accomplished persons
have usually some defect, some weakness in their characters,
which diminishes the lustre of their brighter qualifications.
Tiberius had his forms; Charteris now and then deviated
into honesty; and even Lord Bute prefers the simplicity of
seduction to the poignant pleasures of a rape.   But yours, my
Lord, is a perfect character: through every line of public and
of private life you are consistent with yourself.   After doing
everything, in your public station, that a minister might
reasonably be ashamed of, you have determined, with a noble
spirit of uniformity, to mark your personal history by such
strokes as a gentleman, without any great disgrace to his
assurance, might be permitted to blush for.   I had already
conceived a high opinion of your talents and disposition.
Whether the property of the subject, or the general rights of
the nation were to be invaded; or whether you were tired of
one lady, and chose another for the honourable companion of
your pleasures; whether it was a horse-race, or a hazard-table,
a noble disregard of forms seemed to operate through all your
conduct.   But you have exceeded my warmest expectations.
Highly as I thought of you, your Grace must pardon me when
I confess that there was one effort which I did not think you
equal to.   I did not think you capable of exhibiting the lovely
Thais * at the opera-house, of sitting a whole night by her
side, of calling for her carriage yourself, and of leading her to
it through a crowd of the first men and women in this kingdom.   To a mind like yours, my Lord, such an outrage to
your wife, such a triumph over decency, such insult to the
company, must have afforded the highest gratification.   When
all the ordinary resources of pleasure were exhausted, this, I
presume, was your *norissima voluptas.*   It is of a lasting
nature, my Lord, and I dare say will give you as much
pleasure upon reflection, as it did in the enjoyment.   After
so honourable an achievement, a poet's imagination could add
but one ray more to the lustre of your character.   Obtain a
divorce†, marry the lady, and I do not doubt but Mr.

* Miss Parsons, afterwards Lady Maynard.
† The Duke of Grafton was, subsequently to the date of this letter, divorced
from Miss Liddel, then Duchess of Grafton, and married, not the lady in

Bradshaw will be civil enough to give her away, with an honest, artless smile of approbation.

---

## LETTER XXI.

TO THE PRINTER OF THE PUBLIC ADVERTISER.

Sir,                                                April 23, 1768.

If I were to characterize the present ministry from any single virtue which shines predominant in their administration, I should fix upon *duplicity* as the proper word to express it.

I would not here be misunderstood: I do not by this mean only the little sneaking quality, commonly called double-dealing, which every pettifogging rascal may attain to, but that real *duplicity* of character which our ministers have assumed to themselves, by which every member of their body acts in two distinct capacities, and, Janus-like, bears two faces and two tongues, either of which may give the lie to the other without danger to his reputation.

This is the present catholic political faith, which, unless a man believes, he shall not get a place ; and if people would attend to this, they would be able to account for many of our great men's actions, which are unaccountable any other way.

By this rule a man may say as a judge that the loss of an Englishman's liberty for twenty-four hours only is grievous beyond estimation ; and then as a minister may declare, that forty days' tyranny is a trifling burthen, which any Englishman may bear*.

As a member of parliament, a man may give his word that a certain bill shall be dropped; and the next day, as a chancellor of the exchequer, may bring it into the house.

A first lord of the treasury may declare upon his honour that he has no concern in India stock; but there is nothing in this to hinder him as a private man from having a share with any young lady of *virtue* to the amount of 20,000*l*.

In those cases, you see, the duplicity of character in which

question, but Miss Wrottesley, niece to the Duchess of Bedford. See Junius, Letter 12, vol. i. p. 153.

* In allusion to Lord Camden's opinion upon the power of the Crown to suspend an Act of Parliament. See the subject further discussed in Junius, Letter 60, vol. i. p. 471.

they act covers the parties from all sort of blame; but I will
now do honour to the noble Duke, who, from under the foot-
stool of gouty legs*, has crept into the elbow chair, who,
though green in years, is ripe in devices.   It is he who has
carried this double-faced virtue to its greatest pitch.   He has
not only practised it with great success in public affairs, but
has also lately introduced it into dealings between man and
man.

Everybody knows the story of *nullum tempus*, and the application of it to rob the Duke of Portland of 30,000*l*.   The
Duke of Grafton (as set forth in a case lately published) upon
a representation, before any proceedings were had in the
affair, did actually promise to the Duke of Portland, "That
no step should be taken towards the decision of the matter in
question till his Grace's title should be stated, referred to, and
reported on by the proper officer, and fully and maturely considered by the board of treasury."   Had the Duke of Portland
been fully apprised of the new doctrine of the twofold state of
ministers, he would have considered this promise (as it was
really meant) as illusory, and only an expedient to lull him
asleep while the business was going on.   But his Grace knew
no more of this maxim than if he had been an India director,
and thought that a promise was a promise in whatever character it was given; so while he, in full confidence, was preparing the proofs of his right, the affair in dispute was given
away, and the new grant to Sir James Lowther made out,
signed and sealed in the treasury, without ever "his Grace's
title being stated, referred to, or reported on, by the proper
officer, or fully and maturely considered by the board."

Lest any one should think that I partially ascribe this conduct of the Duke of Grafton to my favourite principle of two
natures, when it ought to be laid to some other of his Grace's
virtues, I shall here quote a reply to the Duke of Portland's
case, lately published (as it is said) under the auspices of the
treasury, where this doctrine is defended with equal modesty
and truth.   The writer begins by admitting the promise,
which he says was *inadvertently* given by the Duke of Grafton ; but then, says he, " since he was the king's servant, and
had no title to the making this promise, he perceived he was

---

* Lord Chatham's.

not in honour bound to adhere to it." Now here is a fair
distinction between the king's servant and the man of honour,
a distinction which, I believe, few people at present are disposed to deny. His Grace (who has undoubtedly very delicate
perceptions) perceived that as a king's minister he was not
bound to keep a promise which he had made as a private
man; and in this (continues the pamphleteer) "he can be
supported by the soundest casuists." I am not deeply read
in authors of that professed title, but I remember seeing Busenbaum, Suarez, Molina, and a score of other *Jesuitical books,
burnt at Paris for their sound casuistry* by the hands of the
common hangman *. I do not know that they have yet found

---

* All kinds of strange conclusions have been drawn from the above
sentence relative to the burning of the Jesuits' books, in reference to who
were likely to have been present as spectators of the conflagration. A decree of the Parliament of Paris, dated August 6, 1761, had ordered that
certain books by Jesuits should be burnt, in the palace yard at the foot of
the great staircase, by the common hangman, "as seditious, destructive of
every principle of Christian morality, teaching a murderous and abominable
doctrine, not only against the safety of the lives of the subjects, but also
against that of the sacred persons of sovereigns." The works condemned
were chiefly those of Busenbaum and his commentator Lacroix. The decree
was executed August 7, 1761. There had been previous burnings of the
books of Busenbaum, namely, in 1757 and 1758, and there may have been
others later than that of 1761. It follows that if Bifrons was Junius,
Junius was in Paris at this date; and if Sir Philip Francis was Junius,
Francis was in Paris. But Francis is not known to have been in Paris that
year; he is known to have been with Lord Kinnoul at Lisbon, from which
city he returned to England in October. Therefore, according to Mr.
Coventry, who first raised the objection, and was followed by Mr. Barker
with other anti-Francisans, Sir Philip Francis could not have been Junius.
But the superstructure falls to the ground at once by removing the foundation.
Is there any evidence that Bifrons was Junius? We believe none; nor has
Mr. Good adduced any. Junius himself has nowhere said that he ever witnessed a burning of books in Paris. Bifrons' epistle has no signs of Junius;
it is loose in style, desultory and unconnected, and has nothing in common
with that great writer, excepting his dislike to the Duke of Grafton. It
may be doubted, indeed, whether Bifrons was an Englishman, or even an
Irishman; he certainly could not have been a British subject in 1761, unless
he was a prisoner of war, for in that year we were at hot war with France.
But if a prisoner of war, how unlikely that he could be at Paris to witness
an *auto da fé* of heretical books; he would have been confined in the interior of the kingdom, not left at large to indulge his curiosity in the capital.
Unquestionably Bifrons is spurious.
Mr. Bohn, the publisher of the present volume, furnishes the following biblio-

their way to England, unless perchance it be to the library of his Grace of Grafton, where they probably stand with the chapter of promises dog-eared down for the perusal of scrupulous statesmen.

This doctrine, once fully established, will add a great facility to business, and prevent unnecessary delays; for example, in former times a minister would have been exceedingly hampered with such a promise as we have here cited: he would have shifted, and delayed, and played the back-game to have got rid of it, or to reconcile the breach to his conscience and reputation; but here you see there was no unnecessary delay: the business went on; and he who acknowledged that he had given his word in a private capacity, brings the book to prove that as a first lord of the treasury "he was not bound to adhere to it,"—and this is sound casuistry. Thus a man who is dexterous in state legerdemain may play his two characters like cups and balls; speak, write, read, lie, promise, swear, and you can never catch him till the box drop out of his hand.

I proposed to have made this a complete panegyric on the Duke of Grafton; but I find it extremely difficult to draw *one* character of a man that acts in *two*. If, however, my poor attempt towards it should find favour in his sight, I hope he

graphical account of these three Jesuits and their books:—Busenbaum's work, entitled "Medulla Theologiæ Moralis," was formerly a text book with the Jesuits, and so popular that it underwent more than fifty editions in less than half a century. It was first published about 1640, in a small duodecimo, and in 1757 was amplified to two bulky folios by Claude Lacroix. This latter edition specially advocated the authority of the Pope, even over the person of kings, and promulgated some doctrines concerning homicide and regicide which were just then particularly obnoxious to Louis XV., on account of the recent attempt on his life by Damien.

In consequence the book was ordered to be publicly burnt, first at Toulouse in 1707, and then at Paris in 1761. Subsequent to this period there are no burnings on record. With respect to Suarez, one of the most learned of the Jesuits, we find no evidence of any of his works having been publicly burnt since 1614. At that date his "Defensio Fidei Catholicæ contra Anglicanæ sectæ errores" was officially burnt at Sens, as it had previously been, by order of James I., in London.

*Molina* died in 1660. His work on "Grace and Freewill," published at Lisbon 1588-9, gave rise to the celebrated congregation *De Auxiliis*, instituted in 1597 by Clement VIII.; but all agitation excited by his writings had ceased long before 1761, nor is there any reason to believe that they were at any time publicly burnt either at Paris or elsewhere.—ED.

will on a future occasion afford me the means of distinguishing
between his two characters, as Moliere's Sosia does between
the two Amphitrious, " c'est l'Amphitrion chez qui l'on
dine."

DIFRONS.

---

## LETTER XXII.

### TO THE PRINTER OF THE PUBLIC ADVERTISER.

May 6, 1769.

*Nil admirari.—Hor.*

Sir,

WHEN the advocates of the ministry assure us that there
never was a set of men more careful of the happiness of his
Majesty's subjects I presume it is Horace's sense of happiness which they would be understood to promote.  If it be
their design to reduce us to a state of resignation in which we
shall wonder at nothing they do, their bitterest enemies must
confess that their endeavours to make us happy have been no
less indefatigable than ingenious.  By a regular progression
from surprise to wonder, from wonder to astonishment, and
so on through all the forms of admiration, they have at last
conducted us to that philosophical state of repose which may
set even the miracles of the present ministry at defiance.  If
the force of example, beyond all ethics, had not made me as callous as a shoeing-horn, the contents of Saturday night's *Gazette* would, I confess, have made me stare.  When his
Majesty (God bless him!) is in perfect health, to be informed
that the first session of a new parliament is to be opened by
commission, is a novelty which, had I been less confirmed in
my principles than I am, would, I own, have filled me with a
certain portion of amazement*.  That the minister himself

---

* *From the London Gazette.—Whitehall, April 30.*  It being His
Majesty's royal intention that the parliament which is summoned to meet on
Tuesday, the 10th day of May next, should then meet and sit, the King has
been pleased to direct a commission to pass the great seal, appointing and
authorizing his royal highness the Duke of Gloucester, his royal highness the
Duke of Cumberland, Thomas, Lord Archbishop of Canterbury, and other
lords, to open and hold the said parliament on the said 10th day of May
next, being the day of the return of the writs of summons.

should have his reasons for not being very desirous to meet a
parliament, or that he should wish to answer for his conduct
by confusion, is not so extraordinary; but that he should give
such advice to a prince, beloved, adored by his people, is a
step, which, in my present condition, does everything but surprise me.   Is it possible, Mr. Printer, that the ministry
should not know what sort of interpretation will be given to
this measure; or did they mean to give the finishing stroke
to Mr. Wilkes's triumph, and to the dishonour which they,
and they alone, have heaped upon the crown?   I protest, Sir,
I had very near betrayed my principles, and suffered an indecent expression of surprise to escape me.   At a time when
the residence of the sovereign was really exposed to violence
and insult *, these worthy ministers gallantly retreated from
the danger; but now, to make amends for that desertion, they
affect a care for the King's security, equally ridiculous and
disgraceful.   What, Sir, is government in their hands really
sunk so low that they dare not hazard a meeting between
their sovereign and his parliament?   Or are they afraid that another language might be held to parliament than that which
they dictate; that some expression of a just resentment of
their baseness should escape; or do they acknowledge to the
world their apprehensions of the populace?   If that be the
case, I can only say, that the infamy of the measure can be
exceeded by nothing but the vileness of the motive.

These distant hints, I hope, Sir, (as I think the ministry
do not pique themselves much upon steadiness) may appear
time enough to induce them to recommend a different system,
more worthy of the crown, though less worthy of themselves.

                                                        C.

---

## LETTER XXIII.

### TO THE PRINTER OF THE PUBLIC ADVERTISER.

Sir,                                              May 12, 1768.
I HAVE read in your paper of this day a second letter in defence of the conduct of the treasury relative to the late extraordinary grant.   That conduct was a specimen of their prin-

---

* See note, vol. I. p. 147, and Miscellaneous Letter, No. 17, ante, p. 164.

ciples. They have now thought fit to give the public a sample of their reasoning.

Their letter *ought* to have been (if it had been what it pretends to be) an answer to the several accusations laid against them in a pamphlet, entitled "The Duke of Portland's Case." Their answer *is* an attempt to prove that the Duke of Portland had no right in law to those lands, of which he and his family have so long continued in possession, and which have been lately granted by the treasury to Sir James Lowther, son-in-law to the Earl of Bute.

I do not mean here to make any reply to the futile arguments by which the ministers, or their advocate, endeavour to establish this point. Because the point itself is, as they know, wholly foreign to the question, and does in no sort concern the public. They shall not be permitted to evade in this manner the real edge of the charge that lies against them.

The charge against them is *not* that they have granted to Sir James Lowther an estate which, in law, is the right of the Duke of Portland; but that they partially, and in many parts of the proceeding, surreptitiously, upon the bare report of a subordinate officer, without suffering his vouchers to be examined, without hearing counsel, or allowing time or means of defence to the party, or of due information to themselves, have violated the equitable and presumptive rights of long and undisputed possession, for the purposes of undue influence at an election, and of paying a base court to a clandestine and dangerous power.

This *is* the charge against them; which they have not attempted to answer; which they never can answer; and which will fix a brand upon their foreheads, that no sophistry will be able to efface, and no veils of ministerial artifice will be thick enough to conceal from the eyes of an indignant and an injured people.

The ministers affect to be surprised that the writer of the Duke of Portland's case has taken no notice of his Grace's title, and has not set forth the surveyor general's report against it: they are at liberty to amuse themselves with such observations. I hope that writer will never give them any disturbance in their learned pleadings on this subject. He has, I trust, too much sense to moot in the public papers the legal construction of a clause in a crown grant.

N 2

It is a matter of perfect indifference to the public, whether the grant, for instance, of the manor of *Dale* is sufficient to convey *Swale* also as its appendant; or whether *Swale* ought specifically to be named. These are not the sort of questions with which we are affected: the ministers may think it wise, perhaps, to hazard the good faith of a crown grant upon such subtle criticisms. Their operation one way or the other (if prescription had not intervened) would not have been a mat ter greatly to concern the public; but it does concern the public, and in the highest degree, whether long, quiet, undis- puted possession, which is the best of titles against the sub- ject, shall or shall not be a title at all against the crown? Whether a treasury, availing itself of a remnant of odious, and for a long time inactive barbarism, shall upon points of legal subtilty endeavour to shake that title? Whether they shall refuse a search of the only material office for settling the doubts that they raised? Whether they shall decline taking the opinion of the king's law servants on such im- portant points of law? Whether they shall refuse to hear the party by his counsel? And whether without any of those forms, some of justice, and all of decency and candour, they shall arm a wealthy and powerful informer with a crown claim to harass and oppress the subject.

These are the points in the Duke of Portland's case, in which the public is concerned. If no prescription is plead- able against the crown, and if the treasury, without hearing, is suffered at pleasure to balloo an informer at your estate, on the bare report of a surveyor's duty, their own creature ; —woe to the property of England! Remember that almost all that property has at one time or other flowed from royal grants. No possessor, no purchaser, no mortgagee is safe ; no further safe than he is covered by the act of James the First, which is now sought to be converted from a temporary regu- lation into a perpetual rule of law.

That truly wise and patriotic bill, which the ministerial gentlemen are pleased to term factious, was what our ances- tors called for, and so far as it regarded themselves, obtained, on the alarm of just such sort of grants as this to Sir James Lowther. They did not contend that the grants should be made, only in cases where the crown had a plausible title. No ; they maintained " that such titles prior to sixty years

should not be set up at all." They demanded that the crown
should litigate with the subject on the same terms of equity
on which the subjects litigated with one another; and that
sixty years of possession should bar a *royal* as well as a *pri
vate* claim.

They lived, indeed, in an age of extravagant prerogative,
and they could not obtain this right fully for posterity; but
they did what they could, and secured it for themselves. The
arguments of the ministry are not against the Duke of Port
land, but against the doctrine of prescription itself; against
natural justice; and against the principles of that wise and
constitutional, though (by the misfortune of its time) imper
fect law, the statute of the 21st of King James the First.

What do we care whether this dormant and antiquated
claim of the crown be well or ill founded in strict law? I
take it for granted that it has no foundation; and make no
sort of doubt that when it comes to trial, it will appear scan
dalously groundless. Besides the favourable presumption
that ought to operate for possession, the whole conduct of the
treasury gives me a right to conclude against them. If they
were so sure of the validity of their claim, why did they not
a little discuss the grounds of the surveyor's report, and order
him to produce his vouchers? How could it hurt this or any
other fair claim (supposing this a fair one) to have the records
in his office inspected? Would a fair claim be hurt by having
it openly and solemnly debated by counsel? Any set of men
who have regard even to decorum in their injustice, could
never have acted with this barefaced partiality to one person,
and with such a scandalous spirit of oppression towards
another.

It was in their official capacity they ought to have seen the
right of the crown to make this grant defended, and the right
of the Duke of Portland examined. They ought to have had
the King's counsel to cover them with their opinions and
arguments in point of law; and not to have first passed the
grant without hearing or examination, and then trusted for
their apology to a legal discussion argued miserably, and
without authority, in a common newspaper. Their arguments
might have been produced with some grace and some weight
to the public, when it was known that they had been officially
considered, and fairly canvassed among all the parties con

cerned *before the act was done;* and that these arguments
were the grounds of their conduct, not excuses for their delinquency. At present they can only excite contempt for
their weak defence of those actions, whose atrociousness had
before merited the abhorrence of all good men.

VALERIUS.

## LETTER XXIV.

### TO THE PRINTER OF THE PUBLIC ADVERTISER.

SIR,                                          May 19, 1768.

AN officer of the guards, on whose veracity I can rely, has informed me that the Secretary at War has thought proper to
write a letter of thanks to the commanding officer of the
troops lately employed in St. George's Fields *. The substance of it, as well as I can remember, is rather of an extraordinary nature, and I think deserves the attention and consideration of the public. I understand that his Lordship
thanks them in the King's name for their good behaviour, and
assures them that his Majesty *highly approves* of their con-

---

* As this letter is frequently alluded to by Junius in the course of the
present work, we shall here insert a copy of it :—

"SIR,                              "War Office, May 11, 1768.
"Having this day had the honour of mentioning to the King the behaviour
of the detachments from the several battalions of foot-guards which have
been lately employed in assisting the civil magistrate and preserving the
public peace, I have great pleasure in informing you that his Majesty highly
approved of the conduct of both the officers and men, and means that his
Majesty's approbation should be communicated to them through you.
Employing the troops on so disagreeable a service always gives me pain,
but the circumstances of the times make it necessary. I am persuaded they
see that necessity, and will continue, as they have done, to perform their
duty with alacrity. I beg you will be pleased to assure them that every
possible regard shall be shown to them; their zeal and good behaviour upon
this occasion deserve it; and in case any disagreeable circumstance should
happen in the execution of their duty, they shall have every defence and
protection that the law can authorize and this office can give.
               "I have the honour to be, Sir,
                    "Your most obedient and most humble servant.
                                        "BARRINGTON.
"Field officer in staff waiting for the
     three regiments of foot-guards.
"Officers for guard on Saturday next,
     Lieut.-Col. Grain, &c., &c."

duct. He further engages his promise that, whatever bad
consequences may ensue, they may depend upon the utmost
assistance and support that his office can afford them *. Without entering into the evidence on which the coroner's verdict
against an officer and some soldiers of the guards was founded,
I shall not scruple to say that this mention of the King's
name is very improper and indecent. The father of his
people undoubtedly laments the fatal necessity which has
occasioned the murder of one of his subjects, but cannot be
supposed to *approve highly* of a conduct which has had dreadful consequences. An event of this shocking nature may
admit of excuse and mitigation from circumstances of necessity, but can never be the object of the *highest royal approbation;* much less was it proper to signify such strong approbation of a conduct which includes a fact still *sub judice*, and
the particulars of which are not yet known with any degree of
certainty.

The secretary at war would have done better in confining
his letter to the expression of his own sentiments. What he
has said for himself, if I am rightly informed, will require
more wit than he possesses to defend. For the mere benefit
of the law, I presume, the prisoners will hardly thank him.
It is a benefit they are entitled to, and will certainly have
whether he and his office interfere or not. If he means anything more, let him look to his words. But I hold it to be
highly unconstitutional as well as illegal, to promise official
support and protection to either party in a criminal case.
wherein the King prosecutes for the loss of his subject. There
is a degree of folly in a minister of the crown signing such a
letter which looks like infatuation; but I hope the Court of

* In the riot here alluded to, which originated from a vast concourse of
people assembled together opposite the King's Bench prison, on May 10, in
the expectation that Wilkes would be liberated from it on this day in order
to take his seat in parliament (it being the first day of its session), about
fourteen persons were shot, and more wounded, by the precipitate firing of
the military. Among the rest was a young man of the name of Allen,
who had taken no part in the tumult, and was slain in an out-house belonging to his father (who lived in the neighbourhood) in the very act of
imploring mercy of the soldiers who shot him. Some of the military more
immediately engaged were secured by the civil power, and were on the point
of taking their trial for the murder; and it is to this transaction the letter
alludes.

King's Bench, or some other court, will let him know what
the law calls *abetment* and *maintenance*, and bring him to *his
senses*.

Yours,

FIAT JUSTITIA*I

---

## LETTER XXV

*For the Public Advertiser.*

July 1, 1768.

TO MASTER HARRY IN BLACK-BOY ALLEY.

—— At tu, simul obligasti
Perfidum votis caput, enigrescis
Atrior multa.——

THE moment I heard you had given a positive promise to
Lord Rockingham in my favour, I did you the justice to be
satisfied that all my hopes and pretensions to succeed Mrs.
—— were at an end.    But a second promise which I understand you have lately given to another, revives my spirits and
makes me flatter myself that you mean me no harm.    I have
one chance less against me than I had, for your last resolution is certainly the one you will not abide by; so that at present there is nothing in my way but your engagement to Lord
Rockingham, the bad effects of which I shall endeavour to
remove by this letter.    I feel as strongly as you how much it
would violate the consistency of your character to keep your
word from any motives of probity or good faith; but if I can
suggest to you the means of performing your first promise to
Lord Rockingham, and yet continuing as great a rascal as you
would wish to be, all objections on the score of integrity will
be removed, and you will owe me no small obligation into the
bargain.    You are a mere boy, Harry, notwithstanding the
down upon your chin, and would do well to cultivate the
friendship of women of experience.    With all due submission

---

' * This and the preceding letters to *Bifrons*, inclusive, are probably by
Junius; at least they are directed to questions on which he was well informed,
and on which he occupied himself afterwards with a more disciplined and
energetic pen.—ED.

to Miss Nancy's * personal knowledge of the world, I believe she has not yet taught you the secret of keeping your word without hurting your principles. This is a science worthy of a superior genius; and without a compliment, Harry, you have talents to improve it into a system of treachery, which, though it may shorten your natural life, will make your reputation immortal.

In the first place, I presume, you will have no difficulty in breaking your word with Mrs. C——y; the whole distress lies in keeping it with your friend the Marquis. My advice is, therefore, that you should order Mr. Bradshaw to write to his Lordship, and assure him in the civilest terms, that " circumstances which you had not foreseen;—that it was with infinite concern;—that his Lordship's recommendation had such weight with you;—that in any other instance;—that you flattered yourself his Lordship would be candid enough to distinguish between the minister and the man;—but that in short you were so unfortunately situated, &c., &c., &c." Mr. Bradshaw's manner will make the message palatable, and it would not be amiss if he were to carry it himself. Having disengaged yourself from Lord Rockingham, you must at the same instant write me a letter of congratulation, and desire me to take possession immediately. By these expedients you will preserve all the duplicity and wayward humour of your character; you will have the merit and satisfaction of failing to two people : you will confer a favour without obliging anybody; and your enemies give you credit for a conduct equally honourable to your morals and your understanding.

Farewell, Harry, and believe me to be, with the most perfect contempt, yours,

POMONA.

P.S. If the place is to be given in trust for Miss Parsons, I beg leave to withdraw my pretensions; for I am determined not to suffer a woman to be quartered upon me in any shape.

* Nancy Parsons.

## LETTER XXVI.

TO THE PRINTER OF THE PUBLIC ADVERTISER.

SIR,                                          July 19, 1768.

THE spirit which once animated the *London Gazette* seems to
have expired with the war.  The learned compiler of that
paper was blest with a genius equal to the description of
battles and victories, but could not descend with dignity to
the pacific annals of domestic economy.  While our troops
were sacrificed abroad, his pen was employed with equal
bravery in murdering our language at home.  He never lost a
consonant from the Elbe to the Weser, or mollified one circumstance in all the guttural pomp of a German campaign.
But, unfortunately for the world, his style perished with his
subject, and we see him now hardly able to support the
fatigue of advertising court-mourning, and introducing foreign
ministers under the auspices of Mr. Stephen Cotterell.  The
gentle slumbers of the ministry prevail over the *Gazette* in
which their dreams are recorded; and if ever we see the
author betray a sign of life, it is only when his principals
turn in their sleep.  I presume we owe the *Gazette* of last
Tuesday* to an *insomnium* with which these gentlemen are
sometimes troubled.  The new commission of trade bears all
the marks of that drowsy wildness which possesses a man,
when he would fain go to sleep, but is so sore all over that he
does not know which side to lie upon.  One day we have a
third secretary of state for a new fancy.  Next day down goes

---

* The following is a copy of the article alluded to :—

"Whitehall, July 12.

"The King has been pleased to constitute and appoint the lord high chancellor; the first commissioner of his Majesty's treasury; the lord president
of the council; the first commissioner of the admiralty; his Majesty's principal secretaries of state; the chancellor of his Majesty's exchequer; the lord
bishop of London; and the surveyor and auditor general of all his Majesty's
revenues in America for the time being; together with Soame Jenyns,
Edward Eliot, George Rice, John Roberts, Jeremiah Dyson, William Fitzherbert, and Thomas Robinson, Esquires, to be commissioners for promoting
trade, and for inspecting and improving his Majesty's plantations in America
and elsewhere.  And his Majesty has thought fit to direct that Wills, Earl
of Hillsborough, one of his said principal secretaries of state, shall duly attend
the meetings of his said commissioners."

poor Lord Clare (not all the softness of his manners nor
modest eloquence can save him) and up gets the new secretary to represent both.  Hence we might have expected a
pause of a few minutes, but these gentlemen are too modest
to be satisfied with anything they do; and now for measures
of vigour with a vengeance!  The chief officers of the
crown having little else to do, are called from their respective
departments; the prayers of a reverend prelate are desired;
Messieurs Rice, Jenyns, Fitzherbert, Eliot, and Robinson still
contribute their mites, and Wills, Earl of Hillsborough, is
*duly to attend the meetings.*  The colonies must be ungovern-
able indeed if such a junto cannot govern them.  In the
last article the writer of the *Gazette* is particularly fortunate,
and avails himself with his usual dexterity of all the advantage of publishing nonsense by authority.  This *due attendance*
will mean anything or nothing, just as the reader chooses.
By the mark set upon Wills, it should seem that the other
commissioners are *not* duly to attend the meetings; or perhaps government, with a laudable caution, means to guard
against any *undue attendance* of the said Wills; they may
possibly mean that Wills alone shall be a quorum; or it may
be——but to guess at their meaning is to reason without data,
so I leave it as they have done, to be explained by contin-
gencies.

After all, Mr. Printer, these are feverish symptoms, and
look as if the disorder were coming to a crisis.  Even this
last effort is the forerunner of their speedy dissolution; like
the false strength of a delirium which exerts itself by fits, and
dies in convulsions.

C*.

---

## LETTER XXVII

### TO MR. WOODFALL.

Sir,                                                  July 21, 1768.
I could not help smiling at your correspondent C.'s dreaming
animadversion, in your paper of yesterday, upon the commis-

* To this letter was given a short answer, which, as it produced a reply
from Junius, is here inserted.

sion of the Board of Trade. He *modestly* fancies himself
awake, while all the ministry are enveloped in darkness and
dreams, and, according to him, only stir to stir no more. Thus
drunkards imagine that everybody reels, and that the world
itself is in disorder.

He owns that his assertions are the result of guess, and
that his reasonings are without the necessary data. He might
have spared himself that trouble; everybody will tell him the
same. Vastly displeased with the compiler of the *Gazette*,
he drops him to abuse his principals; and because they do
not, or choose not, to furnish his empty brain with chat for a
day, or with battles, sieges, and victories in time of peace,
they are therefore doing nothing, or at best are but dreaming
like—*himself*. As he most sagaciously begins without his
data, so he proceeds (as Mr. Locke says) by *seeing a little*,
perhaps like a man half awake, *presuming a great deal, and
then jumping to a conclusion*. This, it is owned, he has admirably well done. He reads in the *Gazette*, that several of
the chief officers of the crown, the Bishop of London, and
some others, are appointed, together with Messieurs Jenyns,
Rice, Eliot, Fitzherbert, and Robinson (whom he very decently
and liberally styles a *junto*) to be commissioners for trade and
plantations, and that the Earl of Hillsborough is duly to attend
their meetings. This throws our gentleman into a trance
(convincing the world that his ignorance and *insomnia* are
well blended), and, fraught with this intelligence, he avers that
all these respectable personages are *new commissioners;*
whereas, in fact, from the original constitution of the Board of
Trade, they have a right to sit there in virtue of their respective offices, though not obliged as Messrs. Jenyns, &c., to *a
due and constant attendance*. In every new commission of
the Board of Trade, these officers for the time being are inserted at length; and at the same time, on account of their
other public avocations, they are therein released from the
obligation of continually sitting at that board. As the business of the colonies has of late years much increased, it was
judged necessary by the Crown to appoint one other principal
secretary of state for the transaction of colony affairs, which
are daily increasing in their importance to this kingdom; and,
perhaps, the noble Lord, who is chosen to this direction, and
whose masterly abilities are the object of your correspondent's

invidious scurrility, is the only man of rank adequate to this arduous task in the present crisis His Lordship is also to preside at the Board of Trade, for the facility and dispatch of business, and will thereby save the government (as he has no salary) the expense of a first commissioner. He is *duly to attend the meetings* of that board, which cannot, as Mr. C. would *wisely* obtrude upon the public judgment, mean anything or nothing at pleasure ; for when there are no meetings his Lordship *cannot attend*, but when there are it is his *duty*. This, every man who is awake can understand ; but as for such dreamers as good Master C., I wish they might sleep more soundly, till the patriotism they attack is extinguished ; and then I believe the world will not be much disturbed with the impertinent visions of such unquiet repose.

INSOMNIS.

## LETTER XXVIII.

### TO THE PRINTER OF THE PUBLIC ADVERTISER.

Sir,                                                                July 29, 1766.

I am willing to join issue with your correspondent *Insomnis*, that one of us is fast asleep, and submit to be tried by a jury of plain Englishmen, who may be supposed to understand their own language. If their verdict be given against him, all I desire is that you will not expose his infirmity to the public, or suffer him to say things in his sleep, which his modesty will blush for when he wakes.

In the first place, I never averred that they were all *new commissioners*, though I spoke of a *new commission*. Is it possible for a man to be awake and not distinguish between these expressions ? But now for a curious discovery : the great officers of state, it seems, are bound and released by one and the same act ; that is, they are bound to the public, and released in private. They figure away as men of business in the *Gazette*, yet by a secret stipulation are relieved from the trouble of attendance. If *Malagrida* had any interest with the present ministry, I should have no doubt that this was one of his subtle contrivances. An ostensible engagement, with a mental reservation, is the first principle of the *morale relachée*, professed and inculcated by the Society of Jesus.

Now, Sir, observe how carefully the example is adapted to the doctrine. The state of the colonies evidently demanded some extraordinary measures of wisdom and of vigour. A pompous list of names is held forth to the public, as if the ministry were roused by the importance and difficulty of the present conjuncture, and were determined to face it with their whole strength and abilities. Such was the appearance which the new commission was intended to convey, and in this light I am very sure it was received by the public : yet *Insomnis* is so candid as to tell us that the ministry meant no such thing; and I believe him very sincerely. A council is instituted which is never to sit, and commissioners are appointed on condition they shall never attend : a common way of throwing dust into the eyes of the public, and frequently practised with success; but I believe it is rather uncommon for a ministerial advocate to make so early and frank a confession of truths, which, though they may answer other purposes, will do his patrons but little honour in point of credit and veracity.

"Go to, go to, you have known what you should not."

A man who talks in his sleep is not fit for a confidential secretary, at least to a ministry who have so many secrets to conceal.

If the duplicity of this contrivance had concerned themselves alone, I should have been contented with comparing it with the rest of their conduct, and thought no more of it. But I own it fills me with indignation to see the name of a reverend prelate so indecently treated. The respect due to his personal character, if not to the sanctity of his station, should have preserved him from so gross an outrage. To see a prelate of the first rank mixed in a low jesuitical farce of imposing upon the public with a great council, when no such matter is intended !—Seriously, Sir, I should not be surprised if his Lordship were to prosecute the writer of the *Gazette* for a libel. For my own part, Sir, I would rather see my name advertised among a company of buffoons at Bartlemy fair, than prostituted in a ministerial junto, to deceive and to cheat my country. A farce upon the stage may amuse at least, if not instruct, but ministerial farces are too dull to please, and seldom conclude without mischief to the audience.

I admit one proposition gravely advanced by *Insomnis*, " that when there are no meetings, Lord Hillsborough cannot attend them ; " but I am not quite so clear about the article of expense. The salary of a first commissioner of trade, at three thousand pounds a year, is saved by appointing a third secretary of state at six or seven, besides all the expense of a new office. But *Insomnis* unfortunately forgets that if Mr. Thomas Townshend, contrary to all expectation, had not refused the vice-treasurership (because the offer of it was attended with an insult) there would have been no room to provide for Lord Clare, consequently he must have remained first commissioner of trade, and all this charming plan of economy, facility, and dispatch, must have waited till another opportunity.

And now, Mr. *Insomnis*, I shall leave you to your repose. Your patrons indeed may turn, and turn, and get no rest ; but what occasion is there for your sitting up to watch them ?

" Thou, quiet soul, sleep thou a quiet sleep."

Above all things let me recommend it to you, never to pretend to be awake for the future. Your eyes and ears, perhaps, are open, but their sense is shut, and really it is not very polite of you to come into company in your night-cap.

C.

## LETTER XXIX.

### TO THE PRINTER OF THE PUBLIC ADVERTISER.

SIR,                                        July 30, 1768.
IT is not many months since* you gave me an opportunity of demonstrating to the nation, as far as rational inference and probability could extend, that the hopes which some men seemed to entertain, or to profess at least, with regard to America, were without a shadow of foundation. They seemed to flatter themselves that the contest with the colonies, like a disagreeable question in the House of Commons, might be put

* Miscellaneous Letter, No. 10.

off to a long day, and provided they could get rid of it for the present, they thought it beneath them to consult either their own reputation, or the true interests of their country.  But whatever were their views or expectations, whether it was the mere enmity of party, or the real persuasion that they had but a little time to live in office*, every circumstance which I then foretold is confirmed by experience.  The conduct of the King's servants in relation to America, since the alteration in 1765, never had a reasonable argument to defend it, and the chapter of accidents which they implicitly relied on, has not produced a single casualty in their favour.  At a crisis like this, Sir, I shall not be very solicitous about those idle forms of respect, which men in office think due to their characters and station ; neither will I descend to a language beneath the importance of the subject I write on.    When the fate of Great Britain is thrown upon the hazard of a die, by a weak, distracted, worthless ministry, an honest man will always express all the indignation he feels.  This is not a moment for preserving forms, and the ministry must know that the language of reproach and contempt is now the universal language of the nation.

We find ourselves at last reduced to the dreadful alternative of either making war upon our colonies, or of suffering them to erect themselves into independent states.  It is not that I hesitate now upon the choice we are to make.  Everything must be hazarded.  But what infamy, what punishment, do those men deserve, whose folly or whose treachery hath reduced us to this state, in which we can neither give up the cause without a certainty of ruin, nor maintain it without such a struggle as must shake the empire?  If they had the most distant pretence for saying that the present conjuncture has arisen suddenly, that it was not foreseen and could not be provided for, we should only have reason to lament that our affairs were committed to such ignorance and blindness.  But when they have had every notice that it was possible to receive, when the proceedings of the colonies have for a considerable time been not less notorious than alarming, what apology have they left?  Upon what principle will they now defend them-

* The Rockingham administration, which lasted from July 10, 1765, to July 30, 1766.

selves? From the first appearance of that rebellious spirit which has spread itself all over the colonies, the chief members of the present ministry were the declared advocates of America. Every art of palliation, of concealment, and even of justification, was made use of in favour of that country against Great Britain. Some there were who did not even scruple to pledge themselves for the future submission and loyalty of the colonies. Every principle of government was subverted, and such absurdities maintained as common sense should blush for. When all these arguments failed, and when the proceedings of the colonies gave the lie to every declaration made for them by their patrons here, still the ministry thought it not too late for further temporizing and delay. Even after the combination at Boston they would not suffer parliament to be informed of the real state of things in that province. They endeavoured to conceal the most atrocious circumstances, and what they could not conceal they justified. Mr. Conway * since last December has, in the face of the House of Commons, defended the resistance of the colonies upon what he called revolution principles; and when a paper, printed at Boston, was offered to the House, as containing matter of the highest importance for the information of parliament, the ministry would not suffer it to be read, because they knew it would be found too bad to be passed over.

If we look for their motives, we shall find them such as weak and interested men usually act upon. They were weak enough to hope that the crisis of Great Britain and America would be reserved for their successors in office, and they were determined to hazard even the ruin of their country, rather than furnish the man † whom they feared and hated with the melancholy triumph of having truly foretold the consequences of their own misconduct. But this, such as it is, the triumph of a heart that bleeds at every vein, they cannot deprive him of. They dreaded the acknowledgment of his superiority over them, and the loss of their own authority and credit, more than the rebellion of near half the empire against the supreme legislature. On this patriotic principle they exerted

* Mr. Conway moved the repeal of Mr. Grenville's Stamp Act, and introduced the Declaratory Act.
† George Grenville.

O

their utmost efforts to defer the decision of this great national cause till the last possible moment. The timidity, weakness, and distraction of government at home, gave spirits, strength, and union to the colonies, and the ministry seemed determined to wait for a declaration of war with our natural enemy, before they attempted to suppress the rebellion of our natural subjects. At last, however, they are compelled to take a resolution which ought to have been taken many months ago, and might then have been pursued with honour to themselves, and safety to this country. How they will support it is uncertain. A resolution adopted by a small majority in a divided council can be but little depended on. It must want the first strength of union, and what effect can we hope for even from a vigorous measure, when the execution of it is committed, most probably, to one of the persons who have professed themselves the patrons of lenient moderate measures, until the very name of lenity and moderation became ridiculous? They will execute by halves; they will temporize and look out for expedients; they will increase the mischief; they will defer the stroke until we are actually involved in a war with France; and when they have made the game desperate, they will resign their places, to save themselves, if possible, from the resentment of their country.

In this situation I am rather afflicted than surprised at the shock which public credit has just received. The weight of the funds is of itself sufficient to press them down. How then should it be possible for them to stand against evils, which separately might overturn the most flourishing state, and which are fatally, at this moment, united against Great Britain: the rebellion of her subjects; the too probable apprehension of a foreign war; and a weak distracted administration at home. Yet, Sir, I hope there is still blood enough in our veins to make a noble stand even against these complicated mischiefs. Far from despairing of the republic, I know we have great resources left, if they are not lost or betrayed. A firm united administration, with the uniform direction of one man of wisdom and spirit, may yet preserve the state. It is impossible to conceal from ourselves that we are at this moment on the brink of a dreadful precipice; the question is, whether we shall still submit to be guided by the

hand which hath driven us to it, or whether we shall follow the
patriot voice * which has not ceased to warn us of our dangers,
and which would still declare the way to safety and to honour.

———

## LETTER XXX.

Sir,                                        August 5, 1768.

An unmerited outrage offered to a great or a good man naturally excites some emotions of resentment even in hearts that
have the least esteem for virtue.  At particular moments the
worst of men forget their principles, and pay to superior
worth an involuntary tribute of sympathy or applause.  We
ought to think well of human nature when we see how frequently the most profligate minds are generous without reflection.  But if a case should happen wherein a character
not merely of private virtue, but of public merit, receives an
insult equally indecent and ungrateful, this common concern
is increased by that share of interest which every man claims
to himself in the public welfare.  A government shameless or
ill-advised enough to treat with disregard the obligation due
to public services, not only sets a most pernicious example to
its subjects, but does a flagrant injury to society, which every
member of it ought to resent.  Reflections such as these
crowded upon my mind the moment that I heard that the
late commander-in-chief in America had been dismissed
without ceremony from his government of Virginia.  I was
grieved to see such a man so treated, but when I considered
this step as an omen of the real resolution of the ministry
with respect to America, I forgot, as he himself will do, the
private injury, and lamented nothing but the public misfortune.  At a time when the most backward of the King's
servants have been compelled to acknowledge the necessity of
vigorous measures, when these measures are held out to the
nation with a declaratory assurance that *now at last we are*

* Mr. G. Grenville's.  See this subject continued in Miscellaneous Letter,
No. 31, and note, p. 198.

*determined,* the resolution to deprive Sir Jeffery Amherst of his post in America cannot but be received as a direct contradiction to all those professions. If they had sincerely meant to do their duty to their country; if they had really adopted measures of vigour, and wished to carry them into execution, instead of depriving him of his post, they would have solicited him to return to America, and take upon him the conduct of those measures. His prudence and moderation are as well known as his spirit and firmness, and who will dare to say that he would have refused an employment which the service of his King and country called upon him to accept? He went to America in circumstances as little favourable as the present; he met an enemy at all times formidable, and at that juncture strengthened by success. He conquered that enemy, and united the dominion of the whole continent to Great Britain. In every light he was the man to have been chosen, if the ministry had really meant to execute their own resolution with vigour. But if it be their design to surrender every point to America, they could not have acted more consistently with such a plan than by dismissing Sir Jeffery Amherst from his post, and appointing Lord Boutetort to succeed him. No collusive bargain could have been made with the former, nor any base unworthy compliances expected from him. He had honour as much as any man to lose, nor even felt the necessity of repairing a broken fortune. Had he been entrusted with a command upon this important occasion, he would have executed the declared, not the secret purpose of the administration. With such a character, it is easy to see how unfit he was to be trusted with the conduct of measures destined to perish at their birth. But, although he might not be entitled to the confidence of the King's servants, in what instance has he deserved such ungrateful treatment? Could they find no other man to mark out to the public as an object of slight and disrespect? Could the wantonness of their power find no other way of providing for a needy dependant? Surely, Sir, the choice was at least injudicious. Lord Hillsborough might have found some more honourable method of distinguishing his entrance into administration; nor do I think it a very favourable omen to Lord Boutetort, that his patrons have

fixed upon Virginia as a retreat for his distresses. Seven
years are too many to spare out of a life of sixty, to say
nothing of the rarity of a man's returning from that country
and surviving the next sessions.

L. L.

---

## LETTER XXXI.

### TO THE PRINTER OF THE PUBLIC ADVERTISER.

Sir,                                             August 6, 1708.

WHETHER it be matter of honour or reproach, it is at least a
singular circumstance, that whoever is hardy enough to maintain the cause of Great Britain against subjects who disown
her authority, or to raise his voice in defence of the laws and
constitution, is immediately pointed out to the public for Mr.
Grenville's friend. From such language one would think
that the order of things was inverted, and that conspiracy had
changed its nature. Mr. Grenville and his friends it seems
are suspected of some dangerous designs, not to destroy but
to preserve the laws and constitution of their country. This
is certainly a reproach of the latest invention. I know there
are men whose characters are safe against suspicions of this
sort, and who form their friendships upon other more useful
maxims. But whether it be owing to the weakness of his
understanding or to the simplicity of his heart, that he pursues a conduct so useful to himself and so suspicious to the
administration, it is surely a pardonable error, and what an
Englishman may yet forgive. It is true he professes doctrines which would be treason in America, but, in England at
least, he has the laws of his side, and if it be a crime to support the supremacy of the British legislature, the Sovereign,
the Lords, and Commons are as guilty as he is. The ministry
indeed have no share in the charge, and it would be uncandid
not to confess that their regard for the honour and interest of
this country is upon the same level with their friendship for
Mr. Grenville *.

* Some speculators have been thoughtless enough to conjecture Mr. George
Grenville to have been Junius. Unluckily for this hypothesis, Mr. Grenville
died in November, 1770, which was soon after Junius began to write under that

For my own part, whatever your correspondents *Moderator*
and *Tandem* may think of me, I shall content myself with
some interior feelings which I fancy they are not much acquainted with; nor will I perplex them with a language they
are incapable of understanding. Whether I am determined by .
motives which an honest man might profess, or by such as
those gentlemen usually act upon, is a point that will not
admit of demonstration. I shall therefore leave their principles out of the question, and try what their arguments
amount to.

*Moderator* and I are, for the most part, agreed. He allows
" that government is sunk into a contemptible state; that
their measures have failed of success, and is convinced that
if the reverse had been practised, the mischief had been
avoided." What conclusion his understanding will draw from
these premises I do not know; but I think the most violent
enemy of the present administration could not have argued
more strongly for a change of hands and a change of measures.

The author of the second letter, finding nothing that will
answer his purpose in the present state of things, is obliged
to carry us back to the original question of the right and ex-

---

signature. Mr. Grenville was a respectable man and statesman, more ex-
emplary for official routine than extraordinary abilities, and had passed
through all the great offices, from that of treasurer of the navy in 1754 to
that of prime minister in 1763. Burke describes him in panegyrical but somewhat exaggerated terms in his speech on American taxation in April, 1774.
" Undoubtedly Mr. Grenville was a first-rate figure in this country. With a
masculine understanding, and a stout and resolute heart, he had an application
undissipated and unwearied. He took public business not as a duty which
he was to fulfil, but as a pleasure he was to enjoy ; and he seemed to have
no delight out of the House, except in such things as some way related to
the business that was to be done within it. If he was ambitious, I will say
this for him, his ambition was of a noble and generous strain. It was to
raise himself, not by the low pimping politics of a court, but to win his way to
power through the laborious gradations of public service, and to secure to
himself a well-earned rank in parliament by a thorough knowledge of its
constitution and a perfect practice in all its business."—After retiring from
the premiership in 1765, Mr. Grenville did not again hold office. This
accounts for the little knowledge Junius admits he had of him ; but he coincided with Mr. Grenville on the right of England to tax the Americans,
dissenting from the metaphysical distinction drawn by Lord Chatham between
the right of the mother country to govern but not to tax the colonies. No
signature is attached to the above communication, and, judging from its
political opinions, it may have emanated from Junius.—ED.

pediency of taxing America. I shall not enter into the
question of right, because it has been already determined
by the legislature, to which an Englishman still owes
some degree of submission. For the matter of expediency,
an advocate for the present ministry seems to me to arraign
his patrons when he argues against it. One part of them
uniformly concurred with Mr. Grenville in forming the Stamp
Act, and in opposing the repeal of it. The other, to serve the
purposes of party, repealed that act, yet showed by their
conduct that they approved of the equitable principle on
which it was founded, that America should contribute a little
to the support of the public expense. The repeal of the
Stamp Act has been followed by other acts more offensive to
the colonies, more directly exerting the right of taxation, and
which will hardly be executed without some extraordinary
efforts on the part of government. Was the act for suspending the assembly of New York recommended by Mr. Grenville? Or was it he who advised the duties on paper, glass,
&c., imported into the colonies? No, Sir, his successors have
paid him the highest compliment by imitating the system
which they had affected to condemn; and in fact they have
carried his principles further than he did, or probably than he
would have carried them. But it is the natural defect of a
weak divided administration, that they can neither resolve
with moderation, nor execute with firmness.

'As to the questions which your last correspondent puts to
me with a sort of heat and petulance not very decent, one
plain answer will, I believe, be sufficient. If the pretensions
of the colonies had not been abetted by something worse than
a faction here, the Stamp Act would have executed itself.
Every clause of it was so full and explicit that it wanted no
further instruction; nor was it of that nature that required a
military hand to carry it into execution. For the truth of
this answer I am ready to appeal even to the Americans themselves. As to the merit of having foreseen the unavoidable
consequences of an inconsistent irresolute system of measures,
I shall place it as low as your correspondent can desire.
Even he might have foreseen what has happened without
waiting for the event. But to foretell those consequences; to
speak truth to the nation; to warn even an adversary of his

danger; to persevere in this upright manly conduct, is indeed
a merit of another sort, and reserved for other virtues *.

Your correspondent confesses that Mr. Grenville is still
respectable; yet he warns the friends of that gentleman not
to provoke him, lest he should tell them what they may not
like to hear. These are but words. He means as little when he
threatens as when he condescends to applaud. Let us meet
upon the fair ground of truth, and if he finds one vulnerable
part in Mr. Grenville's character, let him fix his poisoned
arrow there.

* The following letter from Mr. G. Grenville to Mr. Knox, formerly under-
secretary of state to Lord Hillsborough, is extracted from the second volume
of a small work published by Mr. Knox, entitled "Extra Official State
Papers," and is here copied to give the reader an idea of the political sentiments entertained by Mr. Grenville with respect to America, as developed by
himself in his private correspondence with this gentleman:—

"DEAR SIR,                                     "Wotton, August 28, 1768.
"The account which you gave to me in your letter of the 23rd of this month,
of the late transactions at Boston, seems so natural a consequence of the measures taken in Great Britain, and the state and temper of the government
here, that whatever degree of concern it may give me, I cannot feel the least
surprise at it. If the eyes of those who are most interested in this most
unhappy situation had been sooner opened to the most obvious truths, many
mischiefs might have been prevented; if the authentic proofs which they
have now received of what has happened is not sufficient to convince them, I
will venture to foretell without a spirit of prophecy, *greater calamities will,
when it is too late, rouse them and the whole kingdom from the lethargy, as
to all public measures, into which they have been plunged. I have long feared
that the conduct holden in Great Britain would encourage and delude the
subjects of America, till they would come to extremities of one kind, which
would too probably end in extremities on the other side.* I may appeal to
you, as a private man and as a member of parliament, to my public declarations, that my opinions upon this subject have ever been uniformly the same.
They will still continue to be so until I see much better reasons for changing
them than any which I have yet heard. What prospect there can now be
that they will be attended with success, I cannot pretend to answer; but if
there is no plan formed upon the sound principles of this constitution, supported both by firmness and temper, I can answer that no good success, in
the present difficult situation, can arise from one desultory measure after
another. The respect and affection of its subjects is the basis on which every
wise government must be founded; but if that foundation has been once
overturned, it is not the work of a day to temper the materials so as to unite
and rebuild them, especially if the workmen shall be daily changed, and each
work by a different rule and line from that of his predecessor.
                                                  "I am, &c,
                                                  "GEO. GRENVILLE."

# LETTER XXXII.

## TO THE PRINTER OF THE PUBLIC ADVERTISER.

SIR,                                                  August 10, 1769.

YOUR new correspondent *Virginius* might have saved himself
the trouble of dating his letter from the Carolina coffee-
house. We are a little better acquainted than he imagines
with the style of the secretary of state's office, as well as with
the facts respecting Sir Jeffery Amherst's dismission. When
he calls Lord Boutetort the best of men, I suppose he means
the best of courtiers. If bowing low and carrying the sword
of state constitute merit and services, I confess there are
few men to whom government is more indebted than to his
Lordship. As to those insinuations which *Virginius* calls
malevolent, it would have answered his purpose a little better
if he could have proved them false. Why does he not?
Because they are not only true, but notoriously true. What
say you to the copper mines, *Virginius?* I fancy his Lord
ship would not have been so fond of residing in Virginia, if
he could have continued to reside here either with safety or
convenience. Reflections on characters merely private, ought,
I own, to be discouraged. But let it be remembered that this
courtier might have lived and died in obscurity, if he had not
forced himself into public notice by robbing another man of
an appointment, expressly given him in reward for the most
honourable national services. The discontent of the province
of Virginia at being governed by a lieutenant-governor instead
of a governor, is a mere fiction trumped up by Lord Hillsborough and his secretary to serve this dirty purpose; it was
never heard of before, and if Sir Jeffery Amherst was really
desired to repair to his government, it was not only a most
scandalous breach of conditions with him, but a most impudent mockery. Lord Hillsborough knew it was impossible he
could return to America to be under the command of General
Gage, and that therefore he might put the alternative to him
with safety. By this farce Lord Hillsborough thought he
could throw a colour upon the matter, and that the nation
would be misled by it. What a poor contemptible artifice!
Thus it usually happens with bunglers. They cannot even

be mischievous with dexterity, nor do a public injury without insulting the public understanding.

LUCIUS.

## LETTER XXXIII.

### TO THE PRINTER OF THE PUBLIC ADVERTISER.

Sir,                                                    August 19, 1768.

THE greatest part of my property having been invested in the funds, I could not help paying some attention to rumours or events by which my fortune might be affected ; yet I never lay in wait to take advantage of a sudden fluctuation, much less would I make myself a bubble to bulls and bears, or a dupe to the pernicious arts practised in the alley. I thought a prudent man, who had anything to lose, and really meant to do the best for himself and his family, ought to consider of the state of things at large, of the prospect before him, and the probability of particular events. A letter which appeared some days ago in the *Public Advertiser* revived many serious reflections of this sort in my mind, because it seemed to be written with candour and judgment. The effect of those reflections was, that I did not hesitate to alter the situation of my property. I owe my thanks to that writer that I am safely *landed* * from a troubled ocean of fear and anxiety,

---

* The frequent use of this term by the late Dr. Chalmers was reckoned among his literary peculiarities, but Atticus appears to have preceded him. Since the first volume of Letters was published, a correspondent has suggested a mode for detecting Junius from the intimations in the communication of Atticus.

"It has occurred to me," says he, "that it is worth while searching the list of transferences of stock between the date of the letter alluded to by Atticus and the date of his own. Assuming that Junius was the writer, the insight it would give into his affairs is important."

But the Junius fixed upon in the Essay is not likely to be found signalised by any such weighty transfers of stock as would lead to his identification. Secondly, it is improbable that Atticus was Junius, first, because the shafts of Junius were directed more at *persons* than *things*—disquisitions on fluctuations in the funds, commerce, and the decline of the empire, the favourite themes of Atticus, were not those of Junius. A third objection is that suggested by the *Athenæum*, namely, that an Atticus, either the present or some other, was a frequent writer in the *Public Advertiser* long before and after Junius was known to be a contributor. Finally, it may be added that the test suggested has been applied, and no evidence has been found in the Bank books to unmask Junius.—ED.

on which I think I never will venture my fortune and my
happiness again. Perhaps it may not be useless to individuals
to see the motives on which I have acted.

In the first place, I consider this country as in a situation the like of which it never experienced before, but which
the greatest empires have experienced in their turn. The
successes of the late war had placed us at the highest pin-
nacle of military glory. Every external circumstance seemed
to contribute to our prosperity; the most formidable of our
enemies were reduced, and commerce had promised to increase with the extent of our dominion. But at this point I
fear we met with our *ne plus ultra*. The greatness of a kingdom cannot long be stationary. That of Great Britain carried
in itself an interior principle of weakness and decay. While
the war continued, our superiority at sea gave us an exclusive
commerce with the richest quarters of the world, and supplied
us with wealth to support such efforts as no nation ever
made before. But when the conclusion of peace had restored
our rivals to the enjoyment of their former trade, the very
efforts which had maintained the war rendered it impossible
for us to meet those rivals upon equal terms in foreign
markets. The national debt had risen to a point so far
beyond the reach of economical speculations that the diminution of the principal almost ceased to be a question, and the
ministry found difficulty enough in providing funds for payment of the interest. Here then we find an interior principle
of decay, the operation of which is not less certain than fatal.
The increase of your debt requires a proportionate increase of
trade, at the same time that it not only prevents that increase,
but operates in the contrary direction. A newspaper will not
admit of such a deduction, or I would undertake to demonstrate, that all the profitable part of our foreign trade is lost,
and that in what remains the balance is considerably against
us. But the fact is notorious. The situation of our East-
India trade is so far altered for the better, that we do not send
such quantities of bullion as heretofore to China, and indeed
we have it not to send. Yet the resources of this trade are at the
best but precarious; nor is the balance of it even now clearly
in our favour. A single defeat in India (an event not quite
out of the limits of possibility) would go near to annihilate the
company. But it was in the colonies that our best and surest

hopes were founded.. Their exclusive commerce would have supported our home manufactures when other markets failed, and rewarded us in some measure for that security and extent of dominion which the blood and treasure of this country had purchased for them. Here too our most reasonable expectations are disappointed. Not only the merchant who gives credit on the security of personal good faith is ruined by it, but, in a public view, the sum of the debts of individuals is held out *in terrorem*, to awe us into a compliance with pretensions which shake the foundation of our political existence. We shall be woefully deceived if we form our calculations of the real state of trade on the large commissions, long credit, or extensive enterprises of particular merchants. The commercial prosperity of a nation depends upon the certainty of the return, not on the magnitude of the venture. As things are now managed in the city, the greatest house falls first, and draws with it the ruin of a multitude of little ones. Next to the parties immediately concerned, the public creditors will be the first to feel the consequences of this ruinous system. The funds allotted for their security depend chiefly upon the produce of the customs; these depend upon your trade, and it requires no prophet to foretell, that a false and ruinous system of trade cannot long be maintained. It begins with private beggary, and ends in public ruin. I do not pretend to say that the landholder will be quite at his ease, when public credit is shaken. But his at least is a solid security; the other a mere bubble, which the first rude breath of ill fortune or of danger may reduce to nothing.

I wish it could be proved that any one circumstance in this representation is false or exaggerated. On the other hand, if it be true, the concealment of a moment more or less signifies nothing. It is agreed on all hands that we are in no condition to meet a war. Our enemies know and presume upon it. The experience of many centuries sufficiently proves that their natural restlessness will not long permit them to observe the conditions of any peace. At present they have other additional motives to draw them into action. The articles of the last peace dishonoured them in the eyes of Europe. Necessity alone compelled them to submit to it. As long as the necessity subsists the peace will be maintained. In the mean time, they hazard such strokes as would be a just

foundation of a war, if we had strength or spirits to renew it.
Dunkirk remains undemolished, and Corsica * is added to
the dominion of France.   They know the miserable state of
our finances, the distraction and weakness of our government, and above all, the alarming differences which threaten
a rupture with our colonies.   To suppose that they will not
take advantage of these circumstances, is supposing that a few
years have changed the stamina of a French constitution.   On
the other hand, to say that they are as little in a condition
to make war as ourselves is mere trifling.   Their enterprises
prove the contrary.   Their finances are upon a much better
footing than ours, and at the worst, they have a remedy, which
a British parliament will never make use of but in the last
extremity.   The French apply it without scruple, and, as far
as I can observe, without any bad effect to themselves.   In
short, they consider our weakness more than their own
strength, in adherence to their own policy, *que la foiblesse de
l'ennemi fait notre propre force.*

A prudent man, whose property is in the funds, would do
well to consider the truth of this representation.   What
security has he, when the slightest rumour of bad news from
America robs him of four or five per cent. upon his capital,
when worse news from that quarter is expected every hour,
and when the expectation of a foreign war is founded on facts
and reasoning strong enough to constitute the clearest moral
certainty?   To say that public credit has hitherto passed
safely through the fiery trial of war and rebellion, proves
nothing.   No conclusion can be drawn from a debt of forty-six
millions, at which it stood in 1740, to the present debt of one
hundred and forty millions.   At that time our resources were
hardly known, at this period they are known and exhausted.
We are arrived at that point when new taxes either produce nothing, or defeat the old ones, and when new duties
only operate as a prohibition ; yet these are the times, Sir,
when every ignorant boy thinks himself fit to be a minister †
Instead of attendance to objects of national importance, our
worthy governors are contented to divide their time between
private pleasures and ministerial intrigues.   Their activity is

* See Junius, Letters 3 and 12, vol. i., with the notes.
† The Duke of Grafton was First Lord of the Treasury at this period.

just equal to the persecution of a prisoner in the King's Bench
[Wilkes], and to the honourable struggle of providing for their
dependants.   If there be a good man in the King's service,
they dismiss him of course; and when bad news arrives, instead of uniting to consider of a remedy, their time is spent in
accusing and reviling one another. Thus the debate concludes
in some half misbegotten measure, which is left to execute
itself.   Away they go: one retires to his country-house;
another is engaged at a horse-race ; a third has an appointment with a prostitute; and as to their country, they leave
her, like a cast-off mistress, to perish under the diseases they
have given her.

ATTICUS.

---

## LETTER XXXIV.

### TO THE PRINTER OF THE PUBLIC ADVERTISER.

SIR,                                              August 23, 1768.
AMIDST the general indignation which has been excited by the
marked affront lately put upon Sir Jeffery Amherst, it is odd
to find people puzzling themselves about the motives which
have actuated administration in this extraordinary procedure
Nothing is more short and easy than the solution of this
affected difficulty.   They were *ordered* to act in this manner.
   The public knows and *can* know no other reason.   The
ministry know and *desire* to know no other reason.   They
have not the slightest quarrel with Sir Jeffery Amherst.
They have not the most trivial regard for Lord Boutetort.
Some of them are known even to hate his Lordship; the rest
are scarcely acquainted with him; but they have received the
*order*, and that is enough for *them*.   Their whole political
system is wrapped up in one short maxim—

> "My *author* and *disposer!* what thou bidd'st
> Unargued I obey!"

In this lesson they are perfect to a miracle ; and the signal
proof they have just given of their daring and determined
servility shows them altogether worthy of that confidence
which the favourite so wisely reposed in them (during his

ploasure), the depositaries of his intentions, and the trustees of his power.

But, although it be in vain to seek for any higher principle than blind obedience in the *formal and executive* members of the ministry, it is worth while to examine a little more minutely the motives which might actuate in this affair the secret but *deliberative and guiding* part of administration.

Can we believe from the monstrousness, or can we doubt from the notoriety, of the fact, that the *political principles* held by the present governor of Virginia during the greatest part of his life, and avowed, almost without a mask, could be his sole recommendation to that employment? Can we believe that these *principles* constitute such a transcendent degree of merit as makes it necessary to reward its possessor at the expense of the national honour, gratitude, and safety? Such merit must be served in any way, and at any price. A *peerage*, which every one knows could not be had without the royal countenance, was not sufficient. It was too little that he was put into an honourable employment near the *person* of his sovereign. After an unsuccessful attempt to reward him further by a violation of our laws in an *illegal patent*, he is now to be provided for by the ruin of our affairs in a critical and important government.

As a part of this system, and in order to give it a due roundness and relief, it was thought proper not only to affront living merit, but to insult and trample upon the sacred ashes of the dead. It was not forgot under whose patronage Sir Jeffery Amherst first appeared in the world. It was not forgot that he was one of the many public benefits derived to this country from that great school of military knowledge and loyal sentiments, the family of the late Duke of Cumberland. Here was a glorious opportunity of cherishing a true friend to despotism, and at the same time of insulting the memory of him who had been the heavy scourge, and (it was once hoped) the final destroyer of that cause. This opportunity was not lost.

To return: I have said that the justly obnoxious principles at which I have hinted, constitute, or *seem* at least to constitute, the *sole* merit of the new governor. If the friends of the ministry can discover any other, they would be very kind to mention them. The public looks upon this transaction in

a very serious light. Nothing but the strongest conviction
that the very salvation of America depends upon the abilities
of Lord Boutetort can reconcile them to the affront which has
been put upon Sir Jeffery Amherst.

They derive no consolation from being told that this meritorious commander had received a previous intimation to
repair to his government, with which he showed himself
unwilling to comply. They are as dissatisfied as ever; first,
because the fact itself, standing upon no higher authority than
ministerial assertion, will be disputed. Falsehood is a servile
vice; and to the imputation of that vice people in a slavish
condition, whether low or high (for servitude, as well as hell,
has its ranks and dignities), will always be subject, especially
if ministers are known to have found the dexterous art of
splitting themselves, and possessing one character in which to
promise, and another in which to act *.

But with all the advantage of their supple habits, and of
their double characters, will they venture to assert, that the
arrangement in favour of Lord Boutetort was not determined
upon *before* they had consulted Sir Jeffery Amherst concerning a residence in Virginia? In the next place, did they
not know that his residence in the character of governor
in America, where he had before commanded in chief, was a
thing incompatible with all the ideas entertained by military
men concerning rank and precedence? And if so, was not
the order for residence given (if it was given) that it might be
disobeyed? Is it not a heavy aggravation, instead of the
least excuse, for their offence?

Lastly, the public would be glad to know how it comes that
this grand ministerial reformation was taken up in this single
instance; it made no part of a general arrangement. If it
were done in consideration of the colonies, let me ask,
whether the people of Virginia have lately complained of the
absence of their governor, under which they have acquiesced
upwards of fifty years? If it was done on the part of Great
Britain, again let me inquire whether the lieutenant-
governors, who have acted during those fifty years, have
wanted authority, knowledge, or capacity? If they did, in
what manner is the defect supplied by the new appointment?
Is the new governor invested with any larger powers than the

* See Miscellaneous Letter, No. 21, *ante.*

late lieutenant-governors? Or is he endued with a greater degree of experience, knowledge, or sagacity for the exercise of those powers? No, no; the manner of filling the vacancy made by the removal of Sir Jeffery Amherst sets in the broad glare of daylight the true reasons for making it; it was not done to reform a public abuse, but to accommodate a private job; it was not *Virginia* that wanted a governor, but a court favourite that wanted the salary.

I cannot help observing, in the ministerial writings with which the papers have been lately filled, that much scurrilous abuse has been thrown out against the Whig party and Whig principles. Permit me to congratulate the ministers on this well-chosen topic: the defence is worthy of the cause. They tell us, that all party distinctions ought to be done away, and that men of all kinds ought to have an equal share in public employment. This notion, taken with due corrections, has some sense, but in their application much absurdity. No man would prevent the public from being served by the abilities of any person, because he might have the misfortune in some time of his life to be mistaken in his political opinions or connections. But every Whig thinks it fair, that persons under such circumstances should be obliged to produce some *other* merit besides those *mistakes;* and that they should give some other proofs of their conversion to the principles of our happy establishment, than their necessity, or their desire of partaking in the emoluments which it has to bestow.

This surely is the sentiment and language of candour and moderation. This ought to be the inviolable rule where the question is concerning offices of trust, and which require weight and ability for their execution. When the question is concerning the mere graces of the crown, the rule is to become even more severe; and every lover of the constitution must think it a crime hardly less than treason in those who shall advise a court to discountenance the families which have promoted the revolution, and at the same time to load with its favours those who (reconciled by profit, not by opinion) have ever been the declared enemies both of the revolution and of every benefit we derive from that happy event. You may hear again from

Your humble Servant,<br>VALERIUS.

## LETTER XXXV.

### TO THE EARL OF HILLSBOROUGH.

My Lord,                                        August 29, 1768.

THE honourable lead you have taken in the affairs of America
hath drawn upon you the whole attention of the public.   You
declared yourself the single minister for that country, and it
was very proper you should convince the world you were so,
by marking your outset with a *coup d'éclat*.   The dismission
of Sir Jeffery Amherst has given a perfect establishment to
your authority, and I presume you will not think it necessary
or useful to hazard strokes of this sort hereafter.   It will be
advisable at least to wait until this affair is forgotten, and, if
you continue in office till that happens, you will surely be
long enough a minister to satisfy all your ambition.

The world attributes to your Lordship the entire honour
of Sir Jeffery Amherst's dismission, because there is no other
person in the cabinet who could be supposed to have a wish
or motive to give such advice to the crown.   The Duke of
Grafton and the Chancellor were once Lord Chatham's
friends.   However their views may now be altered, they
must know it would disgrace them in the eyes of the public,
to offer an unprovoked outrage to a man whose conduct and
execution had contributed not a little to their patron's glory.

The Duke of Bedford and his friends have uniformly held
forth Sir Jeffery Amherst as the first military man in this
country; they have quoted him on all occasions when military knowledge was in question, and even been lavish in his
praise.   Besides, they openly disclaim any share in this measure, and they are believed.

The Earl of Shelburne usually finds himself in opposition,
therefore is not too often consulted.   In this instance he certainly did not concur with the majority.   He still is, or pretends to be, attached to Lord Chatham, and I fancy he is not
yet so cordially reconciled to the loss of the American department as to dishonour himself merely to oblige your
Lordship.

You will not venture to insinuate that Sir Jeffery Amherst
was dismissed by the advice of Lord Granby or Sir Edward
Hawke.   Military men have a sense of honour which your
Lordship has no notion of.   They feel for a gallant officer

who had his full share in the toils and honour, and had some
right to a share in the profits of the war. They feel for the
army and the navy. Lord Granby himself has *some* emoluments besides his power, and Sir Edward Hawke has his pension. Nobly earned I confess, but not better deserved than
by the labours which conquered America in America. De-
sides, my Lord, the commander-in-chief is the patron of the
army. It was a common cause which he could not desert
without infamy and reproach. Lord Granby is not a man to
take his tone from any minister. Where his honour is concerned, he scorns to adopt an humble ministerial language ;
he never would say, *that indeed Sir Jeffery Amherst was
rather unreasonable, that his terms were exorbitant, that he
had still two regiments left, and might well be contented.* This
is a language it is impossible he should hold, while he himself
is master-general of the ordnance, colonel of the blues, and
commander-in-chief, with a whole family upon the staff. He
knows the value, and could not but be sensible of the loss, of
those honourable rewards which his distinguished capacity,
his care of the public money, and his able conduct in Germany had justly entitled him to.

I think I have now named all the cabinet but the Earl of
Chatham.

His infirmities have forced him into a retirement, where I
presume he is ready to suffer, with a sullen submission, every
insult and disgrace that can be heaped upon a miserable, decrepid, worn out old man *. But it is impossible he should
be so far active in his own dishonour as to advise the taking
away an employment given as a reward for the first military
success that distinguished his entrance into administration.
He is indeed a compound of contradictions ; but his letter to
Sir Jeffery Amherst stands upon record, and is not to be explained away. You know, my Lord, that Mr. Pitt therein
assured Sir Jeffery Amherst, that the government of Virginia
was given him merely as a reward, and solemnly pledged the
royal faith that his residence should never be required. Lost
as he is, he would not dare to contradict this letter. If he

* His Lordship was less afflicted by age than by hereditary gout. He was
subsequently compelled to retire from his nominal premiership. In the quiet
of unofficial life he recovered, and soon reappeared, like a giant refreshed,
as the leader of the opposition.—ED.

did, it would be something more than madness. The disorder must have quitted his head and fixed itself in his heart.

The business is now reduced to a point: either your Lordship advised this measure, or it happened by accident. You must suffer the whole reproach, for you are entitled to all the honour of it. What then is apparently the fact? One of your cringing, bowing, fawning, sword-bearing brother courtiers* ruins himself by an enterprise†, which would have ruined thousands if it had succeeded. It becomes necessary to send him abroad. Sir Jeffery Amherst is one of the mildest and most moderate of men; *ergo*, such a man will bear anything. His government will be a handsome provision for Boutetort, and if he frets—why, he may have a pension. Your emissaries lose their labour, when they talk with so much abhorrence of sinecures, non-residence, and the necessity of the King's service. You are conscious, my Lord, that these are pompous words without a shadow of meaning. The whole nation is convinced that the fact is such as I have stated it. But to make it a little plainer, I shall ask your Lordship a few questions, to which the public will expect, and your reputation, if you have any regard for it, demands, that you should give an immediate and strict answer.

1. When the government of Virginia was offered to Sir Jeffery Amherst, did he not reply, that his military employments took up all his time, and that he could not accept the government if residence were expected?

2. Did not Mr. Pitt, then secretary of state, assure him in the King's name, that it was meant only as a mark of his Majesty's favour, and that his residence would never be expected?

3. Has there ever been any further mark of favour conferred upon this gentleman for all those important services which succeeded the conquest of Cape Breton?

But now for questions of a later date.

---

* Lord Boutetort, lately Colonel Berkeley, M.P. for Gloucestershire, and groom of the bedchamber. He acted as second to Lord Talbot in his ridiculous duel with Wilkes at Bagshot. According to the account of the affair given by Wilkes in his *Correspondence*, each of the principals discharged a pistol in "exact time." Wilkes then ran up to Talbot, embraced, and retired with him to the Red Lion to discourse of their feat over a bottle of claret.—ED.

† Alluding to the Warmly Company, for converting copper into brass, of which Lord Boutetort was the head.

1. Was not Lord Boutetort's appointment absolutely fixed on or before Sunday the 31st of July?

2. Had Sir Jeffery Amherst the least intimation of the measure before Thursday the 4th of August?

3. Was it not then mentioned to him in general terms, as a measure merely in contemplation, without the most distant hint that Lord Boutetort, or any other person, was actually in possession of his government.

4. Did not Lord Boutetort kiss hands the next day, that is, on Friday the 5th of August?

5. Did you not dare to tell your sovereign that Sir Jeffery Amherst was perfectly satisfied, when you knew your treatment of him was such as the vilest peasant could not have submitted to without resentment?

Finally, my Lord, is it not a fact, that Sir Jeffery Amherst, having been called upon some time ago to give his opinion upon a measure of the highest importance in America, gave it directly against a favourite scheme of your Lordship; and is not this the real cause of all your antipathy to him? Your heart tells you that it is.

Now, my Lord, you have voluntarily embarked in a most odious, perhaps it may prove to you a most dangerous, business. Your Pylades will sneak away to his government; but *you* must stand the brunt of it here. For the questions which I have proposed to you, I must tell you plainly, that they *must and shall* be answered.

You may affect *to take no notice of them*, perhaps, and tell us *you treat them with the contempt they deserve.* Such an expedient may be wise and spirited enough when applied to a declaration of rebellion on the part of the colonies, and God knows it has succeeded admirably. But it shall not avail you here.

Nam negare audes? Quid taces? Convincam si negas.

LUCIUS.

---

## LETTER XXXVI.

### TO THE PRINTER OF THE PUBLIC ADVERTISER.

Sir,                                            August 30, 1768.

I shall not pretend to enter into the merits of Sir Jeffery Amherst's dismission from his government of Virginia. Everybody knows he deserves a great deal of the public; and if

what I have heard be true, even the present administration
do not refuse it him.   But there are a number of busy incendiaries, who use every means to poison the minds of the
good people of England, and to abuse those in power, whoever
they are.   These neither inquire into the truth of the matter,
nor do they fail to show the most disagreeable view of every
action of the ministry.   An impudent varlet, Y. Z., in this
day's paper, talks of forty or fifty lives lost in St. George's
fields.   When was it ?   Others have heaped together a parcel
of ill-natured lies, and given it the name of an account of the
dismission of Sir Jeffery Amherst.

The particulars of Sir Jeffery Amherst's dismission, I am
told, are as follow : for very urgent reasons it had been determined the governor-general of every province in America
should reside.   Upon which Lord Hillsborough wrote a letter
to Sir Jeffery, acquainting him of this resolution  After making very honourable mention of his service in America, how
much his country was obliged to him for that activity, steadiness, and courage, which so eminently distinguished the commander, and which from his example diffused itself through
the whole army, by which means the British arms were
crowned with success, and the war so happily concluded in
that part of the world, he mentioned the very high opinion
his Majesty had of him both as a man and as a soldier, and
how much it would be to his satisfaction, was it suitable to Sir
Jeffery's inclinations and circumstances, to go to Virginia and
take upon him the supreme command in that province : but
if it was not convenient, he might depend on it, that his
Majesty would take the earliest opportunity of doing justice
to his merits, by making him a recompense equivalent at least
to the loss of his government.

This letter was scarce finished when Sir Jeffery Amherst
called at Lord Hillsborough's on some other business.   His
Lordship took that opportunity to explain the intentions of
administration by such a measure, gave him the letter, and
Sir Jeffery seemed to be convinced of the necessity of the
arrangement, acquiesced in the proposals made to him, and
went away to all appearance well satisfied.

If it was next day or not, I know not, but Sir Jeffery very
soon after this demanded an audience of his Majesty, and resigned the command of his regiments.

This not being accepted of, and the ministry willing to

keep such a man in the service, and not wishing to give cause
for his resignation, endeavoured to reason with him; upon
which he (Sir Jeffery Amherst) delivered or sent to the Duke
of Grafton the following articles of accommodation.

1. A British peerage to himself, and failing heirs of his
body, to descend to his brother the colonel.

2. A recompense equivalent to the loss of his government.

3. An exclusive right of working the coal mines at Louisbourg to him and his heirs for ever.

4. A grant of lands in America to a certain extent.

5. And in case it should be judged expedient to create
American peers, that he should have the pre-eminence.

The Duke of Grafton, on receiving this, begged to see Sir
Jeffery, who sent him word, if the interview was intended to
induce him to lower his demands, it was totally unnecessary.
His Grace then went to him, and gave him the following
answers.

1. British peerages were generally given to such whose
opulent fortunes enables them to support that high dignity.
This reason he apprehended Sir Jeffery could not plead.

2. It always had been his Majesty's intentions to make him
a recompense equivalent to his government.

3. Reasons political and commercial forbade the working of
the American coal mines at all.

4. He might have the grant of lands in America when,
where, and to what extent he pleased; but he did not apprehend there was the least reason to make the fifth demand, as
he supposed a creation of American peers would never take
place.

Sir Jeffery Amherst's regiments are not given away.

I shall make no comment on this. I tell it as a fact which
I have heard from what people call good authority. The dismission of an experienced and deserving commander requires
some attention, and there can be no harm in making the
public acquainted with it. The number of falsehoods that
have been spread abroad about this transaction have induced
me to send you this.

I must tell you, however, that my information is second
hand; but it may have this good effect, even if not true, to
induce those who know the contrary to do as I have done. I

shall therefore conclude with this question : are these things
true or not?

CLEOPHAS.

---

## LETTER XXXVII.

### TO THE EARL OF HILLSBOROUGH.

MY LORD,                                              September 1, 1768.

IN the ordinary course of life, a regularity of accounts, a precision in points of fact, and a punctual reference to dates, form
a strong presumption of integrity.  On the other hand, an
apparent endeavour to perplex the order and simplicity of
facts, to confound dates, and to wander from the main question, are shrewd signs of a rotten cause and of a guilty conscience.  Let the public determine between your Lordship
and me.  You have forfeited all title to respect ;. but I shall
treat you with tenderness and mercy, as I would a criminal at
the bar of justice

In your letter signed Cleophas you are pleased to assume
the character of a person half informed.  We understand the
use of this expedient.  You avail yourself of everything that
can be said for you by a third person, without being obliged to
abide by the apology if it should fail you.  My Lord, this is a
paltry art, unworthy of your station, unworthy of everything
but the cause you have undertaken to defend.  While you
pursue these artifices it is impossible to know on what principles you really rest your defence.  But you may shift your
ground as often as you please ; you shall gain no advantage by
it.  Your Lordship, under the character of Cleophas, is exactly acquainted with particulars which could only be known
to a few persons, while you totally forget a series of facts
known to thousands.  You can repeat every article of your
own letter to Sir Jeffery Amherst\*, though your own memory

---

\* This letter was at length published November 2, and is as follows :—

"SIR,                                        "Hanover Square, July 27, 1768.
" I am commanded by the King to acquaint you that his Majesty, upon a consideration of the despatches lately received from Virginia, thinks it necessary
for his service that his governor of that colony should immediately repair to

be too weak to recollect on what day Lord Boutetort's appointment was fixed, on what day he kissed hands, and on what day the design was opened to Sir Jeffery Amherst. These, it seems, are circumstances of no importance; and, to say the truth, I believe they are such as you would willingly forget. I am glad to find, however, that the acknowledgment of Sir Jeffery Amherst's merit and services could not be more full

his government, and at the same time to express to you the high opinion his Majesty has of your ability to serve him in that situation. But it is not the King's intention to press you to go upon that service, unless it shall be perfectly agreeable to your inclination as well as entirely convenient to you. His Majesty does not forget that the government of Virginia was conferred upon you as a mark of royal favour, and as a reward for the very great services you have done for the public, so much to your own honour and so much to the advantage of this kingdom, and therefore his Majesty is very solicitous that you should not mistake his gracious intention on this occasion.

"If you choose to go immediately to your government, it will be extremely satisfactory to his Majesty; if you do not, his Majesty wishes to appoint a new governor, and to continue to you in some other shape that emolument which was, as I have said before, intended as a mark of the royal sense of your meritorious services. It is a particular pleasure to me to have the honour of expressing to you these very favourable sentiments of our royal master. To add anything from myself would be a degree of presumption; I will therefore only request the favour of your answer as soon as may be convenient, and take the liberty to assure you that I am,

"HILLSBOROUGH."

The following short note was published immediately in reply to it :—

"TO THE PRINTER OF THE PUBLIC ADVERTISER.

"SIR,                                    "November 5, 1768.

"To prevent any impression which may arise to the prejudice of Sir Jeffery Amherst from a letter circulated by the Earl of Hillsborough, and now in print, it is only necessary to observe that it is dated the 27th of July, and that the government of Virginia was given to Lord Boutetort on Sunday, the 24th. This being the fact, the humble fawning language of the secretary of state's letter, instead of a compliment, is a real mockery and insult. A true idea of the treatment which Sir J. A. has received can only be had by observing the order of the facts. The government is given away on Sunday; the secretary of state writes his letter on Wednesday; he and Sir J. A. meet on Thursday. Not the most distant hint is given him that his government is actually disposed of, and Lord Boutetort kissed hands next morning. This, Sir, is the treatment which Sir J. A. considers as an affront, not an injury, and which he resents as he ought. If Lord H. had not published his letter, I should not have thought of reviving a question on which the public was before completely satisfied.

"A. B."

and formal than as it is stated in your letter to him.  Upon that point, then, we are agreed.

You say Sir Jeffery Amherst, at your first conversation, seemed satisfied.  My Lord, I must tell you, that when a secretary of state assures Sir Jeffery Amherst that any particular measure is necessary for the King's service, he is too good a subject to set his private interest in opposition to the public welfare.  But did you tell him that his government had been given away four days before?  Did you not speak of it as a measure *in futurum*, which was not to take place till he was perfectly satisfied?  In short, did you tell him that Lord Boutetort was to kiss hands next morning?  Answer these questions like a man and a gentleman.

When Sir Jeffery Amherst found that all this pretended necessity of the King's service ended in a provision for a ruined courtier, he felt the indignation of a man who has received an *affront*, not an *injury*.  Your emissaries affect to say, that he was desired to repair to his government, and upon his refusal was dismissed.  This you know was not the fact, so that every reasoning built upon it falls to the ground.  You never did nor could propose to him to return to America in a rank subordinate to General Gage.  It never was a question; and indeed how should it, when his government was given away on the 31st of July, and he had not the most distant intimation that such a measure was thought of, until Thursday, the 4th of August.  Mark these dates, my Lord, for you shall not escape me.

After the affront had been fixed upon him in the grossest manner, he was desired to consider what satisfaction he would accept of.  He then sent to the Duke of Grafton the demands which you have stated to the public.  These, and the answers to them, shall now be considered.  The word *demand* is peremptory, and unfit to be made use of by a subject in a request to the crown.  It *was not* made use of by Sir Jeffery Amherst, though, for the matter of it, I assert without scruple, that a man of distinguished public merit, who has been signally insulted, is not in the case of a suppliant, but has a *right* to a signal reparation.

The Duke of Grafton's idea of the proper object of a British peerage differs very materially from mine.  His

Grace, in the true spirit of business, looks for nothing but
an opulent fortune, meaning, I presume, the fortune which
can purchase as well as maintain a title. We understand his
Grace, and know who dictated that article. He has declared
the terms on which Jews, gamesters, pedlars, and contractors
(if they have sense enough to take the hint) may rise without
difficulty into British peers. There was a time indeed,
though not within his Grace's memory, when titles were the
reward of public virtue, and when the crown did not think
its revenue ill employed in contributing to support the
honours it had bestowed. It is true his Grace's family derive *their* wealth and greatness from a different origin—from
a system which it seems he is determined to revive. His confession is frank at least, and well becomes the candour of a
young man. I dare say that if either his Grace or your Lordship had had the command of a seven years' war in America,
you would have taken care that poverty, however honourable,
should not have been an objection to your advancement;
you would not have stood in the predicament of Sir Jeffery
Amherst, who is refused a title of honour because he did not
create a fortune equal to it at the expense of the public.

For the matter of a recompense equivalent to his government, he repeatedly told your Lordship that the name of pension was grating to his ears, and that he would accept of no
revenue that was not at the same time honorary. Your
Lordship does not know the difference, but men of honour
feel it.

If reasons political and commercial forbid working the coal
mines in America, *that,* I allow, is an answer *ad hominem.*
It may be a true one; yet I do not despair of seeing these
very mines hereafter granted to support the chastity of a
minister's whore, the integrity of a pimp, or the uncorrupted
blood of a bastard.

His Grace is wonderfully bountiful in the article of lands.
I doubt not he would with all his heart give Sir Jeffery Amherst the fee simple of every acre from the Mississippi to
California. But we shall be the less surprised at his generosity
when we consider that every private soldier who served a
certain time in America was entitled to two hundred acres,
and that not one man, out of perhaps twenty thousand
claimants, has yet settled upon his estate.

As to American peerages, if none are to be created, the request falls of course. But if such a creation had been intended, I call upon your Lordship to point out a man better entitled to precedence upon that list than Sir Jeffery Amherst.

Your last assertion is that his regiments are not given away. It is a matter of perfect indifference; yet the public has reason to believe that Colonel Hotham is now colonel of the 15th regiment, and that the commission of commandant of the royal Americans only waits until it shall be determined whether General Gage shall be recalled or not.

Permit me now to refer your Lordship to the questions stated in my last letter, and to desire you to answer them strictly. If you do not, the public will draw its own conclusions.

Your emissaries, my Lord, have rather more zeal than discretion. One of them, who calls himself *A Considerate Englishman*, could not write by authority, because he is entirely unacquainted with facts. His declamation therefore signifies nothing. In his assertions, however, there is something really not unpleasant. He assures us that your Lordship's great abilities were brought into employment to correct the blunders of Mr. Pitt's administration. It puts me in mind of the consulship which Caligula intended for his horse, and of a project which Duckhorse once entertained of obliging the learned world with a correct edition of the classics.

LUCIUS.

---

## LETTER XXXVIII.

### TO THE PRINTER OF THE PUBLIC ADVERTISER.

SIR,                                        September 6, 1768.

WHEN a worthless administration do a notorious act of *injustice* to a *good man*, which naturally raises the indignation of the public, they are not satisfied with the *first blow*, but their emissaries go to work to *blacken* the character which was *fair* before, in order to justify the measures of their *masters*.

In this light I must look upon the performance of your correspondent *Cleophas, jun.*, in your paper of to-day.

His assertion, "that the Duke of Grafton assured Sir Jeffery Amherst that General Gage should be recalled, if Sir Jeffery chose to go to his government," is an *absolute falsity ;* for (and I speak from *very good authority*) the matter of the *chief* command of the troops never was mentioned, either by the Duke of Grafton or any of his colleagues. Had it been so, Lord Hillsborough in *going his rounds* (his *Lordship understands me*) would not have failed to have expatiated fully thereon ; but the letters of your masterly correspondent *Lucius* have drove his Lordship to the *mean* and *paltry* art of employing some of his *nameless dependants* to throw out *insinuations*, which he knows to be *false*, yet, judging from the general run of mankind, flatters himself that at least part of them will be believed.

My design being only to set the public right in regard to the assertion of Sir Jeffery Amherst's being offered the chief command of the troops, which, in truth, never happened, I shall take no notice of the other part of your correspondent's letter, but leave him and his *bungling patrons* to find in the list of the army an officer so fit as Sir Jeffery Amherst to deal with the *refractory colonists.*

L. L.

---

## LETTER XXXIX.

*For the Public Advertiser.*

September 7, 1769.

Quid enim est minus, non dico oratoris, sed hominis, quam id objicere adversario, quod ille si verbo negarit, longius progredi non possit qui objecerit !—CICERO.

TO THE EARL OF HILLSBOROUGH.

MY LORD,

THE bare assertion of a falsehood requires nothing more than a determined countenance. To maintain a consistent falsehood not only demands a genius of invention, but a faithful memory. In your Lordship's letter, signed *Cleophas, jun.*, you are pleased to assert that the Duke of Grafton offered to recall General Gage in order that Sir Jeffery Amherst might return to America with the chief command of the King's forces. Now, my Lord, I absolutely deny the fact; and as the public will not expect me to prove a negative, I shall leave it to your Lordship to produce your evidence, if you have any.

Really, my good Lord, your letters upon business are drawn up with very little caution. In one article you tell us that the chief command in America was offered to Sir Jeffery Amherst, and in the next that he has been discovered for some time past to entertain a strong partiality for the refractory colonists. If both these facts were true, what an opinion must we conceive of a ministry careless and imprudent enough to intrust a man so biassed with such a command! You see, my Lord, to what an unfortunate dilemma you have reduced yourself by a weak inconsistent defence. The rage of writing letters has brought many a wiser minister than your Lordship to an untimely end.

You seem determined, my Lord, to go through the family of Cleophas. Be it so. If your pedigree extended from Denbigh to St. David's, I would not cease to pursue you from father to son, until I had fairly extirpated the whole family.

LUCIUS.

## LETTER XL.

SIR,                                   September 7, 1768.
As I have not the least intention to enter into any dispute with *Lucius*, indulge me but this once, and give me leave to assure you it shall be the last on the subject from me; and though this man writes so ungenteelly that he scarce deserves an answer, yet I could not help thinking this much necessary, in justice to a nobleman whom he has most shamefully attacked in consequence of my letter, but whose character is above the reach of malice, and who will be respected when such pests of society are no more.

The account I sent you relative to the resignation of Sir Jeffery Amherst I had heard publicly talked of at table, and in a coffee-house; it was told as no secret; but was said to be from very good authority. I sent it as a piece of intelligence, without either adding or diminishing. I made no com-

ment on it, as I intended no offence. Facts were stated as
they were told, and as no dates were mentioned, I gave none.
I left it to the public to form opinions as they pleased; to Sir
Jeffery Amherst's friends to contradict it if they thought
proper; and it has served as a bone for curs of opposition to
snarl at.

Though I do not mean to enter into any dispute with this
fellow, yet I cannot help making a few observations on his
letter. That the government of Virginia was given away four
days before the intention of administration was mentioned to
Sir Jeffery Amherst, I have good ground to believe is not fact;
and if you, *Lucius*, possessed one grain of honesty, and if you
had no other intention but to communicate useful information
to the public, you would have told them so: that it was
applied for even as soon as it was whispered that such a measure was to be adopted, upon the supposition that Sir Jeffery
Amherst would not choose to reside, I can believe; that it
was promised to Lord Boutetort in case he did not, I can
likewise believe; and this might have been four, or even
fourteen days, for aught I know, before it was mentioned;
but pray where is the harm in all this? I fancy no measure
of government is entered into immediately on its being mentioned; it requires some time to digest. And when it was
judged expedient, in consequence of the accounts from that
province, to send the governor-general to reside in Virginia, it
was mentioned in the tenderest manner to Sir Jeffery. No
affront was ever intended. Any recompense (if he did not
choose to go) in the power of administration, or in the gift of
majesty, was offered him. What more could he expect? He
had it in his option to go or not; and if he did not go, he was
promised an equivalent, perhaps more. As soon as this measure was surmised, was there any harm in Lord Boutetort's
application? Was there any fault in Lord Hillsborough's
promising his interest for his friend? But is this an absolute
appointment? No. All the world knows applications are
made long enough before vacancies happen, and preferments
are promised; but everybody, except *Lucius*, can make a distinction between a promise and an absolute appointment. I
dare say there were applications from more than one quarter
before the late archbishop died: and probably it was promised before the event happened; but if the see had not

become vacant, the present archbishop might have remained at Coventry.

But speak out, malevolence—speak, envy, disappointment, and ill-nature. What in the name of goodness could be Sir Jeffery Amherst's objection to Lord Boutetort? Was it because he is a nobleman? Because he has gone to the chapel at St. James's, and has carried the sword of state before his King? Because he never has insulted majesty, but has always behaved himself as a dutiful and loyal subject, and respectfully to his sovereign? Are these the weighty motives for objecting to his succession? Or is it still a greater crime to be poor? And do these make it an *affront*, not an *injury !* Forbid it heaven! Forbid it Sir Jeffery Amherst's better genius! What would you have had, *Lucius !* Would you have wished to have had the naming of Sir Jeffery's successor? What a pity you had not! I declare you deserved it! How could my Lord Hillsborough dare to recommend without your permission!

*Demands*, you say, are unfit to be used from subjects requesting of the crown. Indeed, *Lucius*, you are right; but many subjects now-a-days forget that they are so! And call them by what name you please, I acknowledge these articles of accommodation sent to the Duke of Grafton by Sir Jeffery Amherst, or said to be sent, answer exactly to the ideas I have of *demands*, and pretty peremptory ones too.

It is strange, *Lucius*, that you cannot write one line without abuse. Had you made your remarks upon the Duke of Grafton's answer to the first article without abusing his Grace, it would have been genteel; but the scurrilous language you use, even when your arguments are just, proves that you are equally unacquainted with the gentleman and sense of honour. I believe it is well known that no commander-in-chief ever made less during a long war than Sir Jeffery Amherst did; and I am very sorry indeed that want of fortune, the consequence of honesty and integrity, should ever be assigned as a reason to refuse honours to those who deserve them. The honours of this country and its treasures to support them have often been lavished on many who deserved them less than the conqueror of America. This I think was the only exceptionable answer from the Duke of Grafton. I hope it is not true.

Whatever delicate feelings you, *Mr. Lucius*, may have, I know not; but I am of opinion that sinecure places, non-resident governments, and pensions, are in fact the same, though different in names; nay, the worst of the whole appears to me to be a non-resident governor. The very word implies a necessity of doing something; in fact he does nothing: he therefore is paid for what he does not, though it is his duty to do it. In short he is paid for a neglect of duty; but because our language has not annexed the word pension to such neglect, it does not grate his ears. And, after all, what was Sir Jeffery Amherst but a pensioner of the colony of Virginia? He did nothing for it, and was paid. Our idea of a pension is a reward granted for past services; so was his. Such as you, *Lucius*, such tools of opposition, such state incendiaries, venal mercenary wretches, are glad to receive rewards of your labours infinitely less honourable than either place or pension.

The Duke of Grafton's other answers were unexceptionable. As to the regiments being given away, I did not know it, therefore I am excusable.

And now, *Mr. Lucius*, I'll tell you a secret. Your supposing my letter to come from my Lord Hillsborough, in my opinion did credit to the performance and honour to me; but in justice to him I must declare, that I am not, know not, never saw, nor never spoke to the Earl of Hillsborough in my life—but, just as formerly, I am, &c.

CLEOPHAS.

---

## LETTER XLI.

### TO THE EARL OF HILLSBOROUGH.

My Lord,                                    September 9, 1768.

It is indifferent to the public whether the letters signed *Cleophas* are written by your Lordship or under your immediate direction. Whoever commits this humble begging language to paper, we know to a certainty the person by whom it is held. We know the suppliant style your Lordship has condescended to adopt at routs, at tea-tables, and in bankers' shops. But although you have changed your tone, I am bound in honour not to give you quarter. You have offended heinously against your country, and public justice demands an example for the welfare of mankind.

I foresaw *Cleophas* would soon be disavowed. It seems the poor gentleman never saw, nor spoke to your Lordship in his life, *but just as formerly.* The saving is a good one.

You say your character is above the reach of malice. True, my Lord, you have fixed that reproach upon your character to which malice can add nothing. You say it will be respected when such pests of society as I am are no more. I agree with you that it is very little respected *at present,* and I believe I may unluckily have been the spoil of good company; but I doubt whether *my* death. or even your own, will restore you to your good fame. Your peace of mind is gone for ever.

After the particulars quoted by *Cleophas,* it looks like trifling with the public, to confess that his accounts were collected in a coffee-house, and that he will neither answer for facts nor be directed by dates. These are evasions which I scorn to imitate. My authority is indisputable ; I have stated facts with precision, and marked the dates by which I shall invariably abide, yet *Cleophas* (alias your Lordship) says he has good ground *to believe* that the government was not given away four days before Sir J. A. was apprised of it; he *believes* indeed that it was previously applied for, and that Lord Boutetort had a conditional promise of it. These, it seems, are the articles of his creed ; but, as they are not points of religious faith, to which there might be some merit in sacrificing our understanding, I presume the public is not obliged to conform to them. My questions were put strictly to points of fact and time, and have not yet been answered. Places, 1 doubt not. are often applied for and promised before they are vacant; but I did not expect to bear so indecent a case supposed and urged by a man in your Lordship's station, as that the see of Canterbury was promised to another before the death of the late pious and truly reverend incumbent.

You say that government was ready to make Sir J. A. any recompense ; yet, excepting a grant of lands in a wilderness, every one of his requests was flatly denied.

You ask if there was any harm in this, or any fault in that. What is this but crying *peccavi,* in the very language of misery and despair? It neither suits the spirit which can do wrong with firmness, nor that purity of innocence which is conscious of having done right. If the necessity of sending over a governor to Virginia had really existed, and if your Lordship had thought proper to take an early opportunity of stating that necessity to Sir J. A., if you had previously apprised him of the design of giving him a successor, and if, in conformity to such declarations, a man of business, of judgment, or activity, had been fixed on, you surely could not have paid too great an attention to Sir J. A., and you would have prevented every possible appearance of an intention to affront him. As to the pecuniary injury, I will venture to say there is not a man breathing who would have been more easily satisfied in that respect than Sir J. A. Compare this supposition with your real proceedings towards him, and though you cannot blush, I am sure you will be silent.

Your questions in favour of Lord Boutetort amount to nothing. It is not that he is a bad man, or an undutiful subject. But he is a trifling character and ruined in his fortunes. Poverty of itself is certainly not a crime. Yet the prodigality which squanders a fair estate is in the first instance dishonourable; in the next it leads to every species of meanness and dependence, and when it aims at a recovery at the expense of better men, becomes highly criminal. Will your Lordship, can you, with a steady countenance, affirm that it was the *necessities* of the state, and not his own, which sent him to Virginia?

Your Lordship may give what name you think proper to the requests proposed by Sir J. A. He was desired to specify them to the Duke of Grafton, and they were refused. It is true, he did not confine himself to the idea of a bare equivalent for the pecuniary value of his government. A generous mind, offended by an insult equally signal and unprovoked, looks back to services long neglected, and with justice unites the claim arising from those services to the insult, which of *right* demands a signal reparation.

As you seem, in the Duke of Grafton's answer to the first article, to feel and acknowledge your weakness, I shall not press you further upon it.

The pensions given by the crown have been so scandalously prostituted that a man of any nicety might well be forgiven

if he wished not to have the title of pensioner added to
his name. But I shall not descend to a dispute about words.
I speak to things. If, instead of the government of Virginia,
his late Majesty, on the surrender of Louisbourg, had thought
proper to give Sir J. A. a pension, and if this had been the
declared motive of giving it, he might have accepted it without
scruple, and held it with honour. Instances of pensions so
bestowed are not very frequent. Sir Edward Hawke's is one.
How widely different is the case in question! I will not
pretend to do justice to this good man's delicacy and sense of
honour; but I can easily conceive how a man of common
spirit must be affected, when a place which he possessed on
the most honourable terms is taken from him, without
even the decency due to a gentleman; when he sees it given
to a needy court dependant, and when the only reparation
offered him, is to enroll him in a list of pensioners among
whom an honest man would blush to see his name. If you had
not been in such haste to correct the blunders of Mr. Pitt's
administration, I think your insignificant friend might have
appeared in that list without any disgrace to himself, and his
distresses might have done credit to the humanity of your
Lordship's recommendation.

You did not know that the 15th regiment was given to
Colonel Hotham. Yet your assertion was direct. For shame,
my Lord; have done with these evasions. Poor Pownal* hangs
his head in perfect modesty, and even your *fidus Achates*,
your unfortunate Barrington, disowns you.

I shall conclude with hinting to you (in a way which
you alone will understand) that there is a part of my behaviour to you for which you owe me some acknowledgment.
I know the ostensible defence you have given to the public
differs widely from the real one intrusted privately to your
friends. You are sensible that the most distant insinuation
of what that defence is would ruin you at once. But I am a
man of honour, and will neither take advantage of your imprudence, nor of the difficulty of your situation.

                                        LUCIUS.

* Secretary to the Board of Trade.

## LETTER XLII.

Plerisque moris est, prolato rerum ordine, in aliquem lætum atque plausibilem locum quam maxime possint favor abiliter excurrere.—QUINTILIAN.

TO THE EARL OF HILLSBOROUGH.

MY LORD,                                    September 10, 1769.

YOUR change of title makes no alteration in the merits of your cause. You argued as well, and were full as honest a man, under the character of *Cleophas*, as you are under that of *Scrutator*. The task of pursuing falsehood through a labyrinth of nonsense is, I confess, much heavier than I expected. You have a way with you, my Lord, which blunts the edge of attention, and sets all argument at defiance. But I hold myself engaged to the public, whose cause is united with that of Sir Jeffery Amherst. The people of this country feel, as they ought to do, your treatment of a man who has served them well ; and the time may come, my Lord, when you in your turn may feel the effects of their resentment.

You set out with asserting, that the crown has an indisputable power of dismissing its officers without assigning a cause. Not quite indisputable, my Lord ; for I have heard of addresses from parliament, to know who advised the dismission of particular officers. I have heard of impeachments attending a wanton exertion of the prerogative, and you perhaps may live to hear of them likewise.

Another assertion of the same sort has been thrown out by your emissaries, and is now gravely maintained by your Lordship, viz., that the promise conveyed to Sir J. A. by Mr. Pitt was in itself an absurdity, and that no succeeding minister is bound to make good an engagement entered into by his predecessor in office *. I shall leave my Lord Privy Seal to ex-

---

* The reference is to the letter signed *Scrutator*, in which the writer observes as follows in respect to the subject in question :—" An absurd promise is asserted to have been made to Sir Jeffery Amherst at the time of his appointment to the government of Virginia, that *his attendance on his government should never be required;* and a torrent of obloquy has been

plain to you the motives on which Mr. Pitt acted *.  The
promise arose from his own motion, and if he has not
spirit enough to maintain it, he deserves the contempt with
which you treat him.  In the mean time, I shall presume that
a lieutenant-governor was then thought as *efficient* an officer
as a governor, and that this post was bestowed on Sir J. A.
not as the salary of future duties, but as the reward of services
already performed.  In the second part of your assertion, you
wilfully confound the general measures of government with
the particular promise of a king made to an individual.  Even
ministers, my Lord, might, without any injury to their characters, preserve the faith and integrity of their office.  But
whatever latitude they may claim for themselves, the
honour of a king ought to be sacred, even to his successor.
The proposition that ministers are not bound by the engagements of their predecessors, if taken generally, is false.
There is no breach of public faith which may not be justified on such a principle.  Treaties at this rate may be
violated without national dishonour, and the most solemn
assertions from the throne contradicted without reserve.  You
forgot that you are mixing the permanent dignity of the
crown with the fluctuating interests and views of its servants.
Yet I shall now allow you more, my Lord, than I believe
you expect.  I shall admit, without hesitation, that the
promise made to Sir J. A. could not be so absolute as not to
be revocable in a case of urgent necessity.  If such a case had
been stated, and demonstrated to Sir J. A., he would not
have staid to be solicited.  He would either have gone himself, or cheerfully resigned his government to his Majesty's
disposal.  The question turns then upon the degree of that
necessity.  Make it evident to the public, and I shall then
only complain that you have done a right thing in a manner

poured upon Lord Hillsborough for not keeping a promise which it is not
even insinuated that his Lordship ever made.  I can scarce think that any
man could have been so infatuated as, at any time, to make such a preposterous promise—a promise in itself void by a settled maxim of law, as repugnant to the grant.  But if any man could be so infantinely weak, it is *his*
business alone to answer for the breach."

* Mr. Pitt was at this time Lord Privy Seal, with the title of Lord
Chatham.

the most indecent and absurd. You will remember, my Lord,
how much the issue of this question depends upon Lord
Doutetort's character, for the public will not easily be persuaded that a conjuncture which did not rise beyond the level
of Lord Doutetort's abilities could be difficult, urgent, or important *.

You say the facts on which you reason *are universally
admitted*—a *gratis dictum* which I flatly deny. If, instead of
wandering into wild declamation, you had found it convenient
to answer my questions strictly, we should have joined issue
upon our facts, and the point would long since have been determined. Permit me to refresh your memory with some of
them once more.

1. Was not Lord Doutetort absolutely appointed on the
31st of July?

2. Was it mentioned in any shape to Sir Jeffery Amherst
before the 4th of August?

3. Was it not then mentioned as a measure in contemplation only?

4. Did not Lord Boutetout kiss hands next morning, that
is Friday the 5th instant?

5. Did not Sir Jeffery Amherst's opinion in council defeat
an American scheme formed by you and Lord Barrington, and
is not this the true cause of your rancour against him?

---

* *Scrutator* concludes his letter in the following words:—

"Our vigilant minister is vehemently exclaimed against because he showed
himself prepared on the instant to supply the vacant place of the recreant
knight. According to the ideas of the politicians of the *bon ton*, who always
substitute personal to national considerations, there ought to have been a
decent interval allowed either for the gentleman to repent, or for us, like
fashionable widows, to mourn, before a successor were appointed in his room—
though in that interval the colony should be lost. I honour Lord Hillsborough for having his man ready, ready not only for his place, but for the
province; ready not only to kiss hands, but to take his passage. And from
the watchful activity his Lordship has exerted in every known instance in his
arduous employment, I have not the least doubt but that if Lord Boutetort
had either refused to go, or on any pretext delayed his departure, Lord
Hillsborough had still some third man in his eye, who would have made
ample amends for the deficiencies of both.

"I wish this may prove a lesson to all future ministers of state to keep a
tight rein upon all officers in their departments, lest any one should cry out
and affect to be surprised when suddenly called upon to do his duty as he
prizes his salary."

It is unworthy of the character of a gentleman to endeavour to amuse the public with idle declamations, while such questions as these remain unanswered.

LUCIUS*.

* There were several replies to this letter. One by an *Independent Country Gentleman* just arrived in town, and dated from the *Bell Inn*, and another signed *Chrononhotonthologos*, seem to have obtained some attention from the public; and the latter especially, in consequence of the writer's having discovered that *Lucius* had made a mistake, not in the *facts* of the transaction, but in one of the *dates*, by asserting that Sir Jeffery Amherst came to town on Thursday, August 4, instead of one week earlier, Thursday, July 28. Both these letters were replied to with much spirit by the following, signed *Corrector* :—

"TO THE PRINTER OF THE PUBLIC ADVERTISER.

"Sir,                                                   "September 14, 1769.

"I am not surprised to find the *tools of power* alarmed at the *sensible, pointed,* and *masterly* letters of your correspondent *Lucius;* but the little arts they have as yet used to baffle his arguments have only served to expose their own weakness. I hope the gentleman at the *Bell Inn* took the opportunity of a *dry day* to get to town for further information; for in good truth, if he is still *storm-staid* by the *rainy weather,* he had much better smoke a pipe with Boniface his landlord than trouble the public with *nods,* for such I call his answers to the queries of *Lucius.*

"My troubling you at present is not to answer such a *driveller;* but on reading this morning the letter in your paper signed with the *long name,* I found that, at last, *Mr. Lucius* was catched. Your correspondent, however, deals very tenderly with him, being sensible, I suppose, of the ticklishness of the *ground.* As an admirer of the spirit of *Lucius,* and being thoroughly acquainted with the *times* and circumstances in dispute, allow me to give the true *edition,* by which it will appear that *Mr. Chrononhotonthologos* does not mend the matter by his wonderful discovery.

"*Lucius* begins on Thursday, the 4th of August, whereas in truth it was on Thursday, the 28th of July, that Sir Jeffery Amherst came to town, and finding that Lord Hillsborough had been at his house, he immediately waited on his Lordship, when he had the *first* intimation of his affair, Lord Hillsborough's letter having been sent to Sir Jeffery's house in the country. The very next day, viz. Friday, the 29th, Lord Boutetort kissed hands on his appointment to that government which the day before had been offered to Sir Jeffery; and on the 30th Sir Jeffery sent the *requests* in writing to the Duke of Grafton, which have been by the ministerial hirelings termed *demands,* and which have not been fairly represented. Sir Jeffery did not fix on the *coal mines* as the only *grant,* but left it to administration to give that, or any other which might be more convenient, to enable him to support the dignity he requested; nor did he ask for a *separate* grant of lands as has been asserted. That Sir Jeffery Amherst speaks of Lord Hillsborough in terms like a gentleman I can easily believe, as he is not capable of acting otherwise to a nobleman who has the honour of being one of his Majesty's

## LETTER XLIII.

### TO THE EARL OF HILLSBOROUGH.

MY LORD,                                    September 15, 1768.

THERE is no surer sign of a weak head than a settled depravity of heart. A base action is a disorder of the mind, and next to the folly of doing it is the folly which defends it. Had the letter signed *Lucius* never been answered, you would not have so shamefully betrayed the weakness of your cause, and your silence might have been interpreted into a consciousness of innocence. The question is now exhausted, for the public is convinced. How well or ill we have argued is of infinitely less importance than the integrity of facts. Yet even facts, though separately true, will prove nothing if the order in which they happened be confounded. Take it finally, my Lord, and disprove it if you can. Lord Boutetort's appointment was fixed on or before Sunday. You called at Sir Jeffery Amherst's on the Wednesday following. He was not in town, but you saw him next day (Thursday). You then told him that such a measure was in contemplation, but far from naming his successor, you did not tell him that his successor was appointed. Yet Lord Boutetort kissed hands the next morning (Friday), and the first notice Sir Jeffery Amherst received of his Lordship's appointment was by an express sent to him that evening by his brother.

That you are a civil, polite person is true. Few men understand the little morals better, or observe the great ones less, than your Lordship. You can bow and smile in an honest man's face, while you pick his pocket. These are the virtues of a court in which your education has not been neglected. In any other school you might have learned that simplicity and integrity are worth them all. Sir Jeffery Amherst was fighting the battles of this country, while you, my Lord, the darling child of prudence and urbanity, were practising the

servants; but that he was *pleased* at the treatment he received I absolutely deny, as it must be evident to the world, from what followed the appointment of Lord Boutetort, that he thought himself *grossly affronted*.

"CORRECTOR."

generous arts of a courtier, and securing an honourable
interest in the antechamber of a favourite.

As a man of abilities for public business, your first experiment has been unfortunate.  Your circular letter to the American governors, both for matter and composition, is a performance which a school-boy ought to blush for.  The importance and difficulty of the occasion gave you a fair opportunity
of showing by what talents you were qualified for the station
of a minister.  The assembly of Massachusets Bay, not contented with their own efforts to throw off their allegiance,
solicit the other colonies to unite with them in measures of
the same tendency and spirit.  A resolution of this extraordinary nature demanded the whole attention of government,
and yours in particular.  Let us see how you have treated it.
Instead of a clear precise instruction to each governor—instead of separate instructions adapted to the temper, circumstances, and interests of the several provinces, wherein you
might have shown your political abilities as well as your
knowledge of that country, what have you done?  In a circular letter of twenty or thirty lines (conceived in the same
terms to all the governors) you tell them : —

" That this measure is of a dangerous and factious tendency."
*A most wonderful discovery.*

" That it is calculated to inflame the minds of his Majesty's
subjects."  *What else do you think was meant by it?*

" An unwarrantable combination."  *That's the question
with* THEM, *and why did you not prove it so?*

" That it excites an opposition to parliament."  *What other
design in the name of folly could be proposed by it?*

" That it subverts the true principles of the constitution."
*Which they utterly deny.*

What are these but the loose hackneyed terms of office,
which make no impression because they convey no argument
and hardly a determinate meaning?  You have not suggested
a single motive to any one of the colonies why they should
not unite with the assembly of Boston.  This task you leave
to the governors, and if they find it an easy one, so much the
better.  Your conclusion however is a masterpiece.  You
desire the governors to prevail with their assemblies to take
no notice of the requisition from Boston, *which will be treating it with the contempt it deserves.*  What, my Lord, do you

seriously think that a formal attempt to unite the whole continent of America in rebellion against this country deserves
nothing but the silent indifference of contempt? Is this the
language of business or attention? Your letter, my Lord,
does indeed deserve contempt, but the enterprises of the colonies are of other importance. They call for other measures
and other ministers, and be assured that when parliament
meets, unless you intend to govern without one, neither you
nor your companions will be permitted to ruin this country
with impunity.

LUCIUS.

P.S. A friend of mine has taken the pains to collect a number
of the epithets with which Lord Hillsborough has been pleased
to honour me in the course of our correspondence. I shall lay
them before the public in one view, as a specimen of his Lordship's urbanity and singular condescension :—

1. Wretched scribbler.
2. Worthless fellow.
3. Vile incendiary.
4. False liar, *in opposition to a true one.*
5. Snarler.
6. Contemptible thing.
7. Abandoned tool of opposition, and diabolical miscreant.
8. Impudent scurrilous wretch.
9. Rascal and scoundrel, *passim.*
10. Barking cur, *by way of distinction from*
11. Barking animal, *cum multis aliis.*

To all which I shall only say that his Lordship's arguments
are upon a level with his politeness.

P.S. I acknowledge a mistake the moment I perceive it.
I have advanced the transaction between Lord Hillsborough
and Sir Jeffery Amherst too forward by one complete week.
But the days of the week, the facts, and the order in which
they succeeded one another, are the same. You see plainly
that my arguments are not affected by this mistake. If they
had, I should have acknowledged it without hesitation.

## LETTER XLIV.

MY LORD,                                September 20, 1768.

PERMIT me to have the honour of introducing you to a very amiable and valuable acquaintance. Mr. Ford is the gentleman I mean. Your Lordship will forgive the timidity and bashfulness of his first address, and, considering your quality, condescend to make him some advances. There is a similarity in your circumstances, to say nothing of your virtues and understanding, which may lay the foundation of a solid friendship between you for the rest of your lives. Undoubtedly you are not quite unacquainted with a character on which you appear to have formed your own. His case was singular, my Lord, and cannot fail of exciting some emotions of sympathy in your Lordship's breast. This worthy man found himself exposed to a most malicious prosecution for perjury. A profligate jury found him guilty, and a cruel judge pronounced his sentence of imprisonment, pillory, and transportation. His mind was a good deal distressed in the course of this affair (for he too is a man of delicate feelings), but his character, like yours, was above the reach of malice. Not to keep your Lordship any longer in pain, I have the pleasure of telling you that, when law and justice had done their worst, a lady, in whom he seldom places any confidence at cards, was generous enough to stand his friend. Fortune discovered a flaw in the indictment; and now, my Lord, in spite of an iniquitous prosecution, in spite of conviction and sentence, he stands as fair in his reputation as ever he did. Your Lordship will naturally be struck with the resemblance between your case and his. Facts were so particularly stated against you that they could not be denied; the order in which they happened was demonstrated, and sentence was pronounced by the public. The affair was over, when up gets *Tommy Ford*, and discovers that the whole transaction passed in the last week of July instead of the first in August. This mistake, as it brought the object nearer to us, I called *advancing*. In your Lordship's country I presume it may properly be called a retreat. Here, however, the comparison ends　Your friend escaped by a form of law. But you, my Lord, have been tried at a tribunal of honour and equity. The public, who are your judges, will not suffer my mistake (however it may prove the badness of my heart to acknowledge it) to quash the indictment against you. You are convicted of having done a base and foolish action, in a manner the most despicable and absurd. Your punishment attends you in the contempt and detestation of mankind.

Your Lordship has been pleased to publish a long letter in the Gazetteer, to prove that all Sir Jeffery Amherst's military services are a mere fiction. You did not sign it, indeed, because you had lately signed another, containing the most express and authentic acknowledgment of those services in a style of applause not very distant from flattery. You will not now, it seems, allow him any share in the reduction of Louisbourg, or the conquest of Canada. Perhaps, after all, he never was in America. I am not a soldier, my Lord, nor will I pretend to determine what share of honour a general is entitled to for success, who must have borne the whole blame and disgrace if he had failed. Had the event been unfavourable, his officers, I dare say, would have been willing enough to yield *their* concern in it to their commander-in-chief. As to the rest, I have heard from military men that the judgment and capacity which make resistance useless or impracticable are rated much higher than even the resolution which overcomes it. When you, my Lord, and Mr. Ford are forgotten, this country will remember with gratitude, that Sir Jeffery Amherst had the honour of making sixteen French battalions prisoners of war; that he carried on the whole war in America at an expense less than the fortunes which some individuals had acquired by contracts and management in Germany; and that he *did not* put the savings into his own pocket.

If a British peerage be too high a reward for him, at least do him justice. Do not assure the public that he was not contented with a revenue of four thousand pounds a year, when you know that the income of his government and two regiments did not exceed two thousand three hundred, and that, until he was positively outraged, he never complained. As I profess dealing in facts, take the account :—

|                           |   |   |        |
|---------------------------|---|---|--------|
| Government of Virginia     | . | . | . £1500 |
| Fifteenth regiment         | . | . | . 600  |
| Commandant of the 60th     | . | . | . 200  |
|                           |   |   | 2300   |

As to a peerage, you would have done well to consider upon what sort of people this honour has been conferred for ten years past. Among the rest, we should be glad to know what were your Lordship's services or merits when you were created Baron of Harwich. I take for granted that they were of a different complexion from those of Sir J. A., since they have been so differently rewarded.

Here I shall conclude. You have sent Sir Jeffery Amherst to the plough. You have left him poor in every article of which a false fawning minister could deprive him; but you have left him rich in the esteem, the love, and veneration of his country. You cannot now recall him by any offer of wealth or honours. Yet I foretell that a time will come when you yourself will be the cause of his return. Proceed, my Lord, as you have begun, and you will soon reduce this country to an extremity in which the wisest and best subjects *must* be called upon, and *must* be employed. Till then enjoy your triumph.

LUCIUS.

## LETTER XLV.

### TO THE PRINTER OF THE PUBLIC ADVERTISER.

SIR,                                                    October 6, 1768.

SINCE my last letter was printed*, a question has been stated in the newspapers, which I think it incumbent upon me as an honest man to answer. Admitting my representation of the melancholy state of this country and of public credit to be strictly true, " what good purpose can it answer to discover such truths, and to lay our weakness open to the world?" One would think such a question hardly wanted a reply. If a real misfortune were lessened by concealment; if, by shutting our eyes to our weakness, we could give our enemies an opinion of our strength, none but a traitor would withdraw

* Miscellaneous Letter, No. 33.

the veil which covered the nakedness of his country. But if the contrary be true, if concealment serves only to nourish and increase the mischief, the conclusion is direct. A good subject will endeavour to rouse the attention of his country; he will give the alarm, and point out the danger against which she ought to provide. The policy of concealment is no better than the wisdom of a prodigal, who wastes his estate without reflection, and has not courage enough to examine his accounts.

In my last letter I foretold the great fall of the stocks, which has since happened, and I now do not scruple to foretell that they must and will fall much lower. Yet I am not moved by the arts of stockjobbers, or by temporary rumours, magnified, if not created, for particular purposes in the alley. These artifices are directed to maintain a fluctuation, not a continued fall. The principles on which my reasoning is founded are taken generally from the state of France and of this country. When I see our natural enemy strong enough not only to elude a material article of treaty *, but to set us at defiance while they conquer a kingdom †; and when I combine this appearance of strength with their natural restlessness, I cannot doubt of their taking the first opportunity to recover their lost honour by a fresh declaration of war. On the other hand, considering the hostile temper of the colonies towards us, the oppressive weight of a monstrous debt (to which a peace of six years has scarce given a sensible relief), and, above all, the misery, weakness, and distraction of our interior government, I cannot have a doubt that our enemies now have, or in a very little time will have, the fairest opportunity they can wish for to force us into a war. The conclusion to be drawn from these premises is obvious. It amounts to a moral certainty, and leaves no room for hope or apprehension.

To these, which are the most important circumstances of our situation, may well be added the high price of labour, the decay of trade, and the ruinous system on which it is conducted. Every minuter article conspires against us. The deficiency of the civil list must be paid, and cannot be paid

* His Most Catholic Majesty, being a branch of the Bourbon dynasty—in the refusal of his ministers to discharge the Manilla ransom.
† Corsica.

with less than 700,000*l.* The India Company will yield to
no terms which are not founded on an express acknowledgment of their exclusive property in their conquests in Asia.
How far their pretensions are just, is at least a doubtful question. Whether parliament will divest them of this property
by a mere declaratory law, is a matter of the most important
consideration. It would be a dreadful precedent, because it
would shake every security of private property. Yet, even if
that were determined, another question remains full of difficulty and danger; that is, in what manner the public will
avail themselves of this great right, decided by nothing but a
vote of parliament.

Sir, I am not affected by the rumours of the day. If the
stocks rise or fall upon a report of tranquillity or tumult at
Boston *, I am satisfied that it is owing to the arts and
management of stockjobbers. But I see the spirit which has
gone abroad through the colonies, and I know what consequences that spirit *must and will* produce. If it be determined to enforce the authority of the legislature, the event
will be uncertain; but if we yield to the pretensions of
America, there is no further doubt about the matter. From
that moment they become an independent people, they open
their trade with the rest of the world, and England is undone.

In these circumstances, calamitous as they are, I yet think
the uniform direction of a great and able minister might do
much. His earliest care, I am persuaded, would be to provide a fund to support the first alarm and expense of a rupture
with France. If prepared to meet a war, he might perhaps
avoid it. His next object would be to form a plan of agreement with the colonies. He would consent to yield some
ground to the Americans, if it were possible to receive a
security from them that they never would advance beyond the
line then drawn, upon conditions mutually agreed on. By an
equitable offer of this kind, he would certainly unite this
country in the support of his measures, and I am persuaded
he would have the reasonable part of the Americans of his
side.

These, Sir, unfortunately for us, are views too high and
important even to be thought of while we are governed as we

* See note to Junius, Letter 39, vol. I. p. 293.

are. I would not descend to a reproachful word against men whose persons I hardly know; but it is impossible for an honest man to behold the circumstances to which a weak, distracted administration has reduced us without feeling one pang at least for the approaching ruin of Great Britain.

ATTICUS.

## LETTER XLVI.

### TO THE PRINTER OF THE PUBLIC ADVERTISER.

SIR,                                                October 12, 1769.

I BELIEVE one may challenge any time or country to produce more noble instances of a free and manly spirit than have appeared in several of your late correspondents. Without direction. without information, without promise or hope of reward. without personal friendship, favour, or acquaintance, several heroes of the pen have boldly stood forth and generously dared to defend a great minister of state, although in the plenitude of his power, and invested with the patronage to an infinite number of lucrative offices. This, I say, is true virtue; and this virtue your correspondents, with various hard names, have solemnly assured us they possess.

They have demonstrated to the satisfaction of the public, against the calumnies of a dull writer, called *Lucius*, that every part of the late conduct of Lord Hillsborough with regard to Sir J. Amherst is just what it ought to have been; nothing ill-intentioned, nothing either deficient or redundant; and that it may well serve for a pattern upon all similar occasions.

However, it sometimes happens a little perversely, that the very best actions have every now and then consequences that are somewhat odd—I do not say absolutely bad; but only a little untoward. Thus though Lord Hillsborough has done his duty to a miracle in all parts of this business, and that his character comes like gold out of the furnace of this fierce contest, yet so it happens, that the event, and the sole event, of all this upright intention and wise action is, that the nation has at a critical time lost to her service Sir J. Amherst, and has gained to it Lord Boutetort.

VOL. II.                                                        B

This is a little crooked with regard to the political effect of the measure; but I hope it is set to rights by the moral consequence. Rewards and punishments are so distributed as to point out for the future to all people, in the civil or military lines, the conduct they ought to pursue, in such a manner that it is impossible they should mistake their way. For Sir Jeffery Amherst has lost 2300l. a year by his folly—Lord Hillsborough and Lord Boutetort have each acquired as much by their wisdom. I cannot forbear to congratulate the public upon all these favourable appearances.

I am, Sir,
Your humble Servant,
TEMPORUM FELICITAS.

## LETTER XLVII

### TO THE PRINTER OF THE PUBLIC ADVERTISER.

SIR,                                                   October 15, 1768.

YOUR correspondent, who calls himself *A Friend to Public Credit*, has given us one of the most extravagant conceits that ever entered into the brain of a politician. He assures us that a rupture with France or Spain is highly improbable, because the secretary of state* for that department possesses no share in his master's confidence, and is in open enmity with his colleagues in office. Supposing the argument to be just, let us see how far it will extend. One of his Majesty's ministers is hated and distrusted; *ergo*, a war is improbable. But if two of them should happen to be in that unpleasant situation, the improbability would increase, and so we should proceed to an inevitable conclusion. If all the ministry were separately suspected by their master, and reciprocally detested by one another (which I fancy is not far from the truth), a declaration of war would be the last thing to be expected. At this rate the peace of this country is established upon a foundation equally new and secure—upon the distraction of the councils by which we are governed. What a pity it is that not one article in this pretty syllogism is true! I agree with your correspondent, that when a nation is

* Lord Shelburne.

governed as we are, our constant prayer should be, *Give peace in the time of these ministers, O Lord!* But I fear that the same reasons which ought to keep us quiet will operate in a contrary direction upon our enemies. I fear they only wait until the differences with our colonies and the divisions among ourselves are arrived at a crisis, and that then they will overwhelm us with an open war. In the mean time the House of Bourbon are labouring to unite their strength, and to extend the bounds of their dominion. Their insatiable ambition will not spare even the father of their church, who must be entirely dispossessed of his territories, unless the Protestant powers interpose in his defence. It was and ought for ever to be our policy to support this prince in his temporal power, without any regard to his religion. If he were a Turk, he ought to be protected in the possession of his dominions against the House of Bourbon. Or are we to sink into a lethargic stupidity, while the French conquer Corsica and overrun Italy, and sit with our arms across until they thunder at our gate? There is certainly some dreadful infatuation which hangs over and directs the councils of this country. Our ministers drive us headlong to destruction, while their emissaries insult us with assurances that the divisions among the King's servants form the best security of peace with our enemies. God knows, Sir, it is time to rouse and shake off this lethargy. It is time for parliament to interpose, if yet there be a hope of saving Great Britain. Our last constitutional resource is vested in parliament. By whose advice or neglect the French were suffered to land in Corsica should be one of the first objects of their inquiry, and whether French money has been given or received here. Every measure of government opens an ample field for a parliamentary inquisition. If this resource should fail us, our next and latest appeal must be made to heaven.

BRUTUS.

---

## LETTER XLVIII.

### TO THE PRINTER OF THE PUBLIC ADVERTISER.

SIR,                                                    October 19, 1768.

WE are assured by the advocates of the ministry, that while Lord Shelburne is secretary of state we can have no reason to apprehend a rupture with France or Spain. This proposition is singular enough, and I believe turns upon a refinement very distant from the simplicity of common sense. But, admitting it to be self-evident, the conclusion is such as I apprehend your correspondent, who signs himself *A Friend to Public Credit*, did not clearly foresee. If Lord Shelburne's remaining in office constitutes a security of peace, his being suddenly removed must amount to a declaration of war. Now, Sir, the fact is, that his Lordship's removal has been for some weeks in agitation, and is within these few days absolutely determined *. If I were a party writer, the indiscretion of the ministerial advocates would give me as many advantages as even the wretched conduct of the ministry themselves. But I write for the public, and in that view hold myself far above a little triumph over men whose compositions are as weak as the cause they defend †.

In my former letters I have given you a melancholy but a true representation of the state of this country. Every packet from America and the Continent confirms it. The demonstration of facts follows the probability of argument, and the prediction of the present hour is the experience of the next. If you will now permit me to offer my opinion of the great persons under whose administration we are reduced to this deplorable state, the public will be enabled to judge whether these are the men most likely to relieve us from it. The curiosity of personal malice shall make no part of this inquiry. As public men we have a right to be acquainted with their real characters, because we are interested in their public conduct.

When the Duke of Grafton first entered into office, it was the fashion of the times to suppose that young men might have wisdom without experience. They thought so themselves, and the most important affairs of this country were committed to the first trial of their abilities. His Grace had honourably fleshed his maiden sword in the field of opposition, and had gone through all the discipline of the minority with credit. He dined at Wildman's, railed at favourites, looked up to Lord Chatham with astonishment,

* Lord Shelburne resigned October 21, 1768.
† See Private Letter, No. 5, *ante*, p. 6, In which the author makes a similar remark upon the writers in defence of the then administration.

and was the declared advocate of Mr. Wilkes.   It afterwards
pleased his Grace to enter into administration with his
friend Lord Rockingham, and, in a very little time, it pleased
his Grace to abandon him.   He then accepted of the treasury
upon terms which Lord Temple had disdained.   For a short
time his submission to Lord Chatham was unlimited.   He
could not answer a private letter without Lord Chatham's
permission.   I presume he was then learning his trade, for
he soon set up for himself.   Until he declared himself the
minister, his character had been but little understood.   From
that moment a system of conduct, directed by passion and
caprice, not only reminds us that he is a young man, but a
young man without solidity or judgment.   One day he
desponds and threatens to resign.   The next, he finds his
blood heated, and swears to his friends he is determined to go
on.   In his public measures we have seen no proof either
of ability or consistency.   The stamp act had been repealed
(no matter how unwisely) under the preceding administration.
The colonies had reason to triumph, and were returning to
their good humour.   The point was decided, when this young
man thought proper to revive it.   Without either plan or
necessity, he adopts the spirit of Mr. Grenville's measures,
and renews the question of taxation in a form more odious
and less effectual than that of the law which had been repealed.

With respect to the invasion of Corsica*, it will be matter
of parliamentary inquiry, whether he has carried on a secret
negotiation with the French court, in terms contradictory to
the resolution of council, and to the instructions drawn up
thereupon by his Majesty's secretary of state†.   If it shall
appear that he has quitted the line of his department to betray the honour and security of his country, and if there be a
power sufficient to protect him, in such a case, against public
justice, the constitution of Great Britain is at an end.

His standing foremost in the persecution of Mr. Wilkes,

---

* See notes in vol. i. p. 117.   When, upon the invitation of the Genoese,
the French invaded Corsica, a remonstrance was presented by the English
minister at Paris ; but here the resistance dropped.

† A motion which tended to an inquiry of this kind was made in the
House of Commons by Hans Sloane, Esq.; but the *uninfluenced, unplaced,
unpensioned majority*, thought proper to put a *negative* upon it.

if former declarations and connections be considered, is base and contemptible *. The man whom he now brands with treason and blasphemy but a very few years ago was the Duke of Grafton's friend, nor is his identity altered, except by his misfortunes. In the last instance of his Grace's judgment and consistency, we see him, after trying and deserting every party, throw himself into the arms of a set of men whose political principles he had always pretended to abhor. Those men I doubt not will teach him the folly of his conduct better than I can. They grasp at everything, and will soon push him from his seat. His private history would but little deserve our attention, if he had not voluntarily brought it into public notice. I will not call the amusements of a young man criminal, though I think they become his age better than his station. There is a period at which the most unruly passions are gratified or exhausted, and which leaves the mind clear and undisturbed in its attention to business. His Grace's gallantry would be offended if we were to suppose him within many years of being thus qualified for public affairs. As for the rest, making every allowance for the frailty of human nature, I can make none for a continued breach of public decorum †; nor can I believe that man very zealous for the interest of his country who sets her opinion at defiance. This nobleman, however, has one claim to respect, since it has pleased our gracious sovereign to make him prime minister of Great Britain.

The Chancellor of the Exchequer‡ is a moderate man, and pretends to no higher merit than that of a humble assistant in office. If he escapes censure, he is too prudent to aim at applause. The necessity of his affairs had separated him from earlier friendships and connections, and if he were of any consequence, we might lament that an honest man should find it necessary to disgrace himself in a post he is utterly unfit for. But we have other objects to attend to. It depends greatly upon the present management of the finances whether this country shall stand or fall. A common clerk in office may conduct the ordinary supplies of the year, but to give a sensible relief to public credit, or to provide funds

* See Junius, vol. i. p. 151.
† See Junius, vol. i. p. 166, and Miscellaneous Letter 20.
‡ Lord North.

against a rupture abroad, are objects above him. To remove those oppressions which lie heaviest upon trade, and, by the same operation, to improve the revenue, demands a superior capacity, supported by the most extensive knowledge. To vulgar minds it may appear unattainable, because vulgar minds make no distinction between the highly difficult and the impossible*.

The Earl of Hillsborough† set out with a determined attachment to the court party, let who would be minister. He had one vice less than other courtiers, for he never even pretended to be a patriot. The Oxford election gave him an opportunity of showing some skill in parliamentary management; while an uniform obsequious submission to his superiors introduced him into lucrative places, and crowned his ambition with a peerage. He is now what they call a king's man; ready, as the closet directs, to be anything or nothing, but always glad to be employed. A new department, created on purpose for him, attracted a greater expectation than he has yet been able to support. In his first act of power he has betrayed a most miserable want of judgment. A provision for Lord Boutetort was not an object of importance sufficient to justify a risk of the first impression which a new minister must give of himself to the public. For my own part I hold him in some measure excused, because I am persuaded the defence he has delivered privately to his friends is true, "That the measure came from another and a higher quarter." But still he is the tool, and ceasing to be criminal sinks into contempt. In his new department I am sorry to say he has shown neither abilities nor good sense. His letters to the colonies contain nothing but expressions equally loose and violent. The minds of the Americans are not to be conciliated by a language which only contradicts without attempting to persuade. His correspondence, upon the whole, is so defective both in design and composition, that it would deserve our pity, if the consequences to be dreaded from it did not excite our indignation. This treatment of the colonies, added to his refusal to present a petition from one of them to

* See Lord North's talents further discussed in the Letters of Junius, No. 34, where the writer does not appear to entertain a much higher opinion of them than in his present address.
† Minister for the Colonial Department.

the king (a direct breach of the declaration of rights), will naturally throw them all into a flame. I protest, Sir, I am astonished at the infatuation which seems to have directed his whole conduct. The other ministers were proceeding in their usual course, without foreseeing or regarding consequences; but this nobleman seems to have marked out, by a determined choice, the means to precipitate our destruction.

The Earl of Shelburne had initiated himself in business, by carrying messages between the Earl of Bute and Mr. Fox, and was for some time a favourite with both. Before he was an ensign he thought himself fit to be a general, and to be a leading minister before he ever saw a public office. The life of this young man is a satire on mankind. The treachery which deserts a friend, might be a virtue compared to the fawning baseness which attaches itself to a declared enemy. Lord Chatham became his idol, introduced him into the most difficult department of the state, and left him there to shift for himself. It was a masterpiece of revenge. Unconnected, unsupported, he remains in office without interest or dignity, as if the income were an equivalent for all loss of reputation. Without spirit or judgment to take an advantageous moment of retiring, he submits to be insulted, as long as he is paid for it. But even this abject conduct will avail him nothing. Like his great archetype, the vapour on which he rose deserts him, and now,

> " Fluttering his pennons vain, plumb down he drops." *

I cannot observe without reluctance, that the only man of real abilities in the present administration is not an object of either respect or esteem. The character of the Lord Chancellor† is a strong proof that an able, consistent, judicious conduct depends upon other qualities than those of the head. Passions and party, in his Lordship's understanding, had united all the extremes. They gave him to the world in one moment the patron of natural liberty, independent of civil constitutions, in the next the assertor of prerogative independent of law‡. How he will advise the crown in the present crisis, is of more importance to the public than to himself. His patronage of Mr. Wilkes and of America have suc-

---

\* Milton, Paradise Lost, ii.            † Lord Camden.
‡ Junius, Letter 59.

ceeded to his wish. They have given him a peerage, a pension, and the seals; and as for his future opinions, he can adopt none for which he may not find a precedent and justification in his former conduct.

The Earl of Chatham—I had much to say, but it were inhuman to persecute, when Providence has marked out the example to mankind *!

My Lord Granby is certainly a brave man, and a generous man, and both without design or reflection. How far the army is improved under his direction is another question. His German friends will all have regiments; and it is enough to say of his Lordship, that he has too much good humour to contradict the reigning minister.

The length of this letter will not permit me to do particular justice to the Duke of Bedford's friends; neither is it necessary. With one united view they have but one character. My Lord Gower and Lord Weymouth were distressed, and Rigby was insatiable. The school they were bred in taught them how to abandon their friends without deserting their principles. There is a littleness even in their ambition, for money is their first object. Their professed opinions upon some great points are so different from those of the party with which they are now united, that the council-chamber is become a scene of open hostilities. While the fate of Great Britain is at stake, these worthy counsellors dispute without decency, advise without sincerity, resolve without decision, and leave the measure to be executed by the man who voted against it. This, I conceive, is the last disorder of the state. The consultation meets but to disagree. Opposite medicines are prescribed, and the last fixed on is changed by the hand that gives it.

Such is the council by which the best of sovereigns is advised, and the greatest nation upon earth governed. Separately the figures are only offensive; in a group they are formidable. Commerce languishes, manufactures are oppressed, and public credit already feels her approaching dissolution; yet under the direction of this council we are to prepare for a dreadful contest with the colonies, and a war with the

* His Lordship had resigned his post of lord privy seal three days previous to the date of this letter, and was succeeded in that office, on the 2nd of November following, by the Earl of Bristol.

whole house of Bourbon. I am not surprised that the generality of men should endeavour to shut their eyes to this melancholy prospect. Yet I am filled with grief and indignation when I behold a wise and gallant people lost in a stupidity which does not feel, because it will not look forward. The voice of one man will hardly be heard when the voice of truth and reason is neglected; but as far as mine extends, the authors of our ruin shall be marked out to the public. I will not tamely submit to be sacrificed, nor shall this country perish without warning.

ATTICUS.

## LETTER XLIX.

TO THE PRINTER OF THE PUBLIC ADVERTISER.

Sir,                                              October 26, 1768.

THE great abilities which have distinguished the character of the Earl of Rochford have justly procured him the love of his countrymen, and have entitled him to the favour and protection of his sovereign: it was therefore with universal approbation that the public received the promises of his advancement at this important crisis to the important office of Secretary of State. It was with a degree of hope to which they have long been unaccustomed that they flattered themselves foreign business would now be no longer neglected. They had reason to expect much from a man to whom nature had been lavish, and whose natural talents, great as they were, must have been considerably augmented by a long residence and a constant attention to business in courts which are perhaps superior to all others in the arts and mysteries of negotiation. It was now that they felt themselves secure in the assurance that the correspondences with the courts of Paris, Madrid, and Turin, were to be carried on by a man above all others qualified for so arduous a task; by a man who had gained great reputation as an ambassador in each of them.

It was in vain that the enemies to administration endeavoured to suggest that that nobleman was not singled out on account of his superior abilities, but on account of his neutrality and non-attachment to any particular men or measures; it was in vain that they represented his nomination as a mere act of necessity, resulting from the incapacity of the leaders to promote any other without widening their bottom, which was a measure that, above all others, they most apprehended.

These suggestions had little or no effect; they were either totally disbelieved or disregarded; the consequence was good, and the public were not at all curious to know the cause; their joy, that such a measure was to take place, was only equalled by their surprise; and as their joy proceeded from a reflection of the past, as it related to Lord Rochford, they were inattentive to the present, as it relates to others.

What pity it is that they were so soon disappointed, and that a joy so well founded was destined to be of so short a duration. In proportion as they were elevated with the hopes of his being taken into office, so are they dejected by the manner of his appointment. The course and order of business appears to have been violated, and that vacancy, to which his Lordship ought to have succeeded, and which he was so well qualified to fill, has been suffered to be possessed by another altogether a stranger to the principal wheels of those machines which it becomes his duty to regulate; and the abilities of the Earl have been as far as possible thwarted by his being plunged into a correspondence with courts of whose maxims and interests he is no better qualified to judge than any other of his Majesty's servants who would make use of as much attention, and who may be happily endowed with as much penetration. It is now then that the public have both cause and inclination to ask a question, which they before thought useless and impertinent: it is now that with horror they reflect on the intelligence communicated by your correspondent *Atticus* *; it is now that they tremble at the thoughts of a secret negotiation with the French court in relation to Corsica; and it is now that they ask, why was Lord Rochford appointed Secretary of State, and for the Northern department †?

WHY?

---

* See the preceding letter.
† See this subject further discussed in Junius, Letter 1, vol. I. p. 109.

## LETTER L.

Sir,                                    October 27, 1768.

WHEN an anonymous writer tells the public that a great
minister, who happens to be his particular friend, has given
him assurances of any sort, with regard to state affairs, the
authority is doubly suspicious. In the first place, that such
writers should have such friends is not, in the highest degree,
probable. In the next, it is much to be doubted, whether
ministers of state always tell the truth even to their most
intimate acquaintance. I take for granted, the author of the
letter, signed *Plain Truth and Justice\**, is a modest man,
since he expects an implicit reliance on the bare assertion of
a person entirely unknown to us. But I fear he will find
himself a little disappointed, for the public is not to be
imposed upon by such gross artifices. The letters, in which
your correspondent *Atticus* had foretold the decline of public
credit, seemed to rest upon a very different footing. He made
no assertions of his own, because he neither required nor expected any reliance on his personal credit or authority. He
stated facts too notorious to be disputed, and he reasoned upon
them in a way which there has yet been no attempt to answer.
This is the fair ground on which his opponents ought to meet
him. Vague assertions have no claim to credit, and, if they
had, would amount to no proof. What ministers are pleased
to say, or what their friends say for them, is but of little
moment. A man who in the present crisis would direct his
conduct upon sure grounds, ought to examine the real state
of public affairs, and, according as he finds them, act with
prudence for himself and his family. I know that an artful
combination in the alley may, for a short time, raise or sink
the price of stocks a trifle. But no arts, no combination, can
support them against the reality of national distress. The
maxim holds through life. A beggar may cut a figure for a
day, but his ruin is inevitable, and his creditors perish with
him.

---

\* He alludes to a correspondent in the *Public Advertiser*, who had replied
to his former letter under this signature.

Your correspondent assures us that no money will be wanted for the ensuing year. With all due respect to an anonymous assertion, I should be glad to know by what sort of reasoning he would support it. Do the ministry mean to leave the debt on the civil list unpaid? I will tell him that they cannot, dare not do it. This debt amounts to above six hundred thousand pounds, and if they can pay it without money, so much the better. Have they made any agreement with the East India Company? No. Have they made any provision for outstanding navy and victualling bills? I answer, they must whether they will or no. Have the Bank agreed to continue creditors for the last million they advanced to government? I answer, that the Bank have no confidence in the present administration, and will not trust them. As to taking the four per cents. entirely out of the market. Mr. Grenville, or an able financier who possessed the confidence of the public, might perhaps accomplish it, but it is not an object within the reach of the present treasury board. They talk of it in their dreams, and forget it when they wake*.

These. Sir, are considerations independent of a war, which hangs over us, and of a contest with the colonies, which in no way can end favourably for this country. As to moderate qualifying measures, I know but one which the Americans will accept of, and that is an absolute release from all subjection. They will reject with disdain an offer to be represented in parliament, because they *will* be independent. They found the effect of their last combination, and when they demand a repeal of an act of the legislature, it must be done without conditions. But, in the name of common sense, what useful purpose will our submission answer? Upon the repeal of the stamp act, our exports to America, instead of doubling, as had been promised, diminished considerably. What are we doing, then, but surrendering the first essential rights and principles of the constitution for the sake of a bribe, of which we are cheated at last? We may retire to our prayers, for the game is up.

BRUTUS.

* See Junius, Letter 39, vol. i. p. 299, in which the failure of Lord North to effect this object is censured by the author and explained in a note appended to it.

## LETTER LI.

SIR,                                                   November 14, 1768.

WHEN I foretold the approach of a foreign war, the certainty of a rupture with the colonies, and the decline of public credit, my opinion was chiefly founded on the character, circumstances, and abilities of the present administration. Fortune has but little share in the events most interesting to mankind. Individuals perish by their own imprudence, and the ruin of an empire is no more than the misconduct of a minister or a king. Without the credit of personal reputation, divided as a ministry, and unsupported by talents or experience, his Majesty's servants had left the field of national calamity wide open to prediction. It seems they were determined to accomplish more than even their enemies had foretold. For my own part, I am not personally their enemy, and I could have wished that their conduct had not made the name of friend to the ministry irreconcilable with that of friend to Great Britain.

The most contemptible character in private life, and the most ruinous to private fortunes, is that which possesses neither judgment nor inclination to do right, nor resolution enough to be consistent in doing wrong. Such a man loses all the credit of firmness and uniformity, and suffers the whole reproach of weak or malicious intentions. In politics, there is no other ministerial character so pernicious to the honour of a prince, or so fatal to the welfare of a nation. It is of the highest importance to inquire whether the present ministry deserve it.

The name of Lord Chatham's administration was soon lost in that of the Duke of Grafton. His Grace took the lead, and made himself answerable for the measures of a council at which he was supposed to preside. He had gone as far as any man in support of Mr. Pitt's doctrine, *that parliament had no right to lay a tax upon America, for the sole purpose of raising a revenue.* It was a doctrine on which Lord Chatham and the Chancellor* formed their administration, and his

---

* Lord Camden.

Grace had concurred in it *with all his sincerity*. Yet the first act of his own administration was to impose that tax upon America which has since thrown the whole continent into a flame. A wise man would have let the question drop: a good man would have felt and adhered to the principles he professed. While the gentle Conway breathed into his ear, he was all lenity and moderation. The colonies were dutiful children, and Great Britain a severe parent. A combination to ruin this country was no more than an amicable agreement, and rebellion was a natural right confirmed by the revolution. But now it seems his Grace's opinions are altered with his connections. *The measures of the colonies are subversive of the constitution; they manifest a disposition to throw off their dependence*, and vigorous measures must be enforced at the point of the sword. In vain may we look for the temper and firmness of a great minister: we shall find nothing but the passion or weakness of a boy, the enervated languor of a consumption, or the false strength of a delirium.

The same inconsistency will be found to prevail through every measure and operation of government. Perhaps there may be discovered something more than supineness in the first neglect of Corsica, and something worse than inconsistency in the contradiction given to Lord Rochford's spirited declaration to the court of France*. His Grace has lately adopted the opposite extreme, and scruples not to give an alarming shock to public credit by hints little short of a declaration of war. What is this but the undetermined timidity of a coward, who trembles on the brink until he plunges headlong into the stream?

In one gazette we see Sir Jeffery Amherst dismissed, in the very next we see him restored, and both without reason or decency. The peerage, which had been absolutely refused, is granted, and as in the first instance the royal faith was violated, in the second the royal dignity is betrayed. But this perhaps is a compliment to the Duke's new friendship with the Earl of Hillsborough.

Without approving of Mr. Wilkes's conduct, I lament his fate. The Duke of Grafton, who contributed to his support

* Junius, Letter No. 12, vol. i. p. 160. Lord Rochford acted on the instructions of the Earl of Shelburne, secretary of state, whose conduct was repudiated by his colleagues, and the Earl resigned.—ED.

abroad, has given the mandate for his expulsion. But I trust there is yet a spirit which will not obey such mandates. This honourable enterprise will probably be defeated, and leave the author of it nothing but a distinguished excess of infamy, the last consolation of a profligate mind.

Is it possible, Sir, that such a ministry can long remain united, or support themselves if they were united? The Duke of Grafton, it is true, has no scruple nor delicacy in the choice of his measures. They are the measures of the day, and vary as often as the weather. But his companions had each their separate plan, to which, for the credit of government, and the benefit of this country, they have severally adhered. The intrepid thoughtless spirit of the Commander-in-Chief looks no further than to the disposal of commissions. He is the friend and patron of the military. With this character he suffers the army to be robbed of a regiment, by way of pension to the noble disinterested house of Percy, and Sir Jeffery Amherst to be sacrificed without pretending to the credit of restoring him. His Lordship's conduct perplexes me. I am at a loss which to admire most, the penetrating sagacity with which he understands the rights of the army, or the firmness with which he defends them.

When an ungracious act was to be done, the Earl of Hillsborough was chosen for the instrument of it. He deserved, since he submitted to bear, the whole reproach of Sir Jeffery Amherst's dismission. The gallant knight obtains his price, and the noble Earl, with whatever appetite, must meet him with a smile of congratulation, and, *Dear Sir Jeffery, I most cordially wish you joy!* After all, it must be confessed there are some mortifications which might touch even the callous spirit of a courtier.

The Chancellor of the Exchequer has many deficiencies to make good besides those of land and malt; and to say the truth, he has a gallant way of doing it. He gallops bravely through thick and thin, as the court directs, and I dare say would defend even an honest cause with as much zeal and eloquence as if he were ordered to show his parts upon *nullum tempus* *, or a Cumberland election.

* See Junius, Letter No. 57, vol. i., and note to Miscellaneous Letter, No. 14, *ante*, p. 159.

It would be unjust to the Duke of Bedford's friends to attribute their conduct to any but the motives which they themselves profess. Mr. Rigby is so modest a man that the imputation of public virtue or private good faith would offend his delicacy, if he did not feel, as he certainly does, the genuine emotions of patriotism and friendship warm in his

* breast. They argued not ill for ambition, while they asked for nothing but profit; and when the Duke of Grafton has exhausted the treasury he will find that every other power departs with the power of giving.

In this and my former letters I have presented to you, with plainness and sincerity, the melancholy condition to which we are reduced. The characters of a weak and worthless ministry would hardly deserve the attention of history, but that they are fatally united, and must be recorded, with the misfortunes of their country.

If there be yet a spark of virtue left among us, this great nation shall not be sacrificed to the fluctuating interests or wayward passions of a minister, nor even to the caprices of a monarch. If there be no virtue left, it is no matter who are ministers, nor how soon they accomplish our destruction.

ATTICUS*.

---

## LETTER LII.

### TO THE PRINTER OF THE PUBLIC ADVERTISER.

SIR,                                    November 21, 1768.

IT will soon be decided by the highest authority, whether the justice of our laws and the liberty of our constitution have been essentially violated in the person of Mr. Wilkes†. As a public man, his fate will be determined, nor is it safe or necessary at present to enter into the merits of his cause. We are interested in this question no further than as he is

* Whether or not Atticus was Junius, the reader cannot fail to perceive that the latter availed himself largely of the materials furnished by Atticus and others, his precursors, and wrought them up in superior style and fashion in the columns of the *Public Advertiser.*—ED.

† Upon the issue of the general warrant.

a part of a well-regulated society.  If a member of it be injured, the laws and constitution will defend him.  But where
is the law to enforce the engagements of private faith, or to
punish the breach of them?  Where shall *he* apply for redress with whom all ties of honour, professions of friendship,
and obligations of party have been violated or betrayed?  A
man so injured has no redress or consolation, but what he ·
finds in the resentment and generous sympathy of mankind.

The violation of party faith is of itself too common to
excite surprise or indignation.  Political friendships are so
well understood that we can hardly pity the simplicity they
deceive; and if Mr. Wilkes had only been deserted, he would
but have given us one example more of the folly of relying
on such engagements.  But his, I conceive, is a singular
situation.  There is scarce an instance of party merit so great
as his, or so ill rewarded.  Other men have been abandoned
by their friends: Mr. Wilkes alone is oppressed by them.
One would think that the First Lord of the Treasury* and
the Chancellor† might have been contented with forgetting
the man to whom they principally owed their elevation; but
hearts like theirs are not so easily satisfied.  They left him
unsupported when they ceased to want his assistance, and, to
cover the reproach of passive ingratitude, they pursue him to
destruction.  The bounds of human science are still unknown,
but this assuredly is the last limit of human depravity.
Notorious facts speak for themselves, and, in this case, an
honest man will want no spur to rouse his indignation.  Men
of a different character would do well to consider what their
security is with a minister who breaks without scruple through
all engagements of party, and is weak enough to set all public
shame at defiance.  There is a firmness of character which
will support a minister even against his vices; but where is
the dependence of his friends, when they have no hold either
on his heart or his understanding?  Detested by the better
part of mankind, he will soon be suspected by the worst, for
no man relies securely on another whom he thinks less honest
and less wise than himself.

In the present instance the Duke of Grafton may possibly

---

* The Duke of Grafton.          † Lord Camden.

find that he has played a foolish game. He rose by Mr. Wilkes's popularity, and it is not improbable that he may fall by it.

JUNIUS*.

---

## LETTER LIII.

### For the Public Advertiser.

December 15, 1768.

TO THE RIGHT HON. GEORGE GRENVILLE.

Sir,

If there be anything improper in this address, the singularity of your present situation will, I hope, excuse it. Your conduct attracts the attention, because it is highly interesting to the welfare, of the public, and a private man, who only expresses what thousands think, cannot be well accused of flattery or detraction. If we may judge by what passes every day in a great assembly, you already possess all the constituent parts of a minister, except the honour of distributing, or the emolument of receiving, the public money. These, in the contemplation of the present ministry, are the most essential ornaments of office. They are the *decus et tutamen* of a respectable administration, and the last that a prudent administration will relinquish. As for the authority, the credit, or the business of their offices, they are ready to resign them to you without reluctance. With regard to their appearance and behaviour within doors, these docile creatures find a relief in *your* understanding from the burthen of thinking, and in *your* direction from the labour of acting. This, however, is no more than the natural precedence of

* The date of this short and well-penned epistle, the first bearing the signature of Junius, reminds us that the writer is on the eve of appearing in great figure. It is a genuine sample; has all the neatness and significance of expression, the nice observance and acute knowledge of human nature, that distinguish the authenticated letters. Why Junius did not include it in his collective edition, was probably the thought that his work would more fitly begin with the new year, ushered in by an elaborate and comprehensive exposition of the state of the country and of the characters of the chief members of the ministry. See his Letter, Jan. 21, 1769, vol. i. p. 103.—Ed.

s 2

superior abilities and knowledge. Folly cannot long take the
*pas* of wisdom, and ignorance, sooner or later, must submit to
experience. Yet, considering what sort of heads you have to
deal with, the task of giving them instruction must be a heavy
one. The triumph is hardly equal to the labour which
attends it. To convey instruction into heads which perceive
nothing, is as hard a task as to instil sentiments into hearts
that feel nothing. In both these articles, I think, his Majesty's
present servants are invulnerable. They are of so strange a
composition that knowledge will neither penetrate the substance, nor shame stick upon the surface. They have one
short remedy for every inconvenience, a remedy which tyrants
make use of, and fools profess, without scruple or management. Force is their grand *arcanum imperii*. If this be the
*executive* power of the crown, they possess and exert it to a
miracle. Red and brown makes all the difference. To
Southwark the guards are detached in their uniforms: to
Brentford they march like gentlemen, with orders to change
their colours in the blood of this country. This, Sir, is the
last irresistible arguments of kings; the only one which your
abilities cannot answer, nor your integrity oppose with effect.
In vain shall you demand an account of the most flagrant
waste of public money. The ministry are sure of being protected by the ruffians who received it. The murder of his
Majesty's English subjects calls aloud, but calls in vain, for
justice. To complain is dangerous, to prosecute might be
fatal. We are arrived at that dreadful crisis at which open
murders may well be succeeded by secret assassination. May
heaven avert the omen!

Your weight and authority in parliament are acknowledged
by the submission of your opponents. Your credit with the
public is equally extensive and secure, because it is founded
on a system of conduct wisely adopted and firmly maintained
You have invariably adhered to one cause, one language, and
when your friends deserted that cause they deserted you
They who dispute the rectitude of your opinions admit that
your conduct has been uniform, manly, and consistent. This
letter, I doubt not, will be attributed to some party friend,
by men who expect no applause but from their dependants.
But you, Sir, have the testimony of your enemies in your
favour. After years of opposition, we see them revert to

those very measures, with violence, with hazard, and disgrace, which, in the first instance, might have been conducted with ease, with dignity, and moderation.

While parliament preserves its constitutional authority, you will preserve yours. As long as there is a real representation of the people, you will be heard in that great assembly with attention, deference, and respect; and if, fatally for England, the designs of the present ministry should at last succeed, you will have the consolation to reflect that your voice was heard until the voice of truth and reason was drowned in the din of arms, and that your influence in parliament was irresistible until every question was decided by the sword *.

---

\* The warm attachment of Junius to every part of the conduct of this distinguished statesman may perhaps be conceived to import something more than a mere political concurrence of sentiment, and to indicate an ardent personal friendship. The editor has found it necessary to glance at such an idea on several former occasions. Yet for the honour of Junius it ought to be observed, that there were few political characters of the day who were more entitled to his panegyric; upon which subject the reader will not be displeased at being presented with the following brief sketch of Mr. Grenville's character from the pen of a gentleman to whom these notes have been already indebted, and who had repeated opportunities of forming a correct estimate of his worth. It is extracted from the second volume of Mr. Knox's *Extra Official State Papers*, from which a letter written by Mr. Grenville, on the subject of American politics, has been selected in note to Miscellaneous Letter, No. 31, p. 200. The anecdote respecting Florida and Louisiana is infinitely creditable to his "shrewd inflexible judgment" as a statesman; and his conduct as a minister is, in many respects, not unworthy the imitation of those who hold the same dignified situations in the present day.

"Mr. Grenville, under a manner rather austere and forbidding, covered a heart as feeling and tender as any man ever possessed. He liked office, as well for its emoluments as its power; but in his attention to himself he never failed to pay regard to the situations and circumstances of his friends, though to neither would he warp the public interest or service in the smallest degree. Rigid in his opinions of public justice and integrity, and firm to inflexibility in the construction of his mind, he reprobated every suggestion of the political expediency of overlooking frauds or evasions in the payment or collection of the revenue, or of waste and extravagance in its expenditure. But although he would not bend in any measure out of the strict line of rectitude to gain popularity, he was far from being indifferent to the good or ill opinion of the public; and that tediousness and repetition which his speeches in parliament and his transactions with men of business were charged with, were occasioned by the earnestness of his desire to satisfy and convince those he addressed of the purity of his motives and the propriety of his conduct; and while there remained a single reason in his own mind that he thought would serve those

## LETTER LIV.

TO THE PRINTER OF THE PUBLIC ADVERTISER.

Mr. Woodfall,                                April 12, 1769.

THE monody on the supposed death of Junius is not the less
poetical for being founded on a fiction.   In some parts of it

purposes, he could not be content to rest upon those he had already adduced,
however convinced and satisfied his hearers appeared to be with them.

"Inheriting but a small patrimonial fortune, he had early accustomed himself to a strict appropriation of his income and an exact economy in its
expenditure, as the only sure ground on which to build a reputation for
public and private integrity and to support a dignified independency; and it
was the unvaried practice of his life, in all situations, as he has often told me,
to live upon his own private fortune, and save the emoluments of whatever
office he possessed; on which account, he added, 'The being in or out makes
no difference in my establishment or manner of life.   Everything goes on as
home in the same way.   The only difference is, that my children's fortunes
would be increased by my being in beyond what they would be if I remained
out; and that is being as little dependent upon office as any man who was
not born to a great estate can possibly be;' and he manifested that independence at a time and in a manner but little known; and as the relation
can now do no harm, I shall repeat the account he gave me of it.   He had
accepted the seals of one of the secretaries of state in Lord Bute's administration, and by so doing drew upon himself the resentment and abuse of the
then popular party, and of some of his own nearest relations; his return,
therefore, to them was rendered impracticable upon any occasion, and he had
every motive to induce him to remain with his present connection; notwithstanding which, he very soon hazarded his continuance in office in support of
his opinion of what ought to be done for the advantage of the public, on the
following occasion :—

"While the peace was negotiating, the expedition against the Havannah
was carrying on; and as the chance of its success or failure was not very
unequal, the negotiators agreed to leave it out in their uti possidetis, considering the event as perfectly neutral; so that if, after the preliminaries
were signed, it was found to be taken, it was to be restored without compensation.   Before the preliminaries were signed, however, the account of its
capture was received, and Mr. Grenville immediately proposed that it should
now be included in the uti possidetis, and compensation for it insisted upon;
for as the event was decided before the preliminaries were signed, either
party was at liberty to avail themselves of it.   Lord Bute thought the treaty
was too far advanced to make any advantage of the event being in our favour,
and he feared that our making any fresh demand would not only protract but
break off the negotiation, and prevent the peace taking place immediately,
which he thought so necessary for the nation.   Mr. Grenville was clear in
his opinion of our right to make the demand, and firm in insisting that it
should be made, and proposed two alternatives for consideration: the one,

there is a promise of genius which deserves to be encouraged *.
My letter of Monday will, I hope, convince the author that I

that if we judged it best to get the entire possession of the continent of North
America, France having already agreed to cede all Canada, that we should
insist upon Florida and Louisiana; the other, that if we thought it necessary
to increase our possessions in the West Indies beyond the three neutral
islands which France had also agreed to give us, we should ask Porto Rico
and the property of what we held upon the Spanish main; and he left the
Earl with declaring that he would resign the seals if one of those alternatives
was not adopted and insisted upon. After consulting with Mr. Fox and
Lord Egremont, Lord Bute agreed to make the demand of Florida and
Louisiana, and instructions to that purpose were immediately despatched to
the Duke of Bedford, who made so able and strenuous an application in consequence of them, that the Duke de Choiseul not only consented to cede
Louisiana, but obliged the Spanish minister to cede Florida also, without
sending to his court for fresh orders; and the preliminaries were not delayed
more than a fortnight by the demand and acquisition of that immense
territory."

Mr. Grenville, shortly previous to his death, introduced the Act for determining controverted elections, from a thorough conviction, as he declared to
Mr. Knox, "that the ruin of public liberty must ensue unless some check
was given to the abominable prostitution of the House of Commons in elections, by voting in favour of whoever has the support of the minister." The
good effects of this excellent Act is on all sides the theme of praise so often
as a controversy occasions the necessity for an appeal to its decision, the
impartiality of which has hitherto never been disputed[1].

* These verses were written by Sir John Macpherson, formerly governor-general of India. He was the author of several letters in answer to
Junius, under the signature of *Portikastas*. The lines here referred to were as
follow:—

## A MONODY;

### OR THE TEARS OF SEDITION ON THE DEATH OF JUNIUS.

*Quis tibi Silure furor!*

And are those periods fill'd with tuneful care,
Those thoughts which gleam'd with Ciceronian ore,
Are they, my Junius, pass'd like vulgar air;
Droop'd is thy plume, to rise on fame no more!

[1] The carrying of Mr. Grenville's Election Bill, like the carrying of the
Reform Bill in 1832, is an example that a corrupt legislature will sometimes
reform itself; but on both occasions it may be mainly ascribed to the pressure from without. "So strong," says the *Annual Register*, "was the disposition of the people in favour of the Bill (Grenville's), that very few who had
voted against it could venture to show themselves at the general election."
The Bill was passed in the House of Commons by 250 against 122.—ED.

am neither a partisan of Mr. Wilkes, nor yet bought off by

Thy plume!—it was the harp of song in prose:
 Oft have its numbers sooth'd the felon's ear,
Oft to its tune my Wilkite heroes rose
 With conch'd tobacco pipes in act to spear.

Where now shall stormy Clodius and his crew,
 My dear assembly to the midnight hour,
Ah! where acquire a trumpeter!—since you
 No more shall rouse them with thy classic power.

Accurs'd Silurus! blasted be thy wing!
 That grey Scotch wing which led the unerring dart!
In virtue's cause could all that 's satire sting
 A bosom with corruption's poison fraught!

Impossible!—then hear me, fiends of H—ll,
 This dark event, this mystery unfold:
Poison'd was Junius? No; "Alas, he fell
 Midst arrows dipp'd in ministerial gold."

Then hear me, rioters of my command;
 Condemn the villain to a traitor's doom;
Let none but faithful knaves adorn my band,
 Go, sink this character into his tomb.

Here sunk an essayist of dubious name,
 Whose tinsell'd page on airy cadence run,
Friendless, with party—noted, without fame,
 Virtue and vice disclaim'd him as a son.

                                        POETHASTOR.

Clodius and Silurus, mentioned in the above lines, were at this time
frequent writers in the *Public Advertiser;* the former against administration,
the latter in favour of it. Silurus, assuming a personal knowledge of the
writer of the Letters of Junius, thus describes him :—

"I know Junius, and I am not surprised that he calls aloud for blood.
Bred among the dregs of mankind, he imbibed their vices, and acquired that
hardness of heart which is usually produced by crimes. Possessed of some
ambition, versed in the low arts of adulation, he wrought himself into the
confidence of the vain by unmanly flattery, and rose from obscurity by means
which dishonoured his patrons. Smooth in his language, he gained the ear
without persuading the heart; and by the help of a good memory, some
anecdotes, and trite observations, acquired the reputation of a genius among
some slight characters in the literary world. Dark, cunning, deceitfully self-
denied, he covered himself with such an appearance of openness and candour that even some judges of human nature thought him honest, many
believed him honourable, few suspected the soundness of his head, none the
goodness of his heart.

"Such was Junius before public business called forth the latent and
deformed features of his mind; the real man stood then confessed: his
speciousness was found to be a mask for hypocrisy, his candour a veil for

the ministry [*]. It is true I have refused offers which a more prudent or a more interested man would have accepted. Whether it be simplicity or virtue in me, I can only affirm that I *am in earnest* [†]; because I am convinced, as far as my understanding is capable of judging, that the present ministry are driving this country to destruction; and you, I think, Sir, may be satisfied that my *rank and fortune place me above a* COMMON BRIBE [‡].

JUNIUS.

---

## LETTER LV.

### TO THE MARQUIS OF GRANBY.

MY LORD,                                                    May 6, 1769.

You were once the favourite of the public. As a brave man you were admired by the army, as a generous man you were beloved. The scene is altered; and even your immediate dependants, who have profited most by your good nature, cannot conceal from you how much you have lost both in the affections of your fellow-soldiers and the esteem of your country. Your character, once spotless, once irreproachable, has been drawn into a public question; attacked with severity, defended

---

deceit, his learning discovered to be mere plagiarism, his boasted parts to consist altogether in memory. The flimsy affected, though unaffecting, superficialness of his private discourse was soon traced in the hollow and round period of his public declamations. Detestation took the place of esteem in the minds of many, hatred took possession of a few, and a contempt for him of all. Detected, detested, despised, in his *real* character, he now assumes a *fictitious* name; for Junius cannot deceive but where he is unknown.

"March 27, 1709.                                          "SILURUS."

[*] The letter here referred to is that addressed to the Duke of Grafton, on Mr. Weston's supposed vindication of his Grace, for the pardon of M'Quirk. See vol. i. p. 148.

[†] Private Letter, No. 63.

[‡] This misleading paragraph is very amusing, supposing our demonstration of the authorship to be correct. His first aim was concealment; next, to give weight and authority to his political strictures; and both objects were most likely to be accomplished by artfully representing himself as a man of rank and position, possibly one of the great heads of parties—a Rockingham, Grenville, Temple, Shelburne, or even, as Mr. Macaulay usually calls him, "the great Lord Chatham."—ED.

with imprudence, and, like the seat of war, ruined by the contention. Profligate as we are, the virtues of the heart are
still so much respected that even the errors and simplicity of
a good man are sacred against censure or derision. To a man
of your Lordship's high rank and fortune, is there anything
in the smiles of a court that can balance the loss of that
affection (for surely it was something more cordial than esteem)
with which you were universally received upon your return
from Germany? You were than an independent gallant
soldier. As far as you thought proper to mix in politics, you
were the friend and patron of the people. Believe me, my
Lord, the highest rate of abilities could never have given you
a more honourable station. From the moment you quitted
that line, you have, perhaps, been better able to gratify some
interested favourites, but you have disgraced yourself; and, to
a man of your quality, disgrace is ruin.

You are now in the lowest rank of ministerial dependants.
Your vote is as secure to administration as if you were a lord
of trade, or a vice-treasurer of Ireland; and even Conway, at
your Lordship's expense, has mended his reputation. I will
not enter into a detail of your past conduct. You have enemies enough already, and I would not wish you to despair of
recovering the public esteem. An opportunity will soon present itself. The people of England are good natured enough
to make allowances for your mistakes, and to give you credit
for correcting them. One short question will determine your
character for ever. Does it become the name and dignity of
Manners to place yourself upon a level with a venal tribe, who
vote as they are directed, and to declare upon your honour, in
the face of your country, that Mr. Luttrell is, or ought to be,
the sitting member for the county of Middlesex? I appeal,
*bonâ fide*, to your integrity as an honest man;—I even appeal
to your understanding.

YOUR REAL FRIEND*.

* This is an undoubted Junius. The anxiety Junius felt for its appearance will be seen from his private note, No. 2, *ante*, p. 1, to Mr. Woodfall,
informing him that "the great question [the expulsion of Wilkes] comes on
on Monday, and Lord Granby is *already staggered*." The debate took
place as expected, and the result was as stated in Dr. Good's note—Colonel
Luttrell, with 296 votes, being declared duly elected, and Jack Wilkes, with
1143, rejected. From the *Chatham Correspondence* (vol. iii. p. 356) it
appears that, one week prior to the appearance of the above letter of Your

# LETTER LVI.

SIR,                                          June 6, 1769.

I wish the Duke of Grafton had thought proper to take the opinion of our gracious Queen's solicitor-general * before he pardoned M'Quirk. That worthy lawyer is never at cross purposes with himself, and I dare say would have maintained the same doctrine in his closet which he has delivered in public. He says in his last volume, page 12, " that the pains of death ought never to be inflicted, but when the offender appears *incorrigible :* which may be collected either from a repetition of minuter offences, or from the perpetration of some one crime of deep malignity, which of itself demonstrates a disposition without hope or probability of amendment; and in such cases it would be cruelty to the public to defer the punishment of such a criminal till he had an opportunity of repeating perhaps the worst of villanies."

What would this most respectable of all possible lawyers have thought of granting a pardon to a culprit who had not only been convicted of a repetition of offences, and those not minute but atrocious, but who had actually committed murder? He certainly would have called it something more than *cruelty*

---

*Real Friend*, Lord Granby visited the Earl of Chatham at Hayes, to confer with him on his conduct, especially in regard to the Middlesex election. Of this interview Earl Temple relates, that " Lord Granby has made his report to the Duke of Grafton of what passed with Lord Chatham. His Grace justified himself as well as he could in respect to the different things which he apprehended were found fault with at Hayes—was ready to do as Lord Chatham should direct when he came forth ; but rather wondered that his Lordship should choose to see the King first, as it would be better for them to talk together and settle beforehand." These combined movements, Chatham's interview with Granby and the remonstrative epistle of Junius, had one and the same end in view—to weaken the Grafton ministry, now Chatham had left it, by detaching from it its greatest ornament, the Marquis of Granby. They succeeded at last; the Chatham and Junius pack worried the Marquis into a resignation, and perhaps to death; for he lived unhappily, and died suddenly not long after leaving the King's service. He had distinguished himself in the German war, possessed some talent and a noble heart.—H.D.

* Sir William Blackstone. For the detail of M'Quirk's crime and pardon, see Junius's Letters, No. 8, vol. i. p. 133.

to the public.  His knowledge of the laws would have told
him that the purpose for which this villain was employed by
the ministry was treason against the constitution *; that it
was the highest aggravation of the crimes he committed is
prosecution of it; that murder, simply considered, is only as
injury to the individual who suffers, or, in the most enlarged
sense, to society, in the loss of one of its members; but that
when it is connected with, and founded on, the idea of destroying the constitution of the state (which, as far as Mr. Mac
Quirk's labours could be supposed to operate, was certainly
the case), it then comprehends every quality which can make
an offence of this sort criminal in the eye of the law: the
injury to the individual; a breach of the public peace and
security in a civil light; and a violation of that political
system on which the liberty and happiness of the community
depend.  Mr. Blackstone would have told the fiery Duke,
that to pardon such an offender would not only be a most
scandalous evasion of law and justice, but the grossest insult
to the common understanding of the nation.

His Grace must then have applied to some lawyer of a more
flexible character.  There is a man, for instance, who seems
to have hoarded up a treasure of reputation, not to last him
through life, but to squander away at one moment, with a
foolish indecent prodigality;—who is not ashamed to maintain an oral doctrine directly opposite to that which he had
written, nor to deceive the representative, after instructing
the collective body of the nation.  This man would willingly
have accommodated his authority to the purposes of administration; and as for himself, he could suffer no loss for which
the vanity of an author would not have sufficiently consoled
him.  The respect due to his writings will probably increase
with the contempt due to his character, and his works will be
quoted when he himself is forgotten or despised.

SIMPLEX.

* In reference to Sir W. Blackstone's opinion relating to the Middlesex
election.  See Junius, No. 18, vol. i. p. 185.

## LETTER LVII.

Sir,                                      June 10, 1769.

I am an old reader of political controversy. I remember the great Walpolean battles; and am not a little diverted with the combats of party at this time. They are still carried on with ability and vigour. Long habit has taught me to pass by all the declamation with which the champions parade. I look upon it as no better than those flourishes of the back sword with which the great masters of my time in the amphitheatre entertained the spectators, merely to show their dexterity, but which made no part of the real engagement. I regard as nothing the trappings of panegyric with which they decorate their friends. I entirely overlook the dirt with which they so very liberally bespatter their enemies. Whenever a *fact* is touched upon, there I fix. When a *distinct charge* is made upon a minister, I look for a *distinct and particular answer*, that *denies*, or *admitting*, explains, or in some favourable manner *accounts* for the *fact* charged. If instead of this I find nothing more than a long paper, in which the author of the charge is called a thousand names, and the person accused is lifted up to the skies as a miracle of ability and virtue, I am obliged, as an equitable judge, to consider the cause not as defended, but as utterly abandoned; and the court must enter an admission by his own advocates of the charge against him.

The conduct and character of the Duke of Grafton have been for some time the object of controversy. In what manner have they been attacked and defended? Take as a specimen the controversy of the last week. Junius, whom the ministerial writers appear very much to dread, and affect very much to despise, has made several particular charges upon his Grace. In one column I will state the charges, in the other the reader will see the answers, and he will thereby be the better enabled to judge of the spirit in which this dispute is carried on.

Junius's *charges.*

### First fact.

That Lord Chatham was the first object of the Duke of Grafton's political attachment; yet he deserted him, and entered with Lord Rockingham into an administration in which Lord Chatham refused to engage.

### Answer.

The wicked for the sake of mischief approve of your bold falsehoods, and the envious love a strain of defamation, which brings down to their own mean level the most worthy and most exalted characters in the nation.

### Second fact.

After uniting with Lord Rockingham, the Duke of Grafton deserted and betrayed him.

### Answer.

To retaliate upon you the abuse which you have presumed to throw upon the Duke of Grafton would be raising you into a consequence, to which the meanness of your birth, the depravity of your heart, and the unsoundness of your head, can never have any title.

### Third fact.

That, after entering again into administration with Lord Chatham, the Duke of Grafton forced him (Lord Chatham) to withdraw his name from it.

### Answer

By specious conversation you imposed upon the weak, by open and impudent flattery you gained the confidence of the vain, and you won the favour of the proud by mean unmanly sycophancy.

### Fourth fact.

That the Duke of Grafton is chargeable with great inconsistencies with himself in the frequent variations in his opinions and conduct with regard to America, according

### Answer.

Void as you are of every sense of shame, can you without a blush (but a blush seldom tinges those happy countenances which have been bathed in the Liffy), can you recom-

to the various changes he has made in his connections.

*Fifth fact.*

The Duke of Grafton had been the friend of Mr. Wilkes, and is become his persecutor.

mend to the people of England, as ministers, men whose weakness or villany they have already experienced in office.

*Answer.*

The abilities, the integrity, the dignity of mind, as well as the nobility of family which distinguish the Duke of Grafton, have rendered him superior to your abuse.

The above charges are, with several others, to be found in the last letter of Junius. The ministerial advocate, *Anti-Malagrida* *, has since addressed a letter to him, in which the above paragraphs, in the second column, are the only answers which I could discover. The same charges had been made by Junius and others several times before. Always the same reply. Junius and many others say (and I fancy they speak the sense of the nation) that the Duke of Grafton imposes upon his Sovereign, betrays his connections, persecutes the man who was his friend, idly irritates the colonies, wickedly alienates their affections from their mother country, invades the liberties of the people, abuses the prerogative of the crown, and has actually subverted the constitution; and when Junius civilly asks the reason of all this—Sir (says he) you are a rascal.

Now, Mr. Woodfall, I shall make but one reflection, and that I shall borrow from Sir John Brute:—"This may be a very good answer for aught I know at cross-purposes, but it is a damned whimsical one to a people in our circumstances."

Yours, &c.,

AMICUS CURIÆ.

* A writer in the *Public Advertiser* in favour of administration, but whose letters do not appear to have merit enough to entitle them to be reprinted.

## LETTER LVIII.

LETTER OF JUNIA.

Mr. WOODFALL,                                    September 5, 1769.

AMIDST the great number of correspondents who have raised
*your* paper to a superiority over the rest, I don't remember to
have observed lately any of the *female* sex.  To a woman of
spirit the most intolerable of all grievances is a restraint on
the liberty of the tongue.  I can't bear to see the men have
it all to themselves; and shall certainly burst if I am not
permitted to put in a word.  Much has been said of late about
grievances and apprehensions, instructions and petitions,
elections and expulsions.  Now, Sir, I want to enter the list
with one of the most celebrated of your political correspondents: here I throw down my glove, and am in hopes it will
be taken up by—Junius.  Some people perhaps may blame
me for meddling with politics, a science fit only for the men;
but Junius has no right to find fault, for Junius has been the
aggressor, by making such frequent incursions into scandal,
the natural province of the women.

However, I will do your correspondent Junius the justice
to say, that I think him a very fine writer, a great master of
composition, and indeed, upon the whole, I have not seen a
prettier fellow—upon paper.  His former letters have con-
sisted of general declamation or pointed personal abuse.  In
both of these he has proved himself an adept.  There is a
great deal of oratory in his declamations, though he is perhaps
too flowery and metaphorical, and seems as fond of point and
antithesis as any woman is of point lace and French silk.  As
to his personal attacks, they are irresistible; no character can
stand before him; he is the very butcher of a reputation.
" Heaven preserve the characters of all *my* tribe from Junius!"
In the art of *exaggeration* he has no equal; molehills he
magnifies into mountains, and views your *smallest peccadillo*
through a *double microscope*.  Should there be the least spot
or speck on your reputation, Junius can spread it out (with
the help of a few drops of ink) till it covers you all over, and
makes you as black as a fiend; in short, Junius is chief japan-
ner or calumniator-general to the opposition: he is employed
to besmear the *ministry* with his very best liquid blacking, and

when he has written them out of office, he will no doubt change his colours, take a different brush, and white-wash their successors. I wish he may make as distinguished a figure in the sweet work of panegyric as he has done in the painful task of calumny and detraction!

But of all kinds of abuse, *private* scandal seems to be his *favourite* morsel; Junius lays hold of a scandalous anecdote with as much keenness as a *spider* seizes an unfortunate fly; he crawls forth from the dark hole where he lay concealed; how eagerly he clutches it; with what a malicious pleasure he drags it along; his eyes gloat upon it with cruel delight; he winds it round and round with his *cobweb* rhetoric, and sucks the very heart's blood of family peace!

Various have been the conjectures formed on the question —" Who is this Junius?" I have heard at least twenty persons named whom suspicion points the finger at; nay, I have been assured at different times that each of them was the author in question. They could not *all* be the writer; perhaps none of them is. But in spite of all the curiosity which is imputed to our sex, I declare sincerely, that I would not give a pin for the secret. 'Tis indifferent to me who the man is; and whether he was first dipped in the Thames or the Tweed, the Liffy or the Shannon.

But though I can't tell who Junius *is*, I will tell you what he is *like*. Junius is like a racer in the fields of politics, who walks over the course *alone;* no one venturing to start against him. I have for some time had a violent inclination to enter at the post, although I am sensible the odds at starting would be greatly against the filly; but for all that, perhaps, I should be up with him at the *long run.* But I have run out my simile, and therefore must beg leave to take a fresh one. *Your* paper, Mr. Woodfall, is become the grand political cockpit, and Junius struts about in it like a cock whom nobody can match; suppose that I were pitted against him; how do you think the bets would go? And what are the odds that he does not come off hen-pecked? If I should happen to get the better of him, it will be as much a matter of public wonder as the late affair of the hen in Scotland Yard, who "attacked a prodigious large rat that was carrying off one of her chickens, and after fighting a considerable time, *killed the rat,* to the great joy and surprise of the spectators." And besides, how great will be the honour accruing to our sex from such a victory! It will be recorded amongst the most famous exploits in the anuals of female prowess; and I shall be ranked with the most renowned heroines of antiquity, Thomyris and Semiramis, Judith and Deborah.

But perhaps the defeat of this political Holofernes may not be so very difficult; and indeed on a nearer view he does not appear half so formidable. When Junius stalked upon the heights of *declamation*, he appeared of more than ordinary size, but now that he has descended to the *plain ground* of reason and argument, he appears nearly on a level with common men. His letters on the Middlesex election are most sophistically dull, unless where he throws in some personalities by way of giving spirit and flavour to his political olio. However, I don't believe that with all his sophistry he has made a single convert to his opinion. I fancy there is hardly one cool, moderate, impartial person in England who does not think that the House of Commons are the *only* judges of their own privileges; that no power on earth can force a member upon them, whom they have declared *incapable of being elected;* and, that if any person under such known and declared incapacity happens to have the greatest number of votes, the candidate who has the next greatest number of legal votes must of course be the sitting member. This *opinion* seems to me to be perfectly agreeable to reason, to common sense, and the principles of the constitution, and (notwithstanding the *delusive* appearance of petitions obtained we all know how) I do verily believe it is the opinion of every candid, impartial, unprejudiced person in England; in short, of all those who are not the *tools of faction*, or the *dupes of party*.

I am, Sir,<br>
Your humble Servant,<br>
JUNIA *.

* This letter was claimed, as the production of his own pen, by the late Mr. Caleb Whitefoord.

## LETTER LIX.

### TO THE PRINTER OF THE PUBLIC ADVERTISER.

Sir,                                           September 7, 1769.

I FIND myself unexpectedly married in the newspapers, without my knowledge or consent. Since I am fated to be a husband, I hope at least the lady will perform the principal duty of a wife. Marriages, they say, are made in heaven, but they are consummated upon earth, and since *Junia* has adopted my name, she cannot, in common matrimonial decency, refuse to make me a tender of her person. Politics are too barren a subject for a new married couple. I should be glad to furnish her with one more fit for a lady to handle, and better suited to the natural dexterity of her sex. In short, if *Junia* be young and handsome, she will have no reason to complain of my method of conducting an argument. I abominate all tergiversation in discourse, and she may be assured that whatever I advance, whether it be weak or forcible, shall, at any rate, be directly in point. It is true I am a strenuous advocate for liberty and property, but when these rights are invaded by a pretty woman, I am neither able to defend my money nor my freedom. The divine right of beauty is the only one an Englishman ought to acknowledge, and a pretty woman the only tyrant he is not authorized to resist.

JUNIUS*.

* Junius repented that he had written this letter as soon as it had appeared. He regarded it as *idle and improper;* and it was on this occasion that he addressed to Mr. Woodfall the private note, No. 8, dated September 10, 1769; in consequence of which the following observations appeared in the notice to correspondents in the *Public Advertiser* of the 11th of September :—

"We have some reason to suspect that the last letter signed Junius, inserted in this paper of Thursday last, was not written by the real Junius, though we imagine it to have been sent by some one of his waggish friends, who has taken great pains to write in a manner similar to that of Junius, which observation escaped us at that time. The printer takes the liberty to hint that it will not do a second time."

## LETTER LX.

### AUGUR ON THE GRAFTON MINISTRY.

MR. WOODFALL,                                      September 8, 1769.

IT is hard to determine whether the actions of the present ministry more excite abhorrence and indignation, or the writings of their advocates contempt and ridicule: every action of the former is an invasion of our liberty or our property; every line wrote in their defence by the latter is an insult to our understanding, and a base mockery of our sufferings. I have never yet known a bad cause made better by a bad defence. I cannot conceive what induces his Grace of Grafton to employ such a set of wretches to laugh at us, whilst we are burning at the stake to which he has tied us. It is as void of policy as it is full of inhumanity. Oppression is more easily borne than insult; and the Duke of Grafton, with his new directors, the Bloomsbury gang, may find that it is dangerous to despise those whom he has deeply injured. Why does he let loose upon us his troops of fools and madmen, and buffoons and bullies? He would do more wisely to employ them in their proper places, reserving them to excite the mirth, and add to the wit, urbanity, and elegance of the midnight festivity of his kindred and friends, Weymouth, Gower, and Rigby, at Bedford House.

If the freeholders of this country, alarmed at the invasion of their last and dearest right, the freedom of election, beg in the humblest terms for redress, *Poetikastos* dances before them in a fool's coat, squirts dirty water in their faces, and then cries out to the great joy, and with the loud applause of the *gang*, " You are redressed." To every other complaint, whether of the disgraces which we suffer abroad, or of the oppressions which we feel at home, whether the cry be for property ravished from us, for our liberties infringed, for the laws perverted, for the constitution overturned, we have much the same answer. *Silurus* is let loose from his cell to vent his madness, and covers us with his filth. *Pericles* * stands by him calling out rogue and scoundrel; and then with one voice

* *Poetikastos, Silurus,* and *Pericles* were writers in the *Public Advertiser* in favour of administration.

the minister who employs, and the wretches who are employed, cry out, "We have defeated them; they never dare
appear again; we have hanged them up to public scorn; you
are a coward, cries one; I will cudgel you, says another; I will
lay you a bet of 14,000 guineas, bawls a third."*

Does the Duke of Grafton really think that such actions as
his are sufficiently defended by such arguments as these?
Are those the lawyers whom he has retained against that
dreadful day—for that day will come—when a brave, a haughty,
and a spirited, though patient, people, shall demand vengeance on his head for all the disgraces and injuries which he
has heaped upon theirs? Are these to be his intercessors to
a misguided and betrayed king for mercy? Enjoy with your
associates, my Lord, their buffoonery and their scurrility
whilst you may: the day is not far off—if the Almighty has
not in his wrath given up this country to that worst of punishments, that most intolerable of all tyrannies, the government of insolence without spirit, violence without vigour,
ambition without dignity, obstinacy without resolution, and
ignorance without diffidence—the day is not far off, when
these insults will be retorted most severely, and humanity
itself will not be able to keep them from your head, though
that head should be on the block.

AUGUR.

## LETTER LXI.

### A. B. TO THE DUKE OF GRAFTON†.

My Lord,                                           November 10, 1769.

THE facility with which you abandoned your earliest connections in friendship and politics was, I doubt not, a leading

---

* A challenge had been absurdly given to Junius by several writers in the
*Public Advertiser*, as well as by Sir William Draper; and one correspondent,
as here referred to, had the egregious folly to propose a bet of 14,000 guineas,
being, as he stated, his whole fortune, "that he could produce in six months
a counter-petition, signed by 4,000 freeholders, *all men of sense*, begging his
Majesty to confine the ringleaders of the opposition, and bind them over to
their good behaviour."

† This letter was printed by the desire of Junius in the *Public Advertiser*,
but was not written by him. See Private Letter, No. 11. It was, however,

recommendation to establish your credit at St. James's. A gracious discerning prince, who, even at the moment of his accession, had fortitude enough to get the better of every predilection which he might be supposed to have inherited from his ancestors in favour of the friends of the House of Hanover, must have observed with pleasure that your Grace was equally ready to desert the friends who contributed most to your advancement, and to adopt new principles of government. I will not complain of a change of system, for which you had so powerful a precedent, and which you have found so favourable to your ambition. But there are rules of decency, my Lord, which a wiser man would have observed, even in the grossest violation of morals. There is a certain sort of hostilities which is forbidden by the laws of war between nations, and by the laws of enmity between individuals. The contentions of party have given a fashionable latitude to the principles of modern morality; but still, my Lord, there are some characters too great and venerable to be insulted; there is yet a certain breach of decorum, which the public will not submit to. Was the Duke of Rutland the only man in this country at whose expense you could gratify Lord Denbigh? One would think, my Lord, that if his uniform adherence to the principles of the revolution, his steady attachment to the House of Hanover, and the important services which he and his family have rendered to that House, could possibly be forgotten, there was yet something in his age, his rank, his personal character, and private virtues, which might have entitled him to respect. Was it necessary, my Lord, to pursue him into his own county on purpose to insult him? Was it proper, was it decent, that while a Duke of Rutland is lord lieutenant, the Earl of Denbigh's recommendation should govern the county of Leicester*? Had

___

so generally supposed to have been his, that Junius himself thought it necessary to request the printer to publish the following contradiction in the same journal, November 17. "We can assure the public that the letter signed A. B., relative to the Duke of Rutland, is not written by the author of Junius."

* It refers to certain justices of the peace having been made at the request of Lord Denbigh, by a commission of the Lord Chancellor (Camden) and others, for the county of Leicester, without consulting the Duke of Rutland, who was lord lieutenant, and who, ex officio, ought to have been honoured with the nomination.

Lord Denbigh no friends in Leicestershire but rank Tories to
recommend for the commission of the peace? And is it under
a prince who owes his crown to the Whig interest of England
that a minister dares to send such a mandate to the Duke of
Rutland? I know his Grace's spirit, and doubt not of his returning you an answer proper for you and for himself.

United as you are, my Lord, with men whose concern for
the safety of the church, and whose zeal for the prerogative of
the crown has been so often unluckily mistaken for simple
jacobitism, I take for granted you are as well acquainted with
their history as with their principles. You are able to tell
us, and surely the public has a right to expect it from you,
by what species of merit the Earl of Denbigh has contrived to
make himself so distinguished a favourite at court. Was it the
notorious attachment of his family to the House of Hanover,
or his own personal accomplishments? Was it his fortune that
made him respectable, or his beggary that made him submis-
sive? Was it the generous exertion of his great abilities in
parliament, or the humble assiduity of his attendance at Lord
Bute's levee? Was it the manly firmness of his personal
appearance, or the pliant politeness of his temper? Was it
the independent dignity with which he maintains the rank of
a peer, or the complaisance with which he accepts and executes
the honourable office of a spy? Whatever have been his merits
or services, they are undoubtedly of a complexion very different
from those of the Duke of Rutland.

His Grace has now wisely exchanged that busy scene, in
which he never appeared but with honour, for an hospitable
retirement. His age will not permit us to hope that he can
long be the object of the spite of such a creature as Lord
Denbigh, nor of the scorn and insult of such a minister as your
Grace. But he will leave a family, my Lord, whose principles
of freedom are hereditary, from whose resentment you will
have everything to apprehend. As for himself, I shall only
say, that if it were possible for the views and wishes of the
Tories to succeed, if it were possible for them to place a Stuart
once more upon the throne, their warmest hopes and ambition
might be disappointed. He too, like another judicious prince,
might think it the best policy of his government to choose his
friends and favourites from among the declared, notorious,
determined enemies of his family. The Tories who placed

him upon the throne might be driven disgracefully from his
presence; and, upon the same principle, I challenge your
Grace to point out a man more likely to be invited to the
place of first minister and favourite than the Duke of Rutland.

A. B*.

———

## LETTER LXII.

### ATTACK ON JUNIUS BY MESSALA.

November 17, 1769.

JUNIUS may change his signature, his manner he cannot
change. The far-fetched antithesis, the empty period, the
pert loquacity, distinguish the writer; and the rancorous
and impudent falsehood discovers the man. In vain has he
attempted to conceal himself under initials; he is as invariable in the tenor of his diction as he is in the bias of his
mind.

It was, however, a mark of some judgment in Mr. —— to
use a new signature in your paper of Friday. *A. B.* may
praise the Duke of Rutland, though Junius has infamously
traduced the Marquis of Granby†. By a mean subterfuge,
an appearance of propriety may be preserved among the
superficial; but the generous and discerning must despise and
detest a man who makes the interests of a profligate party
the only standard by which he regulates his encomium as well
as his abuse.

But to set the public right in a matter of fact is the only
design of this letter. The insertion of particular persons by
mandate, without issuing a new commission of the peace, has
been in daily practice; and is an undoubted power lodged in
the great seal; but in that alone; nor can any other servant
of the crown interfere, no more than in a decree of that great
officer, the Chancellor in the Court of Chancery.

———

* The above letter, though avowedly not from the pen of Junius, was
reprinted in the *Public Advertiser* from another journal at his request. It
was replied to a few days afterwards by the letter that follows it, to withhold which would be an act of injustice.

† The Marquis of Granby, eldest son of the Duke of Rutland.

The principles of that noble Lord are as well known as those of the remainder of the King's ministers, who, notwithstanding every aspersion to the contrary from factious artifices, have on every occasion proved themselves to be the supporters of the real liberty of the people, and of the true spirit of the constitution.

Has the Lord Chancellor in any instance deviated from such a character? And yet if Junius, or his shadow *A. B.* were right, this noble Lord would be termed a jacobite: for if there is anything improper in the appointment, he is the man who should be charged, and not the Duke of Grafton, on whom calumny endeavours to fix the mistakes of others.

Junius, in his zeal for his party, defeats the means he uses to serve them. Unfortunately for his cause, the attacks he makes upon, and his charges against, the Duke of Grafton, require only to be fairly stated to confute themselves; and thus (I will do him the justice to suppose) without design he becomes the panegyrist of a character he wishes to ruin in the eyes of the world.

> I am, Sir,
> Your humble servant,
> MESSALA*.

---

## LETTER LXIII.

### X. X. AND MR. ONSLOW.

November 17, 1769.

I WILL not pretend to say that the inclosed letter is a very severe libel on its right honourable author! And yet, Mr. Woodfall, you may safely print it; for though we have laws against self-murder, there are none against self-libelling.

A curious collection of correspondence, both political and amorous, has lately fallen into my hands, with which I shall from time to time furnish you, reserving the most extraordinary of both kinds till the last, *pour la bonne bouche.*

X. X†.

* To this letter *A. B.* gave an answer, but, as it decidedly was not written by Junius, we have omitted it.

† Mr. Onslow was at this time persecuting Wilkes with all the acrimony in his power, in unison with the Duke of Grafton, both of whom had a few

MY DEAR WILKES,

I AM very sorry to have been prevented seeing you to-day;
but I hope to have a good account of you by the return of my
servant who brings you this: perhaps you may be better if
more of your friends besides myself have missed troubling you

years before professed the warmest friendship for Wilkes. Mr. Horne, not
then at enmity with Wilkes, had just published the following letter of a
similar kind, of which Wilkes had given him a copy :—

*To the Printer of the Public Advertiser.*

SIR,                                                     July 14, 1769.

MANY of your readers having seen an abuse on Mr. Horne, for the publication
of a letter from Mr. Onslow to Mr. Wilkes, are desirous of seeing that
original.

COPY OF A LETTER FROM GEORGE ONSLOW, ESQ., TO JOHN WILKES, ESQ.

                                                     "Ember Court,
      "MY DEAR OLD FRIEND,                            "September 21, 1765.

"HAVING been most shamefully silent to you during the remainder of an
opposition which did honour to every man concerned in it, and to the credit
of which you so much contributed, I now begin my correspondence with
you, at my first entering into office with, and under, an administration whose
principles I hope and believe will authorise your giving equal support to in
their very different situation. If they did not, as I know they do, revere
and hold sacred those sentiments they avowed during the last two years,
and in abhorrence those vile and detestable ones of persecution and injustice,
by which the public were so injured in your person, I should be ashamed of
what I am now proud of, bearing the small share I do among them.   Public
marks of this, as well as private ones, I hope will soon take place.

"Honest Humphrey has dined with me here to-day, and we have just
drank your health, as we have often done.   Honest as he is, I never felt
him more so than your last letter to him, which he has just now showed me,
has made him appear to me, in having done justice to my very sincere and
constant regards to, and admiration of you.   Every word of this letter of
yours (dated August 26, from Geneva) I subscribe to, and think and persuade myself the completion of our patriot, not selfish, wishes (for such they
are not) will soon appear among many other proofs of integrity, steadiness,
and virtue, in the present ministry, and of their being as inimical as ever
to those whom they have been opposing, for having acted contrary to all
these principles.

"Your friend, Mrs. Onslow, has been enjoying with us, in infinite mirth,
your last specimens of notes on different parts of great Churchill's works,
viz. Hogarth, Talbot, and the scoundrel Bishop.   They are specimens
indeed of your amazing wit and abilities; and when he has more of them he
has promised me a copy.

"Believe me, my dear John, your mentioning me as you do gratifies my
pride, as it will always do to show myself your friend and humble servant.
I was always so as a public and as a private man.   Our good friend Humphrey

to-day; as I'm sure quiet and keeping down your wonderful flow of spirits must do you good.  To most men in your situation such a caution would surely be needless, because men of less greatness of mind, and of a less noble spirit than yourself, would yield to such a load of damnable persecution from the most dangerous administration that ever was in this country. But honest men like yourself know how to despise *it and them*, and to rise superior to them all.

If I had a mind to raise your indignation, I would bid you think of the similarity of these times to those you and I have talked of with abhorrence; but as I mean always to add to your comfort and satisfaction, I will desire you to think of the similarity of your own circumstances to those of the many great and good men that lived in those times, and suffered as you do now.  Remember how greatly they were thought of, and how their characters are respected now, and remember, and be assured to your comfort, that let the iron hand of power fall ever so heavy on you (it can't fall very heavy, from your innocence) every honest man, and every gentleman, must bestow the same degree of applause on you as they must of abhorrence and detestation on your and their country's enemies.  I will certainly call on you to-morrow morning or evening.  I have nothing new to send you.  I hope it is not *so to you* that I am unalterably,

Dear Wilkes,

Your faithful and affectionate

humble servant,

Curzon Street, Monday Night,                    GEORGE ONSLOW.
    November 21, 1763.

Mrs. Onslow sends you her comps.  I wish you would appoint honest faithful Humphrey to meet me at your house precisely at one o'clock on Wednesday.  I have a thousand things to say to him.

and I are at this moment in your service, and from us both you shall soon hear, particularly as to the contents of your letter of the 26th.  I beg you to believe that I most truly and affectionately am your faithful, humble servant,

" GEO. ONSLOW.

" P.S. Postpone your judgment till you hear again from me, on what I lament as much as you can do, and think of as you do—Mr. Pitt and Lord Temple's being not in employment."

## LETTER LXIV.

### X. X. AND MR. ONSLOW.

November 20, 1769.

I cannot but admire the easy assurance with which that modest gentleman who writes for the *Gazetteer* informs us that he has gained a complete victory over Junius. It is not the first time that the silence and moderation of Junius have been mistaken for submission, nor is this the first blockhead who has plumed himself upon an imaginary triumph over the favourite of the public.—I wish, however, if he be in the secret, that he would tell us plainly whether the officers of the guards are to be tried or not? If they are not, the observations made by Junius upon the conduct of the ministry return with double force. If they are, Junius is right, and acts honourably in not pushing his inquiries further *. As to the facts, it is unnecessary for him to say anything in support of them. They are so notorious that the parties themselves cannot, dare not deny them. If Captain Garth did not wilfully abandon his guard, why does he not demand a court-martial to clear his character? And would not the ministry, for their own credit, take care that Captain Dodd should be brought to a trial if they were not absolutely certain that a court-martial must cashier them? Truly, Sir, these gentlemen have a bitter enemy in *Modestus* †. It appears to me that he has some secret rancour against them, which nothing can satisfy but the loss of their commissions.

X. X.

---

## LETTER LXV.

### Y. Y. IN REPLY TO X. X.

Sir,                                                November 23, 1769.

Junius and his journeymen have engrossed the whole alphabet; but from *A. B.* to *X. X.* the style and manner of the

---

* Junius, in Private Letter, No. 11, assigns the following reason for thus declining it : " The only thing that hinders my pushing the subject of my last letter is really the fear of ruining that poor devil Gansel, and those other blockheads."

† *Modestus*, as before observed, was a Mr. Dalrymple, a Scotch lawyer.

shop are easily discovered. From alpha to omega the same
attention to a period, and the same neglect of good sense,
manners, and propriety. However, *Mr. X. X.* in to-day's
*Public Advertiser* has even out-heroded Herod. It was
certainly unpardonable presumption in the modest gentleman
who writes for the *Gazetteer* to assume the merit of a victory
over the young gentleman who writes for the *Public Advertiser.* But *Te Deums* have been sung before on as slender
foundations. The young gentleman, with that fire and spirit
which accompanies green years, threw down his glove to the
world, and challenged all mankind to contradict the truth of
certain facts, or the justice of certain observations. He proposed, if not a reward to the champion who should vanquish
him, at least a punishment to himself if vanquished; nor that
a slight one, if he were, as *X. X.* says he is, the favourite of
the public. The modest gentleman ventured to take up the
glove, and with a boldness not very consistent with his name,
demonstrated that the narrative was false in every circumstance material to the question; and the observations not only
ridiculous in the view of supporting the conclusion attempted
to be drawn, but in a supreme degree injudicious to the cause
they were intended to promote.

To this Junius, with prudence beyond his years, makes no
reply, and *Modestus,* after a decent forbearance, presumes to
put him in mind of his challenge. This produced the letter
signed Junius, in your paper one day last week; in which, to
speak negatively, he neither supports the truth of his narrative, or the justice of his observations, and in which, to speak
positively, he gives up both. Not fairly, nor with the candour
of a gentleman who is convinced of his rash and dangerous
mistake; but with the struggles and evasions of a culprit who
is convicted of a crime.

Upon this true state of the dispute, *Modestus* most impu-
dently assumed to himself the victory; and I must confess
he seemed to have the appearance of a claim to it. But *Mr.
X. X.* has clearly demonstrated the contrary; and the method
this honourable gentleman has taken to chain victory to the
triumphant car of the public's favourite adds greatly to his
merit.

A person of vulgar understanding would have descended
into a tedious detail; he would have endeavoured to show by

argument and fact that Junius was in the right, and *Modestus*
in the wrong. But *Mr. X. X.*, another Alexander, cuts the
Gordian knot at once, and annihilates the pretensions of *Modestus* with a single word. There is so much energy, so much
eloquence, so much of the polite scholar, the gentleman, and
the patriot, in the term *blockhead*, that if *Modestus* possesses
but a shadow of what its name imports, he must fairly confess himself routed ; and instead of *Te Deum*, I would advise
him to sing *De profundis*.

. It was to be sure the height of insolence in *Modestus* to attack the favourite of the public ; but it may be pleaded in his
excuse, that the public has several favourites who are shrewdly
suspected to be unworthy of its favour; and Junius has staked
and forfeited that favour of which he had much reason to be
proud. But pray, *Mr. X. X.*, have not you been guilty of a
trifling error, by substituting the public in place of the mob ?
You wish to know whether the officers are to be tried or not.
For answer give me leave to ask you whether you have learned
to read ? Had that essential part of your education been attended to, you would not have been so ignorant of what has
been explained again and again, and you would not have been
so illiberal to imagine you could better a bad cause by calling
names, an argument which deserves no answer but the
strapado.

But your education did not depend on yourself, and perhaps
you are left-handed, which I have been told by many intelligent Hibernians, your countrymen, is an insurmountable bar
to scholarship; yet common sense is the portion of the un-
learned as well as of the learned, and though you may be but
an indifferent scholar, there was no occasion to insult her in
the way you have done. The world hitherto has believed that
Junius was rather unfriendly to the officers concerned in General Gansel's rescue, when he publicly aggravated their
offence from a common breach of the peace to an outrage
against the constitution; and it believed that *Modestus* was
not their enemy for endeavouring to show that Junius was in
the wrong, and representing all the circumstances of excuse
which the nature of the case afforded. But here also *Mr.
X. X.* has convinced the world of its mistake: and it stands
on his infallible authority, that Junius is a faithful friend to
these officers, and *Modestus* a rancorous and inveterate enemy,

whom nothing can satisfy but the loss of their commissions. The force of genius is certainly wonderful! It discovers in propositions the very reverse of what they contain. But *Mr. X. X.*, when you address the public again, remember, that though paradoxes astonish, they do not convince against evidence.

However, we are but seconds in the quarrel between *Modestus* and Junius, and we ought not to suffer our principals to proceed to extremities. To soften the rancour of their contention, I would propose that some friendly unfriendly greeting (as Shakespeare calls it) should pass between them. They need not exchange armour, like Glaucus and Diomede (an example which would afford me many choice allusions if I had time to pursue them), but they may exchange names. The propriety of this no man can dispute, for even *X. X.* will agree with me that *Modestus* is a little young, and Junius not a little modest.

> I am, Sir,
> Your humble Servant,
>
> Y. Y.

---

## LETTER LXVI.

### CASE OF GENERAL GANSEL.

SIR,                                    November 25, 1769.

FOR answer to my last letter, in which I asked a very plain question, viz., whether the officers of the guards were or were not to be tried for the rescue of General Gansel? your correspondent *Y. Y.* contents himself with another question, whether I had learnt to read? The question is pertinent enough, and as much to the purpose as if he had inquired the hour of the day. Will this gentleman be so good as to quit all circumlocution, and tell us what we are to trust to? Is Captain Garth, who deserted his guard at noon-day, an equerry to the Duke of Cumberland? Did he not leave the command of his guard to a person who had as little right to take it as Buckhorse, and is he or is he not protected by his Royal Highness? Is not Captain Dodd the old friend of Henry Lawes Luttrell, and the son of the oldest and most intimate

crony of Lord Irnham? Have either of the parties denied
any one of the facts stated by Junius? Has not Colonel
Salter been ordered to hold his peace? Has not William
Viscount Barrington, secretary at war, most infamously neg
lected his duty in not moving the King to order a court-martial for the trial of these offenders? And has not the adjutant-
general publicly and repeatedly, though in vain, represented
that they ought to be cashiered? What will the flat general
contradiction of an anonymous writer avail against circumstances so particular, so well vouched, that the parties most
concerned are ashamed or afraid to deny them? How is
Junius to prove his facts but by such a particularity and precision in the state of them, that no man who knows anything
of the matter will venture to dispute the truth of them? In
this case a negative is as strong as a positive proof, and the
only proof the thing will admit of. It is absolutely incredible
that neither Captain Garth nor Captain Dodd should contradict such facts as lead immediately to their ruin, if justice
were done. Nothing but shame and self-conviction keep
them silent.

As to argument, I should be glad to know why the letter
signed *Moderatus*[*] has not been answered? It has not even
been attempted. Depend upon it, Sir, the silence of Junius
portends no good to the ministry[†]. When he honours them
with his notice it is not a momentary blast. He gathers like
a tempest, and all the fury of the elements burst upon them
at once.

                                                    X. X.

[*] Inserted in the Woodfall edition as Philo-Junius. See Letter No.
31, vol. i. p. 245.

[†] The quotation in the note to the preceding Letter, from Private Letter,
No. 11, is followed by these words : " But as soon as a good subject offers."
This was fulfilled in the attack upon the Duke of Grafton in Letter No. 33,
vol. i. p. 249, for the gift of a patent place, customer of the port of Exeter,
to Colonel Burgoyne, who sold it, with the supposed knowledge of his Grace,
to Mr. Hine for £4000. This Junius deemed so strong a hold upon the
Duke, as to advise the printer, on a threatened prosecution for publishing
this letter, which contains a very severe statement of the fact, " not to show
fear, but to tell them he would justify, and subpœna Mr. Hine, Burgoyne,
and Bradshaw, of the treasury," as that would " silence them at once." See
Private Letter, No. 15.

## LETTER LXVII.

### MODESTUS TO JUNIUS.

Sir,                                November 29, 1769.

Though you may choose to vent your illiberal resentment under the borrowed signature of X. X., I, who think scurrility no disgrace to your real name, shall not affect to make a distinction where there is no difference. For the same reason I do not plead that, Junius having given the challenge, I am not bound to enter the lists against any other. It is a peculiar advantage in this sort of warfare that, when a man is routed in his own person, he can still keep the field under another; and you in particular have a right to the device, *non cultus, non color unus.*

After giving up the question as Junius, you come back upon it as X. X. It would be a labour indeed to answer you the same questions in every form you are pleased to assume. But for once I will take the trouble to repeat what I have already said, not from any merit or novelty in your questions, but to leave you without excuse. Had you turned over to my letter in the *Gazetteer* of the 13th of November, you would have discovered that the gentleman who asked *Mr. X. X.* whether he had learned to read did not put a very impertinent question. It is there stated that Captain Garth was no otherwise concerned in General Gansel's rescue than by being absent from his guard when it happened. This is undoubtedly a military offence; and if the friendship of Junius or X. X. will still insist to have it punished, there is no help for it. But it is not true that Captain Garth left his guard to be commanded by any person; and it is immaterial to the question whether he be equerry to the Duke of Cumberland, or protected by him. If the thing is so, I congratulate him; but surely that honour neither makes him a criminal nor aggravates his supposed crime. With respect to Captain Dodd, you have brought a fresh charge against him, to which there can be no defence. He is, it seems, a companion of Colonel Luttrell, and his father is the intimate friend of Lord Irnham. I am sorry for it; but if he is guilty of such a crime I must give him up; and I do it with the utmost gratitude to the friendly and compassionate Junius, who requires no greater punishment for an offence of this heinous nature than to ruin the fortune and reputation of the person who committed it.

I must also congratulate you upon that candour and moderation with which you declined the contest on this point, lest you should prejudge the trial, civil or military, which I told you was intended. This circumstance affords so striking a proof of your humanity, that you leave me at a loss in what manner to acknowledge it.

But raillery apart. Have you really forgot, or are you so supine, that you could not take the trouble to look over my letter before you crowded together so many ridiculous questions? It is there affirmed that these unfortunate gentlemen would have been immediately tried by military law, unless it had occurred that a trial by court-martial might possibly prejudge the civil action intended to be carried on by the party injured. Some reasons for this were given, and such as ought to have satisfied a patriot at least. But I have learned by much observation that nothing will satisfy a patriot but a place.

Once more I will state those reasons, and though I do not believe you will feel them, yet I am persuaded every man who knows or values our constitution will be convinced of their weight.

By the articles of war a military officer who shall oppose or resist the civil magistrate in the execution of his duty, shall be cashiered; and the only question that remains is, in what manner can the offence be ascertained? I maintain that a court-martial cannot enter into the question of fact by leading evidence to prove that the offence was committed, because this would be to deprive an Englishman of his right of trial for civil offences by jury. The legal and constitutional method of procedure in these cases is a common trial at law for a civil offence, and a conviction of the offender at common law is the only evidence upon which a court-martial can proceed to inflict the military punishment. This being so, had a court-martial been ordered, or were it now ordered upon these gentlemen, it would be a manifest violation of their privileges as Englishmen; because the issue is not yet tried at common law; and till the offenders are tried and convicted at law, there exists no medium on which a court-martial can proceed.

This doctrine may be new to you; but it is not so to any man acquainted with the constitution of which you pretend to be an assertor. The single point in dispute between us is, whether the ministry acted properly or improperly in the affair of General Gansel's rescue? You say the minister ought to have ordered a court-martial to try the officers concerned in it immediately; and because he did not you accuse him to the public. I, on the other hand, affirm that a court-martial ought not to have been called immediately: that the officers could not have been tried consistently with the laws of the land; and if the minister had acted otherwise than he did, he would have been guilty of a very gross violation of our rights. The reasons on which we found this difference in opinion are before the public, and it will judge of them without respect to you or to me. Whether the parties have denied the facts or not, whether Colonel Salter speaks or holds his tongue, are very immaterial circumstances; but if my position is right, Lord Barrington has not neglected his duty in not moving the King to order a court-martial, which the King could not order in the present state of the case consistently with that tender regard which his Majesty has ever shown for the civil rights of his subjects. To answer directly the question you ask, whether or not the officers are to be tried? is impossible. It is a future event, and though the present intention of the ministry is, I believe, favourable to the rancour of Junius, no man can tell what time may produce. But the question is certainly premature, and indeed the whole dispute would have come more properly before the public after the civil trial, which naturally and necessarily must precede the court-martial.

No motive engaged me to enter into this altercation, save an honest indignation excited by your malevolence, ignorance, and misrepresentation. I foresaw the illiberal use to which I exposed myself, and I received it as it deserves to be received. I will not do any of your allies the honour to take notice of them, but I recommend it to you to tie up that over drove animal John Bull, who seems indeed to be stimulated to madness, that he may no longer profane a respectable

name, but own that which he received from his godfathers
and godmothers, viz., Patrick O'Bully.

MODESTUS.

## LETTER LXVIII.

### REPLY TO MODESTUS.

Sir,                                             December 2, 1769.

I NEVER doubted that the unfortunate *Modestus*, if left to
himself, would soon ruin himself and his clients. He has
now fairly clinched the matter. In his letter of this day his
whole defence of the Duke of Grafton, and all the weight of
his arguments against Junius, are made to rest upon a supposed certainty that when the common law has taken its
course, the officers of the guards will be brought to a court-
martial. Here then we join issue with *Modestus*; and
though near ten weeks have elapsed since the rescue of
General Gansel, we are ready to admit that it is not yet too
late for the minister to do his duty; but if, notwithstanding
the assurances given us by *Modestus*, it should appear that
there never was an intention to bring these offenders to a
trial, how will he answer it to the public, that he has dared
to take up such a cause, and to impose so many gross falsehoods upon our credulity? As a friend, I would advise him
to look out in time for some plausible evasion. The ministry have singular reasons for everything they do, and I will
venture to foretell that the officers of the guards will never
be brought to a court-martial, because their offence is so
great that they must inevitably be cashiered.

X. X.

## LETTER LXIX.

### JUNIUS AS DOMITIAN.

Sir,                                             March 5, 1770.

THERE is a certain set of men who, upon almost every action
of their lives, are insulted with the pity both of their enemies

and their friends. They seem to have discovered the art of
doing whatever is base and detestable, without forfeiting their
claim to the public compassion. A bad man, with resolution
and abilities, is a formidable being. His great qualities com
pensate for the absence of good ones, and, though not entitled
to esteem, secure him from contempt. The persons I speak
of are not in this predicament: they have nothing elevated in
their vices. In vain do they labour to distinguish themselves
by the violation of all public duties and private engagements.
They still preserve their natural mediocrity of character, and
have as little chance of being honoured with the detestation
as with the esteem of their country.

I cannot mention the name of Sir Edward Hawke without
concern. How unfortunate it is that a heart unacquainted
with fear should have so little sense of propriety and decorum!
I should be sorry to puzzle him with intricate questions either
of policy or morals, but there are some distinctions within the
reach even of *his* understanding. In his situation, it particularly became him to regulate his conduct by the judgment of
the public. Though not expected to think for himself, he
might have taken a generous part with the friends of his
country, and still have been respected for the integrity of his
intentions. To what a poor insignificant condition has he
now reduced himself! Behold him, at such a conjuncture as
the present, meanly keeping possession of an office which he
owes to Lord Chatham's friendship, and distinguished as the
only surviving minister (of those introduced into the cabinet
by Lord Chatham *) who supports the present administration.
What opinion can he deliver in the House of Commons?
What measures can he maintain in the cabinet? Instead of
the dignity of thundering out secrets of state from the gallery,
we see the First Lord of the Admiralty skulking into the House,
just before a division, as if he thought that everybody had
heard the peremptory message sent him by Mr. Bradshaw.

As to his opinions in council, he must either adopt a new
set of ideas, or, if he presumes to differ from his colleagues,
must silently submit to be overruled. On these terms he
may be permitted to keep an employment which, since he

* See note to Junius, Letter No. 23, vol. i. p. 210.

sold his stock in the beginning of the winter, produces nothing in addition to the salary but the means of providing for his friends. The choice of Commodore Hill and Admiral Geary proves that he can discover latent merit in the most unpromising subjects. By this disposition of the command at Chatham and Portsmouth, he seems to aim at encouraging *future* services, rather than in rewarding the past; and as to his economy, was it possible to give a better proof of it than by turning adrift a multitude of poor artificers to idleness and beggary, on purpose to make up four pounds a day for the use of Mr. Geary?

Admiral Holburne's services in America have also been very properly considered. When so many Englishmen vacate their places, it would be strange indeed if a Scot of such distinguished merit had been left unprovided for. Sir Percy Brett resigns, Mr. Holburne succeeds him, and Sir Edward Hawke is still first lord of the admiralty! Proceed, Sir Edward, in this honourable line. Be a spendthrift of your good name. We shall not quarrel with your prodigality, for you have a right to waste the reputation you had acquired. You once contributed largely to save this country, and have a creditor's claim to contribute to its destruction.

The indigent circumstances of Lord Hertford's family account for and justify their conduct. The same spirit of economy which animated the father to the sale of public employments in Ireland, revives in the son, and finds the best market for the ammunition of the Warwickshire militia *. Lord Hertford, General Conway, and Lord Beauchamp are the very quintessence of courtesy and candour. Undecided in their opinions, disengaged from all attachments, they support no measures without leaving room for explanation, and can reconcile the coldest indifference about the interests of others with the warmest anxiety for their own. It is unluckily the fate of these moderate candid persons to be despised by all parties. In vain does the gentle Beauchamp give the treasury bench the negative assistance of his oratory; in vain does his honest father beg an audience for personal solicitation in

---

* This youth goes by the name of Gunpowder Beauchamp through the whole county.

the closet. General Howard and the secretary at war have still spirit to resist *. The promotion goes in the regiment, and the military achievements of the younger Conway are left for future consideration. Poor Lord Hertford! what is this but a continuation of the Duke of Grafton's tyranny? From one minister we see him regularly kicked down to another. His nephew treats him like a footman, and Lord North, with still greater severity, yokes him with General Græme†.

My sincere compassion for Lord Cornwallis arises not so much from his quality as from his time of life. A young man by a spirited conduct may atone for the deficiencies of his understanding. Where was the memory of this noble Lord, or what kind of intellects must he possess, when he resigns his place, yet continues in the support of administration, and, to show his independence, makes a parade of attending Lord North's levee, and pays a public homage to the deputy of Lord Bute! Where is now his attachment; where are now his professions to Lord Chatham; his zeal for the Whig interest of England; and his detestation of Lord Bute, the Bedfords, and the Tories? Since the time at which these were the only topics of his conversation, I presume he has shifted his company as well as his opinions. Will he tell the world to which of his uncles, or to what friend, to Philipson, or a Tory lord, he owes the advice which has directed his conduct? I will not press him further. The young man has taken a wise resolution at last, for he is retiring into a voluntary banishment, in hopes of recovering the ruin of his reputation. These loose sketches are sufficient to mark to you the kind of character which, with every quality that ought to make it odious, still continues pitiful, and is never important enough in mischief to excite indignation. I would not waste a thought in contriving the punishment or correction of such men; but it may be useful to the public to see by what sort of creatures the present administration is supported. It is unnecessary to enlarge the catalogue. Without name or description, they are distinguished by a certain consciousness

* Lord Hertford not long ago had the modesty to desire that his son, a youth of twenty years old, might be put over the heads of all General Howard's officers.

† Lord Hertford and this worthy Scotchman are spies in ordinary to the minister for the time being.

of shame which accompanies their actions. After deserting
one party, they dare not engage heartily with the other; and
having renounced their first sentiments and connections, are
forced to proceed in the humble track of voting as they are
ordered, without party, principle, or friends,

DOMITIAN *.

## LETTER LXX.

### TO THE PRINTER OF THE PUBLIC ADVERTISER.

SIR,                                                    March 10, 1770.
No man is more warmly attached to the best of princes than
I am. I reverence his personal virtues as much as I respect
his understanding, and am happy to find myself under the
government of a prince whose temper and abilities do equal
honour to his character. At the same time, I confess I did
not hear without astonishment of the answer which some
evil-minded counsellors advised him to return to the sheriffs
of the city of London †. For a king of Great Britain to take

---

* The letters under this signature are recognised by Junius in his Private
Letter, No. 56.

† The following are the particulars of the dispute which occurred in pre-
senting the petition of March 6, 1770 :—

On Wednesday, the 7th, the Sheriffs attended at St. James's, to know his
Majesty's pleasure, when he would be waited on with the city address,
remonstrance, and petition; they were detained till 20 minutes past 2, when,
the levee being over, they, with the remembrancer, were admitted into the
closet, when Mr. Sheriff Townshend addressed himself to his Majesty in the
following words :—

"May it please your Majesty,

"By order of the lord mayor, aldermen, and livery of the City of London,
in common-hall assembled, we have taken the earliest opportunity, as was
our duty, to wait upon your Majesty; but, being prevented from having
immediate access to your Majesty by one of your household, who informed
us that it was your Majesty's pleasure to receive us this day after the levee,
we wait on your Majesty, humbly to know when your Majesty will please
to be attended with an humble address, remonstrance, and petition."

To which his Majesty was pleased to return the following answer :—

"As the case is entirely new, I will take time to consider of it, and transmit you an answer by one of my principal Secretaries of State."

On Thursday evening the Sheriffs received the following letter from Lord
Weymouth :—

time to consider whether he will or will not receive a petition from his subjects, seems to me to amount to this, that

> "GENTLEMEN, "St. James's, March 8, 1770.
>
> "The King commands me to inform you, in consequence of the message which you brought yesterday to St. James's, that he is always ready to receive applications from any of his subjects; but as the present case of address, remonstrance, and petition, seems entirely new, I am commanded to enquire of you in what manner it is authenticated, and what the nature of the assembly was in which this measure was adopted? When you furnish me with answers to these questions I shall signify to you his Majesty's further pleasure.
>
> "I am, Gentlemen,
> "Your most obedient humble Servant,
> "Sheriffs of London. "WEYMOUTH."

On the next day the Sheriffs went to St. James's, and, after waiting some time, Lord Bolingbroke came out, and inquired whether he was to tell his Majesty that they came with a fresh message, or with a message? The Sheriffs answered, with a message. Soon after, the two Secretaries of State, Lord Rochford and Lord Weymouth, came to the Sheriffs. Lord Weymouth asked them, "whether they had received his letter, which was written by his Majesty's order?"

*Sheriffs.* "We have."

*Lord Weymouth.* "His Majesty desires to know whether you come in consequence of that letter, or whether you come on any fresh business?"

*Sheriffs.* "We come in consequence of that letter."

*Lord Weymouth.* "Would it not be more proper to send an answer in writing through me?"

*Sheriffs.* "We act ministerially. As Sheriffs of London we have a right to an audience, and cannot communicate to any other person than the King the subject of our message."

*Lord Weymouth.* "I do not dispute your right to an audience; but would it not be better and more accurate to give your message to me in writing?"

*Sheriffs.* "We know the value and consequence of the citizens' right to apply immediately to the King, and not to a third person; and we do not mean that any of their rights and privileges shall be betrayed by our means."

*Lord Weymouth* then said, "His Majesty, understanding that you come ministerially authorized with a message from the City of London, will see you as soon as the levee is over;" and being introduced accordingly, Mr. Sheriff Townshend addressed his Majesty in these words:—

> "May it please your Majesty,
>
> "When we had last the honour to appear before your Majesty, your Majesty was graciously pleased to promise an answer by one of your Majesty's principal Secretaries of State; but we had yesterday questions proposed to us by Lord Weymouth. In answer to which we beg leave humbly to inform your Majesty, that the application which we make to your Majesty we make as Sheriffs of the City of London, by the direction of the

he will take time to consider whether he will or will not adhere to the fourth article of the Declaration of Rights.  One
would think that this could never have been a question in
the mind of so gracious a prince, if there were not some very
dangerous advice given in the closet.   I now hear that it has
been signified to the sheriffs that his Majesty cannot receive
the petition until he is informed of the nature of the assembly in which it was composed.  A king indeed is not obliged
to understand the political forms and constitution of every
corporation in his dominions, but his ministers must be uncommonly ignorant who could not save him the embarrassment of asking such a question concerning the first body
corporate perhaps in the world.  The sheriffs, I presume,
will hardly venture to satisfy so unusual an inquiry upon their
own bare authority.  They will naturally move the Lord
Mayor to summon another Common Hall to answer for
themselves; and then I doubt not the corporation of the city
of London will fully explain, to those whom it may concern,
*who they are, and what is the nature of their assembly.*  After
all, Sir, I do not apprehend that the propriety of the King's
receiving a petition from any of his subjects depends in the
least upon *their* quality or situation.   He is bound by the
declaration and subsequent Bill of Rights to receive all
petitions from his subjects.   What notice or answer the

livery in common-hall legally assembled.  The address, remonstrance, and
petition, to be presented to your Majesty by their chief magistrate, is the
act of the citizens of London in their greatest court; and is ordered by them
to be properly authenticated as their act."

To which his Majesty replied as follows :—

" I will consider of the answer you have given me."

Whereupon the Sheriffs withdrew.

On the Monday following, the Sheriffs received the subjoined letter.

" GENTLEMEN,                          " St. James's, March 12, 1770.
" The King has commanded me to signify to you his Majesty's pleasure
that he will receive on Wednesday next, at 2 o'clock in the afternoon, the
address, remonstrance, and petition, which you have informed his Majesty is
to be presented by the chief magistrate of the city of London.
                   " I am, Gentlemen,
                        " Your most obedient humble Servant,
" Sheriffs of London.                              " WEYMOUTH."

For further particulars of this contest between the Court and the City, see
Junius's Letter, No. 37, and note vol. i. p. 299.

contents of them may deserve, must be considered afterwards. To refuse the petition itself is against law. I am
persuaded, however, that nothing can be further from the
intention of our gracious Sovereign than to offer a gross
affront to the whole city of London. It is evident that the
ministry either mean to gain time for carrying some poor
counter-measure by means of the wretched dependants of the
court, or to intimidate the city magistrates, and deter them
from doing their duty. I think it therefore absolutely necessary for us to rouse in defence of the honour of the city, and
demonstrate to the ministry, by the spirit and vigour of our
proceedings, that we are not what *they* are pleased to represent us, the scum of the earth, and the vilest and basest
of mankind.

MODERATUS*.

## LETTER LXXI.

### TO THE PRINTER OF THE PUBLIC ADVERTISER.

Sir,                                                    June 26, 1770.

THAT we may be quietly governed is a very proper petition
in the service of the Church of England. If the worst men
should be put in authority under the King, they will think it
politic to counteract the prayers of the people, and indifferently minister injustice, to the punishment of virtue and the
maintenance of vice. The Duke of Grafton has devoted
himself to these principles with all the fervour of an en-
thusiast, nor can we avoid lamenting that so inflexible a
bigot should still have failed of martyrdom. His Grace has
triumphed over the last moments of his power, nor permitted
its extinction till he had dismissed the Chancellor†, and procured a pension, inadequate, indeed, to former merits, for the
truly honest Mr Bradshaw ‡. The first occurrence has been
sufficiently canvassed; the propriety with which his Grace

---

* Letter 31 (vol. i. p. 245), which, in the first Woodfall edition, is signed
*Philo-Junius*, had, when it originally appeared in the *Public Advertiser*, the
signature of *Moderatus* affixed to it.

† The dismissed Chancellor was Lord Camden.

‡ Mr. Bradshaw, as often observed before, was the Duke of Grafton's
secretary.

has effected the second occurrence, cannot possibly be felt through all its force till the deserving object of ministerial gratitude has spoken for himself.

Come forward, Mr. Bradshaw, thou worthy but much injured man, at once convince, and undeceive the public. Tell them, that if a person should exist who dares even to insinuate that the following relation is founded upon stubborn facts he is a gross defamer of unbiassed honour, and would extend that rancorous abuse, which hitherto has preyed upon the fairest and most courtly characters, till it asperse your own.

Mrs. Allenby entered into an engagement with Miss Bradshaw in behalf of Mr. Allenby, her husband. It was stipulated that she should give into Miss Bradshaw's hands the sum of six hundred pounds, which was to have been the purchase-money of the place of surveyor of the pines in America. An application was soon afterwards made for the same place by Captain P——*, who promised that on receiving it he would pay down the sum of eight hundred pounds. In consequence of this promise, the name of Mr. Allenby, already inserted in the list of intended promotions, was erased, and the blank filled up with the name of Captain P——, to which was added a written assertion that his appointment was owing to Mr. Allenby's having chosen to decline going. When this affair was examined at the board of treasury, Mrs. Allenby was asked where her husband was during this transaction. She answered, "In Cumberland, assisting in the support of the Portland interest, when Mr. Robinson and Mr. Jenkinson were doing what mischief they could to oblige Sir James Lowther."

The latter part of Mrs. Allenby's declaration occasioned some little entertainment. She was ignorant that the two intimate friends of the Earl of Bute, whose characters she was then drawing, were actually present. Mr. Bradshaw pleaded in excuse that his sister, a milliner near Moorfields, was solely concerned in this business. When Mr. Cooper mentioned to Mr. Bradshaw an intention of lodging a complaint against him, he burst into tears. They could not have been tears of penitence, or they imply preceding guilt.

---

* Who the person here alluded to is cannot be ascertained.

When Mr. Bradshaw shall have exculpated his conduct,
which cannot be arraigned without injustice, he may perhaps
become a conspicuous instance of the prevalence of example.
The voice of injured innocence may sound within a neigh-
bouring quarter; and, as the ostensible premier may he
questioned on a similar occasion, his Lordship will have an
opportunity to revive this long-forgotten truth.  However con-
temptibly the world may judge of ministers of state, they are
not conscious to themselves of any guilt.

Q IN THE CORNER.*

## LETTER LXXII.

SIR,                                               June 27, 1770.

YOUR correspondent, *A Fellow-Labourer in the public Cause*†,
has a claim to our attention, rather from the liberality and
candour with which he has stated his ideas than from the
force of argument with which he has supported them.   He
seems to have forgotten that the national resentment has not
been so much excited by the exclusion of Mr. Wilkes as by
the insertion of Mr. Luttrell.   He does not seem to be aware
that the discussion of the great question can never be brought
on in a new mode as long as Mr. Wilkes is to be the ground-
work of the debate; that the arguments for incapacitation
of that gentleman were merely personal; that they respected
the member returned, without any reference to the constituents; and, therefore, that the substitution of other constituents can effect no alteration in the case whilst the person
returned continued the same.

* This, with subsequent letters under the same signature, bear marks of the
point, sarcasm, and political antipathies of Junius, and were probably among
his less elaborate compositions in his rural retreat, or excursions in the summer
season.   From May to August he appears this year to have been silent in
the *Public Advertiser* under his more formidable name, and may have
thought to amuse himself by waging a minor warfare as *Q in the Corner*,
and thus keep both himself and the public on the alert against their
common enemy.—ED.

† A letter under the above signature appeared on the preceding day,
recommending Mr. Wilkes to stand forward as a candidate for the city of
London on the death of Alderman Beckford.

Your correspondent would likewise have done well to have borne in mind that the livery of London have, by the most authentic act of the corporation, declared to the world that the intrusion of Mr. Luttrell has *vitiated* the present parliament*. With what consistency then can the same body of

* In such popular detestation was the conduct of the ministry and parliament held, with respect to their proceedings in the Middlesex election, that Mr. Alderman Townshend went so far as to try the legality of the Act of Parliament for raising the land-tax, the Alderman having refused to pay it on the pretence that the intrusion of Mr. Luttrell had vitiated the parliament, and negatived its power.

The trial took place June 9, 1772, and the following account of it is extracted from the *Public Advertiser* of the ensuing day :—

" Yesterday came on in the Court of King's Bench the long-expected cause between Mr. Alderman Townshend and the collector of the land-tax. Lord Mansfield had appointed the trial for 9 o'clock precisely; but he delayed it till near 11, waiting for the Attorney-General, who did not attend. The cause was opened by Mr. Davenport; after which Mr. Sergeant Glynn addressed the jury, and informed them that in common cases it was the custom to content themselves with proving the trespass, and then leave the justification of it to the defendant; but he said the present case required a further discussion from him; that it was an important constitutional point upon which the valuable rights of the whole nation depended. He said he was directed by his client, Mr. Townshend, to conduct the cause as its importance demanded; that therefore he should waive all the informalities in the collector's proceedings; he would admit him likewise to be collector, and that he was authorised by the commissioners; that the single ground of his pleading would be that the commissioners themselves were not authorised: for that a House of Commons, legally chosen by the people, are alone empowered to levy taxes in this country; and he said he insisted, and would prove by evidence, that the persons who passed the Act of Parliament (under which the collector had seized Mr. Townshend's hay) were improperly called a House of Commons, because they were illegally and defectively constituted. He said that to the making of all laws, and the levying of all taxes, it was formerly necessary that every freeholder should assent individually; and especially before a tax was to be levied, the constituents formerly were first referred to, because they were to consent to what they were to pay. Custom and usage (he said) had now made it common for the representatives in parliament to speak for the people, and this was considered the same as the consent of the people, because they were freely chosen by the people for that purpose; and after every election a formal letter of attorney (the indenture) is always given by the electors to the person they have chosen. He said that this implied consent of the people by their representatives depended entirely on their having the free choice of their representatives; for if their freedom of choice was invaded, the reference and implication were destroyed, and the people would no longer have any the least consent in the making of laws or levying of taxes; but that their lives and their property would be absolutely at the mercy of any set of men who

men subscribe to the integrity of the same parliament upon
any other terms than the previous extermination of the con-
taminating object? The introduction of Mr. Wilkes into the

should call themselves a parliament, corrupted by the revenue, and supported by the troops of a weak or a wicked tyrant. He said that this, as
far at least as it related to representation, was the case with the present
persons who call themselves a House; for which, he said, as they were not
chosen, so neither are they acknowledged by the people: the county of
Middlesex, he said, was not represented; that one of the members legally
chosen by the county had been forcibly and illegally excluded, and another
person as illegally and forcibly substituted in his room. Mr. Glynn then
gave a very striking account of the absurdity and impudence of Mr. Luttrell's
pretensions, and of the infamy of our ——, and his abettors and accomplices.
He said, the present pretended House of Commons had superseded the
election of the county by an unwarrantable resolution of their own; and
had, by so doing, seized into their own hands, and for their own use and
emolument, the birthright of all the people of England. He proved in the
clearest manner that the pretence of Mr. Wilkes's incapacity does not exist in
the law; and that the people's right of representation is less than a name if
the House of Commons has an indefinite power of expulsion. Mr. Glynn
said he would produce unquestionable evidence to the points on which he
had rested the merits of his cause; notwithstanding that he thought it
unnecessary, because the facts were so notorious, and so well known to the
jury themselves, that they could of their own knowledge, agreeably to the
laws of the land, give a verdict for the plaintiff even without any evidence.

"As soon as Mr. Glynn had finished his speech, and was directing the
evidence to be called, Mr. Wallace (the King's counsellor) produced a printed
paper, which he said was the Act of Parliament by which the collector levied
the tax. As for the objection that had been made by Mr. Glynn relative to
the seat of one of the members, or of the legality of the parliament, he said
the courts of Westminster Hall had no power to determine.

"Lord Mansfield then rose and said, that he perceived Mr. Glynn wanted
that court to retry the judgment of the House of Commons touching the case
of the Middlesex election; that is, said his Lordship, he wants to prove that
the legislature is dissolved; and that all the Acts of Parliament made since
the year 1769 are void. The evidence which Mr. Glynn wants to produce
is not by law admissible, and I will not suffer it to be given. 'Gentlemen
of the jury, you will find for the defendant.' The clerk then hurried over
the form, and said, 'Gentlemen of the jury, hearken to your verdict, &c.
You find for the defendant, and so you say all.' Whereupon, one of the
jury, Mr. Long, said he did not consent to that verdict. This dissent caused
some embarrassment to Lord Mansfield, which he soon got over by saying,
'Gentlemen, you are sworn to give a verdict according to the evidence; now
no evidence has been produced to you against the defendant; therefore you
must find for him. You cannot try facts by notoriety, that is not law, you
must go by evidence, and you have heard no evidence; you must find for the
defendant.'"

The jury accordingly acquitted the defendant.

House is in itself a circumstance of little importance. If parliament and the county of Middlesex had gone on in an eternal circulation of expulsions and returns, the essence of that assembly would not have been affected. The indispensable point is that the corrupt member should be lopped off; a point that will hardly be compassed by an event of such indifference to the public as the mere seating Mr. Wilkes in the House of Commons a representative of the city of London.

Upon the plan of your correspondent, the prosecutors, indeed, will be changed, but the cause will still be the same. It is in the power of administration alone to vary and extend the cause, by arbitrarily incapacitating *another member* legally elected; a measure which they do in truth "tremble at the thoughts of."

In conclusion: the restoration of parliament must begin in the person of Mr. Luttrell; nor can the injury to the people of England be heightened in the person of Mr. Wilkes. Every county, every borough, is already as essentially affected as the county of Middlesex. It is an eternal truth in the political as well as the mystical body, that "where one member suffers all the members suffer with it."

I am,
A LABOURER IN THE SAME CAUSE.

---

## LETTER LXXIII.

### REPLY TO Q IN THE CORNER.

Sir,                    Southampton Street, Bloomsbury, June 27, 1770.

HAVING, to my great surprise, seen in a letter published in your paper of yesterday, signed *Q in the Corner*, the following paragraph, "When Mr. Cooper mentioned to Mr. Bradshaw an intention of lodging a complaint against him, he burst into tears," I think myself bound in honour and in justice to declare, that the whole of this assertion is false and groundless: I never mentioned to Mr. Bradshaw any intention of lodging a complaint against him; I never heard of any such intention; and I do not know of any circumstance whatsoever that can justify the least imputation on Mr. Bradshaw of the nature intended to be conveyed by the said letter.

I am, Sir,<br>
Your humble servant,<br>
GREY COOPER.

## LETTER LXXIV.

TO THE PRINTER OF THE PUBLIC ADVERTISER.

SIR,                                                    June 30, 1770.

I RECEIVED the circumstance of Mr. Bradshaw's having burst into tears from an authority which I thought at least equal to Mr. Cooper's, and therefore I believed and asserted it. I now perceive that I was mistaken, do willingly give up so *capital* a point in Mr. Bradshaw's case, and join with his honourable friend in declaring that he has not wept at all about the matter.

I have a high opinion of Mr. Cooper's integrity, but a much higher of Mr. Bradshaw's. I find the fair image of truth in the first, in the last I expect to meet an oracle. Why will not Mr. Bradshaw be so obliging as to step forward, and declare upon *his honour*, that *he* " does not know of any circumstance whatsoever that can justify the least imputation on him of the nature which seems to Mr. Cooper to have been conveyed by a letter in this paper? "

I allow Mr. Cooper's evidence, as far as it relates to the falling of some few tears, to be entirely decisive; but I am not so courtly as to infer from Mr. Cooper's absolute ignorance of the subject an equal one in Mr. Bradshaw. It is from Mr. Bradshaw, who must know something more of the matter than Mr. Cooper, that I expect to be told, that no board was ever held at which this particular subject was introduced, and that Mrs. Allenby was not at that time present.

May I presume humbly to inquire of Mr. Bradshaw if Mr. Dyson did not at that time examine Mrs. Allenby; if he did not attempt to browbeat her; and if a noble Lord had not the humanity to interfere?

After all, it may be worth remarking, that Mr Cooper's

VOL. II.                                                    x testimony seems to relate only to *his own intentions* with respect to lodging a complaint, and *his own ideas* of the imputations that should arise from transactions of this nature.

I am, Sir,

Your humble servant,

Q IN THE CORNER.

---

## LETTER LXXV.

### TO THOMAS BRADSHAW, ESQ.

July 7, 1770.

YOUR honourable colleague, Mr. Cooper, bore witness to your innocence. So full a vindication was superfluous. I dare answer for it, that the opinion which the public had conceived of your integrity is still unaltered ; it could not have been lessened although your champion never had appeared ; nor has his entrance within the lists at all increased it. I took the liberty to appeal from his decision to your own : you seem determined to be silent. Perhaps the rigour of your situation deprives you of any choice between the sacrifice of truth and of yourself. You nobly hesitate to make the first, and tacitly confess that in one heedless moment throughout a life of unpolluted honesty you may have been to blame. Perhaps you do not think it quite ineligible to let this matter die away. Consult the feelings of your heart, and they will tell you that the public forms of justice can avail but little. They will not either yield a shelter to yourself, or enable you to direct the storm against another. I have not written from conjecture, nor can you be ignorant that I have drawn my intelligence from its first source, and not the common falsities of the day. There is a place which once was called the House of Prayer ; I leave it to men more versed in Scripture phrases than myself to tell you what it is at present. Should you hereafter think it proper to discuss this subject there, you possibly may find an individual in that virtuous congregation who will assist the hitherto ineffectual inquiries of

Q IN THE CORNER.

## LETTER LXXVI.

SIR,                                                        July 7, 1770.

I FIND myself engaged at once with two antagonists of very different complexions. I must content myself, however, with opposing the same obvious reasoning of a plain man to the cool circumspect address of *The Fellow-labourer in the Public Cause*, and to the rapid, eager precipitation of his supporter. The latter of these gentlemen, with a temperance that does not seem to belong to him, is peremptorily of opinion, " that when a particular injustice is founded on, and supported by, a general principle, the appeal should no longer be made to the passions, but to the wisdom of the people." The reverse is, I believe, invariably true. Prudence may incline us to forget the injury of a moment, the impulse of passion, or the suggestion of caprice. Let the same injury be offered to us with all the insolence of authority, or even let the authority be pretended to without any actual exertion, and wisdom herself shall call forth every passion to resist it.

A simple tax of a few shillings, illegally extorted, was sufficient to enlighten the understandings of the whole nation. Everybody perceived that one such instance, supporting itself on a general claim, was equivalent to, and (like an universal proposition) comprehended a thousand. It did not require the sagacity of a Hampden to deduce the consequences; but it called for all his spirit to oppose them.

I am ready to acknowledge, that " in rigorous consistency the city of London ought not to return any representative " to St. Stephen's Chapel ; I am more ready to dispense with " the attendance of some of the present city members." But I am still willing to admit the necessity of their departing a little from that rigour, *because* I see no medium between such a temporary accommodation, and either the miseries of civil bloodshed, or (what is infinitely more to be deprecated) the established tranquillity of servitude.

The right of resistance on the part of the people is the ultimate sanction of our civil liberties. But God forbid that

X 2

we should be too critically exact in defining the precise boun
dary where the exertion of that right becomes a duty.   The
distresses of an intestine war are known and inevitable; the
event precarious.   It may be better to submit, for a time, to
what even is an irregularity in the most essential part of the
state than instantly to seek redress by violence.   Every
other conceivable method ought first to be eagerly adopted,
and earnestly pursued.   Something may be expected from
time, from importunity, from fear; perhaps something even
from conscience and remorse.   And if, at length, without
coming to extremities, the integrity of the legislature should
be restored, the tyrannical decisions of an unauthorized assembly will of course be abrogated; their useful acts may receive a ratification from a legitimate parliament.

You perceive, Sir, that I am not here maintaining the doctrine asserted in the city remonstrance, but arguing from it.
Yet I must beg leave to observe, that the distinction introduced by this correspondent, between a speculative and a
practical parliament, a parliament *de jure* and *de facto*, is
equally novel and monstrous.   On this account I cannot but
be of opinion that the city should adhere to their constitutional speculation, and insist that Mr. Wilkes is actual representative of Middlesex; although they may without blame,
perhaps, acquiesce, for a time, in the proceedings of an assembly to which they cannot even allow the rank of a convention.

For the sake of peace they may be justified in returning
Mr. Oliver.   For the sake not merely of consistency, but of
the safety and dignity of the state, Mr. Wilkes must not be
allowed to quit "the sure ground on which he stands," to
borrow an expression of his own in an address to his constituents.

But it seems, "if Mr. Wilkes were returned by the city,
and admitted to take his seat, the unconstitutional principle
would be *ipso facto* overturned."   Let us see, then, how the
argument will stand.   If the admission of Mr. Wilkes would
*ipso facto* overturn the unconstitutional principle, undoubtedly
the continuation of Mr. Luttrell must *ipso facto* perpetuate it.
What is this but to make the House of Commons such an absurd monster in politics as has never yet disgraced the reason or the patience of mankind: a legislative body subsisting

by two principles (each in its full force and energy), equal, contrary, and mutually destructive.

The *Fellow-labourer* of this day has, indeed, candidly admitted that the extermination of Mr. Luttrell is the *indispensable point*, if your other correspondent, who absolutely denies the position, will indulge me in the phrase. Mr. Luttrell holds his seat by a very different title from a common determination in the case of a contested return. In the latter instance, the jurisdiction of the House is competent; nor has the constitution hitherto provided an appeal for their decision. In the case before us, a new and unheard-of power is supposed to be usurped, and rights beyond the reach of the whole legislature, I mean the fundamental rights of the people, invaded by a third part of it. By this invasion Mr. Luttrell was seated: upon this principle the return was amended by the House and his name inserted; and it is in consequence of that alteration that he still ranks as a member of parliament. As long, therefore, as he shall be permitted to sit there, so long will the principle be in force. For in the House of Commons, as in every other court, prove the jurisdiction to be incompetent to the case, and the adjudication falls to the ground.

It appears to me that both your correspondents have contemplated this subject in too confined a view. For my own part, I think too highly of Mr. Wilkes's services to the state, and of the sacredness of our common cause, to wish either one or the other to be made a mere engine of party, or a scarecrow of opposition. But since the gentlemen from whom I dissent have delivered their sentiments concerning the effect which the proposed measure would probably produce in the House of Commons and in ministry, I, too, in my turn, will venture to pronounce that nothing is so ardently desired by either, as *a separation between the county of Middlesex and Mr. Wilkes.*

I am, Sir,
Your humble Servant,
A LABOURER IN THE SAME CAUSE.

## LETTER LXXVII.

Sir,                                          November 19, 1770.

A FEW days ago I was in a large public company, where
there happened some curious conversation. The Secretary at
War * was pleased to express himself with unusual simplicity
and candour. He assured us that, after having carefully considered the subject, he did not know a single general officer
(out of near an hundred now in the service) who was in any
shape qualified to command the army ; and, for fear we should
not believe him, repeated and inforced his assertion five several times. You will allow, Sir, that, at the eve of a foreign
war, this is pretty comfortable intelligence for the nation, especially as it comes from authority. He gave us some consolation, however, by assuring us that he and General Hervey
would take excellent care of the army, and compared himself
(not unhappily) to an old woman curing an ague with the
assistance of Dr. Radcliff. I don't so much question Mr.
Hervey's being able to give good advice as that other little
man's being either willing or able to follow it; but I should
be glad to know which of them is to be responsible to the
country for the management of the army, or whether they are
invested with equal powers. Is Lord Barrington the marks-
man and General Hervey only the stalking-horse? Or does
the latter command and that other only do as he is bid? This
point, I think, ought to be explained, for if we don't know
who commands the army, and any mischief should happen,
the Secretary at War and Adjutant General will of course lay
the blame upon each other, and the nation never know which
of them ought to be punished.

                                          TESTIS.

* Lord Viscount Barrington.

## LETTER LXXVIII*.

### TO THE PRINTER OF THE PUBLIC ADVERTISER

SIR,                                        November 24, 1770.

I HAVE never joined in the severe censures which have lately been thrown upon Lord Barrington. The formal declaration he was pleased to make (for the information of the House of Commons and of this country) with respect to the shameful ignorance and incapacity of all the general officers, without exception, may, for aught I know, be extremely well founded; and if it were not so, I do not consider the Viscount as a free agent. He undoubtedly meant no more than, as a dutiful servant, to obey the orders and express the sentiments of his royal master. The Secretary at War, it is true, has a multitude of enemies, but the bitterest of them will not affirm that he is positively an idiot without a single ray of understanding. That would be going a *little* too far. Yet he must certainly be the very weakest of the human species if, without any plan or purpose whatsoever, he loaded himself with the hatred and resentment of so large and powerful a body of men as the general officers. This, I think, is too absurd to be supposed. Yet I do not pretend to deny the fact; on the contrary, I mean to account for it upon clear and rational principles. If it be the King's intention (as we have sufficient reason to think it is) to govern the army himself (by which means the disposal of commissions, like everything else, will ultimately centre in Carlton House), the first step is to possess the public with an opinion that this measure is not of choice but necessity. When the Secretary at War has informed the House of Commons, in the name of his gracious master (for it is not to be suspected that he spoke for himself), that all his general officers were no better than drivellers, it follows of course that the Secretary at War, with the Adjutant General's advice, must be the ostensible manager of the army, and then you see, Sir, every-

* On the outside of Note No. 25, which accompanied this letter, was written, by the author, "the enclosed strikes deeper than you may imagine. C."

thing goes on as her Royal Highness the Princess Dowager of Wales would have it.

Far be it from me to impeach his Majesty's judgment in military matters. Our gracious Sovereign cannot possibly have a meaner opinion of his general officers than I have. Yet I own there is one circumstance that a little surprises me. These poor creatures, it is agreed on all hands, have neither capacity nor experience; but one would think that, as soldiers and gentlemen, they might show a little spirit when they are insulted. What, will they go to court again, to bow, and cringe, and fawn upon * * * * *, who orders his official servant to point them out to their country as a knot of idiots —asses—mules—beasts of burthen !

This affair, Sir (as many other circumstances do, and more important ones may do hereafter), puts me in mind of the sincere, honest, candid character of that pious prince, Charles the First. When a great number of the first people of this country had hazarded their lives and spent their fortunes in his defence, and when, in the last instance, they had formed a convention at Oxford, which, if not a parliament, was at least a meeting highly respectable, what return did they receive from that devout, religious, grateful monarch? He flattered them to their faces, and the next moment wrote to ois wife that they were a base mutinous set of mongrels, whom he was happy to get rid of.

ETSTICULCS.

---

## LETTER LXXIX

TO THE PRINTER OF THE PUBLIC ADVERTISER

Sir,                                                December 8, 1770.

A REPORT prevails that the late premier is very soon to be placed at the head of the admiralty. I thought Junius had fairly hissed him off the stage. But since he adventures again to appear before the public, let me do justice to his modesty, and commend him for his discretion in sinking to an inferior character. I should be sorry to interrupt so natural a descent. By dropping gradually from part to part, he may in time arrive at something that will suit his capacity.

Besides the moral fitness of reducing all men to their proper level, there will be a novelty in the public entertainment, when we see the same wretched stroller, who strutted yesterday in Othello, creeping upon the stage to day in the shape of a candle-snuffer.

In the article of firmness, I think this young man's character is universally given up; but I observe there is still an opinion maintained by some people that, in point of ability, he is not deficient. For my own part, Sir, I never could discover upon what foundation that opinion rested. Let it be fairly tried by the two great decisive tests of the human understanding—*conduct* and *discourse*. These, I know, are sometimes at variance with each other. An ingenious man may act very absurdly, and we frequently see a dull fellow conduct himself with firmness and propriety. It is the Duke's misfortune that he fails equally in both articles—that he neither acts with judgment nor speaks with ability. Look at his conduct from the outset; I mean with a reference not to the treachery, but to the folly of the man. His earliest personal attachment in life was to the Duke of Portland; that friendship he has foolishly dissolved, without succeeding in his purpose, to oblige Sir James Lowther. His first public connection was with Lord Rockingham. That too is lost, together with the friendship of Lord Chatham, for which he sacrificed the Marquis. For the solidity of his union with Lord Chatham he pledged himself to the public by some very uncommon declarations, both abroad and in parliament. Yet from this union, and his subsequent friendship with Lord Granby and Lord Camden, the cajolery of the closet soon seduced him. His easy virtue is not made for resistance. To support his last plan, we have seen him renounce not only all these successive connections, but every political idea, opinion, and principle of his former life, and throw himself, body and soul, into the arms of the Bedfords. Here, at least, he might have stopped, since there was not another party in the kingdom to which it was possible for him to transfer his affections. He had gone resolutely through the whole drudgery of the Middlesex election. He had paid Governor Burgoyne's expenses very handsomely by the sale of that patent to Mr. Hine, which the right honourable the House of Commons have not yet thought proper to inquire into. He had shown fortitude enough to drop the prosecution of Mr. Vaughan, though urged, insulted, braved to it by every *stimulus* that could touch the feelings of a man; and, in conclusion, he had made himself *accessory* to the untimely death of Mr. Yorke;—I say *accessory*, because he was certainly not the principal actor in that most atrocious business. After all, Sir, when it was impossible for him to add to his guiltiness, a panic seizes him, he begins to measure his expectations by the sense of his deserts, a visionary gibbet appears before his eyes, he flies from his post, surrenders to another the reward due to his honourable services, and leaves his King and country to extricate themselves, if they can, from the distress and confusion in which he had involved them.

The danger, as he conceives, being now pretty well over, what plan do you think this worthy, resolute young man pursues at present? While he was First Lord of the Treasury, it is well known (and I speak from knowledge when I assert), that he never treated Lord North even with the common civility due to his clerk. I appeal to Lord North himself, and to every clerk in the treasury (particularly to Grey Cooper), whether it was not known to be a difficult matter for the Chancellor of the Exchequer to obtain an audience even of Mr. Thomas Bradshaw. Would you believe it possible, Sir, that, after these facts, this very Duke of Grafton can be so degraded, so lost to every sensation of pride, of dignity, and decorum, as to be a suppliant beggar for employment to this very Lord North? Yet so it is; and, if I were to tell you with what circumstances of humiliation he accompanies his suit to the minister, the narrative would be nauseous and fulsome. He is so very impatient to be First Lord of the Admiralty, that Lord North can hardly keep the fawning creature from under his feet. Now, Sir, let any man living, I care not whether friend or foe, review this summary of his life, and tell us in what instance he has discovered a single ray of wisdom, solidity, or judgment?

As to the other test of his abilities, I mean his talent for talking in public, I can speak with greater precision, for I have often had the honour of hearing him. With a very solemn and plausible delivery, he has a set of thoughts, or rather of words resembling thoughts, which may be applied indifferently, and with equal success, to all possible subjects.

There is this singular advantage in his Grace's method of discourse, that, if it were once admitted that he spoke well upon any one given topic, it would inevitably follow that he was qualified to deliver himself happily upon every subject whatsoever. He would be *ipso facto* an universal orator. Accept of the following specimen of his Grace's eloquence, and I promise you you will be as well able to judge of his oratorical powers as if you had heard him a thousand times.

" My Lords,

"When I came into the house this day, I protest I did not think it possible, indeed I had formed in my own breast a resolution to the contrary; but, my Lords, I really thought it impossible that I should be compelled to trouble your Lordships with *my* poor thoughts upon the question before your Lordships. I never do presume to trouble your Lordships at any time without always feeling a pain, an internal regret, a degree of uneasiness, which I can with truth assure your Lordships (and I flatter myself that I shall find credit with every noble lord who hears me), it is not easy for me to have the honour of describing to your Lordships. My Lords, I am called upon, as I humbly conceive, and I appeal boldly not only to the candour of noble lords, but to your Lordships' severest judgment, whether I am not compelled to declare my sentiments, as explicitly as I now do, upon the motion upon your Lordships' table. Upon this ground, my Lords, I meet the noble Lord without fear, though I respect his superior abilities, and I pledge *myself* to your Lordships for the truth of what I assert. Otherwise, my Lords, if facts were not as I have stated them, where will your Lordships draw the line? My Lords, I am really *astonished*; yet indeed, my Lords, I ought not to be *astonished*. The question has been handled with so much ability by other noble lords, that I shall content *myself* with this simple, unadorned declaration of my opinion. Yet I could quote cases, my Lords, which I accidentally met with this morning in the course of my readings, which, I doubt not, would convince your Lordships, if conviction were in question. But I fear I have troubled your Lordships too long. I shall therefore return to the leading proposition, which I had the honour of setting out with, and move for an immediate adjournment."

This style, I apprehend, Sir, is what the learned Scriblerus calls *rigmarole* in logic, *riddlemeree* among schoolboys, and in vulgar acceptation, *Three blue beans in a blue bladder.* It is the perpetual parturience of a mountain and the never-failing delivery of a mouse.

> I am, Sir,
> Your humble Servant,
> DOMITIAN*.

--------

## LETTER LXXX.

### *For the Public Advertiser.*

December 13, 1770.

#### CHAPTER OF FACTS, OR MATERIALS FOR HISTORY†.

1. The House of Lords, justly offended at the accuracy and precision with which a certain noble Duke's oration‡ has been delivered to the public, and concluding that the very words must have been taken down in writing, by some foreign enemy, have determined to preserve the honour of their members, and the credit of their eloquence, by ordering *all* strangers to be carefully excluded.

2. But not to give offence. the exclusion is made general ; their Lordships very properly considering that the members of the House of Commons are no more fit to be trusted with the debates of a public assembly than the spies or emissaries of a foreign ambassador, or so many Jesuits in disguise.

3. The right honourable the Speaker of the House of Lords was pleased to summon all the lords to attend on Monday last, on purpose to inform their Lordships collectively in what corner of the house each lord separately might find waste paper for his necessary occasions. N. B. It seems to be the fate of this unhappy paper (which always brings nasty ideas with it) to be produced in a most unseemly manner. In the Court of King's Bench, the introduction of it was allowed to be *irregular, unprecedented*, and EXTRAJUDICIAL. In the House

--------

It has been already remarked that Junius admitted this to be one of his signatures.—Ed.

† By Junius, see note, *post*, p. 319.

‡ See the preceding letter.

of Lords it was only silly and ridiculous. What a strange antipathy some men have to a record! When they dare not *erase* they fairly take post and *travel out of it.*

4. The bill for regulating contested elections was strenuously opposed by Lord North and the rest of the King's servants. Yet every one of the judges who went the circuit last summer, instead of instructing the several grand juries in the old, legal, constitutional way, were ordered to sound the praises of the House of Commons for their singular virtue in passing this and the privilege bill. And now let it be observed that in the first instance of the operation of this new law (the Shoreham election) not one of the ministers attended. Yet, intrusted as they are with the executive power of the state, it is *their* particular duty to attend, to facilitate, and inforce the execution of the laws; and these are the people who deafen us with their complaints of the licentiousness of the times, and the total want of respect into which the laws are fallen.

5. So far from performing this duty, it is a fact notorious that one Purling, a *Caribbee*, has been encouraged by ministry to introduce a third candidate at Shoreham, and to give him *four* of his own votes, in order that by having *two* petitions preferred (a case not expressly provided for by the act), this wise, this salutary law may be defeated in the first instance, and have a contempt thrown upon it.

6. Let it be known to posterity, that when Lord Mansfield was attacked with so much vehemence in the House of Commons on Thursday the 6th instant, not one of the ministry said a word in his defence. Nobody spoke for him but the Carlton House junto, Jenkinson and Sir Gilbert. (N.B. *Mungo is sick*). Even Mr. George Onslow, who in general is not very scrupulous, confined himself to the defence of Mr. Baron Smythe, and did not utter a syllable in favour of poor Mansfield. These facts show plainly: 1st, How the Carlton House connection hangs together. 2nd, That Lord North himself is not over and above pleased with the closet influence of the CHIEF JUGGLER.

The great Lord Camden did yesterday (11th of December, 1770) address himself directly to Lord Mansfield, and declare that he considered the paper delivered in by that Lord as a challenge to himself, which he accepted; that the glove was thrown down, and he took it up. That he was ready to meet him in defence of the laws of this country, and vehemently urged that a day might be fixed for debating the matter. But notwithstanding every possible instance made by the minority Lords, the Chief Justice shrunk from the combat, and would not fix any day.

---

## LETTER LXXXI

*For the Public Advertiser.*

December 14, 1770

SECOND CHAPTER OF FACTS, OR MATERIALS FOR HISTORY.

1. THE Earl of Chatham having asserted, on Tuesday last, in the House of Lords, that Gibraltar was open to an attack from the sea, and that, if the enemy were masters of the bay, the place could not make any long resistance, he was answered in the following words by that great statesman the Earl of Sandwich:—" Supposing the noble Lord's argument to be well founded, and *supposing Gibraltar to be now unluckily taken*, still, according to the noble Lord's own doctrine, it would be no great matter. For although we are not masters of the sea at present, we probably shall be so some time or other, and then, my Lords, there will be no difficulty in re-taking Gibraltar." N.B. This Earl is a privy counsellor, and appeared to have concerted this satisfactory answer with Peg Trentham at the fire-side.

2. Sir Edward Hawke, on Wednesday last, gave the House of Commons a very pompous account of the fleet. Being asked why, if our navy was so numerous and ready for service, a squadron was not sent to Gibraltar and the West Indies? his answer was candid:—" That for his part he did not understand sending ships abroad when, for aught he knew, they might be wanted to defend our own coast." Such is the care taken of our possessions abroad! One great minister tells us they may be easily retaken; another assures us that they cannot be defended. Will that man who sleepeth never awake until destruction comes upon him? Has he no

friend, no servant, to draw his curtain, until Troy is actually in flames?

3. Lord North informed the House of Commons on Wednesday that, although he wished for an honourable accommodation, he thought it his duty to tell the House, that he feared *war was too probable*; that he intended to move for a further augmentation of ten thousand seamen\*, and that, at any rate, he should advise the keeping up the naval and military force upon the augmented establishment, for that, notwithstanding the language held by the French and Spanish ministers, there was, all over France and Spain, the greatest appearance of hostile preparations.

4. The riot in the House of Lords has shocked the delicacy of Sir Fletcher Norton. Upon occasion of some clamour yesterday, he called to them, with all the softness of a bassoon, *Pray, gentlemen, be orderly; you are almost as bad as the other House.*

5. On Tuesday last, Lord Camden delivered into the House of Lords a paper containing three questions, relative to the doctrine laid down in Lord Mansfield's paper, which he

---

\* Both this and the preceding communication were unquestionably from Junius. His industry in collecting information, in attending the debates of parliament, and communicating the results of each through different channels, was indefatigable. In a letter addressed by Mr. Calcraft to the Earl of Chatham, dated December 16, 1770, a similar report is made of the probability of war, and the utterances of Lord North, and which it is likely either Junius had communicated to Calcraft, or Calcraft, who was a member, to Junius. Mr. Calcraft says to his Lordship :—

"First for the land-tax, Lord North alleged the four shillings necessary for the year, in any event. He told us our situation was precarious ; that *war was too probable*; that so many more ships were ordered to be fitted as would take 9000 additional seamen ; and though Spain should come to terms of accommodation, it would be unwise to disarm whilst the warlike preparations of France and Spain continued."—*Chatham Correspondence*, vol. iv. p. 57.

Of the riot mentioned in the next paragraph by Junius, Mr. Calcraft, in the same letter says, " Now for yesterday ! Lord George Germain moved for a conference with the Lords, was seconded by Lord George Cavendish, and most ably supported by Mr. Dunning, Colonel Barré, and Mr. Burke. Their speeches were admirable. Barré described the *riot in the Lords* as a mob broke in, headed by Lords Marchmont and Denbigh, of whose persons he gave the most ridiculous description."—*Ibid*, p. 58.

I have already mentioned the fact that Sir Philip Francis obtained from the late John Calcraft, Esq., all the letters and papers Sir Philip had formerly addressed to his father, the above-mentioned Mr. Calcraft.—ED.

desired that Lord would answer, if he could.  Lord Mansfield
was very angry at being taken by surprise upon a subject he
had never had an opportunity of considering, and that he
valued the constitutional liberty of the subject too much to
*answer interrogatories* \*.

---

## LETTER LXXXII.

### TO THE PRINTER OF THE PUBLIC ADVERTISER.

SIR,                                          December 17, 1770.

As far as assertion goes, no man argues better than your
correspondent *Nerva* †.    If we are contented to take his word

\* *Vide* Lord Mansfield, note, *post*, p. 324.

† *Nerva* was a writer in favour of Lord Mansfield upon the subject of his
conduct in the cause of the King against Woodfall for printing Junius's
Letter to his Majesty ; as well as for his posterior proceeding in the House of
Peers upon the matter of this cause ; in the course of which he thought
proper, as has been observed already, to summons the House specially, in
order to afford him an opportunity of fully explaining himself upon this
point ; an opportunity, however, of which he was even at last afraid to avail
himself.  See Appendix, vol. i. p. 472.

    The letter of *Nerva*, above alluded to, was addressed to Lord Chatham,
and appeared in the *Public Advertiser*, December 14, 1770.  The following
is a copy :—

### " For the Public Advertiser.

### "TO THE RIGHT HON. LORD CHATHAM.

    " MY LORD,                             "December 14, 1770.
" I saw on Monday, in a certain great assembly, the most striking contrast
of character that ever was exhibited on any public occasion.  On the one
hand, decency, propriety, dignity, wisdom, and temper ; on the other, presumption, insolence, absurdity, meanness, folly, ignorance, and rancour.
Your Lordship sat for one of the pictures, and, I am sorry to say, it was not
for the best.  To speak without metaphor, what demon, save the demon of
malice, could inspire you with an objection to the fair, the equitable information which Lord Mansfield offered to the House ?  The proposal itself, the
terms in which it was conceived, would have conciliated a barbarian ; but
your animosity is worse than a barbarian's, and betrays the principle from
which it springs !  In an unprecedented, extrajudicial, captious, and insidious manner, you had taken occasion to censure that great man's opinions in
the court of justice where he presides.  Though you endeavour to take him
by surprise, that you might catch at some unfair advantage from his answer,
you were baffled and disappointed.  He answered you with the noble simplicity of innocence, and the wisdom that never forsakes the *mens conscia*

for proof, Lord Chatham is a hare-brained, desperate old fellow, and Lord Mansfield the very quintessence of integrity,

rreti. He fairly stated his opinions, and the principles on which they were grounded, and, without recrimination, he threw down his glove to you, and to all, daring you to convict him of an error, upon fair and legal argument.

"He did more; to prevent that misrepresentation and misconstruction which might arise from words spoken, he delivered to the House the opinion given by him in court in the case alluded to in writing; candidly and formally declaring, that he meant to ground no motion upon it, but merely for the information of every member, that those who had not steeled their minds against conviction might be convinced how falsely the censure had been made, and that your Lordship and your party might have a more open ground of objection to the doctrine which the writing contained.

"When I give this account of Lord Mansfield's reasons for submitting this paper to the House, I do wrong to the moderation of his expressions; but I speak to a man whose conscience tells him, that the distinction between him and those who are open to conviction is but too well founded. He that as it may, one would have thought you could wish for nothing more than that a person whose doctrines you arraigned should give them under his hand, and dare you to the trial of their truth. Instead of closing with the proposal, you rose up and objected to the delivery of the paper as informal; but it is no new thing with you, after you have made a malicious and groundless attack, when you see it likely to produce consequences, to shrink back, and shelter yourself under some pitiful evasion; catching at form, or any other twig, to save you from the effects of your own folly and ill-nature.

"But if you had made an end here, your audience had gone away, convinced only that you were happy to get out of the scrape into which you had brought yourself by your unprecedented and unjust attack on Lord Mansfield. But, as if you were determined that every man who hears you should bear witness to your rambling inconsistency and ignorance, you did not make an end here. After having affirmed that the paper could not be received—after declaring you knew not what was censured in the proceedings of the courts of justice, nor against whom in particular that censure was directed—after having declared also your ignorance of what the paper contained, you entered into a discussion of its contents. You said the paper contained an extrajudicial and unprecedented opinion, and that the judgment was not warranted by the record, and the two motions on which the judgment was to operate. All this you asserted in terms unbecoming the place in which you stood, unbecoming the person to which they were addressed, and highly improper to be used by one who spoke about what he did not understand. All the world knows that you are ignorant of every science. This country severely smarts, and will long severely smart, for your ignorance in politics and finance. Your ignorance of the law may not perhaps produce such fatal consequences, but it was such on the occasion I speak of that your dependant, the man who has sold himself to you soul and body, who trembles at his tyrant's frown, durst not say a word in defence of your position, nor even by a distinction endeavour to shade the glare of your absurdity.

"I know you are not ashamed of the grossest ignorance and absurdity; but

wisdom, moderation, and firmness.   I wonder he did not
assure us on the same foundation that this worthy judge
never drank the Pretender's health upon his knees; or that
his brother was not secretary to that most Catholic Prince:
or that Peg Trentham's father had not his left foot in the
stirrup in the year 1715, to go off to what he thought the
best side of the question: all this too I suppose we shall be
told is mere fiction, mere inference of law, and the suggestion
of the devil; but, setting aside ornament, let us look a little
to matters of fact.

I would ask you one question.  When the great man, whom you had treated
so injuriously, rose up to explain, and with the most amiable moderation,
and intuitive perspicuity, pointed out your mistake, and rectified your blunder, had you no feelings of remorse for your injustice towards him?  Did you
not *see how lovely virtue was, and mourn your loss?*  Did not the demon of
faction and malice retire dejected from your heart, and leave you in the momentary possession at least of better angels?  If not, you are unhappy indeed!  But I err.  Perhaps your familiar whispered to you, that your opponent's temper was an argument of his contempt; and, to sting you to madness, suggested that your brutal violence was unable to ruffle the steady tenor
of his soul.  I own this were a galling reflection to a man of your pride; but
pride like yours must suffer every indignity.

"If this was his motive for calmness and moderation it was taking indeed
vengeance, but a heroic vengeance.  Were it your fortune to catch him at a
fair advantage (an event which can never happen), how differently would
you use it!  With what vehemence would you not press it home!  How
would you exaggerate a molehill to a mountain, and call heaven and earth
to witness that the nation was ruined and our liberties at an end!  But all
men are not born to be heroes, nor all men candid, just, or wise.  You, my
Lord, have imposed long enough on the world; your faculties have been
greatly misjudged; your organs have been mistaken for talents, your facility
and versatility for parts, your boldness (I could give it a harsher name) for
knowledge, and your precipitation for dispatch.  You are a memorable exception to the general rule of humanity, for years and exercise have not endowed you with experience or wisdom, and you possess, together with the
cold heart of age, the hot brain of rash and intemperate youth.  Already
hath your furious prodigality brought this nation to the brink of ruin.  Do
not persist in your impious intention to accomplish what you have already
well nigh performed.  Retire from the stage, and try in retirement to repent
of the evils you have brought on your country.  If your proud heart cannot
brook the idea of sincere repentance, let the repeated defeats which you have
lately suffered in the prosecution of your outrageous designs teach you to
assume a virtue though you have it not.  By that appearance of contrition,
and by that only, you may soften the odium which must attend you to the
grave, and alleviate the load of indignation which posterity will lay on your
memory.

"NERVA."

For what reason Lord Mansfield laid his paper upon the table, he best knows. He gave none to the House of Lords, except that he thought calling them together was the most compendious way of informing them where each lord might, if he pleased, procure a copy of his charge to the jury in Woodfull's cause. This was the whole, for he made no motion whatsoever, nor did he pretend to say that, in their corporate capacity as a House of Peers, they could take the least notice of the paper. Now, Sir, it remains with Lord Mansfield to give us an example, if he can, of any respectable peer having ever moved for a call of the House for so trifling, so nugatory, so ridiculous a purpose. I think it strongly deserves these epithets, and after much consideration I can find but one possible way of reconciling the fact with the cunning understanding of the man. When he summoned the House, he never meant to do what he afterwards did; some qualm, some terror intervened, and forced him hastily to alter his design, and to substitute a silly, absurd measure in the place of a dangerous one. As for his having dared Lord Chatham to a trial of his doctrines, I should be glad to know by whom the combat was refused. Lord Chatham attacked him directly upon the spot, and on the very next day it is known to the whole world, that the great Lord Camden addressed him in the following words: " I consider the paper delivered in by the noble Lord upon the woolsack as a challenge directed personally to me, and I accept of it: —he has thrown down the glove, and I take it up. In direct contradiction to him, I maintain that his doctrine is not the law of England. I am ready to enter into the debate whenever the noble Lord will fix a day for it. I desire and insist that it may be an early one." The devil's in it if this be declining the trial; but what was the consequence? Lord Mansfield, after an hour's shuffling and evasion, finding himself pushed to the last extremity, cried out in an agony of torture and despair, *No, I will not fix a day—I will not pledge myself* *.

* To what is stated in the Appendix (vol. i. p. 473) it may be added that Lord Mansfield's conduct, on the occasion referred to in the text, was the weakest portion of his public life. His behaviour was pusillanimous in the extreme, and evinced such want of firmness, consistency, and legal competence to maintain his judicial dicta, that he rendered himself an object of pity,

As to Lord Chatham's declarations concerning the irregular production of Lord Mansfield's opinion in the Court of King's Bench, I am sorry to say that your correspondent *Nerva* neither knows the fact, nor understands the argument. He talks of a judgment in a cause where no judgment was ever given. Leaving therefore this poor man to his own unhappy reveries, let me state briefly to the public what was the fact, and what was the irregularity of the proceeding upon it.

The verdict given at *Nisi Prius* in the King and Woodfall was, *guilty of printing and publishing only*\*. A motion in arrest of judgment was made by the defendant's counsel, grounded upon the ambiguity of the verdict. At the same time a motion was made by the counsel for the crown, for a rule upon the defendant to show cause why the verdict should not be entered up according to the legal import of the words. On both motions a rule to show cause was granted, and soon after the matter was argued before the Court of King's Bench. Lord Mansfield, when he delivered the opinion of the court upon the verdict, went regularly through

almost contempt, to the House of Lords. Horace Walpole, who witnessed the scene, says, " The dismay and confusion of Lord Mansfield were obvious to the whole audience ; nor did one peer interpose a syllable in his behalf." He was so closely pressed on the point that he would not answer " interrogatories " by Lords Chatham and Richmond, that the House became desirous the matter should drop, from commiseration of the embarrassment of the Chief Justice, and it was never resumed. Next morning Lord Chatham sent a note to Lord Camden complimenting him on his triumph, and inquiring after his health, and adding, " I think I ought rather to inquire how Lord Mansfield does."—*Lives of the Chief Justices*, vol. ii. p. 489.

Lord Campbell, in his report of the scene, omits the two last questions of Lord Camden.—Ed.

\* The whole of this paragraph is taken by Junius from a speech of Lord Chatham, delivered December 11, 1770, that is, a few days before it appeared in the *Public Advertiser*. Junius long after, in his Preface, quotes the same passage, introducing it with a note which was accidentally omitted in its proper place, p. 95 of vol. i., and acknowledges it to be from a speech of Lord Chatham, and which, in his letter under the signature of *Phalaris*, he omits. " The following quotation," says he, " from a speech delivered by Lord Chatham, is *taken with exactness.* The reader will find it very curious in itself, and fit to be inserted here." He then gives the extract verbatim, as in the above paragraph. It became important afterwards, as one of the means of identifying Sir Philip Francis to be Junius, it being known that Francis reported several of Lord Chatham's speeches and gave copies to Almon, and in consequence was a good judge of the one "taken with exactness."—Ed.

the whole of the proceedings at *Nisi Prius*, as well tho evidence that had been given as his own charge to the jury. This proceeding would have been very proper had a motion been made of either side for a new trial, because either a verdict given contrary to evidence, or an improper charge by the judge at *Nisi Prius*, is held to be a sufficient ground for granting a new trial ; but when a motion is made in arrest of judgment, or for establishing the verdict, by entering it up according to the legal import of the words, it must be on the ground of something appearing *on the record;* and the court, in considering whether the verdict shall be established or not, are so confined to the record that they cannot take notice of anything that does not appear on the face of it; to make use of the legal phrase, *they cannot travel out of the record.* Lord Mansfield did travel out of the record. I affirm therefore with Lord Chatham, that his conduct was *irregular, extrajudicial,* and *unprecedented;* and I am sure there is not a lawyer in England that will contradict me. His real motive for doing what he knew to be wrong was, that he might have an opportunity of telling the public extrajudicially, that the other three judges agreed with him in the doctrine laid down in his charge.

When you have read this paper, I am sure you will join with me in opinion, that to support an uniform system of falsehood, requires greater parts than even those of Lord Mansfield.

PHALARIS.

---

## LETTER LXXXIII.

TO THE PRINTER OF THE PUBLIC ADVERTISER.

SIR,                                             December 24, 1770.

WITHOUT attempting to account for all the political changes which have happened since his Majesty's auspicious accession to the throne, it requires but little sagacity to observe that the general principle from which they have arisen is uniform and consistent with itself. A prince of the house of Brunswick searches for the consolation and endearments of private sociality and friendship in the loyal hearts of jacobites, Tories, and Scotchmen: a devout prince, whose sincere unaffected piety would have done honour even to Charles the First, intrusts the public government of his affairs to Grafton, North, Halifax, and Sandwich. The first choice naturally led to the second. The private convivial hours of Jonathan Wild were happily unbent in the company of the lower adepts in pilfering and petty larceny. In public he resumed his state, and never appeared without an attendant knot of highwaymen and assassins.

I congratulate this country upon the return of the Earl of Sandwich to a station in which he has heretofore given complete satisfaction to his royal master\*. It is the more pleasing because it was unexpected. A gracious and a truly religious prince had often declared that this was the only man in his dominions whom he never would suffer to enter the cabinet. He was tender of the morals of his ministers, and the Bedfords had delicacy enough to acquiesce in the truth of the objection. I feel for his Majesty's distress. To what a melancholy condition must he be reduced, when he is forced to apply to the Earl of Sandwich as the last resource, the only prop remaining to stop the fall of government? Lord Weymouth, it seems, retires perfectly satisfied, and determined to support men and measures as vigorously as if he had continued in employment. Good-humoured creature! What a pity it is that he cannot submit to the drudgery of receiving seven thousand pounds a year! The King presses him to accept of some other post, where there is neither labour nor responsibility; anything, in short, provided he will not fling the public mortification upon his royal master of quitting his service at so critical a conjuncture. Still he resists; still he refuses; but though he quits all connection with ministers and their practices, it is impossible to interrupt his complacency and good-humour. By this nobleman's retreat the nation has made some capital acquisitions. To say nothing of my Lord Sandwich, what do you think of the amiable Mr. Bamber Gascoyne, and that well-educated, gen-

---

\* The office of Foreign Minister, vacant by the removal of the Earl of Rochford to the Home Department, and which, before its occupation by the latter, had been held for two or three years by Lord Viscount Weymouth.

teel young broker, Mr. Chamier*? The first is to thunder
in the senate; the second, in quality of secretary, is to direct
the most secret and important manœuvres of government.
Well done, my Lord Sandwich! Your company, I 'll be sworn,
will be no reproach to you. But was there no employment
to be found for Tommy Bradshaw's sister† as well as his
brother-in-law? She too understands the disposal of places;
at least his fraternal affection has given her the credit of it.

Give me leave, Mr. Woodfall, to ask you a serious question.
How long do you think it possible for this management to
last? How long is this great country to be governed by a boot
and a petticoat?—by the infamous tools of a Scotch exile, and
her Royal Highness the Princess Dowager of Wales?—by
North, Ellis, Barrington, Jenkinson, Hillsborough, Jerry Dyson, and Sandwich? I will answer you with precision. It
will last until there is a general insurrection of the English
nation, or until the house of Bourbon have collected their
strength and strike you to the heart.

DOMITIAN.

P.S. Tell the Duke of Grafton, that if he should dare to
entertain the most distant thought of the Admiralty, the
whole affair of *Hine's patent* shall be revived and published, with an accumulation of evidence. *He* at least shall
be kept under. His Ciceronian eloquence shall not save
him.

---

## LETTER LXXXIV.

*For the Public Advertiser.*

December 20, 1770.

### A CARD.

PHALARIS presents his compliments to Sir —— ——, is
preparing for the press a faithful account of Mr. Justice's
amours with the Lady Williams; and, as he wishes not to give

---

* Chamier was afterwards appointed chief secretary to Lord Barrington,
through the interest of Mr. Bradshaw and his master, the Duke of Grafton,
at that time again in administration, as Lord Privy Seal. See Private Letters, Nos. 52 and 56.

† See Miscellaneous Letters, Nos. 71, *ante*, . 299, and 74, p. 305.

a plain narrative too much the air of a romance, would be very glad to be furnished with any material facts which Mr. Justice may think proper to have inserted; but in order not to give Mr. Justice any unnecessary trouble, *Phalaris* thinks it proper to apprise him of those circumstances, in which he (*Phalaris*) is already particularly instructed, viz., how Mr. Justice was distressed for want of practice; how he was impatient at trying a long cause in a hot day at Hereford; how he made a declaration at a public dinner, confirmed by execrations, that he would marry the devil with money, rather than practise the law without it; how he was introduced to Lady Williams; how, upon sufficient deliberation, he preferred her ladyship to the devil; how he explained his tender passion; how, with a gallant impatience, he hastened the marriage ceremony before he saw the writings of her estate; how he stepped into a hackney coach, one fine morning, in a suit of white cloth lined with green velvet; how he had a levee of visitors at his gate the day after his auspicious nuptials; how Lady Williams complained next morning; how she retired to her country seat near Hereford; how Mr. Justice pursued her in company with a certain strong lady with a strait waistcoat; how both parties, with great cordiality, signed articles of separation; and how Mr. Justice retired to Ireland, without taking leave of his friends.

*Phalaris* hopes Mr. Justice will have no objection to the following motto:

> Felices ter, et amplius,
> Quos irrupta tenet copula.

---

## LETTER LXXXV.

### *For the Public Advertiser.*

#### INTELLIGENCE EXTRAORDINARY.

January 9, 1771.

Sir Edward Hawke resigned this morning. The Earl of Sandwich is to succeed to the Admiralty. His Majesty, who judges of men by their moral characters, has discovered at last that this nobleman is as well qualified for one post as another.

His religion would do honour to a mitre.   If he were Archbishop of Canterbury, the Princess Dowager of Wales could
not do better than make him her father confessor.   In the
spirit of primitive Christianity, *they might confess to one
another*.   Who is to be secretary of state is not yet known,
for we all agree that Lord Suffolk * has too much sense and
spirit to prostitute his virgin character in such a ******* as
St. James's.   When a beautiful woman yields to temptation, let
her consult her pride, though she forgets her virtue.   To be corrupted by such a maquereau as Whately would turn the appetite of Moll Flanders.   This poor man, with the talents of an
attorney, sets up for an ambassador, and with the agility of
Colonel Bodens, undertakes to be a courier.   Indeed, Tom!
you have betrayed yourself too soon.   Mr. Grenville, your
friend, your patron, your benefactor, who raised you from a
depth compared to which even Bradshaw's family stands on
an eminence, was hardly cold in his grave when you solicited
the office of go-between to Lord North.   You could not, in my
eyes, be more contemptible, though you were convicted (as I
dare say you might be) of having constantly betrayed him in
his lifetime.   Since I know your employment, be assured I
shall watch you attentively.   Every journey you undertake,
every message you carry, shall be immediately laid before the
public.   The event of your ingenious management will be
this—that Lord North, finding you cannot serve him, will give
you nothing.   From the other party, you have just as much
detestation to expect as can be united with the profoundest
contempt.   Tom Whately, take care of yourself ! †

## LETTER LXXXVI.

Sir,                                     January 11, 1771.
Your correspondent *W.* is equally unfortunate in his attack
upon Junius and his defence of Lord Mansfield.   Junius does
not enter into the particular merits of the Grosvenor cause,

* See Miscellaneous Letters, Nos. 96, *part*, p. 368, and 97, p. 379.
† Mr Whately had been private secretary to Mr. G. Grenville.

but strikes at the general doctrine delivered by the judge in his charge to the jury; viz., *that in a prosecution for criminal conversation, the jury, when they assess the damages, are not to regard the quality and fortune of the parties, but are to consider the question abstractedly as a question between A. and B.* If this doctrine be true in one instance, it will be applicable to every case of criminal conversation; and the consequences of it will be, that a nobleman with ten thousand a year shall pay no greater damages than a peasant who labours for a shilling a day; or, *vice versâ*, that the seduction of a duchess and of a milliner stand upon the same footing, in regard to the compensation due to the injured husband. In a moral view, I confess, the crime is the same. The punishment annexed to it, though not matter of positive law, cannot be regulated by the rules of morality. It must depend on custom, reputation, and the circumstances of the case. The equity of the verdict must be measured by the distinctions of rank and fortune, admitted and established in society, since it is evident that the penalty or satisfaction sufficient for one man might hardly be felt by another. It is the general doctrine of Lord Mansfield which Junius very truly calls false and absurd; and I know that it was received in Westminster Hall with universal shame and astonishment.

As to the idea of Lord Mansfield's inclining to favour Lord Grosvenor, it is so preposterously false and ridiculous that it would be entirely undeserving of notice, but for one consideration, viz., that, if it were true, it stabs the Chief Justice to the heart. Lord Mansfield is charged with gross and infamous partiality to the defendant; the defence made for him is, that he was grossly and infamously partial to the plaintiff. Let his friends take their choice. Every honest man will equally despise and detest such a judge, whichever way his bad passions incline him.

As to the merits of the Grosvenor cause, they are of no consequence in the present question. If it be necessary, however, I am ready to maintain that the verdict was supported by the evidence, and the damages very moderate. If not, why did not Mansfield order a new trial? When time, and place, and circumstance are proved, there remains but one possible plea for the Duke of Cumberland; and that, by the by, is rather a whimsical one, applied to a boy of one-and-twenty.

Yet, for aught I know, it may be very true, that, with all his attention to the *dear little hair*, he was incapable of taking the fairest opportunity by the forelock.

                                                  ANTI-W.

---

## LETTER LXXXVII.

### TO THE PRINTER OF THE PUBLIC ADVERTISER.

Sir,                                         January, 17, 1771.

If Sir Edward Hawke had followed the advice and example of his friends, he would not have been reduced to the dishonourable necessity of quitting the direction of the English navy, at the very moment it is going to be employed against the foreign enemies of England.   To be left in employment after Chatham, Granby, and Camden had retired; to continue in it in company with Grafton, North, Gower, and Hillsborough; and at last to be succeeded by Lord Sandwich, are circumstances too disgraceful to admit of aggravation.   It is natural to sympathise in the distresses of a brave man, and to lament that a noble estate of reputation should be squandered away in debts of dishonour contracted with sharpers.

His Majesty, God bless him: has now got rid of every man whose former services or present scruples could be supposed to give offence to her Royal Highness the Princess Dowager of Wales.   The security of our civil and religious liberties cannot be more happily provided for than while Lord Mansfield pronounces the law, and Lord Sandwich represents the religion of St. James's.   Such law and such religion are too closely united to suffer even a momentary intervention of common honesty between them.   Her Royal Highness's scheme of government, formed long before her husband's death, is now accomplished.   She has succeeded in disuniting every party, and dissolving every connection; and, by the mere influence of the crown, has formed an administration, such as it is, out of the refuse of them all.   There are two leading principles in the politics of St. James's, which will account for almost every measure of government since the King's accession.   The first is, that the prerogative is sufficient to make a lacquey a prime minister, and to maintain him in that post, without any regard to the welfare or to the opinion of the people. The second is, that none but persons insignificant in themselves, or of tainted reputation, should be brought into employment. Men of greater consequence and abilities will have opinions of their own, and will not submit to the meddling, unnatural ambition of a mother who grasps at unlimited power, at the hazard of her son's destruction. They will not suffer measures of public utility, which have been resolved upon in council, to be checked and controlled by a secret influence in the closet. Such men consequently will never be called upon but in cases of extreme necessity. When that ceases, they find their places no longer tenable. To answer the purposes of an ambitious woman, an administration must be formed of more pliant materials—of men, who, having no connection with each other, no personal interest, no weight or consideration with the people, may separately depend upon the smiles of the crown alone for their advancement to high offices, and for their continuance there. If such men resist the Princess Dowager's pleasure, his Majesty knows that he may dismiss them without risking anything from their resentment. His wisdom suggests to him that, if he were to choose his ministers for any of those qualities which might entitle them to public esteem, the nation might take part with them, and resent their dismission. As it is, whenever he changes his servants, he is sure to have the people, in that instance, of his side.

I love and respect our gracious Sovereign too much to suppose it possible that *he* should be anything more than passive in forming and supporting such a system of government; and even this acquiescence of the best of princes I am ready to attribute to a most amiable quality implanted in him by nature, and carefully cultivated by art—unlimited duty and obedience to his dear mother. Few nations are in the predicament that we are, to have nothing to complain of but the filial virtues of our sovereign. Charles the First had the same implicit attachment to his spouse; but his worthy parent was in her grave. It were to be wished that the parallel held good in all the circumstances.

In respect to her Royal Highness, I shall deliver my sentiments without any false tenderness or reserve. I consider her not only as the original creating cause of the shameful and deplorable condition of this country, but as a being whose operation is uniform and permanent; who watches, with a kind of providential malignity, over the work of her hands, to correct, improve, and preserve it. If the strongest appearances may be relied on, this lady has now brought her schemes to perfection. Every office in government is filled with men who are known to be her creatures, or by mere cyphers incapable of resistance. Is it conceivable that anything, less than a determined plan of drawing the whole power of the crown into her own hands, could have collected such an administration as the present? Who is Lord North? The son of a poor unknown earl, who four years ago was a needy commissioner of the treasury for the benefit of a subsistence, and who would have accepted a commission of hackney coaches upon the same terms. The politics of Carlton House, finances picked up in Mr. Grenville's anti-chamber, and the elocution of a Demosthenes, endeavouring to speak plain with pebbles in his mouth, form the stuffing of that figure that calls itself minister, that does homage to the Princess Dowager, and says, *Madam, I am your man*.

The stage was deprived of a promising actor when poor Lord Hillsborough gave his mind to politics. Yet his theatrical talents have been of use to his fortune. The Princess Dowager saw what part this man was capable of acting; and with regard to himself, it signified but little whether he represented Prince Volscius at Drury-lane, or secretary of state at St. James's.

It is not pretended that Lord Rochford's abilities are of the *explicit* kind. Yet from a *chargé d'affaires* at Turin, the all-powerful guiding hand has raised him to be secretary of state. The Princess Dowager knows, better than we do, what positive good qualities this nobleman possesses. The public only knows that he is a mute in the House of Lords, and that he is destitute of fortune, interest, and connections. To do him justice, he has all the negative qualifications that constitute merit at Carlton House.

The character of third secretary is not yet disposed of. Public suspicion gives Lord Hillsborough a formidable rival. At the opening of the theatre young Suffolk is to be produced. Prince Prettyman can cant very near as well as Prince Vol-

scius. Such a pair of actors make tragedy ridiculous. Our
enemies at least will laugh at the catastrophe. But this
young man shall be left for abler hands. It requires no
vulgar pen to do justice to such a strain of monstrous prostitution.

Why is that wretched creature Lord Townshend maintained in Ireland? Is it not universally known that the
ignorance, presumption, and incapacity of that man have
ruined the King's affairs in Ireland?—that he has, in a great
measure, destroyed the political dependance of that country
upon Great Britain? But he too is an unconnected being,
without any hope of support but in the protection of Lord
Bute and the Princess Dowager.

Why is not a commander-in-chief appointed? Because
there is an insignificant secretary at war, who has no chance
of continuing in the receipt of 2500*l.* a year, but by making
himself the instrument through which the Princess Dowager
disposes of every valuable commission in the army.

Why have we not a master-general of the ordnance?
Because the gentle Conway knows how to be as pliant as
Lord Barrington.

Why is there no chancellor? Partly because there is a
convenience in bribing four of the judges with the emoluments of that office, and partly because no man of credit in
the profession will submit to act with the present infamous
administration.

What merit has Lord Halifax?—The issue of general
warrants; the opposition of his privilege for years together
to the laws of his country; prostitution in private life, and
poverty in the extreme.

Why is the King so fond of having Lord Bristol *about his
person?* If the duties of the noble Lord's office had a closer
connection with the title of it, as usually pronounced, I should
understand his Majesty, and admire his attention in paying
so delicate a compliment to his Lordship's amours. The last
question I would ask is, by what kind of service or ability the
Earl of Sandwich is distinguished? Prostitution and poverty
may be found in other subjects, and appearances saved by a
decent formality of behaviour. The choice and preference of
the most profligate character in the kingdom may suit well
enough with the substantial purposes of Carlton House, but

how does it consist with the hypocritical decorum of Saint James's? What opinion are we to entertain of the piety, chastity, and integrity of the best of princes, when, in the face of England and of all Europe, he takes such a man as Sandwich to his bosom! Let us hear no more of the piety of Saint James's. To talk of morals or devotion in such company is a scandalous insult to common sense, and a still more scandalous mockery of religion.

The Princess Dowager having now carried her plan of administration into effect, it is not to be wondered that she should be very unwilling to expose herself and her schemes to the uncertain events of a foreign war. She knows that a disaster abroad would not only defeat the cunning plan of female avarice and ambition, but that it might reach further. The mothers of our kings have heretofore been impeached; and if the precedents are not so complete as they should be, they require and will admit of improvement.

To maintain this lady in her present state of power and security, there is no insult, no indignity, to which the King of Britain must not submit—no condition, however humiliating, which the King and the nation must not accept of without resentment. At this point, however, her cunning forsakes her. Both she and her ministers deceive themselves grossly, if they imagine that any concessions can secure peace with an enemy determined upon war. She may disgrace the English nation. She may dishonour her son, and persuade him to forfeit his right to precedence among the sovereigns of Europe. The man who receives a blow, and does not return it (whether he be a king or a private person), from that moment stands degraded from his natural rank and condition. If he be a young man, his infamy is immortal. Yet I am ready to confess that where two nations upon the whole are peaceably disposed, there is a degree of slight, and ill humour, and even of injury, which, for the sake of peace, may and ought to be dissembled; but a direct, positive, intended insult must always be resented. To flatter ourselves that the moderation of the Spaniards will be proportioned to our forbearance, or that, because we have submitted tamely to one affront, they will therefore avoid offering us a second, would be arguing in contradiction to all reason and experience. If Falkland Island had never existed, the rancour of the Spaniards would

not have failed to discover itself in some other mode of hostility.   Their whole history, since the accession of Philip the
Fifth, is a continued proof of a rooted antipathy to the name
of Englishman; and I am justified, by a series of indisputable
facts, in affirming that, from the Treaty of Utrecht to this hour,
there has never been a single instance of common justice or
decency, much less of cordiality or friendship, in the conduct
of the court of Madrid towards this country.   Lord Sandwich
declared a month ago in full parliament, that Gibraltar was a
place of no consequence, and immediately afterwards the
Princess Dowager makes him secretary of state.   Whoever
compares the sale of Dunkirk with this nobleman's character,
must be very much of a sceptic, if he entertains any doubt
about the fate of Gibraltar.   But neither this sacrifice, nor
even that of Jamaica, would be sufficient to produce a solid,
permanent union with Spain.   They may despise us more,
but they will never hate us less.

By the Princess Dowager's management, instead of avoiding a war, we make it certain.   A little spirit at first might
perhaps have intimidated the Spaniards.   Our notorious weakness and shameful submission have only served to encourage
and confirm them in their resolution.   In point of honour
we have let the proper moment of resentment pass away.
The royal and national honour is so irretrievably stained, that
it cannot now be recovered by the most vigorous measures of
revenge.   From her Royal Highness's government in time of
peace, we may well conclude in what manner she will conduct
a war.   Gifted as she is, she could hardly fail of success, if
the quarrels of nations bore any resemblance to domestic
feuds, or could be conducted upon the same principles.   The
genius of Queen Elizabeth united the nation, collected the
strength of the people, and carried it forward to resistance
and victory.   When the demon of discord sits at the helm,
what have we to expect but distraction and civil war at home,
disgrace and infamy abroad?

DOMITIAN.

## LETTER LXXXVIII.

### TO THE PRINTER OF THE PUBLIC ADVERTISER.

Sir,                                          February 13, 1771.

I READ with astonishment, and no small indignation, a letter which is at last got into your paper; I mean that from Lord Weymouth to Mr. Harris *  The copy which you have procured

* This letter refers to the much-agitated dispute concerning the Malouine, or Falkland's Islands, which, without any formal recognition, had, for many years after their first occupation by Captain Byron in 1765, been quietly suffered by Spain to remain in the hands of his Britannic Majesty, who had erected a small fort on the coast of the chief of them, named Port Egmont. In June, 1769, however, without any complaint or notice on the part of the Spanish government to the court of St. James's, a forcible debarkation was effected on the coast of Port Egmont, by a Spanish armament from Port Solidad in Buenos Ayres; the whole mass of islands was claimed by the commander of the expedition in the name of his Most Catholic Majesty, whose right was formally asserted to the whole Magellanic region; the small body of English troops stationed at Port Egmont was compelled to submit, and turned adrift from the island in two English frigates which chanced to be in the harbour, to make the best of their voyage home, and relate the history of this extraordinary adventure.

The English ministry heard the account with indignation; and the letter from Lord Weymouth to Mr. Harris, the resident minister at the court of Madrid, referred to above, was the result. The court of Madrid had offered a convention, or conditional restoration, and his Lordship's letter purports to be a reply to such offer; it was dated Oct. 17, 1770, and the following is the most important passage contained in it :—

"His Majesty cannot accept, under a convention, that satisfaction to which he has so just a title, without entering into any engagements to procure it. The idea of his Majesty's becoming a contracting party upon this occasion is entirely foreign to the case; for, having received an injury and demanded the most moderate reparation of that injury that his honour will permit him to accept, that reparation loses its value, if it is to be conditional, and to be obtained by any stipulation whatsoever on the part of his Majesty."

Yet in direct violation of this demand of an unconditional restoration and acknowledged sovereignty, the following declaration and acceptance were mutually acceded to at London, Jan. 22, 1771.

*Translation of the Declaration signed and delivered by Prince de Masserano, Ambassador Extraordinary from his Catholic Majesty, dated the 22nd day of June, 1771.*

His Britannic Majesty having complained of the violence which was committed on the 10th of June, 1770, at the island commonly called the Great Malouine, and by the English Falkland's Island, in obliging by force the commander and subjects of his Britannic Majesty to evacuate the port by

I know to be authentic, having read it amongst the papers laid
by administration before both Houses.   It is the most com-

them called Egmont, a step offensive to the honour of his crown, the
Prince de Maserano, Ambassador Extraordinary of his Catholic Majesty, has
received orders to declare, and declares, that his Catholic Majesty, considering the desire with which he is animated for peace, and for the maintenance
of good harmony with his Britannic Majesty, and reflecting that this event
might interrupt it, has seen with displeasure this expedition tending to
disturb it; and in the persuasion in which he is of the reciprocity of sentiments of his Britannic Majesty, and of its being far from his intention to
authorize anything that might disturb the good understanding between the
two courts, his Catholic Majesty does disavow the said violent enterprise;
and in consequence the Prince de Maserano declares that his Catholic
Majesty engages to give immediate orders that things shall be restored in the
Great Malouine, at the port called Egmont, precisely to the state in which
they were before the 10th of June, 1770; for which purpose his Catholic
Majesty will give orders to one of his officers to deliver up to the officer
authorized by his Britannic Majesty the port and fort called Egmont, with
all the artillery, stores, and effects of his Britannic Majesty and his subjects,
which were at that place the day above-named, agreeable to the inventory
which has been made of them.

The Prince de Maserano declares, at the same time, in the name of
the King his master, that the engagement of his said Catholic Majesty to
restore to his Britannic Majesty the possession of the fort and port called
Egmont, cannot, nor ought, any wise to affect the question of the prior right
of sovereignty of the Malouine Islands, otherwise called Falkland's Islands.
In witness whereof, I, the underwritten Ambassador Extraordinary, have
signed the present declaration with my usual signature, and caused it to be
sealed with our arms.   London, the twenty-second day of January, one
thousand seven hundred and seventy-one.

(L. S.)                   (Signed)   LE PRINCE DE MASERANO.

*Translation of the Earl of Rockford's Acceptance, dated the 22nd day of
January, 1771, of the Prince de Maserano's Declaration of the same
date.*

His Catholic Majesty having authorized the Prince of Maserano, his Ambassador Extraordinary, to offer in his Majesty's name to the King of Great
Britain a satisfaction for the injury done to his Britannic Majesty by dis-
possessing him of the port and fort of Port Egmont; and the said Ambassador having this day signed a declaration, which he has just delivered to
me, expressing therein that his Catholic Majesty, being desirous to restore
the good harmony and friendship which before subsisted between the two
crowns, does disavow the expedition against Port Egmont, in which force
has been used against his Britannic Majesty's possessions, commander, and
subjects; and does also engage that all things shall be immediately restored
to the precise situation in which they stood before the 10th of June, 1770;
and that his Catholic Majesty shall give orders, in consequence, to one of his
officers to deliver up to the officer authorized by his Britannic Majesty the
port and fort of Port Egmont, as also all his Britannic Majesty's artillery,

plete and unanswerable condemnation of the infamous convention with Spain that the mind of man can suggest.    The

stores, and effects, as well as those of his subjects, according to the inventory which has been made of them; and the said Ambassador having moreover engaged, in his Catholic Majesty's name, that what is contained in the said declaration shall be carried into effect by his said Catholic Majesty; and that duplicates of his Catholic Majesty's orders to his officers shall be delivered into the hands of one of his Britannic Majesty's principal secretaries of state within six weeks; his said Britannic Majesty, in order to show the same friendly dispositions on his part, has authorised me to declare that he will look upon the said declaration of Prince de Maserano, together with the full performance of the said engagement, on the part of his Catholic Majesty, as a satisfaction for the injury done to the crown of Great Britain.    In witness whereof, I, the underwritten, one of his Britannic Majesty's principal secretaries of state, have signed these presents with my usual signature, and caused them to be sealed with our arms.    London, the 22nd day of January, 1771.

(L. S.)                                                    (Signed)  ROCHFORD.

These papers, together with the above letter of Lord Weymouth, were laid by Lord North before the House of Commons, Jan. 25, 1771, and on Feb. 4, the two following queries were moved by Lord Chatham, in the House of Lords, for the opinion of the judges:—

1. Whether, in consideration of law, the imperial crown of this realm can hold any territories or possessions thereunto belonging, otherwise than in sovereignty.

2. Whether the declaration, or instrument for restitution of the port or fort called Egmont, to be made by the Catholic King to his Majesty, *under a reservation of a disputed right of sovereignty expressed in the very declaration or instrument stipulating such restitution,* can be accepted or carried into execution without derogating from the maxim of law before referred to, *touching the inherent and essential dignity of the crown of Great Britain.*

"The above queries were not referred to the judges, because Lord Mansfield said that the answer to them was self-evident—that they answered themselves—by which his Lordship was understood to mean that both queries clearly answered themselves in the negative."

On the 13th of February an address of thanks for the communication was voted in both Houses of parliament; that in the Commons, after a very long debate, was carried by a considerable majority, the numbers being for the address 271, against 157, who voted for the amendment.

The address of the Lords was much fuller of approbation than that of the Commons, and was, notwithstanding, carried through with a much greater proportional majority; it was, however, productive of the following nervous and argumentative protest, signed by not less than nineteen peers:—

DISSENTIENT.

1. Because it is highly unsuitable to the wisdom and gravity of this House, and to the respect which we owe to his Majesty and ourselves, to carry up

z 2

whole culprit ministry, together with the King, plead guilty
by their own unanimous voice.  No secretary of state ever

to the throne an address approving the acceptance of an imperfect instrument,
which has neither been previously authorized by any special *full powers* produced by the Spanish minister, nor been as yet ratified by the King of Spain.
If the ratification on the part of Spain should be refused, the address of this
House will appear no better than an act of precipitate adulation to ministers,
which will justly expose the peerage of the kingdom to the indignation of
their country, and to the derision of all Europe.

2.  Because it is a direct insult on the feelings and understanding of
the people of Great Britain, to approve this declaration and acceptance as a
means of securing our own and the general tranquillity, whilst the greatest
preparations for war are making both by sea and land ; and whilst the
practice of pressing is continued, as in times of the most urgent necessity, to
the extreme inconvenience of trade and commerce, and with the greatest
hardships to one of the most meritorious and useful orders of his Majesty's
subjects.

3.  Because the refusing to put the questions to the Judges upon points of
law, very essentially affecting this great question, and the refusing to address
his Majesty to give orders for laying before this House the Instructions relating to Falkland's Islands, given to the commanders of his Majesty's ships
employed there, is depriving us of such lights as seemed highly proper for us
on this occasion.

4.  Because, from the declaration and correspondence laid before us, we are
of opinion that the ministers merit the censure of this House, rather than any
degree of commendation, on account of several improper acts, and equally improper omissions, from the beginning to the close of this transaction.  For it
is asserted by the Spanish minister, and stands uncontradicted by ours, that
several discussions had passed between the ministers of the two courts upon
the subject of Falkland's Islands, which might give the British ministers
reason to foresee the attack upon that settlement that was afterwards made
by the forces of Spain.  Captain Hunt also, arriving from thence so early as
the third of June last, did advertise the ministers of repeated warnings and
menaces made by Spanish governors and commanders of ships of war ; yet so
obstinately negligent and supine were his Majesty's ministers, and so far from
the vigilance and activity required by the trust and duty of their offices, that
they did not even so much as make a single representation to the court of
Madrid ; which if they had done, the injury itself might have been prevented,
or at least so speedily repaired as to render unnecessary the enormous expenses to which this nation has been compelled, by waiting until the blow had
been actually struck, and the news of so signal an insult to the crown of
Great Britain had arrived in Europe.  To this wilful, and therefore culpable,
neglect of representation to the court of Spain, was added another neglect, a
neglect of such timely preparation for putting this nation into such a state of
defence as the menacing appearances on the part of Spain and the critical
condition of Europe required.  These preparations, had they been undertaken
early, would have been executed with more effect and less expense ; would have
been far less distressing to our trade, and to our seamen ; would have author-

did or would write a letter of this sort upon so delicate a matter, without first laying it before his Majesty's most confiden-

ised us in the beginning to have demanded, and would, in all probability, have induced Spain to consent to, an immediate, perfect, and equitable settlement of all the points in discussion between the two crowns; but all preparation having been neglected, the national safety was left depending rather upon accidental alterations in the internal circumstances of our neighbours than in the proper and natural strength of the kingdom; and this negligence was highly aggravated by the refusal of administration to consent to an address, proposed by a noble Lord in this House last session, for a moderate and gradual augmentation of our naval forces.

5. Because the negotiation, entered into much too late, was, from the commencement, conducted upon principles as disadvantageous to the wisdom of our public conncils as it was finally concluded in a manner disgraceful to the honour of the crown of Great Britain; for it appears that the court of Madrid did disavow the act of hostility as proceeding from particular instructions, but justified it under her general instructions to her governors, under the oath by them taken, and under the established laws of America. This general order was never disavowed nor explained; nor was any disavowal or explanation thereof ever demanded by our ministers: and we apprehend that this justification of an act of violence under general orders, established laws, and oaths of office, to be far more dangerous and injurious to this kingdom than the particular enterprise which has been disavowed, as it evidently supposes that the governors of the Spanish American provinces are not only authorised, but required, without any particular instructions, to raise great forces by sea and land, and to invade his Majesty's possessions in that part of the world, in the midst of profound peace.

6. Because this power, so unprecedented and alarming, under which the Spanish governor was justified by his court, rendered it the duty of our ministers to insist upon some censure or punishment upon that governor, in order to demonstrate the sincerity of the court of Madrid, and of her desire to preserve peace, by putting at least some check upon those exorbitant powers asserted by the court of Spain to be given to her governors. But although our ministers were authorized, not only by the acknowledged principles of the law of nations, to call for such censure or punishment, but also by the express provision of the seventeenth article of the treaty of Utrecht, yet they have thought fit to observe a profound silence on this necessary article of public reparation. If it were thought that any circumstances appeared in the particular case of the governor, to make an abatement or pardon of the punishment advisable, that abatement or pardon ought to have been the effect of his Majesty's clemency, and not an impunity to him, arising from the ignorance of our ministers in the first principles of public law, or their negligence or pusillanimity in asserting them.

7. Because nothing has been had or demanded as a reparation in damage for the enormous expense and other inconveniences arising from the confessed and unprovoked violence of the Spanish forces in the enterprise against Falkland's Islands, and the long subsequent delay of justice. It was not necessary to this demand that it should be made in any improper or offensive

tial servants, and taking the King's express orders upon it. It speaks, then, the unanimous sentiments of them all.   His

language, but in that style of accommodation which has ever been used by able negotiators.

8. Because an unparalleled and most audacious insult has been offered to the honour of the British flag, by the detention of a ship of war of his Majesty's, for twenty days after the surrender of Port Egmont, and by the indignity of forcibly taking away her rudder: this act could not be supported upon any idea of being necessary to the reduction of the fort, nor was any such necessity pretended.  No reparation in honour has been demanded for this wanton insult, by which his Majesty's reign is rendered the unhappy æra in which the honour of the British flag has suffered the first stain with entire impunity.

9. Because the Spanish declaration, which our ministers have advised his Majesty to accept, does in general words imply his Majesty's disavowal of some acts on his part tending to disturb the good correspondence of the two courts, when it is notorious that no act of violence whatsoever had been committed on the part of Great Britain.  By this disavowal of some implied aggression in this very declaration, pretended to be made for reparation of the injured dignity of Great Britain, his Majesty is made to admit a supposition contrary to truth, and injurious to the justice and honour of his crown.

10. Because in the said declaration the restitution is confined to Port Egmont, when Spain herself originally offered to cede Falkland's Islands.  It is known that she made her forcible attack on pretence of title to the whole, and the restitution ought, therefore, not to have been confined to a part only; nor can any reason be assigned why the restitution ought to have been made in narrower or more ambiguous words than the claims of Spain, on which her act of violence was grounded, and her offers of restitution originally made.

11. Because the declaration, by which his Majesty is to obtain possession of Port Egmont, contains a reservation or condition of the question of a claim of prior right of sovereignty in the Catholic King to the whole of Falkland's Islands, being the first time such a claim has ever authentically appeared in any public instrument jointly concluded on by the two courts.  No explanation of the principles of this claim has been required, although there is just reason to believe that these principles will equally extend to restrain the liberty and confine the extent of British navigation.  No counter claim has been made on the part of his Majesty to the right of sovereignty in any part of the said island ceded to him; any assertion whatsoever of his Majesty's right of sovereignty has been studiously avoided from the beginning to the accomplishment of this unhappy transaction, which, after the expense of millions, settles no contest, asserts no right, exacts no reparation, affords no security, but stands as a monument of reproach to the wisdom of the national councils, of dishonour to the essential dignity of his Majesty's crown, and of disgrace to the hitherto untainted honour of the British flag.

After having given these reasons, founded on the facts which appeared from the papers, we think it necessary here to disclaim an invidious and injurious imputation, substituted in the place of fair argument, that they who will not approve of this convention are for precipitating their country into the

Majesty pronounces, in common with the rest, his own condemnation in that of this unworthy transaction. The moderate reparation to his Majesty's honour for the injury is not
obtained unconditionally; that is, in the only way which he
himself and his servants thought indispensable. A humiliating stipulation for referring the discussion of the prior
right is a defeasance of the reparation. It wounds irrepar-
ably the honour of the King as a private man, and the glory
of the kingdom; but when that stipulation carries along with
it also a private insinuation or encouragement to the Catholic
King to hope, and most probably, not to say certainly, an

calamities of war. We are as far from the design, and we trust much further
from the act, of kindling the flame of war, than those who have advised his
Majesty to accept of the declaration of the Spanish ambassador. We have
never entertained the least thought of invalidating this public act; but if
ministers may not be censured, or even punished for treaties, which, though
valid, are injurious to the national interest and honour, without a supposition
of the breach of public faith in this House, that should censure or punish, or
of a breach of the laws of humanity in those who propose such censure or
punishment, the use of the peers, as a controul on ministers, and as the best
as well as highest council of the crown, will be rendered of no avail. We
have no doubt but a declaration more adequate to our just pretensions, and
to the dignity of the crown, might have been obtained without the effusion
of blood, not only from the favourable circumstance of the conjuncture, but
because our just demands were no more than any sovereign power who had
injured another through inadvertence or mistake ought, even from regard to
its own honour, to have granted; and we are satisfied that the obtaining such
terms would have been the only secure means of establishing a lasting and
honourable peace.

| | |
|---|---|
| RICHMOND, | AUDLEY, |
| BOLTON, | KING, |
| MANCHESTER, | TORRINGTON, |
| TANKERVILLE, | MILTON, |
| CHATHAM, | ABERGAVENNY, |
| WYCOMBE, | FITZWILLIAM, |
| CRAVEN, | PONSONBY, |
| BOYLE, | SCARBOROUGH, |
| DEVONSHIRE, | ARCHER. |

DISSENTIENT.

Because, though the disavowal may be considered as humiliating to the
court of Spain, the declaration and acceptance, under the reservation of the
question of prior right, do not, in my opinion, after the heavy expenses
incurred, either convey a satisfaction adequate to the insult on the honour of
Great Britain, or afford any reasonable grounds to believe that peace, on the
terms of honour, can be lasting.

RADNOR.

express assurance, that not only Port Egmont now restored
to us, but the whole island, shall in due time, as soon as they
dare, be surrendered to the crown of Spain.  No words can
express the meanness or folly of such a proceeding.  Our
tame submission to France in the Corsican business has
drawn this atrocious insult upon us.  This insult, accompanied with the indignities contained by the minister's own confession in the convention, will renew to us, in the mouths of
the proud and triumphant Spaniards, the ignominious title of
*Gallinas del mar*, and we shall deservedly become a bye-
word of contempt amongst the nations.  The only reparation
which it can be pretended that Spain makes, is the temporary
restitution of Port Egmont.  Restoring to me my possessions
violently seized is an act of justice, not of reparation : but
with what indelible shame shall we be covered, when it is
seen that we pitifully traffic away what was insultingly
wrested from us, and yield the whole to the aggressor under
any pretence or colour whatever?  The insult was committed after repeated notices of our right, in full peace : it
was an insult, not only to the flag of England hitherto spotless, but to the whole majesty of the kingdom, by direct
hostilities committed as in time of actual war, so as to enforce a formal capitulation ; a proceeding till now unheard of,
submitted to with a meanness and treachery on the part of
our rulers, which nothing can now palliate.  We deceive ourselves if we think the peace can be maintained by pusillanimity
and baseness.  Remember "His Majesty cannot accept
under a convention that satisfaction to which he has so just
a title, without entering into any engagements to procure
it."*

> *A Member of one House of Parliament in mourning
> for the honour of his king and country.*

* See this subject further discussed in Junius, Letter 42, vol. i. p. 316,
and notes appended to it.

## LETTER LXXXIX.

### TO THE PRINTER OF THE PUBLIC ADVERTISER.

SIR,                                February 16, 1771.

IT is proper the public should be informed that, upon Lord Gower's election to be a knight of the garter, there were but four knights present, besides the Sovereign, and the Duke of Gloucester was lugged in to be one of them. He intreated, he begged, he implored, but all to no purpose. Poor Peg Trentham was forced to submit to an election, which, by the statutes of the order, is void. Ashmole informs us, that " tc make up a complete chapter of election, there should be assembled six knights companions at the least, besides the Sovereign ; the due observance of which hath been so strict formerly, that elections have been deferred, where chapters have been deficient in that number." *

* The same fact is related, and probably by the same correspondent, in the following article of the *Public Advertiser*, February 15, 1771: —

A correspondent has sent us the following remarks on the *London Gazette*, published by authority.

"This lying paper contains the following unprecedented article:—'St. James's, Feb. 11. This day a chapter of the most noble order of the garter was held in the great council chamber, when Granville Levison Gower, Earl Gower, being first knighted, was afterwards elected and invested with the garter, ribbon, and George, with the usual solemnity.' It is most notorious to a great concourse of nobility and gentry then present, that there were only assisting the best of Kings, the Dukes of Gloucester, Newcastle, and Northumberland ; consequently it is impossible that any election can have been made, the statutes of the order requiring the presence of the Sovereign with six knights. The best of Kings, whose duty it is to preserve the laws inviolable, could, to be sure, on no consideration, not even the election of that most worthy peer the Earl Gower into this noble order, be prevailed upon in the face of all England to set the example of openly violating the statutes which have hitherto been so religiously respected and observed through so many ages. Had there been an election, the *Gazette* would have proclaimed it in the usual form—the knights present would have been enumerated and named. It is impossible that the best of Kings can be a party to the illegally smuggling in a knight upon that most noble order, in the same manner as a knight for the county of Middlesex has been smuggled into the House of Commons. If this article of news could be true, would not the kingdom have reason to lament that all order, decency, and respect for ancient rules and establishment is now broken through by the person whose peculiar duty and interest it is to preserve them? Is the Court itself so unpopular, or is the subject of his Majesty's favour so unworthy, that it was, after ten days waiting, impossible to procure the attendance of more than the King's own

The present way of electing Peg Trentham is, for two reasons, remarkable.  It shows first, in what profound comtempt poor Peggy is universally held.  And secondly, the pious resolution of our gracious Sovereign to introduce a new system of arithmetic.  In the decision of the Middlesex election, it was resolved that 296 were more than 1143, and now we are told that four are equal to six.  This puts me in mind of Lord March's election to the coterie.  All the balls were black; but the returning officer, George Selwyn. thought proper to swear he was duly elected, and he took his seat accordingly.

A. B.

---

## LETTER XC.

### TO THE PRINTER OF THE PUBLIC ADVERTISER.

Sir,                                    February 22, 1771.

THE advocates of the ministry are, in point of ignorance, upon a level with the people whose conduct they defend*.  The questions they ask are suicide to their own cause.  Gibraltar and Minorca were yielded to England by the treaty of Utrecht, to which treaty Spain acceded; and, admitting that they have never given up in form their claim to Jamaica, it is also true, that, since the treaty of Utrecht, they have never asserted such a claim, much less have we allowed it to be inserted in any treaty between the two crowns.  But, Sir, the real question is, not what declarations or pretensions Spain may have thought proper to advance, but, what declarations or preten sions on their part *have we admitted and accepted!*  To sup

brother, the Lord Chamberlain, the Auditor of the Exchequer, and the Duke of Northumberland in flannels 1

"*Rixum tenentis amici !*"

* The following is a copy of the paragraph which occasioned the foregoing essay :—

"People who would cavil, and are clamorous about that part of the Spanish declaration where the King of Spain makes a reservation of a prior claim of right to Falkland Island, would do well to consider that such reservation is only mere matter of form, and is never likely to produce the smallest misunderstanding between the two crowns, especially when they recollect, or may inform themselves, that Spain never to this hour has renounced her formal claim of right either to Minorca or Gibraltar, in the treaties subsequent to our possession of those places."

port a fair comparison between the terms on which we hold
the above places, and those on which Port Egmont is restored,
it should be proved that Spain, in some treaty between us and
it, has asserted its claim of prior right to Jamaica, Gibraltar,
and Minorca, and that we have, with equal formality, accepted
a treaty containing such an express reservation, and declared
ourselves *satisfied with it*. The ministry would then have an
example in point*.

VINDEX.

## LETTER XCI.

### TO THE PRINTER OF THE PUBLIC ADVERTISER.

Sir,                                    March 6, 1771.

PRAY tell that ingenious gentleman, Mr. Laughlin Macleane†,
that when the King of Spain writes to the King of Great Britain, he omits four-fifths of his titles, and when our King
writes to him, his address is always *Carolo, Dei gratia, His-
paniarum, utriusque Siciliæ, et Indiarum Regi Catholico*. It
was reserved for his present Majesty to say, in a public instrument, " Falkland Island is one of my possessions, and yet
I allow the King of Spain to reserve a claim of prior right,
and I declare myself *satisfied* with that reservation." In spite
of Mr. Laughlin's disinterested, unbroken, melodious eloquence, it is a melancholy truth that the crown of England

---

* The printer thought proper at the time, with the consent of the author
(see Private Letter, No. 33), to break off at this point, and to suppress the
remainder of the essay. The autograph of the entire letter is still in the
hands of the proprietor of this edition ; but it would be a breach of confidence
to continue it further. Independently of which, he altogether approves of the
suppression.

† Laughlin Macleane had been under secretary of state during Lord
Shelburne's possession of the office for the southern department. In his defence of the ministry here referred to, he still discovers a hankering after
office, and at least a disposition to forgive them for his dismission. Mr.
Campbell, however, in his life of Hugh Boyd, p. 125, tells us that at this
very period he possessed "a mortal hatred for his Grace (of Grafton), and
indulged his resentment by painting him in the blackest colours ! ! !" See
observations on this subject in the Preliminary Essay, vol. i. p. 78. In
January, in the following year, he received from Lord North the collectorship of Philadelphia, and subsequently an appointment to India, in his
voyage to which he was lost.

was never so insulted, never so shamefully degraded, as by
this declaration, with which the best of sovereigns assures
his people he is perfectly, entirely, completely satisfied.

VINDEX.

## LETTER XCII.

### TO THE PRINTER OF THE PUBLIC ADVERTISER.

Sir,                                                    March 25, 1771

However the Court might have concealed its designs, however it might have deluded those who were disposed to be
deceived, the imposition can exist no longer.    The triplet
union of Crown, Lords, and Commons against England displays
itself with a violence and a candour which statesmen in other
conspiracies seldom have adopted.    It is no more a question
of royal antipathy or feminine unrelenting resentment; it is
not a single inconsequent act of arbitrary power; it is not the
offensive individual, but the free constitution of this country,
whose destruction engages the influence of the crown and the
authority of parliament.

The House of Commons assume a power of imprisonment
during pleasure for actions which the laws have not made
criminal.    They create a crime as well as a punishment.
They call upon the King to support their illegality by a proclamation still more illegal; and the liberty of the press is
the object of this criminal alliance.    They expunge a recognizance; they stagnate the course of justice, and thereby
assume an absolute power over the law and property of Great
Britain *.

* The whole of this requires explanation. The printers of newspapers,
having long intended it, now resolutely determined to report the debates of
both Houses.   Col. Onslow made a motion against them as guilty of a violation of the privileges of parliament, and the printers were summoned to attend.   Wheble and Miller, however, refused to obey the order; and the
minister thought proper to issue a proclamation in his Majesty's name, and
insert it in the *Gazette*, offering a reward of fifty pounds for apprehending
John Wheble, printer of the *Middlesex Journal*, and John Miller, printer of
the *London Evening Post*, for daring to publish certain speeches delivered in
parliament.   In consequence of this proclamation, they were both apprehended—Wheble by a brother printer of the name of Carpenter, who owed
him a grudge; and Miller by William Whittam, a messenger of the House of
Commons. The former was carried before Mr. Wilkes, at that time just

The House of Lords have not been backward in *their* contribution to the scheme of slavery; for they have imprisoned,

liberated from the King's Bench, and, as alderman for Farringdon Without, sitting magistrate at Guildhall; who, denying the legal authority of a mere proclamation, discharged Wheble, and took a recognizance of him to prosecute Carpenter for an assault and unlawful imprisonment. Miller, upon his arrest, sent for a constable, to whom he gave charge of the messenger who arrested him, and immediately carried him to the Mansion House, where the Lord Mayor, Mr. Alderman Wilkes, and Mr. Alderman Oliver jointly heard the cause, discharged Miller, and signed a warrant of commitment of the messenger to the Compter for the assault and false imprisonment; from which, however, he was released upon finding bail. Wilkes, at the same time that these transactions were officially entered by the Lord Mayor's clerk into the Mansion House rota book, addressed a letter to Lord Halifax, one of the Secretaries of State, informing him of the steps he had taken.

All was confusion and uproar. The House of Commons supported the legality of the *proclamation*, issued an *order* to prohibit every kind of prosecution or suit from being commenced or carried on for or on account of the assault and imprisonment of the printers, ordered the clerk to attend who had entered the proceedings in the Mansion House minute book, erased the entire record, and summoned the different aldermen who had officiated to appear at the bar of the House to answer for their conduct.

The City first of all, and afterwards the nation at large, was extremely indignant at such illegal violence. The Lord Mayor's clerk was severely reprimanded, at a general court of aldermen, for suffering the City minute book to be mutilated; the Bill of Rights Society complained vehemently against the outrages committed; Wilkes refused to obey the summons for his attendance; and the Lord Mayor and his other colleagues, upon attending and justifying their conduct, were committed to the Tower for pretended contumacy. It was on this occasion that the Lord Mayor (Crosby) made the following spirited reply:—

"Mr. Speaker,—An honourable gentleman has talked of the lenity to be shown me on account of my health, and my being only committed to the custody of the serjeant-at-arms. I thank God that my health is better than it has been for some time past. I know that I was prejudged on Monday, and that the string of resolutions and warrants is now in the gentleman's pocket. I ask no favour of this House. I crave no mercy from the Treasury-bench. I am ready to go to my noble friend at the Tower, if the House shall order me. My conscience is clear, and tells me that I have kept my oath and done my duty to the city of which I have the honour to be chief magistrate, and to my country. I will never betray the privileges of the citizens nor the rights of the people. I have no apology to make for having acted uprightly, and I fear not any resentment in consequence of such conduct. I will through life continue to obey the dictates of honour and conscience, to give my utmost support to every part of the constitution of this kingdom, and the event I shall always leave to Heaven, at all times ready to meet my fate."

The Lord Mayor was accompanied to the Tower by an immense concourse

and they have fined.   The crime, like the punishment, was in
their own bosom.   They were *ex post facto* legislators.   They
were parties; they were judges; and, instead of a court of final
judicature, acted as a court of criminal jurisdiction in the first
instance.   The three estates, instead of being a control upon
each other, are let loose upon the constitution.   The absolute
power of the crown, by the assistance of the handmaid corruption, puts on the disguise of privilege.   In the arrangement of hostility, the associated senate takes the lead, and
illegal proclamation brings up the rear of oppression.   The
cabal advances upon us as an army once did upon a town—it
displayed before it a multitude of nuns, and overawed the
resistance of the besieged by the venerable appearance.   So

of the livery, as well as of persons not connected with the police of the City,
many of them of the utmost respectability.   He was visited by the Dukes of
Manchester and Portland, Earls Fitzwilliam and Tankerville, Lord King,
Admiral Keppel, Sir Charles Saunders, Mr. Dowdeswell, Mr. Burke, and
many other commoners; as also by the two sheriffs, in order to express their
entire disapprobation of the proceedings that had taken place against them.
And the thanks of the City were voted unanimously, at a meeting of Common Council, holden March 28, to such members of the House of Commons
as had supported the conduct of the Lord Mayor and his colleagues, and
maintained the rights and privileges of the City.   The Common Council
voted that all the expenses of the Lord Mayor's and Mr. Oliver's table, &c.,
&c., should be defrayed by the City.

The magistrates, in order to obtain their discharge, were carried by *habeas
corpus* first before Lord Chief Justice De Grey, and afterwards before Lord
Mansfield; but both judges refusing to discharge them, they were remanded
to the Tower.   In the mean time, in direct opposition to the order of the
House of Commons, the grand jury, at the ensuing quarter-sessions at Guildhall, found bills of indictment against Carpenter, and Whittam the messenger
of the House, for the assault and imprisonment of Miller and Wheble.   The
Lord Mayor and his colleagues remained in the Tower till the 8th of May,
on which day his Majesty, by proroguing the parliament, terminated its power
of confining them any longer.

It is not necessary at this time to enter into the question of the legality or
illegality of the power claimed in this instance by the House of Commons,
under the specious name of parliamentary privilege.   They virtually admitted
themselves to have erred, by their subsequent conduct towards Mr. Wilkes, who,
though by far the most culpable of the whole (admitting culpability of any kind),
was suffered to remain unmolested, except by serving him with three successive summonses to appear at the bar of the House, every one of which he con-
temptuously refused to obey, unless the House would suffer him to take his
place as member for Middlesex.   The result of the contest has terminated
favourably for the public, who have ever since been put into possession of the
debates of both Houses, through the medium of newspaper reporters.

the cabinet puts forth the countenance of parliament, and
marches against the constitution under the shelter of the
hallowed frailty.

What has an Englishman now to hope for? He must turn
from King. Lords, and Commons, and look up to God and himself if he means to be free. He sees the representation of
the kingdom taken from the people, the law dispensed with,
the obligation of a contract erased, the liberty of the subject
invaded, the freedom of the press violated, by the House of
Commons. By the House of Lords he sees liberty, property,
and the freedom of the press assaulted likewise, and the decision * of justice in its last resort a question of influence, not
of law. He beholds three supreme powers instead of one,
and the constitution a separate plunder to each; or rather he
beholds one estate possessed of the power by the profligacy of
the rest. If the cabinet should prevail, we shall not only be
enslaved, but disgraced. The man and means that enslave
us would be an additional dishonour.

*An Englishman, and Enemy to the Cabinet therefore.*

---

## LETTER XCIII†.

### *For the Public Advertiser.*

March 29, 1771.

TO THE LORD MAYOR, MR. ALDERMAN OLIVER, AND MR.
ALDERMAN WILKES.

MY LORD AND GENTLEMEN,
As your conduct in regard to the business of the printers is
become the universal subject of conversation, I will take the
liberty of communicating my sentiments to you in this public

* In the case of Lord Pomfret and Smith.

† There is some doubt as to the genuineness of this as well as of the ensuing letter; but as they are illustrative of one of Junius's most important
letters, No. 44, vol. i. p. 328, as they are excellently composed, and the
subject has been in some measure recently agitated, the editor could not consent to suppress them. The quotation from Hawkins, inserted in the second
letter, will be found adopted by Junius as one of his notes to the letter just
referred to.

manner. The business first opened with a printer's being taken up by virtue of the King's proclamation, and carried before Mr. Alderman Wilkes (who was sitting as a justice of the peace for the city of London) in order to his being committed by virtue of that proclamation *only*. Mr. Wilkes discharged the printer, and upon his complaint, verified upon oath, bound over the apprehender to appear at the quarter-sessions, and the printer to prosecute for an assault. In considering the legality of this proceeding I will totally lay out of the question the privileges and franchises of the city of London, as I think this part of the case does not require any assistance from them, though they may be very material in the subsequent proceedings as to the messenger of the House of Commons. The first consideration then will be, what was the force and effect of the proclamation? In Judge Dalison's Reports, which is a book of authority, p. 20, 2 and 3 Phil. and Mary, it is said, " Note, It was agreed for law, that the king may make a proclamation to his subjects *quo ad terrorem populi*, to put them in fear of his displeasure, but not upon other pain certain, as to forfeit their lands or goods, or to make fine, or to suffer imprisonment or other pain: for no proclamation shall make a law which was not before, but may confirm and ratify an ancient law, but not change it, or make a new one; yet diverse precedents were shewn out of the exchequer to the contrary, but the justices would not have any regard to them, *quod nota*." And in the 12th part of Sir Edward Coke's Report, which is a book of the highest authority, p. 74, in the 8 Ja. 1st (when prerogative ran high), you will find a case, called the case of proclamations, which, amongst other things, contains these resolutions : " That the King by his proclamation or otherways cannot change any part of the common law, or statute law, or the customs of the realm." " That the King cannot create any offence by his prohibition or proclamation which was not an offence before;" and that "that which cannot be punished without proclamation cannot be punished with it." That the King may by his proclamation admonish his subjects to keep the laws, but cannot make a thing unlawful which the law permits. And this, as the learned reporter observes, was well proved by the antient and continual forms of indictments, for all indictments conclude *contra legem et consuetudinem Angliæ*, or *contra leges et statuta, &c.*—" but never was seen an indictment to conclude *contra regiam proclamationem.*"

The learned reporter puts several instances of illegal proclamations, and amongst the rest this: An act was made by which foreigners were licensed to merchandise within London. Hen. IV. by proclamation prohibited the execution of it, and that it should be in suspense *usque ad proximum parliamentum,* which, says the learned reporter, was against law. *Vide* Dors. Claus. 8 Hen. IV.—Proclamation in London. Here give me leave to make one observation, that any proclamation which infringes the ancient customs, privileges, and franchises of the city of London, infringes the statute laws of this land; for the customs, privileges, and franchises of the city of London are confirmed and established by various acts of parliament. The case still goes on, and says that the law of England is divided into three parts, common law, statute law, and custom; "but the King's proclamation is none of them." And the learned reporter concludes in saying: "after this resolution no proclamation imposing fine and imprisonment was made;" and I have no doubt but the learned reporter thought that after this solemn decision no such proclamations would ever be issued in any future times; but alas! he did not see the jurisprudence of the reign of George the Third.

I think I may call this case a solemn determination, because it was settled upon great deliberation by the two Chief Justices, the Chief Baron, and Baron Altham, upon conference betwixt the Lords of the Privy Council and them. When the printer was brought before Mr. Wilkes, Mr. Wilkes acted as a magistrate, and in a judicial capacity; and had he imprisoned the printer, or any other subject of this kingdom upon less evidence than the law required, he would have been highly criminal. And in a case where the liberty of the subject was concerned, it required the best and the highest evidence to justify the deprivation of that liberty. The law and rules of evidence "are part of the common law of the land," and the King cannot "by his proclamation alter or suspend any of those laws or rules;" for that would be to alter the law of the land, and be in direct opposition to those respectable authorities I have cited. It is a law and a rule of evidence, that no judge or justice can judicially take notice

of a private act of parliament, much less can they judicially
take notice of a private order of the House of Commons
relative to two individuals only. Nay, if you add to it the
sanction of the royal proclamation, and consider it as the act
of the King and Commons, does it mend the matter? Does
it give it greater authority in point of legal evidence than an
act of parliament? I should be glad to be informed if the
constitution has given such an arbitrary power of imprisonment to the House of Commons as they claim, why it has
not given them proper officers to enforce it without resorting
to the King? Why has not the serjeant-at-arms a power to
raise the *posse comitatus*? Why are not people punishable
for not giving him assistance? And yet I dare say there is
not a law book that has attributed this power to him, nor did
we ever hear of a person punished for refusing him assistance,
which in my apprehension is a strong argument against the
power claimed by the House of Commons against the printers. I should be glad, too, to be informed what law, usage,
or custom, has made the King the minister to authenticate
the orders of the House of Commons; when it first began, and
where it is to be found. By what writ or authority does the
order come before the King to be authenticated, and where is
it to be found? I never yet saw any statute, case, or even
dictum to authorise this. And if the law has not intrusted
the King with the power of authenticating the orders of the
House of Commons by his royal proclamation, every judge
and justice in this kingdom will do right in paying no regard
to them under such a sanction. I have known trials where
it has been necessary to give in evidence the proceedings and
determinations of the House of Commons, which have always
been done by proving them upon oath to be true copies of the
journals by the witness who examined them. And though
Mr. Wilkes might be convinced in his mind that there was
such an order as stated in the proclamation, he could not in
his judicial capacity take notice of it, as it was not authenticated according to law. This doctrine has been illustrated in
a modern instance. Did not the present Chief Justice of the
King's Bench and his brethren refuse to take judicial notice
of Mr. Wilkes when he surrendered himself in order to the
reversal of his outlawry, because he did not come properly
authenticated before them, although I fancy they had very

little doubt in their minds as to the identity of his person? So upon the same principles Mr. Wilkes was well warranted in rejecting the proclamation; and that being out of the way, I think it will then be so clear that Mr. Wilkes would have done right in committing the assailant upon the printer, if he had not given bail, as not to admit of an argument.

I have two observations to make upon the late attempt of enforcing the order of the House of Commons by the royal proclamation. First, that the calling in the aid of the King upon that occasion was weakening the authority and dignity of the House, and tends to make the execution of the orders of that House dependent upon the pleasure of the King; and in the next place such an interposition on the part of the King carries this appearance with it to the public, that it is not the independence or the just liberties and privileges of the Commons of England that are thus anxiously sought to be preserved, but the gratification of the spleen and resentment (to say no worse of it) of the administration. I shall conclude this letter by saying, and thinking till I am better informed, that the late proclamation was an unwarrantable exertion of power, tending to mislead all judges and justices throughout England, and to put them upon imprisoning an English subject contrary to law, and the rules of evidence, which make part of the law of this kingdom; and therefore I, for one, applaud the conduct of Mr. Wilkes in this instance. In another letter I shall deliver my sentiments as to the proceedings of your Lordship, Mr. Alderman Oliver, and Mr. Alderman Wilkes, when the messenger of the House of Commons was brought before you. I have forborne to take this business up on the same grounds that Mr. Morris has done, as it would only be a repetition of what he has very judiciously before transmitted to the public*. It is sufficient

---

* Robert Morris, Esq., was a member of, and secretary to, the Bill of Rights Society. At their meeting in order to discuss the question of the arrest of the printers, he thus addressed the chairman; and it is to this speech the writer of the above letter refers :—

"Mr. Chairman,—The proclamation issued for apprehending the printers is, on all hands, I think, allowed to be illegal. I do not believe that there is in the whole kingdom a lawyer's clerk who does not know it to be equally repugnant to the spirit and letter of the law and the constitution. The law, though not so well known, is as clear against commitments by the House of Commons. They have nothing to support their pretensions but their own

A A 2

for me to say that I think he has sufficiently demonstrated the illegality of the order of the House of Commons; I only meant to give additional strength to his observations; and if any man will coolly consider the whole case, argument will continually crowd upon his mind to evince the illegality and injustice of the order and royal proclamation.

> I am,
> My Lord and Gentlemen,
> Your most humble Servant,
> G. W.

---

## LETTER XCIV.

### For the Public Advertiser.

April 8, 1771.

TO THE LORD MAYOR, MR. ALDERMAN OLIVER, AND MR. ALDERMAN WILKES.

My Lord and Gentlemen,

IN my first letter I submitted my reasons why Mr. Wilkes could not, in his judicial capacity, take notice of the order of the House of Commons, merely under the sanction of the royal proclamation. If I was right in that, it was totally immaterial whether the order of the House of Commons as to the printers was legal or illegal, for in either case Mr. Wilkes's conduct was agreeable to law. And in either case, the ex-

vote, which certainly is not binding on any but themselves; an act of three branches of the legislature being the only authority that is, besides the common law, acknowledged by England as valid. Matters being thus circumstanced, I am sorry to find that such magistrates of London as belong to this Society do not afford protection to the printers, and rescue them from lawless violence. My concern for this neglect, this fear, or this tergiversation, is the greater, that if the officers of the House of Commons, or any other person but a minister of this city properly authorized, takes these obnoxious men into custody, the rights of the city are violated; it being legally impossible for King, Lords, and Commons, to seize any citizen of London without the consent of its own magistrates. Were they even to make an act for that purpose it could not have any force, because the act made in favour of the city in the reign of William and Mary ought to be considered as a constitution, and as irreversible as Magna Charta—for indeed it is the Magna Charta of the city."

punging of the proceedings taken before him, be it by what
order it may, was a flagrant violation of the law, and a very
dangerous obstruction to the execution of criminal justice.    I
will next consider the subsequent proceedings as to the
messenger of the House of Commons, who was brought before
you, as magistrates of the City of London, and charged upon
oath with having committed a breach of the peace, in assaulting and imprisoning one of your citizens.    The messenger
justified the fact under a warrant signed by the Speaker of
the House of Commons, which I shall state more particularly
hereafter, but at present it is not necessary.

This justification necessarily brought the validity of the
Speaker's warrant *collaterally* in question before you.    Some
people, who have in general applauded your conduct in this
business, have said that you went too far in signing a warrant
of commitment of the messenger, and in obliging him to give
bail.    As you deemed the Speaker's warrant illegal, you could
not do otherwise; it was the necessary consequence and judgment upon the complaint before you.    You would have been
guilty of a breach of duty, as magistrates, if you had adjudged
the messenger guilty of a breach of peace, and not have committed him, or bound him over to answer the offence in a due
course of law.    One of the greatest privileges assumed by
either House of Parliament is that of having their privileges
(as they call them) examined and inquired into in their own
Houses only.    And if this can be established as the law of
England, any subject may be deprived of his life, liberty, and
property, by an arbitrary vote of either House, under the name
of privilege of parliament.    It will be said that this is a foreign
presumption, and that we cannot suppose that those respectable characters in the Houses of Parliament would invade the
liberties of the people.    I must own I think, from some late
exertions, there is no room left for presumptions; but be that
as it may, I think the liberties of England ought to stand
upon a more solid basis than presumptions, or the arbitrary
voice of one branch of the legislature only.

The cases to prove that the assumed privileges of either
House of Parliament are not examinable elsewhere than in
their own Houses, are Lord Shaftsbury's case, 29 Car. 2. in
B. R.; the Queen v. Paty & alias, 3 Ann. in B. R.; and the

Hon. Alexander Murray's case, 24 Geo. 2. in D. R. In all cases adjudged upon constitutional points, regard should be had to the temper of the times when they happened, and the characters, connections, and dependencies of the judges. If these circumstances be attended to in Lord Shaftsbury's case, I am very sure it will be found to be a precedent of no weight or authority. Lord Shaftsbury was a man exceedingly obnoxious to King Charles the Second, having in the House of Lords violently opposed that arbitrary prince, and his attempts to introduce popery into this kingdom. The King's designs were no secret; and the independent members in the House of Commons had meditated means to prevent the execution of them. The King, to frustrate this, prorogued the parliament for fifteen months, within a few days, being the longest prorogation which had been then known. The King had also found means, by pensioning many of the members of the Lower House, to gain a considerable influence in it; and the dissolution of parliament was then (as it is now) a thing earnestly to be sought for. Upon the meeting of the parliament after this long prorogation, a question was propounded in the House of Lords by the country party, whether it was not actually dissolved. Lord Shaftsbury, and others of that party, argued and maintained upon an old statute of King Edward the Third, then in force, which directed that the King should call a parliament once a year, or oftener if need should be, that the parliament was actually dissolved; but the court party strenuously opposed this, knowing that the eyes of the people were opened, and that a new parliament would not be favourable to the King's designs.

This question had made a great noise in the kingdom, and by way of silencing the people, the King's party in the House of Lords voted Lord Shaftsbury, Lord Salisbury, and Lord Wharton, who had maintained that the parliament was dissolved, guilty of a contempt of that House, and sent them to the Tower: that they were sent to the Tower to gratify the King's vengeance is apparent from the words of the warrant of commitment, for it directs them to be kept in safe custody *during his Majesty's pleasure* and the pleasure of the House, for their high contempt committed against that House. Lord Salisbury and Lord Wharton submitted to the House, and

were discharged; Lord Shaftsbury at first refused it, and
sued out his Habeas Corpus, and was brought before the
King's Bench with the warrant of his commitment.

The warrant was glaringly illegal and unconstitutional, and
seems to be admitted by all judges in that case to be so, particularly Mr. Justice Wylde, who said the return no doubt was illegal. This was a critical case; in fact, it was the King's cause,
and the judges to determine it at that time held their offices
during the pleasure of the crown, so that they were reduced
to an awkward dilemma; however, they found means to extricate themselves from it by determining that though the commitment was illegal they could not examine into it, and so
Lord Shaftsbury was remanded; and the three puisne judges
on the case of the Queen v. Paty & alias, as also the judges in
Mr. Murray's case, seem implicitly to have followed the determination in Lord Shaftsbury's case, and therefore if that
determination be overthrown, the other two must sink of
course.    In the case of the Queen v. Paty & alias, 3 Ann. the
defendants having been committed to Newgate by a warrant
of the Speaker of the House of Commons, signed Robert
Harley. Speaker (a fatal name to liberty), were brought by
Habeas Corpus into the Queen's Bench, and prayed to be discharged upon the illegality of the commitment. The three
puisne judges refused to interfere upon the authority of Lord
Shaftsbury's case, and the prisoners were remanded, contrary
to the opinion of Lord Chief Justice Holt, one of the ablest
judges that ever presided in that court.    He was of opinion
that what the House had called a breach of privilege was not
a breach of privilege, nor could their judgment make it so, nor
conclude that court from determining contrary; and he says,
"When the House of Commons exceed their legal bounds
and authority, their acts are wrongful and cannot be justified
more than the acts of private men: that there was no question
but their authority is from the law, and as it is circumscribed,
so it may be exceeded.    To say they are judges of their own
privilege and their own authority, and nobody else, is to make
their privileges to be as they would have them.    If there be
a wrongful imprisonment by the House of Commons, what
court shall deliver the party?    Shall we say there is no
redress, and that we are not able to execute those laws upon
which the liberty of the Queen's people subsists?    To con-

clude, all courts are so far judges of their own privileges, and
entrusted with a power to vindicate themselves, that they may
punish for contempts; but to make them, or any court, final
judges of them, exclusive of everybody else, is to introduce a
state of confusion by making every man judge in his own
cause and subverting the measures of all jurisdictions." What
says another learned lawyer, Mr. Serjeant Hawkins, in his
Pleas of the Crown, p. 110?—In commenting upon Lord
Shaftsbury's case he says, "But if it be demanded in case a
subject should be committed by either of those Houses for a
matter manifestly out of their jurisdiction, what remedy can
he have?  I answer, that it cannot well be imagined that the
law which favours nothing more than the liberty of the subject
should give us a remedy against commitments by the King
himself, appearing to be illegal, and yet give us no manner of
redress against a commitment by our fellow-subjects, equally
appearing to be unwarranted."  To this I may add the dictum
of the present Speaker of the House of Commons when
counsel*, who is reported to have said, that had he the
honour to preside in any court of justice, he should no more
regard the resolutions of that House than the resolutions of a
set of drunken porters.  Some apology may be made for the
judges in the case of the Queen v. Paty & alias.  They might
connive at a stretch of power in the House of Commons, for
fear of weakening the dignity and independence of the House:
and if ever that can be justifiable, it was so then, because the
House was truly honourable and independent; for no placeman or pensioner was then capable of sitting in that House.
Very different is it at this time: the House swarms with
placemen and pensioners, and the people want a barrier to
guard them from the invasions of their own representatives.

But if such a dangerous position is to be established as that,
though the order of the House be apparently illegal, no court
of magistrates can give redress, a door will be opened through
the House of Commons to elude all those excellent laws
which our ancestors have procured for the preservation of our
liberties, and to overturn the fundamental principles of the
constitution.  But let us hope that by such weak authorities
as the three cases cited, the liberties of England are not to

* Sir Fletcher Norton.

be determined.  In another letter I will trouble you with my
sentiments upon the privileges of the House of Commons,
and the warrant of commitment*.

I am,

My Lord and Gentlemen,

Your most humble servant,

G. W

———

## LETTER XCV.

### TO THE PRINTER OF THE PUBLIC ADVERTISER.

SIR,                                                        April 9, 1771.

THE arguments used in defence of the late proceedings of
the House of Commons would have a considerable weight with

---

* This promised letter did not appear, though the same subject is pursued
in the following letter, as well as under the more dignified signature of
Junius, and occurs in the letters with this subscription, No. 44, vol. i.
p. 328.

To the arguments and opinions both there and here cited upon the authority of royal proclamations, and powers of privileges of parliament, the editor
will, on this occasion, take the liberty of adding the following decision on
the same point by that great and constitutional judge, Lord Chief Justice
Holt.

"In the reign of Queen Anne, in 1704, several freemen of the borough of
Aylesbury had been refused the liberty of voting at an election for a member
of parliament, though they proved their qualifications as such ; the law in
this case imposes a fine on the returning officer of £100 for every such offence.
On this principle they applied to Lord Chief Justice Holt, who desired the
officer to be arrested.  The House of Commons, alarmed at this step, made
an order of their House to make it penal for either judge, counsel, or attorney, to assist at the trial.  However, the Lord Chief Justice, and several
lawyers, were hardy enough to oppose this order, and brought it on in the
King's Bench.  The House, highly irritated at this contempt of their orders,
sent a serjeant-at-arms for the judge to appear before them ; but that resolute defender of the laws bade him, with a voice of authority, begone ; on
which they sent a second message by their Speaker, attended by as many
members as espoused the measure.  After the Speaker had delivered his
message, his Lordship replied to him In these remarkable words :—' Go back
to your chair, Mr. Speaker, within these five minutes, or you may depend
on't I'll send you to Newgate.  You speak of your authority ; but I tell you
I sit here as an interpreter of the laws and a distributer of justice, and, were
the whole House of Commons in your belly, I will not stir one foot.'  The
Speaker was prudent enough to retire, and the House were equally prudent
to let the affair drop."

me, if I could persuade myself that the present House of Commons were really in that independent state in which the constitution meant to place them.  If I could be satisfied that their resolutions were not previously determined in the King's cabinet, that no personal resentment was to be gratified, nor any ministerial purpose to be answered, under pretence of asserting their privileges, I own I should be very unwilling to raise or encourage any question between the strict right of the subject, and that discretionary power which our representatives have assumed by degrees, and which, until of late years, they have very seldom abused.  While the House of Commons form a real representation of the people, while they preserve their place in the constitution, distinct from the Lords, and independent of the Crown, I think to contend with them about the limits of their privileges would be contending with ourselves*.  But the question will be materially altered if it should appear that, instead of preserving the due balance of the constitution, they have thrown their whole weight into the same scale with the Crown, and that their privileges, instead of forming a barrier against the encroachments of the other branches of the legislature, are made subservient to the views of the Sovereign, and employed, under the direction of the minister, in the persecution of individuals, and the oppression of the people.  In this case it would be the duty of every honest man to stand strictly to his right; to question every act of such a House of Commons with jealousy and suspicion, and wherever their pretended privileges trenched upon the known laws of the land, in the minutest instance, to resist them with a determined and scrupulous exactness.  To ascertain the fact, we need only consider in what manner parliaments have been managed since his Majesty's accession.

He found this country in that state of perfect union and happiness which good government naturally produces, and

---

* The necessity of securing the House of Commons against the King's power, so that no interruption might be given either to the attendance of the members in parliament or to the freedom of debate, was the foundation of parliamentary privilege; and we may observe in all the addresses of newly-appointed Speakers to the Sovereign, the utmost privilege they demand is liberty of speech and freedom from arrests.  The very word privilege means no more than immunity, or a safeguard to the party who possesses it, and can never be construed into an active power of invading the rights of others.

which a bad one has destroyed. He promised to abolish all
distinctions of party, and kept his word by declaring Lord
Bute his favourite and minister, by proscribing the whole
Whig interest of England, and by filling every place of trust
and profit under his government with professed Tories, notorious Jacobites, and Scotchmen of all denominations. He
abolished no distinctions but those which are essential to the
safety of the constitution. King, Lords, and Commons, which
should for ever stand clear of each other, were soon melted
down into one common mass of power, while equal care was
taken to draw a line of separation between the legislature and
the people, and more particularly between the representative
and the constituent body of the Commons. The Lower House
distinguished themselves by an eager compliance with every
measure that could be supposed to gratify the King personally,
or to humour the vindictive passions of his royal mother.
[When Mr. Wilkes was to be punished, they made no scruple
about the privileges of parliament; and although it was as
well known as any matter of public record and uninterrupted
custom could be, *that the members of either House are privileged, except in cases of treason, felony, or breach of the peace,*
they declared without hesitation *that privilege of parliament
did not extend to the case of a seditious libel;* and undoubtedly
they would have done the same if Mr. Wilkes had been prosecuted for any other misdemeanor whatsoever.] It was
upon that occasion that Sir Fletcher Norton, the patron of
privilege, declared in the House that, if he were a judge
in Westminster Hall, he should regard a vote of the House
of Commons no more than a resolution of a company of
drunken porters. To show us his politeness he preserves
his style; to show us his morality he changes his opinions.
    The House of Lords have not been less pliant in surren-
dering the rights of the peerage, whenever it has suited the
purposes of the cabinet. They joined heartily in the vote
above-mentioned, and when they were called upon to support
that enormous violation of all law, truth, and reason, which
was perpetrated by the House of Commons in the case of
the Middlesex election, they gave up that reciprocal check and
control by which the balance between the three estates can
alone be preserved, and were content to bury their own privi-

leges under the ruins of the constitution.  The influence of
the crown over the resolutions of both Houses continues to
operate with equal force, though now it assumes a different
appearance.  The liberty of the press, besides giving a daily
personal offence to the Princess of Wales, must always be formidable, therefore always odious to such a government as the
present.  Prosecutions had been attempted without success.
The privilege of parliament, which had been so shamefully
surrendered to answer one ministerial purpose, must now be
as violently asserted to answer another.  [The ministry are of
a sudden grown wonderfully careful of privileges which their
predecessors were as ready to invade.  The known laws of the
land, the rights of the subject, the sanctity of charters, and the
reverence due to our magistrates, must all give way, without
question or resistance, to a privilege of which no man knows
either the origin or the extent.  The House of Commons
judge of their own privileges without appeal ; they may take
offence at the most innocent action, and imprison the person
who offends them during their arbitrary will and pleasure.
The party has no remedy ; he cannot appeal from their jurisdiction ; and if he questions the privilege, which he is supposed to have violated, it becomes an aggravation of his
offence.  Surely, Sir, this doctrine is not to be found in
Magna Charta.  If it be admitted without limitation, I affirm
that there is neither law nor liberty in this kingdom.  We
are the slaves of the House of Commons, and through them
we are the slaves of the King and his ministers.]
     The mode in which the House have proceeded against the
city magistrates can neither be reconciled to natural justice,
nor even to the common forms of decency.  They begin with
shutting the doors against all *strangers*, the usual name by
which they describe their constituents.  Some of their debates appear in the public papers.  The offence, if any, is
certainly not a new one.  We have the debates as regularly
preserved as the journals of parliament* ; nor can there be
any honest reason for concealing them.  Mr. Onslow, however, thinks it necessary to prosecute the press, and the

---

* Grey's *Collection of Debates*, in ten volumes, was published under the
direction of the late Arthur Onslow, Esq.

House of Commons is mean enough to take part in his caprices. Lord North, who had so lately rewarded the Reverend Mr. Scot with the best living in the King's gift, for heaping invectives equally dull and virulent upon some of the most respectable characters in this kingdom, is now shameless enough to support a motion against the liberty of the press with the whole influence of the crown. [That their practice might be every way conformable to their principles, the House proceeded to advise the crown to publish a proclamation universally acknowledged to be illegal. Mr. Moreton publicly protested against it before it was issued; and Lord Mansfield, though not scrupulous to an extreme, speaks of it with horror. It is remarkable enough that the very men who advised the proclamation, and who hear it arraigned every day both within doors and without, are not daring enough to utter one word in its defence, nor have they ventured to take the least notice of Mr. Wilkes for discharging the persons apprehended under it.]

The pretended trial of the Lord Mayor and Mr. Oliver resembled the dark business of a Spanish inquisition, rather than the fair proceedings of an English court of judicature. These gentlemen, as magistrates, had nothing to regard but the obligation of their oaths, and the execution of the laws. If they were convinced that the Speaker's warrant was not a legal authority to the messenger, it necessarily followed that, when he was charged upon oath with a breach of the peace, they *must* hold him to bail. They had no option. Yet how have they been treated? Their judges had been partially summoned by treasury mandates, pressing attendance, and demanding a vote of condemnation. They were tried and condemned at midnight, without being heard by themselves or their counsel, on the only point on which their justification could possibly depend. In short, Sir, a question, strictly of jurisdiction, was referred to numbers, and carried like a common ministerial measure. Their next step was to force the Lord Mayor's clerk, by the terror of a prison, to erase the record of a judicial proceeding, held regularly before the chief magistrate of the city. Lord North himself made the motion, and declared that the constitution could not be safe, until it was carried into effect. They then resolved that all prosecutions for the assault (which, though charged upon

oath, they call a pretended one) should be stopped.  I wish
that grave and sober men would consider, independently of
the other questions before us, how far this particular precedent may extend.  If the House of Commons may interpose
in a single instance, between the subject who complains and
the laws which ought to protect, I see no reason why they
may not, at any time, by their vote, stop the whole course of
justice through the kingdom.  Besides the injury done to the
subject, their granting a *noli prosequi* is in effect an encroach-
ment upon the royal prerogative [*].

Many circumstances of insult have been mixed with these
measures of violence.  Their pretended lenity to the Lord
Mayor, which he nobly refused to accept of, amounted only to
an offer of the garrets of the House for the place of his con-
finement instead of the Tower; and, though it be of less
moment, it is still worth observing, that the indignity offered
to the city is aggravated by the time expressly chosen for imprisoning their chief magistrate.  Not content with interrupt-
ing all city business, they fixed upon Easter, because it is the
chief city festival, and found a contemptible gratification in
putting a stop to the amusements usual at this season, and
depriving a public charity of the customary collections, which
they knew must be reduced to nothing by the absence of the
Lord Mayor.

Nothing remained but to keep up a terror and alarm through
the kingdom by appointing committees of inquiry.  This
double star-chamber was moved for long after midnight, and
lists partially sent round by the messengers of the treasury.
Where will these arbitrary, iniquitous proceedings end?  The
ministry, I doubt not, have a plan prepared, but it is such a
one as they neither dare openly avow nor uniformly adhere to.
One day they appoint committees of inquisition to sit *de die*

---

[*] The following is a copy of the minutes of the House of Commons, of
March 20, 1771, here referred to:—

"That James Morgan, clerk of the Lord Mayor, do at the table expunge
the minutes taken before the Lord Mayor, relative to the messenger of this
House giving security for his appearance at the next general quarter-sessions
of the peace; and he accordingly at the table expunged the same.

"Motion made, and question proposed,

"That no other prosecution, suit, or proceeding, be commenced, or carried
on for, or on account of the said pretended assault, or false imprisonment.

"It passed in the affirmative."

*in diem;* the next thing we hear is that the committees are adjourned, and the members of them dispersed into the country. After advising the King, very unnecessarily, to go to parliament, they come to him while his equipage is in waiting, contradict their own advice, and endeavour to stagger his resolution at the moment when he has most occasion for it. They alone are answerable for all the indignities heaped upon the King's person, since they could not but foresee that the people would take the earliest opportunity of resenting the imprisonment of their magistrates.

When the Princess of Wales was named in the House of Commons, where was that zeal which some people boast of for their royal master? The mother of their Sovereign was branded by name as the authoress of all our calamities, and the assertion passed without censure or contradiction.

Sir, I most truly lament the condition to which we are reduced, and the more so, because there is but one remedy for it, and that remedy has been repeatedly refused. A dissolution of the parliament would restore tranquillity to the people, and to the King the affections of his subjects; the present House of Commons have nothing to expect but contempt, detestation, and resistance. This violent state of things cannot long continue. Either the laws and constitution must be preserved by a dreadful appeal to the sword, or (what probably is intended by the present system of measures) the people will grow weary of their condition, and surrender everything into the King's hands, rather than submit to be trampled upon any longer by five hundred of their equals.

A WHIG*.

* The passages in this letter which are placed within brackets, are retranscribed by the author, and added as notes to his Letter 44, vol. i. p. 325, published in his own edition, under the signature of Junius, where the reader will still find them.

The messengers were indicted in defiance of the resolutions of the House of Commons, and true bills were found against them, but further proceedings were stopped by the Attorney-General entering a *noli prosequi*. As the arguments urged by Mr. Adair, who was of counsel for the printers, on showing cause against this measure, are extremely curious, and not generally known, we shall subjoin them for the information of the reader, and for the better elucidation of this and other letters upon the subject of this important dispute.

Mr. Adair, in pursuance of notice, attended the Attorney-General, Mr. De

## LETTER XCVI.

### *For the Public Advertiser.*

April 15, 1771.

#### HENRICUS TO THE EARL OF SUFFOLK.

My Lord,

THE singularity of your late conduct seemed to claim some attention from the public, which you do not, I presume, think

Grey, on the 17th of May, 1771, and after the indictment and an affidavit of the defendant had been read, spoke as follows :—

"It requires no arguments to show, that though the entering a *noli prosequi* on prosecutions at the suit of the King only is an undoubted prerogative of the crown, yet, like all other prerogatives, it is intended for the general good of the subject, and not for the hindrance or interruption of public justice.

"It is indeed a discretionary power, but it is to be exercised, not according to an arbitrary, but a sound and legal discretion. It is for this reason, Sir, that it is not left to the wanton caprice of a favourite, or the arbitrary will of a minister, to be executed at pleasure, but it is deposited as a public trust in the hands of the Attorney-General, that the exercise of it may be directed by his knowledge of the laws and constitution of the kingdom.

"Many reasons may be suggested why this power should be most sparingly exercised in cases of prosecution by indictment.

"Though the King's name is necessarily used as the general guardian of the laws, there is another party concerned in indictments, the injured party, who is for the most part the real, as the King is the nominal prosecutor.

"The practice, too, of entering a *noli prosequi* on indictments is but of modern date.

"In the case of Goddard and Smith in the 6th Mod. 262, Holt, Chief Justice, said, 'He had known it thought very hard that the Attorney-General should enter *noli prosequi* upon indictments, and that began first to be practised in the latter end of King Charles the Second's reign ; and he ordered precedents to be searched, if any were, in Mr. Attorney Palmer, or Nottingham's time ;' and at another day he declared, 'that in all King Charles the First's time there was no precedent of a *noli prosequi* on an indictment.'

"I therefore submit to you, that (sitting here to determine upon the application of a power so recent in its commencement, and of which we are told by so respectable an authority, that it has been looked upon as a hardship in itself,) you will require the most cogent reasons to induce you to exert it upon this or any other occasion.

you have entirely escaped; but since by their silence they
either think you superior to shame or below the dignity of

"These reasons must arise either from the conduct of the prosecutor, the
personal situation and circumstance of the defendant, or the subject-matter of
the prosecution.

"I do not find from the affidavit of the defendant, which is the only
information I have had of the grounds of his application to you, that he
complains of any particular hardships or oppression, arising either from unnecessary delay, unusual rigour, or any other misconduct in the prosecutor:
he must therefore expect the extraordinary interposition of the prerogative in
his behalf, in this instance, either from something peculiarly favourable in his
personal situation, which entitles him to the protection of the crown, or from
the charge against him being totally groundless and unfit to be discussed in a
court of justice.

"As to the first of these points, if we consider Mr. Whittam not being a
magistrate's constable, or any other officer intrusted with the execution of
the laws, but acting merely in a private capacity, as wantonly assaulting
one of the King's subjects, in his own house, who was not even accused of
any crime, and violently attempting to deprive him of his liberty; if, I say,
we consider him in this point of view, he can hardly be thought a fit object
of the royal favour and protection; but if we view him in the light in which
he has thought proper to place himself by his own affidavit, he will be found,
if possible, still less entitled to that exertion of prerogative for which he has
applied. He tells you, Sir, that he is a messenger of the House of Commons;
that in that character, and acting under the express orders and authority of
that House, he did the fact with which he is charged in the indictment.
Does he mean, Sir, that you should consider this as a reason for granting a
noli prosequi? When was it heard before that an exertion of prerogative was
necessary to support the authority and privileges of the House of Commons?
When was that House known to sue to the servants of the crown to screen
their officers from the laws, or protect them from the indignation of an inconsiderable printer?

"I believe when any of their privileges have been really invaded, they
have never been found wanting either in power or inclination to support
them; and I am satisfied that if the House were now sitting, Mr. Whittam
would not have dared to make an application so manifestly tending to expose
their privileges and authority to ridicule and contempt. But, Sir, I am persuaded that the honour and dignity of the House of Commons are safe in
your hands, and that you will suffer no act to proceed from you that can
throw even an oblique imputation upon them.

"If there is for these reasons nothing in Mr. Whittam's personal situation
or circumstances which can entitle him to an extraordinary interposition in
his favour, it remains only to be considered whether any motive can be suggested from the subject-matter of the prosecution to induce you to put a stop
to it by an exertion of the royal prerogative.

"The charge set forth in the indictment, and not denied by the defendant's affidavit, is for assaulting and imprisoning the prosecutor, Mr. Miller.
It will not be contended that there appears anything upon the face of the

revenge, I cannot help giving to them what I owe on this occasion, which, had I only considered the gratification of a

indictment oppressive, illegal, unfit to come before a court of justice, or which affords any motive whatsoever for granting the *noli prosequi;* the reason, therefore, if any, must arise from the matters set forth by the defendant's affidavit.    The affidavit states, that the defendant is one of the messengers of the House of Commons; that the Speaker's warrant for apprehending the prosecutor was issued by order of the House, and that, in consequence thereof, the defendant, to whom the warrant was delivered, did make the arrest with which he is charged in the indictment, and that he used no violence in so doing, other than seizing Mr. Miller by the arm, as is usual in arrests.

"I apprehend it is not incumbent upon me here to consider, as I submit it is not competent for you, Sir, to determine in this summary manner, whether the matters here set forth do or do not amount to a good defence, or legal justification.    We are not now to try the cause; but you, Sir, I am confident, will not interpose the prerogative of the King to prevent our trying it in the regular course before the proper jurisdiction, unless the prosecution, as it now appears before you, is so clearly and manifestly groundless, and unfit for discussion in a court of law, that it would be an abuse and mockery of public justice to bring it to a trial.    If the authority under which Mr. Whitam alleges himself to have acted was not competent to authorise the fact which he committed, or if that authority never was in fact delegated to him, in either of those cases the prosecution is well founded in law.    If any doubt or question can be raised on either of these points, it is not so clearly groundless as to justify the putting a stop to it by prerogative before those questions are legally determined.

"It might well be questioned, whether the House of Commons has any power, by the laws or constitution of this kingdom, to authorise the issuing of such a warrant as that under colour of which Mr. Miller was apprehended.

"It might be said, and supported too by the greatest authorities, that they cannot, by any act of theirs singly, create any new power or privilege to themselves; that there was a time when they evidently neither possessed nor claimed any such power as that in question; and when the authority of an Act of Parliament was thought necessary to punish even so undeniable a breach of privilege as the assaulting the person of a member attending upon his duty in parliament.    The statute, Sir, which I here allude to, is the 11th of H. VI. c. 11, which was made to extend the provisions of 5th H. IV. c. 6, for punishment of assaults on the servants of members of parliament when attending on their masters in their duty, to the persons of the members themselves.    It might be urged, that the power in question has never been given them by any Act of Parliament, and that if there ever was a time when they did not possess it, they can by no other means have legally acquired it.    All this and much more might be said, if it were necessary to dispute the authority of the House of Commons to issue the warrant for the commitment of Mr. Miller; but it is sufficient for me at present to contend, that whether they had or had not the power, they never did in

passion, I should have sooner done. I own I now do it with some distrust of my own abilities, in doing justice to the un-

fact give the defendant any authority whatsoever to make the arrest in question.

"The warrant, Sir, under colour of which Mr. Whittam acted, is a warrant purporting to be issued in pursuance of an order of the House of Commons, and signed Fletcher Norton, Speaker. But, Sir, the order of the House, as it is recited in the warrant itself, is for taking Mr. Miller into the custody of the serjeant-at-arms or his deputy; and Mr. Whittam is described in the direction of the very same warrant to be neither the one nor the other of these. No authority whatsoever can be conveyed to Mr. Whittam, by virtue of an order in which he is not named, and which particularly points out certain persons, in contradiction from all others. This warrant, therefore (so far as it relates to Mr. Whittam), appears to be issued by the Speaker, merely of his own authority, unauthorized by any order of the House of Commons. Has the Speaker any power to commit, unless he derives it from the orders of the House? If he has not, which must be granted, he is bound strictly and literally to pursue that order which creates his authority: as far as he exceeds it, he acts without authority himself, and most clearly can convey none to any other person. Mr. Whittam therefore, in this case, acting without any legal authority whatever in the arrest of the prosecutor, a prosecution grounded upon that cannot be considered as totally void of foundation. But supposing for a moment that the prosecution was frivolous and ill-grounded, I submit that that alone would not be a reason for the extraordinary interposition of the crown. If it would in this case, it must in every other; every defendant who fancied himself unjustly prosecuted would apply for protection to the crown, and almost every indictment must first be tried by the attorney-general before it could come regularly into a court of justice. I presume you will conceive it was not for these purposes that this prerogative was vested in your hands, and that there must appear some strong reasons peculiar to the case to show why it is improper and unfit for public discussion, besides merely that of the prosecution being ill-grounded to induce you to make this extraordinary interposition. I submit to you, Sir, with great deference, that there appears no such reasons in this case. Every motive of policy and prudence seems to weigh on the other side. The question to be tried is the most important that can well be conceived. The privileges of the House of Commons on the one side, and the liberties of the people of England on the other, are said to be materially affected. Perhaps, indeed, it might have been wished that this great question had never been started, or brought to the public view, by issuing the warrant in question. But when it has been already so much agitated, and has engrossed the attention of the public, it seems necessary, for the satisfaction and quiet of the kingdom, that it should proceed to a solemn and legal determination in a court of justice. If, therefore, Sir, the House of Commons had no authority by law to authorise Mr. Whittam to make the arrest upon the prosecutor, or if, in fact, no authority was delegated to him, in either of these cases he has illegally assaulted an innocent man, and deprived him of his liberty; and the entering a *noli prosequi* would be an obstruction of public justice. If, on the other hand,

dertaking.  Your Lordship must be aware that it is generally
a matter of some degree of delicacy to undertake the discussion

the House of Commons had a legal authority, and regularly delegated the
execution of it to Mr. Whittam, the public should be convinced of it by a
discussion and determination in a court of law; and the granting the *noli
prosequi* in that case would tend to mislead many people into an opinion
that it was done to screen an offender from the laws, who had no legal justification in a court of justice: I therefore submit to you, Sir, for these reasons,
that you, as Attorney-General, will not think proper in this case to grant a
*noli prosequi*."

Mr. *Attorney-General.*—" Do you produce any evidence?"

Mr. *Adair.*—" We offer no other evidence than what appears in the affidavit of the defendant himself, and the warrant to which it refers."

Mr. *Attorney-General.*—" You are extremely right in this, that it is not at
all a fit thing for the Attorney-General to try either the fact upon which the
defendant is indicted, or to determine the law.  The only question is this,
whether it is fit for the King to interpose as the prosecutor of this offence?
That, I take it, should be the ground of your argument, and the point upon
which I expected satisfaction.  The affidavit itself states the messenger of the
House of Commons to be acting under the authority of the House of Commons;
and if this was the only way in which that question could be brought before
a court of law, I should be obliged to give an opinion whether it ought or
whether it ought not.

" The only point I have to consider is, whether it be fit for the name of
the crown to appear in prosecuting one who appears to be the messenger of
the House of Commons, and to be armed by the authority of that House for
doing the very thing he has done under the orders of the House?  I don't
mean to pass over the objection which has been made, that the Speaker of
the House, by orders of the House, directing the warrant to a person not
named in such order, whether that order extends only to arresting the prosecutor, and taking him into the custody of the serjeant-at-arms, or his deputy:
I dare say I take Mr. Adair's objection perfectly right; the order of the
House is for taking him into the custody of the serjeant-at-arms, or his deputy; and the objection is, that the person in whose custody the prosecutor
was originally taken is neither the serjeant-at-arms or his deputy.  And
the doubt you raise upon it is, whether the Speaker of the House of Commons can authorize another person to arrest and bring him into the custody
of the serjeant-at-arms or his deputy; for the serjeant-at-arms, or his deputy,
is the proper and the only custody I know of belonging to the House; and
the gentleman's argument is, that in point of the arrest it cannot be made
without the serjeant, or deputy-serjeant, with respect to the orders of the
House of Commons, and the direction of the warrant by the Speaker, which
is a question of law to be sure.  It has been constant in point of practice for
the messengers to be employed (in the orders of the House, and for other
than messengers to be employed) upon the very same occasion.  There is
nothing so constant as the messengers all to be employed; there are some
few instances where more than the messengers have been employed upon
these occasions.  The difficulty upon it was, whether they should or not be

of any part or system of politics, as it is of some difficulty to
avoid the share of imputations which are indiscriminately

inserted in the warrant; or whether, if they were not inserted in the warrant,
it could be construed under the general description of the serjeant-at-arms or
his deputy; or whether that authority could go to warrant those which might
be appointed by the serjeant-at-arms or his deputy upon that occasion. It
was thought more proper to make a warrant directed to the person to be employed, though it was mentioned in the orders of the House that the custody
was to be that of the serjeant-at-arms, or his deputy, according to the usual
form of their orders.

"But the only point for me to consider is, how far it is fit the King should
be the prosecutor of a servant of the House of Commons, in the execution of
a privilege which they now claim, which they have claimed for ages, and have
been in the possession of for ages; and that the King should be brought into
a proceeding against the servant of the House as a prosecutor. The *noli
prosequi* is called a prerogative right of the crown; it amounts to no more
than this, that the King makes his election whether he will continue or not
to be the prosecutor upon an indictment, and the *noli prosequi* is entered in
the same words in case of the crown as of a private person. The entry upon
the record is exactly the same by the Attorney-General as by a private plaintiff upon record in any civil suit.

"I did expect that you would have given me some reason for entertaining
an opinion that it was decent and fit for the crown to continue and stand
forth as a prosecutor of the messenger of the House of Commons, acting
under their direction, in maintenance of a privilege they have claimed and
held so long. That is the only point I put it upon. The affidavit, as made
by the defendant, makes it necessary to consider him as an officer of the
House.

"I did not indeed expect any disputes upon it, or that it would be put
upon so small a ground; the reason I expected was, that it was becoming an
officer of the crown, in the name of the crown, to continue a prosecution by
the crown, against the messenger of the House of Commons, acting under
the authority of the House of Commons."

*Mr. Adair,* expressing a doubt whether it would be proper for him to
make any reply to this, the *Attorney-General* said he should be glad to hear
him.

*Mr. Adair.*—"With regard to what you have suggested, it is true the
entry upon record is the same in the case of the crown as of a private person;
yet in a prosecution by indictment the crown is not solely concerned. To
make the case exactly similar, it should be an information *ex officio*, or any
other really and truly a crown prosecution; and then the entering *noli prosequi* upon that would be the same as upon private actions. But in the case
of indictments, the King being in fact a nominal prosecutor, though his name
is necessary, yet the injured party being the true prosecutor (who applies to
the laws of his country for justice against the offender, who has violated those
laws and particularly injured him), if in that case the King puts a stop to the
prosecution by withdrawing his name from it, it is the same in effect, though
not in form, as if he sent his mandate and said that prosecution should not go

thrown on all who submit their anonymous opinions to the public. Though these reproaches may fall on those whose names would give some credit to their assertions, yet while they adopt the common method of hirelings, their writings must expect the same treatment. With whatever circumstances

on; because if he withdraws his name from it, that prosecution cannot, by the laws, go any further—the prosecutor himself cannot proceed in his own name; the withdrawing that name has the same effect as the actual interposition of prerogative by the Attorney-General, and operates the same as a pardon. Mr. Whittam being alleged to have acted under the authority of the House of Commons, to have had a warrant directed to him, the question is not whether the warrant is legal or not, but whether it is proper for the crown to put a stop to that prosecution, and whether, the privileges of the House of Commons being said to be concerned, any interposition of the crown be necessary to support their authority. If Whittam has acted in pursuance of the order of the House, if those orders are such as the House has a competent authority to make, I submit that it cannot be a doubt that that matter, pleaded or brought in a regular manner before a court of justice, would be a sufficient defence. If the courts of law are of opinion that the House has that authority, and that it was regularly delegated to Whittam, they would necessarily be of opinion to acquit him; and upon that ground there appears to be no necessity for the crown withdrawing itself from a prosecution which by no possible means can prove oppressive or injurious to the defendant. If he has acted under a legal authority, he must be legally acquitted in a court of justice. But if the authority is not sufficient, or not regularly conveyed, it is proper, for the sake of justice and the liberty of the subject, that judgment should be pronounced upon it in a court of law. I believe the prosecutor does not contend that the defendant has been guilty of that kind of offence for which he means to prosecute him with any rigour; he don't mean to oppress him, or proceed for the sake of punishment only. Whether it is five pounds or five thousand is indifferent to him; the only thing he wishes, is to have the question decided by a legal competent jurisdiction. If it comes regularly before the court, though perhaps upon this indictment it could not, but if it does, the question is, whether the Speaker of the House of Commons had a sufficient legal authority to authorise that arrest, or whether the defendant has actually acted under that authority, such as it was. And I submit to your consideration whether, upon that point, such interposition appears to be necessary in this case, either upon behalf of the defendant, or of the privilege of the House of Commons."

Mr. *Attorney-General.*—" I don't put it upon the tenderness to Mr. Whittam, or the point of privilege of the House of Commons, but merely upon the foot of decency, as the circumstance of the crown taking a part in the prosecution (which they must do if they go on with it) against the messenger of the House of Commons, acting under the authority of the warrant of the Speaker, pursuant to an order of the House."

Mr. De Grey, the Attorney-General, was afterwards Chief Justice of the Common Pleas, and Mr. Adair subsequently Recorder of London.

any object of my notice might be attended, I should expect criticism, and I hope I could bear it with temper. I cannot, however, help considering it as a lucky circumstance, that the first production I ever ventured to give to the public excludes the possibility of any imputation, as the actions I shall condemn admit not the possibility of defence. Before I arraign your subsequent conduct, which I mean to do pretty freely, I must admire the simple *candour* with which you have declared yourself without principle. In the most destructive administrations, composed of men perhaps more profligate than your Lordship, care has generally been taken to save, in some measure, appearances with the public; and although the destruction of this constitution has been pretty clearly their object, they have never ventured openly to avow it: even the Duke of Grafton did not condemn his own principles, though he avowed and gloried in such measures as no man with principle could undertake. Your Lordship is the first man who ever saved others the trouble of accusation. Your protests must remain to all posterity a monument of your infamy; and one would almost imagine you designed they should. You are young, my Lord: you thought it was necessary for a man of fashion to engage in public business; and as some of your private connections happened to be in opposition, you went with the stream and opposed. Apparently attached to that party, you perhaps thought it a civility to adopt and pursue their measures, whatever they were, of opposition; and your vanity was afterwards tickled with an offer from administration which your civility would not permit you to refuse. You did not reflect, or perhaps you did not know, that you was catching at an object which was not attended even with the usual appearance of honour; and you did not then consider (for I am sure you must now recollect), that you was attaching yourself to men from whose connection that protest, which will now be transmitted down with ridicule to your posterity, ought to have excluded you for ever;—or perhaps, to speak more fairly or more fashionably, you thought the force of such declarations was no longer of consequence when the purpose was answered for which they were made. These reasons are so much below a schoolboy, that I am sure your Lordship would not be willing to allege them; and if you have in the world a friend, he will not wish you should: but unhappily friendship is not one of

those ruling objects which you have been solicitous to preserve,
however fortunate you may *formerly have been* in obtaining it.
The man who, without honour to support any administration
from principle, has still craft enough to betray all, may perhaps
be solicited by every succeeding minister, or perhaps their credulity may be deceived into his friendship; but the poor un-
taught villain, who can neither support with consistency, nor
betray with decency, will be *despised* by those whom he deserted,
and ridiculed by the very men to whom he has made so capital
a surrender.   Your Lordship, I believe, sees with some uneasiness the truth of the observation, and I will give your
conscience credit for the feelings it must produce.   I would
therefore consider you, what you seem willing to be considered,
an object of pity rather than of reproach.   The situation in
which you appeared before a whole House of Peers, and the
trial you then underwent, might be an object of triumph to some
men; but I hope all hearts were not shut to the feelings of
compassion.   I am willing only to extend reproach to those
who seem proud of receiving it.   The criminal who is executed
at the gallows ought not to excite the anger, much less the
exultations, of the public whom he has defrauded : but the
villain who has seduced him to the commission of the crime
for which he suffers, and who glories in his impudence, has a
claim to all we can give him—our detestation and our curses.
The comparison I think you understand, and I believe you
have sensibility enough to feel it ; indeed you testified it sufficiently to those who could observe you wished to justify, or at
least to excuse, so extraordinary a change of principles and conduct : your courage forsook you, and you did not dare to rise.
The Duke of Grafton, when he deserted those principles and
those connections to which every sentiment of honour ought to
have allied and bound him, seemed happily to have lost all that
*mauvaise honte* with which young adventurers like his Grace
were usually attended, and he creditably told us that he gloried
in his situation.   Your Lordship's prostitution was not attended
with those peculiar circumstances which attended his.   You
felt the sacrifice you had made ; your conscience forced your
silence, and every man was confounded : administration looked
for a notable advocate, but were deceived with a reproach which
cut them to the quick.   For your own sake, my Lord, let me
advise you to consider your own plan, and let me appeal to

your understanding for its acquittal. Your situation by birth
is such as put it in your own power to have acquitted yourself
in life respectably, and your connection with such men as Lord
Rockingham, Sir George Saville, the Duke of Portland, and
the Duke of Richmond, were no disgrace to you. Was your
fortune encumbered with debt, or sold through extravagance?
Had you a numerous family to provide for, whose support you
could not command from your own establishment? Had administration reversed its order of governing, and given you any
security for the preservation of our rights, and redress of our
grievances? If any private assurance of this sort has been
given you, I shall think your conduct has been consistent,
though it will still be disgraceful with respect to your friends
in opposition. You will not answer any of these questions in
the affirmative; nor is it necessary you should answer them at
all. The two first propositions I know to be false. The third,
if it had existed, would before this time have been declared.
Thus we see a hopeful young peer, possessed of an independent
fortune, with an only child, a daughter, connected with the
most honourable characters in this kingdom, prostituting his
honour, and every valuable consideration of the public for that
of an office, independent even of those sweet allurements which
could, one would imagine, make the bitter pill go down. For
shame, my Lord, to throw yourself away under such circumstances, at the discretion of *such* an administration! Had you,
like poor Whateley, been reduced from a state of independence
to the humiliating necessity of soliciting your support from
administration, our reproach would be only turned against
those who creditably took advantage of such a situation, and
gratified themselves with the purchase of an honest man's reputation; and though we congratulated them on the acquisition
which they had prudently secured, we should sincerely pity the
object of their triumph. I am neither surprised nor shocked
at any inconsistency in Mr. Wedderburne: his profession sets
his principles at auction, and it is reasonable that the highest
bidder should command them: but that the Earl of Suffolk
should act such a part, I own astonished me—a man who had
everything to lose, and nothing to gain by prostitution: that
an independent peer of England should voluntarily pledge
himself to his country for the exertion of every right
and every power with which the constitution had vested

him for their service, and should after this betray every interest of the public, and desert that service—that he should in one session repeatedly declare to this purport, if not to this tenour, that he would *never hereafter* be induced, for *any* consideration, to herd with men whom he considered as enemies to their king and country, and in the next deliver over his conscience, his right and his powers into their hands at their discretion, and thereby include himself in every odious term of reproach which he had so liberally bestowed on them.    There seems something at least extraordinary in such conduct; and we are induced, with some curiosity, to inquire, for God's sake, Sir, from what consideration could Lord Suffolk be induced to take so strong a part with opposition, if he intended the next session to betray it?    Or if he was then sincere in his attachments and his professions, what views could he have in deserting them?    These are reasonable, and I think natural questions.    We cannot but commiserate the mortifying state of human nature, when we are answered the truth, and informed of the circumstances attending it.    Had you, my Lord, been entrapped, like poor Yorke, by the prevailing force which was contained in the personal entreaties and solicitations of Majesty, and had your honour been seduced and struck into compliance, though we should abhor the act, we should acquit at least *you* of the guilt, and you would have had a just claim to our pity unmixed with our contempt.    But, my Lord, what are we to say, when we see a man in your Lordship's situation stooping to so humiliating a consideration as to *entreat* a connection in office with those very men whom you had before reviled and despised ?    That you should, after being answered, with an air of superiority, that you was at least the third to be considered—that you should wait with patience and resignation, and see three men successively refuse such a connection, and then accept it under such circumstances !    The conclusion which we are to draw, I leave to your Lordship's feelings to determine.    You have had time to reflect on your situation, and I would not wish to add more to embitter the sweets of office.    Had this address appeared sooner, while you was *fortunâ dulci ebrius*, you would perhaps have laughed with Lord Sandwich at the undertaking of one who endeavoured to prove that honesty and virtue had any real existence.    You would, like the Duke of Grafton, have perused it at your tea-table,

and perhaps taken a pride, like Lord Hillsborough, that you
was dignified with an enemy, though you had not, like him,
preserved a friend. But I think, my Lord, a sufficient time is
elapsed, during which some intervals of private reflection and
remorse must have interfered, and the flattery of those who
purchased must have subsided, and left your conscience and
Mr. Grenville to reproach you. For I still believe you to consist of that composition which, without virtue enough to avoid
prostitution, has still feeling enough to be ashamed of it.

Yorkshire, March 7, 1771.                                    HENRICUS.

[This letter has been misplaced, or would have appeared
sooner.]

---

## LETTER XCVII.

### HENRICUS TO THE EARL OF SUFFOLK.

My Lord,                                                    May 21, 1771.

In my last address to your Lordship, I spoke to your feelings.
I thought your conduct was such as could afford no very pleasing reflection, and I readily believed that you was willing to
consider the tenderness which had been preserved on the occasion with that silent gratitude which refined and delicate
feelings must naturally suggest. It was acknowledged that
Lord Suffolk acted without virtue, or without reflection; and I
believe most men concurred with me in supposing that you had
feeling enough to be ashamed of a transaction which you had
not courage to avoid. The resignation with which you seemed
to submit to your ignominy was some pledge of your delicacy,
if not of your integrity. You was pitied, I believe, by all mankind, and perhaps by some you were forgiven: the transaction
sunk, as it might be supposed you wished it should, in silence
and obscurity. It was not, I believe, imagined that you would
ever be found hardy enough to renew the consideration of an
affair which every man who felt for you must wish to be forgotten. It was not conceived that so short a time would have
reconciled you to a measure which no man of understanding
could view without ridicule. But we live in an age where no
inconsistency is irreconcilable, and are governed by men with
whom no villany is inconsistent. They have, I suppose, my

Lord, made a convert of your understanding as well as your integrity, and you may be indebted to the piety of Lord Sandwich for a system of ideas more conformable to the plan you have pursued. He may have taught you, that to repent of successful villany is still greater folly than to preserve integrity. I congratulate you on the connection you have formed, and the acquisition you have secured; especially since you have lost nothing but your honour—a term "more adapted to Roman barbarism than to the civilized regulations of English (I beg pardon—Scotch) policy." Your Lordship, I believe, recollects the inconsistency which occasions this address. Your speech on the Duke of Richmond's motion in the House of Lords was a pretty remarkable adventure. Had you contentedly and professedly resigned yourself, without attempting to reconcile your present with your former system, your conduct, believe me, would never have called out a second attack on so truly contemptible a being. It is the singular immodesty of your behaviour which I own has tempted me to expose you, as you are willing to be an object of public detestation and disgust. There are few men, except Mr. Wedderburne and your Lordship, who would have gone through the difficulty of exposing themselves to those who had such evidence against them, with that happy indifference which we have experienced from you both. To preserve the hypocrisy of patriotism, after you had openly made your compact with corruption; to profess consistency in adhering to the words of a protest, on the tenour of which your whole conduct is the grossest ridicule; and to possess the characteristical firmness of administration in reviving so ignominious a consideration, requires more courage and intrepidity than most men have the good fortune to possess: but I allow your friend Wedderburne has outstripped you. He has modestly ventured not only virtually, but directly, to attack opposition for measures which he himself concurred in promoting; and hears himself despised, execrated, detested, without fear, and without anger. Let him excuse me when I assure him, with some very allowable pride, that I do not think he has a claim to any notice beyond my advice to consider, that the power from whence he derives very superior abilities will expect, and must receive, an account to what purposes they have been employed. You will now, perhaps, ask me, in all the hypocritical simplicity of St. James's, what part had I to act, after making a traffic of my abilities, which might not have given offence? I justified before all mankind the protest which I had signed, and the pen of satire has been busy to condemn me. Had my conduct been different, would it have been consistent? Would it have been satisfactory? To this I must answer, you had brought yourself, my Lord, into that odious situation where you could neither retreat with decency nor persevere with integrity. But to have retired from the curses of your countrymen would have been remembered, I believe, more to your credit as a man, if not as a minister. But I make too great allowance, I find, for human nature. I have not reflected that the only valuable consideration is interest; and I have forgot that influence to which Mr. Yorke is indebted for a very hazardous eternity. For the future I shall learn to view things with less *candour*, and observe villany, if not without mortification, at least without surprise. I shall now take my leave of your Lordship, probably for ever. But I must congratulate you, my Lord, on that ambition which has led you to inquire into those desirable *arcana* of a court by which you have learned a sort of loyalty distinct from duty to his Majesty, or affection to his family; by which you have found that it will be for your interest, and consequently for your honour, to attach yourself hereafter to men who, while they act directly contrary to the interest of their countrymen, and are indifferent with regard to their confidence or esteem, can hug themselves among the highest of mankind, and ridicule the contemptible folly of those whose virtue has excluded them from their share in the plunder of the public.

HENRICUS.

---

## LETTER XCVIII.

### DOMITIAN TO THE PUBLIC ADVERTISER.

Sir,          June 28, 1771.

In answer to the card repeatedly addressed to *Domitian*\*, he

---

\* The following is a copy of the card :—

" 19 *June*, 1771.

" TO DOMITIAN.

" In your second letter is this remarkable promise—' Tell the Duke of

desires it may be observed that although he has not altered his sentiments with regard to the Duke of Grafton, the case has not happened in which he thinks himself bound, either by the letter or the spirit of his promise, to the public.   The Duke *is not* First Lord of the Admiralty*, nor is he actually in any post in which patents can immediately be sold by himself, or by Tommy Bradshaw, or by Miss Polly Bradshaw, who, like the moon, lives upon the light of her brother's countenance, and robs him of no small part of his lustre.   The fact was notorious.   The sale of that patent to Mr. Hine (the only man of merit whom the Duke of Grafton ever provided for), so far from being denied, was publicly defended.   Yet the House of Commons, who pretend to be the grand inquest of the nation, suffered this infamous breach of trust to pass by without censure or examination.   For the present, therefore, it would answer no good purpose for *Domitian* to produce his evidence.   But perhaps the day of inquiry is not far off.   In the meantime, to show the Duke that *Domitian* does not speak at random, he begs leave to remind his Grace that there are three such persons in the world as *Ross*, the agent; *Taylor*, the house-builder; and *Taylor's little boy.—Verbum sat.*

*Domitian*, upon the whole, thinks he may venture to leave the Duke of Grafton, or, if there be one more odious, more base, and more contemptible person of rank in the kingdom, that he may safely leave them both to the care of *Junius*†.

Grafton, that if he should dare to entertain the most distant thought of the admiralty, the whole affair of *Hine's patent* shall be revived, and published with an accumulation of evidence.   He at least shall be kept under.   His Ciceronian eloquence shall not save him.'

" As the Duke of Grafton has got an higher and more lucrative office, it is expected by the public that you now *fulfil your promise.*"

*   His Grace had now rejoined the ministry, and held the office of Lord Privy Seal.

†   He refers to Junius's two letters to the Duke of Grafton, Nos. 49 and 50, dates June 22 and July 9, 1771, vol. i. pp. 350 and 355.

## LETTER XCIX.

### TO THE PRINTER OF THE PUBLIC ADVERTISER.

SIR,                                                        July 5, 1771.

EVENTS and characters of a similar nature recur so often within the compass of a few centuries, that history is in effect little more than a repetition. The scenes and names of the performers are changed, but the fable is the same. I was led to this observation by a passage I lately met with in a modern French author. The account he gives us of the Emperor Valentinian the Third deserves our notice:—"Le premier soin de cette princesse fut d'inspirer à son fils l'horreur de l'hérésie et le respect pour l'église; qualités très estimables dans un souverain, mais qui ne purent couvrir le vice d'une éducation molle et efféminée. Sa mère travailla plus à former sa croyance que son esprit ni ses mœurs; aussi fut-il toujours très Catholique, sans être jamais Chrétien." For the benefit of my Lord Suffolk, I shall give you a translation. Mr. Wheatley, I hear, has got the start of his master, and, with the help of a dictionary, may do it into English for himself:—"The Princess Dowager made it her first care to inspire her son with horror against heresy, and with a respect for the church; qualities much to be esteemed in a sovereign, but not sufficient to conceal the defects of a soft effeminate education. His mother took more pains to form his belief than either his morals or his understanding, so that he was always an excellent Catholic without ever being a Christian." I do not mean to apply the passage, but merely to save some future historian the trouble of drawing a new character.

I am, Sir,
Your humble Servant,
AN INNOCENT READER.

## LETTER C.

### TO THE PRINTER OF THE PUBLIC ADVERTISER.

SIR,                                          October 16, 1771.

IF the pert youth who calls himself *An Old Correspondent* *, and who makes free with Junius, does not know the difference between *contact* and *collision*, nor between the *friction* which produces the electrical powers, and the action of flint and steel which produces sparks of fire, his ignorance must be deplorable. But what right has he to change the terms? Why say *contact* when Junius says *collision?* When this pert youth asks what virtue there is in Mr. Wilkes, I wish he would tell us what fire there is in flint and steel. It is action that makes them sparkle, and, if there be anything combustible in the passions of Mr. Nash, a single spark may set him on fire.

Again, Junius admits the strict right of pressing seamen, but denies the King's right to arm his subjects in general, excepting in the case of an invasion. This my pretty *Black Boy* calls a retractation of Junius's first concession, and applies to his aged father for an old woman's proverb. Junius speaks of *softening the symptoms of a disorder.* The *Black Boy* changes the terms again, and destroys the allusion. The rest of his letter is of a piece with these instances; a misrepresentation of Junius, equally pert, false, and stupid. *Ex his disce omnia.*

I know nothing of Junius, but *I see plainly that he has designedly spared Lord Holland and his family* †. Whether Lord Holland be invulnerable, or whether Junius should be wantonly provoked, are questions worthy the *Black Boy's* consideration.

ANTI-FOX.

* A letter under this signature appeared in the *Public Advertiser* in answer to Junius (Letter No. 59, vol. i.), and was by him attributed to Mr. Fox, Lord Holland's second son. That Junius was inclined to favour, or rather, in the words of the concluding paragraph of this letter, to spare Lord Holland, is obvious throughout these letters; but will be more particularly seen by a reference to Private Letter, No. 5.

† This sentence has been often cited, and Dr. Francis, who was Lord Holland's chaplain, and indebted to his Lordship for valuable church preferment, was first fixed upon as Junius by Mr. Taylor. Why Anti-Fox, who

## LETTER CI.

### TO THE PRINTER OF THE PUBLIC ADVERTISER.

Sir,                                                      November 5, 1771.

Junius, I see, has got my Lord Mansfield upon the hip, and fairly driven the Scotch out of their discretion, and almost out of their senses. The change in the apparent position of their cheek bones is very remarkable. The complacent, insidious smile has universally given way to a ghastly grin of rancour and despair. Your correspondents *Anti-Junius* and *One of the Bail* actually foam at the mouth*. But calling *liar* and

It is likely was Junius, should notice the connection, seems curious. But it was doubtless intended for mystification, and to divert any suspicion that the author of the sharp reply to *Black Boy*, supposed to be Lord Holland's son, was in any way connected with his Lordship's family.—ED.

* The following are copies of the letters here alluded to, which certainly evince no small degree of acrimony :—

"TO THE PRINTER OF THE PUBLIC ADVERTISER.

"Nov. 4, 1771.

"Sir,—You have inserted, in your paper of Saturday last, a short but infamous paragraph, addressed to Lord Chief Justice Mansfield, and signed Junius, alleging that his Lordship had admitted to bail a man at the intercession of three of his countrymen, who Junius presumes is also a Scotchman.

"In justice to his Lordship (although without his consent, approbation, or knowledge), I hereby declare, that he did not know who were the bail for Mr. Eyre, nor did any of them ever make any prior application to his Lordship, nor were they personally acquainted with him, though 'tis probable his Lordship might have seen them on juries. I also declare that Mr. Eyre is not a Scotchman, but an Englishman ; and from what I can guess of Junius, he is worse than either, viz. an Irishman, a liar, and a jesuit.

"None of the three gentlemen who bailed Mr. Eyre ever saw him till the morning they went to Lord Mansfield's, at Cane Wood, to bail him. This they did purely to oblige an intimate friend who was connected with him by marriage, without any other motive whatsoever.

"Whether the noble Lord, whose very great abilities have brought upon him, though unjustly, the envy and malice of such assassins as Junius, was right or wrong, I leave to the learned in the law to defend ; and have no doubt his Lordship has acted in this matter according to his usual ability in law affairs, and rather with a view to enlarge than contract the liberty of the subject. At the same time, Mr. Printer, I should wish to be certain who this Mr. Junius is who stabs all good characters in the dark. My reason is, I should be glad of an opportunity of using such a lying, infamous, cowardly scoundrel as he ought to be ; for which purpose (if he chooses it) I have left my name with the printer.

"*One of the three who bailed Mr Eyre.*"

*scoundrel* is no answer to Junius. He did *not* assert that
the thief was a *Scotchman* \*; he only *presumed* it, from the
circumstance of his being bailed by three of that country. It
appears now that the thief was *closely connected* with Scotland.
These sweet-blooded children, even when they bail an *Englishman*, adhere to their principles. If the devil himself, connected as he is with an ancient nation, were taken up for
felony, I do not doubt that all Scotland, to a *mon*, would
readily be his security.

Junius did not blame the *bail* for interesting themselves in
favour of their friend, countryman, or associate. Yet he
might have done it with propriety. The thief was not
charged on *suspicion*, but taken in the fact. He was, *ipso
facto*, a felon, and to bail him required all the natural bene-

" TO JUNIUS.

"Nov. 4, 1771.

" You seem to delight most in traducing the most exalted and most respectable characters.

" You say, Lord Mansfield bailed Mr. Eyre at the *intercession* of three of
his countrymen.

" *I* say, that is *false ;* and that what he did was his duty to do as Lord
Chief Justice of England, and perfectly agreeable to law and to constant
practice.

" You *say*, that you presume Mr. Eyre is a *Scotchman*.

" *I* say, the culprit is an *Englishman*.

" You *say*, his bail were all *Scotchmen*,

" *I* say, they were. And how did that happen? Because a Scotchman is,
by marriage, unhappily allied to him. And why should it be deemed a reproach that they joined in doing a good-natured office at the request of a
countryman? Or that they contributed to alleviate the distress of an innocent woman, who, though unfortunately connected with the criminal, had not
a participation in his guilt? Dost not thou know, thou slanderer, that the
offence, though felony by law, was of the slightest kind? And wouldst thou
not, had that able and amiable judge (whose name will be an everlasting
honour to this country) refused to admit Mr. Eyre to bail, have traduced his
Lordship for that very refusal, and charged him with executing the law with
wanton rigour because *he was an Englishman?*

" Mr. Eyre *has* been brought to trial, and has pleaded guilty. *I* say, nevertheless, that the offence by the laws of England *is bailable ;* and I pledge
myself, before God and my country, to prove that Lord Chief Justice Mansfield acted in this matter agreeable to law, and that Junius has shown himself
in this, and many other instances, a *public incendiary* and a *liar*.

"ANTI-JUNIUS."

\* His words are, " At the intercession of three of your countrymen you
have bailed a man who, *I presume*, is also a Scotchman." See *Junius*, Letter 65.

volence of Scotland. Either he had no English friends, or they were ashamed to acknowledge any connection with him.

Instead of meeting Junius upon the strict question of law, these *loons* wander into circumstances of no moment, or defend Lord Mansfield by apocryphal assertions, which, if true, would be nothing to the purpose. One says that he has surrendered and taken his trial, the other that no intercession was made with Lord Mansfield—one says that the felony (for which the culprit is unluckily transported) was of the *slightest* kind, the other says that Eyre is an Englishman. Now the plain matter of fact is this: a thief taken in the fact is refused bail by the Lord Mayor of London; three *Scotchmen* take the said thief or felon before another *Scotchman*, who bails the said felon. The single question arising from the fact is, *was he or was he not bailable by law!* For my own part, until I hear good reasons to the contrary, I shall abide by Junius, because I am persuaded he would not hazard his credit so unnecessarily if he were not very sure of his law.

A. B.

---

## LETTER CII*.

November 13, 1771.

Sir,

I beg your Royal Highness's acceptance of my sincere compliments of congratulation upon your auspicious union with the daughter of Lord Irnham†, and the sister of Colonel

---

* Of this letter Junius writes, " Cumbriensis has taken greatly." Private Letter, No. 43.

† The marriage of the late Duke of Cumberland was first announced to the readers of the *Public Advertiser* in the following communication, obviously from the pen of Junius :—

" INTELLIGENCE EXTRAORDINARY, THOUGH TRUE.

" We can assure the public that his Royal Highness the Duke of Cumberland is happily married to Mrs. Horton, sister of Lieutenant-Colonel Luttrell, the worthy nominee of Middlesex. The new-married pair are now celebrating their nuptials in France, where the Duchess of Cumberland receives all the honours due to her high rank and new relation to the House of Brunswick. This match, we are informed, was negociated by a certain duke (Grafton), and his cream-coloured parasite (Bradshaw), by way of reward to

Luttrell.   For the present you will have so few of these compliments paid you, that mine, perhaps, may be thought worthy
your attention.   I do assure your Royal Highness, with great
sincerity, that, when I consider the various excellencies which
adorn or constitute your personal character—your natural
parts—your affable, benevolent, generous temper—your good
sense, so singularly improved by experience—and, above all
the rest, the uncommon education which your venerable
mother took care to give you—I do not think it possible to
have found a more suitable match for you than that which you
have so discreetly provided for yourself.   What you have
done, will, I am sure, be no disgrace to yourself or to any of
your relations.   Yet I must confess, partial as I am to you
for the sake of that good prince of whose resemblance you
carry some cutting traces about you, I could wish you did not
stand quite so near as you do to the regency and crown of
England.   God forbid I should ever hear your royal nephews
say, as Edward the Fifth does in the play, *But why to the
Tower, uncle!*—*Or why should you lock us up, aunt!*—I mean
their uncle Luttrell and aunt Horton.

   But, my good youth, let no considerations of this sort interrupt your pleasures.   Your amiable spouse is as much Duchess
of Cumberland as our gracious Queen is Queen of Great
Britain; and of course she is the *second* woman in the kingdom.
Your *papa* Irnham must at least take rank of Lord Mansfield;

Colonel Laurell. [*Vide* vol. i. p. 443.] It is now, happily for this country,
within the limits of possibility that a Luttrell may be king of Great Britain.   There was no court yesterday." [1]

---

[1] Henry, Duke of Cumberland, commemorated above, was one of the three
surviving brothers of George III.   His marriage with Mrs. Horton had been
privately solemnized, October the 4th, at her house in Hertford Street, May-
fair.   When the match was publicly announced the King forbad them the
court.   But the royal displeasure did not prevent the Duke of Gloucester, in
the ensuing spring, from avowing as his consort the Countess Dowager of
Waldegrave, whom he had privately married in April, 1766.   The marriages
gave rise to the Royal Marriage Act of 1772, which disqualified the descendants of George II. from contracting marriage without the previous consent of
the Crown, unless above twenty-five years of age, and then not without
twelve months' prior notice to the Privy Council, and the implied consent of
both houses of Parliament.   These restrictions were rigorously but in-
effectually opposed in Parliament.—ED.

your brother Henry of the Princes of Mecklenburg; and your sister Miss Luttrell of Madam Swellenburgh. As to the King's not acknowledging the Duchess, or forbidding her the court, it signifies nothing. Her marriage is good in law, and her children will be legitimate. She may order plays, keep a court of her own, and set the Princess Dowager at defiance. But you need have no fear of being ill used. Your brother Harry has a dagger at the throat of a certain person, and swears he will let the cat out of the bag about the Middlesex election. So far from offending Harry, I should not wonder to see him *aide-de-camp* to the King, and, in a little time, commander-in-chief.

Whenever you want a divorce, you need only leave your spouse alone for an hour or two with *** ******.* When he performed the office of father to *Poll Davis*, and gave her to his infatuated friend, he contrived to send the young man upon a fool's errand, and that very night consummated with her himself. You, I know, Sir, will never go upon a fool's errand, and I suppose it may be equally certain that your papa, if he had an opportunity, would not ****** ** ** **†.

CUMBRIENSIS‡.

## LETTER CIII.

### TO THE PRINTER OF THE PUBLIC ADVERTISER.

Sir, November 19, 1771.

I HAVE great faith in Junius, and wish the friends of the cause would leave Lord Mansfield entirely to *his* care§. It is not fair to anticipate his arguments, or to run down the game which *he* has started. Junius, I dare say, has it as much at heart to sacrifice Mansfield, with his own pen, as Achilles had

* Doubtless Lord Irnham, afterwards Earl of Carhampton, of whom see Junius's note, vol. l. p. 443.—ED.

† The omitted words are probably, "commit incest."

‡ This letter is indirectly acknowledged by Junius in his private correspondence, No. 43.

§ A great number of letters appeared in support of the doctrine maintained by Junius on the subject of the bailment of Eyre. But the authors could not have been lawyers any more than Junius. The question is settled on high authority, in the Inquiry into the Authorship of Junius.—ED.

to prevent any other of the Grecian army from killing Hector. The passage I allude to is one of the finest in the Iliad.

> " Λαῶων δ' ἀνίνη ααρήστι δἴος 'Αχιλλεὺς
> Οὐδ' Ἰια Ἰμαναι ἐπὶ Ἕκτορι πικρα βέλεμνα·
> Μένη αὐδος ἄρωτο βαλὼν, ὁ δὲ δεύτερος Τιδὺς."
>
> 22 B. line 205.
>
> Divine Achilles, lest some Greek's advance
> Should snatch the glory from his lifted lance,
> Signed to the troops to yield his foe the way,
> And leave untouched the honours of the day.—POPE.

Yours,

ANTI-BELIAL*.

---

## LETTER CIV.

### TO THE PRINTER OF THE PUBLIC ADVERTISER.

SIR,                                                December 4, 1771.

Your ingenious correspondent, *Anti-Junius*, has too much wit and taste to be easily satisfied. It is really a misfortune to be born with such exquisitely fine feelings. If, now that he is well fed and clothed, he cannot endure the severity of a southern breeze, what would become of him upon his native mountains? Junius can never write to please him. If he receives the least mention of *past enormities*, what is it but *"cold scraps, baked meats, political fiddling,* and the *voice of the charmer!"* hashed mutton, and *Dutch music* with a vengeance! If, on the contrary, he lays any new villanies before the public, then, one and all, the hungry pack open upon him at once: *"Here's invention for you!—What an abominable liar!—Why does he not stick to his facts! Does he think us such idiots as to swallow wit for truth!"* In short, Sir, the Scotch have strange qualmish stomachs; it is not in the art of cookery to please them. Nothing will go down but oatmeal and brimstone.

*Anti-Junius* is not so explicit as I could wish. 1. What intercourse was that between Lord Irnham and his daughter,

---

\* The letters of Anti-Belial, and the next, from Juniper, are doubtless from the varied and prolific pen of Junius. They are minor Philo-Juniuses, to explain, defend, and support the reputation of the principal.—ED.

which he says has been *so long interrupted?* I mean no offence to the lady, but really the word *intercourse* is a little equivocal. 2. What was *that purpose* for which Sir James Lowther's grant was obtained, and which, *Anti-Junius* says, has been long since defeated? 3. Who does he mean by *a man ever burthensome to every administration?* I hope he does not mean the Duke of Grafton's friend, Sir James Lowther, or at least that he does not give the Baronet this pretty character by order of the Duke of Grafton.

After all, I really think that Junius, called upon as he is by so able an antagonist, cannot do less than discover himself. He must be woefully given to suspicion, if he has the least doubt of the tender mercy of the Scotch, or of the forgiving piety of St. James's.

JUNIPER *.

* The following are the passages in *Anti-Junius's* answer to Junius, Letter 67, to which a reply is more particularly given in the above :—

" Had Junius a single friend in the world whom he dared trust or consult, his performance of yesterday, so uninstructive to your readers, so fatal to his reputation, would surely have never found its way to the press. His invective has neither novelty nor variety to recommend it; the public palate must nauseate at the insipidity of his repeated abuse, and loathe the repast which his miserable thrift has attemoted to furnish forth from the cold scraps and baked meats of his former scurrilous entertainments. In vain does this political fiddler labour for the public attention, by thrumming the worn-out strings of Middlesex election, Whittlebury timber, Hine's patent, and the long-forgotten rule made absolute against Mr. Vaughan. The voice of the charmer himself can no longer charm with these sounds; these chords so repeatedly struck fall flat, even upon the ear of envy itself.

* * * *

" With the recriminating malice of antiquated virginity, he endeavours to sully the daughter's innocence with the father's crimes, suppressing a well-known circumstance, viz. that all intercourse between that father and that daughter has long been interrupted.

* * * *

" Sir James Lowther's nonsuit is in the eye of the heaven-reading Junius another visible operation of retribution, not on the King, indeed—he does not seem to be affected by it, any farther than as it has introduced the parenthesis of the Luttrell alliance—but on the poor Duke of Grafton, whose days are anxious, and whose nights are sleepless, because a grant, obtained to serve a purpose long since defeated, and to gratify the importunities of a man ever burthensome to every administration, is adjudged invalid. For this the Duke of Grafton wears the dismal countenance of solitary sorrow ; for this does he fruitlessly look round for consolations ; for this does Mr. Bradshaw shed the April showers of lambent lamentation. Surely Junius thinks to mislead rea-

## LETTER CV.

### VETERAN TO LORD BARRINGTON.

MY LORD,                                        January 28, 1772.

IT is unlucky for the army that you should be so thoroughly con
vinced as you are how extremely low you stand in their opinion.
The consciousness that you are despised and detested by every
individual in it, from the drummer (whose discipline might be
of service to you) to the general officer, makes you desperate
about your conduct and character. You think that you are
arrived at a state of security, and that, being plunged to the
very heels in infamy, the dipping has made you invulnerable.
There is no other way to account for your late frantic resolution of appointing *Tony Shammy* your deputy-secretary at war.
Yet I am far from meaning to impeach his character as a
broker. In that line he was qualified to get forward by his
industry, birth, education, and accomplishments. I make no
sort of doubt of his cutting a mighty pretty figure at Jonathan's.
To this hour among bulls and bears his name is mentioned with
respect. Every Israelite in the alley is in raptures. *What, our
old friend, little Shammy!—Ay, he was always a tight, active
little fellow, and would wrangle for an eighth as if he had been
born in Jerusalem. Who'd ha' thought it! Well, we may now
look out for the rebuilding of the temple.* My Lord, if I remember right, you are partial to the spawn of Jonathan's.
Witness the care you took to provide for Mr. Delafon-
taine in the military department. He limped a little when
he left the alley *, but your Lordship soon set him upon his
legs again. This last resolution, however, approaches to mad-

son, and annihilate common-sense, by the use of a few ridiculous half-
meaning epithets.
                    *          *          *          *

"If you are really the honest state-gardener you would be thought, and
not the malicious discontented impostor I think you, away with your shuffling well-worded delays. The noisome plant that has brought forth such
bitter fruit is surely now ripe enough to be plucked."
    * The transactions here referred to in respect to Delafontaine and Chamier,
or Shammy, as he was called in the alley, are more particularly noticed in
the Private Letters, Nos. 52 and 56. Chamier was successor in the War
Office to Mr. D'Oyly, who was discarded to make room for him.

ness.  Your cream-coloured Mercury * has over-reached both
you and himself; and remember what I seriously tell you, this
measure will, sooner or later, be the cause, not of your disgrace (that affair's settled), but of your ruin.  What dæmon
possessed you to place a little gambling broker at the head of
the War Office, and in a post of so much rank and confidence
as that of deputy to the Secretary at War?  (I speak of your
office, not of your person.)  Do you think that his having been
useful in certain practices to Lord Sandwich gives any great
relief to his character, or raises him in point of rank?  My
Lord, the rest of the world laugh at your choice; but we
soldiers feel it as an indignity to the whole army, and be
assured we shall resent it accordingly.  Not that I think you
pay much regard to the sensations of anything under the degree of a general officer, and even that rank you have publicly
stigmatized in the most opprobrious terms.  Yet still some of
them, though in your wise opinion not qualified to command,
are entitled to respect.  Let us suppose a case, which every
man acquainted with the War Office will admit to be very probable.  Suppose a lieutenant-general, who perhaps may be a peer,
or a member of the House of Commons, does you the honour
to wait upon you for instructions relative to his regiment.
After explaining yourself to him with your usual accuracy and
decision, you naturally refer him to your deputy for the detail
of the business.  *My dear General, I'm prodigiously hurried.
But do me the favour to go to Mr. Shammy ; go to little
Waddlewell; go to my duckling; go to little three per cents
reduced; you'll find him a mere scrip of a secretary; an
OMNIUM of all that's genteel; the activity of a broker ; the
politeness of a hair-dresser; the— the— the— &c.*

Our general officer, we may presume, being curious to see
this wonderful Girgashite, the following dialogue passes between them:—

*Lieut.-Gen.*  Sir, the Secretary at War refers me to you for
an account of what was done—

*Waddlewell.*  Done, Sir!  Closed at three-eighths!  Looked
flat, I must own; but to-morrow, my dear Sir, I hope to see
a more lively appearance.

* T. Bradshaw, whose absurd elevation has been already noticed, and will
occasionally be found observed upon again.

*Lieut.-Gen.*    Sir, I speak of the non-effective fund.

*Waddlewell.*    Fund, my dear Sir!  In what fund would you
wish to be concerned?  Speak freely: you may confide in your
humble servant—I'm all discretion.

*Lieut.-Gen.*    Sir, I really don't understand you.  Lord Barrington says that my regiment may possibly be thought of for
India—

*Waddlewell.*    India, my dear Sir!  Strange fluctuation!
from fourteen and an half to twenty-two—never stood a moment, but ended cheerful: no mortal can account for it!

*Lieut.-Gen.*    Damn your stocks, Sir!  Tell me whether the
commission—

*Waddlewell.*    As for commission, my dear Sir, I'll venture
to say that no gentleman in the alley does business upon easier
terms.  I never take less than an eighth, except from Lord
Sandwich and my brother-in-law; but they deal largely, and
you must be sensible, my dear Sir, that when the commission
is extensive, it may be worth a broker's while to content himself with a sixteenth.

The general officer, at last, fatigued with such extravagance,
quits the room in disgust, and leaves the intoxicated broker to
settle his accounts by himself.

After such a scene as this, do you think that any man of
rank or consequence in the army will ever apply to you or your
deputy again?  Will any officer of rank condescend to receive
orders from a little whiffling broker, to whom he may formerly,
perhaps, have given half-a-crown for negociating an hundred
pound stock, or sixpence for a lottery ticket?  My Lord, without a jest, it is indecent—it is odious—it is preposterous.
Our gracious master, it is said, reads the newspapers.  If he
does, he shall know minutely in what manner you treat his
faithful army.  This is the first of sixteen letters addressed to
your Lordship, which are ready for the press, and shall appear
as fast as it suits the printer's convenience

                                                    VETERAN.

## LETTER CVI.

SIR,                                                February 6, 1772.

THERE is one general, easy way of answering Junius, which his
opponents have constantly had recourse to since he first began
to write, or they to answer him. They either misquote his
words and misstate his propositions, or they laboriously employ themselves in refuting doctrines which he has not maintained, or maintaining others which he has not disputed *.
This has been particularly their practice in all the argument
about the bailment of Eyre.

1st. Junius has never affirmed that the judges of the Court
of King's Bench were named, or specially comprehended, in
the statute of Westminster, or any other of the old statutes
preceding the *Habeas Corpus* Act. The design of those quotations was to prove the meaning and intention of the legislature
with respect to the right of bailing a person under the circumstances of Mr. Eyre. This meaning and intention, once
clearly proved, he affirms, is the direction and land-mark to
the judge in the exercise of that discretionary power which
the law has left with him.

2nd. Junius has not denied that the judges of the Court of
King's Bench have a discretionary power to bail in all cases,
*according to the circumstances of the cases.* But does it follow
that they may legally bail when *no circumstances whatsoever*
are alleged on one side to alleviate the force of the positive
charge of *felony* made on the other? If it does, their power
of bailing is *arbitrary,* not *discretionary.* Discretion implies
consideration; but if no allegations whatsoever be made in
behalf of the prisoner, they have then nothing to consider.
The warrant of commitment expresses a positive charge of
felony. If nothing be alleged in behalf of the prisoner, the
judge has then no subject whereupon to exercise his discretion.
He has no choice: he *must* remand the prisoner.

---

* This letter is more particularly designed as a reply to a very long and
elaborate one published the preceding day in the *Public Advertiser*, and addressed—Justinius to Junius. It is certainly well written, but unquestionably labours under the defects here complained of.

3rd. Junius does not insist upon the case of Eyre so much on the score of its own enormity, as because it establishes a dangerous doctrine, applicable to all crimes, however indisputably proved, and gives the judges an *arbitrary* power which the laws never meant to give them. As for Lord Mansfield, it is probable that Junius would not have attacked him in the manner he has done if this had been the only instance of his misconduct. In truth, it is one out of a multitude.

I beg leave to conclude with asking this wicked judge two plain questions :—1. Is there, or is there not, any difference between offences *bailable* and offences *not bailable?* and if there be, what is it? 2. When the legislature, in the *Habeas Corpus* Act, do specially, and by name, forbid the judges of the Court of King's Bench to proceed to the bailment of the prisoner, if it shall appear to them that he is committed for such matters or offences *for the which by the law the prisoner is not bailable*, have they any meaning, or have they none at all? Let it be remembered that Junius never pretends to be a better lawyer than Lord Mansfield. On the contrary, he takes every opportunity to acknowledge the superior learning and abilities of that wicked judge; and in the present instance particularly insists, not that he was ignorant of the law, but that he sinned against his own certain knowledge and conviction.

ANTI-BELIAL *.

## LETTER CVII.

### VETERAN TO LORD BARRINGTON, NO. II.

My Lord,                                         February 17, 1772.

In my last letter I only meant to be jocular. An essay so replete with good humour could not possibly give offence. You are no enemy to a jest, or at least you would be thought callous to reproach. You profess a most stoical indifference about the

---

* The points in this explanatory letter are admirably put—neatly, forcibly, and unequivocally. It is a dexterous effort of Junius to escape from the false position into which he had fallen in denying the power of the Chief Justice to bail Eyre. I suspect Anti-Belial has escaped the notice of Lord Campbell; and I doubt whether the present successor of Lord Mansfield would find it easy to answer the first question of Junius in the concluding paragraph.—Ed.

opinion of the world, and above all things make it your boast
that you can set the newspapers at defiance. No man, indeed,
has received a greater share of correction in this way, or profited less by it, than your Lordship. But we know yon better.
You have one defect less than you pretend to. You are not
insensible of the scorn and hatred of the world, though you
take no care to avoid it. When the bloody Barrington, that
silken fawning courtier at St. James's—that stern and insolent minister at the War Office—is pointed out to universal
contempt and detestation, you smile indeed, but the last ago-
nies of the hysteric passion are painted in your countenance.
Your cheek betrays what passes within you, and your whole
frame is in convulsions. I now mean to be serious with you,
but not to waste my time in proving that you are an enemy to
the laws and liberties of this country. The very name of Barrington implies everything that is mean, cruel, false, and contemptible. The Duke of Newcastle's livery was the first habit
you put on. What an indefatigable courtier at his levee!
What an assiduous parasite at his table! Was there a dirty
job to be performed—*away went Barrington*. Was a message
to be carried—*Who waits there? My Lord Barrington*. After
ruining that brave and worthy man, General Fowke *, under
the auspices of the Duke of Newcastle, who saved you from
destruction, you deserted to Mr. Pitt the moment he came
into power. Before the late king's death you secured a footing
at Carlton House; and were prepared to abandon your last
patron the moment Lord Bute assumed the reins of government. From Lord Bute to Mr. Grenville there was an easy
transfer of your affections. You are the common friend of all
ministers, but it is not in your policy to engage in overt acts
of hostility against those who may, perhaps, be next in turn to
patronise Lord Barrington. *My dear Lord*, or *my dear Sir*,
are titles with which you have occasionally addressed every man

---

* General Fowke, who was then stationed at Gibraltar, received Instructions in several letters from Lord Barrington, shortly after his appointment
to be Secretary at War, in 1760, under the Duke of Newcastle's administration, which produced measures that had nearly effected the loss of that
important post. Lord Barrington, on perceiving the blunder he had committed, most ungenerously prevailed on General Fowke to take the chief
blame upon himself, under a promise of indemnification. The result was,
that Fowke was ruined, and Barrington liberated.

who ever had an office, or the chance of an office, in this kingdom. Even the proscribed John Wilkes, the moment he was
sheriff, had a claim upon your politeness. Your character was
a little battered by the frequency of your political amours, when
Lord Rockingham took you into keeping. While you existed
by *his* protection, you intrigued with the Duke of Grafton.
Another change succeeded. Your mind was open to new lights,
and, *without a doubt, Lord Chatham was the only man in the
kingdom fit to govern a great empire.* Still, however, your
opinions of men and things were not perfectly settled. When
the Duke of Grafton took the lead, the pliant Barrington, of
course, saw things in a different point of view. There is nothing in your attachments that savours of obstinacy. When
his Grace resigned, you soon discovered that to establish government upon a solid footing, the minister's presence was
indispensable in the House of Commons. Lord North was
then the man after your Lordship's own heart. In *your* ideas
the First Lord of the Treasury for the time being is always
perfect—*but every change is for the better.* With all your
professions of attachment to this temporary minister, I tell
him, and I tell the public, that at this very hour you are cabal-
ling with the Duke of Grafton and the Bedfords to obtain the
recall of Lord Townshend, and to drive Lord North from the
Treasury. But they all know you. In the inventory of the
discarded minister's effects, Lord Barrington is always set
down as a fixture.

By garbling and new modelling the War Office, you think
you have reduced the army to subjection. *Walk in, gentlemen!
Business done by Chamier and Co.* To make your office complete, you want nothing now but a paper lanthorn at the door,
and the scheme of a lottery pasted upon the window. With
all your folly and obstinacy, I am at a loss to conceive what
countenance you assumed when you told your royal master that
you had taken a little Frenchified broker from 'Change Alley,
to intrust with the management of all the affairs of his army.
Did the following dialogue leave no impression upon your dis-
ordered imagination?—You know where it passed.

*K.* Pray, my Lord, whom have you appointed to succeed
Mr. D'Oyly?

*B.* Please your M—, I believe I have made a choice that
will be highly acceptable to the public and to the army.

*K.* Who is it?

*B.* Sire, it s'appelle Ragosin. Born and educated in 'Change Alley, he glories in the name of broker; and, to say nothing of Lord Sandwich's friendship, I can assure your M— he has always kept the best company at Jonathan's.

*K.* My Lord, I never interfere in these matters; but I cannot help telling your Lordship, that you might have consulted my honour and the credit of my army a little better. Your appointment of so mean a person, though he may be a very honest man in the mystery he was bred to, casts a reflection upon *me*, and is an insult to the army. At all events, I desire it may be understood, that I have no concern in this ill-judged, indecent measure, and that I do not approve of it.

I suppose, my Lord, you thought this conversation might be sunk upon the public. It does honour to his Majesty, and therefore you concealed it. In my next I propose to show what a faithful friend you have been to the army, particularly to old worn-out officers.

VETERAN.

## LETTER CVIII.

VETERAN TO LORD BARRINGTON, NO. III.

MY LORD,                              February 27, 1772.

THE army now, according to your own account of the matter, is under a very creditable sort of direction. If we may rely upon the Secretary at War's opinion, solemnly and deliberately expressed before the House of Commons, there is not a single man in the profession who is in any shape qualified for commander-in-chief, at least none whom you would think it safe to recommend to his Majesty. If your judgment upon this subject had been better founded than it is, I do not understand that a Secretary at War has any right to pass so disgraceful and precipitate a sentence upon so many of his superiors. Believe me, my good Lord, there is not one of those officers whom you dared to stigmatize in that infamous manner who is not qualified to be your master in the art military, notwithstanding all the experience you got in St.

George's Fields\*, when you urged and exhorted the guards to
imbrue their hands in the blood of their fellow-subjects.
While that bloody scene was acting, where was the gentle
Barrington? Was he sighing at the feet of antiquated beauty?
Was he dreaming over the loo-table, or was he more innocently
employed in combing her Ladyship's lap-dog? But, my Lord,
when you paid that pretty compliment to the body of general
officers, had you no particular apologies to make to General
Conway, to Lord Albemarle, or to Sir Jeffery Amherst? Did
General Harvey deserve nothing better of you than a ridiculous
nickname, which, like Lord Mansfield's secret, he must carry
with him to his grave? In lieu of a commander-in-chief, you
have advised the King to put the army into commission. *A
graduate in physic, an old woman, and a broker from 'Change
Alley.* The doctor prescribes, the old gentlewoman ad-
ministers, and little *Syringe,* the apothecary, stands by the
glisterpipe. This, you tell the King, is making himself commander-in-chief, and the surest way to preserve the affections
of the army. It may be so, my Lord, but I see no right you
had to give the nickname of *Doctor Radcliffe* to so brave a
man as General Harvey. Though his natural sweetness of
temper may induce him to pass it by, it must always be mortifying to a brave adjutant-general, when he marches into St.
James's Coffee-House, to hear the ensigns of the guards
whisper to one another, *here comes the Doctor;* or when he
marches out, *there goes the Doctor.* I dare say he has furnished
work enough for the surgeons, but, until you so politely
pointed it out, I cannot say I ever saw anything medical in
his appearance.

After treating the most powerful people in the army with
so much unprovoked insolence, it is not to be supposed that
field officers, captains, and subalterns have any chance of
common justice at your hands. But that matter shall be the
the subject of another letter, and every letter shall be concluded with a conversation piece. The following dialogue is
not imaginary:—

SCENE—WAR OFFICE.

*Enter* Barrington, *meeting* Waddlewell.

*B.* My dear friend, you look charmingly this morning.

---

\* Alluding to the suppression of the riots, for which see *ante,* p. 183.

*W.* My dearest Lord—the sight of your Lordship— *Here they embrace, Waddlewell's thoughts being too big for utterance.*

*B.* When did you see my *Pylades,* our dear *Bradshaw?*

*W.* Ay, my Lord, there is a friend indeed—firmness without resistance, sincerity without contradiction, and the milky way painted in his countenance. If I could ever reconcile my mind to the distracting prospect of losing your Lordship, where else should we look for a successor! But that event, I hope, is at a great distance. *Late, very late, Oh may he rule us!*

*B.* Ay, my dearest Waddlewell, but we are sadly abused, notwithstanding all our virtues.

*W.* Merit, my dear Lord, merit will for ever excite enmity. I found it so in the alley. I never made a lucky hit in my life, that it did not set all Jonathan's in an uproar. If an *idea* succeeded, my best friends turned against me. Judas and Levi, Moses and Issachar—people with whom I have been connected by the tenderest ties—could not endure the sight of my prosperity. The ten tribes of Israel united to destroy me, and for two years together were malicious enough to call me *the lucky little Benjamin.* Friendship, among the best of men, is little better than a name.

*B.* Why, my dear deputy, it is not that I regard the contempt and hatred of all mankind.—I never knew it otherwise. No man's patience has been better exercised. But what if the King should hear of it?

*W.* Ay, there's the rub!

*B.* If the best of princes, who pretends to be his own commander-in-chief, should hear that the name of Barrington is opprobrious in the army—that even he himself is not spared for supporting me—

*W.* (*weeping*)—Oh, fatal day!—Compared with this, what is a *viscounter!* Alas, my dearest Lord, you have unmanned your deputy. I feel myself already at ten per cent. discount, and never shall be at par again.

*B.* Something must be done. Let us consider.

*W.* Ay, my dear Lord, for heaven's sake let us speculate.

*Exeunt disputing about precedence.*

VETERAN.

## LETTER CIX.

MY LORD,                                    March 10, 1772.

I AM at a loss for words to express my acknowledgment of the
signal honour you have done me.   One of the principal purposes of these addresses was to engage you in a regular public
correspondence.   You very justly thought it unnecessary to
sign your name to this last elegant performance.   *Novalis**
answers as well as Barrington.   We know you by your style.
This is not the first of your epistles that has been submitted
to the criticism of the public.   While yet, like poor *Waddlewell*, you were young in office, your letters to General Fowke
were considered as the standard of perspicuity†.   You are
now *very old* in office, and continue to write exactly as you
did in your infancy.   I do not wonder that the extremes of
your capacity should meet in the same point, but I should be
glad to know at what period you reckoned yourself in the
prime and vigour of your official understanding.   Was it when
you signified to the third regiment of guards his Majesty's
gratitude and your own for their alacrity in butchering their
innocent fellow-subjects in St. George's Fields‡?   Was it
when you informed the House of Commons that *you* and the
*doctor* were equivalent to a commander-in-chief?   Or when
you declared that there was not a man in the army fit
to be trusted with the command of it?   Or when you established that wise and humane regulation, that no officer, let his
age and infirmities be ever so great, and his services ever so
distinguished, should be suffered to sell out unless he had
bought all his former commissions?   Or, in short, was it when
you dived into *Jonathan's* for a deputy, and plucked up
*Waddlewell* by the locks?   When you answer these questions,
I shall be ready to meet your Lordship upon that ground on

---

* The name subscribed by a writer who undertook the defence of Lord
Barrington, and whom our author, according to his usual custom, here identifies with the noble Earl.

† See note to Letter 107, *ante*, p. 397.

‡ See note to Miscellaneous Letter, No. 24, *ante*, p. 182, in which the
letter here alluded to is inserted.

which you think you stand the firmest.  In the meantime, give me leave to say a few words to *Novalis*.

You are pleased to observe that my three first letters are filled with low scurrility upon hackneyed topics collected from the newspapers.  Have a little patience, my dear Lord; I shall soon come to closer quarters with you.  As for those dialogues, which you are pleased to say have neither wit nor humour in them, I can only observe that there are many scenes which pass off tolerably well upon the stage, and yet will not bear the examination of the closet.  You and *Waddlewell* are excellent performers.  Between a courtier and a broker *words* are the smallest part of the conversation; shrugs and smiles, bows and grimaces, the condescension of St. James's, and the pliant politeness of 'Change Alley, stand in the place of repartee, and fill up the scene.

You intimate, without daring directly to assert, that *you did not fix* that odious stigma upon the body of general officers.  Have you forgot the time when you attempted the same evasion in the House of Commons, and forced General Howard to rise and say he was ashamed of you?  These mean, dirty, pitiful tricks are fitter for Jonathan's than the War Office.

*You have more experience than any of your clerks, and your great abilities are acknowledged on all sides.*  As for your experience, we all know how much your conduct has been improved by it.  But pray who informed you of this *universal acknowledgment* of your abilities?  The sycophants whose company you delight in are likely enough to fill you with these flattering ideas.  But if you were wise enough to consult the good opinion of the world, you would not be so eager to establish the credit of your understanding.  The moment you arrive at the character of a man of sense you are undone.  You must then relinquish the only tolerable excuse that can be made for your conduct.  It is really unkind of you to distress the few friends you have left.

To your Lordship's zeal to discover and patronise *latent* merit, the public is indebted for the services of Mr. Bradshaw.  Pray, my Lord. will you be so good as to explain to us, of what nature were those services which he first rendered to your Lordship?  Was he winged like a messenger, or stationary like a sentinel?

" Like Maia's son he stood
And shook his plumes ;"

*videlicet*, at the door of Lady ——n's cabinet. His zeal in
the execution of this honourable office promoted him to another door, where he also stands sentry,

" Virgáque levem coercet
Aureâ turbam."

That he has ably served the state, may be collected from the
public acknowledgments the ministry have made him. Fifteen
hundred pounds a year, well secured to himself and his family,
will acquit the King of any ingratitude to Mr. Bradshaw. It
is by mere accident that Sir Edward Hawke and Sir Jeffery
Amherst are no better provided for.

But we are indebted to your Lordship for another discovery
of merit equally latent with Mr. Bradshaw's. You have a
phœnix of a deputy, though yet he is but young in his nest.
He has hardly had time to clear his wings from the ashes that
gave him birth. This, too, was your Lordship's apology for
ruining General Fowke. You gave it in evidence that you
had been but four months in office, and now you tell us that
your deputy also is in the same unfledged state of noviciate;
though for abilities and knowledge of the world, neither *Jew*
nor *Gentile* can come up to him! For shame, my Lord Barrington ; send this whiffling broker back to the mystery he was
bred in. Though an infant in the War Office, the man is too
old to learn a new trade. At this very moment they are calling out for him at the bar of Jonathan's—Shammy! Shammy!
Shammy! The house of *Israel* are waiting to settle their
last account with him. During his absence things may take
a desperate turn in the alley, and you never may be able to
make up to the man what he has lost in half-crowns and six-
pences already.

                                        VETERAN.

## LETTER CX.

VETERAN TO THE PUBLIC ADVERTISER.

SIR, March 23, 1772.

I DESIRE you will inform the public that the worthy Lord Barrington, not contented with having driven Mr. D'Oyly out of the War Office, has at last contrived to expel Mr. Francis*. His Lordship will never rest till he has cleared his office of every gentleman who can either be serviceable to the public or whose honour and integrity are a check upon his own dark proceedings. Men who do their duty with credit and ability are not proper instruments for Lord Barrington to work with. He must have a broker from 'Change Alley for his deputy, and some raw, ignorant boy for his first clerk. I think the public have a right to call upon Mr. D'Oyly and Mr. Francis to declare their reasons for quitting the War Office. Men of their unblemished character do not resign lucrative employments without some sufficient reasons. The conduct of these gentlemen has always been approved of, and I know that they stand as well in the esteem of the army as any persons in their station ever did. What then can be the cause that the public and the army should be deprived of their service? There must certainly be something about Lord Barrington which every honest man dreads and detests. Or is it that they cannot be brought to connive at his jobs and underhand dealings? They have too much honour, I suppose, to do some certain business by commission. They have not been educated in the conversation of Jews and gamblers; they have had no experience at Jonathan's; they know nothing of the stocks; and therefore Lord Barrington drives them out of the War Office. The army indeed is come to a fine pass, with a gambling broker at the head of it! What signifies ability, or integrity, or practice, or experience in business? Lord Barrington feels himself uneasy while men with such qualifications are about him. He wants nothing in his office but ignorance, impudence, pertness, and servility. Of these com-

---

* Francis, afterwards Sir Philip, and D'Oyly, were chief clerks in the War Office. The displacement of D'Oyly to make room for Chamier has been already noticed in Letter 105.

modities he has laid in a plentiful stock, that ought to last
him as long as he is Secretary at War. Again, I wish that
Mr. Francis and Mr. D'Oyly would give the public some account of what is going forward in the War Office. I think
these events so remarkable, that some notice ought to be
taken of them in the House of Commons. When the public
loses the service of two able and honest servants, it is but
reasonable that the wretch who drives such men out of a public office should be compelled to give some account of himself
and his proceedings.

VETERAN.

---

## LETTER CXI.

### SCOTUS TO LORD BARRINGTON *.

MY LORD,                                               May 4, 1772.
I AM a Scotchman, and can assure your Lordship that I do
not esteem my country, or the natives of it, the less because
we are not so happy as to be honoured with Lord Barrington's
favourable opinion. From a pamphlet, which lately fell in
my way, I perceive that there is something in the temper of
the Scots that does not suit the manly, sterling virtue which
distinguishes your own worthy character. We are too insolent to those beneath us, and too obsequious to our superiors;
and with such a disposition must never hope to find favour
with Lord Barrington!  "And Cockburne, *like most of his
countrymen*, is as abject to those above him as he is insolent
to those below him." These are your words, given under
your hand, as the solemn, deliberate opinion of his Majesty's
Secretary at War. Such a censure, coming from a man of
honour, good sense, or integrity, might, perhaps, have some
weight with the thoughtless or uncandid. But when it comes
from a man whose whole life has been employed in acting the
part of a false, cringing, fawning, time-serving courtier—from
a man who never had a different opinion from the minister for
the time being, and who has always contrived to keep some lucrative place or other under twenty different administrations,

---

* The original copy of this letter is still in the hands of Mr. H. D. Woodfall, the printer of the present edition.

—I am not so much offended at the reproach itself, which you
have thought proper to throw upon the Scots, as I am shocked
at the unparalleled impudence of applying your own individual character to a whole nation. It seems my countrymen
*are abject to those above them.* Pray, my good Lord, by what
system of conduct have you recommended yourself to every
succeeding minister for these last twenty years? Was it by
maintaining your opinion upon all occasions, with a blunt,
firm integrity, or was it by the basest and vilest servility to
every creature that had power to do you either good or evil?
*But we are insolent to those below us.* Indeed, my Lord, you
paint from your own heart. There is courage at least in *our*
composition. It is the coward who fawns upon those above
him. It is the coward that is insolent, wherever he dares
be so. You have had some *lessons* which have made you more
cautious than you used to be. You have reason to remember
that modest humble merit will not always bear to be insulted
by an upstart in office. For the future, my little Lord, be more
sparing of your reflections upon the Scots. We pay no regard
to the calumny of anonymous writers, and despise the malignity of John Wilkes. But when a man, so high in office as
you are, pretends to give an odious character of a whole nation,
and sets his name to it, we should deserve the reproach, if we
did not resent it. You are so detested and despised by all
parties (because all parties know you), that England, Scotland,
and Ireland have but one wish concerning you, and that is,
that as you have shown yourself a fawning traitor to every
party and person with which you ever were connected, so all
parties may unite in loading you with infamy and contempt.

SCOTUS*.

## LETTER CXII.

TO THE LORDS OF THE ADMIRALTY.

My Lords,                                    May 6, 1772.
Having seen in last Saturday's paper that Mr. Bradshaw was
appointed to be a member of your board, give me leave to con-

* It is almost needless to add that Scotus is Junius. His letter is referred
to in a private note, *ante*, p. 59.—Ed.

gratulate your Lordships on the event, as a person of Mr. Bradshaw's birth and talents may be of the greatest use to you on many occasious, besides adding infinitely more weight and dignity to the board; I was therefore a good deal surprised at the simple manner in which his *well-merited* promotion was announced to the public, but must attribute it either to *his own modesty*, or the printer's ignorance: but, whatever be the cause I think it necessary to acquaint you, his brother Lords, with a little of his history.

It is needless to trouble your Lordships with an account of his birth or education, as the first might be a very difficult task, and the latter your Lordships may see has not been neglected. His first appearance in the *great world* was as one of Lord Barrington's domestics, from whence he moved to Ireland, set up a shop, and under the influence of a happy planet returned to England, where, by means of his uncommon address in administering to the *pleasures of the great*, he was appointed one of the secretaries to the Treasury, which office he held during the Duke of Grafton's administration, and by exerting his happy talents between his Grace and the celebrated Nancy Parsons, he so far ingratiated himself with the Duke, that he became his chief confident, and was privy to the whole of his *generous treatment* of that young lady, and of course became his Grace's *bosom friend*; for which service he first received a pension of *fifteen hundred pounds a year for three lives*, and, that not being sufficient, is now made *one of you*. I cannot avoid again congratulating you on the acquisition of such *a brother member*, as it is to be hoped he will assist any of your Lordships with his good offices upon all occasions.

I have the honour to be,
My Lords,
Your Lordships' most humble
And obedient servant,

Pall-Mall.                                    ARTHUR TELL-TRUTH.

## LETTER CXIII.

### NEMESIS TO THE PUBLIC ADVERTISER*.

SIR,                                    May 12, 1772.

I AM just returned from a visit in a certain part of Berkshire, near which I found Lord Barrington had spent his Easter holidays. His Lordship, I presume, went into the country to indulge his grief; for whatever company he happened to be in, it seems his discourse turned entirely upon the hardship and difficulty of his situation. The impression which he would be glad to give of himself is, that of an old faithful servant of the crown, who on one side is abused and vilified for his great zeal in support of government, and at the same time gets no thanks or reward from the King or the administration. He is modest enough to affirm in all companies, that *his* services are unrewarded; that *he* bears the burthen; that other people engross the profits; and that *he* gets nothing. Those who know but little of his history may, perhaps, be inclined to pity him: but he and I have been old acquaintance, and, considering the size of his understanding, I believe I shall be able to prove, that no man in the kingdom ever sold himself and his services to better advantage than Lord Barrington. Let us take a short review of him from his political birth.

On his entrance into the House of Commons he declared himself a patriot; but he soon found means to dispose of his patriotism for a seat at the Admiralty-Board. This worthy man, before he obtained his price, was as deeply engaged in opposition to government as any member of the *Fountain Club*, to which he belonged. He then thought it no sin to run down Sir Robert Walpole, though now he has altered his tone. To oppose the measures of government, however dangerous to the constitution, or to attack the persons of ministers, however justly odious to the nation, is now *rank faction*, in the opinion of the pliant Lord Barrington. His allegiance follows the descent of power; nor has he ever been known to dispute the validity of the minister's title, as long as he continued in possession.

---

* This letter was advertised under the title of *Memoirs of Lord Barrington*, in compliance with the request of the author. See private note, No. 62.

His Lordship remained at the Admiralty, until long servility and a studious attachment to the Duke of Newcastle had engaged his Grace to recommend him for Secretary at War. When the Duke resigned, in the year 1756, he, of course, expected that Lord Barrington would have followed him. But his Lordship's gratitude to his patron was not quite heavy enough to weigh against two thousand five hundred a year. He knew the value of his place, and kept it by making the same professions to Mr. Pitt and Lord Temple by which he had deceived the Duke of Newcastle. Before the late King's death he had taken early measures to secure an interest at Carlton House; and when his present Majesty could no longer bear him as Secretary at War, he found means to ingratiate himself so far with Lord Bute, that for some time he was suffered to be Chancellor of the Exchequer; and when that post appeared to be not tenable, he still had art and contrivance enough to secure himself in the lucrative office of Treasurer of the Navy. In 1762 he was the most humble servant of Mr. Fox. In 1763 and 1764 he was no enemy to Mr. Grenville In 1765 he gave himself back, body and soul, to the late Duke of Cumberland and Lord Rockingham. The last manœuvre restored him to the War Office, where he has continued ever since, with equal fidelity to Mr. Pitt, the Duke of Grafton, and Lord North; and now he modestly tells the world *that he gets nothing* by his services.

Besides the singular good fortune of never being himself a moment out of place, he has had extraordinary success in providing for every branch of his family. One brother was a general officer, with a regiment and chief command at Guadaloupe. A second is high in the navy, with a regiment of marines. A third is a judge, and the fourth is a bishop. Yet this is the man who complains *that he gets nothing*. At the same time his parliamentary interest is so inconsiderable that, ever since his canting hypocrisy and pretended attachment to the dissenters was discovered at Berwick, he has been obliged to the influence of government for a seat in the House of Commons, which he holds without its costing him a shilling.

Having given you a short account of the emoluments he has received from government, I should be very glad to see as faithful an account of his services. Some of them are probably of a secret nature, of which we can form no judgment. His ostensible services, in the public opinion at least, have been considerably overpaid. At his very outset, the blundering orders he sent to Gibraltar might have occasioned the loss of that important place. When the fate of Gibraltar was at stake, we had a Secretary at War who could neither write plain English nor common sense. But he compensated for his own blunder by ruining the worthy General Fowke, whom he and a certain countess (taking a base advantage of the unhappy man's distress) prevailed upon to write a letter, the recollection of which soon after broke his heart. In the House of Commons, I think, the noble Lord was never reckoned an able debater. Poor B—ch, for many years was his nickname. His time-serving duplicity is now so well known, that he seldom speaks without being laughed at. Sometimes his folly exceeds all bounds; as, for instance, when he traduced the whole body of general officers, which, I presume, they will not readily forget. In the War Office he has made it his study to oppress all the lower part of the army by a multitude of foolish regulations, by which he hoped to gain the reputation of great discipline and economy, but which have only served to make him as odious to the military as he is to every other rank of people in the kingdom. With respect to the public in general, I presume there never was a man so generally or so deservedly detested as himself. The people of this country will never forget nor forgive the inhuman part he took in the affair of St. George's Fields. Other Secretaries at War have ordered out troops to assist the civil magistrate: for this man it was reserved to give it under his hand, that he rejoiced and exulted in the blood of his fellow-subjects. This stroke alone would be sufficient to determine his character. Yet, so far from having done the King any service by his officious zeal upon this occasion, I am convinced that no one circumstance has so much contributed to throw an odium upon the present reign. I will not suppose it possible that the best of princes could be pleased with the treason, but I am sure be has reason enough to hate the traitor.

Such are the services which, in his Lordship's opinion, can never be sufficiently rewarded. He complains that he gets nothing, although, upon a moderate computation, he has not received less of the public money than fifty-three thousand pounds, viz.:

| | |
|---|---|
| Ten years Lord of the Admiralty . . . . . | £8,000 |
| Eighteen years either Secretary at War, Chancellor of the Exchequer, or Treasurer of the Navy, at £2500 per annum . . . . . . . . . . | 45,000 |
| | £53,000 |

It is not possible to ascertain what further advantages he may have made by preference in subscriptions, lottery tickets, and the management of large sums lying in his hands as Treasurer of the Navy. Mr. Chamier, if he thought proper, might give us some tolerable account of the matter. When a Secretary at War chooses a broker for his deputy it is not difficult to guess what kind of transactions must formerly have passed between them. I don't mean to question the honour of Mr. Chamier. He always had the reputation of as active a little fellow as any in Jonathan's. But putting all things together, I think we may affirm that, when Lord Barrington complains of getting nothing from government, he must have conceived a most extravagant idea of his own importance, or that the inward torture he suffers, from knowing how thoroughly he is hated and despised, is such as no pecuniary emoluments can repay.

NEMESIS*.

* William Windham, the second Viscount Barrington, whom, under this signature, and that of A Veteran, Junius so bitterly persecuted, had served under almost every variety of ministry since 1746. In that year he was a Lord of the Admiralty; in 1754 Master of the Wardrobe; in 1755 Secretary at War; in 1757 Chancellor of the Exchequer; in 1762 Treasurer of the Navy; and in 1765 again Secretary at War. Lord Barrington, in early life, had been groom of the bedchamber, and appears to have been an easy, good-natured man of the world. If neither his virtues nor abilities were of a high order, he does not seem to have overrated himself. The following is an extract from a letter dated March 23, 1761, addressed to his friend Sir Andrew Mitchell, long the British resident at Berlin:—

"Our friend Holdernesse is finally in harbour: he has four thousand a-year for life, with the reversionship of the cinque ports, after the Duke of Dorset, which he likes better than having the name of pensioner. I never could myself understand the difference between a pension and a sinecure place. The same strange fortune which made me Secretary of War five years and a half ago, has made me Chancellor of the Exchequer; it may perhaps at last make me pope. I think I am equally fit to be at the head of the church as of the exchequer. My reason tells me it would have been more proper to have given me an employment of less consequence when I was removed from the War Office; but no man knows what is good for him." [Lord Barrington died in 1793, in his seventy-sixth year.—ED.]

# APPENDIX.

PRIVATE LETTERS OF JUNIUS TO LORD CHATHAM.

*(From the Chatham Correspondence. Edited by the Grandsons of the Earl of Chatham.)*

### JUNIUS TO THE EARL OF CHATHAM.

"*(Private and secret: to be opened by Lord Chatham only.)*

"MY LORD,                                         "London, January 2, 1768.

"IF I were to give way to the sentiments of respect and veneration which I have always entertained for your character, or to the warmth of my attachment to your person, I should write a longer letter than your Lordship would have time or inclination to read. But the information which I am going to lay before you will, I hope, make a short one not unworthy your attention. I have an opportunity of knowing something, and you may depend on my veracity.

"During your absence from administration, it is well known that not one of the ministers has either adhered to you with firmness, or supported, with any degree of steadiness, those principles on which you engaged in the King's service. From being their idol at first, their veneration for you has gradually diminished, until at last they have absolutely set you at defiance.

"The Chancellor, on whom you had particular reasons to rely, has played a sort of fast and loose game, and spoken of your Lordship with submission or indifference, according to the reports he heard of your health ; nor has he altered his language until he found you were really returning to town.

"Many circumstances must have made it impossible for you to depend much upon Lord Shelburne or his friends ; besides that, from his youth and want of knowledge, he was hardly of weight, by himself, to maintain any character in the cabinet. The best of him is, perhaps, that he has not acted with greater insincerity to your Lordship than to former connections.

"Lord Northington's conduct and character need no observation. A singularity of manners, added to a perpetual affectation of discontent, has given him an excuse for declining all share in the support of government, and at last conducted him to his great object—a very high title, considering the species of his merit, and an opulent retreat. Your Lordship is best able to judge of what may be expected from this nobleman's gratitude.

"Mr. Conway, as your Lordship knows by experience, is everything to everybody, as long as by such conduct he can maintain his ground. We have seen him in one day the humble, prostrate admirer of Lord Chatham ; the dearest friend of Rockingham and Richmond ; fully sensible of the weight of the Duke of Bedford's party ; no irreconcileable enemy to Lord Bute ; and, at the same time, very ready to acknowledge Mr. Grenville's merit as a financier. Lord Hertford is a little more explicit than his brother, and has taken every opportunity of treating your Lordship's name with indignity.

" But these are facts of little moment. The most considerable remains. It is understood by the public, that the plan of introducing the Duke of Bedford's friends entirely belongs to the Duke of Grafton, with the secret concurrence, perhaps, of Lord Bute, but certainly without your Lordship's consent, if not absolutely against your advice. It is also understood, that if you should exert your influence with the King to overturn this plan, the Duke of Grafton will be strong enough, with his new friends, to defeat any attempt of that kind ; or if he should not, your Lordship will easily judge to what quarter his Grace will apply for assistance.

" My Lord, the man who presumes to give your Lordship these hints, admires your character without servility, and is convinced that, if this country can be saved, it must be saved by Lord Chatham's spirit—by Lord Chatham's abilities*.

" To the Earl of Chatham,
      " &c. &c. &c. &c.,
" At Hayes, near Bromley, Kent."

### "JUNIUS TO THE EARL OF CHATHAM†.

[From the original in his handwriting.]

" (Most secret.)
      " MY LORD,                              " London, January 14, 1772.
" CONFIDING implicitly in your Lordship's honour, I take the liberty of submitting to you the inclosed paper, before it be given

---

*. " It may be remarked that this panegyric on Lord Chatham adds considerable weight to an opinion entertained by many persons ; namely, that some of the Miscellaneous Letters inserted in Woodfall's edition of Junius are erroneously attributed to that distinguished writer. The five letters written on the 28th of April, the 28th of May, the 24th of June, and the 19th of December, 1767, and that on the 16th of February, 1768, under the signatures of Poplicola, Anti-Sejanus Junior, Downright, &c., are conceived in a spirit of bitter animosity to that nobleman ; and it is incredible that the same individual should anonymously and *privately* address a minister in terms expressive of " respect and veneration" at the very time that he was endeavouring to destroy that minister's influence by *publicly* ridiculing his infirmities, and giving to the world anonymous libels on his character and conduct."—*Note by the Editors of the Chatham Papers*, 1839.

† This letter was forwarded to Lord Chatham at Burton Pynsent, with proof sheets of those addressed to Lord Chief Justice Mansfield and Lord Camden, and which were about to appear in the *Public Advertiser*. They

to the public. It is to appear on the morning of the meeting of parliament. Lord Mansfield flatters himself that I have dropped all thoughts of attacking him, and I would give him as little time as possible to concert his measures with the ministry. The address to Lord Camden will be accounted for, when I say, that the nation in general are not quite so secure of *his* firmness as they are of Lord Chatham.

"I am so clearly satisfied that Lord Mansfield has done an act not warranted by law, and that the inclosed argument is not to be answered (besides that I find the lawyers concur with me), that I am inclined to expect he may himself acknowledge it as an oversight, and endeavour to whittle it away to nothing. For this possible event I would wish your Lordship and the Duke of Richmond to be prepared to take down his words, and thereupon to move for committing him to the Tower. I hope that proper steps will also be taken in the House of Commons. If he makes no confession of his guilt, but attempts to defend himself by any legal argument, I then submit it to your Lordship whether it might not be proper to put the following questions to the judges. In fact, they answer themselves; but it will embarrass the ministry, and ruin the character which Mansfield pretends to, if the House should put a direct negative upon the motion :—

"1. 'Whether, according to the true meaning and intendment of the laws of England, relative to bail for criminal offences, a person positively charged with felony, taken *in flagrante delicto*, with the *mainœuvre*, and not making any defence, nor offering any evidence to induce a doubt whether he be guilty or innocent, is *bailable* or *not bailable?*

"2. 'Whether the power exercised by the Judges of the Court of King's Bench, of bailing for offences not bailable by a justice of peace, be an absolute power, of mere will and pleasure in the Judge, or a discretionary power, regulated and governed in the application of it by the true meaning and intendment of the law relative to bail?'

"Lord Mansfield's constant endeavour to misinterpret the laws of England is a sufficient general ground of impeachment. The specific instances may be taken from his doctrine concerning libels,—the Grosvenor cause ; his pleading Mr. De Grey's defence upon the bench, when he said, *idem fecerunt alii, et multi et boni;* his suffering an affidavit to be read, in *the King against Blair*, tending to inflame the court against the defendant when he was

were published on the 21st of January, and were the last efforts of this celebrated writer under the signature of Junius.—*Editors of the Chatham Papers.*

See the private notes of Junius to Mr. Woodfall, Nos. 48 and 49, p. 52, which refer to the subject of the letter to Lord Chatham.

brought up to receive sentence ; his direction to the jury, in the cause of Ansell, by which he admitted parol evidence against a written agreement, and in consequence of which the Court of Common Pleas granted a new trial ; and lastly, his partial and wicked motives for bailing Eyre. There are some material circumstances relative to this last, which I thought it right to reserve for your Lordship alone.

" It will appear by the evidence of the gaoler and the city solicitor's clerk, that Lord Mansfield refused to hear the return read, and at first ordered Eyre to be bound only in 200*l*. with two sureties, until his clerk, Mr. Platt, proposed 300*l*. with three sureties. Mr. King, clerk to the city solicitor, was never asked for his consent, nor did he ever give any. From these facts I conclude, either that he bailed without knowing the cause of commitment, or, which is highly probable, that he knew it extra-judicially from the Scotchmen, and was ashamed to have the return read.

" I will not presume to trouble your Lordship with any assurances, however sincere, of my respect and esteem for your character, and admiration of your abilities. Retired and unknown, I live in the shade, and have only a speculative ambition. In the warmth of my imagination, I sometimes conceive that, when Junius exerts his utmost faculties in the service of his country, he approaches in theory to that exalted character which Lord Chatham alone fills up and uniformly supports in action.

"JUNIUS."

---

## LETTERS OF COLONEL BARRÉ.

COLONEL BARRÉ was a man (as already observed, Essay, p. xxxi) of remarkable abilities and remarkable history. He was a native of Dublin, of humble parentage, born about the year 1726. He entered the army at an early age, and gradually rose to the rank of colonel. After the death of General Wolfe, his commander and friend, he addressed a letter to Mr. Pitt, then Secretary of State, describing his services and want of interest with people in power, and soliciting his aid. He was then a major, and the following is a copy of his letter, from the *Chatham Papers.*

"SIR,         "New York, April 23, 1760.

" If I presume to address myself to the first minister of my country, it is under the sanction of a name which is still grateful to his ear. General Wolfe fell, in the arms of victory, on the plain of Abraham. I received near his person a very dangerous wound, and, by the neglect I have since met with, I am apprehensive that my pretensions are to be buried with my only protector and friend. The packets bring no directions concerning me ; so that I remain as adjutant-general with General Amherst, by his desire; though with a very bad prospect of ever being taken notice of.

"From power I have not interest enough to ask favour; but, unless the discernment of my late general be much called in question, I may claim some title to justice. If my demands appear reasonable, an application to Mr. Pitt cannot be charged with great impropriety.

"For want of friends, I had lingered a subaltern officer eleven years, when Mr. Wolfe's opinion of me rescued me from that obscurity. I attended him as major of brigade to the siege of Louisburg, in which campaign my zeal for the service confirmed him my friend, and gained the approbation of General Amherst. When the expedition to Canada was determined upon, General Wolfe got his Majesty's permission to name me his adjutant-general. Upon this occasion, I only got the rank of major in America, and captain in the army; my being still a subaltern was the reason assigned for such moderate honours. Thus my misfortune was imputed to me as a fault, and though thought worthy of that high employment, the rank of lieutenant-colonel (so necessary to add weight to it) was refused, although generally given in like cases, and in some instances to younger officers.

"My conduct in that station was so highly approved of by the General, that when the success of the campaign seemed doubtful, he regretted his want of power to serve me, and only wished with impatience for an opportunity to make me the messenger of agreeable news. This last honour the battle of Quebec deprived me of [*]. After the defeat of his Majesty's enemies, the trophies I can boast only indicate how much I suffered; my zealous and sole advocate killed, my left eye rendered useless, and the ball still in my head.

"The presumption in appealing to you, I hope, will be pardoned when I affirm that I am almost utterly unknown to the Secretary at War. Besides, Sir, I confess it would be the most flattering circumstance of my life to owe my preferment to that minister who honoured my late general with so important a command, and which I had the pleasure of seeing executed with satisfaction to my King and country. I have the honour to be, with the most profound respect, Sir,                "Your most devoted humble servant,
                                "ISAAC BARBÉ."

This application was refused by Mr. Pitt on the ground that senior officers would be injured by the promotion, and in a subsequent letter Barré expressed himself satisfied, and "bound in the highest gratitude" for the attention he had received. Afterwards he appears to have considered himself neglected, and obtaining a

* In the following September, Barré was the bearer of the despatches announcing the surrender of Montreal.

seat in Parliament through the interest of Lord Shelburne, in the following year, he made a violent attack on Mr. Pitt. It is likely this maiden outbreak was the result of inexperience as well as pique; at all events it was in bad taste. Describing the oratorical manner of Mr. Pitt, he said,—" There he would stand, turning up his eyes to heaven, that witnessed his perjuries; and laying his hand in a solemn manner upon the table—that sacrilegious hand that had been employed in tearing out the bowels of his country." A few years later the Colonel and Lord Chatham became good friends, for in politics there seems neither friendships nor enmities —only interests. Lest too unfavourable an impression should be left by this incident in Barré's career, and the better to elucidate the obscure history and character of a meritorious man, I insert two letters from Colonel Barré, written in France in 1764, and contained in Mr. Burton's late publication of " Letters of Eminent Persons addressed to David Hume," the historian :—

" DEAR HUME,                        " Rochefort, August 3, 1764.

" When you joked me about my native country, as you was pleased to call it, I did not imagine that it was likely to produce any other good to me but a little amusement, and the pleasure of meeting you in Paris. However, since my arrival in this part of France, I find that an uncle of mine (younger, and only brother to my father) died lately, possessed of about ten thousand pounds sterling, which (as there was no will) has been very rapidly divided amongst a number of very distant relations, who supposed me dead. I don't know all the particulars as yet, but intend to set out for the very spot to-morrow morning early, and after getting all the information I can, I shall go to Bordeaux, where I shall state the whole affair to some able lawyer, and be directed by him how to proceed. Forgive me if I trouble you upon this occasion ; you see it is a serious one. First, let me know what the law, custom, or court opinion is as to the right of succession in an Englishman to an inhabitant of this country. Next, pray prepare yourself to support me with all your influence, if it comes to any trial. I only ask justice ; but you'll perhaps tell me that I am very unconscionable. I would not have you speak of this, till I can write to you more fully ; but, in the meantime, you may, perhaps, be able to send me some recommendation at Bordeaux, which may be of use to me in this affair : I mean in the law way. This will, probably, break through my proposed plan, and keep me longer at Bordeaux than I at first intended. However, the object is to me important. Indeed, if it had not been so, I should not have given you any trouble. Believe me most sincerely yours,

" Direct to me, at Messrs. Ainsley's, Bordeaux."      " I. BARRÉ.

"DEAR HUME,                              "Toulouse, September 4.

"I thank you for your last letter from Paris, which I received just
as Smith and his *élève*, and L' Abbé Colbert were sitting down to
dine with me at Bordeaux. The latter is a very honest fellow, and
deserves to be a bishop; make him one if you can. I stated my
case (or, rather, my father's) to a lawyer at Bordeaux, who thinks
he has no right; and grounds his opinion upon several of the
King's declarations; and particularly upon one of the 27th of
October, 1725. He makes the whole turn upon my grandfather's
being a Protestant. This I have alleged (though without any
positive proof) to be the case. May I beg of you to take some
lawyer's opinion, at Paris, simply upon this case as I state it,
viz.:—Barré dies in France about twenty-five years ago, leaving
two sons, Peter and John; Peter went over to Ireland about the
year 1720 or 22, young and unmarried, but afterwards married and
settled there. John, being upon the spot at the time of his father's
death, divided the property very nearly as he thought proper.
John dies in September, 1760, intestate and childless. Bonnomeau,
a maternal uncle of his, takes possession of his estate as nearest
heir. This Bonnomeau died in the month following, and his whole
fortune was divided between sixteen nephews or nieces, who stood
in the same degree of relation to him as the deceased John Barré
did. At the time of John's death it had been reported that Peter
and his children were dead. Now, I wish to know what right
Peter has to the estate of his brother John, considering the circumstances of his having left France, and his living so long in
Ireland, professing the Protestant religion, and whether that right
is affected by his father being a Protestant. John was generally
thought to be a Protestant, though his heirs contrived to have him
buried as a Catholic. When you get an opinion, pray send it to
Foley's, who forwards all my letters, and knows where to find me.
Why will you triumph and talk of *platte couture?* You have
friends on both sides. Smith agrees with me in thinking that you
are turned soft by the *délices* of a French court, and that you
don't write in that nervous manner you was remarkable for in the
more northern climates. Besides, what is still worse, you take
your politics from your Elliots, Rigbys, and Selwyns!!! A bad
politician tells me just now that we are to have war. Impossible.
Adieu."

---

## DUEL BETWEEN MR. HASTINGS AND SIR PHILIP FRANCIS.

The circumstances attending the personal rencontre between
these two eminent persons were somewhat peculiar, and may deserve
more particular notice than is given in the Essay, p. l.

B B 2

From the first landing of the new councillors in India, there had been misunderstandings—disputes on matters of etiquette, number of discharges of salute guns, receptions, and first visits. It was manifest the two divisions of the Supreme Council, Messrs. Clavering, Francis, and Monson on one side, and Messrs. Hastings and Barker on the other, were resolved not cordially to amalgamate. At the council-board altercations were incessant; conflicting opinions and recriminations were entered on the minutes; till at length, from daily bickerings, the exasperation between Francis and Hastings became so embittered that the latter seems to have been determined to bring their differences to a short issue by converting them into a personal affair.

Mr. Hastings caused the following minute to be entered in the council-book, and communicated the same to Mr. Francis on the evening of August 14, 1780 :—"My authority for the opinions I have declared concerning Mr. Francis depends on facts which have passed within my own knowledge. I judge of his public conduct by my experience of his private, which I have found to be *void of truth and honour.* This is a severe charge, but temperately and deliberately made, from the firm persuasion that I owe this justice to the public and myself, as the only redress to both, for artifices of which I have been a victim, and which threaten to involve their interests with disgrace and ruin. The only redress for a fraud for which the law has made no provision is the exposure of it."

Next day they met as usual at the council-board. No notice was taken of this communication till after the conclusion of the business of the day, when Mr. Francis desired to speak to Mr Hastings in private. They withdrew into an adjoining room, when Mr. Francis adopted the unusual course of giving a verbal challenge to Mr. Hastings, which was accepted, and the meeting fixed for an early hour next morning. It was altogether "a silly affair," as Mr. Hastings admits in the account he gave of it to a friend, and cited in his "Life" by Mr. Gleig. A native old woman, Mr. Hastings says, happened to be standing near the spot, and seemed astonished at the strange scene that passed before her, enacted by two Europeans. Two gentlemen meet, take their stand at a measured distance, deliberately fire their pistols at each other; one gentleman falls, and the other runs up to tender him assistance. The ball struck Francis just below the right shoulder, passing out at the lower part of the abdomen. Next day Mr. Hastings sent a messenger to inquire after his health, and expressed a desire to pay a visit of condolence. This civility Mr. Francis politely declined, expressing a due sense of his kindness, and, not to be outdone, assured him that nothing which had passed would, on his part, leave anything like feelings of personal rancour in their future meetings at the council-board.

## MR. SERGEANT ROUGH TO MR. BARKER.

"Serjeant's Inn, Chancery Lane, April 12, 1827.

"DEAR SIR,—I hasten to acknowledge your letter, with the printed papers accompanying it, delivered at my chambers by Mr. Maxon. I am sorry, however, that I can render you so very little service in respect of the subjects on which you write. The Letters of Junius to Mr. Wilkes passed through my hands to Mr. Woodfall, and are those which appear in his edition of 1812. They belonged to Mr. P. Elmsley, the late Principal of St. Alban's, who, as I believe, possessed them as executor to his father. His knowledge of me as a brother-Westminster with me and the circumstance of my having married an acknowledged daughter of Mr. Wilkes, induced him to decline letting Mr. Woodfall have them without my assent. They came to me, from my friend Mr. Hallam, to whom they were afterwards returned for Mr. Elmsley. Mr. Wilkes used, I have been told, to say that *he* knew who the author of Junius was—that it was *not* Rosenhagen; but he never said it was *not* Sir P. Francis. The latter used to dine at Kensington frequently, and once cut off a lock of Mrs. Rough's hair (she was then quite a girl). *She had an obscure imagination that her father once said, she had met Junius.* All this is too slight, I admit, to build any conclusion upon. In the letters, I fear I have to answer for the striking out of a line or two in which the late king was spoken of, upon alleged personal knowledge, with an expression of much bitterness. It was an idle precaution on my part, inasmuch as Junius's opinions could have done little harm to any one, and were sufficiently avowed in other letters. I have never seen the letters about which you enquire, *since* they were given back by me to Mr. Hallam for Elmsley. I may mention here, that some letters of Mr. Wilkes's, forming a part of his correspondence with his daughter (Mary), and published by Longman and Rees, 1804, also passed through my hands. They were purchased of Sir Robert Baker, Bart., then of Richmond, for £300, by Mr. Hatchard, jointly with Longman and Rees. I was induced to superintend the publication with a view of serving Mr. Hatchard, and of guarding against anything appearing in the letters unpleasant to the feelings of my wife. She was a natural daughter of Wilkes. With *him* I never was in company; he was dead before I knew his daughter. Of that daughter our dear Dr. Parr thought with veneration. For myself, life has never been what it once was, since I lost her.

"There is nothing secret in what I have thus communicated.

"I am yours truly,

"To E. H. Barker, Esq"                "W. ROUGH."

# INDEX.

**Longfellow's Poetical Works**, complete, including The Wayside Inn. Twenty-four page Engravings, by Birket Foster and others, and a new Portrait.

———; or, without the illustrations. 3s. 6d.

——— **Prose Works**, complete. Sixteen page Engravings by Birket Foster and others.

**Marryat's Masterman Ready**; or, The Wreck of the Pacific. 93 Engravings.

——— **Mission**; or, Scenes in Africa. (Written for Young People.) Illustrated by Gilbert and Dalziel.

——— **Pirate and Three Cutters**. New Edition, with a Memoir of the Author. With 20 Steel Engravings from Drawings by Clarkson Stanfield, R.A.

——— **Privateer's-Man One Hundred Years Ago**. Eight Engravings on Steel, after Stothard.

——— **Settlers in Canada**. New Edition. Ten fine Engravings by Gilbert and Dalziel.

**Maxwell's Victories of Wellington** and the British Armies. Illustrations on Steel.

**Michael Angelo and Raphael, their Lives and Works**. By Duppa and Quatremère de Quincy. With 13 highly-finished Engravings on Steel.

**Miller's History of the Anglo-Saxons**. Written in a popular style, on the basis of Sharon Turner. Portrait of Alfred, Map of Saxon Britain, and 12 elaborate Engravings on Steel.

**Milton's Poetical Works**. With a Memoir by James Montgomery, Todd's Verbal Index to all the Poems, and Explanatory Notes. With 120 Engravings by Thompson and others, from Drawings by W. Harvey. 2 vols.

Vol. 1. Paradise Lost, complete, with Memoir, Notes, and Index.

Vol. 2. Paradise Regained, and other Poems, with Verbal Index to all the Poems.

**Mudie's British Birds**. Revised by W. C. L. Martin. Fifty-two Figures and 7 Plates of Eggs. In 2 vols.

———; or, with the plates coloured. 7s. 6d. per vol.

**Naval and Military Heroes of Great Britain**; or, Calendar of Victory. Being a Record of British Valour and Conquest by Sea and Land, on every day in the year, from the time of William the Conqueror to the Battle of Inkermann. By Major Johns, R.M., and Lieutenant P. H. Nicolas, R.M. Twenty-four Portraits. 6s.

**Nicolini's History of the Jesuits**: their Origin, Progress, Doctrines, and Design. Fine Portraits of Loyola, Lainez, Xavier, Borgia, Acquaviva, Père la Chaise, and Pope Ganganelli.

**Norway and its Scenery**. Comprising Price's Journal, with large Additions, and a Road-Book. Edited by T. Forester. Twenty-two Illustrations.

**Paris and its Environs, including Versailles, St. Cloud, and Excursions into the Champagne Districts**. An Illustrated Handbook for Travellers. Edited by T. Forester. Twenty-eight beautiful Engravings.

**Petrarch's Sonnets, and other Poems**. Translated into English Verse. By various hands. With a Life of the Poet, by Thomas Campbell. With 16 Engravings.

**Pickering's History of the Races of Man**, with an Analytical Synopsis of the Natural History of Man. By Dr. Hall. Illustrated by numerous Portraits.

———; or, with the plates coloured. 7s. 6d.

*.* An excellent Edition of a work originally published at 3l. 3s. by the American Government.

**Pictorial Handbook of London**. Comprising its Antiquities, Architecture, Arts, Manufactures, Trade, Institutions, Exhibitions, Suburbs, &c. Two hundred and five Engravings, and a large Map, by Lowry.

This volume contains above 900 pages, and is undoubtedly the cheapest five-shilling volume ever produced.

**Pictorial Handbook of Modern Geography**, on a Popular Plan. 3s. 6d. Illustrated by 150 Engravings and 51 Maps. 6s.

———; or, with the maps coloured. 7s. 6d.

Two large Editions of this volume have been sold. The present New Edition is corrected and improved; and, besides introducing the recent Censuses of England and other countries, records the changes which have taken place in Italy and America.

**Pope's Poetical Works**. Edited by Robert Carruthers. Numerous Engravings. 2 vols.

——— **Homer's Iliad**. With Introduction and Notes by J. S. Watson, M.A. Illustrated by the entire Series of Flaxman's Designs, beautifully engraved by Moses (in the full 8vo. size).

——— **Homer's Odyssey, Hymns**, &c., by other translators, including Chapman, and Introduction and Notes by J. S. Watson, M.A. Flaxman's Designs beautifully engraved by Moses.

9

**Pope's Life.** Including many of his Letters. By ROBERT CARRUTHERS. New Edition, revised and enlarged. *Illustrations.*

*The preceding 5 vols. make a complete and elegant edition of Pope's Poetical Works and Translations for 25s.*

**Pottery and Porcelain, and other Objects of Vertu** (a Guide to the Knowledge of). To which is added an Engraved List of all the known Marks and Monograms. By HENRY G. BOHN. *Numerous Engravings.*

———; *or, coloured.* 10s. 6d.

**Prout's (Father) Reliques.** New Edition, revised and largely augmented. *Twenty-one spirited Etchings by Maclise.* Two volumes in one, 7s. 6d.

**Recreations in Shooting.** By "CRAVEN." New Edition, revised and enlarged. *62 Engravings on Wood, after Harvey, and 9 Engravings on Steel, chiefly after A. Cooper, R.A.*

**Redding's History and Descriptions** of Wines, Ancient and Modern. *Twenty beautiful Woodcuts.*

**Robinson Crusoe.** With Illustrations by STOTHARD and HARVEY. *Twelve beautiful Engravings on Steel, and 74 on Wood.*

———; *or, without the Steel Illustrations.* 3s. 6d.

*The prettiest Edition extant.*

**Rome in the Nineteenth Century.** New Edition. Revised by the Author. *Illustrated by 34 fine Steel Engravings.* 2 vols.

**Southey's Life of Nelson.** With Additional Notes. *Illustrated with 64 Engravings.*

**Starling's (Miss) Noble Deeds of** Women; or, Examples of Female Courage, Fortitude, and Virtue. *Fourteen beautiful Illustrations.*

**Stuart and Revett's Antiquities of** Athens, and other Monuments of Greece. *Illustrated in 71 Steel Plates, and numerous Woodcuts.*

**Tales of the Genii; or, the Delightful** Lessons of Horam. *Numerous Woodcuts, and 9 Steel Engravings, after Stothard.*

**Tasso's Jerusalem Delivered.** Translated into English Spenserian Verse, with a Life of the Author. By J. H. WIFFEN. *Eight Engravings on Steel, and 24 on Wood, by Thurston.*

**Walker's Manly Exercises.** Containing Skating, Riding, Driving, Hunting, Shooting, Sailing, Rowing, Swimming, &c. New Edition, revised by "CRAVEN." *Forty-four Steel Plates, and numerous Woodcuts.*

**Walton's Complete Angler.** Edited by EDWARD JESSE, Esq. To which is added an Account of Fishing Stations, &c., by H. G. BOHN. *Upwards of 203 Engravings.*

———; *or, with 26 additional page Illustrations on Steel.* 7s. 6d.

**Wellington, Life of.** By AN OLD SOLDIER, from the materials of Maxwell. *Eighteen Engravings.*

**White's Natural History of Selborne.** With Notes by Sir WILLIAM JARDINE and EDWARD JESSE, Esq. *Illustrated by 40 highly-finished Engravings.*

———; *or, with the plates coloured.* 7s. 6d.

**Young, The, Lady's Book.** A Manual of Elegant Recreations, Arts, Sciences, and Accomplishments; including Geology, Mineralogy, Conchology, Botany, Entomology, Ornithology, Costume, Embroidery, the Escritoire, Archery, Riding, Music (instrumental and vocal), Dancing, Exercises, Painting, Photography, &c. &c. Edited by distinguished Professors. *Twelve Hundred Woodcut Illustrations, and several fine Engravings on Steel.* 7s. 6d.

———; *or, cloth gilt, gilt edges,* 9s.

## II.

## Bohn's Classical Library.

UNIFORM WITH THE STANDARD LIBRARY, AT 5s. PER VOLUME (EXCEPTING THOSE MARKED OTHERWISE).

**Æschylus.** Literally Translated into English Prose by an Oxonian. 3s. 6d.

———, **Appendix to.** Containing the New Readings given in Hermann's posthumous Edition of Æschylus. By GEORGE BURGES, M.A. 3s. 6d.

**Ammianus Marcellinus.** History of Rome from Constantius to Valens. Translated by C. D. YONGE, B.A. Double volume, 7s. 6d.

*.* This is a very circumstantial and amusing history. Gibbon expresses himself largely indebted to it.

Apuleius, the Golden Ass; Death of Socrates; Florida; and Discourse on Magic. To which is added a Metrical Version of Cupid and Psyche; and Mrs. Tighe's Psyche. *Frontispiece.*

Aristophanes' Comedies. Literally Translated, with Notes and Extracts from Frere's and other Metrical Versions, by W. J. Hickie. 2 vols.
    Vol. 1. Acharnians, Knights, Clouds, Wasps, Peace, and Birds.
    Vol. 2. Lysistrata, Thesmophoriazusae, Frogs, Ecclesiazusae, and Plutus.

Aristotle's Ethics. Literally Translated by Archdeacon Browne, late Classical Professor of King's College.

——— Politics and Economics. Translated by E. Walford, M.A.

——— Metaphysics. Literally Translated, with Notes, Analysis, Examination Questions, and Index, by the Rev. John H. M'Mahon, M.A., and Gold Medallist in Metaphysics, T.C.D.

——— History of Animals. In Ten Books. Translated, with Notes and Index, by Richard Cresswell, M.A.

——— Organon; or, Logical Treatises. With Notes, &c. By O. F. Owen, M.A. 2 vols. 3s. 6d. each.

——— Rhetoric and Poetics. Literally Translated, with Examination Questions and Notes, by an Oxonian.

Athenæus. The Deipnosophists; or, the Banquet of the Learned. Translated by C. D. Yonge, B.A. 3 vols.

Cæsar. Complete, with the Alexandrian, African, and Spanish Wars. Literally Translated, with Notes.

Catullus, Tibullus, and the Vigil of Venus. A Literal Prose Translation. To which are added Metrical Versions by Lamb, Grainger, and others. *Frontispiece.*

Cicero's Orations. Literally Translated by C. D. Yonge, B.A. In 4 vols.
    Vol. 1. Contains the Orations against Verres, &c. *Portrait.*
    Vol. 2. Catiline, Archias, Agrarian Law, Rabirius, Murena, Sylla, &c.
    Vol. 3. Orations for his House, Plancius, Sextius, Coelius, Milo, Ligarius, &c.
    Vol. 4. Miscellaneous Orations, and Rhetorical Works; with General Index to the four volumes.

——— on Oratory and Orators. By J. S. Watson, M.A.

——— on the Nature of the Gods, Divination, Fate, Laws, a Republic, &c. Translated by C. D. Yonge, B.A., and F. Barham.

Cicero's Academics, De Finibus, and Tusculan Questions. By C. D. Yonge, B.A. With Sketch of the Greek Philosophy.

——— Offices, Old Age, Friendship, Scipio's Dream, Paradoxes, &c. Literally Translated, by R. Edmonds. 3s. 6d.

Demosthenes' Orations. Translated, with Notes, by C. Rann Kennedy. In 5 volumes.
    Vol. 1. The Olynthiac, Philippic, and other Public Orations. 3s. 6d.
    Vol. 2. On the Crown and on the Embassy.
    Vol. 3. Against Leptines, Midias, Androtion, and Aristocrates.
    Vol. 4. Private and other Orations.
    Vol. 5. Miscellaneous Orations.

Dictionary of Latin Quotations. Including Proverbs, Maxims, Mottoes, Law Terms and Phrases; and a Collection of above 500 Greek Quotations. With all the quantities marked, & English Translations.

———, with Index Verborum. 6s. Index Verborum only. 1s.

Diogenes Laertius. Lives and Opinions of the Ancient Philosophers. Translated, with Notes, by C. D. Yonge.

Euripides. Literally Translated. 2 vols.
    Vol. 1. Hecuba, Orestes, Medea, Hippolytus, Alcestis, Bacchæ, Heraclidæ, Iphigenia in Aulide, and Iphigenia in Tauris.
    Vol. 2. Hercules Furens, Troades, Ion, Andromache, Suppliants, Helen, Electra, Cyclops, Rhesus.

Greek Anthology. Literally Translated. With Metrical Versions by various Authors.

Greek Romances of Heliodorus, Longus, and Achilles Tatius.

Herodotus. A New and Literal Translation, by Henry Cary, M.A., of Worcester College, Oxford.

Hesiod, Callimachus, and Theognis. Literally Translated, with Notes, by J. Banks, M.A.

Homer's Iliad. Literally Translated, by an Oxonian.

——— Odyssey, Hymns, &c. Literally Translated, by an Oxonian.

Horace. Literally Translated, by Smart. Carefully revised by an Oxonian. 3s. 6d.

Justin, Cornelius Nepos, and Eutropius. Literally Translated, with Notes and Index, by J. S. Watson, M.A.

Juvenal, Persius, Sulpicia, and Lucilius. By L. Evans, M.A. With the Metrical Version by Gifford. *Frontispiece.*

11

**Livy.** A new and Literal Translation. By Dr. Spillan and others. In 4 vols.
Vol. 1. Contains Books 1—8.
Vol. 2. Books 9—26.
Vol. 3. Books 27—36.
Vol. 4. Books 37 to the end; and Index.

**Lucan's Pharsalia.** Translated, with Notes, by H. T. Riley.

**Lucretius.** Literally Translated, with Notes, by the Rev. J. S. Watson, M.A. And the Metrical Version by J. M. Good.

**Martial's Epigrams, complete.** Literally Translated. Each accompanied by one or more Verse Translations selected from the Works of English Poets, and other sources. With a copious Index. Double volume (660 pages). 7s. 6d.

**Ovid's Works, complete.** Literally Translated. 3 vols.
Vol. 1. Fasti, Tristia, Epistles, &c.
Vol. 2. Metamorphoses.
Vol. 3. Heroides, Art of Love, &c.

**Pindar.** Literally Translated, by Dawson W. Turner, and the Metrical Version by Abraham Moore.

**Plato's Works.** Translated by the Rev. H. Cary and others. In 6 vols.
Vol. 1. The Apology of Socrates, Crito, Phædo, Gorgias, Protagoras, Phædrus, Theætetus, Euthyphron, Lysis.
Vol. 2. The Republic, Timæus, & Critias.
Vol. 3. Meno, Euthydemus, The Sophist, Statesman, Cratylus, Parmenides, and the Banquet.
Vol. 4. Philebus, Charmides, Laches, The Two Alcibiades, and Ten other Dialogues.
Vol. 5. The Laws.
Vol. 6. The Doubtful Works. With General Index.

**Plautus's Comedies.** Literally Translated, with Notes, by H. T. Riley, B.A. In 2 vols.

**Pliny's Natural History.** Translated, with Copious Notes, by the late John Bostock, M.D., F.R.S., and H. T. Riley, B.A. In 6 vols.

**Propertius, Petronius, and Johannes Secundus.** Literally Translated, and accompanied by Poetical Versions, from various sources.

**Quintilian's Institutes of Oratory.** Literally Translated, with Notes, &c., by J. S. Watson, M.A. In 2 vols.

**Sallust, Florus, and Velleius Paterculus.** With Copious Notes, Biographical Notices, and Index, by J. S. Watson.

**Sophocles.** The Oxford Translation revised.

**Standard Library Atlas of Classical Geography.** Twenty-two large coloured Maps according to the latest authorities. With a complete Index (accentuated), giving the latitude and longitude of every place named in the Maps. Imp. 8vo. 7s. 6d.

**Strabo's Geography.** Translated, with Copious Notes, by W. Falconer, M.A., and H. C. Hamilton, Esq. With Index, giving the Ancient and Modern Names. In 3 vols.

**Suetonius' Lives of the Twelve Cæsars,** and other Works. Thomson's Translation, revised, with Notes, by T. Forester.

**Tacitus.** Literally Translated, with Notes. In 2 vols.
Vol. 1. The Annals.
Vol. 2. The History, Germania, Agricola, &c. With Index.

**Terence and Phædrus.** By H. T. Riley, B.A.

**Theocritus, Bion, Moschus, and Tyrtæus.** By J. Banks, M.A. With the Metrical Versions of Chapman.

**Thucydides.** Literally Translated by Rev. H. Dale. In 2 vols. 3s. 6d. each.

**Virgil.** Literally Translated by Davidson. New Edition, carefully revised. 3s. 6d.

**Xenophon's Works.** In 3 Vols.
Vol. 1. The Anabasis and Memorabilia. Translated, with Notes, by J. S. Watson, M.A. And a Geographical Commentary, by W. F. Ainsworth, F.S.A., F.R.G.S., &c.
Vol. 2. Cyropædia and Hellenics. By J. S. Watson, M.A., and the Rev. H. Dale.
Vol. 3. The Minor Works. By J. S. Watson, M.A.

XII.

## Bohn's Scientific Library.

UNIFORM WITH THE STANDARD LIBRARY, AT 5s. PER VOLUME
(EXCEPTING THOSE MARKED OTHERWISE).

**Agassiz and Gould's Comparative Physiology.** Enlarged by Dr Wright. Upwards of 400 Engravings.

**Bacon's Novum Organum and Advancement of Learning.** Complete, with Notes, by J. Devey, M.A.

**Blair's Chronological Tables, Revised and Enlarged.** Comprehending the Chronology and History of the World, from the earliest times. By J. Willoughby Rosse. Double Volume. 10s.; or, half-bound, 10s. 6d.

**Index of Dates.** Comprehending the principal Facts in the Chronology and History of the World, from the earliest to the present time, alphabetically arranged. By J. W. Rosse. Double volume, 10s.; or, half-bound, 10s. 6d.

12

**Bolley's Manual of Technical Analysis.** A Guide for the Testing of Natural and Artificial Substances. By B. H. PAUL. 100 Wood Engravings.

**BRIDGEWATER TREATISES.** —

—— **Bell on the Hand.** Its Mechanism and Vital Endowments as evincing Design. *Seventh Edition Revised.*

—— **Kirby on the History, Habits,** and Instincts of Animals. Edited with Notes, by T. RYMER JONES. *Numerous Engravings, many of which are additional.* In 2 vols.

—— **Kidd on the Adaptation of** External Nature to the Physical Condition of Man. 3s. 6d.

—— **Whewell's Astronomy and** General Physics, considered with reference to Natural Theology. 3s. 6d.

—— **Chalmers on the Adaptation** of External Nature to the Moral and Intellectual Constitution of Man. 5s.

—— **Prout's Treatise on Chemistry,** Meteorology, and Digestion. Edited by Dr. J. W. GRIFFITH.

—— **Buckland's Geology and** Mineralogy. *With numerous Illustrations.* [*In Preparation.*

—— **Roget's Animal and Vegetable** Physiology. *Illustrated* [*Shortly.*

**Carpenter's (Dr. W. B.) Zoology.** A Systematic View of the Structure, Habits, Instincts, and Uses, of the principal Families of the Animal Kingdom, and of the chief forms of Fossil Remains. New edition, revised to the present time, under arrangement with the Author, by W. S. DALLAS, F.L.S. *Illustrated with many hundred fine Wood Engravings.* In 2 vols. 6s. each.

—— **Mechanical Philosophy, As-**tronomy, and Horology. A Popular Exposition. 182 *Illustrations.*

—— **Vegetable Physiology and** Systematic Botany. A complete Introduction to the Knowledge of Plants. New Edition, revised, under arrangement with the Author, by E. LANKESTER, M.D., &c. *Several hundred Illustrations on Wood.* 6s.

—— **Animal Physiology.** New Edition, thoroughly revised, and in part re-written by the Author. *Upwards of 300 capital Illustrations.* 6s.

**Chess Congress of 1862.** A Collection of the Games played, and a Selection of the Problems sent in for the Competition. Edited by J. LÖWENTHAL, Manager. With an Account of the Proceedings, and a Memoir of the British Chess Association, by J. W. MEDLEY, Hon. Sec. 7s.

**Chevreul on Colour.** Containing the Principles of Harmony and Contrast of Colours, and their application to the Arts. Translated from the French by CHARLES MARTEL. Only complete Edition. *Several Plates.*

—— ; or, with an additional series of 16 Plates in Colours. 7s. 6d.

**Clark's (Hugh) Introduction to** Heraldry. *With nearly 1000 Illustrations.* 18th Edition. Revised and enlarged by J. R. PLANCHÉ, Esq., Rouge Croix. Or, with all the Illustrations coloured, 15s. [*Just published.*

**Comte's Philosophy of the Sciences.** Edited by G. H. LEWES.

**Ennemoser's History of Magic.** Translated by WILLIAM HOWITT. With an Appendix of the most remarkable and best authenticated Stories of Apparitions, Dreams, Table-Turning, and Spirit-Rapping, &c. In 2 vols.

**Handbook of Domestic Medicine.** Popularly arranged. By Dr. HENRY DAVIES. 700 pages. With complete Index.

**Handbook of Games.** By various Amateurs and Professors. Comprising treatises on all the principal Games of chance, skill, and manual dexterity. In all, above 40 games (the Whist, Draughts, and Billiards being especially comprehensive). Edited by H. G. BOHN. *Illustrated by numerous Diagrams.*

**Hogg's (Jabez) Elements of Experimental** and Natural Philosophy. Containing Mechanics, Pneumatics, Hydrostatics, Hydraulics, Acoustics, Optics, Caloric, Electricity, Voltaism, and Magnetism. New Edition, enlarged. *Upwards of 400 Woodcuts.*

**Hind's Introduction to Astronomy.** With a Vocabulary, containing an Explanation of all the Terms in present use. New Edition, enlarged. *Numerous Engravings.* 3s. 6d.

**Humboldt's Cosmos;** or Sketch of a Physical Description of the Universe. Translated by E. C. OTTÉ and W. S. DALLAS, F.L.S. *Fine Portrait.* In five vols. 3s. 6d. each; excepting Vol. V., 5s. *.* In this edition the notes are placed beneath the text. Humboldt's analytical Summaries and the passages hitherto suppressed are included, and new and comprehensive Indices are added.

—— **Travels in America.** In 3 vols.

—— **Views of Nature;** or, Contemplations of the Sublime Phenomena of Creation. Translated by E. C. OTTÉ and H. G. BOHN. A fac-simile letter from the Author to the Publisher; translations of the quotations, and a complete Index.

**Humphrey's Coin Collector's Manual.** A popular introduction to the Study of Coins. *Highly finished Engravings.* In 2 vols.

13

Hunt's (Robert) Poetry of Science; or, Studies of the Physical Phenomena of Nature. By Professor HUNT. New Edition, enlarged.

Index of Dates. *See* Blair's Tables.

Joyce's Scientific Dialogues. Completed to the present state of Knowledge, by Dr. GRIFFITH. *Numerous Woodcuts.*

Knight's (Chas.) Knowledge is Power. A Popular Manual of Political Economy. *[Just Published.*

Lectures on Painting. By the Royal Academicians. With Introductory Essay, and Notes by R. WORNUM, Esq. *Portraits.*

Mantell's (Dr.) Geological Excursions through the Isle of Wight and Dorsetshire. New Edition, by T. RUPERT JONES, Esq. *Numerous beautifully executed Woodcuts, and a Geological Map.*

———— Medals of Creation; or, First Lessons in Geology and the Study of Organic Remains; including Geological Excursions. New Edition, revised. *Coloured Plates, and several hundred beautiful Woodcuts.* In 2 vols., 7s. 6d. each.

———— Petrifactions and their Teachings. An Illustrated Handbook to the Organic Remains in the British Museum. *Numerous Engravings.* 6s.

———— Wonders of Geology; or, a Familiar Exposition of Geological Phenomena. New Edition, augmented by T. RUPERT JONES, F.G.S. *Coloured Geological Map of England, Plates, and nearly 200 beautiful Woodcuts.* In 2 vols., 7s. 6d. each.

Morphy's Games of Chess. Being the Matches and best Games played by the American Champion, with Explanatory and Analytical Notes, by J. LÖWENTHAL. *Portrait and Memoir.*

It contains by far the largest collection of games played by Mr. Morphy extant in any form, and has received his endorsement and co-operation.

Oersted's Soul in Nature, &c. *Portrait.*

Rennie's Insect Architecture. *New Edition.* Enlarged by the Rev. J. G. WOOD, M.A. *Shortly.*

Richardson's Geology, including Mineralogy and Palæontology. Revised and enlarged, by Dr. T. WRIGHT. *Upwards of 400 Illustrations.*

Schouw's Earth, Plants, and Man; and Kobell's Sketches from the Mineral Kingdom. Translated by A. HENFREY, F.R.S. *Coloured Map of the Geography of Plants.*

Smith's (Pye) Geology and Scripture; or, The Relation between the Holy Scriptures and Geological Science.

Stanley's Classified Synopsis of the Principal Painters of the Dutch and Flemish Schools.

Staunton's Chess-player's Handbook. *Numerous Diagrams.*

———— Chess Praxis. A Supplement to the Chess-player's Handbook. Containing all the most important modern improvements in the Openings. Illustrated by actual Games; a revised Code of Chess Laws; and a Selection of Mr. Morphy's Games in England and France. 6s.

———— Chess-player's Companion. Comprising a new Treatise on Odds, Collection of Match Games, and a Selection of Original Problems.

———— Chess Tournament of 1851. *Numerous Illustrations.*

Stöckhardt's Principles of Chemistry, exemplified in a series of simple experiments. *Upwards of 270 Illustrations.*

———— Agricultural Chemistry; or, Chemical Field Lectures. Addressed to Farmers. Translated, with Notes, by Professor HENFREY, F.R.S. To which is added, a Paper on Liquid Manure, by J. J. MECHI, Esq.

Ure's (Dr. A.) Cotton Manufacture of Great Britain, systematically investigated; with an introductory view of its comparative state in Foreign Countries. New Edition, revised and completed to the present time, by P. L. SIMMONDS. One hundred and fifty Illustrations. In 2 vols.

———— Philosophy of Manufactures; or, An Exposition of the Factory System of Great Britain. New Ed., continued to the present time, by P. L. SIMMONDS. 7s. 6d.

## XIII.

## Bohn's Cheap Series.

Barber, The; or, The Mountaineer of the Atlas. A Tale of Morocco, by W. S. MAYO, M.D. 1s. 6d.

Boswell's Life of Johnson. Including his Tour to the Hebrides, Tour in Wales, &c. Edited, with large additions and Notes, by the Right Hon. JOHN WILSON CROKER. The second and most complete Copyright Edition, re-arranged and revised according to the suggestions of Lord Macaulay, by the late JOHN WRIGHT, Esq., with further additions by

Mr. CROKER. *Upwards of 40 fine Engravings on Steel.* In 4 vols. cloth, 4s. each, or 8 parts 2s. each.

*.* The public has now for 16s. what was formerly published at 2l.

Boswell's Johnsoniana. A Collection of Miscellaneous Anecdotes and Sayings of Dr. Samuel Johnson, gathered from nearly a hundred publications. *A Sequel to the preceding, of which it forms vol. 5, or parts 9 and 10. Engravings on Steel.* In 1 vol. cloth, 4s., or in 2 parts, 2s. each.

14

**Cape and the Kaffirs.** A Diary of Five Years' Residence. With a Chapter of Advice to Emigrants. By H. WARD. 2s.

**Carpenter's (Dr. W. B.) Physiology** of Temperance and Total Abstinence. On the Effects of Alcoholic Liquors. 1s.; or, on fine paper, cloth. 2s. 6d.

**Cinq-Mars; or a Conspiracy under** Louis XIII. An Historical Romance by Count Alfred de Vigny. Translated by W. HAZLITT. 2s.

**Dibdin's Sea Songs** (Admiralty Edition). *Illustrations by Cruikshank.* 2s. 6d.

**Emerson's Orations and Lectures.** 1s.

—— **Representative Men.** Complete. 1s.

**Franklin's (Benjamin) Genuine Au-**tobiography. From the Original Manuscript. By JARED SPARKS. 1s.

**Gervinus's Introduction to the His-**tory of the 19th Century. From the German. 1s.

**Guizot's Life of Monk.** 1s. 6d.

—— **Monk's Contemporaries.** Studies on the English Revolution of 1648. *Portrait of Clarendon.* 1s. 6d.

**Hawthorne's (Nathaniel) Twice Told** Tales. 1s.

—— the Same. Second Series. 1s.

—— **Snow Image** & other Tales. 1s.

—— **Scarlet Letter.** 1s.

—— **House with the Seven Gables.** A Romance. 1s.

**Irving's (Washington) Life of Mo-**hammed. *Portrait.* 1s. 6d.

—— **Successors** of Mohammed. 1s. 6d.

—— **Life of Goldsmith.** 1s. 6d.

—— **Sketch Book.** 1s. 6d.

—— **Tales of a Traveller.** 1s. 6d.

—— **Tour on the Prairies.** 1s.

—— **Conquests of Granada and** Spain. 2 vols. 1s. 6d. each.

—— **Life of Columbus.** 2 vols. 1s. 6d. each.

—— **Companions** of Columbus. 1s. 6d.

—— **Adventures of Captain Bon-**neville. 1s. 6d.

—— **Knickerbocker's New York.** 1s. 6d.

—— **Tales of the Alhambra.** 1s. 6d.

—— **Conquest of Florida.** 1s. 6d.

**Irving's Abbotsford and Newstead.** 1s.

—— **Salmagundi.** 1s. 6d.

—— **Bracebridge Hall.** 1s. 6d.

—— **Astoria.** 2s.

—— **Wolfert's Roost,** and other Tales. 1s.; fine paper. 1s. 6d.

—— **Life of Washington.** Authorized Edition (uniform with the Works). *Fine Portrait, &c.* 5 parts, with General Index. 2s. 6d. each.

—— **Life and Letters.** By his Nephew, PIERRE E. IRVING. *Portrait.* In 4 parts. 2s. each.

*** For Washington Irving's Collected Works, see p. 4.

**Lamartine's Genevieve; or, The** History of a Servant Girl. Translated by A. R. SCOBLE. 1s. 6d.

—— **Stonemason** of Saintpoint. A Village Tale. 1s. 6d.

—— **Three Months in Power.** 2s.

**Lion Hunting and Sporting Life in** Algeria. By JULES GERARD, the "Lion Killer." *Twelve Engravings.* 1s. 6d.

**London and its Environs.** By CYRUS REDDING. *Numerous Illustrations.* 2s.

**Mayhew's Image of his Father.** *Twelve page Illustrations on Steel by* "PHIZ." 2s.

**Modern Novelists of France.** Containing Paul Hoet, the Young Midshipman, and Kernock the Corsair, by Eugène Sue; Physiology of the General Lover, by Soulié; the Poacher, by Jules Janin; Jenny, and Husbands, by Paul de Kock. 2s.

**Munchausen's (Baron) Life and Ad-**ventures. 1s.

**Preachers and Preaching.** Including sketches of Robert Hall, Newman, Chalmers, Irving, Melvill, Spurgeon, Bellew, Dale, Cumming, &c. 1s. 6d.

**Sandford and Merton.** By THOMAS DAY. *Eight fine Engravings by Anelay.* 2s.

**Taylor's El Dorado; or, Pictures of** the Gold Region. 2 vols. 1s. each.

**Willis's (N. Parker) People I have** Met; or, Pictures of Society, and People of Mark. 1s. 6d.

—— **Convalescent; or, Rambles** and Adventures. 1s. 6d.

—— **Life Here and There; or,** Sketches of Society and Adventure. 1s. 6d.

—— **Hurry-graphs; or, Sketches** of Scenery, Celebrities, and Society. 1s. 6d.

—— **Pencillings** by the Way. *Four fine plates.* 2s. 6d.

15

www.ingramcontent.com/pod-product-compliance
Lightning Source LLC
Chambersburg PA
CBHW021936110726
47901CB00003B/862